The Fence

Gary Yeagle

Words Matter Publishing
P.O. Box 1190
Decatur, Il 62525
www.wordsmatterpublishing.com

ISBN 13: 978-1-958000-88-5

Library of Congress Catalog Card Number: 2023946311

Dedication

I would like to dedicate *The Fence* to Walter, our crazy cat who sleeps next to me on his chair in my office while I go about the business of writing.

Acknowledgments

I would like to thank my wife for the countless hours of proofreading as she continues to correct all my flaws of being an author.

CHAPTER ONE

The short walk from his college dorm to Mussleman Stadium only took Max ten minutes. As a rule of thumb, he didn't enjoy most sports. The only sport he had been involved in as a youth had been little league and high school baseball down in South Carolina. His roommate, a muscular lad from the Southern Tier of New York State, was a second-string lineman for the Gettysburg Bullets. He had been invited to the game and Max could hardly refuse. Besides, it was Saturday night, and he didn't have anything else planned so, it was off to a night of small-town college football.

Shirk Field was centered in the stadium, surrounded by a well-maintained six-lane turf running track flanked on either side by tall metal bleachers. The stands were already filling up quickly with students and local football fans. Sitting on an end seat five rows up, he found himself seated next to three young female students. Two of the three reminded him of the typical young college girls he had seen around campus: far too much makeup, fashionable jeans, stylish hairdos, expensive designer sneakers, and purses.

The third female of the trio whom he was seated next to stood out like a sore thumb with long blond hair, fixed in a grandmother-style bun, a long black dress buttoned up to the neck that ran down to just above her ankles, and a pair of plain, ankle high, black lace-up shoes. She wore no jewelry and carried no purse. Wrapped around her neck was a hand-crocheted off-white scarf. Max was about the farthest thing from being a ladies' man one could imagine but he couldn't help thinking about how this girl looked plain; a *plain Jane*. If his mother told him once she told him a hundred times while growing up that it was unwise and foolish to judge another person by their appearance alone. First impressions could be very misleading.

He had been staring too long when the girl, her hands folded neatly at her thin waist, turned slightly and gave him a gentle smile. His previous opinion of her being plain was quickly altered as he gazed at the angelic face of a China doll complexion: rosy cheeks, deep hazel green eyes, and full lips. This girl was anything but plain. She appeared pure, wholesome, and downright beautiful in its simplest form. A more pronounced, genuine smile formed on her lips when she nodded again in his direction. Smiling, he nodded back but then felt awkward for thinking she was plain.

Turning his attention back to the field, he thought about how difficult it was to not judge people. It seemed like a natural reaction. Wanting to gaze at the girl's face once again, but not desiring to be too obvious, he focused on the players who were busy preparing themselves for the upcoming gridiron contest.

Minutes later, Gettysburg kicked off to their opponent, and three plays later following a long downfield pass, Gettysburg's football team found themselves trailing early in the game by a score of 6-0. Watching Franklin and Marshall's placekicker drop the ball perfectly between the uprights of the goalpost, the score was now 7-0.

Max found it difficult to concentrate on the game as he had no interest in football. He looked off into the distance, not even a mile away from where he saw the lights of town—at one time, one hundred and forty-nine years in the past Gettysburg had been a small rural, somewhat religious farming community surrounded by the gently rolling hills of the Pennsylvania countryside. Today, Gettysburg was no longer considered a small farming community, but a thriving small city, actually a borough, complete with everything people needed to survive. Gettysburg, the county seat of Adams County, had its hospital, Walmart, drugstores, car washes, churches, restaurants, and all the other service-related businesses people required.

Gettysburg was one of those towns that wherever you went and whoever you talked to was well known, a town steeped in the history of the Civil War, namely the epic battle between the North and South referred to as the turning point of the war. On July 1st, 2nd, and 3rd back in 1863 over fifty thousand soldiers had lost their lives within a few miles of where he now sat.

Gettysburg was also known for the immortal speech that Lincoln gave; The Gettysburg Address. He remembered how back when he was in junior high, he had to memorize the famous speech for a school play where he had portrayed Abraham Lincoln. Thinking back to that time, which was just eight years in the past, he recalled how proud his mother had been of him as he stood before the crowded auditorium at Charles B. Debose

Middle School in Summerville, South Carolina while reciting Lincoln's famous words without missing a beat. His father had agreed with his great performance but said the play was out of sync with the way Lincoln looked.

Max, at that time, was one of the shortest students in his class and quite frankly looked ridiculous standing up there on the stage in that long oversized black coat and tall stovepipe hat. His father meant no offense but said Max looked like some sort of overgrown gnome. Max hadn't taken offense or concern with his father's observation and despite the fact he had done an excellent job in reciting the "Address" he had to go along with his father on how ridiculous he looked in the *wanna-be* Lincoln costume. During his high school years, he had shot up like a weed and now stood at just over six foot in height and weighed in at a trim one hundred and seventy-two pounds.

Another roar from the opposite side of the field where the Franklin and Marshall fans were seated brought his attention back to the game. Gettysburg's opponents scored for the second time and following the extra point increased their lead to 14-0. Looking around at the Gettysburg students, he noticed how they were still cheering for *their school!* His roommate, a somewhat obnoxious young man in his opinion, had explained to him that it was important as a student to attend the game and support the school team.

At the moment he wasn't feeling the desire to jump up and down and yell, 'Let's go Gettysburg' along with the line of enthusiastic cheerleaders down near the edge of the field. What did they expect from him? He was just a freshman. He had only been at school for two months. He was still in the process of trying to acclimate himself to college life. He couldn't see how rooting for *his school* was in any way going to assist him in getting passing grades. He had four years of schooling ahead of him and was determined to get his degree in finance. He was here to learn and the idea of rooting for his school's team who at the moment were getting their butts kicked seemed like a waste of time and energy. Suddenly, a hot dog and a cup of hot chocolate sounded good. Getting up he made his way down the bleachers and to the concession stand at the other end of the stadium.

While standing in a short line at the food stand, the familiar sound of the Battle Hymn of the Republic from his cell phone got his attention. Digging the small device from his jacket pocket he ran his finger across the screen and answered, "Hello!"

The sound of his mother's voice, "Hello, Max," made him smile.

"Hello, Mom, what's new down there in Summerville?"

"Same ol', same ol'. We haven't talked since last week. Are you getting settled in up there in the cold north?"

"Yes, I'm slowly getting used to college life, but I still haven't quite gotten used to the winter weather here in Southern Pennsylvania. Like right now. I'm at a school football game in mid-November and the temperature according to the scoreboard is hovering just above 42°. One of my professors earlier today in class said it was unseasonably warm for this time of year. What's the temp down there in good ol' Summerville?"

"Right now, it's about 63°. I just finished up this week's grocery shopping at Publix. I'm out here in the parking lot at the moment loading up the car. Everyone is walking around in shorts. Listen, I hope you're not having second thoughts about going to school up there in Gettysburg because of the weather?"

Max laughed. "No, I'll be fine. It's just that up this way winter is more than just a word. It's an actual season, a notable change in the temperature from late October until early April. What's Dad been up to?"

"He's been getting a lot of work done on the house down at Fripp. That storm we had last summer knocked off some of the roof shingles and the gutters need to be replaced. Two of his Civil War buddies are down there helping him with the repairs. That reminds me. Are you planning to go with your father next spring to a reenactment?"

"No, I think I'll have to take a pass what with year-end exams and all. I'll miss going along with him and his cronies. Have they decided where they're going this coming year?"

"Your father and I were just discussing that very topic last night while we were having dinner at the Dockside. He said he and the group were undecided. They considered going to Shiloh for the 150th reenactment but they've already been there twice so they are considering either McDowell, Virginia on May 5th or Hartford, Indiana on May 12th. I guess he and his pals are having a meeting next week to decide which event they want to attend. Of course, come next July he and the group will be making their yearly journey to Gettysburg for the annual reenactment."

"How long has Dad been making the yearly visit to Gettysburg?"

"Ya know, I'm not sure. I know he was a Civil War reenactor long before we ever met. I think he went with your grandfather for years before Gramps passed away. I bet it's close to thirty years that he's been a reenactor. It's a passion for your father. Do you think you'll go along with him to Gettysburg this year or not?"

"I can't say right now. In the past whenever he took me along it was something I looked forward to each year, but now, going to school and living here, I can just drive over to the battlefield whenever I choose. So, coming back here with Dad might not be as exciting as it has always been in the past. I'll just have to wait and see."

Max's mother probed, "How is the job search going?"

"Quite well. I only went to one place. I saw a NOW HIRING sign in the window at Burger Palace, went in, and filled out an application. The manager just happened to be in that day and decided to interview me on the spot. He told me he'd probably give me a call later this week. He said he was looking for someone who could give him about thirty part-time hours a week, evenings, and weekends. It's ten dollars an hour so when and if he gives me a call, I'm on board. Your son, a future financial advisor might be flipping burgers for the next couple of years."

"There's nothing wrong with that, son. When I attended college over in Savannah, I worked my way through school at a fast food fish place. At times, I considered the job a pain in my backside, but the extra money I had coming in from that weekly paycheck was nice. Listen…are you still driving down for Christmas."

"Yes, that's the plan. Are we celebrating Christmas in Summerville or down on Fripp?"

"It's going to be Fripp. Your father said we haven't done that for the last three years and he thought it would be a nice change. Depending on when you leave you may have to drive directly to Fripp rather than Summerville."

"Okay. Tell Dad I said Hey and I'll see you guys next month."

After dumping a spoonful of relish on his hot dog he added a squirt of mustard and then ketchup. He took a large bite and, satisfied with the taste, grabbed his hot drink, and started back for his seat when a loud cheer went up from the crowd. Max looked at the scoreboard and noticed that Gettysburg had scored a touchdown, the score was now 14-7. Approaching the bleachers, he was glad he had gotten up and gone to the concession stand because now, as he returned to his seat, he would be able to look at the strangely dressed but beautiful girl without being too obvious. Walking up the elevated metal steps he noticed the girl staring *at him*. He made eye contact with her, but after what seemed like a prolonged stare, he looked back at the field and sat down. He wasn't sure but he felt her eyes were still on him. Nervously, he turned and sure enough, those deep green eyes were staring directly at him. He felt like he should say something; but what?

Suddenly the girl spoke up as she gestured at the hot dog. "Does that taste good?"

Max held up the hot dog and responded, "This hotdog…yes. There's nothing like a good hot dog."

The girl frowned slightly as she commented, "I've never had one."

Somewhat amazed, Max gestured with the hot dog and asked, "You've never had a hot dog?"

"No…never!"

For some reason, Max felt he should apologize. "Well, if I had known that I would have brought you one back. I can go get you one right now if you want."

The girl bent down and removed a folded ten-dollar bill from her shoe and announced in a sweet voice, "That's all right…I have my own money. Where do I go to get one?"

Awkwardly Max pointed toward the concession stand with his drink as he answered, "Right down there at the end of the field."

The girl stood and excused herself. "If you'll just let me by, I think I'd like to go down there and get…a hot dog."

Max stood as the girl moved out in front of him, her face just inches away from his. She looked directly into his eyes, and he felt like his legs were going to buckle. Watching her descend the metal steps, he asked himself a silent question. *What is going on? Why do I feel like this?*

When she reached the base of the bleachers, she made a right and started toward the concession stand with a very slight but noticeable limp, the ten-dollar bill clutched in her right hand. He watched her for a few seconds when someone in the next row asked him to please sit down. Apologizing, he returned to his seat when another roar went up from the crowd as Gettysburg kicked a field goal, the score now 14-10. Max tried to focus on what was going on down on the field, but his mind couldn't shake off the thoughts of the strange girl.

Gettysburg kicked off and Franklin and Marshall received the kick and marched down the field in seven straight plays. Gettysburg stopped them on the twenty-yard line, and it looked like their opponents were going to have to settle for a field goal. The kick was long enough but to the left. The referee signaled that the kick was no good and it was first and ten for Gettysburg. There was only one minute left until half-time.

Before Max realized it the strange girl was making her way back up the bleachers, a hot chocolate in her right hand, a hot dog in her left. Max stood and allowed her to pass by, that pleasant smile still on her face. Seated, she sat her drink on the edge of the seat and took a dainty bite from the hot dog, chewed, swallowed, and nodded in approval as she spoke to Max, "This hot dog…is very good."

Max, not quite sure what to say, agreed, "Yes, very good."

The strange girl continued to take small bites of her dog as Gettysburg continued to push the ball down the field with two consecutive first downs. With five seconds on the clock, Gettysburg's quarterback threw a long pass down the sidelines that the right end snagged and outran three defenders to the end zone. Gettysburg had now taken a 14-16 lead. When the ref signaled touchdown the students and fans in the stands went haywire, jumping up and down and yelling. The strange girl, likewise, caught up in the excitement, jumped up, and knocked her hot drink down onto Max's lap. The burning sensation caused him to jump up as he dabbed at his soaked pant leg with a napkin. The girl was instantly embarrassed as she apologized, "I'm so sorry! Please forgive me! Is there anything I can do?"

Seeing the girl was upset Max tried to calm her as he gestured at his leg. "It's not that bad. I'll be fine."

The girl, obviously upset with her actions, stomped her right foot, and buried her face in her hands, "I'm so clumsy! I just knew I shouldn't have come tonight. Once again, I'm so sorry. Can I at least pay to get your pants cleaned? I feel so bad!"

Max placed his hand gently on the girl's shoulder and explained, "It's no big deal. It was just an accident. You didn't do anything wrong."

The girl looked into his eyes and pleaded, "Please, there must be something I can do."

Those green eyes seemed magnetic, and he felt himself being drawn to this girl. Without even realizing what he was saying he blurted out, "Go to dinner with me."

The girl instantly withdrew as she placed her hands beneath her neck and over her chest. "I just can't do that…heavens no! I'm so sorry. Please forgive me but I can't go to dinner with you…I just can't!"

Realizing he had crossed some sort of line, Max backed off and apologized, "I'm sorry…I shouldn't have asked you that. I've never in my life asked a girl to dinner. Why I just did, well, I don't know why. Look, I've got to go. It was nice to meet you!"

With that, Max was down the bleachers, across the lot, and down a long grassy slope where he stopped and looked back at the stadium. *What an odd evening,* he thought. He had every intention of watching a football game but instead had been captivated by the beauty of this strangely dressed female student. At least, he thought she was a student, He thought how his final statement of how it had been nice to meet her was ridiculous. He hadn't said more than a hundred words to her. He hadn't introduced himself, and he never found out her name, where she was from, was a student… nothing! He looked at the glowing face of his watch, almost eight o'clock. Too early to go back to his dorm. Looking toward the lights of Gettysburg, he decided to take a stroll downtown.

On Washington Street, he thought again about the strange girl at the football game. *Who was she? Where was she from? Why was she dressed so differently than everyone else?* Maybe she was from another country. After all, out of the twenty-seven hundred students enrolled there were students from forty-three states and thirty-five countries. Come to think of it she did have a very slight accent…like maybe German or Dutch. Crossing Buford Boulevard, he came back to his senses saying to himself, "Forget it, Max! A girl that beautiful is way out of your league. You're not even in the same ballpark."

Ten minutes later he made a right onto Baltimore Street and three blocks later he found himself in one of his favorite parts of town. Both sides of the street were lined with quaint gift shops and businesses. Further down the street, he could see where some of the damage that had been done to the buildings was still evident a century and a half after the Battle of Gettysburg.

Passing three different gift shops he stopped and looked in the window of the Blue and Gray Gift Shop, one of his father's favorite places to visit during his yearly trip to Gettysburg. His father always purchased something, usually a book on the Civil War. Back home in Summerville, his father had an extensive collection of not only books but movies on the Civil War along with other assorted historical paraphernalia he had collected over the years. Sitting on a bench in front of the shop, he thought about his father. When it came to the Civil War there wasn't too much his father didn't know about this important time in American history.

He continued to think about his father—a boy who had grown up on a rural Central South Carolina farm. Max's grandfather, according to his father had been a harsh man, a man who never graduated from high school, but despite his lack of basic education still turned out to be a relatively successful tobacco farmer. Max's father had many a conversation with Max about his boyhood days working the one hundred thirty-six-acre tobacco farm with his grandfather. He no sooner graduated from high school when he moved to Charleston where he got a job with a landscaping company.

Three years later, after learning the trade, he moved to Summerville where he opened a small landscaping business—his first year resulted in nothing but cleaning up local yards or businesses after storms and planting occasional trees and plants for customers. As time went on, he eventually purchased a backhoe and a new truck and things just kind of went from there.

Today, and for many years now Max's father owned *Miller's Landscaping*, the largest landscaping and construction company in Dorchester County. For just a South Carolina country boy with a high school education, his father had done all right for himself. He admired his father. He was a good man. In some ways, he was downright intelligent. Over the years of studying the Civil War Max's father knew more about the events of the past war than most college professors or historians. Max's father was known as quite the expert on the war and had been invited many times to speak at Civil War gatherings and seminars.

Max continued down Baltimore Street and turned onto Steinwehr Avenue, another one of his favorite streets. Two blocks up he passed McClellan's Tavern, a known hangout for college students. He had never gone there but heard they had good food.

The tavern was named after George B. McClellan and according to Max's father had been but just one of Lincoln's *do-nothing generals*. Earlier in the year, just one week before when he had headed out for college, Max had attended a seminar his father had spoken at in Charleston at the Citadel. His father had gone on to explain in front of a packed auditorium how frustrated Lincoln had been during the war because his generals could never seem to get a leg up on the Confederacy.

From the very beginning of the war, Lincoln experienced a steady stream of unsuccessful generals. The first general to disappoint Lincoln had been Irvin McDowell who had been appointed as Brigadier General over the Union army in May of 1861 at the outbreak of the war. Two months later that same year in late July the first major battle of the war was fought on the hills and fields around Manassas, Virginia. McDowell's strategic battle plan was far too complex and unimaginative. General Stonewall Jackson not only defeated McDowell and his Union forces but drove them nearly back to Washington. Lincoln was amazed and embarrassed that the United States Army could be defeated so soundly and quickly replaced McDowell with George B. McClellan.

McClellan, known as *Little Mac,* was known for his meticulous planning and preparation but these very tactics hampered the ability of his forces to function in fast-moving battlefield situations, thus the Battle of the Seven Days in July of 1862, what was thought to be an obvious victory for the north turned out to be a partial Union defeat.

Lincoln, dissatisfied with McClellan's performance replaced him with John Pope, the new Commanding General of the Union Army. In August of that same year, Pope went up against Robert E. Lee and Stonewall Jackson and was defeated soundly at the Second Battle of Manassas. Lincoln still baffled that he could not find a general who could lead the northern troops to victory, handed the reins of command back to McClellan for the second time. In September of '62 at the Battle of Antietam, Lee once again could not be corralled, and after a battle that was considered a draw Lee escaped with his army intact.

Lincoln turned command of the army over to Ambrose Burnside who was known to be overly confident. During the winter of '62 in mid-December Burnside ordered several frontal attacks against well-entrenched Confederate troops at Fredericksburg, Virginia resulting in massive losses by the Union Army. It was reported to Lincoln the battle could only be described as *Butchery!*

In January of '63, Burnside was replaced by General Joseph Hooker, who winds up facing Lee at the Battle of Chancellorsville in Virginia. Lee was severely outnumbered but as always seemed to outfox the Union generals, in this case, Hooker, flanked his army and ran them back across the Rappahannock River. At this point, Lincoln probably wondered if there was a general in the entire Union Army who could defeat Lee and the Confederacy.

Hooker was severely criticized for his lack of performance at Chancellorsville and eventually stepped down and resigned his command. On June 28th, 1863, just days before the Battle of Gettysburg would take place George Meade assumed command of the Union forces. During the three days of battle, Meade accomplished his greatest victory and his greatest mistake. Lee had made some tactical blunders that nearly annihilated his southern troops but on July 4th he managed to escape with the remnants of his army. Meade was harshly judged by Lincoln for not pursuing Lee and bringing the war to an end. Because this was not done the war would rage on for two more bloody years.

In the spring of 1864, Lincoln finally located a general who understood the mathematics of war and appointed Ulysses S. Grant head of the Union Army. Max's father had gone on to explain that Grant was willing to sacrifice a great number of his men to accomplish his goal of crushing Lee and the Confederacy. Through a series of bloody battles: The Wilderness, Spotsylvania Courthouse, and Cold Harbor, Grant lost massive amounts of soldiers but was relentless as he continued to push Lee further down into Virginia. Grant had Lee on the run, and it was just a matter of time before Lee stood his ground at Petersburg, where he found himself practically surrounded, outgunned, and outnumbered.

In April of '65, Lee surrendered to Grant at Appomattox Courthouse and the war finally came to an end. During these final months, Grant had lost over half of his army and unfortunately, this was the mathematics required to defeat Lee. Max could appreciate the mathematics of war because he was a mathematician. He understood how math worked and that a mathematical computation could not be disproven.

His father's past seminar talk had been on his mind for the last half hour as he had walked back up Washington Street. He was now back on campus and in the distance could see the lights from the stadium. He could hear no cheering, so he figured the game had ended. He wondered if Gettysburg won.

The temperature had dropped steadily, and it was beginning to spit snow, something he had never seen while growing up in Summerville. Stopping at the student canteen, he purchased a cup of coffee and decided to sit outside and watch the snow for a while. Sitting on a bench he sipped the wonderful coffee and watched the snowflakes begin to increase in size. Sitting there under a streetlight with his coffee, which seemed like a friend in the night, was a comforting feeling.

He thought about the girl he had met at the football game. He wondered where she was at the moment. Was she somewhere on campus getting ready to turn in for the night? The campus itself was two hundred twenty-five acres and if she was a student that meant she was close by. He felt foolish, in an odd sort of way. Here he was thinking about her, and he had no doubt she was not thinking about him.

Why should she? He was just another male student who no doubt had been struck by her beauty. He had seen good-looking girls before, not only on campus but back when he was in high school. For the most part, they never gave him a second look. They knew they were attractive, and he had to face the facts; he was no prize package. But then he remembered how the girl had stared at him with those fantastic green eyes. Taking the last swallow of his drink he shrugged off the thought of her and decided to go back to his room and hit the hay. Tomorrow would come and like everything else in life what happened today would have nothing to do with the next day. He'd probably never see the girl again.

CHAPTER TWO

Seated in an uncomfortable wooden chair, Max stared out the fourth-floor window of Glatfelter Hall to the southwest, beyond the town limits of Gettysburg. It was out there in the rolling hills where he and his father had spent many an afternoon walking the famous battlefield sites: Culps Hill, Little Round Top, The Peach Orchard, and Devil's Den. When, in the past, he had toured these and many other historical Civil War sites with his father, his dad had explained in great detail what had transpired on those blood-soaked fields and hollows a century and a half ago. The way his father explained the intricate movements of past battles made them seem like they just occurred yesterday. Listening to his dad go on and on about a particular battle, you could almost hear the cannon fire and the screams of men on both sides of the conflict. It was like stepping back in time.

He closed the book he had been studying; *The Principles of Mathematics* and made a final note on the legal pad he brought along, got up, placed the book back on the shelf, put the pad into his briefcase, and stretched while rotating his neck. He had been studying for the past two hours in the small student library. It was almost eleven o'clock and his next class was scheduled for one-thirty on the other side of campus. He had two hours to kill. Maybe he'd grab some lunch and just relax.

Max took the elevator to the third floor and walked down the remaining three floors using the grandiose staircase leading to the main floor. As he stepped out the massive front door the bell from the one hundred- and forty-three-foot bell tower began its hour on the hour chiming of the time. Looking up at the tower, he admired the building; deep red and gray brick constructed in a Romanesque Revival style. It not only housed the mathematics department, but anthropology, computer science, political science, and sociology departments. Whenever he had an opportunity to study in the fourth-floor library, he always enjoyed the time spent there. Just walking into the marvelous structure made one feel more intelligent.

It had been a week since he had attended the football game. The weather over the past few days had been what he considered tolerable. Growing up in South Carolina, this time of year the temperature was always in the low to mid-sixties. The grey, overcast sky threatened snow or rain. It had snowed on three different occasions the past week, but so far: no accumulation. Walking down a long sidewalk he smiled to himself and thought, the first major snowfall we get where there is any accumulation, I'm going to go outside, make up some snowballs, and toss them at something; maybe a tree. Here he was, nineteen years old, and had never experienced snow, except for the past few days when a few flakes had fallen to the ground.

Arriving at the college dining center, he entered and walked to the rear of the hall where several stainless steel and glass display cases offered anything from a sandwich to a full meal. Grabbing a ham and cheese sandwich, a bag of chips and a flavored tea he paid for his purchase then went back outside and sat beneath a grove of tall oak trees at one of the scattered picnic tables.

He had no more than took his first bite when he was interrupted by a soft voice, "Excuse me!"

As he turned, he couldn't imagine who was speaking to him. The only friend he had made during his first few weeks at school had been his pain-in-the-ass roommate. He couldn't believe it. There she stood! The beautiful girl from the football game.

When it was apparent, he was not going to speak the girl stepped closer, her hands folded at her waist. "I hope you remember me from the other night at the game."

Max swallowed the bite he had in his mouth and then spoke, "Yes, I do remember you. How could I forget?"

"I suppose it is easy to remember a person who spills a hot drink on them. Once again, I apologize."

Max struggled for the right words as he stammered, "It really…wasn't that big of a deal…As I said…before. It was just…an accident. There's no need for an apology."

The girl gestured at the table, and asked politely, "May I sit?"

Jumping up Max apologized, "I'm sorry. How rude of me. Please… please have a seat."

The girl hesitated while looking at his open sandwich wrapper. "If I'm interrupting your lunch we can always talk later."

With an odd face, Max pushed the chips and unfinished sandwich to the side. "What this…it's just a little snack. You're not interrupting anything."

As the girl seated herself directly across from him, he noticed she was dressed much the same as the first time he had seen her. She wore the same type of dress but this time it was dark blue rather than black. Her long blond hair was still worn in the conservative bun style, partially encased in a white bonnet and she had what appeared to be a well-used brown jacket covering the upper half of her body. The one thing that indeed had not changed was her beautiful face that at that moment was looking right at him. Moments of silence ticked by, and he tried to think of what he should say next when she finally broke the ice while extending her right hand. "My name is Elizabeth King."

He took the girl's hand and gently responded, "I'm Max, actually Maxwell…Maxwell Miller. My friends call me Max."

"Nice to meet you for the second time, Max." Without waiting for him to reply she went right on, "I've been looking around campus all week for you. Since I did not have your name or even know if you were a student I was just about to give up. But I guess today is my lucky day. I'm on my way to a class and here you sit."

Pushing his tea to the side, Max probed, "I'm a little confused here. Why on earth would you be looking for me?"

"Because there is something I want to say to you. I should have said it the other night at the game, but I was so surprised when you asked me to dinner."

"Oh that," said Max. "Look, like I told you that was the first time in my life I have ever asked a girl to dinner. I guess when it comes to that sort of thing, I'm not very polished. I apologize if I seemed too forward."

"There is no need for you to apologize. It is I who overreacted. Later that night when I got back to my dorm room, I started thinking about how unkind I had been to you. You see, we are kind of alike. That was not just the first time you asked a girl to dinner, but it was the first time I have been asked. It must have been awkward for you. I know it was for me. I thought about how I refused you and the way you must have felt. I prayed about it that night and the next day I promised myself if I ran into you, I would ask you the question."

Lost, Max raised his hands and inquired, "What question?"

"Well, I was wondering if that dinner invitation is still open, I would be glad to have dinner with you?"

Flabbergasted, Max responded with a wide grin plastered across his face. "Of course, the invitation is still good. We can still go. I'd love to take you to dinner."

A slight breeze blew across campus, several stray blond hairs blowing across her face. This disarray of hair made her even more attractive as she brushed the few rebellious strands back behind her ears and smiled. She remained silent when Max suddenly realized he should say something. "Well, I guess we better set a date then. Would tomorrow night be too soon?"

"No, that would be fine."

"Would six o'clock be all right?"

"Yes, I think six would be all right."

"Where do I pick you up?"

"I'll meet you out by the large fountain at the entrance to the campus. Do you know where that is?"

"Yes…the large fountain. I'll be there at six on the nose."

The girl looked across a large section of grass as she stood. "I'd best be on my way, or I'll be late for class. One more thing, Max. There are two conditions for our dinner arrangement. First, it has to be somewhere we can walk to, and second; I have to be back at my dorm by ten o'clock."

"Okay," said Max. "Six o'clock at the fountain, somewhere we can walk to and then you're back here by ten. I can handle that."

She started to walk away but then turned back and gave Max one of those heart-melting smiles. "I'm really glad I found you again. Thank you for being so patient with me. See you tomorrow evening."

Max watched her walk up the long walk, once again with that slight limp. When she was no longer in sight, he got up and sat on the end of the wooden table and spoke out loud to himself, "What just happened here? What just happened?"

An hour later, in an Applied Mathematics class, Max sat in the third row near a set of large windows while the professor went on and on about business and mathematics. Suddenly his lack of attention was noted as his name was announced loudly, "Mr. Miller!"

Turning toward the professor Max noted the unfriendly scowl on his face. "Mr. Miller…if your future intention is to be a member of the financial world, I would strongly suggest you focus your attention on what is being said rather than gazing out the windows of this class."

Max instantly apologized, "I'm sorry Sir. I seem to be preoccupied with other thoughts this afternoon. I was thinking about mathematics. Something happened to me just before class that doesn't seem to add up."

"Would you care to share this mathematical dilemma with the class?"

"No, I would not, Sir. Please go on with whatever you were talking about. I'm with you now!"

The professor frowned and added a touch of humor to his classroom. "I'm sure we all feel better. Let's continue."

The remainder of his day passed by quickly. Following his afternoon class, he walked to the indoor gymnasium the campus offered where he swam laps in the Olympic-sized pool, walked three miles on the indoor track, and spent an hour peddling a stationary bike. After a long relaxing shower, his mind once again returned to thoughts of Elizabeth King and how she had sought him out. He wasn't all that sure about what had happened or even why it had occurred. The more he thought about it the more he realized he wasn't going to be able to figure the situation out. *Why even try to figure it out? He was going to have dinner with a beautiful and strange girl.* He had to admit he was looking forward to tomorrow evening.

The next morning, he was up early, jogged down to the rec center, swam for an hour, had a light breakfast then knocked out his two morning classes, followed by lunch, then his early afternoon class. Walking out of the last class of the day it was two o'clock and he had four hours before meeting the mysterious Elizabeth King at the fountain. Despite the fact it was a cold blustery afternoon he decided on a bike ride out Emmitsburg Road to the battlefield where he would turn around at The Peach Orchard and pedal back to campus. He'd then grab a relaxing shower, study for maybe an hour, and then it would be time for his first rendezvous with a member of the opposite sex. He was rather concerned about what he should say or even do during the upcoming evening but then remembered that according to her this was her first male-female encounter as well.

Max stood in front of a full-length door mirror and inspected himself, rust-colored V-neck sweater, button-down Oxford blue shirt, casual khaki dress pants, grey argyle socks, and shiny Cordovan loafers that he only wore to weddings and funerals. Checking the time on his wristwatch he noted the time: 5:15. In forty-five minutes he was scheduled to meet Elizabeth. It was only a fifteen-minute walk to the fountain and if he left now he'd be a half hour early. *Perfect,* he thought. He'd never been late for anything in his life and his habit of being punctual would continue this day. Slipping on a brand-new Navy P-Coat his mother had purchased for him to wear in the cold north, he was out the door.

Outside on the sidewalk, he pulled the collar of his coat up around his neck to combat the stiff breeze and occasional snowflakes. Looking up at the dreary sky he passed an outdoor school bulletin board where he saw a temperature gauge mounted on the side. The thin red line of mercury was just below the thirty-five-degree level. To date, this was the coldest day he had ever experienced in his young life. He couldn't recall it ever being this cold in Summerville.

Minutes later he arrived at the three-tier fountain and took a seat on one of four wooden benches that surrounded the centerpiece of the main entrance to the campus. Gazing at the cascading water his mind quickly associated what he was looking at with numbers. Being a mathematics student and to date, a lifelong lover of the way numbers related to life, he surmised. It was said that water would freeze at 32° Fahrenheit. This was not exactly true. The freezing process depended on the ambient air pressure, and the purity of the water, both chemical and nuclear. That being said, at normal pressure pure water would freeze at 32°.

His mathematical musings were interrupted by Elizabeth's voice as she approached unnoticed. "Hello Max…I think I'm a few minutes early."

"Hey there…Elizabeth. I was just looking at the fountain and thinking that later on tonight when the temperature drops below freezing the water will freeze. Where I'm from, down in South Carolina, that's something that would more than likely never happen. At least I've never seen it."

Dressed in a similar outfit that she had been wearing the previous day, she looked up at the sky and commented, "If it's too cold out for you maybe we should go when it's a little warmer."

Max, trying his best to be what he thought was manly, stood in defiance of the cold wind and stated, "I'll be fine. I'm looking forward to our dinner but if you think it's too cold, I guess we could go another day."

"Nonsense," said Elizabeth. "I'm used to the winters here in Pennsylvania. I grew up on a farm in Lancaster County. There have been many a winter day as a young girl when I had to get up at four in the morning and trudge through deep snow down to the barn to help milk our cows. Then there's the livestock to feed, the cleaning out of the stalls, and the gathering of eggs from the chicken coup. Life on the farm continues despite the cold weather."

"All right then," said Max as he gestured at the street that ran in front of the campus. "Let's head down Washington Street. There's a small café in town where they have great Italian food, and their soup is really good."

Elizabeth agreed, "This cold weather does make for a great soup day."

Side by side they walked, Max sticking his hands deep into the pockets of his new coat as he asked, "This farm you grew up on. Is it far from here?"

Elizabeth responded, "Lancaster is about a three-hour drive from Gettysburg. It's Northeast of where we are now, about three hours west of Philadelphia."

Max continued the conversation, "I've always heard that being a farmer is a hard way to earn a living. Have you always lived on this farm?"

"Yes…born and raised right there on the family farm. Our farm is located near several other farms. It's kind of a community, all of the families helping each other if need be."

"You said you had to get up early to milk the cows, so I assume your farm is a dairy farm."

"No, we're not that type of farm. We only have six cows. My father's farm is one of the larger farms in the area where we live. We have just over a hundred acres where we grow corn and tobacco. My father is also a cabinet maker. He and two other men from the community design and create custom cabinetry. Between his cabinet business and the money we get after harvesting our crops, we always seem to get by. Aside from that our farm is self-sustaining. From our small herd of cows, we make our milk, cheese, and butter. We butcher our hogs, and the chickens supply us with eggs. My mother makes her bread, and we have a five-acre garden that yields us ample vegetables. We have grape vines and a four-acre apple orchard. My mother cans fruits and vegetables so during the winter months we have much to eat."

Interested, Max asked another question, "Do you have any brothers or sisters?"

"Yes, I have three sisters and twin brothers. The boys just turned six and two of my sisters are in their early teens. My older sister got married two years ago and is about to have her first child."

"Does she live in Lancaster?"

"Yes, she and her husband have a small farm a few miles down the road from where our farm is located."

Max was about to pop his next question but didn't have the opportunity as Elizabeth asked a question of her own. "You said you were from South Carolina…correct?"

"Yes, that's right. We live in a town about the size of Gettysburg, maybe larger, called Summerville. It's known as one of the friendliest cities in the south. It's somewhat of a tourist town and there are many people who, after visiting, wind up retiring there. Summerville is located in what we call the Lowcountry. Everything is below sea level so there are a lot of streams and rivers in the area not to mention vast salt marshes. Summerville is only about a thirty-minute drive from the ocean."

Stopping at Buford Blvd for several cars to pass by Elizabeth stated with a tone of sadness, "I've never been to the ocean. I've always heard it's beautiful. I've seen photographs of the ocean. I sure would like to go sometime before the Good Lord calls me home."

"I assume you're talking about your future death. My mother told me to never ask a woman her age but I'm guessing you're about the same age as me. I'm nineteen. My point is this, I don't think the Good Lord as you have stated is going to take you any time soon."

"Perhaps you're right. I'm eighteen and I'll be nineteen in two months. The Bible tells us we can live to be seventy to eighty years of age if we have the strength. If I make it to that age of life that means I'll have fifty to sixty years to see the ocean."

Max crossed the street and nodded affirmatively. "You really should go some time. I've lived near the Atlantic Ocean now for almost two decades and I still find it amazing." His mathematical mind clicked in, and he went on, "The Atlantic covers around forty-one million square miles and 20% of the earth's surface and about 29% of the earth's water surface. It is connected to the Arctic Ocean to the north, the Pacific to the southwest, the Indian Ocean to the southeast, and the Southern Ocean to the south. The average depth of the Atlantic is about eleven thousand, eight hundred feet deep, and the deepest is thought to be over twenty-seven thousand feet in a place called the Puerto Rico Trench. Scientists estimate there are over nine million species of plants and living creatures living in the ocean that have not been discovered. I find that amazing!"

He stopped talking when he noticed that Elizabeth was not at his side but had stopped and was staring at him with an odd look. Before he could say another word, she held out her hands and stated humbly, "I'm afraid I don't understand a single thing you just said."

Max apologized, "I'm sorry, it's just that I have always been obsessed with numbers and how they work. I've been that way ever since I was knee-high to a grasshopper, so my parents tell me. That's why I'm here studying at Gettysburg. They have one, if not the best mathematics courses in the country. My major is Applied Finance and Mathematics. Someday after I graduate, I plan on having my own financial business."

Elizabeth smiled as if she understood and then asked, "How far is this café you told me about?"

"It's just up the street," said Max. "One more block and then down the street. I think you'll enjoy this place. C'mon." Reaching out he took her hand, not in an affectionate way, but more along the lines of leading her down the street. Holding his hand, she gave him a brief look of reluctance but then gently squeezed his hand as they proceeded.

Minutes later, he opened the old wooden door of Vanuccis Restorante and gestured for her to step through. A passing waitress approached and asked politely, "Will there just be the two of you this evening?"

"Yes, just two," said Max. "Could we have a table by the front window?"

"Yes, you may. We have two available at the moment." Placing two menus on the table the waitress inquired, "And what are we drinking tonight?"

Max thought for a moment and then requested a glass of sweet, iced tea. Elizabeth ordered a glass of iced water and a cup of black coffee. Max gave her an odd look then sat back and commented, "I've never run into a female our age who drinks coffee, and at that without cream or sugar."

"It's one of the things I miss most about being back home on the farm. In the early morning when I would go to the barn with my father for milking time, he would always give me a cup. I've been drinking black coffee ever since I was twelve. This is something my mother never knew. It was just a special time between me and my father. What do you miss most about this Summerville you're from?"

Max ran his hand across his chin as he thought and then answered, "There are so many things I miss from back home. First of all, there's the weather. I miss the warm temperature. I miss all the great seafood that is available, and I also miss going with my father down to Fripp Island where we spend time fishing and crabbing and walking on the beach right next to the ocean."

Interested, Elizabeth probed, "This Fripp Island, you speak of, I assume since you call it an island that it is surrounded by water. Is that where you walk on the beach next to the ocean?"

"That's just one of the places I can go. My two favorite places to walk on the beach are Fripp and then another Island before you get to Fripp called Hunting Island. Besides the home my parents own in Summerville we have a second home on Fripp. It's more of a rental property than it is a residence. Once in a while, if we don't have someone on vacation renting the place we may go down there for a weekend or a day relaxing on the beach. When we go, we usually drive but if we're going to be doing some fishing my father takes the family down in his boat. Ever since I was a small boy, I have always enjoyed the boat rides down to Fripp."

His explanation of Fripp was interrupted when the waitress returned with their drinks. Politely, she asked, "Are we ready to order?"

Max picked up one of the menus and answered, "We haven't had a chance to look at the menu yet. Could you give us a few minutes while we decide?"

Understanding, the waitress replied, "Of course. Take your time."

As she walked off, Max noticed that every person in the place was staring in their direction. Leaning forward, he whispered to Elizabeth. "Is it just me or does everyone in here seem to be staring at us?"

Elizabeth gently patted his left hand. "This is nothing to be concerned over. They are not looking at *us!* They are staring at me! Over the years I've gotten used to people staring."

Embarrassed, Max gave her a sad look. "You mean like the way I stared at you at the football game?"

Elizabeth, not the least bit upset, looked at him across the table and inquired, "Tell me, Max. Why did you stare at me? Was it because of the way I was dressed? You can be honest with me."

Max thought for a moment and then replied, "Yes, at first but only because you were dressed so differently than any other girl I've ever seen. But then…I looked into your face and my opinion of your simplistic dress attire was replaced with your beauty… your wholesomeness. I guess I was just captivated by your eyes, your skin. It was so refreshing. I don't know how else to explain the way I felt. It's the same way I feel at this very moment. How you dress makes no difference to me. To be honest, I feel honored to be with you this evening."

Elizabeth smiled graciously at the couple at the next table and nodded gently. The couple, realizing their staring had been too obvious, went back to eating their meals as Elizabeth turned her attention back to Max. "People have always stared at me ever since I was little. One of the main reasons for their staring is because of the way I dress. I suppose there are other reasons but that's the first thing that gets their attention. Let me explain. You see, I'm Mennonite. Everyone in my family, actually in our entire community back in Lancaster dresses very plain."

Max, trying his best to understand, held up an index finger to make a point. "Mennonite! I remember during my senior year in high school which was just this last spring we studied various religions. The Mennonites were mentioned and if I recall they are similar to the Amish. Am I correct?"

"You are correct. And what did you learn about the Amish?"

"Well let's see. I learned they are very religious and live in a completely different world than most folk. For instance, if I remember correctly, they do not drive cars but travel around in horse-drawn buggies. I don't think they have telephones or indoor plumbing and there's a bunch of other stuff I can't remember."

Elizabeth confirmed what Max had said with a nod of her head and then went on to explain, "The Mennonites are similar in many ways to the Amish, but in many ways, we are quite different. We are very religious and live our lives according to the word of God. We are known as a peace church and as pacifists. We, like the Amish, are also not all that worldly. There are many different sects of both Amish and Mennonite. The Mennonite community I was raised in is known as Black Bumper Mennonites."

Giving Elizabeth a strange look, Max repeated, "Black Bumper…now you've got me confused. What does that mean?"

Without missing a beat, Elizabeth went on to explain, "The Mennonite community I belong to is more worldly than most Amish or other Mennonite groups in Lancaster County. Unlike many Mennonite groups who refuse to own or even ride in an automobile, the sect I belong to will own and operate a car, truck, or tractor. The reason we are called Black Bumpers is because we paint every inch of an automobile that we may own completely black. This includes shiny bumpers, wheel covers, and so on. My father owns a black Chevrolet with black bumpers. It's one of the ugliest cars you'll ever see. Unlike many Mennonite families who refuse to have a telephone, my family does have one, but it is not in the house. It's out in the barn. We also have indoor plumbing. We had it installed back when I was just five years old. The one thing we have stuck to is how we dress. Ever since my descendants migrated here from Central Europe over a century ago, we have continued to dress as what the world calls…*plain.*"

Max, looking across the room at a party of six who were staring their way turned back to Elizabeth and stated, "Well I don't care what other people think. Sitting here and talking with you, I find you to be anything… *but plain!*"

The waitress returned with her order pad and pen in hand. Max apologized to the young girl. "I'm afraid we still haven't looked at the menu. Tell you what…I'm going with the spaghetti and meatballs and a cup of your minestrone." Gesturing at Elizabeth he asked, "Do you still need some time to go over their choices?"

Elizabeth pushed her menu to the side and spoke softly, "I'll just have the same thing."

The waitress finished writing down their orders and then announced she would be back with hot rolls.

Max took a drink of his tea and changed the subject. "So, what is your major here at school?"

Fingering the rim of her coffee cup, Elizabeth answered, "I'm taking nursing. I want to help people who are recovering from illness. Ever since I was a small girl I've always been concerned about the health of my family and our neighbors as well. There are several Mennonite colleges I could have attended but Gettysburg not only has an excellent nursing program, but I don't have to travel that far from where I was raised. Because of the way we as Mennonites view the world, it's pretty unusual for a young Mennonite woman to go off to college. Most Mennonite girls my age are being courted or preparing themselves to become a wife. From the moment as a young girl of just four or five years of age a Mennonite female begins to learn the process of becoming a future wife. By the time Mennonite girls reach my age they are well prepared to marry a young Mennonite man."

Interested, Max inquired, "If I could ask, what does this, I guess you could say training involve?"

"I can cook, sew, bake, plant, and tend a garden; I can fruit and vegetables, I can drive our tractor, and know how to till and plow a field. I can butcher a hog, milk cows, and any other thing that needs to be done on a farm."

"I find that amazing," remarked Max. "Why I bet 99% of the girls here on campus can't do most of the things you've mentioned. I know I can't! When it comes to cooking my mother tells me I can't boil water. I can't ever remember my mother sewing my clothing. If something I was wearing got torn or ripped, we would always just replace it with new clothing. The only thing I know about gardening is how to pull weeds. I've never even been on or near a tractor. I can't imagine butchering a hog. We always just go to the grocery store if we need meat or anything else for that matter. As far as milking cows is concerned, I don't know one end of a cow from the other. I guess that's the difference between being a small-town boy and a country girl."

Elizabeth cocked her head and gave him one of her heart-melting smiles. "You make it sound like I'm multi-talented, when in fact, my skills and talents are strictly farm-related. There's a lot more to the world than just the farm or the Mennonite community I was raised in. There's an entire world out here that I am just now being exposed to. You, on the other hand, have lived in a world I don't know for nineteen years. The number of things you can do is far greater than what I've done in my life. You can drive a car, you've seen the ocean, and you tell me you're good at fishing and crabbing and that you're good at mathematics. And those are just a few things you have grown up with that are a world away from how I was raised. Especially mathematics. The daily duties on a farm have little if nothing to do with the mathematics of life."

Max hesitated as if he were not sure how to respond, then finally spoke, "Look, I know this is the first time I've ever spent an evening with a female and I wouldn't want to say anything to destroy the time we've spent together tonight, but I have to disagree with you on farm life having nothing to do with numbers. Most people don't even realize how numbers affect our everyday lives. Numbers dictate time, dates, weights, and measures, and too many other things to even mention. Numbers indicate when the sun rises and sets daily, *and* those times are constantly changing. From where I'm from and many other shoreline places around the world numbers through time determine when the tide rises and when it falls." Stopping himself, he realized he was getting off track. "Let's get back to life on the farm. You said earlier you had to get up at four in the morning on the farm to milk the cows. That means daily you had to get out of bed…what, around three thirty…quarter to four, every day without fail. Is this correct?"

Not sure where Max was going, Elizabeth answered, "Yes that is correct."

"What would happen if everyone overslept and didn't go out to the barn until…let's say five o'clock?"

"That would never happen because the cows would get the jitters. They know they are on a schedule."

Max further explained, "I bet your mother has breakfast prepared at a certain time give or take a few minutes. It's probably the same way for lunch and supper. You told me you have acres of corn and tobacco. I don't know anything about planting any type of crop, but I imagine there is a particular time of the year to plant and then a time to harvest those crops. If you don't get enough rain or maybe even too much then your crops fail. Even if your crops get the proper amount of sunshine and rain not every single seed will take hold. It's all about the numbers…even in farming."

Elizabeth nodded in agreement and stated, "I think I see what you're saying. I've never given it much thought, but I guess numbers or mathematics are an important part of life. Like this evening. We met at the fountain at six o'clock and we have to return by ten." Picking up one of the menus she went on, "And look at this menu. All the prices are printed for the benefit of the customer."

The waitress returned to their table pushing a small cart on which sat two heaping plates of spaghetti and a large bowl of sauce. Placing the bowl and plates on the table she explained, "Be careful because these plates are hot." Pointing at the red sauce she went on. "We are quite famous for our spaghetti sauce. It's a little spicy but folks seem to like it. Will there be anything else?"

Looking across the table at Elizabeth, Max shrugged, "No I think we have everything we need at the moment. I would like a refill on my tea."

Elizabeth held up her glass of water and replied, "I'm fine…thank you." She then stared at her plate of noodles and then at the bowl of red sauce. "Do you remember when at the football game when I said I never had a hotdog before?"

"Yes, I do remember that," said Max.

"Well, I've never had spaghetti either, at least in this form. Back on the farm, we have noodles quite often. They are different from these noodles. The ones my mother makes are flat and thicker than these. We would have them with brown gravy or maybe even just heavy butter."

Max pointed at the sauce and suggested, "Well then maybe you should try just a little bit of sauce with some noodles to see if you like it that way."

She reached across the table for Max's hand and spoke softly, "Let's bless our meal."

Grasping her dainty hand Max could feel the light callouses on her palm from working on the farm.

Taking in a deep breath as if she were inhaling the very presence of God, she began. "Dear Lord, Heavenly Father, we thank You for this meal You have placed before us, and we ask that You bless the hands that prepared it. We also ask that You bless our families back in Lancaster and down in this…Summerville. Remember those who are less fortunate. In Jesus' name, we pray…Amen!"

The blessing complete, Elizabeth asked politely, "Would you please pass that bowl of sauce to me so I can try some?"

Max pushed the bowl across the white tablecloth and then began to butter one of the rolls that had been brought to their table. Elizabeth, using a ladle placed a small amount of sauce at the corner of her plate and then pushed a small forkful of noodles into the thick sauce. Max watched with great interest as she took the spaghetti to her lips. She swallowed a small bite, then smiled, and commented. "This is good. I think I'd like to have more of the sauce."

As they approached the fountain Max looked at his watch and remarked, "Nine forty-five. I've got you back on campus with fifteen minutes to spare."

Elizabeth nodded toward the north side of the campus. "My curfew for my dorm is ten and I've still got a five-minute walk, so I best be on my way. I had a wonderful evening with you." Large white snowflakes began to gently fall as she held out her hands and stated. "Good night, Max and thank you for the nice dinner."

Max stepped forward and suggested, "Perhaps I should walk you back to your dorm."

"No that won't be necessary. It's just a short walk and there are plenty of lights along the way." Elizabeth slowly turned and started to walk away when she stopped and turned back. "Max, you haven't asked me why I limp. Did you not notice?"

"Yes, I did see that you limp, but I didn't think it was proper for me to ask why."

Giving him one of her great smiles she explained, "It was a bull on our farm. We've had him for years. He weighs over a ton. When I was seven years old, he stepped on my foot and my ankle got injured. It never completely healed so during the winter months when it gets cold like this I tend to limp. During the summer…I'm fine. I just thought you'd like to know."

Max waved her explanation off as he remarked with confidence. "Thank you for sharing that with me but it does not change the way I look at you. You are still the most beautiful girl I have ever seen. I don't suppose that… maybe next week we could go to dinner again. We don't have to do Italian again. Why we could go for Chinese, burgers, or maybe fried chicken. What do you say?"

"I'd like that Max. We could meet right here at the fountain next Wednesday at six."

"Next Wednesday it is then. Looking forward to it."

He stood and watched until she walked around the corner of a building. For some reason, he felt better than he had in quite some time. Sitting on one of the benches he leaned back allowing the snowflakes to melt on his smiling face.

CHAPTER THREE

Elizabeth tore off the corner of a blueberry muffin and gazed out the front window of a quaint downtown Gettysburg coffeehouse. "It looks like you're going to get your wish, Max. I heard on the radio early this morning in my room that we could receive as much as five inches of snow today."

Max sipped at a hot chocolate and looked out at the large white flakes falling from the gray sky. "I hope so. I'm still looking forward to making my first snowball. I've been here now for almost three months and still, no significant snowfall. One of my professors was talking earlier this week in class saying, that so far, it was an easy winter."

"Your professor is right," said Elizabeth. "Normally this time of year in Pennsylvania we've already had several snow days. I think today is going to be our first accumulation of the year. If we get enough snow, we might even be able to make a snowman."

"That would be great," beamed Max. "I've seen snowmen in the movies on television but never an actual one. How many inches of snow will it take to make one?"

"It doesn't quite work that way," pointed out Elizabeth. "We could get a foot of snow and still not be able to build a snowman or even make a single snowball. It has to be the right type of snow…heavy, wet snow. If it comes in the form of light crystals, then it will not pack correctly." Looking out the window again, she gestured with a nod of her head. "Those flakes that are falling appear to be heavy and if this keeps up, you'll be able to make your snowball."

Max placed his hand on the windowpane and fingered three untouchable individual snowflakes on the opposite side of the glass. "Look at these snowflakes. Each one has a very distinct design of its own, different from the others." The heat from the inside of the café quickly melted the flakes which were rapidly replaced with others. "Each one of these flakes looks so harmless and fragile but yet given enough time after billions or even trillions of flakes fall to the ground we could wind up with numerous inches or feet of snow. Once again, the mathematics of life are intriguing."

Elizabeth changed the subject. "Later today, both of us will be heading home for the Christmas holiday…me off to Lancaster and you down to South Carolina. This is …the fifth time we have shared a meal of sorts over the past few weeks. In all that time you never mentioned what faith you and your parents practice."

"I never said anything about that because it never came up in all the things we've discussed. I mean, that's something most people just don't talk about. I can't imagine myself after meeting someone blurting out that I happen to be Catholic, Lutheran, or Baptist. That doesn't seem to be a topic of interest for most folks."

"So, which one are you, Catholic, Lutheran, or Baptist?"

Max shook his head in amusement and quickly responded, "Actually, none of those. My parents are Methodist, so I guess I'd have to say I am too. We've been attending the same Methodist Church in Summerville for as long as I can remember. I mean we don't attend every week, but it's pretty rare for us not to be there on Sunday morning. From the way you explained your family, I can tell you this. Your family is far more religious than mine. You have told me how your father reads the Bible to the family for a half hour after breakfast and how Sunday in your community is a day of worship. Back home, Sunday at our house aside from going to church is just another day. We have a large white Bible on our coffee table in the living room. I can't recall the book ever being opened. I asked my mother about it one time and she told me it had been a wedding gift. Even though my folks don't talk about God that much, I know they believe in His existence. I believe in God myself. I guess I've just never thought much about how He may be involved with my life."

Now it was Max who went in a different direction. "Let me ask you. Do Mennonites celebrate Christmas?"

"Some do and some don't," said Elizabeth. "The old order of Mennonites does not honor Christmas as a holiday but focuses totally on the fact that this is the day when Christ was born. We, as Black Bumpers do celebrate Christmas, but we stay away from all the commercialism your world offers. We do not display our home with Christmas lights and decorations. We do not put up a tree or listen to holiday music. We attend church on Christmas Day and then the rest of the day is spent with family. There is a lot of singing of religious hymns and we usually have a big meal. We do celebrate the act of giving but only for the small children. Most families set out a large bowl filled with candies and small gifts. Aside from that, life on the farm continues. The cows still need to be milked, the stalls cleaned out and so on. How does your family celebrate Christmas?"

"Well," said Max, "first of all Christmas in my world, as you put it, is more than just Christmas day. For some folks, it starts in late October while others seem to wait until the day after Thanksgiving. Christmas, it would seem, over the years has grown into a season because it can and often does last for two to three months. Right after Halloween all the retail stores and gift shops scramble to get all their Christmas wares on the shelf. That always seems so ridiculous to me and yet people flock into the stores to buy Christmas items before they run out. That being said, the day after Thanksgiving is called Black Friday because it is the biggest shopping day of the year. Stores have special prices on certain items and people line up at the front door the night before to take advantage of the Christmas bargains. Around town, you see places where they have live Christmas trees for sale.

"At about this time, the malls and radio stations start to play constant Christmas music. But in the south, that's normally where the celebration ends. Most people in Summerville will put up a tree but not many will decorate the house with lighting like they do here in the north. My father never really gets all that excited about Christmas and to tell you the truth I'm the same way. Now my mother…that's a completely different story. We have an artificial tree she decorates on Thanksgiving Day. She hangs a colorful Christmas wreath on our front door and makes my father place a string of colorful lights across the front porch. On Christmas day we exchange gifts in the morning and then later on in the day we have a large meal, sometimes down on Fripp Island. It's just a relaxing day where we eat far too much. We usually watch a couple of football games on TV. To tell you the truth, I'm glad when it's all over. By the time New Year's Day rolls around I'm ready to move on with the next year."

Elizabeth gave him an odd look as she tilted her head sideways and bit her lower lip as if she were thinking, then asked, "When you go home for Christmas break are you going to tell your parents about me?"

Max confirmed, "Most definitely! My mother is scared to death that some college girl who has been around the block a few times might get her claws into me and lead me down the road to corruption. I think she will be quite relieved when I explain to her that you are Mennonite. My father probably won't care one way or the other but I'm sure he and my mother will have many questions about you and our short relationship so far. How about you? Will you tell your parents about me?"

Sitting back as if what Max had said was taboo, Elizabeth placed her hand over her mouth and then responded, "Oh heavens…no!"

The look that came over Max's face indicated confusion.

Elizabeth leaned forward and not wanting to offend Max, she spoke softly, "It's not that there is anything wrong with you, it's just that…well, let me explain." Making herself comfortable she sipped her black coffee and began, "My parents…especially my father would not understand our relationship or even our level of friendship. You see, Mennonite girls my age, maybe even slightly younger are prepared to be a Mennonite wife…to a Mennonite man.

"As young Mennonites, boys and girls do not see each other or date as it is referred to in your world. If a Mennonite boy wants to spend time with a Mennonite girl, it must be arranged and approved by both sets of parents. The boy would approach, most likely his father, and explain that he desires to court the girl. The parents, or in many cases, the father will approach the girl's parents and explain his son's interest in the girl. If the girl's parents approve, then the boy is brought to the girl's farm and they are introduced. Most of the time the girl and boy already know each other from school or just being part of the community.

"During the courtship, however long it may last, the couple is never left alone for any great amount of time. If they go on a buggy ride or for a walk there is always an adult nearby. Kissing and hand holding for the most part is forbidden and only acceptable if the girl has agreed to marry the young man. On the other hand, if the girl does not enjoy the young man's company, she will make this known to her father, who more than likely will put an end to the courtship. The young man according to our standards for courting will understand and move on. So, you see I could never, at least at this point, tell my parents about you. Young Mennonite girls around my age do not in general have male friends unless they are being courted.

"If I were to tell my father about you, he will ask me if I have intentions of marriage with you. We've only known one another for a few short weeks.

When I would tell him I was not considering marrying you he would then ask me why I was spending time with you. The old order of Mennonites would never permit a Mennonite girl to see a boy like you. My parents come from a more modern Mennonite viewpoint of the world. That being said, I'm not sure how my parents would look at the relationship we have. My father is very strict and if he found out about you and the fact, we have been seeing one another, even if it is just a few meals, he might drive over here to the school and take me back home…never to return to college again."

Max let out a long breath as he responded, "I think I understand how your culture looks at male-female relationships, but I don't understand why you sought me out and accepted my first proposal of the two of us having dinner, especially if you knew your father would not approve."

"I don't think my father would disapprove of you because he is not a man who judges others. He tries to live his life and guide his family by the Holy Bible. The Bible tells us 'Judge ye not lest ye be judged!' My father would not judge you because we are seeing each other but he would question why I have chosen to spend time with you. It would all be on me…not you! You may be sitting there thinking I have gone against the male-female rules of the Mennonite community, but I do have a mind of my own. In a way I have followed what my father taught me over the years as a young girl growing up. He always taught me to look into a person's eyes and more times than not I would be able to get a good grasp on the type of person they are. When I first saw you at the football game and looked into your eyes, I saw a young man who was caring and trustworthy. And, after spending time with you over the past few weeks I find you are indeed a good man."

Feeling as if he had been complimented, Max held out his hands and shrugged. "I can't remember a time in my life when someone told me I was good! Then, on the other hand, I've never been referred to as bad either. I always viewed myself as just…sort of normal. Let me ask you this. Has a Mennonite boy ever requested to court you?"

"Yes, a boy by the name of Eli Hoffman. My father was leery of allowing Eli to court me because Eli's father has a reputation in our community for not being very respectful to his wife and daughters. He is not all that well-liked in the community. With reservations, my father agreed to Eli coming to our farm to spend an afternoon with me. We sat on our front porch on an old swing and drank sun-brewed tea. Eli was quite the braggart, and it was hard for me to even get a word in. That evening after he left, I told my father I had looked into Eli's eyes and didn't like what I saw. That put an end to Eli's courtship as far as my father was concerned. My rejection of Eli didn't sit too well with his father, but the rules of our community gave me the right to accept a Mennonite man or not. That was almost a year ago and whenever my family was around the Hoffman's you could just feel the tension. In a way, I'm glad I'm three hours away from all that nonsense now."

"So, what ever happened to this Eli character?"

"I received a letter from my mother shortly after enrolling here at school. Eli took a liking to one of my best friends, Ellen Stotz. She has accepted a marriage proposal from Eli, and they plan on being wed soon. Looking back, I'm glad I'm not in her shoes."

Elizabeth waved off the subject of Eli and Ellen. "When we leave for Christmas break, we won't see each other for two weeks until we get back to school. I think this is a good thing. It will give us both time to consider if we want to continue our relationship. How do you feel about that?"

Max glanced at his watch and answered Elizabeth's question. "Well, there doesn't seem to be all that much for me to think about. Going to college here in Gettysburg has been rather awkward for me. It's the first time I've been away from home for an extended amount of time. Aside from you, I haven't made many friends so far. Before we met the only enjoyment I experienced was driving or biking out to the battlefield where I could relax and feel like I was a part of anything. College is much different than high school. The professors here at school could care less if you show up for class and they treat you like you're just another run-of-the-mill student. What I'm saying is that you have been like a breath of fresh air for me since I arrived here on campus. I'm going to be thinking about you a lot during Christmas break. I can't see how spending two weeks completely away from you will make me rethink our friendship. I'll be glad to see you when we get back."

Max looked out at the falling snow and commented candidly, "That being said, we have to leave before we can get back. What time is your father picking you up today?"

"At ten this morning. That gives me two hours to get back to my dorm room and get packed. My father is very punctual and if I'm not ready to go when he shows up, he'll be upset. I guess you better walk me back to campus." Taking a final sip of coffee, she stood and inquired, "When are you heading down to South Carolina?"

"Late tonight, probably sometime after ten o'clock. I have to work the late shift at Burger Palace. I'll have my car packed and as soon as we close up shop I'll be heading south."

Elizabeth gestured toward the door and confirmed, "Well then I guess we had better get moving."

Placing two cheeseburgers in foil wrappers of a red and yellow Burger Palace sack, Max scooped up a batch of hot fries, placed them in a small cardboard container, added them to the sack, and spoke to Cindy, a young girl at the front counter. "This order gets a large orange drink." Turning to another employee who was flipping several burgers on a long grill, he gestured toward a large walk-in freezer. "We're getting low on fries. I'm gonna grab two more five-pound bags. Be right back."

Just as he was opening the stainless-steel freezer door, he looked at the clock on the wall in the manager's office; just after eight o'clock. They'd be closing in two hours, then following clean-up which normally took about an hour or so he'd be on the road to South Carolina and warmer weather. He was looking forward to spending time with his parents. This year, Christmas dinner would be celebrated on Fripp Island at their rental property which, at the moment, was unoccupied. He was looking forward to walking on the beach. He thought about Elizabeth and the fact she had never seen the ocean. For some reason, he couldn't wait to tell his parents about this wonderful girl he had met.

According to Elizabeth, her father was to pick her up at ten. That was over ten hours ago, and she was no doubt at that very moment back on the farm, away from the worldly ways of college life. Picking up two sacks of frozen fries he smiled at the thought of her. He was glad they had met. She was so different from all the other students he had seen around campus or had sat next to in his classes. At times over the past three months, he wondered how serious many of them were about getting an education. They skipped classes from time to time, partied at night, and in general seemed to care less about the fact they were in college. Elizabeth was quite serious about attending her classes and becoming a nurse. If he had to describe her in a single word it would have to be *genuine!*

He no sooner walked past the front counter when in the door walked his roommate Brad and three of his football-playing companions. Their brash and loud entrance captured the immediate attention of the three couples seated in the dining area.

Brad approached the counter and laughing loudly waved his arms back and forth which resulted in his right arm knocking over a counter display, brochures and coupons scattering across the floor. Staring at Max and Cindy, he placed his hand over his mouth and rolled his eyes, stating sarcastically, "Oops! Looks like you're going to need another display."

One of the other boys stepped forward and pushed Brad to the side in a comical manner. "Get out of the way, dumb ass!" Bending down he began to pick up some of the coupons but fell over due to his obvious excessive drinking. The other three boys laughed as they leaned on the counter.

The tallest boy in the foursome looked directly at the girl and announced boldly, "We'd like to get a late-night snack…maybe some burgers." Using a smart assed tone he inquired, "You do have burgers here…right?"

The relatively new girl looked at Max as she answered, "Yes, we have burgers."

One of the other boys leaned close to the girl and gave her a stupid grin when he spoke, "She's not only pretty, but she's smart too!"

Brad pushed the boy to the side and looked up at the overhead menu board. "I'm ordering first." Reaching out he touched Cindy's right hand and asked, "I don't suppose you're on the menu tonight." All four of the boys laughed.

Max, sensing trouble informed the girl to go clean up the fallen display and that he would take their order. Cindy gladly backed away from the counter as Max stepped forward and in a friendly voice proclaimed, "All right guys. Let's get your orders rolling!"

Cindy was no sooner around the counter when one of the boys, a good two hundred and fifty pounder knelt next to her and suggested, "Here let me help!" His alcohol breath caused her to back away as she made a disgusting face.

Max calmly told her to go clean some of the dining room tables and that he would get the mess cleaned up. The boy in a drunken stupor leered at her as she walked off, then proceeded to scoop up all the coupons and the display itself which he placed on the counter in a sloppy pile. Waving his hand, he commented in a slurred voice. "There ya go…problem solved!"

A couple entered the restaurant but then turned and left when they witnessed the four drunken football players. Max figured the sooner he took the boys' orders, the sooner they would eat and then leave.

Max was in the process of taking the last player's order when the boy spoke up and he pointed at Max. "Hey, Brad! This dude behind the counter. Isn't he your roommate?"

Brad, who was a few feet away at the drink machine finished filling his cup and then walked to the counter. "Yep, me and 'ol Max bunk together. We're about as opposite as you can get. I play football and Max counts things."

The tall boy remarked, "That doesn't make sense. What do ya mean…. counts things?"

Brad held up his hands in a mocking and pompous fashion and answered, "He's a mathematical genius. According to Maxwell, everything in life is connected to numbers."

The tall boy responded as he addressed Max, "Well if that's true then you better get crackin' so we can get our burgers before this damn joint closes!"

All the boys laughed loudly as they walked to the drink machine. Cindy approached Max and whispered, "I called Jim, our manager. He's supposed to be coming in about nine to help us close up. I told him we had a group of troublemakers in here. He told me to let everyone know to just ignore them and go about business as usual. He said he'd handle things if need be when he gets here."

The four boys gathered at a table by the front window one of the boys grabbing a chair from a nearby table where a couple sat eating. Rudely, he commented, "I'm taking this chair. Hope ya don't mind because if you do well it doesn't make any damn difference."

The couple looked at one another in amazement, not believing the crass behavior of the boy and realizing that objecting to his actions would only lead to trouble, they got up from their table and exited the building.

Cindy bumped Max on his arm and remarked with a tone of disbelief, "Your friends are going to run all of our customers off!"

Max shot the girl a confusing look. "Those boys are not what I would call *my friends!* I just happen to have the misfortune of rooming with one of them. That's where it ends."

An older man who had been sitting by a window table got up and approached the counter. "I come in here every Wednesday night for a burger and a Coke. I've been doing this for years and this is the first time I have not enjoyed myself. Those boys have had way too much to drink. I think you should call the police before they get completely out of hand. Is the manager in tonight?"

Before Max could respond, the girl answered, "We gave him a call. He's on his way in."

The man looked back at the loud foursome, then turned back, and spoke to Max directly, "I still think you should call the police."

"I'm not the manager or even in control of anything. I'm just a part–time shift manager. We'll wait for the manager and let him decide what needs to be done."

The old man turned and started to leave but then stopped and walked over to the boys. "You boys need to settle down. This is a place where families and people come to relax and enjoy a nice meal. You have run three couples off since you came here, including me! Why don't you do us all a favor and leave?"

Brad looked at his teammates in wonder, stood, and got in the man's face. "Look…you old fart. Why don't you get the hell out of here and mind your own business!"

The man gave Max a sharp look, turned, and walked out the door just as a cook from the back yelled, "Orders up!"

The counter girl grabbed one of the two trays the orders had been placed on. Max grabbed the other tray and suggested, 'When we get over to their table just set down your tray and then go back to the counter. I'll take care of drink refills and anything else they need."

Cindy trailed Max across the dining area, set her tray on an adjacent table to where the boys were seated then walked back to the counter while Max addressed the four unruly customers. "Okay, who gets the cheeseburger with extra onions and pickles?" After distributing the orders, Max held out his hands and asked politely, "Will there be anything else gentlemen?"

Brad winked at his cronies, leaned over, and whispered to the tall boy seated next to him. "Watch this!" Taking a large bite from his burger he wiped the side of his mouth with his hand and spoke in a cocky fashion as he smiled at his companions. "So, tell me, Miller. How is that little Amish broad you're dating?"

Deciding to ignore Brad's question, Max responded, "If there's nothing else, I've got to get back to the counter."

Max turned to walk off but was stopped by Brad's loud, demanding voice. "Miller! You didn't answer my question. Are you too good to talk with us? How is that Amish stuff? She's a strange girl. I said hello to her the other day, and she just ignored me. I guess she's too good for my type." Bumping one of his friends on his shoulder, Brad raised his eyebrows and grinned in an evil clown gesture. "I bet underneath those weird clothes she wears there's a real tiger...isn't there!"

For some reason, Max just couldn't walk off. Walking back to the table, he leaned forward and spoke directly to Brad. "First of all, we're not dating and secondly she happens to be Mennonite."

Brad blew off Max's comments with a wave of his hand. "Amish, Mennonite...what's the dif. She's a religious chick. I had a goody-two-shoes Catholic girl when I was a senior in high school last year. She was a handful...a wild one! I bet this Mennonite broad is the same. I figure underneath those weird duds she wears she's a wildcat!"

Max knew he should just walk away, but inside he was seething with anger. Looking at all four boys he stood his ground and pointed at Brad. "You have a big mouth Brad and someday it's going to get you in trouble."

Brad stood in defiance and glared back at Max. "Well today isn't that day and you're not the one who is going to give me any trouble."

Don't do anything stupid, Max told himself.

In the next second Brad picked up his burger and threw it at Max, the bun, burger, and fixings, splattering his white shirt and then falling to the table.

Giving his friends a cocky smirk Brad ordered Max. "Looks like I dropped my burger. Why don't you just mosey back on over behind the counter and rustle me up a fresh one."

All of the boys laughed loudly as Max turned to walk away but was stopped again when Brad tossed a handful of fries hitting him on the back of his head. Before Max could even turn back around Brad bellowed, "Tell ya what. When you're finished up with that Amish-Mennonite chick or whatever the hell she is let me know. Maybe I'll just take a crack at that!"

That's it! thought Max. Walking back to the table he stopped, stared at Brad then drew back his right hand, clenched his fist, and jammed it into Brad's nose and upper lip. Brad instantly fell back over his chair. The other three boys stared in amazement at what had happened to their companion. The tall boy blocked Max from walking away as he got in Max's face. "That was uncalled for. You didn't have any reason to hit him."

Max shoved the boy to the side as he exclaimed, "Get out of my way!" The boy stumbled back into a chair but quickly recovered and pushed Max in the back causing him to tumble over a chair and a table. By the time Max got back to his feet, the tall boy picked him up and threw him into another set of chairs. Max got up slowly and yelled toward the counter, "Call the police…now!"

The tall lad approached again as Max picked up a chair to defend himself. Realizing the boy was not going to back off, Max backed away but fell over a chair. The next thing he knew he was being picked up by the large boy and hoisted high into the air. The boy, laughing loudly spun Max around once and then tossed him like a rag doll. The last thing Max remembered was the sound of shattering glass.

The distinct odor of smelling salts brought Max back to his senses as he shook his head and wrinkled his nose at the nauseating aroma. Looking at the pleasant face of a female hovering above him, he asked, "Where am I? Who are you?"

The woman smiled as she placed the used smelling salts in a small disposable plastic bag. "At the moment you're lying on the sidewalk in front of Burger Palace. My name is Barb and I'm a local paramedic. And before you ask your next question, which will probably be *what happened,* I'll fill you in. You were thrown through the front window of Burger Palace. Do you recall that happening?"

Max pushed himself up on his elbows and responded, "Not really. The last thing I remember was the sound of shattering glass." Looking to his left at the front of the restaurant he noticed the four inches of fresh snow that had fallen throughout the day. Noticing the reflection of numerous sections of broken glass sticking in the snow he remarked, "There's glass everywhere. I've got to help clean up this mess. I'm the shift manager. It's my responsibility."

Suddenly another face, this time a familiar face appeared. It was Jim, the manager. "They tell me you're going to be okay, Max. Don't worry about the clean-up. We'll take care of that. You need to go with the paramedics to the hospital and get checked out."

Concerned, Max tried to sit up but then raised his hand to his forehead. "I feel kind of dizzy."

The paramedic gently pushed him back to the ground. "It's going to take a few more minutes before you're back to normal. Just try to lie still and we'll get you loaded up in the ambulance for a short ride to the hospital."

"Why do I have to go to the hospital? Is there something wrong with me?"

"At this point…nothing serious or life-threatening. You have quite a few cuts and bruises on both of your arms and hands. You have a laceration on your neck and two abrasions on your left cheek. We also need to run some simple tests to make sure you don't have a concussion."

Once again concerned, Max probed, "And how long will all this take? I'm supposed to leave right after work for South Carolina for Christmas. Please don't tell me I'll be spending a few days at the hospital."

"That's for the doctors and the medical staff to decide but to be honest with you, I think after they get you stitched up and tested, you'll be on your way later this evening."

Jim placed his hand on Max's shoulder and spoke. "The police told me they are probably going to send someone by later to the hospital to ask you some questions about what went on here tonight."

Max looked in the direction of the restaurant and asked, "What happened to those football players? Did they run off?"

"No, they did not run off. A better way to put it would be to say they were hauled off…by the police. They are going to be spending the night in our local jail. They are being charged with disorderly conduct, public intoxication, possibly assault and battery."

Fifteen minutes later, with the help of the two paramedics Max was helped into the back of the ambulance. He wanted to sit on a seat next to a removable medical gurney, but the paramedic who remained in the back with him insisted he lay down until he was examined by a doctor at the hospital emergency room. Max reluctantly lay on the gurney and asked, "I thought you said my injuries were nothing serious or life-threatening!"

Gently pushing him back, the paramedic explained in a calm voice, "Believe me, you'll get released from the hospital a lot quicker than if you're admitted through the mainline of the hospital. You did say you wanted to be on your way later tonight…right?"

"Yes, I did say that."

"Well, then you just lay back and let me and my partner do our job. We've been doing this for years and I know what I'm talking about." She looked at a watch on her wrist. "It's almost nine o'clock. We'll get you checked in, stitched up, and run a few simple tests to make sure you didn't suffer a concussion. I'll bet you a dime to a dollar that you're on the road before midnight."

At eleven forty-seven Max found himself seated in a foyer just off the emergency waiting room. The cab company he had called said they'd have a taxi to pick him up in ten minutes. Sipping on a cup of hot chocolate he gazed out at the snow that was still falling but now much lighter than earlier in the evening. He watched while a man was rolled through the front double doors in a wheelchair. He thought about how the evening had turned out a lot differently than he had planned. If it hadn't been for the unfortunate altercation with the drunken football players at the Burger Palace by this time, he'd be nearly two hours down the road on his way to South Carolina.

Smiling, he thought, the paramedic had been right. She had stated he'd be on his way before midnight. The last two-plus hours had been anything but boring. After being admitted he was wheeled to a room where he was quickly examined by a doctor, then moved to a small operating area where his wounds were tended to. The only stitches required were for the cut on his neck. The cuts on his arms and hands, along with the abrasions on his cheek were sterilized and medicated. Then, they ran some tests which indicated he had not suffered a concussion. This was followed by a visit from two Gettysburg Police Officers, who after asking him some questions about the unpleasant events at Burger Palace, took some notes, wished him well, and were on their way.

Max decided on some fresh air. Stepping outside beneath an overhang he waited for the cab. In the next few minutes his ride pulled up, the driver hopped out and asked him if he had called a cab. Nodding, Max climbed in the back and gave the driver directions to Burger Palace which was only five blocks away. Seated in the back of the cab he gazed out the window. Despite that it was after midnight the five inches of snow that had fallen seemed to brighten up everything it touched: lawns, sidewalks, the roofs of the houses.

Surprisingly the wet streets were clear of the white covering. He looked at his watch: 12:10. He wondered what Elizabeth was doing at that moment. Probably fast asleep in her bedroom on the farm in Lancaster. He smiled as he thought about her; about how she would no doubt be getting up with her father in a few short hours, walking out to the barn and having black coffee while she helped her father milk their cows. He thought about the fact that when they both returned from Christmas vacation, he was going to have to tell her about his run-in with the football players.

Gettysburg was a small college and news traveled swiftly across the campus daily. If he didn't tell her she would eventually find out through the campus grapevine about the fight at Burger Palace. He wondered how she would view his actions. She had stated that she and her family were pacifists. Looking back on that moment when he had made the split-second decision to strike out at his roommate, it was almost as if he couldn't control himself. He was sure Elizabeth would think he should have just walked away, but he didn't see it that way. The world he lived in was so very different from how she was raised.

His thoughts were interrupted as the cab driver pulled the cab to the curb and stated, "Burger Palace."

Max leaned forward and asked, "What do I owe you?"

The driver checked his meter and replied. "Just short of five dollars."

Feeling generous, Max handed the driver a ten and smiled, "Merry Christmas…keep the change." Standing on the sidewalk Max watched the cab slowly move up the street and then make a left leaving him alone in the cold night. Pulling the collar of his jacket up around his neck, he crossed the street and there in the parking lot behind the Palace sat his green Jeep which, at the moment, was partially covered in white snow.

One of the large front windows of the Palace where he had been tossed through was boarded over. Looking up and down the street there was not a soul out. He looked at the streetlamp and watched as specks of snow continued to fall. He started to cross the lot when he thought, Snowball! Reaching down he scooped up a handful of the heavy snow and formed it into a baseball-sized sphere. Spotting a stop sign at the intersection he paced off the approximate distance between home plate and the pitcher's mound. Looking over his shoulder at an imaginary runner on first base, he assumed the pitcher's position and checked the invisible runner again.

Bringing the snowball to his chest, he wrapped his fingers around the white ball of snow and threw a split-finger fastball at the red sign. The snowball hit the lower left-hand corner and exploded into several smaller sections. Max shouted up the empty street, "Strike three…you're out!" Thinking about his past days of being a pitcher for the Ashley High School Swamp Foxes he walked across the lot to his car. If he drove straight through to Fripp which was a twelve-hour drive with stops for gas and food, he'd arrive on the island around one to two tomorrow afternoon. He had a lot of time between now and then to figure out how he was going to explain to his parents the stitches and bruises on his neck, face, and arms.

CHAPTER FOUR

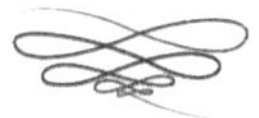

Max checked the time on the dim green dashboard clock: 3:30 in the morning. He had been on the road for three and a half hours. He was tired and hungry, but not quite ready to pull over for a break. Cruising down Rt. 95 at seventy miles an hour he passed a green road sign that read:

THIS EXIT- COLD HARBOR CIVIL WAR BATTLEFIELD SITE

Max thought back to eight years in the past when his father had taken him and his mother along on a trip where his father was to participate in the Civil War reenactment of the Battle of Cold Harbor. They had arrived in Cold Harbor two days before the event and thanks to his mother procuring a room at the local Day's Inn months ahead of time, she and Max had a place to stay. Every available room in the surrounding area was spoken for as the reenactment promoters were expecting thousands of visitors for the staged historical battle.

Max's father wouldn't think of staying in a motel room during a reenactment event. He along with hundreds of Civil War reenactors representing the North and the South would converge on Cold Harbor where they would sleep out on the battlefield in authentic tents and cook their meals with Civil War-era pots, pans, and utensils. Max's mother always told Max his father and the other reenactors went to extremes to relive the past as it was but, in all actuality, it was two make-believe armies playing war games. She then backed this statement up saying if that was the worst thing his father did, she was all right with it. Max's father didn't gamble, drink, use drugs, or run around with women so she was perfectly willing to go along with the make-believe battles.

Max thought back to that time when he was eleven and his father and he walked every inch of the Cold Harbor Battlefield while reading the various inscriptions on the monuments and metal markers explaining the events of that time one hundred and forty years in the past. As usual, his father's detailed rendition of the battle went far beyond what the markers revealed. His father had stated the actual battle of Cold Harbor took place near Mechanicsburg in 1864 and lasted from May 31st through June 12th, the most significant and deadly part of the thirteen-day conflict being fought on June 3rd. The Battle of Cold Harbor was part of what was referred to as The Overland Campaign as Ulysses S. Grant, Commanding General of the Union Army, staged an elaborate, unrelenting attack on Robert E Lee's Confederate Army as Grant pushed the southern army farther south.

Following battles at the Wilderness and Spotsylvania Courthouse, the casualties on both sides were mounting. Since the beginning of May Grant had lost fifty-one thousand men and Lee's losses stood at thirty-nine thousand. At this point, Lee was conducting a defensive strategy while Grant was the aggressor realizing if he kept up the pressure Lee would eventually be forced to fold as the mathematics of war would take over. Despite the fact Grant was losing more men than Lee, every Union soldier who was killed could be replaced while resources of manpower in the South had diminished. It had gotten to the point where it was said that Richmond, the capital of the Confederacy, was guarded by old, gray-bearded men in their seventies along with young boys as young as fourteen to fifteen years of age. No one at this juncture could have known what thoughts were on Lee's mind, but many in the north knew the devastating war was coming to an end. The South was running out of men and supplies. It was just a matter of time.

On May 31st Grant's Calvary arrived and seized a crossroads at Cold Harbor. Throughout the day they pushed back repeated attacks by the Confederates until Union infantry arrived. The next day, June 1st, two more Union corps arrived on the scene and that evening they advanced on the Confederate lines west of the crossroads, experiencing moderate success.

June 2nd arrived and re-enforcements for both armies brought the strength of the Union army to one hundred and seventeen thousand while the Confederates mustered sixty-two thousand.

Outnumbered practically two to one Lee has his men construct seven miles of trenches that were well-fortified. At dawn on June 3rd, Grant ordered three corps to advance a full-frontal attack on the southern end of the entrenchments. The Union forces were repulsed easily with extremely heavy casualties. When it was all said and done Grant was labeled as the *Butcher.* Max's father said years later, Grant in his memoirs stated he regretted having made the final advance which resulted in a massive loss of life in his ranks while the Confederates held their ground. Over the next few days, there were skirmishes here and there, but the main battle was over and Lee had conducted a great defensive victory. It was to be his last as by the next spring Lee surrendered to Grant bringing an end to the war. Max's thoughts about the battle of Cold Harbor were interrupted when he noticed a flash of distant lightning off to the west followed by light rain. Turning on the windshield wipers he rubbed his eyes and realized that soon he was going to have to pull off and take a break from driving.

Pulling off Rt. 95 South just north of Fayetteville, North Carolina, he parked in the huge dirt lot of a truck stop, stepped out of his Jeep, stretched, and yawned. The surrounding parking lot lights penetrated the early morning darkness. Locking his vehicle he started across the lot. He had driven through Maryland and Virginia into North Carolina with little difficulty. The further south he drove the less snow there was on the ground. The parking lot was devoid of any trace of snow but there was still light rain falling. Adjusting the collar of his jacket up around his neck he headed for the bright neon sign that read: RESTAURANT. He had planned on driving straight through, eating in the car, but the night driving had taken its toll and now he needed a break, a splash of cold water on his face, then a good sit-down breakfast with a cup of coffee. He figured he'd be on his way by six-thirty.

He nodded at a group of truckers huddled beneath an overhang of the restaurant as they smoked cigarettes and swapped war stories about their over-the-road experiences. He no sooner entered the eatery when he saw a handwritten sign:

PLEASE SEAT YOURSELF

Taking a window seat, he picked up a bent and food-stained menu and looked at the raindrops running down the windowpane.

An older waitress with stringy blond hair approached his table and held up a pot of coffee. "Start ya off with a cuppa?"

Max slid a ceramic mug on the table to the edge and replied, "You betcha!"

Pouring the hot liquid, she inquired, "Breakfast with that coffee?"

Max opened the menu. "What's good here?"

"Honey, we're open seven days a week, twenty-four hours a day. You can get breakfast, lunch, or dinner anytime you please. What are ya in the mood for?"

He saw a waitress at a nearby table deliver two large plates of food to a bearded trucker which caused Max to ask, "What's that fella getting?"

"That'd be the trucker's special. We're famous for that one. Ya get three eggs, your choice of bacon or sausage, hash browns, toast and a stack of buttermilk pancakes, juice, and all the coffee ya can swill down."

Max motioned toward the men's room. "I'm gonna mosey on over there and freshen up. Why don't you put me in for the special; eggs over easy and I'll have bacon, make that orange juice."

The waitress wrote his request on an order pad and remarked, "Be about ten minutes. We're really busy tonight."

Max removed his jacket and hung it over the back of the chair then walked to the restrooms located on the opposite side of the restaurant. After tending to his business, he splashed cold water on his face and examined himself in the mirror above the sink. The cuts and abrasions on his arms, hands, and face even though medicated had become dark in color and ugly looking. He was even getting a black eye. He couldn't recall getting hit by a punch. Maybe it was just the way he landed. Either way, he was a sight.

Back out in the restaurant, while passing a display of assorted snacks he noticed that his jacket was missing. It was no longer hanging on the back of the chair. Walking up to his table he gazed around the large room. Truckers were seated at the counter and five different tables; people were checking out at the register while others shopped at the various displays. He thought about running out into the parking lot, but thought, *What's the use? Who-ever took that coat is probably long gone!*

Seated again, he thought about the fact someone had not only stolen his coat but that earlier in the evening he had been thrown through a plate glass window, resulting in his Christmas vacation getting off to a rough start.

The waitress, carrying a tray, placed a plate with pancakes and the other plate of bacon and eggs in front of him. Without asking she refilled his half-empty cup, gave him the once over and commented as she nodded at the cuts on his arms and face. "I'm sorry…it's probably none of my business, but you look like a dog that's been in a catfight."

"I've just had sort of a bad day," said Max. "These cuts and bruises happened where I work but that's not the only thing that has happened to me today. While I was in the restroom someone stole my coat. I left it hanging right here on this chair and when I came back out…it was gone. You didn't happen to see anybody around my table, did you?"

"No, I didn't, but then again, I wasn't paying all that much attention. Unfortunately, at this time of night, we get an occasional undesirable in here." Nodding toward the counter she went on, "There happens to be two state troopers over there having coffee. I can say something to them if you want me to."

Max gently objected. "No that won't be necessary. Besides, what could they do? I'm sure they have more important things to do than investigating a stolen coat."

The waitress laid the bill on the table and touched him on his shoulder, remarking, "I hope the rest of your day turns out better."

The minutes passed as Max enjoyed the trucker's special while watching as one truck after another pulled in and out of the massive parking lot. Dipping a piece of toast into egg yolk his solitude was interrupted by a deep voice, "Excuse me, sir!"

Max was surprised when he saw the two state troopers standing next to his table. He laid down the toast and replied. "Good morning, what can I do for you gentlemen?"

The taller of the two officers, holding his hat in his hands gestured toward the counter and explained, "Marge, our waitress, informed us someone may have stolen your coat. Is that correct?"

"Yes, it would appear that way, but I'm sure there is little you can do at this point."

The other officer gave Max the once over and spoke up, "Are you okay this morning, sir?"

Max grinned and sat back. "Now I see. You fellas didn't come over here to solve the mystery of the stolen coat…you came over here because of the way I appear." Holding up his bruised hands and nodding at his arms he went on, "I realize that I look anything but normal, no doubt like one of those criminals you see on wanted posters, but I can assure you these cuts and bruises are from an accident I experienced earlier in the evening. If you have any doubts, you can call The Burger Palace in Gettysburg, Pennsylvania, and speak with Jim Stedman…he's the manager." Reaching for his wallet, Max explained, "I have his number here if you'd like."

"Gettysburg," replied the tall officer. "I've been there on the battlefield with my family. Why that's a good five, six-hour drive from here."

"That's right and since I left right about midnight I've been driving through the night and decided to stop and take a break for about an hour and then hit the road again."

The other officer almost in an apologetic manner asked, "And where are you headed?"

"Fripp Island, South Carolina, down near Beaufort. I'm a college student at Gettysburg College and I'm on my home for Christmas break."

The other officer nodded, "We're sorry about your coat. You'll probably never see it again. Drive safe and have a nice Christmas."

Max half saluted the two men as they walked off when Marge approached and spoke, "I'm sorry…I just thought maybe they could help you out. Was everything all right?"

"Everything was fine. Could I get a coffee to go? I need to hit the road."

"Sure, I'll have it waiting for you at the register."

Max paid for his meal and then walked out the entrance of the restaurant finding that the rain had stopped. Starting across the lot he noticed a pop-up tent next to the restaurant with a hanging banner:

AMISH FRUITS AND VEGETABLES

A young Amish woman dressed completely in a black dress and white bonnet was instructing two young children who were dressed the same about how to arrange some produce. The woman looked about the same age as Elizabeth, the children maybe nine or ten years of age.

Approaching the tent Max examined two baskets of apples as he spoke, "Good morning."

The young woman smoothed her dress and replied, "And a good morning to you, Sir. Would you like some apples?"

Picking up one of the shiny apples, Max examined the piece of fruit. "I think I may. You see I'm on my way home for Christmas and my mother…

well, she always bakes a couple of pies. I was thinking some fresh apples night make for a good pie. I see you have two kinds here. Which one would be the best for baking?"

Pointing at the first basket the young woman explained, "These are Red Delicious and would be better for baking than the Winesap," as she gestured at the second basket.

Max was about to speak when one of the young girls pointed at a wooden shelf near the back of the tent and commented, "We have three kinds of pie: peach, cherry, and Dutch apple. My momma baked them early this morning."

The other little girl grabbed one of the pies and laid it on the table. "This is not only Dutch apple but it's deep dish…my favorite."

"Deep dish apple pie…fresh baked," said Max. "Tell you what. If you have a box for that pie, then it's a sale!"

The other girl grabbed a box from a stack and presented it to the other girl as she stated in a sweet voice, "We have boxes."

Max complimented the young woman, "You have quite the two salesladies here. How much for the pie?"

The young woman answered, "That will be nine dollars."

Max opened his wallet and handed her a ten as he remarked, "A good pie is at least worth ten dollars. Keep the change. Thank you. My family will enjoy this dessert." Taking the boxed pie from one of the girls Max looked directly at the woman. "You remind me of someone I met in college. She's Mennonite and comes from Lancaster, Pennsylvania. Are there any Mennonites here in this area?"

"Not that I know of. Our farm is up the road about three miles where there is a small Amish community." Another customer approached and the woman nodded graciously at Max. "Drive safe and have a blessed day."

The bright December early morning sun was up and shining intensely on the driver's side window when he pulled back onto Rt. 95. Looking down at the pie box he placed on the front passenger seat he noticed some bold black magic marker writing on top of the square white container: God Bless! This was accompanied by a crude drawing of a happy face. The simplistic message caused him to think about Elizabeth and what she might be doing at that very moment on her father's farm in Lancaster.

Elizabeth stood in the large country kitchen and finished drying a plate with a dish towel. As she was placing it up onto a shelf in some long oak cabinets, her mother who was in the process of washing another plate asked, "You haven't said nary a word about your schooling since you've been home."

Reaching for another plate in a handmade wooden dish draining rack, Elizabeth answered the question. "During milking early this morning Father asked me the same and I told him all about my first four months at Gettysburg. I figured he'd go over all that with you."

Elizabeth's mother dipped a plate into the soapy water in the sink and gave her daughter a look of doubt. "Come now…do you think your father has changed his stripes since you've been away to school? You know he is a man of few words and tends to not pass on to others what he is told."

Elizabeth looked out the window at the snow-covered fields behind their farmhouse. "One would think as his wife you would be the first to hear what's on her husband's mind."

"When it comes to your father, what might be on his mind is not always what comes out of his mouth."

"Well then," said Elizabeth, "I guess I'll just have to tell you the same things I discussed with Father out in the barn. Ask your questions."

Elizabeth's mother picked up a coffee cup and nodded in satisfaction. "Have you made any new friends at this school?"

Elizabeth instantly thought about Max and just like she had told him she was not about to tell her mother or father about their relationship. Looking directly at her mother she said, "I have met many students on the campus going to and from classes. I have exchanged hellos and nods with many but as far as friends go, I have only made two. One is my roommate who is from India. Her name is Adai Bagdi. She is very dark-skinned but has different facial features than African Americans I've seen on campus. Adai feels they roomed us together because we are from different cultures than most of the students.

"My other new friend is from Japan and her name is Lin So Huira. She is in one of my classes and rooms just down the hall from Adai and me. We've become the best of friends. At first, Adai and Lin So had so many questions for me about the American way of life. They were surprised when I told them as a Mennonite that my people were not of the world but just in the world and I was not the typical United States student they would run into. Adai is studying to become a chemical engineer and Lin So is in pharmaceutical medicine. They are both extremely intelligent. Lin So has a beautiful voice and sings in the school choir. Adai is quite talented and is an artist. She does body art, mostly hands and arms."

Elizabeth's mother gave her daughter a strange look, asking, "Are you saying she is a tattoo artist? You know the way our people feel about the human body being a temple of the Lord." Placing her right hand on her hip she raised her left and quoted, "The Bible states very clearly in Leviticus 19:28, 'And a cutting for the dead you will not make in your flesh and writing marks you will not mark on you, for I am the Lord."

"It's not like that, mother. The art she practices is called Mehndi, more commonly known here in America as Henna. According to Ahai the art of Henna is taught to many a young girl from India. It's not an ink but a paste made by mixing hot water with the crushed leaves of the Henna plant. This creates a black or blue substance that can be drawn on the skin. It only lasts for seven to fourteen days then, turns to a pale pink or orange, and then fades away. I've seen some of her work. It is quite beautiful."

"Are you saying this is not a sin?"

"No, I'm not saying that…it's just part of Ahia's culture. I have not tried it and have no intention of doing so."

"This Ahai and Lin So. Do they have a walk with the Lord our Savior?"

"The three of us have had many a conversation about the different cultures we come from. One evening we had a long discussion about religion. They knew nothing of the Mennonite faith. Ahai is a Hindu and Lin So practices Buddhism They believe in the same God as we do. They just have a different way of worshiping the Almighty than we as Mennonites. I think one of the reasons we get along so well is because we have accepted one another as we are."

Getting off the subject of religion, Elizabeth added, "We stay up late at night talking about how we grew up, the customs and traditions of our families, even the different foods we eat. That reminds me, I have to bake two shoofly pies to take back with me to school."

"Just be careful," warned her mother. "When your father and I agreed to allow you to go off to college we had a long talk about if it was the right thing to do. I was concerned once you were exposed to the world outside of our faith you might be led astray. Your father informed me that both he and I have done a good job of raising you as a God-fearing young woman and we need to trust that you would always do the right thing." Placing her hand on Elizabeth's shoulder, she went on, "You are indeed a good young woman and I know you will always make the right decision based on your faith."

Their conversation was interrupted by a female voice from the other side of the kitchen, "Good morning, everyone!"

Turning, Elizabeth and her mother saw a young Mennonite woman framed in the doorway. Elizabeth immediately dropped her dish towel and ran across the room to embrace their guest. "Ellen…It's so good to see you!"

Ellen held Elizabeth at arm's length and looked her up and down. "College life has not changed you one bit. You are still the most beautiful girl in our community. So, tell me, are you glad to be back home?"

Elizabeth placed her arm around her childhood friend while speaking to her mother. "If it's all right, Ellen and I are going out to the barn. We have so much to catch up on. Besides, I have to clean out the stalls."

"Don't worry over the cleaning out of the stalls. Your brothers can see to that chore."

"No, I'd rather do it. All the years I spent as a young girl cleaning the barn and often wishing I did not have to. Now that I've been away from the farm, I realize there are things about my past life I miss and one of those, believe it or not, is cleaning the stalls. Father has always said it's important to never forget where you come from, so we're off to the barn!" With that, she and Ellen turned and exited the kitchen.

Elizabeth opened a side door that led into the massive two-story barn, slipped into a pair of rubber boots, and placed worn gloves on her hands. Ellen climbed up two bales of straw stuck a loose strand in her mouth and asked, "Do you miss cleaning the stalls?"

Walking into a large stall Elizabeth gently slapped the rump of a large, dark brown draft horse as she ordered the animal, "Back Jacob…back!"

The horse began to slowly back out of the stall at which point Elizabeth led him to an adjacent stall. While repeating the process with the second horse, Elizabeth answered Ellen's question, "I do miss working out here in the barn. It might sound crazy, but the smell of the manure, straw, and dirt makes me feel at home."

She picked up a short-handled shovel and a dented metal bucket and entered the empty stall as Ellen asked her a question, "I can't wait to hear about your experiences at school. You know, you're the talk of the community. Everyone thinks going to college away from our way of life will change you…and not for the best. So, tell me…what's it like at this school?"

Thirty minutes later after explaining to Ellen everything from her new roommates to her professors to some of the new foods she had tried and on and on, Elizabeth emptied the last bucket of manure into a wheelbarrow. She leaned the shovel against the side of the stall and placed her index finger over her lips indicating silence as she walked to the barn door, opened, looked out then shut the door. Climbing up the wood ladder leading to an overhead loft, she signaled for Ellen to follow. "Let's go on up. I have a secret to share with you like when we were little. Do you remember?"

Ellen giggled as she followed Elizabeth up the ladder. "Yes, I do. We shared many a secret up in this loft."

Seated on a small barrel Elizabeth watched as her best friend made herself comfortable on the partially straw-covered wood slat floor. Sitting Indian style in the corner of the loft, Ellen asked with great excitement, "We haven't shared a secret for quite some time. What have you to tell me?"

Elizabeth folded her hands properly on her lap and then answered, "I've met a boy while away at college."

Ellen shot Elizabeth a strange look and then inquired, "A Mennonite boy?"

"No, he's not Mennonite. He is a member of the Methodist faith. His name is Maxwell. He goes by Max, and he lives down in South Carolina in a town by the name of Summerville. He lives about thirty miles from the ocean and enjoys fishing with his father. He also knows a lot about the Civil War which was fought in our country nearly a century and a half ago."

"And you have told this to no one other than me?"

"Yes, that's why it is and must remain a secret between just you and me."

"I agree," said Ellen. "If the community or especially your father found out, it might not go well for you. Being courted by a boy outside of our faith would be frowned upon. How did this happen? How did you meet this Max?"

"First of all, this boy is not courting me. We happened to meet quite by accident at a school football game. He asked me to dinner which I refused but then later that night after I prayed about it I decided if I ran into him again at school then I would accept the dinner offer. Later in the week I ran into him on campus and told him I'd be glad to go with him. We've been to dinner and lunch a few times. Aside from that we have met at the school fountain and have sat and had long conversations and we've taken long walks around campus and the town."

"It has been said, "remarked Ellen, "that outside of our faith when a boy and a girl desire one another's company it is called dating or seeing each other."

"Look, I don't know much about this dating business, but seeing each other seems to describe our relationship so far. I don't even know that much about the way we as Mennonite's court either. Remember, I've only been courted once and that was by Eli, who is now your husband."

"I also have only been courted by one boy and that also was Eli. I remember the day after you told your father you were not interested in Eli. About how you looked into his eyes and did not like what you saw."

Elizabeth could see their conversation was heading in a direction she did not want it to take. "Ellen, I mean no disrespect towards you or your husband. Eli was just not the man for me."

"I understand what you're saying Elizabeth and I have taken no offence by what you have said. You and I, well the entire community are well aware of the bragging ways of Eli Hoffman, but still, I think despite his high opinion of himself he is indeed a good man. We've been married now for going on six months. At times he is a man who is hard to live with, but he is a good provider. I have a secret, two secrets to share with you."

Ellen looked down over the edge of the loft to make sure they were alone in the barn and placed her right hand partially over her mouth as if what she was about to say should not be spoken. "Here's the thing about Eli. He is without a doubt the biggest braggart I have ever encountered, but when you take the time to think about it he can back up his claims of superiority. He is the fastest runner; he can plow a field faster than any other man in the community and he can toss bales of hay long after the strongest amongst our men are tuckered out. But the truth be known I have discovered something where Eli falls short of the mark." Almost in an embarrassing tone, Ellen leaned forward and in a soft voice announced, "In the bedroom, Eli is not all that proficient!"

Elizabeth looked at her friend with a combination of shock and amazement and remained silent.

Ellen responded to the stare with, "What?"

"What!" exclaimed Elizabeth. "You're talking to me about something

I know nothing of. I've never been with a man. I've no idea as to what proficient is."

"Believe me," said Ellen. "When that time comes, you'll know. My mother told me this is just something a woman knows."

"This is an awkward thing to talk over but let me ask. How do you know Eli is not proficient if you have nothing to compare it to?"

"Eli is the only man I've even been with, so you're right in what you say. I went to my mother shortly after Eli and I were married and told her I felt my husband was not that proficient in the bedroom. After explaining to her how he conducted himself she agreed with me and told me my father was quite proficient. She said she was sorry but that as a wife I might just have to overlook the pleasure of any bedroom activity and concentrate on bearing children, which led to my second surprise. Despite Eli's lack of proficiency in the bedroom I have still managed to become pregnant and that's the second secret." Gently rubbing her stomach Ellen smiled, "I'm only three months along. I haven't even told my mother the good news yet. I was thinking I would announce to Eli and our families about the baby on Christmas Day."

"I'm sure Eli will be quite pleased."

"I'm sure he will," agreed Ellen. "I can just hear him now as he will no doubt start bragging about how beautiful the baby will be if it's a girl and how strong the child will be if a boy."

"Speaking of his bragging ways has he changed since being married?"

"Yes and no. For the first two months after the marriage, he was attentive and polite, but then one evening when I didn't get supper on the table at the usual time, he became angry and told me that he was a hard-working husband and deserved his supper on the table on time and would not put up with a wife who could not do so. I apologized and told him I was sorry, but I had lost track of time. He just wouldn't let up and he kept yelling and then he took me by my shoulders and yelled in my face, 'Do you understand?'

"I don't know what got into me but at that moment I picked up one of my cooking pans and hit him squarely on top of his head. He got this dazed look on his face and fell to the floor in a sitting position. Getting down on my knees I waved that pot in his face and told him I would not have a violent man in my house. Later that night when we went to bed, he told me he was sorry and I forgave him. I believe that was the night I became pregnant.

Ever since that moment in the kitchen, he's been kind as can be."

Elizabeth shook her head in wonder and replied, "I guess maybe no one before you ever stood up to him."

Ellen stood, went to Elizabeth, and hugged her. "I've got to be going. I've got a lot of baking to do. See you on Christmas day."

CHAPTER FIVE

Max checked the gas gauge. Realizing he was down three-quarters he needed to fill up. Pulling over at a combination gas station and country store, he parked beneath an overhang that housed three sets of ancient, faded red gas pumps. It was almost two o'clock in the afternoon. He had driven through the long night and was now just eighteen miles from Fripp Island. He stepped out of the Jeep, unscrewed the gas cap, and inserted the nozzle of the pump into the tank opening. Watching the rapidly, rotating numbers on the pump he looked around the familiar area; Niebocks Sea Island Market. How many times over the years had he and his parents stopped by the market on Ladies Island on their way down to Fripp to gas up?

It was hard to believe he was only twelve hours from the cold and snowy weather of Gettysburg, and yet here in South Carolina there was not a flake of snow to be seen, the temperature was 72°. It was good to be home away from the cold north. He was looking forward to the next ten days, walking on the beach and around the island, maybe playing a round of golf or doing some fishing with his father. Later on in the week, he would dine with his family at one of his favorite local seafood restaurants, and then there was his mother's cooking which he had not experienced for the past few months. The thudding sound of the pump indicated his tank was full. Placing the nozzle back into the pump he started across the lot to the rustic building nestled in a group of tall oak trees. A twelve-ounce fountain Coke sounded good.

He entered through the double glass doors and looked around Niebocks. He hadn't been in the store for nearly a year, but it looked just the way he recalled. The wooden counter on the right backed up with shelves of handmade sweet grass baskets, the back wall was lined with glass wall-to-ceiling coolers containing varied beverages from milk to iced tea to beer, wine, and sodas. The middle of the store had two long rows of shelves stocked with chips, pretzels, and other assorted snacks. The front wall was lined with other grocery and household products. Max walked to the far wall and spotted what he needed. Next to three coffee dispensers, there was a large machine that offered fountain drinks. Selecting a Styrofoam cup, he filled it to the brim, took a short swig, and then topped off the drink. Grabbing a plastic lid and a straw he headed for the front of the store.

At the front counter, he saw his friend, seventy-three-year-old Frederick Niebock. Freddy, as he was called, and his wife Cela owned the market for as far back as he could remember. Frederick and his wife were members of an elite group of African Americans who were descendants of the Charleston slave trade back in the mid-1700s. They became known as the Gullah people. The Gullahs were extremely intelligent and highly skilled and were not used as most slaves had been. They had worked as foremen or held indoor plantation jobs. Their language even still today could only be described as unique, a combination of Creole mixed with African phrases combined with a slight Southern drawl. Waving at his friend, Max offered an enthusiastic greeting, "Freddy…it's so good to see you. How's the wife?"

Flashing Max a wide, toothy grin, the old black man responded, "She be gone ta da big store up da road." Before Max could speak, Freddy went on, "I see ya bok frum de north."

"Yes, I'm back ten days for Christmas break. I'm headed down to Fripp to celebrate the holiday with my folks."

Freddy confirmed Max's statement as he nodded. "Yer mum and dad, da cum by ta see me an' Cela two day ago."

Max laid two one-dollar bills on the counter next to his drink, but Freddy pushed the money back. "Drink on de house as dey say. Merry Tismas!"

"Thanks, Freddy, and a Merry Christmas to you and your wife. I'd like to stay and talk but I've been driving all night. I need to get down to Fripp."

Max turned to leave but was stopped when Freddy held up his right hand and with his left reached beneath the counter and placed a foil-wrapped object on top of the counter. "Cela, she bak sum o' her nana nut bread. You take dis for yer Tismas meal."

Picking up the loaf, Max replied, "I've had Cela's banana nut bread before. This is some good eatin'."

Freddy tilted his head to the side as he looked at the cuts and bruises on Max's face and arms. Taking on a serious tone he remarked in wonder. "What happen at dis school ya go ta in da north? Look like herd o' cattle rund ober ya!"

Max started for the exit. "Nothing to worry over. Just an accident where I work. I'll drop by to see you and Cela before I head back to school. Enjoy the holiday."

Max took a long swig of his drink as he pulled out onto Highway 21 South. He thought about the twenty-minute ride down the Sea Island Parkway as it was referred to. For the past nineteen years, he and his parents had traveled down the parkway countless times on their way to Fripp. He knew every inch of the road that led across St Helena, Harbor, and Hunting Islands. Soon, he would be passing many of his favorite Lowcountry haunts: the Marsh Walk, Boondocks, Johnson Creek Café, the Crab Shack, and the entrance to Hunting Island State Park. Taking another drink he thought, *It's sure good to be home.*

The two-lane highway that led from Ladies Island to Fripp was straight as an arrow except for a long sweeping curve after crossing the Harbor Island Bridge, then it was a straight two-mile stretch. Passing the Hunting Island State Park Entrance Max looked out at the vast salt marsh on his right that faded into the distance. Within ten minutes he'd be pulling up to his parents' Fripp Island getaway.

When he crossed the bridge that spanned Fripp Inlet, he looked at the ocean on his left. The tide was in, and the inlet was dotted with two-foot whitecaps. A group of pelicans swooped down and over the bridge just before he stopped at the guard shack. After swapping some pleasantries with the officer he proceeded down the paved road flanked on both sides with tall palm trees and Palmetto bushes. Aside from an occasional deer or two grazing in the grass next to the road, the area seemed to be deserted. *It's winter here on the island,* thought Max. There were probably few if any vacationers on the six-and-a-half-square-mile island. The island was occupied with just over fourteen hundred homes, most of which were utilized as rental property. He recalled his father telling him there were only about four hundred permanent residents on the island. A golf cart coming in the opposite direction passed by as he waved at the driver. Further down the road a dump truck filled with discarded tree limbs and brush passed.

Slowly driving down Tarpon Blvd, the main road on the island, he looked to his right and left as he drove by numerous homes all of which he had seen countless times over the years. He had his favorites, like the oriental one-story home that seemed to go on forever as it blended back into the trees and thick island foliage. Then there was the two-story home that sat back from the road fronted by a long row of low pier abutments. His favorite was the huge three-story white house which resembled a miniature version of the White House. It was thought to be one of the most expensive homes on the island.

Now on the southwest side of the island, he was on the last stretch of Tarpon where three houses from the end of the island, he pulled into the gravel driveway of his parents' second home. Parking his car beneath the elevated beige-sided ranch, he walked up the wood steps, opened the door, and entered the kitchen where he saw his mother standing at the sink peeling potatoes. Clearing his throat to gain her attention, he announced while raising his hands to his waist when she turned around. "Ta…Dah. Nanook from the north has returned!"

His mother, wiping her hands on an apron, was about to speak but then stared at his face and then his arms. Following what seemed like seconds of silence, she placed her hands on her hips and asked. "What in the world happened to you? You look like you went through a meat grinder. I send my son away to college and he returns to me months later looking like he went to war!"

Max held out his hands and explained, "It's not as bad as it looks. This happened at work. They took me to the hospital where I got stitched up and medicated. They ran some tests to make sure I didn't suffer a concussion. Everything turned out all right and I was released. Where's Dad?"

Amazed that he had changed the subject so rapidly, his mother answered, "He's at a homeowner's association meeting. He said he'd be back around four. According to your father, they are having a problem with the alligator population here on the island. They are meeting with a man and his sons from Savannah. They specialize in moving or relocating gators if need be."

Max shook his head in wonder and comically remarked, "Relocating alligators! Now there's a job I definitely would not want to do. Listen, if you don't mind, I'm going to take my bag up to the spare room and then take a leisurely walk down on the beach. I might just walk up to Ocean Point." Curious, he asked, "What's on the grill tonight?"

Picking up a potato, Max's mother answered her son's question. "We're going to have steaks with some fresh shrimp. I'm also whipping up some potato salad and baked beans. How's that sound?"

Max headed for the stairway and gestured with his right hand, "That sounds incredible. I haven't had a home-cooked meal since I left for college in August." Hesitating at the bottom of the stairs, he reassured his mother, "If it's all the same I'd rather wait and explain my minor injuries when Dad gets back. If I explain the entire situation to you now, then I'll just have to repeat it all when he shows up."

In agreement, Max's mother held up a paring knife. "Don't be on the beach too long. We'll be eating around five."

Minutes later, sporting his Gettysburg Bullets ball hat, old windbreaker, and flip-flops, he stepped out onto the attached screened-in deck that ran the length of the back of the house. Opening the screen door, he walked across a short elevated three-foot-wide walkway to a set of weathered wood steps that led down to the beach. Placing the flip-flops on the bottom step he stepped onto the beach and wiggled his toes in the semi-warm sand. Taking a long deep breath he breathed in the salty air and looked out at the vast Atlantic spread out before him. High tide was in and the walking area on the beach had been reduced to a six-foot-wide area separating the incoming sea from the twelve-foot stone seawall embankment that protected the homes from storm surges throughout the year. Looking to the east he started up the beach; Ocean Point, his goal, three miles off.

A few yards down the beach he bent down and picked up a seashell that had washed up onto the sand. Inspecting the opposite side of the shell he admired the pinkish-red color of the interior, then flicked the shell back out into the sea. He thought about the shell collection he had back in his room in Summerville. Over the years he had found several unique shells on the beach. Anymore, at least for the past ten years or so, it seemed like Fripp Island had become less of a beach where one could find very many shells. His favorite was the sand dollars. It was a rare occasion to find a sand dollar that was not broken.

Further down the shoreline, the homes were separated from the beach by a wide stretch of dunes and vegetation. Passing by a three-foot high dune Max noticed the remains of a turtle nest. The Loggerhead turtle that had used the nest had long since returned to the sea and hopefully all of her young as well. His mother belonged to the turtle preservation club and when she was on the island walked daily to inspect the nests. How many times had he and his mother walked the beach from June through October saving countless newborn turtles that could not make it to the ocean from the nest? It was now late December and the Loggerhead turtles had returned to the sea until next year when the cycle would repeat itself.

He looked out at the horizon and saw three fishing boats bobbing up and down on the ocean waves. A Navy jet flew over in the distance, no doubt headed for the air base just north of Beaufort. He was more tired than he realized and decided not to walk to Ocean Point. Sitting on a large tree trunk that had been washed up onto the beach, he thought about Elizabeth and how she had told him she had never seen the ocean. Suddenly, he got an idea. Before he left Fripp, he would place some seawater in a small jar along with some sand in another and take it back for her. Maybe he'd even gather up a few shells. If she couldn't come to the ocean, then he would take a small sample of it back for her.

Seated in the sand he leaned back against the old tree, closed his eyes, and relaxed as the late afternoon South Carolina sun beat down on his face. Maybe he'd just take a short beach nap.

The buzzing of his cell phone brought Max back to life as he looked at his watch. It was 3:42 and he had been sleeping on the beach for the last twenty minutes. Retrieving his phone from his jacket pocket he answered, "Hello!"

The familiar voice on the other end replied, "Max…it's Jim…Jim Steadman. I just wanted to call and make sure you got home okay."

Realizing he needed to start back down the beach, Max stood as he confirmed, "Hey Jim…thanks for the call. I did get home all right. I happen to be walking on the beach as we speak. How did everything turn out at Burger Palace…?"

A quarter mile from his parents' house he had to cut through John Fripp condos since the ocean water from the high tide was now three feet deep and crashing into the stone wall. He was now going to have to walk down Tarpon to get back home. Fifteen minutes later he crossed the grass next to their driveway, washed the sand from his bare feet using a water hose, climbed the steps, and entered the kitchen where he heard the music from a radio. Walking through the kitchen and the living room he saw his parents on the screened-in deck, his dad flipping a steak on the grill, his mother going about setting the table. Deciding on a quick shower he went upstairs and disrobed. He had a lot of thinking to do. He had been prepared to tell his parents all about his run-in with Brad and his cohorts at Burger Palace but since Jim's phone call on the beach, now he had some additional information to share with his folks he was not looking forward to.

His shower complete, he threw on a gray sweatshirt, a pair of fresh jeans, and deck shoes, and down the stairs to dinner he went. Entering the screened-in deck, his father was the first to notice his arrival. Pointing a spatula at his son, he remarked, "Ah…Max, your mother told me you were home." Turning one of the steaks on the grill he added, "I hope you're hungry. We'll be ready to eat in less than five minutes. Your mother tells me you have some interesting information about those cuts on your face and arms."

Before Max could respond his mother suggested, "Max, would you be so kind as to go back into the kitchen and bring out the pitcher of iced tea I left on the counter."

Max, not even getting an opportunity to speak since he had stepped out onto the deck nodded and went back inside to retrieve their evening dinner beverage. Back outside he placed the pitcher in the middle of a picnic table next to a bowl of baked beans his mother was stirring.

Stepping back, she inspected the table and motioned for Max to have a seat. "We'll be eating soon." Turning to her husband she asked, "How are those steaks coming?"

Cutting into the side of one of the one-pound, cut slabs of beef, Max's father replied, "I think they're just about done. Within the next couple of minutes, we should all be sinking our teeth into U.S. Certified Grade A medium rare steak."

Max's mother seated herself and followed her husband placing a platter of meat on the table. She bowed her head and blessed the food while Max and his father looked on. Passing the baked beans to Max his father remarked comically, "Your mother told me you wanted to wait until we were all together before you give us an injury report. So, what's the deal?"

Max plopped a scoop of beans on his plate, stabbed one of the steaks, and took a drink of tea. "I already told mother it's not as bad as it looks. It was an accident at work but it's more along the lines of an unfortunate mishap at Burger Palace I came out on the crappy end of. It was the last night of work before I was to head down here. It was around eight o'clock and in walks my roommate Brad and three of his football buddies…"

Interrupting Max, his father spoke up. "You say your roommate Brad. Didn't you tell us right after you found out you were bunking together that he was a bit of an ass?"

"I did say that, but now I have to restate the way I feel about him. "He's a total ass and when I finish up with what happened I hope you'll agree with me."

Max's father cut into his steak and grinned, "Well let's have it then!"

Reaching for the potato salad Max continued with his story. "Anyway, they had all been drinking and it was obvious they had too much. They were loud and obnoxious. They even knocked over a counter display and within the next few minutes ran all of our customers off. I figured the faster I got Brad and his friends their food, the sooner they would eat and leave. Their orders finally came up and I delivered their food to their table. The girl I had working at the counter was rather new and quite frankly scared to death about waiting on them, so I told her to stay at the counter.

"After they got their meals, and everything seemed to be all right, I started to walk off when Brad started in on me telling his cronies that I was a mathematics geek and in general making fun of me. I figured it was just liquor talk so I decided to ignore the comments and walk away but then he said something that was really out of line about a friend of mine. I turned back around and told Brad he had a big mouth and someday someone was going to close it. He stands up and gets in my face and tells me today is not that day and I'm not the one who is going to do it. I could see things were getting out of hand, so I followed your advice, Dad; about how it takes more of a man to walk away from a fight than it does to argue and continue to make things worse. So, as I'm walking away Brad decides to throw his burger at me…"

Max's mother was about to take a bite of steak when she hesitated and spoke in amazement. "This Brad threw food at you?"

"Yeah, he did but I just kept walking away and the next thing I know I'm being pelted with fries."

Max's father chimed in, "And you just kept walking off?"

"That's right, but then Brad made another lewd comment about this friend of mine, and I guess what he said hit me the wrong way because, in the next second, I turned *and hit him!*" Holding up his right hand for effect Max went on, "I hit ol' Brad right on the nose. My hand still hurts. I never knew there was so much blood in one's nose. His face exploded in blood, and he went down like a sack of potatoes. Before I know it I'm tangling with the other three. Tables and chairs were flying and at some point, during the scuffle, I got this black eye. It all happened so fast. I remember being picked up by this one large player, who spun me around and then tossed me into the air. The next thing I know I'm going through Burger Palace's front window.

"I must have passed out because the next thing I can recall is when I woke up on the front sidewalk with a local paramedic jamming some smelling salt under my nose. She informed me I had to go to the hospital to get stitched up and that they were also going to run some tests on me." Pointing at his neck, Max explained, "I had to get five stitches here on my neck. The rest of the cuts and bruises were medicated, and they ran their tests which resulted in me receiving a clean slate. I was released and I drove through the night and now I'm here." Cutting into his steak he took a small bite, sat back, and looked at both of his parents.

Max's parents looked at one another for a second, then Max's father waved his fork at Max and inquired, "I have a question about this friend of yours whom Brad insulted. Who is this friend? Is he one of your classmates? What's his name?"

Max swallowed a bite of steak and replied, "First of all my friend is not a he. My friend happens to be a girl."

Before he could explain further his mother spoke up in amazement, "Hold on here for just a moment. I've been sitting here listening to how you clubbed this Brad character for saying something detrimental about this friend of yours who I just assumed was a male and I couldn't seem to figure out why you would hit your roommate for saying something about another male student. But now it's clear. You say your friend is a girl. When you add those two words together you come up with *girlfriend!* So, I guess your father and I can assume you now have a girlfriend? Not that there's anything wrong with that. I mean you're nineteen years old and in college. I knew at some point you would begin to show interest in the opposite sex."

Max's father jumped in on the revelation. "The situation now does make more sense. You popped this Brad on the kisser to defend the honor of this girl you are dating!"

"Yes, I did but it's not what you guys think. We met at a football game on campus, and I asked her to dinner. She refused but later in the week we ran into each other, and she agreed to go. We're just good friends. We've gone out to eat I guess it's four or five times. We've gone on some long walks around town, and we have quite a bit in common. Her name is Elizabeth, she is studying nursing, and she lives on a farm in a town in Pennsylvania called Lancaster. This is the first time either one of us has been away from home and neither one of us has made a lot of friends. Believe me, it's not a girlfriend-boyfriend situation. Oh, and one other thing about her. She happens to be Mennonite."

Both of his parents stared blankly across the table at him and remained silent until his mother asked, "Mennonite...aren't they religious people, sort of like the Amish?"

Max confirmed, "Yes. The Mennonites are quite religious and are kind of like the Amish but different in many ways. Elizabeth comes from a group called the Black Bumpers which means they can have cars and telephones. In other words, they are more worldly than the Amish or other Mennonite sects. Elizabeth dresses very plainly, kind of like the Amish. She is very beautiful and if you ever get the chance to meet her, I'm sure you would both approve. She can cook, sew, bake, butcher a hog, till a field and several other amazing things that I for one cannot do."

Next, it was Max's father who said, "And where do you think this relationship or friendship, as you call it is going? I mean to hear you talk she sounds like the perfect wife, that is if you're a Mennonite or live on a farm."

"We've already talked about our futures, about how I plan to have my own financial business and how after she graduates, she will return to her community as a nurse but will still no doubt, marry into the Mennonite way of life."

"How do you think she feels about you putting the hurt on this Brad to defend her honor?"

"I'm sure she doesn't even know it happened. Her father picked her up earlier in the day before the incident at Burger Palace occurred. She probably won't find out what happened until she returns to school. When you take the time to think about it, my friendship with her might come to an end. She has told me the Mennonites are opposed to fighting of any sort. They are pacifists. I guess I'll find out when I go back to Gettysburg."

Holding up her glass of tea Max's mother said, "Well I guess now we know what happened and why you look the way you do. By the way, do you know what happened to this Brad and his chums?"

"Just before they loaded me up for my ride to the hospital Jim Steadman, that's my manager, let me know the police arrived on the scene and hauled Brad and the others off to jail, which leads me to the second part of this unbelievable tale. On the drive down here, I had a lot of time to think about what happened and also about what the ramifications would be when I returned to school. I remember thinking it would be nice if this all just disappeared and nothing more was said or done about it.

"To tell you the truth I have no idea what will be waiting for me when I go back to school. But then, when I was out walking on the beach earlier, I received a call from Jim who clarified what it might be like when I return. One of the reasons Jim called was to see if I got home okay, which I told him, I did. He also told me Brad and the other three football players were released on bail and had all gone home for Christmas vacation. He also went on to inform me he had to call the incident into Burger Palace's home office which is in Nashville. He tried his best to explain to his superiors that as far as he was concerned, I had acted in self-defense. They told him they'd get back with him."

Max continued and pushed his plate to the side. "Jim told me he no sooner finished his call with his boss when he got a call from a man by the name of Harmon Sykes who happens to be Brad's father. Harmon Sykes some twenty-five years ago was a student at Gettysburg. He was the star quarterback on the Gettysburg football team four years running, was president of the student council, editor of the school newspaper, and a bunch of other illustrious positions around campus. He was the golden boy on campus back then and still in certain circles is held in high esteem. He graduated first in his class with a degree in business and went on in life to be highly successful. He owns a chain of department stores scattered across the country and also owns several large manufacturing plants. He is said to be a millionaire many times over.

"According to Jim, Brad's father over the years has donated millions of dollars to the college for their building fund. This Harmon goes on to inform Jim that he is now in the process of acquiring a team of lawyers to bring lawsuits not only against Burger Palace but me as well regarding what happened to his son, Brad. He told Jim we would be hearing something from his lawyers after the first of the year, which is right around the corner."

Max's father was about to say something, but Max raised his hand signaling he was not finished. "Right after Jim was finished listening to Brad's father, he gets another call. This one was from his district manager who had been contacted by Burger Palace's home office. Jim went on to tell me he had been instructed to let me go because Burger Palace has a hands-off policy when it comes to their customers. Jim said he hated to let me go because I was the best shift manager he ever had. He said he was sorry but that I might be able to get a job with Battlefield Pizza right there in Gettysburg which is owned by a friend of his. He said he would put a good word in for me if I was interested. Oh, and one other thing I forgot to mention. On my way down here, I stopped at a truck stop for a bite and while I was using the restroom, someone stole that new Navy P-coat you bought me, Mom. Aside from all that, I'm home and things are looking up!"

Max's father laid down his fork and got up from the table. "I don't know about anybody else but I'm getting a beer."

"Make that two," said Max's mother.

During his father's short absence, Max's mother sat back and looked out at the ocean and then back to her son. "Boy, you're just full of surprises. I'm upset because someone stole your coat but at the moment that seems to be the least of your problems. I can't believe they fired you from your job."

Max's father, who was now back on the deck and had overheard the tail end of his wife's comment walked over and handed her an open beer. "Your stolen coat is not that big of a deal and as far as losing your job goes, well that's life. You can always get a new coat and another job, but this lawsuit business has me concerned. You say this Jim stated Brad's father and his team of lawyers could be meeting with you after the first of the year. Like you said, that happens to be right around the corner. No son of mine is going to walk into a meeting that includes Brad, his father, and a team of slick lawyers. If you attend this meeting without legal counsel, they'll chew you up and spit you out. We need to get you in touch with a lawyer and I know just the person, Rich Mathers."

Max's mother jumped in on the conversation, "Where have I heard that name before? Isn't he one of your Civil War friends?"

"Yes, he is. You remember Rich. We went to an outing at his house this past summer over in Mt Pleasant."

"Yeah, now I remember him. He has the twin girls…right?"

"That's right. He is not only a good attorney but is a partner in a large law firm in Charleston. I'm going to give him a call and see if we can get together before you head back to school. While I'm thinking about it, I'm going to give him a call right now. I guarantee you, son. You're not going to have to face this situation alone. When the time comes, we'll be there with you."

CHAPTER SIX

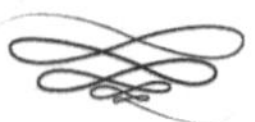

The morning sun passing through the partially open Venetian blinds created a striped effect on the dark bedroom wall. Max sat on the edge of his bed, stretched, and yawned, then slipped on a pair of socks he had draped over the bottom of the footboard. He got up, went to his dresser, and threw on a sweatshirt, then walked to the door that led out to the second-floor veranda of his parent's Summerville home. Stretching again, he sat in a wicker rocker and looked across the backyard where a neighborhood park butted up to their property. Between the tall pines, he could see several locals, walking their dogs, riding bikes, or just out for a morning stroll. According to the weatherman he had watched the previous evening before turning in, the forecast for the day was clear skies and a temperature in the mid-seventies. He imagined that back in Pennsylvania there was a drastic difference in the weather conditions: snow, ice, cold winds, and freezing temperatures.

His daydreaming was interrupted by his mother's voice when she stepped out on the veranda. "Good morning, son. Looks like it's going to be a lovely day." Sitting in a matching wicker chair she offered Max one of two cups of coffee. "Here; I thought you might like a cup."

Max yawned and asked, "What time is it?"

"Just after eight. You slept longer than usual. Don't forget you and your father have an appointment with that attorney Mr. Mathers this morning."

"That's not scheduled until eleven. That's almost three hours from now. I've got plenty of time to get ready."

Max's mother walked to the railing, turned, and faced her son while taking a sip of coffee. "In one sense you're correct in what you say about having plenty of time and then on the other hand, you don't have all that much time."

In confusion, Max stared back at her. "Either I'm not fully awake yet or I don't understand what you're saying."

"What I'm saying is you do have enough time to get ready for your meeting with this lawyer today, but what about this other meeting that is to take place right after the start of the year…the one with Brad's father and his team of lawyers? It's now December 27th, two days after Christmas, and in less than a week, it'll be the New Year. You'll be heading back to Pennsylvania on January 2nd without even knowing when the meeting up there is to take place. You could be facing the possibility of being sued the first week in January or it might not take place until later in the month or maybe even the next month. My point is, your father and Rich Mathers only have a few days to prepare a defense."

Max waved off his mother's concern. "I'm sure before I leave for Gettysburg, we'll have a plan put together. I'm not worried. Dad claims Mathers is a good attorney. I think we'll be ready for Brad's father and his lawyers when the time comes."

Max's father glanced at his watch as he pulled out of their subdivision. "It's just after ten-thirty. Our meeting with Rich is scheduled for eleven at the Navy Pier for lunch."

"The Navy Pier," exclaimed Max, "one of my favorite restaurants in Charleston. I hope they still have their French onion soup. Mom and I were talking this morning. She feels like we don't have much time to come up with a solid defense."

"I think we'll be fine. I talked with Rich the other night on the phone for over an hour. He told me he has a couple of ideas, but he needs to get all the information as to what happened before he can put together a plan. That's what the meeting today is about, so make sure when he asks you questions that you don't leave anything out. If we expect to go up against Brad's father and his attorneys with a loaded gun, we're going to need all the ammunition we can muster."

Parked in a municipal lot one block from the Navy Pier, Max and his father walked down Concord Avenue then up the wide, slightly elevated concrete walkway leading to the popular downtown restaurant. Inside the front entrance, they approached a hostess stand where a young girl greeted them. "Good day, gentlemen. Will there just be the two of you?"

Max's father answered, "Actually there will be three of us. We are meeting our third party here at eleven. He might already be here. His name is Richard Mathers."

The hostess grabbed two menus and gestured for them to follow. "I believe Mr. Mathers is already seated out on the deck. If you will follow me."

Out on the sprawling deck, they trailed the girl to the far corner where a tall, suited man with long hair fashioned in a ponytail stood and waved. "Charley…Max!" Looking at his watch he went on, "Right on time." Shaking Max's father's hand and then Max's, Rich commented, "What's it been since I've seen you two…five months?"

Charley took a seat at the oval wooden table and responded, "I guess that's about right. Let's see, it was back in the last weekend of July when you and I went with the rest of our reenactment regiment up to Georgia and then two weeks later our family attended the bar-b-que at your place."

Rich looked Max up and down and complimented him, "You look like you're doing well. I'm a little jealous. Gettysburg happens to be one of my favorite towns. I so enjoy going there for their annual reenactment. Now, that you are attending college there you can just stroll on over to the battlefield anytime you choose."

Max, taking a seat at the table glanced out at the Charleston River. "I never really thought about it quite that way, but I guess you're right. It is the perfect place to live for a Civil War buff."

Seated, Rich gestured at the table. "I took the liberty of ordering us a pitcher of iced tea. If you care for something else to drink, we can call our waiter over."

Charley, who was now seated waved his hand. "Iced tea is fine with me."

Max agreed as he poured himself a glassful. "Tea it is then."

Rich pushed a menu off to the side and remarked. "I thought maybe we could get started on Max's situation first, then later on we can order lunch, that is unless you two are hungry now."

Charley tapped his stomach. "Max and I had breakfast a couple of hours ago so if we eat later, it won't be an issue. So, where do we get started on this?"

Rich lightly clapped his hands once and then rubbed them together as he addressed Max. "Your father and I had quite the conversation the other evening. He told me everything that happened. That being said, I would like to hear your version of the incident in your own words. It's not that I question your father's information, it's just that whenever someone passes on something they have been told they tend to change the story just a tad here and there. This is not done on purpose, it's just a natural reaction to place one's spin on what they hear."

Placing a small recorder on the table, Rich went on to explain, "I intend to record your entire recap of the incident and related topics so I can then with your help put together an action plan to combat this Brad Sykes and his father. Now, I need you to tell me everything that happened from just before Brad and his buddies entered the Burger Palace, your confrontation with these boys followed by your unfortunate flight through the front window, your trip to the hospital, and what went on there. I also need to hear about how you felt during the drive down here to South Carolina and finally, the call you received on the beach where you learned about the fact you lost your job and that you could be sued. Be as detailed as you can. I am going to need every shred of evidence we can come up with to use against this Brad character."

Max looked at his father, swallowed a swig of tea, and then began, "Well, it was a typical weeknight at the Palace. Not all that busy, just a steady flow of customers. I remember looking at the clock when Brad and his cronies strolled in. It was 8:05. They were loud and it was obvious they had been drinking…"

Thirty-five minutes later Max ended his run-down of the entire situation. "After I received the call on the beach about the potential lawsuit from Jim Steadman, my manager, I walked back home and laid all this crap on my parents. My dad suggested I might need some legal help, so…here we are!"

Rich turned off the recorder and remarked, "What you have told me pretty much is in alignment with what your father revealed to me." Tapping the recorder, he continued, "Hopefully, this information will assist us in putting together a solid legal plan. I say this with reservation because the way I see this the cards are kind of stacked against us."

"I don't understand," said Max. "How could anything in this situation be against us…or I guess I should say…me? I was just doing my job when Brad and his so-called friends walked in. They were drinking…I wasn't! They were loud and obnoxious…I wasn't! For crying out loud. I was thrown through a plate glass window! How could anything be in Brad's favor? I acted in self-defense!"

Rich took on a tone of professionalism as he answered, "You would think with all things being equal the result of doing what's right would fall in your corner, but in this case, all things are not equal. We have to consider who this Brad Sykes is and that is based on who his father is. Harmon Sykes is not just a Gettysburg College alumnus…he is one of the most important alumni the school has. Some twenty-five years ago he led their school football team to four undefeated conference seasons, which led to two state championships. He truly is, as you have stated, the golden boy of the school.

"After graduating he went on to be quite successful in business and today is a millionaire many times over. He has contributed millions of dollars to the school over the years which gives him a say on how the school is run… to a point. In some cases, if Harmon Sykes says jump the school is going to say…how high? What I'm saying is the school administration is not going to throw Brad Sykes under the bus. This does not mean they are going to run roughshod over you either, but they are not going to give you any special considerations."

"I get that," said Charley, "but we are still talking self-defense here. Doesn't that stand for something?"

"Normally," said Rich, "yes. But in this case, it doesn't hold much water. Let me explain what self-defense is. First of all, it's a term or phrase we the public toss around all the time. Self-defense is an action taken by an individual triggered by an emotion of fear of being harmed. In other words, we feel our life is in danger, so we strike out to protect ourselves. Let me ask you this, Max. At what point during this confrontation did you feel your life was in danger? Was it after Brad threw food at you or after he made the comments about this Elizabeth King?"

"Neither," remarked Max. "The moment when I was hoisted into the air and then tossed toward the front window, I had a brief moment of being harmed, but other than that, I never feared for my life."

"That's my point. If this case goes before a judge and we plead self-defense, based upon what happened the judge will not rule in your favor. You claim you felt your life was in danger just before you went through the window. Correct me if I'm wrong, but this happened after you hit Brad Sykes. And while we're on this particular subject, even if you felt like your life was in danger from food being tossed at you, that boat would not float either. In my mind, the only manner in which food is thrown at someone that would endanger their life would be if they were tied to a tree and stoned, so to speak, to death with apples. Being pelted with a cheeseburger and a handful of fries does not constitute one's life being in danger. And, another thing, you can't plead self-defense because of the comments he made about Elizabeth King. In short…you screwed up when you decided to hit Brad. You should have just kept on walking away. I realize you may have not been thinking clearly at the moment and reacted out of frustration to not only what was said but everything that happened since Brad and his cronies walked into the place."

Charley spoke up and sat back in wonder. "You make it sound like we don't have a snowball's chance in hell of not being sued!"

"To be honest with both of you," said Rich, "the way things stand, you very well may get sued…but for how much? That's the quandary we face."

Max, in disbelief, spoke up, "So what you're saying is we can't win."

"In a sense…yes. You hit a person out of frustration, and they are not going to have any problem proving that. Let me explain. By Burger Palace letting you go, well that's not going to bode well for you. Sykes' lawyers will be armed with the paperwork they acquire from Burger Palace stating they fired you. A judge would have to agree that even your employer felt what you did was wrong. Why else would they let you go? But, let me say this. There may be a course of action we can pursue which may level the playing field."

"Sounds like you have something up your sleeve," said Charley.

"Up my sleeve! Now there's a term that does not and never has applied to my legal abilities. What I have in mind is not illegal, shady, or underhanded. What I am proposing is we take the information we possess, even though it may not be the greatest, and utilize it to our advantage. It's not always the truth that wins a case but at times it's the perception of the events as they took place."

Max looked at his father and then at Rich. "I don't quite understand."

"It's a rather simple approach, but before I get into exactly what I think we should do let me ask? Why do you think Brad's father, this Harmon Sykes, a man who has made millions in the business world be interested in suing a college freshman, namely you?"

Max thought and then answered, "I suppose because I hit his son?"

"Yes, but there is probably more to it than that. He'll sue Burger Palace because they are a national company with ample money in their coffers.

Large companies, in most cases, will want to avoid having their name on the front page when it comes to something like this. It's just easier for them to settle out of court and then go on with business. When it comes to the reason for the lawsuit against you it's a matter of who he and his son are and who *you are!* Harmon Sykes was without a doubt the man about campus, a star to say the least when he attended school at Gettysburg. His former college days combined with his business success label him as a man, who for lack of a better phrase, wears armor that is untarnished and not dented in any form. When you hit his son, whether you realize it or not you tarnished his armor, put a serious dent in it, so to speak. He can't and won't accept that…hence he threatens you with a lawsuit."

Charley moved uncomfortably in his chair as he inquired, "How much can Brad's father sue my son for?"

"When it comes to lawsuits there are no specific guidelines. When people are being sued or are attempting to sue someone else the figure that normally comes to mind is one million dollars. In Max's case, no judge would award that amount based on what happened. Harmon Sykes and his lawyers can't sue you because Brad has suffered a loss of income from a job because he probably doesn't even have a job. I'd say there's a better-than-average chance he is living off his father's money. You can't be sued because Brad cannot play football, whether he is suspended for several games or because of his injuries. Playing college football does not fall into the category of a job position. The only thing Sykes is going to be able to sue you for more than likely are his son's medical expenses."

Max held up his right hand. "And what could that amount to?"

"I can't say for sure, but we do have an idea. I took the liberty of calling my wife's sister who happens to be a nurse here in Charleston. I asked her to give me an estimate on what medical expenses would be to repair a broken nose. She went on to say the expenses could vary depending on the severity of the injury. For instance, the nose is near the eyes, the jaw, and even the teeth. What she is saying is when you popped Sykes on the nose you very well could have caused damage to one or both of his eyes. You could have broken his jaw or created dental problems. As far as repairing a broken nose is concerned it could run from a few grand up to twenty thousand. When you consider the possibility of some of the other potential injuries she mentioned, we could be talking forty-fifty grand, maybe a hundred thousand. It depends on the damage resulting from your fist slamming into Brad's face.

Look, a hundred thousand dollars to Harmon Sykes is chump change but to folks like you and me, that's quite a financial hit. What we need to do is come up with a plan that will diminish or cut down on the amount a judge will award them for damages."

Charley, concerned over possibly being sued for a hundred thousand let out a long breath and then asked, "And how do we go about cutting into this amount?"

"It's very simple and therefore my idea might just work. Max, you said this Brad character is a constant wiseass, always making off-color comments, being rude, and the like. What we have to do is turn his smartass demeanor into an advantage for us. We accomplish this by making him look worse than he is. For instance, his father and his lawyers will admit Brad was drinking. What we have to do is escalate this admission from simply drinking to being drunk. They will claim Brad was loud. We have to change from loud to rude and obnoxious. Do you see where I'm going here?"

"I think I'm starting to get the idea. We need to take mischievous and turn it into really bad…even horrible actions on his part."

"That's exactly right. Whatever Brad's lawyers come up with we need to keep going back to the fact that Brad and his friends provoked the entire situation. Didn't you say Brad knocked over and destroyed a counter display?"

"Yeah, he did, but he could say it was an accident."

"Yes, he can, but it still shows he had no regard for Burger Palace's property. In all actuality, he destroyed public property. It's a small insignificant matter but when we add that to everything else, he did while there it just adds another log to the fire. You said the counter girl Cindy, got to the point where she was afraid to come out from behind the counter because of the way Brad and the others were acting and what they were saying… correct?"

"Yes, she was scared to death. I wouldn't be surprised if she quit. She was new and had only been on the job for less than a week."

"We have to establish from the moment Brad and the other three football players entered Burger Palace that they created a mood of discomfort for all who were there. Didn't you say that a family came inside the Palace but upon seeing and hearing Brad and his friends turned around and left? Correct me if I'm wrong but you also stated when these boys were seated, they took a chair from a nearby table that was occupied and informed those sitting there they were taking it and it didn't make any difference what they thought. Then there was that old man, a regular customer who approached Brad and told them he thought they should leave. Brad gets up and gets in the man's face calls him an old fart and tells him to get the hell out of the restaurant."

"Yes," said Max. "Those instances are all true."

"These moments, if presented properly might convince a judge that Brad and the others were a public nuisance, combined with disorderly conduct and public drunkenness." Snapping his fingers, Rich continued, "We could also counter-sue Brad. We can sue him for your loss of employment. And there are your medical expenses. Let's not forget that you were thrown through a plate glass window. That falls under aggravated assault, yet another charge. You had to be taken to the hospital where you were stitched up and medicated. They had to run tests on you to make sure you did not suffer a concussion. Your medical expenses may not equal Brad's, but they can cut into the amount he may be awarded. Who knows, if we go after Brad the judge may call the entire situation a wash and you might walk out of there without having to pay a cent. This is the best defense I think we have. If we try and go the self-defense route, we'll get eaten alive."

Charley gave his son a look of approval at which Max simply nodded.

Rich, in his desire to assure Max that they had a good plan in the works confirmed. "It's now December 29th and in four days you will be heading back to Gettysburg. I know I just threw a lot of legal jargon at you so let me take two days and put all this together. We can meet again on the thirty-first to go over everything so that when you go back to school you'll be prepared for when you are notified about the upcoming meeting with Brad's attorneys. Speaking of that you are going to have to prepare yourself for a different school environment."

Confused, Max probed, "What do you mean…different?"

"What I mean is just this. Gettysburg is a small community as is the college. At one time I suppose Gettysburg was considered to be a quaint town but through the years it has grown. That being said, it is still a somewhat small community and when something happens it stands to reason everyone in town will find out. The same is true of the campus. When something like what you have just gone through happens it can spread across campus like wildfire. I mean…think about it. A regular in-line student, in this case, a mathematics student punches a football player in the face and takes him out with one blow. This is highly unusual, to say the least. I know this because I played football in both high school and college. College schools can have up to one hundred and twenty-five active players on their football team. These players form a bond; they train together, eat together, many of them live together, they win and they lose together. In other words, they are like a giant family. They support one another in every aspect of their lives unless a player does something highly illegal. The Gettysburg football players are not going to ostracize one of their own because he was simply drinking, knocked over a display, and was rude. What I'm saying is you could have an entire football team that will not look upon you favorably. Didn't you say you were rooming with Brad?"

"Well, I was when I left. I'm not sure about now."

"If he is still staying in the same room you are going to return to, well that can't be. This can only lead to further verbal confrontations or maybe even additional physical problems between the two of you. I'll make some phone calls to the college and see what I can find out. If Brad has moved out, then fine. If he hasn't then you'll have to move. Something else. Is Brad in any of your classes?"

"No, he is not."

"Other than in your room, do you have occasion to run into him around campus?"

"That depends. There are days when I run into him three or four times and then there are three or four days in a row when I don't see him."

Rich raised his hand to make his next point, "You must avoid contact with him. If you see him around, then you need to go in a different direction. If he approaches you and wants to talk, just tell him you have nothing to say. From the moment you step back on campus, you need to avoid him. And what about this Elizabeth King? You stated that she couldn't possibly know about what went on at the Palace."

"That's correct. Like I said, she's a Mennonite. She does not have a cell phone and the only phone on the farm where she lives is out in the barn. I couldn't contact her by phone if I wanted to."

"Let me ask you this? When is she returning to school?"

"We talked about that the day she left to head back home. She will be returning on January 1st, the day before I get back."

"This could pose a problem. It would be better if we could contact her and let her in on what happened, but you claim that isn't possible."

"That's right. I only know she lives in Lancaster on a farm. I don't know the address or where it's located. Besides that, that would not go down well. She has not told her parents about our relationship, as innocent as it is. If I were to contact her it would only cause problems for her with her family. I guess I'll just have to wait until we meet after we're both back."

"You do realize," emphasized Rich, "that by her arriving back on campus the day before you get back, there is a distinct possibility she will find out what happened at the Burger Palace before you have an opportunity to speak with her. If this occurs, she may get a shadowed or disguised version of what happened. Like I said before, Gettysburg is a small conservative college and when the news about what happened between you and Brad leaks out and I'm sure it already has, it will be what students talk about. Let me ask you, Max, during this what you claim to be an innocent friendship, have you two been seen together around campus?"

"Of course, we have. We usually meet at the large fountain at the main entrance. This is an area where a lot of students congregate. I have no doubt we've been seen together there as well as walking around the school grounds. We've probably been seen downtown at different restaurants. Like I said, it's all very innocent."

"That's not my point," said Rich. "What people see and what is going on can be two very different things. You and the King girl may be just great friends, but other students may view you as a couple. Perception can be a very misleading thing. I just hope by the time you get to speak with her she hasn't been poisoned by school rumors or the spin others will no doubt place on what happened at the Burger Palace. I mean, think about it. She goes back home for Christmas break and then returns unaware of what happened between you and Brad. She could get blindsided with what others have heard which may not be that accurate. By the time you get to speak with her, she may have already formed an opinion, especially if she hears you hit your roommate because of what he said about her. She may wind up feeling somewhat responsible."

Max objected as he held up his right hand. "I don't think she'll form an opinion until she speaks with me. She happens to be very level-headed and is not one to judge others. On the other hand, as a Mennonite, she has been raised as a pacifist. The Mennonites do not believe in violence of any nature so I'm not sure how she will view the fact I clobbered Brad Sykes. Even though I defended her honor, my pugilistic actions at Burger Palace might put a damper on our relationship."

"Well, whenever you wind up finally speaking to her, you need to make her realize even though she is not the one being sued she still has to travel the same road you are, at least until this upcoming meeting has taken place. She, like you must avoid contact with Brad Sykes and talking with others about the situation."

Picking up one of the menus Max stated, "After I discuss this with her, I'm sure she'll understand and if there is nothing else then I say we order some lunch."

On the outskirts of North Charleston Max's father turned onto Route 26 North while asking his son. "So, tell me. What did you think about our meeting with Rich? Do you feel it was productive? How do you think it went?"

Max looked at Charley and gestured in doubt. "I think the meeting went okay. It was different, but I think we made some progress. I have to admit it was strange. We have both sat through various types of meetings but never one where you have to come up with a defense because you're in danger of being sued. I guess the number one thing about the meeting is that I feel better about going back to school and having to face Sykes and his lawyers. I'm kind of concerned over Elizabeth returning before I get back and possibly receiving bogus information about what happened."

Charley adjusted the sun visor as he asked, "What are your plans for the rest of the day?"

"I thought I might take a drive over to Folly Beach and walk for a couple of hours. I've got a lot to think about. When I get back to Gettysburg if I do any walking it will no doubt be in freezing temperatures in slush or snow. Once back at school I won't be back home until spring break so I want to get as much beach time in as I can before I leave."

CHAPTER SEVEN

Max drove over the Maryland-Pennsylvania Border, or what was more commonly referred to as the Mason-Dixon Line, an imaginary border separating not only the two states but the north from the south. According to history, back in the late 1700's Charles Mason and Jeremiah Dixon surveyed the area to resolve a border dispute between the two states. Later on, before the war, the Mason-Dixon Line was a demarcation separating the northern free states from the southern slave states. Not even a mile into Pennsylvania it started to spit snow and Max nodded his head in confirmation that he indeed was back in the cold north, the warm weather, and pleasant beaches of South Carolina hours behind him.

Within the next hour, he would be arriving in Gettysburg. For the past eight hours, he had done a lot of thinking. He and his father had met with Rich Mathers on the thirty-first as planned to go over their defense against Harmon Sykes and his lawyers. He still had no idea when the meeting with them was to take place, but Rich and his father had assured him when the call came, all he had to do was notify them and they would be on the first possible flight to Harrisburg where they would rent a car and then drive to Gettysburg. Rich told him not to worry; they had his back. Rich had some good news to share with him, explaining he had contacted the housing administration office on the Gettysburg campus, who as it turned out was aware of the confrontation between Max and Brad. Rich's concern over the two freshmen rooming together was put at ease when the administration director explained that Brad's father had phoned the school and requested his son be moved to other living quarters.

His thoughts turned to the fact that Elizabeth had arrived on campus yesterday, the day before he was to return. He realized all of the students would not be back on campus, but it only took one person to inform her about the incident between him and Brad. She was so innocent and would be an easy target for lies and rumors. Even if she learned the truth about what happened he was not sure how she was going to react. There was nothing he could do to prevent any of that at the moment. He would just have to wait until they met as planned tomorrow afternoon at the fountain.

Suddenly, it occurred to him that he hadn't given Brad all that much thought during his short stay in South Carolina. He, his father, and Rich had mainly focused on Brad's father, his team of lawyers, and the upcoming lawsuit. He hadn't thought about it but the potential lawsuit might not have even been Brad's idea. It might all be his father's doing. He wondered what Brad could be thinking?

Brad reclined in a comfortable brown cushioned chair while sipping a Coke. Dressed in a pair of sweatpants and flip-flops, a large towel was draped around his neck and partially covered his bare muscular chest. Adjusting a pair of expensive sunglasses on his face he gazed out of the elevated glassed-in swimming pool of the Cayuca Country Club. The Cayuca Lake spread out to the east and west, a large section of the immense body of water was frozen over and cordoned off where skaters moved here and there.

Taking another drink, Brad noticed one of his former high school friends approaching his table. The boy, sporting a Cornell University sweatshirt gave Brad a casual wave and took a seat on the opposite side of the table.

Reaching across he greeted his longtime friend. "Brad, heard you were back for Christmas break. The word around the club is you had some sort of accident down there in Pennsylvania."

Brad removed the sunglasses while displaying his face; both eyes blackened, a bandage taped over his discolored and bruised nose. "It happened at a burger joint near campus. I got into an argument with, believe it or not, my roommate. I threw a cheeseburger at him, and he sucker-punched me. I didn't have a chance, Ted. My nose is broken and because of my injuries, I can't play football for at least the next four games. The doctor said depending on how the healing goes I might have to sit the rest of the year out."

"That's too bad," said Ted. "You and I have been playing football ever since we played Pop Warner back when we were seven. We played high school ball together and then after we graduated, I stayed right here in Ithaca and went to Cornell on a scholarship, and you went off to Gettysburg College. When you think about it we've been playing ball for eleven years. That's over half of our life to date."

"You were the lucky one," said Brad. "You got to stay right here in Ithaca and my father shipped me off to Pennsylvania to play at the school he attended."

"That's right, I forgot. Your dad was the starting quarterback for Gettysburg for four years. Gave the school two state championships. Those are hard shoes to fill."

"I'll never be the player my father was and that's not the main reason why he sent me off to further my education. If he's told me once he's informed me a hundred times, it's imperative I get my business degree and then after I graduate from college, I'll be working for him at one of his many businesses. He is quite adamant that down the road I'll be prepared to step in and run his business affairs after he is no longer able to do so."

"So, what happened to this roommate of yours who popped you on the kisser?"

"I'm not sure. I haven't seen him since our altercation. I assume he went home for Christmas break. My father has every intention of suing him for damages."

"Really. How much is he suing for?"

"I don't know. Right now, that's between my father and his lawyers. They haven't filled me in on that part of the process. They did say they'd let me know before a settlement meeting they are planning to have with my attacker, but I gotta tell ya. I don't care how much they sue that bastard for hitting me. That won't satisfy me. If it's the last thing I do, I intend to get even."

"Is that a wise choice? That could lead to even more trouble. If I were you, I'd just go with the lawsuit and move on. Why would you even worry about this so-called roommate of yours? Think about it! Your folks live in a three-million-dollar lakefront mansion, and they have more money than the man on the moon. You're driving a brand-new Corvette, have the best clothes money can buy, and speaking of money, you've always got plenty of cash in your pocket. It sounds to me like your father has a rather successful future planned for you. Why worry about this guy? I say sue him and move on."

"That's easy for you to say. You weren't there, Ted, and besides, that's not all there is to it. You're a football player. You know how it is. Playing football is a man's game. You hit and you get hit. It's a rough game and you and I have been at it now for over a decade. Do you remember in high school how all the girls wanted to date us...and why? Because they placed us up on a pedestal. We as football players were the tough ones and nobody messed with us. It's the same way in college...you're on a pedestal. Back down there in Gettysburg when my roommate, this mathematics clown, took me out with one punch he knocked me off my pedestal. Back there on campus, I'm a joke and the other players on the team laugh at me. I've got a score to settle with Max Miller and like I said. I'm going to make sure he pays and pays dearly. I have no doubt my father and his lawyers will sue Miller, but that's not good enough for me. I want personal satisfaction."

Ted stood, reached out, and shook Brad's hand. "I've known you since you were three years old. When you set your mind to something you always accomplish it. Just be careful. I've got a scheduled tennis match at one o'clock. I better get moving. I'll see you next time you're in town."

Brad watched his friend walk off. Reaching into his sweatpants he withdrew a sliver whiskey flask and poured a small portion of alcohol into his remaining Coke. Thanks to his father's large liquor cabinet which housed an ample supply of bourbon, Brad smiled and thought, *You've got something coming, Max Miller. I'm not sure exactly what, when, or how I'm going to get even...but it's coming!*

It was just after six o'clock when Max pulled through the main gate of the college. The further he had driven into Pennsylvania the more evident the presence of winter became, six inches of snow covering the ground, icicles hanging from gutters and tree limbs. Parking in the large student lot he grabbed his small suitcase and began the walk to his dorm just up the street. From the small number of cars in the lot and the lack of students walking about on the campus grounds it was evident most of the students had still not returned. A stiff wind blew down the street as he adjusted the collar of his new Navy P-coat. His mother, feeling bad because of the theft of his coat, purchased him an after-Christmas gift with the new coat.

It wasn't even three minutes when he walked through the large wooden door of his dorm. The main lobby was devoid of any students and reminded him of a ghost town. Normally the dorm lobby was filled with male students sitting on chairs and couches as they read books, gazed at laptops, or talked on cell phones. Climbing two flights of stairs he made a right, walked down three doors, and was about to remove his room key from his pocket when he noticed the door slightly open. Max's head dropped in despair. The only other key holder to the room was his former roommate. The last thing he needed was a confrontation with Brad Sykes.

He opened the door slowly and peered into the room where he saw someone with their back to him standing by Brad's bed. From the back, it appeared to be Brad but then he noticed the shaggy blond hair and realized that the intruder was not Brad. Clearing his throat to get the stranger's attention, the blond-haired individual turned, smiled, and approached Max with an extended hand. "Why hello there. I'm guessing you're Max Miller."

Before Max could say anything, the muscular lad grabbed his hand and pumped it twice. "Name's Scott Cable…your new roommate. You are Miller, I assume?"

Max released his hand and spoke, "I am Max Miller and that's one hell of a handshake you've got there."

"Sorry," said Scott. "Sometimes I forget my strength. I'm a wrestler and keeping in tip-top shape has been a way of life for me since I was in Junior High."

Max walked to his bed and tossed his suitcase on the mattress while removing his coat. "Well, if you're staying here at this dorm, you must be a freshman…just like me. I don't recall ever seeing you around campus."

"That's because today is my first day here at Gettysburg. I transferred in from Hofstra University."

Max opened the suitcase, removed a small stack of socks, and then walked to a nearby dresser. "I've heard of Hofstra. That's a pretty good school…isn't it? Where is it located?"

"It's in Long Island, New York. That's where I'm from. They gave me a full scholarship for four years for wrestling. Don't mean to blow my own horn but last year I was the New York State High School Wrestling Champ. My two older brothers wrestled at Hofstra so when it came time for me to go to college, I thought I'd just keep my further education in the family. Besides, the wrestling coach who recruited me coached my brothers. Then, out of nowhere, he is accused of molesting a young girl years ago. There was quite the scandal around school and well you know how things go. Because of what our coach had done years in the past, we, the entire wrestling squad, were not well received around campus. This went on for about a month and

I decided to transfer here to Gettysburg where they happen to have a pretty decent wrestling program. That's my story…what's yours?"

Placing some tee shirts and briefs in the dresser, Max responded, "I'm from down near Charleston, South Carolina. I'm a mathematics student and you are now one of a small number of students who know me by name. After I graduate, I plan on opening my own financial business. So, tell me, aside from wrestling what are you majoring in?"

"I'm hoping to get a degree in business. I don't want to wind up like a lot of college athletes who spend four years at college and then graduate with no skill set." Snapping his fingers Scott tapped himself on his forehead. "I almost forgot. I wasn't even here in the room for maybe ten minutes or so when some girl dropped by asking for you. She said her name was Elizabeth. I have to admit she was quite unusual. I think she may have been Amish. She had these magnificent eyes. Anyway, she gave me a note to give to you. I put it over there by the television."

"What did the note say?"

"I don't know. Figured it wasn't any of my business. Just laid it over there."

Max walked over and scooped up a folded piece of paper from the top of the television, unfolded it, and silently read the printed note.

Max,
I must see you as soon as possible. Come see me at my dorm!
Elizabeth

Putting his coat back on Max placed the note in his pocket and apologized, "I'm sorry Scott. I'm going to have to cut our conversation short. I need to get in touch with Elizabeth and straighten something out. Tell you all about it when I get back."

"Don't worry about it," said Scott. "Over the next few days, weeks, and months we'll have plenty of time to talk."

Minutes later, Max walked past the fountain where he was supposed to meet Elizabeth tomorrow at noon. She had made it clear in the note he contact her as soon as possible. It seemed obvious she had been exposed to the unfortunate matter between him and Brad. Kicking a small piece of ice, he watched as the frozen object skidded up the sidewalk. Sticking his hands deep into his coat pockets he thought, *What could Elizabeth be thinking? What did she hear? How was she going to feel about him now?*

Arriving at Elizabeth's dorm building Max took the length of concrete steps in four strides, hesitated at the front door, ran his fingers through his hair, and smoothed his coat. Next, he took a deep breath and then pressed a buzzer at the side of the door. Seconds passed when a pleasant female voice answered, "May I help you?"

"Yes, you may," said Max. "My name is Max Miller, and I am here to see Elizabeth King. I believe she is expecting me."

The voice responded, "One moment please."

A full minute passed which seemed to Max like an eternity when a buzzer sounded followed by the voice. "You may enter, Mr. Miller."

Max stepped inside the door and found himself in a marble-tiled foyer, a glass chandelier dangling above his head. He spotted a desk to the right of the large room topped with a sign that read:

INFORMATION

He proceeded as he looked around the neat-as-a-pin room. There were only three girls present at the moment, two seated on a couch and the other reading a book in a large comfortable-looking chair in the corner. All of the girls glanced at him but then went back to what they were doing. Crossing the room, he approached the desk and was feeling just a little out of place. He did not doubt that at the moment there was a very distinct possibility he was the only male in the building. Stopping at the desk he noticed a girl with long brunette hair seated at a computer. Removing fashionable glasses from her pleasant face she inquired, "Mr. Miller?"

"Yep, that's me…Mr. Miller. What do I do now?"

The girl nodded toward the center of the room. "If you will just have a seat Elizabeth will be down directly. Would you care for some coffee or a bottle of water?"

"No, I'm fine. I'll just wait over there." He walked across the room and seated himself in a cushioned green chair next to a large window. The girls were no longer paying him any attention and it became evident from time to time that male visitors were a common sight at the dorm. Pulling back a lacy curtain he looked out at the street in front of the dorm and could tell from the light from a nearby streetlight that it had started to rain.

Turning his attention back to the room, he saw Elizabeth as she descended a stairway on the left. Her long blond hair was fashioned as usual in a bun style. Her dress attire was something he had grown accustomed to, a dark brown long dress, buttoned up to the neck and stopping just above her ankles. Black lace-up shoes completed her outfit.

Holding a dark coat folded over her left arm she slowly limped across the carpet, and stopped in front of him, those deep green eyes of hers putting him at ease. "Hello there Max. I see you got my note. I couldn't wait to speak with you at the fountain tomorrow as planned. Something came up I need to discuss with you."

He looked past her and noticed the two girls on the couch as they stared in his direction and leaned toward each other, holding their hands to their mouths as if they were sharing some sort of secret. Did they know he was Max Miller, the mathematics student who had taken down the mighty football player, Brad Sykes?

One of the girls giggled and Elizabeth held out her hand for Max to get up. "Come on, we can't talk here. Let's go somewhere."

Max looked at the window and spoke in a low tone. "It's starting to rain. If we try to walk downtown, we'll be soaked to the skin, but I have an idea where we can go; Glatfelter Hall. This time of year, they always have a fire going in their huge fireplace on the first floor. There's a small café there where we can get something warm to drink if you'd like."

Elizabeth agreed. "That sounds nice. Let's go."

Outside, as they started down the steps she asked, "How far is it to this Glatfelter place?"

"Less than ten minutes. We should be all right. It's not raining that hard."

Walking down the sidewalk, Max asked, "How was your Christmas over there in Lancaster…on the farm?"

"It was very nice to go back home," said Elizabeth. "I got to do many of the things I've grown used to over the years, helping my father with the milking, cleaning out the stalls, helping my mother around the kitchen. I even did some baking. That reminds me. I baked two shoefly pies. I brought one back for my two friends and one for you. I left yours up in my room. I'll give it to you later this week."

Max gave her an odd look. "Shoefly pie. I've never heard of that. What is it?"

"Well, let me see. It's got a cakey texture. It's got a crumb top and it's very gooey…and sweet. My mother says I make the best shoefly in our community. I think you'll like it." Further up the sidewalk, she went on, "Aside from that I did get to spend some time with my best friend Ellen."

"I recall when you spoke of her before. Isn't she the one who married Eli Hoffman, that boy who courted you unsuccessfully?"

"Yes, that's her."

"Did you happen to run across ol' Eli when you were home?"

"Yes, I did. Every year the community celebrates Christmas day at one of the farms in the community. This year it was held at Hoffman's place. According to Ellen, Eli has calmed down quite a bit. A lot of that probably has to do with the fact that she is pregnant, which my father talked with me about for nearly a half hour on the way back here to school. He claims all of my childhood friends are married and are starting to raise families of their own and here I am going off to school, placing myself in danger of being caught up in the ways of this world. If it were not for my mother's support in attending college, I'm not so sure my father would have agreed to my going off to school. How was your short vacation down in Summerville?"

Not wanting just yet to divulge the fact he had not only learned during his short stay in South Carolina about the loss of his job but the fact he was going to be sued, he kept his answer simple. "I spent a few days down on Fripp Island where I celebrated Christmas with my folks then we drove over to Summerville. I spent some time on the beach and enjoyed some great seafood. The thing I liked the most about the time away from school was the warmer weather down south. But now it's the New Year and it's time to get back to my studies. Speaking of that do Mennonites celebrate New Year's Day?"

"Not really, I mean not the way your world does. We don't set off firecrackers and shoot off guns or drink champagne. It's simply just another year. Another cycle in our life. It's another year of plowing the fields and then there is spring planting and on and on."

Max agreed with Elizabeth. "I never thought about it but you're right in what you say. It is simply just another year. On December thirty-first we realize that it is the last day of the year and then later on that day we get down to the last hour, minute, and finally the last second of the year, and then in the blink of an eye it's no longer 2012, but 2013 and what has changed? You and I will be attending the same classes as last year with the same professors and teachers, people who are married are still married to the same spouse, they still have the same job, live in the same house, and drive the same car. It's really all in our heads. Businesses and people alike in October and November always say 'Well, let's wait until the beginning of next year,' before they have to do something or make a decision. It's kind of like a do-over for most folks. People always have these New Year's resolutions they promise themselves they are going to accomplish. People say they are going to stop smoking or lose weight and get in shape, but then a few days, weeks, or sometimes if they are lucky months, they go back to their old ways of smoking or eating everything they can get their hands on.

"When you think about it, it's all pretty ridiculous. Once again, it's all about the mathematics of life. The New Year is just another round of numbers that will pass by, twelve months, three hundred and sixty-five days, twenty-four hours a day, sixty minutes in an hour, sixty seconds in a minute, and so on. And when it comes to the numbers it's the same for all of us whether we live on a farm in Lancaster, Pennsylvania, or in a house in Summerville, South Carolina." Realizing he was rambling, he apologized, "I'm sorry, guess I got off on a tangent. Anyway, here we are, Glatfelter Hall."

Elizabeth followed Max up a short set of steps as she looked up at the towering bell tower. "I've never been in here before."

Max opened the door and explained, "I come here quite often to study in their library."

Once inside Max closed the door and looked across the main room where he saw a maintenance man placing a log on the roaring fire housed in a twelve-foot floor-to-ceiling stone fireplace. The man, while jabbing the fire with a metal poker turned as Max and Elizabeth approached. He gestured at the fire. "You two look like you've been out in the cold rain. Please, have a seat here in front of the fire and get warmed up."

Max walked over and placed his hands in front of the flames. "That's what we had in mind. Been many students in today?"

"Not as many as I thought there would be. I guess most of the student body will be returning in the next day or two." Looking around the empty room, the man remarked, "Looks like you've got the fire all to yourselves… enjoy."

As the man started to walk off, Max inquired, "Is the café still open?"

"Yes, it is, and it'll be open until nine this evening."

Gesturing at the edge of a large couch centered in front of the fireplace, Max addressed Elizabeth. "Why don't you get comfortable here on the couch and I'll get us some hot drinks. Hot chocolate for me and I guess for you…black coffee."

Elizabeth rubbed her hands together as she answered, "Hot coffee sounds good right now."

It wasn't but a few minutes when Max returned with the hot drinks. Placing Elizabeth's coffee on an end table he commented, "This is hot. You might want to wait a bit before you try taking a drink." Sitting on the couch and leaving a space between them Max crossed his legs and took a short sip of the chocolate then looked directly at Elizabeth. "Your note said you wanted to see me as soon as possible. I can only assume you have something you'd like to discuss that couldn't wait until tomorrow." Slightly cocking his head, he waited for her response.

She folded her hands on her lap and cleared her throat, then began, "I wasn't even back on campus but a few minutes when my roommate told me something she heard involving you. She said she had heard you and your roommate, Brad, had gotten into a fight at Burger Palace. She said the story is you hit Brad right in the mouth, clobbered him with one punch, and then you were thrown through the front window of the Palace." Giving Max a blank stare she asked, "Is what I heard true?"

"Two things," said Max. "First…I had a feeling this is what you wanted to speak with me about and second, it is true, but I think you should hear the entire story rather than what someone else heard because there is a reason why I hit Brad."

Elizabeth sipped at the coffee. "Okay then, if you want to share what happened with me, I think that's a good thing."

"All right, here it is. I was working the late shift at the Palace and toward the end of the evening Brad and three of his friends walk in…"

Minutes later, Max finished up, "…After they released me from the hospital, I drove home to South Carolina…spent ten days down there and now I'm back."

Elizabeth sat in silence and drank more coffee. The silence went on for a few seconds when Max broke the ice, "Your silence concerns me. Now that you've heard the whole truth what are you thinking? How do you feel about what happened?"

A few more seconds of silence passed when Elizabeth finally spoke, "This is a lot to take in…"

Before she could finish the sentence Max interrupted, "I realize that, and I also realize you are of the Mennonite Faith. You told me, as a Mennonite you were raised as a pacifist and your faith does not believe in fighting…for any reason. I need to know how you feel about this."

Elizabeth shot Max a quick smile and then explained, "If my father were here, he would not have the slightest hesitation in telling you what you did was wrong. My father was raised in our faith as an old-line Mennonite, and he has never changed. If our farm was invaded by men who meant his family harm, if his entire family was murdered and the farm burnt to the ground and all the livestock destroyed, my father would not even consider retaliation or revenge. He would forgive those responsible and move on. But I, on the other hand, am not my father. In today's world, the Mennonite community has become more exposed to the world. My father has always been very strict with his children but has also taught me to think for myself. Since I've been here at school, I've come to realize that just because my faith, the Mennonite faith, believes life should be lived according to our doctrine, that does not mean people of other faiths or cultures are necessarily wrong in the way they think."

Now it was Max who took on the role of silence. Elizabeth, desiring to offer Max a level of comfort, reached across the couch and touched his right hand. "I feel what you did was wrong, but yet according to you, you hit Brad not because he threw food at you but because of what he said about me. We can still be friends and continue to see one another. I guess in a way I feel indirectly responsible for the incident with your roommate."

"That's ridiculous. Why you were not even there when it happened."

"I am partially responsible for this. Think about it, Max. If we hadn't met at that football game and if I hadn't stupidly knocked my hot chocolate on your lap, none of this would have happened. It was I who sought you out and agreed to go to dinner with you after I initially said no. We were seen together around campus and downtown dining together. I know how people think. They think that we are a couple. If all of the things I mentioned would not have happened, then Brad would have had no reason to say these things about me. So, you see I am responsible. How could I possibly be upset with you for defending my honor when I am the very reason for you striking out at Brad?"

"Look, I can understand the way you must feel, but it was I, not you, who lashed out at Brad Sykes. Looking back, it's hard to explain the reaction I had to Brad's behavior."

Elizabeth agreed and then spoke, "All of my life to date I have been raised by parents who strongly believe in the Holy Bible. You claim everything in life is about the numbers, but I was raised with the belief everything is Bible-related. Like, this situation between you and Brad. It reminds me of the story of David and Goliath. Have you ever heard the story?"

"Yes, I have. Twice, once when I was six years old when I attended Bible school at the church we attend and then ironically just last year at the same church where our pastor preached on the story. When I first heard the story in Bible school it had more of an impact on me than our pastor's rendition. Back in Bible school our teacher, Mrs. James told our class the story. She was very animated. She used a Velcro board and figures while explaining what happened. That was a long time ago and I can't recall everything said but the gist of the story was that David, a mere shepherd boy, was sent by his father to a battlefield where the Israelites and the Philistines were at war.

"David had some brothers who were in the Israelite army. While visiting his brothers he hears this great Philistine warrior; Goliath, a giant of a man standing almost ten foot tall. This Goliath defies the Israelites and informs them to send out a warrior to face him in battle. The entire Israelite army flees in fear because they know they have no one who can stand against Goliath. Much to the surprise of everyone present David walks out onto the battlefield and confronts Goliath and rather than running away he runs toward this giant and with one stone hurled from a slingshot he takes Goliath down. I'm sure there is more to the story than that, but that's what I remember. Let me ask. How does that story relate to my confrontation with Brad Sykes?"

Shaking her head in wonder, Elizabeth replied, "You can't see this? It's so obvious. You have described yourself as a mere mathematics student. David was a mere shepherd boy. Brad, as described by you, is the football player no one messes with. Goliath, the mighty Philistine warrior was an individual no one wanted to deal with. You have stated that Brad is a loud-mouthed bully who does and says what he pleases and just like Goliath who defied the entire Israelite army, Brad defies practically everyone he comes in contact with. David defeated Goliath with one stone from a slingshot. You defeated Brad with one punch. How can you not see the similarity? And because of what David accomplished he found great favor in the eyes of most people. They even made him a king."

Max nodded his head in agreement. "If I do have to say so myself that was a great analogy. And now that I think of it, I have a more modern analogy that runs along the same lines. You mentioned before about how Eli Hoffman, a Mennonite lad who courted you turned out to be a brash individual who was a braggart, who according to you didn't have a lot of respect for anyone else, let alone women. You said he was difficult to be around and that you were done with that nonsense. It's the same thing with me and Brad. Brad Sykes is the Eli Hoffman in my life. The way he was always acting it was just a matter of time. If I hadn't knocked him down a peg eventually someone else would have. But here's the thing. David turned out to be quite popular and you say they made him a king. The result of all this is even though some students may look at me as a hero of sorts, in the end, I'm not going to fare that well."

Elizabeth seemed confused, "Whatever are you talking about?"

"There is another part to all of this that I'm sure no one on campus may know about. When I first arrived on Fripp Island at my parents' place, I took a long walk on the beach. On my way back to the house I got this phone call from my manager at Burger Palace. He proceeded to tell me despite the fact I'm the best shift manager he ever had he was instructed by his district manager to let me go. The company has a hands-off policy when it comes to customers and because I hit Brad on company property, I can no longer work for them."

Elizabeth, setting down her coffee exclaimed, "They fired you? I can't believe that."

"Well, that's not all that happened on the beach. Jim, my manager, goes on to tell me he received a call from Harmon Sykes, Brad's father and goes on to tell him he is not only going to sue Burger Palace but me as well. He told me this Mr. Sykes said there was going to be a meeting sometime after the first of the year to discuss the issue. So, unlike David who defeated Goliath, I may have defeated Brad Sykes, but it doesn't appear I'm going to be rewarded by becoming a king or anything even close. I've lost my job and I'm going to be sued."

Elizabeth lowered her head and remained silent. Max realized he had spoken out of line as he apologized, "I'm sorry, that didn't come out quite the way I wanted it to. I didn't mean to insinuate you are in any way responsible for the loss of my job or the lawsuit."

"I know, it's just that I do feel responsible." Looking into the dancing flames of the fire, she asked, "I assume you told your parents about all of this. What do they think?"

"My father said I needed legal counsel…an attorney. He has a friend who is an attorney and we met with him recently. We have come up with a defense plan, but the attorney said more than likely I would get sued."

"My people, the Mennonites do not believe in lawsuits against anyone for any reason, but sitting here and listening to you explain what happened at the Burger Palace, it's hard for me to imagine how this Harmon Sykes could sue you. It sounds to me like his son provoked you into hitting him. Isn't that self-defense?"

"One would think so but that's not the way the law looks at it. You can't hit someone unless you feel your life is in danger and another thing. You cannot hit another individual because of something they say. I guess I should have just kept walking away but when he started to talk about you in a degrading manner I just couldn't hold back."

The conversation was interrupted when two college girls walked by the fire, gave them a look, and then approached the couch. The taller of the two girls, a skinny blond looked directly at Elizabeth and commented, "You surely must be Elizabeth King!"

Elizabeth, taken by surprise answered humbly, "I am Elizabeth."

The other girl, much shorter addressed Max while extending her hand. "And you must be Max Miller."

Max shook the young lady's hand and responded, somewhat skeptically, "Yes, I'm Miller."

The girl looked at Elizabeth. "You're very lucky to have a man like Max here; a man who stands up for his woman. We need more upstanding young men like Max on campus."

Before Max or Elizabeth could speak the tall blond explained, "I wasn't even here at school for a month when I went to a party here on campus. Brad Sykes was there, and he asked me to dance. Trying, as usual, to be friendly I said yes, and before I knew it during the song, he had his hands all over me, kissing my neck. I pulled away and told him to stop. He just laughed and grabbed me, pulling me close saying, 'Don't worry, it's just a harmless dance.' He continued to grope me, so I slapped him at which point he shoved me into a nearby chair and called me a bitch! Then, on top of that, he picks up a drink from a table and throws it at me. He just laughed and walked off and not one person did anything. I, for one, say Brad Sykes got what was coming to him when you smashed him in the face at the Palace." Pointing at Elizabeth the girl went on, "You've got a good man here. Hold onto him because they are hard to come by." With that, the two girls walked across the room and exited the hall.

Elizabeth gave Max a half smile as she stated, "So, I guess now I'm your woman!"

Max objected firmly, "Those were not my words. That was their opinion."

Elizabeth stood and smoothed her long dress. "It's getting late. I better get back to my dorm."

Minutes later, standing at the main door of the dorm, Max asked, "Are we still on for dinner this week?"

Elizabeth reached for the door, "Of course, but it can't be tomorrow. I just signed up for the school choir. We have our first practice tomorrow evening. If you don't have any plans I can go on Thursday."

"Sounds good. We'll meet at the fountain at six as usual." Turning to leave, Max turned back and added, "One more thing. I had hoped I could explain the situation with Brad to you tonight. To be honest I think I could have done a better job of it."

Elizabeth flashed one of her magnetic smiles and then spoke, "I understand how awkward it must have been for you tonight. Don't worry…we're still good Max."

Max backed away as he said, "Good night."

He was prevented from leaving as Elizabeth spoke again, "Max, I've been thinking about what those two girls back at the hall said. I guess everyone here on campus thinks we are dating, that we're a couple."

"Well, they can think what they want. We know differently. We're just friends."

Elizabeth reached for the door again and as she opened it, she remarked, "Maybe we are dating, and we just don't know it!"

After she closed the door Max stood for a moment and thought about what she said. Smiling to himself he started the walk back to his dorm. It was starting to rain again.

CHAPTER EIGHT

Max opened his eyes, turned his head, and stared at the glowing red numerals on his alarm clock radio: 8:10. He had slept longer than planned. Sitting on the side of the bed, he yawned and looked across the room for his roommate. The bed was empty. *Probably down at the school gym.* Getting up he walked across the room and drew back the drapes. Earlier in the week the local weatherman had forecast a highly unusual warm trend in the weather for mid-January in Southern Pennsylvania. It was Saturday and the forecast for the day was mid-fifties with plenty of sun, and no rain or snow. The snow and ice that had covered Gettysburg like a white blanket for the past two weeks was gone. Moving to the bathroom, he splashed cold water on his sleepy face and thought, *Spring is just around the corner.*

He put on a pair of well-used jeans, a flannel shirt, and heavy wool socks, then slid his socked feet into a set of well-used walking shoes, grabbed his P-coat, gym bag, towel, and swimsuit, and headed for the door. He had no classes over the weekend and his first enjoyable task for the day was an hour's swim in the Olympic-sized pool the college offered. Reaching for the doorknob he noticed a section of white paper sticking out beneath the bottom of the door. Opening the door, the section of paper turned out to be a letter-sized envelope with his last name, *Miller!* typewritten on the front. He leaned against the hallway wall, opened the envelope, and removed a folded sheet of paper. Typed in all caps, the contents of the message read:

THIS IS FAR FROM OVER!

Another student who was walking down the hall was stopped by Max who asked, "Did you see anybody hanging around my door this morning?"

The answer was short and to the point. "Nope…just got up."

Max locked the door and then stuffed the envelope and the note in his shirt pocket. The negative message was not going to mess up his free weekend.

He read a thermometer attached to the outside wall of his dorm; the temperature was right at 41°. Walking down the sidewalk he couldn't even remember the last time he had ventured outside while at school over the last two months when it had not been below freezing. He thought about how down on Fripp Island at that very moment it was probably 60°. For him, the beach and warmer temperatures of South Carolina were nearly four months away.

His thoughts quickly turned to the disturbing note that had been left for him. It had to have come from Brad. Who else? During his first two weeks back at school he had seen Brad around campus but had managed to keep his distance, thus avoiding any awkward moments and conversation. If Brad's father or his attorneys had given Brad the same advice Rich had given him he was not following their suggestion. The message had been typed. Smart! Handwriting could be traced or proven. If push came to shove Brad could always deny delivering the troublesome note to his room. The note had to have been generated by Brad. Who else would have a reason to leave the threatening message? He was going to have to contact Elizabeth and not only tell her about the note but show it to her.

The last time they had been together was last Wednesday evening when, after meeting at the fountain, they had walked downtown for dinner. Their next scheduled get-together had been planned for Saturday evening. He'd show her the note then. He would be meeting her as usual at six. That was ten hours off. There didn't seem to be any reason to contact her immediately regarding the message. What could happen between now and then? After all, he was the one who had clobbered Brad, not her. No, he would wait until later and tell her then.

He entered the large sports complex, walked down a long hall on the right, and entered the men's locker room where he located an empty locker at the end of the third row. Hanging his coat in the locker he sat on a floor-attached bench and began to unlace his shoes when he was roughly pushed from behind. He turned and noticed two large male students both well over six feet in height towering over him.

Staring at the human wall of flesh Max quickly estimated their combined weight to be somewhere around five hundred and fifty to six hundred pounds. Both students wore swimsuits, the taller of the two was baldheaded and bare-chested, the other boy's upper torso covered with a grey Gettysburg football jersey. Max surmised that he had been confronted by two of the one hundred and twenty-five football players on the school team.

The baldheaded youth thumped Max on his shoulder and asked rudely, "You Max Miller?"

Max, feeling as if he were at a disadvantage answered politely, "Yes, I'm Miller."

Bumping the other player on his arm the baldheaded boy went on sarcastically, "I told you Miller was a twerp! It's hard to believe this little weasel took out Sykes with one punch."

The other boy leaned down and sneered in Max's face. "Some say you're kind of a hero, but I say you're a weakling. Some say you sucker punched Brad. That has to be the truth because after seeing how puny you are there is no way you could have taken out Brad Sykes in a fair fight." The boy stepped back and braced himself as he offered. "You wanna take a crack at me?"

Max remembered what his attorney had told him. *Try not only to avoid Brad but other players on the team and do not discuss what happened between you and Brad with anyone before the meeting with Sykes's lawyers.* Calmly removing his shoes, he turned his back on the two players and spoke in a normal tone, "I'm not looking for any trouble."

The baldheaded boy stepped over the bench and slammed the locker shut while giving Max a cocky smile. "Maybe you're not looking for trouble, but you sure found some!" Making sure no one was watching, he bent down, picked up Max's gym bag, and threw it violently down the aisle, the bag just missing a student who was walking around the corner.

The student looked down the aisle at Max and his two unwelcome visitors. Without saying a word, he picked up the bag, walked down the aisle, and handed it to Max. "I believe this is yours. The last time I saw you this morning you were fast asleep."

The student stepped directly in front of the bald player and despite the fact he was considerably shorter looked up into the boy's face and spoke with an air of confidence. "My name is Scott Cable. You've probably never seen me before because I'm new around campus. Just transferred in from New York about two weeks ago. Max and I just happen to be roommates.

He told me all about this business with Brad Sykes and because of that, he had to be careful around football players. Over the last two weeks, I've heard a lot of talk about what went on at the Palace and I've come to the conclusion this Brad character got what he had coming to him. Another thing, I happen to be on the school wrestling team and I've yet to see a football player who could take down a wrestler. Now, why don't you two goons just move on!"

Max could tell from the change of expression on the bald boy's face that he was intimidated. Not so, the other player who stepped close to Scott while clenching his fists as he proudly announced, "You do realize I could crush you into a fine powder."

Scott never even flinched as he responded calmly, "Well then…make your move. I'll have you on the floor in three seconds and put you in an arm lock accompanied by pain you can't even imagine. Now, do you want to be taken down or do you want to walk away?"

The bald youth took his partner by the sleeve and spoke as if it were not an issue. "Com'n…this is a waste of time. Let's hit the pool."

The two players walked slowly down the aisle as if to silently indicate they decided to leave, not Scott. Scott trailed them down the aisle and watched as they walked down the intersecting aisle and then entered through a door that read: Pool Entrance. Joining Max on the bench Scott asked, "Coming or going?"

Max removed his shirt and opened the locker door. "I just got here a few minutes ago when those two idiots showed up."

Scott looked back down the aisle. "Then you're still planning on swimming. You know those two went into the pool area."

Hanging up his shirt Max sat back down and removed his jeans. "Yeah, I am. I'm not going to allow those two jerks or anybody else to control the way I live my life and besides that, there will be too many people in the pool area for them to try anything."

"Just be careful," said Scott. "I'd stick around but I have to meet two of my wrestling buddies for some weightlifting and then it's off to lunch. Don't forget what I told you earlier in the week. If anybody messes with you…let me know."

"Thanks for the support, but I think I'll be fine at the pool."

Scott got up and started down the aisle as he gave a sloppy wave. "See ya later!"

The pool, as usual on a Saturday morning, was busy. Students swam laps, sat leisurely by the pool, or just congregated around the edge of the water. Out of the eight lanes available, lane number three was not being used. Max draped his towel over the edge of a lounge chair, walked to a metal ladder that led down into the pool, and entered the seventy-two-degree water. He rinsed off his goggles, placed them over his eyes went under, came back up, and made an adjustment. On the far right of the pool, he saw the two players who had given him a hard time in the locker room. They were gathered around a table with three girls and two other rather large males. At the moment they were not looking in his direction. Beneath the water, he sank to the bottom and relaxed as he thought, Despite the presence of the annoying football players in the next hour I'm going to get my mile of swimming in!

On the surface he pushed off with his feet and began the repeated process of a conventional breaststroke, his face in the water, then every fifth stroke coming up for air. Forty-one strokes later he reached the opposite end of the pool, pushed off the concrete wall, and started back in the opposite direction. Five minutes later he stopped, pushed the goggles back on his head, and rested at the edge as he chanced a quick look at the players. They hadn't even noticed him when he entered the pool while they went about their conversations. Just as well. He didn't need any more trouble. Putting the obnoxious players out of his mind he pushed off and started another five-lap series.

An hour and a half later following a hot shower, Max got dressed, and was on his way to his next stop for the day, the campus café where he would grab a hot chocolate for the walk back to the dorm.

Checking his cell phone, he noticed the temperature had risen to an uncommon 49°. The sun felt good on his face as he passed the fountain where he was to meet Elizabeth later in the day. It was just after ten o'clock and he had eight hours before they met up for dinner. Moving to the side of the walk so a cyclist could pass by, Max thought, A bike ride sounds good. Maybe I'll just take a ride over to the battlefield…maybe Little Round Top.

Max replaced his Navy P-coat with a Fripp Island sweatshirt and a Gettysburg College ball hat, walked to the corner of his room, removed the cover from his ten-speed bike, proceeded out to the hall, locked the door, then it was down the hall, through the lobby and out to the street. He started to peddle toward the main campus entrance as he passed the fountain where he saw several students out walking, jogging, and like him, out for a bike ride. It seemed everyone was out enjoying the break in the winter weather.

On Baltimore Street, he turned onto Middle Street, then went right on Steinwehr Avenue where he stopped at Duff's Bakery for a bacon, egg, and cheese bagel and an apple juice. Sitting at a wrought iron table in front of the tiny bakery he ate his breakfast and checked the time: 10:25. It was a four-mile jaunt from town out to Little Round Top and he estimated his arrival time on the battlefield site somewhere between 10:45 and 11:00. He took the last bite of his sandwich and washed it down with a final gulp of juice and was on his way once again as he made a left onto Pa. 134. Two more right-hand turns and he found himself on Sykes Avenue which led directly past Little Round Top.

This was the first time since his encounter with Brad Sykes that he had gone out to the battlefield. He had traveled down Sykes Avenue more times than he could remember over the years with his father while touring the battlefield. But now Sykes Avenue took on a whole new meaning. The street was named after one of the Union generals who had fought at Gettysburg, Major General George Sykes, who according to one of his father's many Civil War history lessons, graduated from the United States Military Academy in 1842.

As a military man, he had been involved in many conflicts: The Second Seminole War, the Mexican-American War, and of course the Civil War where he had led Union troops at Bull Run, Antietam, Fredericksburg, Chancellorsville, and Gettysburg. He commanded the Union V Corps at Gettysburg and performed well at the Wheatfield and Little Round Top, but later that year was questioned about his performance at The Battle of Mine Run and in 1864 was sent to Kansas for the remainder of the war. He survived the war and died in 1880.

All in all, the way his father had talked about George Sykes, he thought the general sounded like an upstanding individual. Now, peddling down Sykes Avenue, Max wondered if the general was a distant relative of Harmon Sykes and his son, Brad. Guiding the bike to the side of the road, he arrived at the parking area at the base of Little Round Top. Chaining the bike to a nearby tree, he spun the dial on his bike lock, turned, and looked up through the trees that shielded the top of the long hill.

He stood at the beginning of the trail leading to the top of the famous hill and read the square metal marker:

LITTLE ROUND TOP

Starting up the four-foot-wide dirt path he stepped up onto the first of many cut railroad ties that had been imbedded into the earth at intervals to prevent erosion from the one hundred and fifty-foot steep grade. On his left, the landscape was covered with low to medium-height vegetation, while on the right of the path, it was heavily wooded. Large boulders were scattered here and there on both sides. Having climbed the path before he knew it would be a good twenty minutes before he arrived at the top. Passing three more metal informational markers describing various movements the Confederates had made during the assault, he finally stood on the crest.

Taking a deep breath, he turned and looked back down through the trees he had just passed on the way up. Sitting on one of two benches he closed his eyes and sat back. Every time he had come to Little Round Top, especially if he was alone, despite how much bloodshed had been spilled during the battle a century and a half ago he always felt so relaxed here. Looking up through the tall trees surrounding him the problem of Brad Sykes and his father seemed a world away.

He picked up a small twig and began to dig at some dirt that had caked on his left shoe. Just up the path that ran between Little and Big Round Top, he saw an older man appear as he emerged from the trees. Walking very slowly the man moved forward, old hickory wood walking stick clutched in his right hand, grey pants tucked into old high-top hiking boots, checked blue-flannel shirt, wide red suspenders, faded green knapsack on his back, a battered fishing hat topped off his clothing.

As he approached Max noticed a wide grin through the bearded and wrinkled face. The man stopped at the bench and pointed the walking stick down the path at a large oak tree as he spoke in a deep voice. "I gotta make it down to that old tree. That's where I always turn around. After that, I'm going to join you here on the bench if you don't mind." He didn't wait for a response but walked another ten yards, tapped the trunk of the oak with his walking stick, turned and walked back, stopped at the bench, removed his knapsack, and placed it on the ground. Stretching, he looked down into the trees below, then sat. Extending his right hand, he introduced himself, "Name's Kellem McCulhay. Nice to meet you."

Taking the man's hand, Max answered, "Max Miller."

The old man opened the knapsack and removed an old canteen and a paper sack. "After walking an hour and a half I need some nourishment." Holding up the canteen he went on, "Got me some grape Kool-Aid. Care for a swig?"

Max declined. "No thanks…I'm good."

After three long gulps, the man laid the canteen on the bench and opened the sack. "I also packed a tuna fish sandwich along with an apple and a banana, I always take two pieces of fruit with me when I go out for my daily walk. I only ever eat one and today I'm going with the apple." Unwrapping the sandwich, he offered, "That means I'm gonna have this banana left over. Maybe you'd like it. It'd be nice to have someone share my lunch with me. Usually, I sit up here on the hill and eat lunch all by myself." Holding out the yellow fruit, he grinned, "Whadda ya say?"

For some reason, Max took an instant liking to the old fella. "I can't recall the last time I had a banana." Taking the fruit, Max removed the top half of the peel and took a bite. "I almost forgot how good bananas taste. Thank you."

Kellem took a bite out of his sandwich and asked, "Have you ever been up here before…I mean up here on Little Round Top?"

"Plenty of times," said Max. "My father is a reenactor and he and his regiment from South Carolina have been coming here for nearly thirty years in July on the anniversary of the battle of Gettysburg. He started bringing me here when I was seven. When I turned fifteen, I joined the regiment and have come here the first week of July for the past four years. Two years ago, we reenacted Little Round Top. How about you? You come up here often?"

Washing down a second bite of the sandwich with another shot of Kool-Aid, Kellem cleared his throat and then replied, "Twice a week for over fifty years. I live on a farm with my two older brothers. It's about two miles east of here. Every day, without fail, I hike out here to the battlefield. Some days I walk down to Devil's Den or the Peach Orchard, Culp's Hill, or some other battlefield site. Up here on Little Round Top…well that's my favorite. I walk up here, turn around at that tree, sit on this bench, enjoy my lunch, relax for maybe an hour, then I head back to the farm."

Max inquired. "You said you have two brothers."

"That's right. Joseph is the oldest at eighty-six and then there's Seth who is eighty-four. At eighty-two I'm the baby of the family. Maybe you've heard of our farm. McCulhay's Tree Farm. It's about a mile and a half out of town on Chambersburg Pike. Me and my brothers have seventy acres where we grow Christmas trees. I thought maybe you heard of the farm?"

Max pointed at his hat and explained, "Aside from coming here in the past during the July reenactment I now attend Gettysburg College. I'm a freshman so this is my first year here at school. Besides hiking or riding my bike out here to the battlefield or walking downtown, I haven't ventured too far outside the town limits."

Interested, Kellem asked, "What is your major at school?"

"Mathematics. Numbers have always intrigued me. Like the battle that took place right here on Little Round Top. When it was all said and done numbers determined the outcome of that day a hundred and fifty years ago."

"What do you mean?"

Max stood and walked to the edge of the path and pointed to the ground while walking a few yards to the west. "On July 2, 1863, Colonel Joshua L. Chamberlain in command of the 20th Maine, positioned his men along this line extending out to the left. They were on the extreme left flank of the Union Army and were told in no uncertain terms that they could not retreat under any circumstance. Chamberlain had to hold this position to the last man. The 20th Maine, along with the 83rd Pennsylvania, 44th New York, and the 16th Michigan regiments quickly constructed a two to three-foot high wall of small boulders and logs right along the edge of this path that was not present back then. As you can see most of the original wall has been destroyed by the weather or sadly by tourists. Amazingly after all this time, you can still make out where the wall was. It was at the end of this wall where Chamberlain placed the 20th Maine."

Max, placing his hands on his hips walked a few paces down the path, stopped, and then explained, "Chamberlain was a very unusual officer. He did not possess a military background and sat out the first two years of the war. Before joining the Union Army, he was a professor at the prestigious Bowdoin College in Maine. He was a professor of rhetoric and modern languages. He was not only fluent in English but Greek, Latin, Spanish, French, German, Italian, Arabic, Hebrew, and Syriac. At one time he had taught every subject the school offered except science and mathematics. Now, based upon the outcome of the Battle of Little Round Top, as a mathematics student, I believe Chamberlain understood mathematics quite well."

Max walked back to the bench, sat, and crossed his legs as he kept talking, "Chamberlain and the 20th Maine along with the other supporting regiments arrived here just minutes before the Confederates attacked their position. In short, Chamberlain, who controlled the left flank of the entire Union Army had little time to plan his defense. Looking back on this battle it's easy to say it was chaotic, but in all actuality, it was a series of patterns involving numbers. If history tells us anything about the Civil War, in most battles fought, the South was always outnumbered, but despite what seemed like an unfair advantage, under the leadership of Robert E. Lee, they were the victors in most of the conflicts. The Battle of Little Round Top was just the opposite with Lee holding the advantage as far as the number of fighting men."

Swallowing the last bite of the banana, Max continued, "Earlier in the day the Union troops positioned on this hill had been pulled out prematurely leaving the hill undefended. Lee, who was a wizard of troop movement on the battlefield discovered that Big Round Top only held a few Union signalmen and Little Round Top was not protected. If he could take Little Round Top, he could then skirt Big Round Top and take the Union army from behind. Lee immediately sent five regiments to take this hill, the 4th and 5th Texas along with the 4th, 15th, and 47th Alabama.

"Now right here is where the patterns of numbers began to form. It is estimated that in each one of these Confederate regiments, there were six to eight hundred men which means the Confederates had plans of sending anywhere from twenty-four hundred to four thousand determined grizzled veteran soldiers up this hill.

"Besides the 20th Maine and their three supporting regiments, there were additional Union regiments to Chamberlain's right which meant that Little Round Top was defended by about three thousand Union troops. It was a great opportunity for Lee as he held the mathematical advantage of manpower. But here's the reality about numbers. Just because the numbers seem to be leaning in your favor cannot make up for the raw emotion of the men in your command. Lee's troops had been on a long-forced march before arriving in Gettysburg and it has been said they were, at least for that day…fought out! On the other hand, Chamberlain and the 20th Maine were fresh and ready for the fight."

Kellem held up the sandwich indicating that he wanted to speak. "In all the years I've been coming up here I've heard countless stories about what happened on this hill, and yet even though monuments are honoring the other Union regiments who participated in the battle, Chamberlain and the 20th Maine are what people always talk about. Why do you suppose that is?"

"To be honest with you, I believe Chamberlain's dominance, as far as history is concerned, is based on some of the battlefield decisions he made, that in all actuality saved the day. When Chamberlain arrived, he quickly surveyed the situation and deduced that Lee's main objective was to flank him on the left. During the ongoing battle, the greatest pressure was placed on the 20th Maine.

"Chamberlain knew he had to concentrate his defensive efforts on his left where he had no men. He had to prevent the Confederates from going around him. He probably, at first, had no idea how many regiments Lee would send up the hill, but he knew the numbers had to be substantial. He had at the ready three hundred fifty-eight men in his regiment. When asking one of his officers how they were set on ammunition he was informed each man had about sixty rounds.

"Chamberlain figured that was sufficient. Think about it. Three hundred and fifty-eight men with sixty rounds each equal, let's see." Doing some quick addition in his head, Max quickly calculated, "That equates to two thousand, one hundred forty-eight rounds." Fashioning a make-believe musket with his hands he pointed the invisible gun down the hill in the direction of the trees pulled the invisible trigger with his index finger and stated, "Now, that's a lot of firepower. Chamberlain's men were well rested, well-armed, and protected behind the wall they had constructed."

Max looked down the steep hill and continued, "All of Chamberlain's initial thoughts came to him shortly after he arrived here. Lee's five regiments were already halfway up the hill by the time Chamberlain and the 20th Maine were on the scene. It must have been a frightening sight for Chamberlain and his men as they looked down the hill. At first, they must have heard the oncoming Confederate troops, twigs snapping under their feet, the sound of clanging equipment. The next thing they saw were the actual men as they emerged from the trees right down there.

"Three-quarters of the way up the hill the 4th and 5th Texas regiments crashed through the trees as they went to the double-quick. I have tried to imagine how the Union troops up here must have felt as they viewed the long lines of gray uniformed soldiers as they advanced, Confederate flags hoisted high combined with the horrifying Rebel yells that normally sent chills down the backs of the Union troops. The Texans were met with a galling return of fire from the 20th Maine and within a few minutes the Southern regiments retreated accompanied by cheers of victory from Chamberlain's men. This celebration was short-lived as within the next few minutes the Confederates had reformed and were advancing up the hill for another try. This second assault and a third attempt were also repulsed."

Max pointed far down to the left near a small gully as he elaborated, "While the Texans continued to pressure the 20th Maine, behind the cover of the front lines the 15th Alabama moved perpendicular up the hill trying to get around the left flank. Chamberlain, not one to be outmaneuvered, quickly reacted to Lee's flanking movement, and immediately extended his line of defense to the left, leaving his original defensive position weak. But he didn't have a choice. The men who moved to the left had no wall for cover as they formed a line of defense, some kneeling, a second-row standing. Within the next ninety minutes, the Alabama boys got within thirty yards of the 20th and on one attempt got close enough where there was hand-to-hand combat, but once again they were beaten back.

"Chamberlain quickly assessed his dire situation and realized his men could not hold off another attack. They could not retreat, they were out of ammunition, so therefore they could not make a standing fight. His only other option was to have his remaining men charge downhill and hopefully take the Confederates by complete surprise. It was a gamble, to say the least. Nearly half of his regiment were down leaving him with around two hundred men to attack an opposing force of somewhere between six hundred to nine hundred men just thirty yards away. With bayonets attached to their guns, the order to charge was given and down the slope they went and once again the numbers dictated the outcome. The front line of the Confederates managed to get one volley fired off but then the screaming, bayonet-wielding Union forces were on them. Chaos set in and the front line of the Confederates caved, and they started to run down the hill, causing those behind them to do the same. The entire remaining Confederate forces on the hill were routed and about four hundred men were taken captive. Hence, the battle of Little Round Top was a Union victory."

Kellem sat in silence as if he were thinking, then asked, "Your version of the attack on Little Round Top from a numbers aspect is something I've never heard before but still it has always puzzled me how and why the Rebs fell apart at the end of the day."

"My father," said Max, "who seems to know every detail about every battle that was fought during the Civil War claims there are a half dozen reasons for the Confederate collapse that day up here on Little Round Top. First, you have to consider the weather. It was July and it was the hottest part of the day. It has been said the temperature was hovering in the mid-eighties. Combine the heat of the day with the heavy wool uniforms that were standard at that time, why the heat must have felt oppressive as the Confederates charged up the hill.

"Second, by the time Lee's regiments got to Little Round Top they were already played out as they say. They had fought their way through Devil's Den and then Plum Ridge and now they are ordered up Little Round Top.

"The third reason for their failure was the terrain itself. Up until two years back when my reenactment regiment stormed up Little Round Top, I had only heard about how difficult the advance was. The southern regiments had to advance through thick vegetation, around boulders and trees. The uphill footing was not that great.

"Fourth comes the fact they had made numerous attempts at breaking the Union line and had been repulsed every time. When you combine this fact with the heat, the uphill climb, and their exhaustion they must have been demoralized. The fifth reason comes in the form of their surroundings and their emotions. They were exhausted, and confused amid the heat, smoke, and noise, not to mention dead or wounded comrades lying everywhere.

"Then there is the final nail in the coffin. The bayonet charge itself. The Alabamians were only thirty yards from the top when the order was given by Chamberlain to charge. Two hundred screaming, yelling men, bayonets at the ready charging downhill. The front line of the Confederates got off a few rounds but had no time to reload so within seconds the Union boys were on them.

"When I made the reenactment charge up the hill and the Union reenactors charged down the hill at us it was a very helpless feeling. I turned and ran just like those Alabama boys did. I also was captured just like many of them were on that fateful day. Even though Lee held the mathematical advantage of more men on the field, Chamberlain and his two hundred brave men defeated nearly six hundred Confederates. So, as they say, two and two do not always equal four. I'm sure there is a lot more I could say about that day but if I keep on talking why we could be up here for the next week."

Kellem took a swig of Kool-aide, replaced the lid on the canteen, and then asked, "Did you ever consider becoming a battlefield tour guide here in Gettysburg? If you know as much about the other battle sites in the area, I think tourists would enjoy listening to you."

"The thought of becoming a guide has never entered my mind, but it sounds like something I would enjoy."

"I think you'd be good at it. While you were telling me the story of Little Round Top, even though I have heard the story countless times, you had my interest. I would have to say when you tell a story you put a little extra jam on the bread!"

Max laughed at Kellem's analogy.

Kellem looked off into the trees and asked, "You ever seen any ghosts anywhere on the battlefield sites here in Gettysburg?"

Max gave Kellem a strange look. "No, can't say I have. I mean when you're alone at one of the sites you hear things like a snapping twig or the wind blowing in the trees. I can honestly say I have never encountered a ghost, apparition, or spirit anywhere here in the six-thousand-acre park. Needless to say, there are hundreds of ghost stories associated with the Battle of Gettysburg. My father and I have discussed this very topic.

"As knowledgeable as he is about what went on here at Gettysburg he does not believe in ghosts. He feels the reason why so many people feel the Gettysburg battlefield is haunted is due to the incredible carnage that happened here on these fields and hills. It is a known fact those who believe in ghosts think wherever there has been violent death that the spirits of those involved are earthbound. My father once told me because of the raw emotion of the men who fought here on both sides that they have left invisible footprints on the battlefield which are merely memories and not ghosts. How about you? Ever see anything odd or spooky while you're out here walking around?"

"Well, like you, I have heard things like the snapping of twigs or the wind blowing but more than that, I have heard on occasion, the clanging of equipment, like maybe a canteen banging against the side of a musket... things like that. One time down on Plum Ridge I thought I saw the rear end of a brown horse disappear behind a tree. The strange thing was the animal never appeared on the other side. I questioned myself silently and wondered if I had seen what I thought I did. Similar things have happened on occasion at different spots in the park. When I think back on those moments, they are just kind of unexplainable."

Kellem placed the canteen into his knapsack as he went on, "With that being said there happens to be two instances where I feel a ghost...of sorts appeared on our farm, which as I told you earlier is about two miles from here. It sits right on the edge of the battlefield. The house and barn were built by my grandfather and his son, my father back in 1932. I was born in '35 and have lived there for over eighty years. My grandfather, at the time, had lost his wife a few years prior. He lived there at the farm until '37 when he passed away at the age of seventy-nine.

"Years passed and well, I guess I must have been about eight years of age. My father, one evening sat me and my two older brothers down and told us something we found hard to believe. According to my father, he claimed he had seen a ghost on our farm the year after my grandfather died. That would have been back in 1938. He told us that on July 2nd as he was coming out of the barn, he saw this young man standing next to an old fence he and Grandpa had built. This fence sits right at the edge of our property and separates our farm from the battlefield. Anyway, he goes on to describe the young man, eighteen, nineteen, maybe twenty years of age, in a typical Confederate gray uniform, musket in his right hand, wounded in his right upper arm and lower left leg. My father said he could see the blood on the uniform. He had this strange canteen with him. It was wooden and it was suspended in place using what appeared to be old rope.

"Seeing as how it was the second day of the 75th reunion of the Battle of Gettysburg my father figured it was a Confederate reenactor. He said he started across the backyard to approach the young lad when the boy turned and limped off into the trees just beyond the fence. The next day my father said he read in the paper that there were only twenty-five Civil War veterans at the three-day event. Their average age was ninety-four, plus there were about two thousand family members of the soldiers who had fought there. My father then said the young boy could not have been a veteran but an over-zealous spectator, but still it seemed very strange."

Max interrupted Kellem as he asked, "That makes sense but what about these wounds...this blood. That doesn't make any sense. Maybe it was not an actual wound, therefore proving the over-zealous young man theory."

"That's the exact thing we said to our father. Then, jokingly he said. 'Well, maybe it was just a ghost!' We all just laughed and forgot about the whole thing."

With a look of confusion, Max pointed out, "You said you had two ghost-related instances. You've only shared one with me and it doesn't sound like you and your brothers were convinced that it was a ghost."

"Back then we didn't think it was a ghost. Time passed and eventually, our folks died and the three of us continued to work the farm. When I say time passed, I mean thirty-one years passed by when it happened again! The year was 1969 and I was forty years of age. My brothers and I, why we were just three bachelors working the farm. We never married so there were no wives or children on the farm…just the three of us.

"So, here I am walking out of the barn when low and behold there he is…the young soldier standing by the fence. We just stood there and stared at one another for maybe a full minute. I didn't know what to think or do. The young soldier fit my father's description of the boy he had seen thirty-one years in the past to the tee. Eighteen, nineteen, maybe twenty years old, grey Confederate uniform, musket held in his hand, and the same old rope-suspended wooden canteen. The blood stains were also there on his upper right arm and lower left leg. In my mind, I went over what my father had told me that day over three decades in the past, and yet here stood what I thought was the same boy, who hadn't aged one single day."

Highly interested, Max added, "And you thought this boy was a ghost?"

"Not at first, but then I realized it was July 2nd…the 106th anniversary of the Battle of Gettysburg. All the veterans of the war long past were all gone now."

Max jumped in and stated, "Maybe you saw a Confederate reenactor."

"I considered that, but why the same wooden canteen, and then there were those wounds. Well, anyways, I started across the yard toward this fella, and just like the boy my father had seen he limps back into the tree line beyond the fence. Not to be put off, I ran and jumped over the fence to follow the boy. I took one step toward the trees and then the strangest feeling I have ever experienced in my life came over me. I can't explain the exact feeling, but it was like I shouldn't be there. A chill ran down my spine and back over the fence I went. Ever since that day and now decades later not a day passes when I don't think about that young soldier. He had to be a ghost or some sort of spirit. What other logical explanation could there be?"

Max grinned and replied, "Talk about putting a little extra jam on the bread. Your compelling story is hard to disagree with or disprove. I'm not saying I believe in ghosts, but it gives you something to think about." Standing, Max held out his right hand. "Listen, I've got to head back to school. I have a dinner engagement with a beautiful young lady this evening."

Kellem stood and grabbed Max's hand. "It was a pleasure to meet you, Max. I best be on my way back myself. Who knows? Maybe we'll meet up again somewhere out there on the battlefield."

Shaking the old man's hand he remarked, "I think I'd like that."

Kellem picked up the knapsack and threw it over his shoulder. Walking back up the path, he spoke, "If you're ever in need of a Christmas tree stop by the farm. I'll make sure you get a great tree and a good deal!"

Max stood and watched as the old man disappeared into the trees. Turning, he started down the path that led to the bottom of Little Round Top. An enjoyable and yet very strange afternoon!

CHAPTER NINE

Max nodded at two of his fellow freshmen as he walked his bike across the main floor of the dormitory. His attention suddenly shifted to the opposite side of the room where a male student, who was manning the information desk, summoned him, "Hey…Miller! Some dude dropped a letter off here for you about an hour ago."

Max approached the desk, asking, "When you say 'dude' I assume you mean the mailman. Seems awful early for the mail on a Saturday."

The boy at the desk held up a white envelope as he replied, "The person who dropped off this letter was no mailman. He looked to be in his late twenties. He reminded me of one of those brand-new lawyers who just passed the bar exam, clean-cut, preppy-looking sort of fella. Shiny shoes, starched white shirt, pin-striped three-piece dark blue suit, complete with red power tie and London Fog trench coat. He strolled up to the desk and asked if you were in. I told him you had left earlier in the morning. He then opened what appeared to be a new black briefcase and removed this envelope. He lays it on the desk and explains to me that it is of the utmost importance that you receive it as soon as you return. I had to sign for it. With that he thanked me and out the door he went. It was all…very professional." Laying the envelope on top of the desk the boy patted it and stated, "There ya go."

The only mail Max ever received was a monthly letter from his mother. No, this had to be the notice from Sykes' lawyers he had been expecting. His suspicion was verified as he read the return address in the upper left-hand corner of the envelope: The Law Offices of Dolstrum, Eichman and Dunn 317 Baltimore Street Gettysburg, Pa.

Max walked the bike through the door, and down the hallway to his room. Inside, he threw the cover back on his bike and then made himself comfortable on the edge of the bed. With the aid of his trusty Swiss Army pocketknife, which he always carried with him, he carefully sliced open the envelope and removed a folded sheet of expensive rag-content paper. The top of the document was a duplicate of the name and address of the Gettysburg law firm on the envelope.

The one-page typed information began with: To Maxwell Miller. The upper right-hand corner was dated January 17, 2013, which meant the document had been generated just yesterday. The contents of the letter was professional, short, and to the point, ending with a typed name: Micheal P. Dolstrum accompanied by a matching penned signature. He read the letter again and then laid it on the bed. No more guessing or wondering when the meeting was to take place. He had been officially notified. His first response to the letter was that he needed to contact his father immediately and update him on the situation. Walking to the window of his room he pulled out his cell phone and dialed his father's number.

Charley Miller sat on one of his three backhoes as he stared out into the Atlantic Ocean while taking a bite of one of two sandwiches he had packed for lunch. Swallowing, he answered his phone that he always kept hanging from the rearview mirror. "Hello!"

Max, glad to hear his father's voice, said, "Hey Dad. What's up down there?"

Charley, equally happy to hear from his son, replied, "Taking a lunch break at the moment. My crew just started working on the foundation for that new strip mall I told you about over here in Mt. Pleasant. What's going on up there in Pennsylvania?"

The pleasantries of the conversation over, Max broke the news, "I just received notice from Sykes' lawyers about the upcoming meeting. It is to be held next Saturday, a week from today. Surprisingly, it is to be held right here in Gettysburg at some law firm by the name of Dolstrum, Eichman and Dunn. Their office is down on Baltimore Street. It's scheduled for ten in the morning. The letter suggests I bring legal counsel with me. I guess we need to contact Rich and let him know."

Charley agreed, "You're right. Here's what we'll do. Where are you right now?"

"I'm in my dorm room."

"Okay then…just sit tight. I'm going to give Rich a call. I'm sure he'll want to call you about the notification. After he contacts you call me back so we can get on the same page about when Rich and I plan on flying up there. I'm going to hang up now but before I go how has everything else gone since you returned to school?"

Max thought about mentioning the 'This is far from over' note and also his encounter with the two football players but thought better of it for now. He already knew what Rich would say. 'There is no proof Brad Sykes generated the note and as far as the football players are concerned, they may have not been sent by Brad.' Max replied with a simplistic answer, "Everything has been fine. Listen, I'll talk to you after I hear from Rich. Tell Mom I said Hey."

Tossing his phone on the bed he checked the time: 11:47. He had a little over six hours before he was to meet with Elizabeth. He had planned on having their normal pleasant dinner conversation but now he had three things to share with her. The potential threatening note, the two menacing football players, and the meeting with Brad's lawyers.

One of the things he wanted to talk over with Elizabeth was the pleasant but strange afternoon he had spent up on Little Round Top with Kellem McCulhay. He wasn't too sure about how he felt about this ghost business Kellem had shared with him. He wanted to get Elizabeth's take on ghosts. Coming from a Mennonite background she always had such a different way of looking at things than he did. When he considered everything, he now had to share with her Kellem's ghost story would no doubt be placed on the back burner. He wasn't nervous about the upcoming call from Rich but more along the lines of unsettled.

As a mathematics major, he didn't enjoy what he called gray areas. For him, a situation either had to be black or white. In applying math to his way of thinking there was always a mathematical answer, plus or minus, large or small. There was never a gray area when it came to numbers. Picking up a book he was in the process of reading—How Numbers Affect Life—he sat in an old Lazy Boy chair in the corner. Reading always relaxed him.

He hadn't even finished a page when his cell rang. The familiar voice on the other end was just who he expected, "Max, it's Rich. Just got off the phone with your dad. He tells me you received the notice about the meeting."

"That's right," said Max. "Just got it about an hour ago. I didn't get to meet the messenger. It was dropped off at the dormitory desk."

"Okay, here's what we're going to do. I'm going to turn on my recorder and you're going to read the letter to me word for word. After that when we are finished, I want you to make a copy of the letter then I want you to have the original sent to me overnight mail. This way I'll be able to review what the letter says and maybe we can get a better feel for what direction these lawyers are headed. Let me know when you're ready to begin."

Max cleared his throat and answered, "Okay…turn on the recorder."

Following a brief moment, Rich spoke, "It's on…go!"

"The letter starts with the name of the firm: Dolstrum, Eichman and Dunn…thirty seconds later Max finished up, "…it's signed by Micheal P. Dolstrum."

"Perfect," said Rich. "It sounds to me since they mentioned the possibility of a settlement in the letter that they want to avoid a court case. We'll stand a better chance of cutting our losses if we stay out of court. Who knows, we might even come out on the winning end of this thing. I think we have a strong case. We just have to stick to the plan we agreed on. Your father said nothing unusual has happened since you went back to school."

Once again, avoiding the recent events he had gone through, Max replied, "Yep, nothing unusual. What's next?"

"You should be receiving a call from your dad later on this afternoon. When our recent conversation ended, he said he was going to call the airport and get us a flight into Harrisburg. He said he was going to try and get a flight out early on Friday so we could meet with you the day before the meeting. Other than that, as I said, get a copy of the letter made and then mail me the original…overnight mail."

Max felt better after talking with Rich. "As soon as we hang up, I'll get that done. I guess I'll see you and dad then next Friday. The sooner this is over the better."

In the next five minutes, Max was once again walking his bike across the main floor of the dorm. The boy manning the desk commented, "Leaving again? You just got back!"

Giving the boy a thumbs up, Max announced, "Busy man!"

It only took ten minutes to peddle downtown to the post office which was on Buford Avenue. The office wasn't busy, and he got the letter mailed off to Rich in no time at all. Unlocking his bike from a metal bike rack,

Max was prevented from climbing on when his cell buzzed. He guessed the call was from his father…which it was. "Max, just got off the phone with the airlines here in Charleston. Rich and I are booked on Southwest Flight 714, leaving at 9:15 next Friday morning. We fly to Atlanta where we have an hour's layover then it's on to Harrisburg. We plan to rent a car and then drive to Gettysburg. We should arrive sometime in the afternoon. Plan on having dinner with Rich and me Friday night there in town. We can go over our plan of defense again so when we walk into the meeting we don't look like fools. I'm confident this whole thing will work out."

Max asked, "How does Mom feel about all of this?"

"Look, you know how your mother is when it comes to anything out of the ordinary which the situation between you and this Brad Sykes certainly falls into. She is not concerned about the fact you could be sued for a few thousand dollars. She is afraid you may have to serve some jail time or that the college might reprimand you in some way. I assured her Rich is not going to allow those types of things to happen. Don't worry…she'll be fine. She's a mother and that's what mothers do. You're her only son so it stands to reason she would be concerned. Before you know it, this whole thing will blow over and things will get back to normal. Listen, I've got to get back to work. I'll see you in Gettysburg next Friday. Stay out of trouble."

A man walking a dog passed by and smiled at Max as he commented, "Nice day huh? They say it's going to reach 53 today. In this part of the country in mid-January, that's almost like a heat wave."

Max had to agree with the man and started to peddle down Buford. He still had over five hours before he was to meet up with Elizabeth. Turning the bike toward the downtown section he decided to ride down to the town square and then around town for an hour or so.

A few minutes later he found himself by the town square, a circular road, intersected by four different streets: Baltimore, York, Carlisle, and Chambersburg. Located smack dab in the center of the circular pavement there was a tiny park decorated with varied plant life, two benches, four streetlights, and a town clock supported by a wrought iron post. Peddling into the fifty-foot square center of attraction the town offered, he leaned his bike up against one of the benches and decided to walk across the street and grab a coffee at Starbucks.

Inside the glass-fronted popular business, there were a few couples seated at small tables and three couples standing at the counter. Waiting patiently for the next available counter person, he was taken by surprise when one of the male customers turned and grimaced when he saw him. Max froze, standing no more than two feet from Brad Sykes. Max thought instantly about turning and leaving but he just couldn't bring himself to do so. In his mind that would be giving Sykes a form of satisfaction in front of his friends.

Brad tapped a girl he was standing next to on her shoulder as he spoke sarcastically, "Well look who we've got here. Max Miller, the mathematic whiz." His cutting remark caused the other four students to turn and stare at Max as Brad kept on talking, warning the group. "Better be careful. One minute you can be standing there and the next ol' Max here will sucker punch you."

With six sets of eyes staring at him, Max couldn't think of an appropriate response, so he simply stepped down to the end of the counter and spoke to the salesgirl standing there. "I'd like to order a small decaf to go please."

Brad moved down the counter next to Max, leaned over, and looked directly into his face. "I guess you and I will be seeing one another this coming Saturday. Hope you have a good lawyer. I do!" With that, he laughed and suggested to the group. "Com'n, let's blow this joint before Max here goes off and clobbers somebody!"

As Brad and his friends filed out of the store, the counter girl who had witnessed the strange behavior of Brad, placed a small cup of decaf on the counter in front of Max and skeptically asked, "Friends of yours?"

Max laid a five on the counter and replied emphatically, "Not hardly!"

Back at the bench next to his bike, he removed the top of his coffee and was about to take a drink when an old, battered pickup truck pulled next to the circular curbing. The driver's side window slowly lowered and out the open window leaned none other than Kellem. "Howdy there Max. Seen any ghosts since we talked up on Little Round Top?"

Surprised to see the old codger in town, Max replied, "Nope, nary a one! What brings you to town?"

Kellem angled his thumb toward the back of the truck and grinned. "Just pickin' up a few things I need from the hardware store." The car behind him honked and Kellem pulled off as he shouted, "Don't forget…you ever need a tree stop by the farm."

As the old truck rumbled down York Street, Max thought, what a day. I wonder who I'll run into next!

Reclining on his bed, he looked at his watch: 2:15. He had three hours before he had to freshen up and then meet Elizabeth for dinner. For some reason, he felt exhausted. Setting his alarm for 5:15 he laid back and closed his eyes. A three-hour nap sounded like a good remedy.

The familiar sound of his alarm never sounded as Max opened his eyes, reached over, and turned it off. He sat on the edge of the bed, stretched, and rubbed his hands over his face and through his hair. The power nap he had planned on had turned into a three-hour deep sleep. He felt refreshed and ready for whatever the remainder of the day held. Walking into the tiny bathroom, he ran a cold washcloth up and down his arms and then dabbed at his face. Running a comb through his slightly disheveled hair, he stared at his reflection in the mirror that looked back at him. Satisfied, he thought, All I need now is some deodorant and a fresh shirt and soon I'll be on my way to a lovely evening with Elizabeth.

At exactly five-thirty, he exited the dormitory and made his way down the sidewalk that led to the main entrance of the campus. The temperature was fifty-four and it seemed like everyone was out enjoying the unusually high level of warm weather for this time of year.

As he walked along, he wasn't all that confident the upcoming evening with Elizabeth was going to be as lovely as he hoped it would be. Based on the list of negative events that had occurred during the day he could not be sure how she was going to react. Elizabeth, he had learned, in the short time he knew her, was a great listener and not an individual who judged others. Once again, he asked himself the same question he had asked himself several times over the past few weeks. Because of her religious and strict Mennonite upbringing would she eventually become overwhelmed with all the worldly problems he seemed to be plagued with and end the platonic relationship they shared?

Max made a right at an intersecting street not far from the fountain just up the way. As he approached the popular campus gathering spot, he couldn't help but notice the warm weather had brought everyone out of their rooms. Students were congregated around the concrete edging surrounding a small pool that housed the three-tier operating fountain. All four benches were occupied, some students lounging on blankets in the grass. Other students were riding bikes, skating, or just out for a walk. Seating himself on a large boulder across the walk from the fountain area, he didn't want to be that noticeable. It seemed like over the past two weeks wherever he went on campus someone was staring at him or making some kind of unknown remark to those they were with.

Thinking about the upcoming meeting he realized that soon all this nonsense would be over and the student body, in general, would move on to something else. He checked his watch. He was twenty minutes early. Elizabeth was always right on time, never late. At times, she was even a few minutes early. Gazing in the direction of where her dormitory was located, he saw her as she slowly limped up the sidewalk. Today was one of those days she was going to be early.

Max walked across the street to meet her. He knew Elizabeth could care less about what others thought of her, but it bothered him that other students were always staring at them. When she saw him approaching, she smiled and waved.

Gesturing at the bright sun Max enthusiastically asked, "What about this sunshine we have today? It doesn't seem like January…does it?"

Elizabeth folded her hands at her waist and agreed, "In my eighteen years of life I have never experienced a day in January where it has been this warm."

Max guided her down the walk toward the main road out of campus while asking, "Where would you like to eat this evening?"

"I'm really in the mood for a good meal. Sort of a meat and potatoes meal. Is there a place like that in town?"

"I know the perfect place for just that kind of food. It's on the other side of town so we'll have to walk a little farther than we normally do, but it's so nice out. It's a small mom-and-pop diner where my father always takes me when we come for the reenactment. It's called the Peach Orchard. It's named after one of the famous battle sites here in Gettysburg."

Elizabeth gave him one of her great smiles and simply said, "And?"

Max, not understanding her one-word response, asked, "And…what?"

"Come now, Max. Every time you mention something about what went on here in Gettysburg regarding the three-day battle that took place here, you always, without fail, give me a short history lesson on that event.

So, go ahead and tell me about this Peach Orchard. It sounds like a lovely place. We have a peach orchard on our farm. When I was a little girl, I always used to go out into the orchard and sit by the trees and daydream. It was always so peaceful there."

"The orchard I am referring to before the second day of battle back in July of 1863 here in Gettysburg was peaceful. Back in those days most of the people who resided here in the area were farmers. At that time, the rolling hills of Gettysburg were known for their delicious peaches. I'm not going to bore you with all the statistics on the second day of battle, like what generals or regiments were involved or who decided what, but the Union forces advanced on the Peach Orchard because it represented higher ground which was easier to defend and a great place to position artillery. The Union troops no sooner took possession of the orchard when they were bombarded from two directions by Confederate cannons. This was followed by an assault by Confederate troops causing the Union boys to retreat. Not to be denied, the Union lines reformed and attacked and once again took control of the orchard. This resulted in the Confederates realigning their lines and attacking again. Back and forth the fighting raged, one side taking the field only to be beaten back, then returning to beat their opponents back. Back and forth they went, fighting bitterly for hours. The Confederates eventually won the day at the Peach Orchard but at a loss of many a good Southern man. It was estimated on the second day of battle in Gettysburg that around twenty-thousand men lost their lives, many falling in the Peach Orchard.

"My father told me a story years ago about something he had read about one of the last reunions held here in Gettysburg for veterans who were still alive. Back in 1938 at the annual reunion of survivors of the war which ended in 1865, out of the one hundred and sixty thousand men who fought here in Gettysburg, there were only twenty-five remaining.

"One of the Confederates, a man who, at the time was ninety-four, said he had fought at the Battle of the Peach Orchard. Sadly, he told the crowd of onlookers that after the war ended, he never had another peach. This wonderful, juicy fruit just reminded him of the bloodshed and the carnage he had witnessed on the field. Hence, the Battle of the Peach Orchard."

"So, what happened to the orchard? With all the cannon fire and the fighting for hours, the peach trees must have been ruined."

"They were not all ruined but most of the trees and the ground itself were damaged. The orchard was owned by a farmer by the name of Joseph Sherfy. After both armies pulled out leaving the entire Gettysburg area in a state of agricultural turmoil, Sherfy went to work to bring back the orchard and restore it to its original fruit-bearing ways. It took a few years but eventually, he started to sell delicious Gettysburg peaches once again. Sales were quite good. Sherfy was able to advertise that his peaches came from the original trees that were there during the horrific battle."

Elizabeth joked, "You know a lot about the Civil War, but I bet I know more about peaches than you do."

"Well, I'm not going to argue with that. After all, you said your family had a peach orchard. The closest I've even been to a peach is out of a can."

"I think I can explain my knowledge of peaches from a mathematical point. Remember after we first met you explained to me that even on a farm numbers matter. When I was a little girl, we had thirty-six mature peach trees. Over the years some have died off either from the weather or from disease. I think as it stands right now, we still have twenty-seven healthy trees standing. Each tree can yield from three to six bushels. A bushel contains about one hundred and fifty peaches weighing about fifty pounds. When you multiply the number of trees, we have which is twenty-seven you come up with approximately, four bushels times twenty-seven trees which equals six hundred peaches per tree for a total harvest of somewhere in the area of sixteen thousand peaches! You said The Battle of the Peach Orchard was fought on July 2nd. It just so happens peaches in Pennsylvania are normally picked in late July. This can only mean the peaches in Sherfy's orchard were close to being harvested, but as you say the orchard was ruined. This must have been heartbreaking for this farmer...Sherfy."

Max took two quick steps and turned around facing Elizabeth while he walked backwards. Holding out his hands he blurted out. "I concede. You know more about peaches than I do. Sixteen thousand peaches! Let alone how do you manage to get them picked, after that what do you do with thousands of peaches? You told me you have two sisters and young twin brothers still living at home. Including you and your mother and father then means you have seven people to do the picking. That sounds like a lot of work for seven people."

"We always have a lot of help. When it's time to harvest the peaches it's a community event. Everyone pitches in, and each family in the community gets their fair share of peaches. It's the same with apples. Ellen Stolz, my friend, well her family has a huge apple orchard. We no sooner finish up picking peaches in late July when in mid-August everyone helps the Stolz's to pick their apples. I remember as a little girl when I and my sisters would walk around the trees and pick up fallen peaches or apples. Then, when we were older, we would pick the lower fruit from the trees. The adults always harvest the higher fruit."

"Sounds like there's never a dull moment in your community. What do you do with all these peaches and apples?"

"A lot of them are sold at three different farmer's markets in Lancaster. Other than that, we bake peach and apple pies, we make peach cobbler and peach honey. One of the first things my father always does with the peaches, and this happens each year, in August in the dog days of summer when the heat is stifling is he makes homemade ice cream.

"We have an old-fashioned hand crank ice cream maker. My father would dump in the ice, salt, and cream and then I remember me and my sisters sitting for hours turning the crack as we churned the concoction into ice cream. My father would add fresh-cut peaches toward the end of the long process…the result was the best peach ice cream that ever passed over your lips and down your throat. To this day my mother claims I could eat more peach ice cream than anyone in the community. When I think back to all the ice cream I ate as a youngster I should weigh five hundred pounds."

Max held up his right hand. "We've arrived. With all this talk about pie and ice cream, I'm going with a dessert of some kind after dinner."

They hesitated in a small lobby while reading the specials written in chalk on an eye-level easel board. Max immediately spoke up. "I'm going to go with the pork chops with the two sides. Anything look good to you?"

Elizabeth scanned the white writing and then responded, "Meatloaf…I'm having the meatloaf."

Another metal stand sign just inside the small restaurant read: Please seat yourself.

Max motioned at a table against the wall on the left, Elizabeth following him across the room. Pulling the chair out for her, Max looked around the eatery, noticing just two other seated couples. "They don't seem very busy tonight."

Elizabeth fingered an ornamental peach arrangement on the table while admiring the décor of the restaurant. "I love the theme they have chosen.

Everything is about peaches from their tablecloths to the lighting. I especially like the large mural of that peach orchard."

"Believe it or not that is the modern version of the Peach Orchard where the battle I told you about took place."

A waitress approached and politely spoke, "Good evening. Can I start you folks off with something to drink?"

"Yes," said Max. "I would like some of your freshly brewed peach tea." Speaking to Elizabeth, he pointed out, "If you like tea, they have a great peach tea here. I highly recommend it."

"All right," said Elizabeth. "Peach tea it is then."

Before the waitress could run off Max added, "We already know what we'd like to order. I'm having the pork chops with mashed potatoes and the green beans, and she'll have the meatloaf with…"

Elizabeth finished the sentence, "With mashed potatoes and creamed corn."

The waitress nodded while writing on her pad, "I'll put your orders in, and I'll be right back with house salads. We have four different dressings which are on the table."

Elizabeth placed a cloth napkin on her lap and asked, "We last talked on Wednesday. Anything interesting happened since then?"

"It's funny you should ask because several things have happened to me this past week and all of them happened today! Mathematically speaking up until meeting you for dinner this evening I've experienced five different situations of which four were on the negative side. That means up until we met tonight, I'm having an 80% bad day."

"I'm glad you said up until we met. I'd hate to think I am in any way part of a bad day for you. So, what happened?"

"It all started early this morning when I got up. I'm on my way out of my room on the way to the pool for a morning swim when I find this under my door." Reaching into his pocket he removed the envelope containing the note and slid it across the table.

Elizabeth was about to pick it up when the waitress returned with a pitcher of tea and two glasses. She placed the glassware on the table and announced, "Free refills. Your meals should be out in about ten minutes."

Max poured tea into both empty glasses as he suggested, "Go on, open it."

Elizabeth read his name on the front and then opened the envelope and extracted the folded note. Laying it on the table she smoothed out the edges and read the note in a low tone of voice, "THIS IS FAR FROM OVER!" Folding the note back up she placed it back in the envelope and pushed it to the side. "I assume the note is from Brad Sykes. I mean…who else could it be from?"

"That's the same thing I thought," said Max "I don't have any proof Brad wrote it, but when you consider what happened at the Palace it seems logical he is the creator of the negative message."

"What do you think it means?"

"I've thought about that, and it could mean one of two things. It could be Brad is referring to the upcoming meeting with his lawyers or it could also mean he is planning something on his own, possibly in the future…a way to get even with me."

"Did you contact your father or your lawyer about this?"

"No, I did not. I, or no one else for that matter, can prove Brad is behind the note. Depending on how things go at the meeting I may bring it up. I'm not sure."

Elizabeth tapped the envelope with her left hand and remarked, "The words in this message seem threatening. Doesn't that bother you?"

"In a way it does but then in another way it doesn't. It bothers me Brad might be planning an unpleasant event for me in the future and short of just being careful of where I go and what I do there is nothing I can do about it. On the other hand, it might just simply be a scare tactic. If he is planning on doing something I don't think he'll try anything before the meeting. I think he'll wait until I'm not expecting something or until I let my guard down. If he has something in mind, it may not happen for months. If he feels he has an axe to grind with me, I'll just have to deal with that when the time comes."

Elizabeth pushed the envelope back across the table. "That's one negative item out of the way. You said you had four other moments. What happened next?"

Max placed the envelope back in his jacket pocket and explained, "I wasn't about to allow this note to ruin the day so off to the pool I went just as planned. I'm at the sports complex in the locker room for no more than a few minutes when two, what I assume were school football players approach me and, how can I put this…they gave me a rough time. They accused me of sucker punching Brad and one of the players even suggested

I try and take him on. I tried my best to ignore them but one of them slams my locker shut and tosses my gym bag down the aisle. If my roommate, Scott, who I told you is on the wrestling team, would not have happened by, I think I would have gotten my butt kicked. He stood up to them and ran them off, so I guess you could say I dodged a bullet."

Elizabeth scooted forward as she asked, "Do you think Brad sent them to bother you?"

"In the back of my mind, based on the note it would be easy to say he was behind those two players confronting me, but in the end, I can't prove it. If it came down to it if I reported this to the school or my lawyer, the players could deny it ever even happened. It would be my word, and Scott's against theirs. These types and future run-ins with Brad's friends might be part of his threatening note."

"I take it from what you said you didn't mention this football player incident to your lawyer either."

"No, I haven't mentioned it to anyone but you. I'm going to keep this incident along with the threatening note close to the vest, as they say. I may be able to use these two negative moments, if need be, during the meeting."

"Two down and three to go." said Elizabeth. "What happened next?"

"The next thing I did turned out to be the one incident during the earlier part of the day that was rather pleasant. I decided to take a bike ride out to Little Round Top, one of the Gettysburg battle sites. I won't bore you with stats about that particular battle, but I will say I climbed up Little Round Top and sat on a bench they have up there for tourists. I always have enjoyed going up there. It's a place where you can go and relax. Ya know… just sit there and enjoy the peace of nature. Well, there I am just staring off into the woods when down the path strolls this older man. He joined me on the bench, and we had quite the conversation, but before I get into that I want to tell you about the other two unpleasant moments of my day. We'll get back to Little Round Top later."

Elizabeth tugged at her right ear. "Still listening!"

"When I got back to the dorm from Little Round Top, I was notified by our on-duty desk man someone had dropped a piece of mail off for me…and here it is." Max withdrew the legal envelope from his pocket and slid it across the table.

Elizabeth read the name of the law firm, frowned, and then opened the envelope and removed the document. She read it silently, then laid it to the side. "No more guessing about when the meeting is to take place. By this time next Saturday, it should all be wrapped up."

Max reached over and placed the envelope and letter back in his jacket. "The term, 'wrapped up' could mean any number of things, but from what my attorney has said all along we'll probably lose, and I'll wind up being sued for thousands of dollars." Giving her a look of hopelessness, Max sadly joked, "Starting next week after the meeting I might not be able to afford to take you to dinner."

She placed her hand over his and spoke with confidence. "I don't know much about the law but from where I sit it sounds like you've already given up. Maybe you should start thinking more positively. You said yourself your lawyer feels you have a good case."

Max sat back and shook his head. "We'll see!"

Elizabeth crossed her arms across her chest. "I'm ready for the last unpleasant thing that happened to you today."

"Unlike the first two things that happened which I have chosen to not reveal to my lawyer yet, I did call him and tell him about the notice of the meeting. He told me to make a copy and send him the original, which I did as soon as we finished talking. While I was downtown, I decided to ride around a bit and wound up at the town square. I then went to Starbucks for a coffee and low and behold who do I run into…Brad Sykes and some of his friends. Being Brad, he just couldn't let it go so he started to make some snide remarks about me, which I ignored. Before he left, he moved down the counter to where I was standing. He leans over close to my face and in a cocky sort of way says, 'Hope you have a good lawyer…I do!' Then he and the others walked out. This incident, I also did not tell my lawyer about. And that in a nutshell sums up my day…well that is until now."

The waitress returned to their table and placed their meals in front of them and asked if they needed anything else. After she walked off, Elizabeth commented, "That was perfect timing. Now you can tell me all about your pleasant day at Little Round Top over dinner. I believe you said an older fella joined you on a bench and you had quite the conversation. Let's bless this food and then pick it up from there."

The blessing complete, Max cut into his chop and then took a bite of potatoes. "We talked about the historic battle for an hour or so when suddenly he asked me if I had seen ghosts anywhere on the battlefield. His question took me totally by surprise and I answered by saying I couldn't remember ever seeing a ghost anywhere, let alone here in Gettysburg. He went on to tell me he had seen what he thought were ghosts a couple of times in the area and we both agreed at times in life some things happen that are kind of unexplainable. He then proceeds to tell me about two times in his past life where there was a possible ghost that had entered his life and still today, he cannot say what he was told or what he had seen was not true."

Max chewed on a bite of pork and continued to expand on Kellem's strange story. "Kellem said his father had told him and his two older brothers when they were about ten years of age about a time when he saw a Confederate soldier who appeared at the fence near the back of their property on their farm. It was a young man, maybe in his late teens or early twenties, dressed as a Confederate soldier from the Civil War, off-gray wool uniform with a matching battered hat, musket, and canteen. The strange part about the soldier was that he was bleeding, more than likely from a wound. But this would have been impossible because if the boy was a reenactor he couldn't have been wounded as reenactors never use live ammunition. His father said he approached the lad, but he limped back off into the trees up a small rise beyond the fence. Kellem said that over the years he forgot about the strange meeting but then thirty-one years later the soldier appeared again. He said by that time their father had passed on and he and his two brothers were working the farm.

"Kellem claims he was walking out of the barn and there, standing by the fence is this young soldier. He recalled the story his father had shared with him years in the past. Standing there, he just couldn't believe what he was seeing. Over three decades had passed, and there in his backyard stood this Confederate soldier who fit the description of the soldier his father had seen some three decades in the past, gray, wool uniform, the musket in his hand, the old canteen, and the wounds. Kellem said he started to walk across the yard toward the boy when he up and limped off into the trees just like the boy his father had seen did. Kellem said he jumped over the fence and had every intention of following, what he thought could be a reenactor, but when he got on the other side of the fence, he got the strangest feeling like he wasn't supposed to be there. Kellem was convinced he had been in the presence of a ghost...what other explanation could there be?"

Elizabeth was about to take a forkful of corn to her mouth but hesitated and laid the fork back on her plate. "I don't know how to answer your question. Sitting here listening to you go on about what this Kellem told you I can't offer you a reasonable explanation. As a Mennonite, growing up in our community I have always and still to this day do not believe in ghosts. Now, saying that our religion teaches us that angels do exist. I can say in my eighteen years of life I have never seen an angel…or a ghost."

"You bring up an interesting point," said Max. "Is there a difference between a ghost and an angel?"

"Since I have never seen either, how can I answer that? In your world, the world I'm taught to try and steer clear of, what do you see as the difference between ghosts and angels?"

"Like you, I also have never seen an angel or a ghost. The church my parents and I have attended since I was born, which is about nineteen years, has had three different pastors. They all, at one time or another, preached about angels. Based on their teachings I believe angels are messengers of God sent to earth to protect us from evil and destruction. Like I said, I've never seen an angel but, like most Christians, I associate angels with something good.

"On the other side of the coin, many people claim there are ghosts. It has been my experience in life that ghosts are associated with evil or not-so-good. So, if there are angels, I feel they are from God and if there are ghosts, I feel they may be of the ol' devil himself. The world I live in celebrates Halloween every year at the end of October. Often, parents dress their children in outfits ranging from ghosts to witches, to devils and all sorts of creatures. This is all done in fun, but I don't feel it's the work of God."

Swallowing some corn, Elizabeth agreed, "You're exactly right in what you say. As Mennonites, we do not celebrate Halloween. We view it as a pagan holiday. Dressing your children up to appear as a ghost or a witch is simply inviting evil into one's life. As far as your friend Kellem's ghost story goes I think you're correct in saying it may just be one of those things in life that are unexplainable. When you take the time to think about it what difference does Kellem's story make in our lives?"

Max was quick with an answer, "None…absolutely none!"

"That's right and at the moment and for the next week you have something else you need to focus on, and that's this upcoming meeting."

"Speaking of the meeting next Saturday. My father and my lawyer are going to arrive here in Gettysburg sometime on Friday. I'm sure we'll meet up and go over how we intend to handle Brad, his father, and their lawyers.

I'm not sure you and I will be able to meet for dinner as usual next Saturday. Depending on how things go I may have to have dinner with my dad and my lawyer."

"Don't worry about that…or even me. You need to do what you have to, to prepare for this meeting. When you get everything straightened around, I'll still be here." Cutting into her meatloaf, she pointed her fork at Max and stated, "Two things, first of all, I'll be praying for you and that God will have His staying hand on the meeting and second…you need to eat that pork chop before it gets cold!"

CHAPTER TEN

Max, seated in his business and accounting class, looked at the circular clock centered over a wall-mounted chalkboard: 2:10 in the afternoon. Professor Langston's class was scheduled to start at precisely 2:05, but the professor who was well up in years had a habit of always arriving a few minutes late.

The male student seated next to Max leaned over and tapped him on the shoulder. "Miller…the word around campus is you are going to court tomorrow over this business with Sykes."

Max couldn't see any harm in answering the question. "You heard wrong. It's just a meeting with Sykes and his lawyers to discuss what happened between Brad and me. We'll never see the inside of a courtroom. It'll be settled out of court."

"Well, for what it's worth, you have more people around here who support you than you probably imagine. Sykes happens to be in one of my classes. I've never spoken to him, but it's easy to see he's one of those spoiled rich kids who thinks he can do or say whatever he pleases. Money can go a long way in covering up or maybe even excusing one's faults. Good luck tomorrow!"

Max's cell phone buzzed as he raised his right hand to interrupt the student. "Excuse me, but I've got to take this call." Stepping out into the hallway he leaned against the wall and answered, "Hello."

A sense of relief flooded over him when he heard his father's voice, "It's me, Max. Rich and I just pulled into Gettysburg. We're getting a room at the Holiday Inn. Where are you now?"

"I'm just about to enter my last class of the day. It should end around three to three-fifteen. After that, I'm free for the rest of the day."

"Good, let's plan on the three of us having dinner at the Peach Orchard this evening at about five. Can you make that?"

"Yes, I can. You better call ahead and get reservations. With it being Friday night every restaurant in town will be crowded."

"How is everything going?"

"Fine, Dad. Listen, I've got to run. My class is about to start." The call over, Max noticed Langston slowly walking down the hall.

The old professor, seeing Max leaning against the wall stopped and adjusted a set of ancient glasses held together with a small section of Duct Tape. Looking Max up and down, the professor cleared his throat and asked in a rude tone, "Will you be joining us this afternoon, Miller?"

Cordially, Max opened the door and spoke politely, "After you, Sir."

For the second time in the past seven days, Max walked into the Peach Orchard. Before the hostess could utter a word, he inquired, "Do you have a reservation for the Miller party?"

She scanned a clipboard and replied, "We have a Charley Miller and two guests."

"That would be my father. He and his other guest should be arriving in the next few minutes. Can I be seated, or do I need to wait until they arrive?"

She nodded and grabbed three menus. "If you will please follow me we have your party over there by the front window."

At the table, she announced their waitress would be Carolyn and that she would be right over. She no sooner left when a young red-headed girl Max had seen around campus walked up and introduced herself, then asked, "Would you care to order a drink, or do you want to wait for the rest of your party?"

Max quickly answered, "I think I'll just go ahead and order a peach iced tea with lemon."

By the time she returned with the drink, Charley and Rich followed her across the room to the table. Charley pulled out a chair and seated himself while speaking to the girl. "I'd like a glass of your peach tea. How about you Rich? What are you drinking?"

"Tea sounds fine to me, and I would also like a cup of coffee."

Charley held up his index finger, addressing the waitress, "Then let's just make that a pitcher of tea."

Rich rubbed his hands together and looked around the small restaurant. "I hope the food here is as good as your father claims it to be. Right now, I'm in the mood for a cup of hot coffee and a hearty, warm meal." Angling his thumb toward the window, he elaborated, "It's only 29 out there. When we left Charleston this morning it was almost fifty. I don't know if I could function day in, day out in this cold weather."

"That was my first reaction," said Max, "but you get used to it. Besides, with any luck you two should be heading back to sunny South Carolina tomorrow afternoon."

"Let's talk about that," said Rich. "Has anything unusual happened since we last talked?"

"Yes, I did have something happen during my last class earlier today. One of the students in my class mentioned to me the word around campus was I was going to court tomorrow over this Brad Sykes situation. The only person who I told about tomorrow's meeting was Elizabeth and I guarantee you; she hasn't said a word to anyone about the meeting. Brad, no doubt has made it known around campus about the meeting. Other than that, things seem to be pretty normal."

"I did a little checking on this law firm who is representing Brad Sykes. Dolstrum, Eichman and Dunn have only been in existence since 2003, which means they have been in business for nine years. Now, Michael P. Dolstrum, one of the partners who signed your notification has been in the legal business for twenty-five years, graduating with a law degree from, you're not going to believe this, but Gettysburg College back in 1992, the year Brad's father, Harmon Sykes also graduated from good 'ol Gettysburg. Turns out they were the best of friends in college. Harmon, graduating with a degree in business, went on to become a very wealthy entrepreneur while his close friend, Dolstrum, passed the bar and became a lawyer.

"Michael Dolstrum's father, Tilton Dolstrum at the time owned a very prestigious law firm in Harrisburg, the state capitol, just up the road not an hour from where we now sit. At one time, Tilton was the mayor of Harrisburg, eventually ran for the state senate and was defeated. He returned to his law practice and when his son, Michael, graduated from law school, he went to work for his father.

"A few years down the road ol' Tilton died, and his son Michael took over the business. In 2003 he joined forces with two other high-profile lawyers, Eichman and Dunn and they retained their office in Harrisburg and opened offices in Lancaster, Pennsylvania, and here in Gettysburg. According to the Pennsylvania Board of Law firms, Dunn and Bradstreet and the local Better Business Bureau, Dolstrum, Eichman and Dunn hold an excellent A-1 credit rating and are highly regarded in the industry. In short, these people are not what I would call ambulance chasers we are dealing with. Between their three offices, they have a working staff of thirty-three lawyers, who specialize in everything from corporate law to accident and injury, to divorce matters, and on and on. We're going to be going up against some major leaguers when we walk into tomorrow's meeting. Just saying!"

Max looked at his father and then to Rich, "You make it sound like we are inferior to Dolstrum and his staff."

"We're not inferior to them," pointed out Rich, "they just happen to be very good at what they do. In the legal business, legitimate law firms like Dolstrum, Eichman and Dunn have nothing to hide. I can assure you the people we are going to meet tomorrow are above board. We don't have to concern ourselves with them pulling any tricks or doing something that is not ethical. They will present their case to the letter of the law. I called their firm and talked with Michael Dolstrum. He couldn't have been more cooperative over the phone. We briefly discussed the case and he said he and his staff were looking forward to meeting us. He told me he is confident we can come to a mutual agreement and keep the situation out of court.

"Now, that being said. Some lawyers, not all, but some operate like politicians. They say one thing and then do another. When we meet up with Dolstrum tomorrow morning we'll know within the first few minutes what type of lawyers we're dealing with. Either way, we stick to the plan we discussed. Remember, we're going to be on their turf. We cannot allow them to dominate or control the meeting at all times. We have to walk in there with confidence knowing we can win this thing. Any other attitude than that and they will eat us for lunch, as they say. We have to look, act, and think sharp."

Max, in wonder, asked, "How do you know all this information?"

"Easy," said Rich. "Every law firm, including the one I work with always has someone who does their investigative work. It could be a local detective or someone on the police force. In our case, I happen to be friends with a detective with the Charleston Police. He made a few phone calls and, bingo, we get the lowdown on Dolstrum, Eichman and Dunn."

"If that's the case, then they must know about your law firm as well."

"Maybe, maybe not. Remember we had an entire week of notification as to who they are. I didn't phone Dolstrum until Thursday afternoon, just yesterday. More than likely, they probably didn't have enough time to find out that much about me or our firm."

"Speaking of looking sharp," said Charley. "Your mother had me purchase you a brand new dark blue suit, conservative gray tie, white shirt, and new shoes. She didn't want these northern lawyers to think you are some swamp-running, backwoods kid from the south. I guess it's her way of supporting you since she can't be here. So, how do you feel about tomorrow?"

"I guess I feel pretty good. I'm not 100% sure we are going to walk out of there with a victory. I'm not even sure I'm at fifty-fifty. You said yourself, Rich, there is a good chance we'll lose, but be able to cut our losses to a minimal amount. I kind of feel like we're sailing into uncharted waters."

"That's a good way to put it," said Rich, "but it's not like I've never sailed a boat before. We'll put our boat in the water tomorrow and I think no matter what they throw at us we'll manage to stay afloat. Remember this, they can't be sure what we are going to bring to the table. In the end, whichever boat can take on the most water and remain afloat will come out of the meeting ahead."

Charley stood and motioned at a long buffet table toward the back of the restaurant. "All this talking is making me hungry. I'm going with the buffet."

Max nodded and agreed, "It's the buffet for me too."

Rich stood. "Let's make it unanimous then!"

It was a miserable kind of morning, the mixture of snow, sleet, and rain making for an unpleasant start to the weekend. Charley parked the rental car in a paved lot next to a two-story creek stone home that at one time had been an expensive residence but now housed the law firm of Dolstrum, Eichman and Dunn. Rich checked his watch as he held his hands over the heater vent. "It's quarter to ten. I know we're a little early, but I say let's go in and relax for a few minutes before this thing kicks off."

As they walked across the slush-covered pavement, Rich pointed at a row of cars parked near the back of the lot, a black Mercedes, a silver Cadillac, a dark blue Corvette, and three conservative compact cars. "You can tell a lot about whether a law firm is making big money or not by looking at their employee parking. Those three luxury cars no doubt are owned by Dolstrum and his partners, the other three vehicles probably belong to secretaries or lawyers who haven't reached the level of success where they can afford anything but a conservative car."

Max, moving up next to Rich, stated, "I've always been under the opinion that all lawyers are rolling in the cash."

"Not so. In the legal business, the twenty-eighty rule comes into play as it does in most business. When it comes to lawyers, 20% of them make 80% of the money and the remaining 80% of barristers scramble for the remaining 20%." Gesturing toward the expensive vehicles, Rich grinned, "It's easy to see that Dolstrum, Eichman and Dunn are in the lower percentage of lawyers making the higher percentage of money. What I'm saying is these guys have been around the block a few times. They are not going to be pushovers."

Walking up classic marbled concrete steps flanked on either side by life-size concrete lions, Rich opened a massive eight-foot-high walnut door and then followed Charley and Max into an eight-by-ten-foot foyer leading to a spacious waiting room. An attractive secretary with long blond hair was seated behind a large walnut desk. Upon seeing the three arrivals she politely asked in a sweet voice, "May I help you, gentlemen?"

Rich approached the desk and introduced himself while handing her a business card. "Yes, my name is Richard Mathers and I am representing Maxwell Miller. We have a ten o'clock meeting with Michael Dolstrum."

The secretary glanced at the time on a grandfather clock in the corner of the room while checking a ledger on her desk. "Yes, here it is. If you'll just have a seat Michael will be right with you." Gesturing at an antique walnut buffet she explained, "We have coffee, sodas, juice, and water. Please help yourself. It'll be a few minutes before the meeting will begin."

Following Rich to the beverage selections, Charley and Max stared at several eight-by-ten framed photographs hung on a wall to the right of the beverage buffet. Rich poured himself a cup of coffee, added cream and sugar then walked to the wall.

Charley sat on an expensive black leather couch while Max grabbed a bottle of water and then joined his father. Staring at a huge crystal chandelier, the rosewood paneling, and the plush deep green carpet, Max whispered, "This place bespeaks of a great deal of money. I'm beginning to understand what Rich was talking about before. It's like waiting to see God! It's rather intimidating."

After two minutes of silence, Rich sat on a matching black leather chair across from Charley and Max. Placing his coffee on a nearby small coffee table he revealed something he had discovered. "Those photos over there on the wall number over twenty. They are all dated by year and location. They are all fishing trips up to Canada. On close examination, at the bottom of each photo, there is a list from right to left of those in each picture holding up fish they caught. Some of the photos list John Eichman and Authur Dunn. *All of the photos* have Harmon Sykes and Michael Dolstrum in them. The investigator we used to get the lowdown on Dolstrum, Eichman and Dunn informed me Sykes and Dolstrum were old college buddies and have remained friends over the years, at least according to the pictures. It would only make sense Brad's father would turn to his close friend Michael Dolstrum, who just happens to be a highly successful lawyer to represent his son. It's a safe bet to say Dolstrum reviewed the case thoroughly before taking it on. If he didn't think Harmon Sykes and his son had a chance to win this thing, he'd tell them upfront. Let's face it, Dolstrum doesn't need to take on this case, because when you think about it, it boils down to two young men barely out of high school who get into an argument which results in one hitting the other. Dolstrum doesn't need that type of penny-penny business. I'll tell you why he took on this case. He took it on as a favor to his longtime friend, Harmon Sykes. I guarantee you he has probably told Sykes this is a slam dunk in their favor. When this thing starts, he'll pull out all the stops to prove that you… Max are in the wrong."

Max took a short swig of water and then asked Rich, "Aren't we doing the same thing? My father, just like Brad's, wants the best for his son. You and my father, just like Harmon Sykes and Michael Dolstrum have been friends for years. He turned to you, just like Brad's father did for his son. What's the difference?"

"The difference is that Michael Dolstrum is going into this without one single shred of doubt that they can win, or he would not have taken the case. I told you right up front we'll probably lose. I'm just trying to keep your losses as low as possible. If we can manage that then in a sense, we've won."

Max took another drink of water and then spoke, "I had lunch with Elizabeth this past Wednesday. She told me she was praying for me and about this meeting. She quoted me a Bible verse from the book of Proverbs that pretty much sums up what we're faced with. *The axe may be dull, its edge unsharpened but with skill and strength success can still be achieved.* I've thought about that verse every day since. We may be headed into this meeting with a dull axe, but with your skill and strength Rich, we can still succeed even though they may be wielding a razor-sharp chainsaw. I think there is a possibility we could win this thing."

Charley lightly punched his son on his shoulder, "They say attitude is everything. If that is true, then I say let's swing our axe with confidence!"

Rich checked the time. "It's past ten now. It's five after. Their plan is already underway, and the meeting hasn't even started. We show up early and they make us wait. It's a silent message that they are in control. When we get in there, they'll try to control the entire meeting. We cannot allow this to happen. We need to counter and chip away at everything they throw at us."

The secretary walked over to the couch and professionally announced, "If you gentlemen will follow me into the conference room."

Max, Charley, and Rich followed the woman across the room and down a hall lined with well-maintained tropical plants in brass planters. The walls were decorated with various framed documents of achievement and polished wooden plaques complete with raised gold embossed lettering. At the end of the hall, they made a right and entered what, at one time, had no doubt been a large formal living room. Another crystal chandelier, larger than the one in the outer office, was centered in the ten-foot-high ceiling, and a twelve-foot walnut table complete with fourteen chairs with inlaid dark green velvet was spaced evenly around the table. At the far end of the room, there was a large floor-to-ceiling, burning fireplace surrounded by rows of walnut shelving containing law books bound in a deep green and trimmed in gold. The woman walked to the center of the room and gestured for the three visitors to be seated on the right. Max seated himself between Rich and Charley as he gazed around the magnificent room. "Whoever lived here in the past was a very wealthy person."

Rich opened his briefcase and stated, "We're going to have our hands full today. Now, before they get in here. I'll do most or maybe even all of the talking. If they ask either one of you a question look at me first and I'll give you a nod if you should reply. They are going to be throwing a lot of one-hundred-mile-an-hour fastballs at us. We need to be able to hit the ball back at them with greater speed than it comes at us…"

Rich's explanation of what was about to transpire was interrupted when a short parade of five males and one female entered the room. The female who was wearing a pin-striped business suit sat at the head of the table while placing a manila folder on the table. She looked at Max, Charley, and Rich and smiled pleasantly. The five males continued down the side of the table, where a young man in the lead stopped two chairs from the end. The other four males, one of whom happened to be Brad, turned and faced Max and his small team. Brad had a snide grin on his face as he stared directly at Max but remained silent. The second man in line, a very distinctive gray-haired gentleman who was wearing a custom black, three-piece suit extended his hand while introducing himself. "Welcome, my name is Michael Dolstrum, one of the partners here at our firm."

Rich instantly stood and took the man's manicured hand as he responded, "Richard Mathers of Mathers and Wilts out of Charleston, South Carolina." Turning to Charley and Max, Rich continued, "This is my client, Maxwell Miller, and his father Charles."

Dolstrum smiled broadly and stated, "Yes, I believe we spoke on the phone, what was it, this past Thursday. Allow me to introduce you to the others on our side of the table. The young man on my left is Stanley Finch, who is on our legal staff. He has been practicing law for the past seven years. The lawyer on my right is the newest addition to our firm; Lance Redmond, who just passed the bar exam two months back. The two gentlemen standing next to Stanley are my client, Bradley Sykes, and his father Harmon." Everyone reached across the table and shook hands except for Brad who sat down, leaned back, and crossed his arms in defiance.

Max watched as his father and Brad's father engaged in a friendly handshake, two very distinctly different men there on behalf of their sons. Charley Miller, a high school graduate who owned a construction company and made his living digging in the dirt, a man who at the end of a day's work came home filthy. A man who wore his best and only suit for the meeting; a plain gray affair that he had owned for years and only wore to weddings and funerals.

Harmon Sykes, a self-made millionaire stood across the table from Charley, a tailored Italian suit fitting his medium frame perfectly, French Cuffs with inlaid gold cufflinks, and a gold Rolex watch peeking out from the edge of the sleeve of his suit coat. The two men smiled at one another, but what could they be thinking? The same was true of Micheal Dolstrum and Rich Mathers as they clasped hands. He did not doubt that Rich was a good lawyer, but he got the feeling that Rich, his father, and even himself were outmatched.

Dolstrum spread out his hands as he addressed everyone present at the table. "Before we begin I'd like to lay down some basic ground rules so we can move the process along. I would suggest if anyone needs to use the restroom facilities they do so now. If anyone needs to get a coffee or beverage that also needs to be taken care of at this time." Hesitating, he looked up and down the table; not one individual budged. Dolstrum then seated himself as he offered, "Well then let's be seated and get the meeting started."

After everyone was seated, he folded his hands on top of the table and continued to dominate the conversation as he gestured at the woman at the end of the table. "Mrs. Chambers, who is one of our in-staff paralegals will be reading the deposition given to us by our client, Brad Sykes. If at any time during the reading, counsel for Mr. Miller can feel free to speak up with any objections, additions, or deletions he feels are necessary." Motioning to the lawyer on his left, he went on, "Mr. Finch will be recording our conversation for the records so there can be no future discrepancy as to what was discussed here today. There are legal pads and ink pens at each seating location for anyone who wants to take notes." Looking at Rich, Dolstrum inquired, "Any questions at this time?"

Rich opened his briefcase while speaking, "No questions, but we as counsel for Mr. Miller will be recording also. Any objections?"

Dolstrum flashed a healthy-toothed smile and replied, "No objections, and that being said if there are no other questions then Mrs. Chambers can begin the reading of the deposition."

Opening the manila folder, the female paralegal balanced a set of reading glasses on her short nose, softly cleared her throat and then began, "This deposition number 517-S was taken by Dolstrum, Eichman and Dunn Law Firm located at 317 Baltimore Street, Gettysburg, Pennsylvania on January the 22nd, 2013 starting at 7:04 P.M. and ending at 7:37 P.M. The client, Bradley F. Sykes gave this deposition in the presence of Michael P. Dolstrum and Stanley Finch, attorneys at law, along with Harmon Sykes, the client's father and Glenda Chambers, paralegal. The deposition reads as follows: On Tuesday evening December 21st, 2012 Brad Sykes and three other students, namely, Walt Krenshall, Matt Hughes, and Edward Levoy entered The Burger Palace located at 214 Steinwehr Avenue shortly after eight o'clock. Brad and his companions approached the counter where they were met by a counter girl by the name of Cindy Wells and a shift manager by the name of Max Miller. After placing their food orders they proceeded to the drink dispensers and then seated themselves in the dining area…"

Seconds later, Rich lowered his head and shook it slightly then raised his hand while speaking, "There seems to be a problem with the deposition. I know there is much more that happened leading up to the confrontation between our client and yours, but it would appear that we are off to a questionable start. I have in my nearly thirty years as an attorney sat through many a deposition. A simplistic deposition is much different than sitting on the witness stand in court where an individual, regardless of who they may be must swear to tell the truth, the whole truth, and nothing but the truth. Most people do not realize it, but these are three different things. Now, your client, Brad Sykes, may be telling the truth, but he has not told the whole truth and is nowhere near divulging nothing but the truth."

Dolstrum, not the least bit intimidated by Rich's profound statement leaned back in his chair, ran a finger across his pencil-thin mustache, and smiled, "Please, go on."

"I intend to," stated Rich. "First of all, the beginning of this entire ordeal didn't take place sometime shortly after eight o'clock. The time was exactly 8:05."

"That hardly seems like an issue to be concerned over Mr. Mathers. The time frame here has nothing to do with what went on minutes later."

"I agree, but we just want counsel to know we have done our homework on this case and we will not accept anything but the absolute truth."

Nodding at Finch, Dolstrum in a commanding sort of way suggested, "Make a note of the exact time, Stanley."

"And that's not the only discrepancy in your deposition," said Rich. "When Brad and his companions entered Burger Palace, they just didn't simply enter and approach the counter. Anyone with half a brain who was present at the time could tell these four young men had been drinking. They were loud, boisterous, and a nuisance to everyone working and dining in the establishment." Sorting through a small stack of documents Rich held up a sheet of paper and explained, "Here is a copy of the police report filed after Brad and his companions were arrested and charged with underage drinking, public intoxication, disorderly conduct, destruction of company property and last but not least, assault and battery."

Dolstrum turned again to Finch and asked, "Do we not have a copy of the arrest report?"

Finch, right on top of things produced a duplicate document that Rich had presented. Rich, now on a roll and in his mind in control of the meeting laid the document down and spoke again, "Wait, there's more! Brad and his three cohorts, because of their loud and unruly behavior ran off four groups of customers who were in the restaurant at the time of their arrival. One customer, an older gentleman who is a regular at the Palace, suggested to Max he should call the police. Max explained that the manager had already been contacted and was on his way and that he would make that decision. The old man proceeds to Brad's table and tells the boys they need to settle down." Looking directly at Brad, Rich emphasized, "Your client, Brad Sykes stands up and gets in the man's face, calls him an old fart, and tells him to get the hell out of the restaurant and mind his own business. Just previous to this conversation one of the other boys grabs a chair from a table where a family was seated and tells them he is taking it and doesn't care if they mind."

Dolstrum sat forward as he spoke to Finch, "Are you getting all this?"

Finch who was writing as fast as he could responded, "Yes sir!"

Max, who was enjoying Rich's attack on the first part of the deposition looked at Brad's father who was giving his son a not-so-friendly look.

Rich leaned forward and spoke directly to Dolstrum. "Your client may have told the truth, but we bring the whole truth and nothing but the truth to the table. That's all we have at the moment."

Dolstrum raised his eyebrows, no doubt relieved that the counterattack had come to an end. Reaching over, he took the police report from Finch, laid it in front of himself tapped it with his right hand, and explained, "We concede our client was drinking and was underage to consume alcohol. We also concede he and those with him were loud and boisterous as you point out. The fact that some of the customers decided to leave due to the fact they may have felt uncomfortable has no bearing on the fact that *your client, one Max Miller* hit *Brad Sykes* without provocation. Just because someone is drunk gives no one the right to attack or hit them. Just because someone makes a nuisance of themselves also does not give anyone the right to punch someone in the face. We're not implying our client was not without fault on this particular night. What we are stating is Max Miller had no right to lash out at Brad Sykes. That's the law! Any other objections at this point?"

Rich shrugged, smiled sarcastically, and answered, "No more objections at this time. Let's continue with the reading. I think it will be very interesting."

Dolstrum nodded at Mrs. Chambers. She took a long drink from a glass of water and then began. "Okay, we left off with Brad and his friends seating themselves in the dining area. Continuing, Bradley states a few moments passed when Cindy and Max approached their table with their food orders. Cindy returned to the counter and Max remained at the table asking if there was anything else we required. It was at this point we engaged in swapping some pleasantries. A couple of joking statements were made that rubbed Max the wrong way. He looked directly at me and said, 'You have a big mouth, Brad, and someday it's going to get you in trouble.' He then turned and started to walk away. I have to apologize that I did not appreciate what he had said about me, so I did something foolish. I threw a cheeseburger at him. This did not faze him so then I threw French fries at him. Suddenly, without any warning, he turns and hits me with a clenched fist in the nose. I must have blacked out because the next thing I remember was being in the hospital.

"Later, when the police talked with me, they told me Max had gotten into a fight with my three friends which resulted in Max being thrown through the front window. All we wanted to do was get something to eat. We were not looking for any trouble. However, I do apologize to Burger Palace for any of their property that was destroyed. The above explanation is what happened on the evening of December 21st at Burger Palace to the best of my knowledge." Mrs. Chambers looked up from the document smiled at everyone and then ended the reading, "Signed Bradley F. Sykes."

Satisfied with the completion of the reading Dolstrum gestured toward Rich. "Well, that's it, counselor. Any comments…questions?"

Giving Dolstrum a genuine smile Rich spoke calmly, "There are always two sides to every story as you well know, Michael. Most of the time the stories are quite opposite, which means someone is lying. In this case, I'm not saying Brad has lied during the deposition, but in his mind, I suppose he's telling the truth. I think in all actuality what your client has done is cherry-picked the events of the evening at Burger Palace. We have already pointed out the misstatements made during the first part of the deposition. The second part which we just heard is also full of holes and does not hold much water. Let's start with when Cindy Wells and Max Miller brought the meals out to your client's table. Cindy did not return to the counter of her own accord but was told to do so by Max. Max told me when Brad and his friends approached the counter some things were mentioned to her that made her feel nervous, like one of the players asking if she was on the menu.

She had only been on the job for one week and was in training. Since that evening Max has been contacted by his manager at the Palace and was told Cindy was so upset because of what she had to go through that night that she quit her job. I won't dwell on that because you will no doubt point out to me that has no bearing on what happened later. So, moving right along."

Rich hesitated for effect as he stared at Dolstrum and then at Mr. Sykes. "Brad mentions in his disposition there were some pleasantries, and let me emphasize, his own words, joking comments made. The only pleasantries expressed were when Max asked Brad and his friends if there was anything else they needed. He turned to go back to the counter when Brad began a tirade of lude, unsavory, comments about a girl who happens to be a good friend of my client."

Dolstrum for just a brief second looked over at Harmon Sykes, who, in turn, gave his son a poker-faced glance.

Rich, picking up on the rapid, but strange behavior of his opponents clapped his hands once and raised his voice, "Just like I thought. You gentlemen are not aware of what these *joking comments were*…are you?"

Harmon gave Rich a deadpan look while Dolstrum could only answer, "No I guess we have not, and I can only assume you are going to tell us what was said at that table."

"I am…I am indeed. Now, I don't know how you treat ladies up here in the north but down south we respect our females and therefore I would suggest that perhaps Mrs. Chambers would prefer to leave the room before I reveal Brad's lack of respect for women."

Dolstrum waved his hand at Mrs. Chambers and asked calmly. "If you care to leave the room, you may."

Mrs. Chambers removed the glasses from her face, sat back, and looked at the men around the table. "I've been taking depositions for nine years and have sat through countless meetings where it seems like everything under the sun had been brought up; some good, some bad. So, if it's all the same I'll stay."

Dolstrum turned his attention back to Rich. "Very well then. You heard her counselor. Let's have it."

"Okay, but before I begin let me first set the stage for the type of girl my client, Max is friends with. She is from Lancaster Country right here in your state and she happens to be Mennonite. According to Max she is one of the nicest people he has ever met, doesn't have an unkind word to say about anyone, and wouldn't hurt a fly." Looking across the table, Rich asked Dolstrum and his team. "Are you familiar with the Mennonite faith?"

No one answered except Dolstrum who replied, "Yes, I am familiar with these people."

"Good," said Rich, "then let's continue. As Max turned to walk away from the table, your client, Brad, remarks, I quote this from a deposition taken from my client." Holding up a sheet of legal paper Rich laid it on the table and read, "While I was leaving the table Brad speaks up and says, 'So, Miller! How is that little Amish broad you're dating?' Max, not wanting any trouble ignored the comment and said, 'If there is nothing else, I've got to get back to the counter.' He started to walk away but was stopped by Brad's loud voice. Here is what was said: 'Miller! You didn't answer my question. Are you too good to talk with us? How is that Amish stuff? She's a strange girl? I've said hello to her before and she just ignored me. I guess she's too good for my type. I bet under her weird clothes there's a real tiger…isn't there?'

"Max walked back to the table and spoke directly to Brad. 'We're not dating and she happens to be Mennonite.' Brad came back with 'Amish… Mennonite what's the difference? She's a religious chick!' Then Brad goes on to explain, 'I had me a goody two shoes Catholic girl last year in high school. She was a handful…a wild one! I bet this Mennonite broad is the same. Beneath those weird duds she wears she's a wildcat!' Max knew he should walk away but Brad's comments angered him. He pointed at Brad and said, 'You have a big mouth Brad, and someday it's going to get you in trouble!' Brad stands up and replies, 'Today isn't that day and you're not the one who is going to give me any trouble.' Max recalls thinking to himself about not doing anything stupid, so once again he walks away. It was then that Brad threw his burger at Max hitting him in the chest area. Brad then makes a snide comment about how he dropped his burger and that Brad better rustle him up another.

"Brad turned and walked off while all four boys were laughing loudly. The next thing that happens is Brad throws a handful of French fries that hit Max in the back of his head. Still…still after all that had happened Max continued to walk off but then Brad yelled out, 'Tell ya what! When you're finished up with that Amish-Mennonite chick or whatever the hell she is, just let me know. Maybe I'll take a crack at that!'

"Max thought *that's enough!* He stops in his tracks, turns, walks back, and pops ol' Brad here right on the kisser! And that moment…right there is the moment that you gentlemen seem to be focused on. Everything that happened and everything that was said up until that moment is not considered in the equation. I am well aware of the law and that an individual cannot hall off and hit another person no matter what was said or what happened, provided feeling that their life was threatened. Before you ask, let me state at no time up until this point did my client feel threatened."

"If you are admitting," said Dolstrum, "that your client at no time felt as if his life was in danger then there is no argument your client was at fault. Despite what you term as bad behavior on the part of Brad and his friends it was your client who was the aggressor. He was the one who stated Brad had a big mouth and that it was going to get him in trouble. He was the one who put his hands or hand on Brad by hitting him. Furthermore, even after Brad was knocked unconscious, according to depositions we took from the boys who were present, one of the boys, Levoy, I believe it was stated he stood up and said to your client that hitting Brad was uncalled for and there was no reason to hit him. Your client once again placed his hands on one of the boys, this time Levoy, shoved him and told him to get out of the way. After that, all hell broke loose and your client winds up getting thrown through the plate glass window. The entire incident was unfortunate, and was caused by your client breaking the law and hitting our client and physically pushing one of his friends."

Dolstrum turned to Finch and snapped his fingers as he asked, "Please give me the document from Burger Palace."

Finch quickly rifled through a small stack of papers until he came to the document requested. Handing the paper to Dolstrum, the attorney waved it at Rich and stated, "This document, at our request was sent to us from Burger Palace's headquarters in Nashville. It states very clearly that one Max Miller was terminated from their employment as he had broken a hands-off company policy when it comes to customers. What more proof is required? Even the company your client worked for stated he broke the law by attacking our client. Now, we intend to sue Mr. Miller for all medical expenses to repair not only our client's broken nose but dental work as well. He also suffers from spells of dizziness." Slamming the document down on the table, Dolstrum blurted out, "Case closed!"

Following Dolstrum's final tirade, Rich sat back as if he had been defeated.

Max leaned toward Rich and whispered, "I would like to say something if it's all right."

Rich gave him a look of hopelessness and then relented, "Go ahead."

Max straightened his tie, scooted forward, and looked at Brad and the four men seated across from him. "I have something that needs to be said. First off, I am sorry I hit Brad. I know it was wrong, but there have to be times in life when doing the wrong thing is the right thing to do. I didn't hit Brad because he and his friends were drinking. I didn't hit him because he made Cindy Wells nervous. I didn't hit him because he knocked over a counter display. I didn't hit him because he and his friends ran off all of our customers. I didn't hit him because he threw food at me. I hit him because of what he said about my female friend. I felt that because of what he said I had to protect her honor. If it happened again, I'd do the same thing. In this world doing the right thing is not always popular, but I feel it is important to always do the right thing regardless of what others think. That's all I have to say. Now, if I have to serve time in the local jail, well then so be it. If I have to pay for Brad's medical expenses, well then okay. At least I can know in my heart I did the right thing considering the circumstances." Finished, Max looked at his father, smiled, and sat back.

Everyone remained silent, Dolstrum finally breaking the silence as he spoke, "That was quite the speech…"

Harmon Sykes, who had remained silent throughout the meeting raised his hand interrupting his attorney. "I'd like to say something myself. When I came here today, I didn't know what type of person to expect regarding Max Miller. My son described Max as a mathematical geek, so I guess I expected to be sitting across the table from a skinny sort of fella with thick glasses and twenty ink pens in his coat pocket. But it appears Max is anything but that. I have found him to be dressed impeccably, well-mannered, and well-spoken. I also agree with what his attorney Mr. Mathers said about the truth, the whole truth and nothing but the truth being three different things.

"After hearing everything said here today, I believe I may have come to this meeting unprepared. In doing so, I believe I have given information to Dolstrum, Eichman and Dunn that may have caused their law firm to come here today…also unprepared. I am not an expert when it comes to the law, but I have always thought if an individual speaks before they have all the information, they can wind up looking like a fool."

Harmon stood and ran his right hand across the back of his neck. "I don't know about the rest of you but if I sit for over an hour I tend to get stiff." Walking to the fireplace he held his hands over the fire while rubbing them together. Turning back, he leaned on the large wood mantle facing the table and continued. "Please be patient with me as I would like to share a short story with you. Back, let's see I guess it would be twenty-five years ago I was a freshman right here in town at Gettysburg College. I was a nineteen-year-old kid who loved the game of football, but I had bigger plans for my life. I wanted to be a businessman, I wanted to become a millionaire. As you probably all know I was quite good at football and this in itself became a distraction from my ultimate goal of becoming a wealthy man. Then, I met a young woman, also a freshman. Her name was Susan. It's strange how meeting someone in your life can change the way you think. I dated Susan for four years straight while in college and we married the first year after we graduated. I can say without any reservation she is the reason for the success I have gained and still enjoy to this day. Over the years I have established a reputation in business as a tough and shrewd negotiator. I have gained many friends over the years, and I suppose created some enemies as well. The one thing I am proud of is the fact I have always been honest with anyone I had business dealings with. Back in my college days and even today my wife, Susan, is the love of my life. When I was here at Gettysburg if anyone would have made similar comments about my Susan that my son, Brad made about this girl Max here is friends with, I have no doubt whatsoever I would have not hesitated to punch that person right in the mouth. Listening to what was said here today I think Max Miller displayed incredible patience during the ordeal at Burger Palace that night."

Walking back to his chair, Harmon seated himself and looked across the table at Max. "I think I have a solution to the problem we are faced with here today. I feel that within the next few minutes, we can all walk out of here and put this all behind us. Here is my solution. I now realize why Max hit my son and even though according to the law what he did was wrong I feel he acted correctly. If Max is willing to stand up before this panel and apologize to my son, then we will drop the lawsuit and speak of this no more."

Brad was livid as he stood and pointed at his father. "What in the hell are you doing? You can't let him get away with this. Look at me! My nose is broken! I need dental work! I can't play football and I'm the laughingstock of the school! You can't allow him to just walk away from this!"

Harmon stood and gave his son a stern look. "Sit down, Son. You're making a fool of yourself. Sit down...now!"

Straightening his suitcoat Harmon addressed. Max. "Well, what's it going to be son?"

Max looked at Rich and asked? "What do you think?"

Rich didn't even hesitate in his answer. "You're not going to get any better deal than that."

Max smiled at his father, stood, took a deep breath, and faced Brad, who at the moment was glaring at him. Folding his hands in front of himself, Max began his apology. "Brad, I am deeply sorry for hitting you. I guess I just lost my temper and took it out on you. I'm sorry about your broken nose and I also feel bad because you can't play football right now." Leaning across the table Max extended his right hand and continued, "Please... forgive me!"

Brad crossed his arms across his chest and remained seated in defiance. Max felt awkward standing there with his outstretched hand while Brad remained seated.

Harmon stood and pounded his fist on the table. "Do you mean to tell me that a son of mine is not going to accept this apology?"

Brad gave his father a stern look and replied loudly, "That's correct, Father! I do not intend to stand and shake the man's hand who broke my nose. I can't believe you're letting him off the hook. If you will not sue him...then I will!"

Harmon's face turned to a sad grin as he spoke again to his son. "Brad, think about what you're saying. The sad truth is you're not going to sue anyone. You don't have any money. If it wasn't for your mother and I, you wouldn't have anything. We paid for the clothes on your back, the shoes on your feet and the food in your belly. That new car you drive and your college education have all been paid for by your mother and me as well. Without us, why you don't have a pot to piss in. You've never worked a day in your life. I can't even begin to tell you how disappointed I am in you at this moment!"

Turning to Rich, Charles, and Max, Harmon apologized. "I am sorry we have wasted your time today. The lawsuit I had in mind will be dropped. I will take care of my son's medical expenses." Sitting down he calmed himself and stated, "The matter is concluded."

Max and Charley began to stand but Rich prolonged the meeting when he spoke, "I don't mean to upset the apple cart here but there is one more thing that I think needs to be discussed."

Dolstrum who was already on his feet, asked, "And what would that be?"

Rich raised his hands slightly as he explained, "Well, I was just thinking what with the somewhat negative attitude Brad has displayed here today regarding my client's apology what guarantee do we have your client or members of the football team will not retaliate against my client in the future?"

Harmon was quick with a response. "I can't guarantee you what other people other than my son may do or say. I can't guarantee that my son will abide by my final decision here today, but let's do this." Opening his wallet, he removed a business card and handed it to Max. "If you have any trouble that is spearheaded by my son, give me a call and I will deal with him. In short, I can only hope my son has learned a valuable lesson here today and that he will conduct himself as a gentleman for the remainder of his college career."

Rich looked at Max who nodded in approval, at which point Rich agreed. "Well, I guess that's it then.

Within the next few seconds, everyone filed out of the room, Brad remaining in his chair as his angry eyes and set jaw followed Max.

Outside, standing in the parking lot in the cold early afternoon weather, Rich gave Max a high five as he grinned, "Well, we pulled it off…didn't we?"

Charley, reaching for the car door handle suggested, "The first thing I'm going to do is call your mother, Max. She will be so relieved at the outcome. It's just twelve-thirty now. I say we spend the rest of the afternoon visiting some of the great museums they have here in town and then we finish up the day with celebratory steak dinners at Mic's Steakhouse?"

Heading down Baltimore Street Max sat in the backseat and thought, *I can't wait to call Elizabeth and give her the good news!*

CHAPTER ELEVEN

Max stood in the parking lot of Denny's and waved goodbye to Rich and Charley. Following an early morning breakfast his father and his attorney were on their way to Harrisburg where they would catch a flight back to Charleston. Before leaving, Charley offered to drop him back off at campus, but Max declined, saying it was only a half-hour's walk back.

On Carlisle Street, he buttoned up his P-coat. It was a chilly morning; a crisp sort of day; a clear sky, and no snow forecast for the next few days. He felt a sense of freedom he hadn't experienced since he had been notified about the meeting with Harmon Sykes and his lawyers. But that was all behind him now as he had been exonerated from slugging Brad Sykes. For weeks he had gone to his classes and walked around campus wondering if he would be sued, but now that had been resolved and he could move on with his life.

He recalled the sour look on Brad's face when the intense meeting came to a close. Even though both sides had come to a mutual agreement and Harmon Sykes had tried to guarantee his son would not retaliate against him in the future, he was not convinced Brad Sykes was going to just move on and forget that evening at Burger Palace. Reaching in his coat pocket he removed the envelope containing the threatening note. that at least in his mind Brad had slipped under his door. Taking the note out of the envelope he read it to himself; THIS IS FAR FROM OVER!

Despite the fact he had not been sued and was considered free of any wrongdoing by the powers to be, the note still sent a shiver down his back. Thinking back to the meeting, he had every intention of bringing the note up as well as the confrontation with the football players at the gym, but with the way everything went, the note had not been required. Slipping the note in the envelope he placed it back in his coat. His father and Rich still were not aware of the note, and he intended to keep it that way for now. Why rock the boat? They had walked out of the meeting victorious. His father was always saying, 'If it ain't broke don't fix it!'

Passing a Methodist Church, he thought about Elizabeth and how she always spent Sundays on campus reading her Bible and praying. He had every intention of calling her after the recent meeting but by the time dinner with his father and Rich was over it had been too late to contact her. Maybe he'd wait until later in the day and drop by to see her at her dorm. He was excited about telling her about the wonderful outcome of the meeting and he knew she would be equally happy.

Max watched as two couples entered the church. He felt guilty because he hadn't attended church one single time while at college. The last time he had stepped into a church had been when he had gone home for Christmas and he and his parents had attended a midnight Christmas Eve service. The college had a small non-denominational church on campus. He had heard from one of his fellow roommates at his dorm who had attended and said it was not all that crowded. He figured he was not that different from many of the students on campus. Most of them, especially the freshmen, were away from home for the first time in their life and experiencing a level of freedom away from living under their parent's rule.

He moved on but he then stopped and looked back at the church. It wouldn't do him any harm to go to church. After all, he had a lot to be thankful for. Elizabeth had told him she was going to pray for him and about the meeting and God had been listening and had answered her prayers. *I'm going in!* thought Max as he climbed the concrete steps and walked through the massive oak double doors.

Inside, he walked through a small reception area, took a church bulletin from a small table, and shook the hand of a greeter who welcomed him. The church was full and rather than walking up the aisle and awkwardly searching for a seat he decided to just take a seat three rows from the back. Sitting on a cushioned oak pew, he checked his watch: 8:55. The service, according to the sign on the right side of the entrance door, started at nine. He took a hymnal from a wood rack in the seat in front of him, opened the well-used book, and scanned the first few songs. Putting the hymnal back he smiled to himself. Why had he taken a hymnal? He never sang while in church. He thought about his parents. His mother always sang while his father never opened his mouth. When it came to church, he was more like his father. His mother had always been more religious, and his father told him on more than one occasion that he had married up! If it wasn't for his mother, he wasn't so sure he and his father would even attend church.

The minister walked across the red-carpeted altar while the twelve-person choir belted out an uplifting song he had never heard before. Following another, slower song, a man seated on the front row walked to the podium and gave the standard church announcements, parishioners who needed prayer, the results of a recent fund-raising dinner, and church events for the upcoming week. Following a few opening comments and remarks by the minister, he held his hand out over the congregation and asked them to offer a sign of peace to those around them. This was a practice Max was accustomed to as he shook hands with three people seated in front of him and then with those on his right and left. Getting ready to be seated he felt someone tap his shoulder. Turning he noticed a young girl, about his age, who extended her right hand, smiled, and shook his, "Peace be with you."

Max, taking the young lady's hand, responded, "And you also."

The girl, staring at his face did not release his hand as quickly as he thought she should have. Finally, she released her soft grip. Max turned around and faced the altar. *Strange!* he thought.

Familiar with the Methodist concept of worship Max relaxed as the service moved right along. Two different readings from the Bible, another song by the choir, and then the sermon given by the minister. Ironically the sermon was about turning the other cheek. As Max listened to the man of the cloth go on, he thought, *how appropriate!* It was as if the minister was speaking directly to him. Max thought about how he had managed to turn the other cheek during his encounter with Brad and his cohorts at the Palace, at least up until the point when he had enough, turned and lambasted Brad squarely on the nose. He also thought about the moment when Harmon Sykes had relented during the meeting and said there would be no lawsuit. Brad, his son, had reacted negatively and had at that moment no intention of turning the other cheek. Max was so caught up in his thinking that before he knew it the sermon ended, and the collection plate was being passed down each row of pews. An older woman seated next to him passed him a wicker basket into which he dropped two one-dollar bills.

Another song was sung during communion time. Max was glad when they passed a tray of thin wafers and then another tray of small plastic cups of grape juice down each row. He was relieved he didn't have to get up, move out into the aisle, and proceed to the altar to receive communion. He didn't want to be one of the people whom the regular parishioners would look at and think to themselves, *Who is this new person?* In his home church back in Summerville whenever someone he had never seen before walked down the aisle for communion, he always wondered who they were or where they were from. Placing one of the wafers in his mouth he washed it down with the purple juice.

After communion, there was yet another song followed by the minister blessing the congregation and telling them to go in peace. Max stood to leave but was prevented from doing so as the woman seated next to him introduced herself as Mildred and then asked if he was new to the church. After explaining he was a student at Gettysburg College, and this was his first time at the church she introduced her husband as Wilbur. By the time Max stepped out into the aisle most of the congregation had emptied.

In a gathering area outside the church, Max saw the strange young girl who had sat behind him. She approached him and asked, "You're Max Miller…correct?"

Max, taken by surprise, answered, "'Ah…yes…I'm Max Miller. Do I know you from somewhere?"

The girl smiled graciously and introduced herself, "No, we've never met before, but I have seen you around campus. My name is Celia Crawford. I'm a freshman at Gettysburg. I live in the same dorm as Elizabeth King."

Walking up the street next to Celia, Max felt more at ease. "Then you know Elizabeth?"

"Yes, I do. She is one of the nicest people I have ever met. I room just down the hall from her. I'm one of her closest friends at school. There are six of us who kind of pal around together. Elizabeth, being Mennonite sets her apart from most of the girls, not only in the dorm but on campus. Some people draw a circle around themselves and therefore they are hard to get to know. In Elizabeth's case, the circle around her has been placed there by her Mennonite faith, the way she dresses, and what she believes in. We met a few days after we first got here last fall. I sat next to her one day down in the dorm lounge and we got to talking. I told her I was Methodist, and we discussed the differences in our religious beliefs. I guess I connected with her as most of the girls on campus are not what you would call religious. I guess it was around two months later or so when she told those of us who are close to her that she had met a male student on campus." Celia gently touched him on his right arm. "And that would be you…Max Miller! She told us all how strange it was for her, a young Mennonite girl to be involved in any fashion with a man who was not of her faith. As the weeks passed, she never really went into any great detail about her relationship with you. She did say you were a mathematics student and a Methodist from South Carolina. I remember telling her that if you were a Methodist then you were probably a decent person."

Max, enjoying the conversation with Celia, asked, "Where are you from, and what is your major here at school?"

"I'm from upstate New York… a town in the Western Tier of the state called Ithaca. It's a college town that sits right on one of the Finger Lakes."

"Ithaca" repeated Max, "Isn't that where Cornell University is located?"

"Yes, it is. Like Gettysburg, Ithaca is a college town. It's also home to Ithaca College. To answer your second question, I'm a psychology major."

"So, if I could ask how, did you wind up here in Gettysburg?"

"Interesting story," said Celia. "From the moment I was born my parents had it in mind that I was going to go to college. My folks were middle class and still are today. We never had much money, but we got by. Over the years they saved every penny they could so I could go to college when the time came. When I was seven years old, I started to play the flute and by the time I hit high school, I was better than average and qualified for a full college scholarship in music. My parents and I agreed even though I could remain right there in Ithaca and attend Cornell or Ithaca College it might be better if I go away somewhere to school. I had lived in Ithaca for the first eighteen years of my life and it seemed like a good idea for me to start getting out into the world, so they shipped me off to Pennsylvania and here I am. Second seat in the flute section of the Gettysburg College Orchestra."

Celia continued their conversation as they crossed Buford Boulevard, "Believe it or not you and I share more in common than just the fact we are both friends with Elizabeth."

Max stepped up onto the curb. "How's that?"

"If Elizabeth has told me once she has told me several times after spending time with you how you are very knowledgeable about the Civil War and that you are always telling her interesting stories about the war. She also told me you and your father are reenactors. My father just happens to be a Civil War reenactor himself. Of course, living in New York State he is a Yankee reenactor. I suppose because you are from the South you are a Confederate. One of the reasons why I decided on Gettysburg as my college choice is because this happens to be one of my father's favorite reenactment sites. He and a group of men from not only Ithaca but from some of the surrounding towns get together and attend the Gettysburg reenactment every year."

In amazement, Max stopped. "Small world…huh! Maybe our fathers know one another. What's your father's first name?"

"Clark…Clark Crawford."

Before Max could give Celia his father's name, she went on to explain, "There's something else you and I have in common. I hate to bring it up because I know it must be a sore subject to you, but I know Brad Sykes quite well. He and his family live on Cayuca Lake just north of Ithaca. We grew up in the same town."

Max's amazement elevated as he stammered, "Then…you know Brad pretty well?"

"I guess you could say that. I never really got to know him that well until my junior year in high school. His parents sent him to an upscale elementary and junior high school. It was a school that I nor any of my friends could afford to go to. The story is his parents always had problems with him while he was growing up. Always getting into fights, back-sassing teachers, cheating on tests, and on and on. When it became time for him to go to high school his father decided to send him to an elite military school. His father never had any intention of his son eventually joining the military, but he thought the discipline and the strict standards of the institute would straighten his son out. Not so! For two years he defied the other students and professors as well. It got to the point where he became uncontrollable, so the school phoned his father and told him to come get his son. He was being expelled from the academy. His father had no choice but to enroll him at Ithaca High School for his junior and senior years."

Interested, Max probed, "What was that like…I mean going to school with Sykes?"

"I didn't have that much interaction with him. He ran with a different group of students than I did. Two different groups. He hung with the rich kids and the roughnecks. He always had money and was a real pain in the ass if I do say so myself. I never had any direct dealings with him. I'd see him around school. I was always polite and said hello to him. He usually nodded back. Other than that, we never really spoke to one another. Like most of the kids, we tried to steer clear of Brad. He was trouble from the word go! His father planned on sending him to Cornell, but the school would not accept him. Brad's father, a wealthy man to say the least, despite the unsavory behavior of his son, always bailed him out of whatever trouble he got into. What other choice did he have? Brad was his son. Harmon Sykes, a couple of decades or so in the past had attended Gettysburg College and was quite the football star here on campus. Over the years he donated large sums of money to the school so when he sent his son here for a college career, they could hardly say no. By the time I found out Brad was going to the same college as I, well, it was too late. All in all, his presence hasn't affected me that much. I see him around school, and he says hello to me. Once again, just like in high school, I intend to keep my distance. I already know about the trouble you had with him at the Palace, and I say he got what he deserved."

She looked at the bell tower of Glatfelter Hall in the distance, lowered her head, and spoke softly, "It's a shame Elizabeth had to leave school. We, I mean all of her friends, were really upset. I'm sure you feel the same."

Max stopped dead in his tracks and just stared at Celia. Finally, he managed to link together a few words of disbelief. "What do you mean… leave school? I just talked with her last Wednesday. I was planning on dropping by her dorm later today to speak with her."

Celia apologized, "I thought you knew she went home. I'm sorry you had to hear about the news secondhand."

Confused, Max asked, "Why would she just up and leave and go home? I don't understand."

"We all…all of her close friends, thought she told you. Early this morning she received a call from some friends of her family. She was informed her father had taken a nasty fall in their barn. I think she said he had a broken wrist and suffered a broken leg and an injured knee. He also has a severe cut on the right side of his face and may have suffered a concussion. He was admitted to the hospital and is going to recover but it could take three to four months to heal up. Her mother requested Elizabeth come home immediately. A man and a woman who are close friends with the family were driving over to take her back to Lancaster. After she received the call the first thing she did was she told us she was going to go to your dorm and let you know she had to leave. That's why I took it for granted you already knew."

"Of course, she tried to contact me," said Max. "I was having breakfast with my father and one of his friends downtown when she probably showed up at the dorm. She must have been so disappointed when I wasn't there. I feel so helpless like there is something I should be doing to help her out, but I don't have a phone number for her or even know exactly where she lives."

Celia snapped her fingers. "Look, I know the way she feels about you and I'm sure she wouldn't just leave without at least leaving you a note. When you get back to your dorm, I bet there will be a message there for you."

Max wasn't quite sure what to do as he asked, "Did she say how long she would be gone? I mean, she is coming back to school…right?"

"Yes, that's her intention. She contacted the school administration and explained her family situation. They told her she could most definitely go and that she needed to take as much time as possible to take care of whatever she needed to do. The last thing she told us was she might only be gone for a week or two, but then again depending on what she found out it might be a couple of months. She said she might be back after spring break, or she might have to wait until the fall semester. Either way, the school officials understood and said she could catch up on her studies when she returned."

Max, now standing at the main campus entrance took Celia by her shoulders. "I'm going to go back to my dorm and see if she left me a message. In the meantime, if you hear any news, please get hold of me. If I happen to hear anything I'll get in touch with you as well. With that, he turned and ran up the sidewalk.

It only took two minutes to run down the street and around the corner to his dorm. Taking the steps in three long strides he entered the front door and looked at the front desk. It was unmanned; it was Sunday. Bending over he placed his hands on his knees and caught his breath. The dorm lounge was empty. It was just after ten and most of the other students probably were not even up yet. Walking quickly across the room he opened the residence door, climbed the flight of stairs to the second floor, and walked down the hall to his room where he found the door slightly open. Earlier in the morning after he got up and left for breakfast he had closed and locked the door. At that time, his roommate, Scott was still asleep. Why was the door now not only unlocked but open? Scott always locked the door when he left for the day.

Opening the door slowly, he carefully looked into the room. The thought of the revenge-minded Brad Sykes lurking around campus bent on getting even with him was a concern. Looking around the door he saw Scott lying on the floor as he did a series of body crunches. Bringing his knees up to his chest he clutched a fifty-pound barbell in his hands. Following three repetitions, he lay on the floor in a prone position and let out a long breath. The short break from his exercise was interrupted by Max's voice. "Good morning. I see you finally decided to get up and join the world of the active!"

On his side, Scott pushed the heavy metal barbell away, sat up, and leaned against the wall. Sitting there in bare feet, wearing a pair of old grey sweatpants, he grabbed a towel draped over a nearby chair and rubbed it across his sweaty bare chest. Gulping water from a plastic bottle he wiped his face with the towel and grinned at Max. "I was wondering when you'd get back here. Last night when you got back, I must have been in the shower. You were already in bed and asleep when I came back out here. I was interested in how your meeting with the lawyers went, but I decided rather than waking you I'd wait until morning. By the time I got up you had once again flown the coup! That reminds me. Elizabeth dropped by to see you, I guess it was around seven thirty. She seemed stressed out and was disappointed because you weren't here. I asked her if there was something wrong and she went on to tell me there had been an accident involving her father back on their farm and she had to leave school and head back home. I told her I would let you know as soon as you got back but then she said she'd rather leave a note. I gave her one of your envelopes, a sheet of paper and a pen. She sat right there at your desk and wrote out the note. She placed it on your bed and said she had to go because some friends from her community back home would soon be there to pick her up. She was out the door, and that was it."

Next to his bed, Max confirmed, "There was an accident on her farm."

Scott stood and asked, "If you already knew about the accident then why would she leave you the note?"

"She didn't know I knew…that's why she came by to see me." Max sat on the bed, opened the envelope, and read the short message. After reading what was written he folded the paper, placed it back in the envelope, and looked across the room at Scott who was now seated in a chair by the window. Picking up the envelope Max pointed it at Scott and explained, "The note verifies everything I was told."

"Told…told what," said Scott.

"I found out about the farm accident from a girl I met in church this morning."

Scott laughed, 'Since when did you start going to church?"

"That's not important. What is, is that I did go this morning and I ran into one of Elizabeth's friends from her dorm. After church, I walked this girl back to campus and during our conversation, she dropped a bomb on me and told me Elizabeth had to go home." Holding up the note, he went on, "This note pretty much verifies what I was told. Elizabeth got a phone call from someone in her community back home to let her know her father took a nasty fall in the barn not only injuring his wrist but also his leg and knee. He might even have a concussion. He was hospitalized and it will take a few months for him to completely recover. Therefore, Elizabeth had to go back home and be with her family. The note states she might come back to school after a couple of weeks, or she might not even return until after spring break. She even writes that it might be next fall when school starts up again."

Max sat in a chair on the opposite side of the room and shook his head in wonder. "Life sure can be strange. I mean, here I am at school…a freshman. First time away from home for an extended amount of time, not knowing exactly what to expect, and then wallah! I meet this strange girl, a Mennonite girl who despite the different worlds we come from become close friends. Over the past few months, we've gone to lunch or dinner every Wednesday and Saturday. Turns out, we have a lot in common. Just when I think we're getting along fine…poof, she up and goes back home… just like that. How do you explain things like that?"

Scott took another drink of water and answered, "I don't know."

"It's just like the meeting I had with Sykes and his lawyers," said Max. "There we sat, me, my father, and my lawyer across the table from Brad, his father, and their three lawyers. Back and forth the lawyers bantered. It seemed like their side had an answer for everything we brought up and it appeared we were on our way to losing, which would result in my being sued. But then, toward the end of the ordeal Harmon Sykes, Brad's father, had a change of heart when he discovered his son had not been as truthful as he should have been while explaining the events that took place that night at the Burger Palace. Long story…short. Mr. Sykes dropped the lawsuit providing I apologize to his son. I stand up and go through the process of apologizing to Brad who refuses to stand and shake my hand. This made his father even more upset. The result of the meeting was that I walked out of there, and at least, according to my lawyer, we scored a victory. It's the same thing as this Elizabeth situation. One minute she's here and the next she's gone. One minute, I feel like I'm going down the drain at the meeting, and then, just like that, I come out on top. Go figure!"

Scott stood and walked over to where he left the barbell. Picking up the heavy iron object he started a series of arm curls while asking. "What was Brad's reaction to his father backing off on the lawsuit?"

"Believe me," said Max. "He was anything but happy. Like I said he refused to shake my hand and told his father if he would not sue me then he would!"

"Do you think he will?"

"According to what his father said…no. Brad Sykes has never worked a day in his life and any money he does have is supplied by his parents. In short, he does not have the money to sue me. But that's not what bothers me. If you could have seen the look on Brad's face when we filed out of the meeting. I think he means to get even with me. Now, exactly what that means I'm not sure. My lawyer brought this very point up at the meeting. He directly asked Brad's father if he could guarantee Brad would not retaliate against me in the future. Mr. Sykes said he couldn't guarantee what other people may do but as far as his son was concerned, he gave me one of his business cards and told me if Brad tried to get back at me to just give him a call and he'd take care of it."

Scott stopped lifting for a moment and asked, "Do you think Brad will abide by his father's wishes?"

"No, I don't think he will. I think he'll back off for now, but at some point down the road, and by down the road I'm talking weeks or months from now. Hell, he might even wait until this fall when we come back to school from summer vacation. He can afford to be patient, which is of great concern to me. I, on the other hand, will always have to be looking over my shoulder. Months could pass by and then there could be a moment when I let my guard down and bam…Brad strikes!"

"But if that happens all you have to do is call his father…right?"

"That's what was said, but if enough time passes his father may not live up to his guarantee. Besides, when and if Brad does strike back at me, depending on what takes place I may have a difficult time proving he was even involved. He could arrange to have someone else do the deed."

"You don't think he'd lash out at Elizabeth…do you?"

"I've thought about that. The more I think about it the more I realize that is a possibility. He could try to even the score by harming someone close to me. I have no idea what he may have in mind for me, or Elizabeth. Something could happen to either one of us that may appear to be an accident, but in all actuality is generated by Brad. It's almost like he's a snake hiding in the grass. He could strike at any moment and then slither away never to be caught."

Lifting the barbell, Scott breathed deeply. "So, what's your plan from here on out?"

"All in all, the same plan I had when I first came here to college. Keep my nose to the ol' grindstone as they say for the next four years, graduate with my degree in financing, and move back to South Carolina where, more than likely, I'll land a job with some financial firm. Then, at some point, after I get a few years of experience under my belt, I'll open my own financial business. Other than that, I guess somewhere along the line I'll get married, buy a house, and have some kids. Ya know, the good ol' American dream."

Scott laughed. "It's hard for me to imagine myself being married, living in a house with the proverbial white picket fence, and having a bunch of kids. That seems like a world that's far off for me." He lowered the weight to his side and lifted it to his chest. "How does Elizabeth fit into your plans?"

Max gave Scott a look of hesitation, then answered, "Until you just mentioned it, I never thought about that. I suppose as long as both of us are going to school here we'll remain friends. Elizabeth is one of those types of people my mother told me I would run across during my life, meaning from time to time, someone steps into your life, be it for a few seconds, minutes, weeks, months, or even years, and then they go on their way, and you never see them again. Like you and me for instance. If things work out the way I think you and I will remain friends here at school for the next four years. After we graduate, we'll both move on with our lives going in different directions and there's a good chance our paths will never cross again. I guess that's life."

"So, you don't think you and Elizabeth would ever get married?"

Surprised, Max blurted out, "Good Lord…no! She could never marry a man like me…or you or for that matter anyone who is not a Mennonite. We've talked about our futures; about how after we graduate, I'll be heading back down to South Carolina where eventually I'll have my own financial business and she'll take the nursing skills she'll learn here at school back to her community where she has stated she'll wind up marrying a Mennonite man. Besides that, let's just say we do fall in love, or however, that kind of stuff works. It would be difficult for her to survive in the world you and I are accustomed to." Max laughed. "And I could never move back to her community and become a Mennonite. Are you kidding me? Can you see me…Max Miller milking cows at four in the morning, picking apples, plowing fields, and planting corn? Talk about farm failure! I would no doubt wind up being the first Mennonite farmer whose family starved to death. No, when this is all over, I mean when both she and I graduate we'll go our separate ways. It's safer and more comfortable for someone like her to live with her people. Just sitting here right now thinking of her back on her farm she's better off. It's a crazy world out here. In a way, I think she'd fare better if she didn't return, but then on the other hand I kind of miss her. I'll be glad to see her when she gets back, whenever that happens to be."

Scott laid the weight down "The next thing on my agenda for the day is a five-mile run. Care to tag along?"

"No thanks. "I might head on over to the gym and get a few laps in. I guess I'll see you later."

Scott toweled his sweaty chest off, took a fresh t-shirt from a dresser, slipped it over his muscular torso, grabbed a hooded sweatshirt, walked to the door, and saluted Max. "See ya!"

Alone in the room, Max reopened the envelope from Elizabeth and read it again. Bending down, he slid his old gym bag from under his bed, opened it, and checked the contents, goggles and a bottle of swimmer's shampoo. All he needed was a towel and a pair of swim trunks and he too, would be out the door.

With everything he required for his swim, he picked up the bag and reached for the door when his cell phone buzzed. Taking a quick mental inventory of those who might give him a call he thought, *Rich, my dad, or more than likely…Mom. It had to be her. Didn't his father say he was going to give her the good news about the outcome of the meeting?* Digging the phone out of his pocket he answered enthusiastically, "Hello there, Mother!"

The female response was not who he assumed it to be. "Max…it's Elizabeth."

"Elizabeth! Where are you calling from? Are you in Lancaster?"

"Yes, I'm on the farm. I'm calling you from the barn."

Max, recalling one of their many conversations responded, "That's right…you did say your folks had a phone in the barn."

"I'm not on the barn phone. I'm using a cell phone."

Amazed, Max asked, 'Where on earth did you get a cell phone?"

"It belongs to my friend Ellen. I mentioned her to you before. She decided to get one a few weeks ago and showed me how to call you. I wanted to call you and let you know I was all right."

Max breathed a sigh of relief knowing Elizabeth was back home. "I knew about your going back home before I ever got the note. I went to church this morning and ran into one of your friends…Celia. She told me you had gone back home because your father had an accident. How is your father?"

"My mother and I just got back from the hospital. The doctor told us he had broken both of his wrists and had a broken right leg, and his left kneecap was busted. He has some nasty cuts on his face but at this point, they don't think he suffered a concussion. Other than that, the doctor said my father is as strong as an ox. They have him on some pain medicine right now and starting tomorrow or the next day they will begin a series of operations to put him back together. The entire healing process could take four to six months. They said he might be able to come back home in three weeks, but he won't be able to do much of anything. The doctor said it was important he take the medicine he was given. My father isn't much on doctors so he hasn't been very cooperative with getting shots and taking pills, but my mother and I convinced him to cooperate and that the sooner he did the sooner he could get back to normal."

"How did the accident happen?"

"Well, we can only go with what my father said. He was alone in the barn up in the loft when one of the floor slats gave way causing him to fall forward. He reached out for the railing, but it gave way and down he went onto the floor below. He tried to lessen the fall with his hands but broke both wrists. He said he tried to get up but blacked out. He's not sure how long he was out but he finally came around and crawled across the barn floor to a warning bell most of the farms around here have. He tugged on the rope. My mother was the first to arrive and then shortly after that friends and neighbors started to show up. We called an ambulance and took him to the hospital."

"How is your mother taking all of this?"

"She is a strong woman, but I know inside she has to be feeling a little insecure. She and my father have been married now for twenty-four years and there has not been one single day until this accident where they have been separated. She told me she was so relieved I came home."

"Is there anything I can do? I feel like there is something I should be doing."

"No, aside from praying for a complete recovery for my father. Remember, my folks do not know you even exist. You have always offered me a sense of security in the world outside of how I was raised, and I wish I could see you and just sit and talk, but right now that is impossible. Enough about me and my family. How did the meeting go?"

"It went well. God answered your prayers. Brad's father turned out to be a decent man and after discovering his son was not completely truthful about what happened he changed his mind and dropped the lawsuit, so I'm off the hook." Max reversed the conversation back to Elizabeth and her dilemma. "Are you and your mother going to be able to keep the farm running with your father laid up?"

"Heavens…yes! When something like this happens the rest of the Mennonite community pitches in. The other men in our community will be by each day for milking and anything else that has to be done daily. The women, all of our neighbors help with cleaning and cooking. We have more food here now than you can imagine. Listen, there's something I need to tell you. The way it's starting to look I may not be back at school until the fall semester in August. I wish things were different, but they are not."

Doing some simple math Max added, "That's over seven months from now. I hope this doesn't put a damper on our friendship."

"I've thought about that as well. I don't want to wait seven months to talk with you again. If it would be all right with you, I'd like to call you every Wednesday and Saturday, just like we've been meeting. Would that be okay?"

"Of course. That goes without question. More than that, you can call me anytime you want."

Elizabeth's voice rose as she replied, "I've got to go. Ellen is watching the barn door, and two men are coming this way. I can't be caught on the phone. There will be questions. I'll call you next Wednesday. Goodbye, Max."

By the time Max began to speak, she had already disconnected. Staring at the silent phone, he spoke out loud to himself, "Talk to you then!"

CHAPTER TWELVE

Max parked his Jeep Renegade on the side of the road walked across the snow-covered grass and wiped two inches of fresh snow from a wooden bench facing the huge rock formations of Devil's Den. Staring at the labyrinth of twenty-foot-high boulders intertwined with deep crevices he removed the metal top from a thermos his parents had given him for Christmas and poured hot chocolate into the top which also served as a cup. He thought about how cold it was. The weatherman stated earlier in the morning that the high for the day was a bone-numbing nineteen degrees. Following a refreshing Saturday morning swim and two hours of relaxing reading he decided on a winter's drive out to the battlefield. It was ten fifty-five. Six days had passed since he learned of Elizabeth's sudden and unexpected return to the Lancaster farm country. The last time they had spoken was just four days past when she called him as promised. It was good to hear her voice and just as they agreed she would be calling today at noon.

Since he entered the battlefield acreage, he had only seen one car, February, not the most ideal time to visit the historical battlefield sites surrounding Gettysburg. Looking at the foreboding outcrop of gray boulders, he thought about the many soldiers on both sides of the conflict who lost their lives on July 2nd, 1863. The overshadowing boulders of Devil's Den were one of, if not the most eerie places on the battlefield. He recalled the ghost stories his father had shared with him about this deadly place.

Back in 1939, some tourists reported seeing two men walking down the road north of Devil's Den. They were walking arm in arm as if they were injured. They were carrying muskets and wearing what appeared to be old-fashioned, ragged grey military uniforms. When the tourists pulled over and asked them if they needed help the men explained their friend had been shot and was wounded, leaning against a tree. The tourists walked back down the road and just like the two men said there was another man in ragged grey clothing propped up against a tree. The tourists could see the man was bleeding and told the other two men they were going to drive into town and get some help. A short time later, the tourists pulled into a filling station and told one of the attendants about the three men. The attendant didn't even bat an eye and explained there was no reason to go back...*the men would not be there. They were simply the restless dead of Gettysburg.*

Max gazed across the road and thought of yet another ghost story his father had shared with him. Getting up he crossed the road and entered a rock-strewn gorge called The Slaughter Pen where there had been intense and brutal fighting, an area where many a Confederate and Union soldier lost their life on that hot July afternoon. Stepping over and around rocks of varied sizes and shapes he crossed the gorge and came to a small stream of water called Plum Run or Bloody Run as it had been tagged because of the amount of blood filling the stream that day long ago. Standing next to the babbling brook, he watched as the water gurgled and moved around partially water-covered rocks. This was the focal point of the other ghost story he had heard. Frequently, tourists have reported being approached by a barefooted old man wearing shabby clothes and a ragged hat as he points toward Plum Run and says, "Over there...that's what you're looking for." In the next few seconds, the old man is gone. Over the years his mysterious appearances at Devil's Den have garnered him the nickname of The Happy Hippie.

On the other side of the stream, Max stared up into the trees, where hidden five hundred yards, just five football field lengths up the steep incline The Battle of Little Round Top had taken place. Sitting on a small boulder he took a sip of his hot drink and thought about all the death and carnage that took place between Little Round Top, The Slaughter Pen, Devil's Den, the Peach Orchard, and The Wheatfield. These five battle sites were now and had been known for over a century as The Valley of Death where on a single day approximately seventy-nine hundred men had breathed their last. For some strange reason, despite the fact so many lives had been lost during the three-day Battle of Gettysburg he always enjoyed sitting and relaxing at the various battle sites, but the current cold temperature and occasional bitter wind caused him to get up and make his way back across the road to the bench where he refilled his cup.

He thought about the ghost stories of Devil's Den which caused him to think about the old fella he had met days ago up on Little Round Top and the strange story he had told. Kellem McCulhay, *an odd sort*, he thought. An eighty-two-year-old codger who lived on a nearby farm and liked to hike out onto the battlefield daily. The ghost story he had shared occurred in 1938 and then recurred again in 1969; with the sighting of a young Confederate soldier standing by a fence on his farm.

Even though thirty-one years had passed since the original sighting had taken place, over three decades later, the same soldier appears and has not aged one bit. *Difficult to believe,* thought Max, but then again, it was just one of those things that are difficult to explain. *Hell,* maybe Kellem McCulhay was a ghost himself. *He couldn't be!* The old man had sat right next to him and even shared part of his lunch. The banana he had eaten was real. He had sat there for over an hour and discussed the Battle of Little Round Top with Kellem. He couldn't be a ghost! Hadn't he seen him later at the town square where Kellem had pulled up in an old pickup truck and talked with him? No, Kellem McCulhay was no ghost. Screwing the lid back onto the thermos he decided to go back to his Jeep and await the call from Elizabeth.

Max placed the thermos on the console, turned on the ignition, and adjusted the heater to medium-high. The warm heat from the vent felt good as it ran up his arms. Looking out the side window he saw a deer drinking cool water from Plum Run and then jump across the stream and disappear in the trees. His view of the wonder of nature was interrupted when his cell phone buzzed. Picking it up on the second familiar buzz, he answered, "Hello!"

Just as he thought, his suspicion that it was Elizabeth calling was verified while he listened to her voice, "Hello Max...It's Elizabeth. Where are you?"

"Gettysburg."

"I know that. But what are you doing?"

"Right now, I'm over here at the battlefield at a place called Devil's

Den watching a deer drink water from a stream. Oh yeah, and I'm drinking hot chocolate. We had two inches of snow last night and it's really cold out today."

"Devil's Den," repeated Elizabeth. "You've mentioned that spot to me before. I miss having you tell me about the Civil War facts and statistics you know so well. Maybe when I get back to school you could tell me all about this Devil's Den."

Max watched the deer walk off into the woods again. "I look forward to that. How is your father doing?"

"My mother and I just got back from the hospital about an hour ago. He's made quite a bit of progress since he was first admitted. This last week they set both of his wrists and his right leg. He now has a knee brace and they discovered he has a fractured rib. The nurses and the doctors agree the sooner he is released the better. He hates the hospital food and gives the hospital staff a hard way to go when it comes to getting shots. It's always a problem when he has to take his medications. The doctor we talked with today said next week they'd be getting him up and around so he can be fitted for and start to use crutches. They said he could probably come home in two weeks. Between a visiting nurse and all the help from our community, we should be fine."

"Sounds like things are moving right along. Do you have any idea when you'll be returning to school?"

"We talked about that very thing at the hospital. My parents said it was up to me, but I think underneath it all my mother wants me to stay until the fall semester, so I've decided that's what I'm going to do."

"That means we won't see each other until the end of August."

Elizabeth changed the subject and asked, "I guess in the next few weeks you'll be heading back home to South Carolina for Spring break."

"That's correct. Spring break starts on March 7th and goes through the 14th. I plan on leaving here from Gettysburg on March 6th, which falls on a Friday. My last class of the day will be over at two o'clock, I'll throw a few things in my Jeep and then I'll be on my way for a week of South Carolina sunshine and of course, some serious beach time and great seafood. After that, it's back to school for almost three months and then the end of May rolls around, and I'll be beach-bound until August when we meet up again."

Elizabeth's voice took on a tone of sadness. "That's six months…half the year. I'm going to miss our Wednesday and Saturday get-togethers. I hope when I return, we can pick things up where we left off."

"The same thought crossed my mind. I would be greatly disappointed if our friendship came to an end."

There was an awkward moment of silence on both ends of the conversation when Max finally spoke up, "I just got a crazy idea. When I leave school for Spring break, I could take a side trip and drive down to Lancaster and maybe we could spend some time together. What do you think?"

"That sounds wonderful, but you wouldn't be able to come to the farm. Remember, my folks don't know anything about you. The last thing I need to do is stress my father any more than he already is."

Max apologized. "I'm sorry. I feel like I'm putting you on the spot."

"It's not that I don't want to see you. It's just so hard for me to get away from the farm. I can't drive my father's car and my friend Ellen does not drive as well. The only time I leave the farm is on Friday when a group from our community goes to Roots Farmers Market where we have a booth where we sell baked goods and such. We are usually there from nine in the morning until eight at night. It wouldn't do you any good to come there because I along with other members of our community have to work the booth. I wouldn't be able to get away and spend time with you."

Another moment of silence followed when Elizabeth seemed to cheer up. "There might be a way on Saturday when we could meet. Ever since I was about ten years old, whenever I want some alone time, I tell my folks I'm going to walk down to the pond which is about a mile from our farm. The pond is off the road, back in the woods. In all the years I've been going there I've never run into anyone else. It's like my private plot of ground where I can always go and just get away from things. If you are still interested in coming in Friday or even on Saturday, I can give you directions and we could meet there and spend a few hours together."

"That sounds great," said Max. "How do I find this pond?"

"That's easy. I'll give you directions and also Ellen's phone number. I'll make sure I take her phone with me. If you get lost, you can just give me a call and I can guide you there. So, you think you can do that?"

"Piece of cake! Just let me get my pen and some paper and you can give me directions."

Moments later, with the simple directions written on an index card, Max placed the square white card up behind his visor. Elizabeth's voice sounded again as she asked, "Any problems with Brad Sykes…"

Ten minutes passed when Elizabeth said she had to go back to the house to help with some baking for the upcoming day at the market. "Okay then," said Max. "I'll be leaving about two-thirty or so on Friday, March 6th. I should arrive in Lancaster around five and then I'll get a motel room. Then, on Saturday, the seventh, following your directions, I'll meet you at this pond at noon. We'll talk again on the phone over the next two weeks and I'll see you on the seventh of March."

The next two weeks seem to fly by rapidly and Max found himself walking out of his last class of the day, Friday, March 6th. The temperature was hanging in the mid-twenties, the roads were clear of snow and the forecast for the day was clear skies. The time was 2:05 and within the hour he would be on his way to Lancaster. All he had to do was pack a bag, gas up the Jeep, grab some chow and he would be on the road.

After gassing up, he selected a deli sandwich, bag of chips, and a cold drink from the station, pulled out onto Route 15 North, and was on the first leg of his journey. Leaving the Gettysburg town limits he reviewed the directions Elizabeth had given him. Take Route 15 North, bypass Harrisburg on Route 76, and then get onto Route 283 South which would take him right into Lancaster. It was a seventy-four-mile trip that could be knocked out in an hour and a half. Taking a bite out of his sandwich he figured after spending a couple of hours with Elizabeth on Saturday he would then be on his way to Summerville for Spring break.

Nearly a half hour passed when Max found himself driving across a large bridge spanning the Susquehanna River. Route 15 bypassed the greater part of Harrisburg and within a few short minutes, he was passing through a suburb named Camp Hill. Max recalled a few years in the past when they had been at a reenactment in Gettysburg when his father had talked about Harrisburg, which at the time of the Civil War was the state capital of the second largest state in the Union. Because of the numerous railroads passing through the city, Harrisburg became extremely important to the Northern Army. Tens of thousands of recruits were trained and drilled at or near Camp Hill, not to mention that the state capital was also a valuable and main supply route. Robert E Lee, well aware of the importance of the city, decided to invade and capture Harrisburg in 1862 during what was called The Maryland Campaign. Because of the Battle of Antietam Lee had to cancel the taking of Harrisburg and eventually retreated to Virginia. A second attempt to overtake Harrisburg occurred in June of 1863. On June 29th, just three days before the Battle of Gettysburg kicked off, Southern General Richard S. Ewell and two divisions approached Harrisburg from the southwest while General Jubal Early crossed the Susquehanna at a town called Wrightsville, Pennsylvania, planning to take Harrisburg from the rear at Camp Hill. General Couch, the Northern General in command at Harrisburg ordered fortifications constructed along the river. The attack was canceled by Lee as he needed Ewell and Early to pull back to a place called South Mountain as massive Union troops were on the move. This resulted in the Battle of Gettysburg.

Ewell, redeploying his divisions left two cavalry units behind at a place called Sporting Hill just west of Camp Hill. Northern General William F. Smith sent two infantry units to stave off the Confederate cavalry which resulted in the Battle of Sporting Hill, which is known as the farthest battle into the north. Before Max knew it, he had driven through Camp Hill and was now about to exit onto Route 76 East.

He was only on 76 for a few minutes when he saw the exit for 283 South where a standard green road sign read: Lancaster- 38 Miles. Looking at the bright early March sun he figured that within the next hour, he would be in Lancaster, just a few miles from Elizabeth's farm.

Passing through a community called Middletown, Max thought with all those deaths that occurred in a five square mile radius at Gettysburg was there any wonder of the number of ghost stories that abounded on the fields and roads on the battlefield? Maybe that man at the filling station back in 1939 was right, *The restless dead of Gettysburg!*

On the other side of Middletown, the countryside took on a different look, vast fields, scattered farms here and there, herds of cattle grazing in the distance. The next thirty minutes of pleasant driving took him through the small towns of Elizabethtown and Mount Joy and eventually, he saw the first exit for Lancaster. The next exit: Hempfiekd Township was the exit he wanted. Getting off the main highway he pulled into an area where there were two motels available: Motel 6 and Days Inn. Parking the Jeep at the main entrance of Days Inn, he hopped out and walked through the lobby door where he saw a young lady sporting a long ponytail who was manning the check-in desk. Smiling pleasantly at Max the young woman spoke, "Good afternoon, sir. Do you require a room?"

"Took the words right out of my mouth," said Max. "I'll just need a single for one night; first floor, no smoking."

The girl checked a computer screen as she replied, "I think we can handle that. If you'll just fill out one of our registration cards then that will be fifty-eight dollars for the night. Will that be cash or credit card?"

Max flipped open his wallet, removed his MasterCard and laid it on the counter.

The girl quickly ran his card, handed it back and took the registration card. Laying a key card on the counter she stated, "That will be room number twenty-seven. It's down near the end. We have a continental breakfast starting at six in the morning. I hope you have a pleasant stay."

Max turned to walk back out to his Jeep but then asked, "I don't suppose you could tell me anything about the Roots Farmers Market…could you?"

"Roots…one of my favorite places to go. My husband and I go there every other week. We do a lot of our grocery shopping there. They have wonderful fruits and vegetables. They have Amish cheese and baked goods and some of the best honey you've ever tasted."

"I've heard of this Roots, and I was thinking about going over there tonight."

The girl looked at a clock on the wall as she responded, "It's just after five. If you left now, you could be there in about twenty-five minutes."

"Ya know…I think I will take a drive over there. You said it's about a half-hour drive…right?"

"That's correct."

"And how do I get there from here?"

"That's easy. The road right out in front of the motel is Route 72. What you do is when you leave the lot make a left and head up 72. In a few miles, you'll be in a town by the name of East Petersburg. Drive right through town and keep going for I'd say three or four miles when you'll come to Lititz Road. Take a left there and in a couple of miles you'll come to Gravestone Road. Take a right on Gravestone and a quarter of a mile or so down the road you'll come to Roots. You can't miss it. There will be tents and buildings on the left side of the road and large fields on the right filled with cars. At this time of the day on a Friday, they'll be really busy so you might have to park pretty far out. One other thing, with all the rain and snow we've had lately it might be kind of muddy over there"

Giving the young woman a thumbs up, Max replied, "Thanks!"

"One other thing," said the girl. "Have you had dinner yet?"

"No, I haven't."

"They have some great food over there. Whenever we go, we always get the fish sandwich at Heitzelman's. It's the best fish sandwich in the county."

"Thanks again," said Max. "Looks like I'm on my way to a great dinner!" He parked at the end of the building, got out, and inspected the room which appeared to be a normal motel room, neatly made bed, mid-sized television, chair, dresser, and nightstand. He peeked in the bathroom that looked spic and span and out the door he went. His next stop, Roots Farmers Market.

After he passed through East Petersburg Max saw a road sign for Landisville Road. This was the road he was to take to get to the pond, but that was tomorrow. Right now, he was focused on getting to the market. Just like the girl at the motel said Lititz Road was three miles past East Petersburg. Making a left on Lititz he realized he was deep in farm country. The farms here appeared much different than those he had seen in South Carolina. The farms he was passing, especially the barns, were neat as a pin, bright white paint with gleaming silver-topped silos surrounded by sturdy fencing. The barns back down in South Carolina were weathered and at times partially covered with vines and rickety fences, some of the barns appearing as if they could collapse at any second.

He drove by a few more farms when he came to an intersection with a stop sign, its black metal pole overgrown with three-foot-high weeds. A small green sign on the opposite side of the road indicated this was what he was looking for: Gravestone Road. Making a right-hand turn, he wasn't on the road for a full minute when he saw the tents he had been told about. A man standing by the side of the road signaled him to pull into a field and stop. The man motioned for Max to roll down his window and instructed him there was parking at the back of the field. Driving over bumps and ruts on a man-made dirt road that was now mostly mud, Max found a spot in the last row. Opening the door, he noticed the ground was saturated with moisture from either melting snow or a recent rain; a field of mud just like the girl back at the motel said. Not desiring to have his good running shoes saturated with mud he reached under the passenger seat and pulled out a pair of old battered work boots. Changing his footwear, he climbed out of the Jeep and sloshed up the muddy road, the grassy area on either side oozing like a South Carolina marsh.

On the other side of the paved road, he came to the first row of tents separated by an eight-foot-wide straw-covered path. Walking along he noticed that the mixture of straw and mud created a mucky concoction that stuck to his boots. The first three tents on the right offered furniture made out of whiskey barrels, a tent full of old wagon wheels, and another with lamps made from old horseshoes. The tents on the left were custom-made jewelry, handmade baby clothes, and a variety of hats and sweatshirts. Passing several other tents, he stopped at a tent that appeared to have either Amish or Mennonite workers. Approaching the ten, Max inquired, "Amish or Mennonite?"

An older woman dressed in plain clothes similar to what Elizabeth wore gave him an odd look and answered, "We're Amish. The Mennonites are at the end of the row. Make a right. They've got ten or twelve tents down there."

Max slopped through the muddy straw, turned at the end of the row, and saw more tents to the left. He stopped at the first tent and asked a young girl about the same age as Elizabeth. "Are these all-Mennonite tents down through here?"

The girl, who was busy placing a cake in a box answered, "This whole row is Mennonite."

Max leaned on a fold-up table and asked his next question. "Is the King family in this row somewhere?"

The girl pointed down the row and answered, "Next to the last tent on the left. That's where you'll find the Kings."

Thanking the girl Max trudged on through the mud but slowed down as he approached the King's tent. He didn't want to startle Elizabeth as she was not expecting him at the market. Moving to the opposite side of the path he hid behind a row of portable bathroom facilities and tried to see if he could see her. Quite a few customers were standing at the tent and passing by. All of the women in the tent were clothed in the plain black style of dress he had come accustomed to. Peering in between passing people he thought he caught a glimpse of her but wasn't sure. He walked around the bathrooms, crossed the path went around the last tent, and approached the King's tent from the rear where there were no customers.

Casually looking around the back corner of the tent he scanned the group of Mennonite men and women walking back and forth and talking with customers. Suddenly he saw her as she handed a customer a jar of honey, took the money, and walked to a register. Melting into the group of customers he slowly made his way to the front of the tent and waited until he could get her attention. Selling two more jars of honey and some cupcakes, she stuffed the money into an apron she was wearing and looked up at the next customer. Her mouth dropped open and her eyes grew in size as she stared at Max. Following two seconds of silence, Max asked, "Cat got your tongue?"

Elizabeth nodded for him to move down toward the end of the tent as she followed and then spoke in amazement. "Max, what are you doing here? We're not supposed to meet until tomorrow."

"I know," said Max, "but when I checked into my motel room and found out how close the market was, I decided to drop by and see you, even if it's just for a few minutes." Realizing it might appear odd if they just kept talking, he suggested, "Maybe I should buy something like I'm a customer." He opened his wallet, laid a ten on the table, and put his hand over it. "Maybe I should buy a pie."

Elizabeth casually reached down and patted his hand twice and then laid her hand over his. "That won't be necessary. I am glad you came but this might not be the best time to talk."

Max placed his other hand over hers and apologized, "I'm sorry if I've upset you in any way. I just wanted to see you...that's all."

From the back of the tent, a large, bearded man wearing a black shirt, pants, and a straw hat placed his right hand on Elizabeth's left shoulder and looked down at her hand partially covered with Max's. Giving Max a stern look he then asked Elizabeth. "Is there some sort of problem?"

Elizabeth gently pulled away from Max's hand and spoke to the large man calmly. "No...there is no problem, Simon. This customer was just deciding what type of pie he wanted to purchase."

Max, realizing something was wrong added, "Yes, I can't decide whether I want the blueberry or the apple. I think I'll just go with blueberry." Removing his hand from the table he displayed a ten-dollar bill. "Will ten cover it?"

Elizabeth spoke up, "I owe you a dollar and a blueberry pie."

While she walked to the back of the tent to a rack of pies the man continued to give Max a dirty look. Max tried to smile back at the man, but he was just too intimidating. The man leaned forward inches from Max's face and spoke roughly. "I don't like anyone touching my woman."

Max couldn't think of anything to say other than, "I just wanted to buy a pie. I'm not looking for any trouble."

Elizabeth returned with the boxed pie and handed it to Max, all the while the man never took his piercing eyes off Max.

Max gave Elizabeth a blank look, thanked her, turned, and walked up the path. He no sooner got twenty feet when someone tapped him on his arm.

Turning, he saw Elizabeth, who didn't allow him to speak. "You forgot your dollar. Back there…what happened is not what it looks like and don't take any stock in what that man said. He can be short-tempered. I'll explain all this tomorrow when we meet at the pond. Now get out of here before he sees us talking." With that, she turned and ran back down the path.

Max watched her as she disappeared into the crowd. Confused, he looked at the pie in his right hand and then down at his mud-caked boots as he thought, *What the hell is going on?*

He stopped when he saw Heitzelman's fish tent where the two rows of tents intersected. *Might as well get that fish sandwich.* Only one couple was standing at the tent as they ordered. Max stood next to the couple when a young man wearing a ball hat and a food-stained apron addressed him. "What can we get for you, sir?"

Max put his pie on the counter, opened his wallet, and took out a twenty. "I'd like one fish sandwich please."

The young man turned and yelled to a girl standing toward the back of the tent, "One fish dinner!" Turning back to Max he explained, "That comes with fries and coleslaw…that okay?"

"Sure, how much do I owe you?"

"Twelve dollars will do it."

As Max handed a twenty to the young man, he noticed the intimidating man who had placed his hand on Elizabeth's shoulder standing with two other men at the side of the tent. All three were sporting the standard Mennonite attire, black clothing, and straw hats. The trio of large identically dressed men reminded Max of one of those bizarre tag team wrestling matches he had seen on T.V. He received his change from the young man along with a sack with an explanation, "There's ketchup, salt, pepper, tartar sauce, a fork, and napkins in there with your dinner. Thank you and have a nice evening."

Max shot another look at the three men who had moved farther down the side of the tent in his direction. Without any hesitation, he turned and walked quickly up the path toward the road. *They can't be following me… that's ridiculous!* His efforts at walking at a fast pace were hampered by the weight of the mud caked on his boots.

Reaching the road, he turned and looked back. The three men were trudging through the mud as fast as they could go without running. Jogging across the road Max couldn't believe what was happening. *What have I gotten myself into?* Running as best he could through the muddy parking area, he realized the only light in the field was from the distant pole lights back where the tents were. He looked around the dimly lit field and there was no one else in the lot at the moment. Around a corner of parked cars, he headed for the back where he had parked but then decided he needed to do something drastic as he had no idea what was going to happen. He cut in between two parked cars, laid the pie and the sack on the hood of a white compact Ford, ran out into the darkness of the two-foot-high weeds a few yards, and crouched down while keeping his eye on the three men as they stopped at the car where he had left his purchases.

He listened while they spoke, one of the men asking, "Do you think this is his car?"

Another man responded. "No…there's no one inside." He picked up the pie as if it were a frisbee and tossed it out into the field then dropped the fish dinner to the ground and stomped it with his boot. "He's close by. Spread out. He can't leave this lot. Keep your ears open for any cars starting up."

Max watched the three walk off in different directions, one walking out into the field, stopping just a few feet from where he was. The man turned on a flashlight and moved it back and forth across the weeds, the light passing two feet above where he lay. Laying as flat as he could, he could feel the oozing mud covering his fingers and then his hands. The front of his shirt was soaking up the wetness of the ground as Max thought, *It's Spring break for crying out loud! I should be on my way to the sunny beaches of South Carolina but no, here I am lying in some muddy field in the middle of the Pennsylvania farmland!*

The man turned off the light and moved back to the parking lot. Max stood, crouched, and made his way through the weeds until he came to the last row of cars. He wasn't exactly sure how far down the Jeep was, but he knew it was at least nine or ten vehicles. Moving slowly down the row of parked vehicles he kept his eyes on the men. The man who had slung his pie was walking back toward the road. The man with the flashlight was searching the row of cars he had first ducked behind. The third man, at the moment, had disappeared somewhere in the maze of parked vehicles. Seven cars up, he came to the Jeep. Touching the rear of his vehicle he couldn't ever remember being so glad to see the Jeep. Now, all he had to do was climb in and drive off. A car in the next row down about twenty yards backed out from a parking spot and started down the muddy road but was stopped by the man with the flashlight. Seeing the driver was not who he was looking for he apologized and told the driver he was just looking for someone who had lost their wallet.

Max realized that he was going to have to get in his Jeep differently than he was used to which amounted to him pressing his key fob, which would unlock the driver's side door at the same time the horn honked once, and the lights flashed twice. He duckwalked up the side of the Jeep, reached up, and inserted the key into the lock. Following a low click the door unlocked. He checked for the men once again and then slowly opened the door sat in the driver's seat and closed the door, which was followed by a low thud, which made him wince. He saw the man he had lost track of as he walked down a row searching each car's interior with a flashlight.

All three men now were wielding lights, and he knew he couldn't stay put as it would just be a matter of time before he was discovered. He couldn't go back out the same way he had entered the lot because that was blocked by one of the men. He placed the key into the ignition and thought, *I sure hope there's another way out of this lot!* Then, he saw a set of red taillights of a car leaving in a different direction. *Here goes!* He turned the key and just like always the Jeep came to life. He pulled out slowly to the right keeping his headlights in the off mode as he slowly drove up the muddy road. Rolling down the window, he watched and listened. At first, there was silence but then a yell. "Over there…a Jeep…come."

The road was filled with not only mud but numerous ruts which made driving any faster than fifteen miles an hour difficult. The rear taillights he saw before stopped, then made a left and sped off. Going through a deep rut he was jerked to the side as he thought, *I hope that's Gravestone up ahead.*

He saw one of the men on his left about twenty yards away as he weaved in and out between parked cars. Looking in the rearview mirror he saw the second man thirty yards behind him as he ran up the road. He couldn't locate the third pursuer. The tents were on the other side of the road. He was just a few yards from escaping when the Jeep slid to the right. Max had to hit the brakes, which allowed both of the men to close the distance. Hitting the accelerator, the back tires spun in the mud. He backed up and then put the gearshift back into first gear as he hit the gas. The car rocked forward but then back to the hole he seemed to be in. The man from the back was almost at his bumper when Max floored the gas pedal, the Jeep jolting out of the muddy hole, splattering the man with mud. The man from the right side reached for the door handle but by that time the Jeep jumped up onto the pavement of Gravestone Road where suddenly the third man appeared, shining the flashlight directly into the windshield. Blinded, Max floored the gas pedal, laid on the horn, and turned on the high beams. The man jumped out of the way at the last second as Max blasted down the road and made a left onto Lititz Road without stopping for the stop sign. Looking in the rearview mirror it didn't appear he was being followed. He took a deep breath and eased off on the accelerator. Wiping mud from the side of his face he wondered, *What the hell was that all about?*

By the time he got back to his motel, he had calmed down but was still quite confused. Parking in front of his room he got out and noticed from the bright lights in the lot that he was covered in mud. Walking down to the main lobby he entered and walked up to the counter. The same girl who had checked him in stared at him in disbelief. "Mr. Miller, isn't it?"

"Yep, it's me. I might look a little different than when I checked in but yes it's still me!"

"What on earth happened to you? Did you go to Roots?"

"Yes, I did and as you can see I brought back half of the mud you told me about over there. Listen, I was wondering if you have any large plastic bags I can put these muddy clothes in after I shower?"

"Yes, if you look at the bottom of the dresser in your room, you'll find three large plastic bags for dirty clothes. Here, let me get you a couple of extra towels. Looks like you're going to need them. What on earth happened over there?"

Max gladly took the towels and tried to explain without going into any great detail. "I purchased a blueberry pie and one of those fish sandwiches you recommended. My pie was thrown out in a field, and someone smashed the crap out of my fish dinner. There's a lot more to it than that, but I'd just as soon forget it."

"Do you want me to call the police?"

"Heavens no! I'm sure they have more important things to do than track down a pie and a smashed fish sandwich. It's not that big of a deal. I'd just like to go down to my room and crawl out of these filthy duds, take a shower, and then I'm going to slip into some dry clothes, walk over to that McDonald's across the street, and get me two fish sandwiches. Not exactly the best fish sandwich in the county but it'll have to do. Look, I know that being next to the highway you probably from time to time get some real weirdos in here. So, with that, I'll say thanks for the towels, and I hope the next person you meet isn't as weird as I seem to be."

CHAPTER THIRTEEN

Max threw his travel bag into the back of his jeep, walked down to the motel lobby, and entered a small room off to the side. It was ten o'clock and the continental breakfast that was offered expired at eleven. He had plenty of time to eat and drive to Elizabeth's Pond. He grabbed a Styrofoam plate and a set of plastic utensils as he surveyed the assortment of breakfast foods. Opening a plastic see-through cover of a stainless-steel buffet server, using a serving spoon he placed a scoop of scrambled eggs and then three strips of crispy bacon on the plate and poured himself a glass of apple juice. Next, he prepared a cup of coffee and filled a bowl with corn-flakes which he topped with a sliced banana. He sat at one of six tables and watched the local news while enjoying his breakfast.

The weather report, given by a spunky, thirty-ish-year-old woman was an encouraging forecast, not only for the day but the upcoming week. No precipitation in the next few days, cloudy, and slightly above normal tem-peratures, adding that it looked like an early spring. Taking a bite of eggs Max thought. *How appropriate! March 7th…the first day of Spring break.*

He'd probably finish up his breakfast around ten-thirty, check out, gas his Jeep up, and be on his way to the pond no later than eleven. Elizabeth said she would meet him there at noon. Since he had never been to this pond or even on Landisville Road, he planned on giving himself some extra time.

Max stood at the gas pump at ten-forty-five. Spotting a nearby car wash he thought his ol' Jeep deserved a good rinsing off following the previous night's romp through the muddy parking lot at Roots. He pulled across the street into a bay, inserted the number of quarters required, and began to spray off the caked-on mud from the tires, bumper, and frame. Finished, he pulled out of the bay and saw a Mennonite man walk across the lot and nod at him. The thought that he was still being followed was erased. The man was wearing the same get-up as the three men from last night but was wearing glasses and was shorter. Pulling out onto Route 72, he smiled to himself. *Stop being so paranoid!*

He drove through East Petersburg and made a left onto Landisville Road as instructed. The town wasn't very big and within two minutes he found himself passing several farms flanking both sides of the road. According to Elizabeth, their farm was about three miles west of town, the address 3015 Landisville Road. The white fencing surrounding the third farm on the right seemed to be endless, with hundreds of dairy cows scattered across the vast fields. Two farms up, indicated by the number 3015 on a plain black mailbox on the left, he passed what he thought was the King's farm. Just like all the other farms he had seen it looked clean as a whistle!

The next thing he was to look for was an old-fashioned covered bridge spanning a local creek. On the other side of the bridge, there would be a gravel area where he could park, then he was to follow a path downstream that ran perpendicular to the creek until he came to a downed tree. It was here he was supposed to follow what Elizabeth referred to as a barely recognizable deer path.

Two farms past the King's place Max stared in amazement as a late model vehicle pulled out of the dirt lane and entered onto the paved road. Elizabeth had been right on the money when she had explained the meaning of Black Bumper Mennonites. The car itself was not only black but the bumpers, wheel covers and anything that at one time had been chrome had been painted a flat black. It was the ugliest car he had ever seen. She had told him the pond was about a mile away from her farm, so he expected to see the bridge within the next minute or so.

Maneuvering around a long sweeping curve he crossed the wooden bridge and pulled into a gravel area next to the water. He got out, locked the Jeep, and started down the path. Elizabeth had explained that the downed tree would be about fifty yards or so down the creek side path. As he walked along, he thought about how awkward it might be if he ran into some Mennonite men fishing, but the possibility of that happening seemed unlikely. It was early March and it seemed too cold for fishing.

He walked around a short bend in the creek when he saw the fallen tree that blocked the path and formed a makeshift bridge across the water. Looking to his left he saw somewhat of a path, the tall weeds on both sides leaning to the side. Walking through the low underbrush after a few yards he came to a small clearing. On the other side of the clearing, according to Elizabeth, he should look for a bird feeder she had placed there as a little girl years in the past. Approaching a stand of trees he saw the feeder, weather-beaten and falling apart but it was still there. From here he was to follow a dirt path for about a hundred yards where he would come to a break in the woods and there, he would not only find the pond, but Elizabeth as well. Walking slowly through the tall trees he had to agree with what Elizabeth said about the pond being in the middle of nowhere.

He thought the dense trees were spooky, the branches of the leafless trees reaching outward up toward the grey sky like evil tentacles, the soft moss at his feet feeling as if it would give way and swallow him up like quicksand. Old vines hung from the trees, adding to the eerie woods. He stopped for a moment and listened, not a sound. Then, the pleasant chirping of a nearby bird high up in a tree gave him reassurance there was something alive…and harmless in the surrounding forest.

Up ahead he thought he saw the edge of a clearing, the sun peeking through the clouds shining off of shimmering water. Pushing through the trees a few yards more his eyesight had not failed him. It was water…a pond. The circular pond was surrounded by trees and was no more than thirty to forty feet across and equally as wide. At the far end of the pond there sat Elizabeth on the trunk of a tree that had fallen at some point. Her back was to him, and she appeared quite different than what he expected. She was wearing the traditional long black dress which he had grown accustomed to, but she was not wearing her bonnet, the short stains of blond bangs he had seen peeking out from the bonnet turned out to be a full head of flowing hair stopping a few inches past her shoulders.

Not wanting to startle her by shouting her name he picked up a golf ball-sized stone and tossed it toward the center of the quiet pond.

The sound of the gentle splash caused her to look at the pond as the ever-growing circle of ripples spread. Turning, she saw Max standing at the edge of the trees. Instantly, she stood and ran toward him as she responded to his appearance in an excited, elevated tone of voice, "Max…you're here!" She skirted the edge of the pond and stopped just short of running into him when she reached down and took both his hands in hers. Squeezing his hands gently, she looked into his face and gave him one of her smiles that always seemed to erase anything else on his mind.

Looking into those deep green eyes he had seen for the first time at that football game last fall, he remained silent and just relished in the moment.

Elizabeth led him around the edge of the water and stated, "I see you didn't have any problems finding my pond."

"No, I didn't. Your directions were easy to follow. Although, I was a little concerned while walking through the trees. I wasn't sure if I was going in the right direction, but here I am!"

When they got to the downed tree trunk she sat and offered, "Please have a seat."

Max sat next to her and gazed out at the circular pond. "So, this is, I believe you said, your special place."

"Yes, it is. Like I said. In all the time I've been coming here I've never run into anyone. A lot of the men in our community fish but no one seems to come back in here. Mostly they stay out by the creek. I've never even seen any fish in this pond. About the only thing I see on occasion are some deer who come here for a drink. They always look at me and then go about their business. I guess they sense I'm harmless and they are in no danger."

"I have two places where I go when I want to get away from things," said Max. "Back in Gettysburg it's over at the battlefield and when I'm at home in South Carolina it's the beach. It is nice here. I can see why you like coming." Straddling the tree Max asked, "I've been meaning to ask you something. I see you're not wearing your bonnet. You always wear it, wherever we go."

Elizabeth picked up the white bonnet and explained, "It's called a Prayer Kapp and as a Mennonite woman it's an important part of how we are required to dress, especially in public. If my father were here right now, he'd tell you no self-respecting Mennonite woman would ever be caught dead outside of her home without her Prayer Kapp on her head. In our faith wearing the bonnet is Biblical. In 1 Corinthians it reads: *For if a woman does not cover her head, she might as well have her hair cut off, but it is a disgrace for a woman to have her hair cut off or shaved, then she should cover her head.*" Quoting another verse, Elizabeth went on without missing a beat, "Also, in 1 Corinthians 15:11 it states: *But if a woman has long hair, it is a glory to her, for her hair is given her for a covering.*" Holding up her bonnet she further explained, "The Prayer Kapp is a sign of modesty and humbleness before

God. The only time a Mennonite woman would be without the bonnet would be inside her own home, and even at that when she is bathing or getting ready to lie down with her husband for the night."

"I'm confused. First of all, when it comes to the Bible, I know very little about scripture. Other than the Lord's Prayer which I know is in there somewhere I can't think of any other verse. I have sat in church with my parents many a Sunday and listened to our preacher go on and on about the Bible and to be honest with you it seems to go in one ear and out the other, while you on the other hand apply what it says in the Bible to your everyday life. In one way I feel honored that you would go against wearing your Prayer Kapp in my presence but then on the flipside of the coin I feel because of the relationship we have I may have caused you to go against one of your religious beliefs. I feel a person should believe in what they think and not be swayed by others. I realize I was raised in and come from a different world than you were brought up in and it was never my intention to change your religious values. If I have done so, then please forgive me as it was never my intention to do so."

Elizabeth took his right hand in her left and explained. "Not wearing my bonnet today here at the pond is something I do quite often when I come here. It's just kind of a way of letting my hair down, as they say. I thought about leaving the bonnet on, but I wanted you to see me as I am. I wanted you to see that I am more than just a Mennonite girl. I guess I just wanted to let you know that I am a woman. Do you understand?"

"I think I do understand but when I think of the word *woman,* I think about my mother or some of the females who are professors back at college. I have, ever since we first met considered you a beautiful girl, or I guess a better way to put it would be a beautiful young woman. Since we've been seeing one another, I often ask myself how could a girl this beautiful possibly be interested in me. There are times when I am with you, I feel I'm out of my league and you deserve a man who is better than me."

Elizabeth raised her hand and placed her index finger over his lips. "Enough of this talk. You have stated that I am a beautiful young woman and I, in turn, feel you are a good man. I've already told you that, so let's just leave this alone for a bit. There's something else I want to talk about and that is what took place last night at the farmer's market. You must have left there not understanding what went on. I wish to clear this up, so you are not confused about what went on or was said."

Without allowing Max to speak she continued, "I was not expecting you to show up at the market so you can just imagine how surprised I was. I tried my best to not let on, we knew one another when you approached the tent and I don't think anyone suspected anything. If you could have just purchased that pie and moved on there would have been no confusion. But unfortunately, Simon interrupted our conversation. What he said was not true and it was also inappropriate. When he gave you what must have seemed to you, a dirty look, and then spoke, his choice of words were misused. When he told you he didn't like anyone touching his women, what he should have said was our women. In the Mennonite community someone like you is considered an outsider and not permitted to touch a Mennonite woman, even if it is an innocent gesture. The truth is a Mennonite woman should only be touched by her husband or possibly a man who is courting her. When Simon looked down and saw your hand over the top of mine, he acted correctly but he also should not have laid his hand on my shoulder and stated I was his woman. I have never been, nor do I have intentions of ever being his woman."

"Well, that does clear things up somewhat, but why would he refer to you as his woman, when in fact…you are not?"

"It's a long story, but it needs to be told."

Max tugged at his right ear. "My mother has always told me I'm a great listener, so please, continue."

"Okay, this Simon is a member of our community. His full name is Simon Baumer. He is a farmer, a very successful farmer. When you came down Landisville Road earlier do you recall seeing a really large farm on the right?"

Max thought and then replied, "I did. I passed a farm that had a long white fence that ran along the side of the road. It must have been at least a mile long."

"It's a mile and a half stretching from the East Petersburg town limits to the edge of our farm. Simon owns the largest dairy farm in the county, maybe the state. He also farms more tobacco and corn than anyone in the area. He owns a lumber company, a farm supply, and a convenience store in town. To say Simon Baumer is wealthy is an understatement. It has been said he is a millionaire many times over. For a Mennonite farmer, it is highly unusual to have that much wealth.

"Now, backing up here a little bit going back about a month, my father was over at Baumer's Lumber Company picking up some wood for some custom cabinets he had to make for a family over in Manheim, one of the local towns nearby. Over the years Baumer and my father have become good friends. While paying for the lumber, Simon and my father got to talking and Simon asked my father if he could have permission to court me. My father gave him approval, but at the time this decision was made, I was at school in Gettysburg. Two weeks later when my father had the accident and I had to return home the first thing I did was go to the hospital to visit him. My mother, sisters, and brothers were all there. My father seemed to be in good spirits especially after I showed up. After I guess, it was maybe two hours or so my father asked to speak to me privately. I had no idea what he wanted to speak with me about. After everyone left the room, he explained to me that what he was about to say had already been approved by my mother. This didn't surprise me as my mother normally goes along with whatever my father says."

Elizabeth kicked a twig at her feet and continued, "My father explained to me the conversation he had with Simon Baumer over at the lumber yard and that he had permitted Simon to court me. Needless to say, I was shocked. I knew who Baumer was and certainly had no interest in being courted by him but at the time was in no position to refuse my father. He was in enough pain, and I didn't want to stress him out any more than he already was so I just remained quiet and went along with the way he wanted things to go, although I had no intention of ever marrying Simon Baumer. Besides that, my father is quite interested in getting me married. In our community, it's not good for a father to have a daughter who is of age who is not married or at least being courted. I had already turned down Eli Hoffman and my father agreed that was the correct thing for me to do. He told me there was talk in the community I may have been too hasty in turning down Eli and that I should have been more patient with him. After all, he wound up marrying my best friend, Ellen and it looks like Eli is turning out to be a decent husband. If I refused Simon Baumer's eventual proposal I may be looked at as too picky or too good for anyone which would be a bad reflection on my family. So, you see I had to go along with Simon's courtship, at least for the time being. Does this make any sense to you?"

"Yes, I can understand how difficult it may be to go against the grain of the way your community functions. Let me ask you. How old is this Simon? When I first came into contact with him at the market, he stuck me as much older than you."

"He is older than me. He's thirty-two…thirteen years older than I. In our Mennonite culture, it is not uncommon at times for a young girl like me to marry an older man. Besides, there are not that many, if any available Mennonite women who are not married who are in their thirties. As a Mennonite woman by the time you reach, let's say thirty, you've been married for nine to ten years with no less than two, three, maybe four young ones you're raising. Simon Baumer has not always been a single man. I remember when I was nine he married a beautiful young woman in our community by the name of Suzanna. She was nineteen and he was twenty-two. I remember our family attending their wedding and my mother telling me how much they were in love. You would think that any young couple getting married would be in love, but this is not always the case. Many Mennonite marriages are based on convenience rather than love. That's not a road I want to go down. I want to marry a man I am in love with despite what my father or the community may think.

"Anyway, getting back to the story. Suzanna becomes pregnant and then down the road when it's time for the baby to be born there are complications. She loses the baby and then passes on herself. It was very tragic, and Simon didn't take it well. Following six months of mourning, the elders sat down with Simon and advised him he had to move on with his life. It was at that time that Simon decided to put his nose to the grindstone and get back to work. And the work he did! Here it is, over a decade later and he is the wealthiest Mennonite not only in the county but the state. Earlier this year Simon decided it was time for him to find a wife. He knew I was available; he talked things over with my father and the wheels of motion were put in place. My father thinks Simon would make a great husband and I would be foolish to not consider being his wife due to the fact he has more to offer than any other Mennonite man I may meet in the future."

Max looked out at the pond and asked, "I still do not understand why after courting you for what, a few weeks, this Simon would refer to you as his woman."

"That's easy to figure out," said Elizabeth, "The very first night after my father told me Simon was interested in courting me he showed up at our farm for supper. He told us he was going to be at the farm quite often, probably every day. He and some of the other local men from the community would be dropping by to help with the milking, repairs to the barn and outbuildings, and getting the fields ready for Spring planting; things my father would normally be doing but will not be able to do for quite a few months. That first evening at supper, after we finished up, Simon asked me to sit on the porch with him. He was very pleasant, unlike Eli Hoffman who was a total disaster when it came to communicating. Every day now for the past few days he has been at our farm doing various chores around the place. He eats at least one meal a day with us, be it breakfast, lunch, or dinner. He spends no less than an hour with me every day. He is quite the gentleman, a good listener, who doesn't talk much about himself but is interested in what I think. He has in that time never forced himself on me. We have taken a few walks and buggy rides. Aside from the incident at the market, he has never touched me in any way, be it a kiss or any hand-holding. I never really did anything to encourage him but then again, I never said anything to make him feel unwelcome. For this reason, I can only assume he feels the courting is moving along well. But when August arrives and it's time for me to return to school that will all come to an end. I'm hoping because he won't be able to see me daily his idea of courting me will fade and he'll move on. I even told him a few days back I was planning on finishing up my four years of schooling before I would consider marriage. I would have thought this would have discouraged him, but he told me if things worked out between us, he would be willing to wait until I graduate for us to marry. He even suggested if we were to marry before I graduated, I could still go to college and he would buy me a nice house in Gettysburg to live in while there and he would even pay for my entire education. It turns out that even though Simon Baumer appears to be a very patient man he is used to getting his way and will not accept an objection to anything he wants. So, now you know why things went the way they did at the market, which I apologize for. I hope you can understand why I have to grind my way through this situation until it's time for me to go back to school."

"I do understand," said Max, "but there happens to be more to this story than you may realize. After you followed me and gave me back my change at the market and I was on my way something else happened that turned out to be unpleasant."

Giving Max an odd look, Elizabeth asked, "Whatever are you talking about?"

"On my way out of the market, I decided to stop at Heitzelmans Fish Tent."

Elizabeth lit up. "Really…they have the best fish sandwich I've ever had. Did you enjoy it?"

"I never had an opportunity to enjoy it. It was destroyed!"

"What do you mean…destroyed?"

"I'll explain that later. While standing at the tent waiting for my order I look up and who do I see standing at the back corner near the tent? None other than Simon Baumer and two other Mennonite men, who believe it or not were even bigger than Simon. The three of them were giving me looks that made me feel threatened. They started to move down the side of the tent in my direction and I knew I had to get out of there. Why, I wasn't sure. I knew I just needed to go!"

Elizabeth held up her left hand. "The two men with Simon sound like his brothers; Rupert and Thaddeus. It's been said around the community if you mess with one of the brothers then you will have the other two to contend with as well. So, what happened next?"

"I paid for my sandwich and started to walk toward the parking lot. I didn't get very far when I had a very distinct and uneasy feeling that the three men were following me. Walking by the last few tents of the market, I turned and looked back. Sure enough, there they were all three of them trudging through that muddy straw. From the looks of determination, they had on their faces I realized they were not a welcoming committee.

"When I got to Gravestone Road I started to run and quickly entered the parking lot which was a sea of mud. I knew there wasn't enough time for me to get to my Jeep and drive off before they were on me, so I ducked in behind the first row of cars I came to, placed my pie and fish sandwich on the hood of someone else's car, ran into the adjacent field and hid in the weeds. From where I was, I could still see the lot. When they saw the pie and the sack my sandwich was in, good 'ol Simon tossed the pie out into the field and proceeded to stomp my fish dinner into the mud. I was close enough so I could hear them talking. Simon said the car was not mine and that I shouldn't be allowed to leave the lot. He told his brothers to spread out and search the entire parking area. That allowed me to get to my Jeep, but I had to stay in the field which was about as muddy as you can imagine. By the time I found the Jeep, I was covered in mud. I hopped in, started the Jeep up, and pulled out leaving my headlights off.

"I was confident at that point I was going to escape whatever Simon and the other two had in store for me. Not so! They spotted the Jeep and began to close in. I couldn't drive that fast because of the mud and the ruts in the lot, but it looked like I was going to make it before they reached me.

Then I got stuck! I jammed the gearshift in reverse and then forward trying to rock out of the rut, but the Jeep was not cooperating. On my second attempt, the Jeep spun out of the rut and splattered one of the men who was just about to grab the back of the Jeep. A Second man was just a few yards away when I finally made it to the pavement on Gravestone. I turned left to get down to Landisville Road when the third man, I'm not sure which one jumped out in front of me. I turned on my high beams, laid on the horn, and floored the gas pedal. I almost ran over him, but he jumped out of the way at the last second. Twenty minutes later I pulled into the Days Inn realizing I had dodged a bullet."

Elizabeth placed her left hand over her mouth and stared at Max in astonishment. Lowering her hand she spoke with great concern, "I had no idea Simon and his brothers followed you. I am so sorry that happened. What could they have had in mind?"

"That's pretty easy to figure out. I'm sure they were not just going to talk things over with me. I think they were out to teach me a lesson."

"I can't believe this. I feel like I should say something to my father… maybe even the elders."

"We both know that cannot happen. Right now, your mother and father are not aware of who I am, let alone the fact, that we are, I guess you could say, very close friends. If you were to tell him what happened at the market, that would only lead to other questions that eventually would reveal our relationship, and that would not bode well for you. I think we just need to let sleeping dogs lie. Come next August when you return to school, this business with Simon's efforts to court you will no doubt come to an end and our lives will return to normal. In the meantime, we can continue to speak over the phone every Wednesday and Saturday just as we planned. Who knows, if you agree I can always stop by here and meet you at the pond on my way back to school next week."

Elizabeth stood and walked to the edge of the calm water and looked out into the surrounding trees. Turning back, she addressed Max in a serious tone. "What you call normal as far as our relationship is concerned may be changing."

"What do you mean?" asked Max.

Elizabeth walked back and straddled the tree while facing him. "Seven years ago when I was eleven years old, I remember one evening while helping my mother with the dishes I asked her how it feels to be in love. She gave me a strange sort of look but then answered. She went on to say being in love is a feeling that comes from the heart. It's a feeling toward another person and in my case someday in the future, it would be a Mennonite man probably from our community. She described this feeling as very deep and emotional. She said a day would come when a Mennonite man would come into my life who would cause me to have this feeling; a feeling of wanting to be near him all the time; a feeling of great joy when I am in his presence. A feeling of wanting to spend the rest of my life with this man. I did not experience those feelings when I was in the presence of Eli Hoffman and not even in the presence of Simon Baumer. I have lived in our community long enough to know a lot of Mennonite marriages are based on convenience… not love. When I do get married, I want it to be a man I am truly in love with. I've never been in love so I can only base how I may feel on what my mother told me. I'm not sure how to say this, Max, but I think I may have those very feelings toward you."

Now it was Max who was astonished. "I'm not sure how I am supposed to respond to what you just said. Maybe I've seen too many love stories at the movies or on television but I'm pretty sure if someone indicates they love you, then in return you are to answer with 'I love you too.' I, like you, have never been in love either, but I do have to admit I have some of those feelings toward you that your mother talked about. Let's back up here for a moment. Are you saying you love me?"

"I'm not sure. All I know is I've never felt this way before about any-one…and now…I do!"

"When I came here today to meet you I never expected to have this kind of a conversation. Why, we've only known one another for what… maybe four months. Until today, we've never even held hands. We've never even kissed and here we sit talking about the possibility of being in love with each other. How can this be? Maybe we've just been kidding ourselves in saying we're just friends."

Elizabeth looked deeply into Max's eyes as she scooted closer, reached up with her hand gently ran her fingers across his lips, and whispered, "We have been kidding ourselves. You've been courting me ever since we first met at that football game." She moved closer and her face was inches from his. Then…in a magical moment, she caressed the side of his face and gently kissed him full on the lips. Max responded and following a few seconds pulled away and looked into her green eyes.

"Do we even have any idea what we're getting into? Are you sure you want to go down this road? I feel like I'm leading you down the wrong path, away from your Mennonite beliefs, away from how you were raised. I find myself in a situation that I have sort of told my parents about, but you cannot tell your folks about me. Down the road, this could be a problem for us. When we get back to school if our feelings are as they seem to be now, or possibly even get stronger, at some point, we are going to have to face our parents…and your community. Is that something you will be prepared to do if necessary?"

She held both of his hands in hers and smiled. "If it's God's will that we are to be together, then so be it. It doesn't make any difference what people in this world think of me. It's what God knows about me…and that's important. I may be breaking the rules of my community, but God knows what's on my heart. I am a good person, a strong woman, and I deserve to fall in love with whoever I choose…not my parents or my community." Giving him a short peck on his cheek, she stood, "It's been three hours since I left the house, I better be getting back. I have to help my mother with supper for tonight. I hate to end our wonderful afternoon on a sour note but Simon will be eating with my family this evening."

Max stood and stretched, "I guess I best be on my way also. I've got a long drive ahead of me. Can I drive you back to the farm?"

Elizabeth bent down, allowing her long hair to drop forward over her face. She spoke while using both hands and the aide of some pins she removed from a pocket on her dress. "You can only walk me back as far as the creek. From there on I'm on my own. We can't be seen together." Scooping up her hair she weaved it into a tight bun which she tucked beneath her bonnet. She held her hands out to her sides. "There you go. Back to the girl you're used to seeing." She held his hand and led him by the pond as they stepped into the woods.

Skirting a large tree Max asked, "Has your hair always been that long?"

"It was down to my waist but when I decided to go to college I decided to cut about twelve inches off. I'm probably leaving it this length until after I graduate then I'll let it grow out again." She noticed that Max suddenly seemed nervous. Bumping him on his arm, she asked, "Is there something wrong?"

Staring out into the trees up ahead, Max replied. "I was just thinking how horrible it would be to see Simon and his two brothers suddenly jump out of the trees."

"Stop worrying about them. You'll probably never see them again as long as you live."

Minutes passed and they stepped out of the tree line next to the bubbling creek. Smoothing out her dress, Elizabeth commented, "Looks like this is where we part ways."

She gave Max a quick kiss to which he responded, "This kissing business could turn out to be a pleasant habit."

"Let's hope so. Go on, get out of here, I'll call you this coming Wednesday. Have a great Spring break. Maybe we can meet at the pond again… soon."

Max started up the path next to the creek and looked back. "Let's plan on it. Talk to you Wednesday."

Twenty yards up, the creek took a bend to the right. Max stopped and looked back at Elizabeth who had removed her shoes and was wading in the shallow water. He waved one last time and then walked up the path.

Back at the clearing he started the Jeep, pulled back onto the road but decided to go in the opposite direction he had come. He drove for about a quarter mile and then turned around in a long dirt lane that led to one of the local farms. Going back toward the bridge he was hoping to see Elizabeth as she walked down the road. Crossing the bridge slowly he looked for her at the creek; nothing!

Further down Landisville Road he didn't even get a quarter mile when he saw her walking next to the road. He slowed the Jeep to a crawl and when he pulled up next to her he rolled down the passenger side window, leaned across the seat, and shouted, "Can't wait to see you again!"

She looked up and down the road to make sure no one was in sight, ran to the Jeep, and took Max's right hand in hers. "I forget to tell you. Tomorrow is my birthday."

Somewhat surprised, Max responded, "Why didn't you say something when we talked on the phone? I would have gotten you as a gift."

"It's all right. Not to worry. Seeing you at the pond today was the best gift I could receive. Be safe, Max. Talk to you Wednesday! Now…scoot!"

Max gave her a thumbs up and pressed down on the accelerator, the Jeep speeding down the road. He watched in the rearview mirror while Elizabeth became smaller and smaller until she disappeared. Turning his attention back to the road, he thought about how strange life could be. Here he was on his way to a week of fun in the sun in South Carolina while

Elizabeth was back there on that country road on her way home where later tonight her family would be entertaining a dinner guest, Simon Baumer; the pie-throwing, fish stomping, ill-mannered dairy farmer from East Petersburg, Pennsylvania.

CHAPTER FOURTEEN

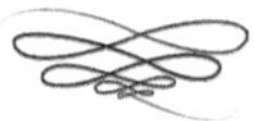

It was 3:10 in the morning when Max pulled into his parent's driveway in Summerville. Getting out of his Jeep he noticed the dim blue light that filtered through their living room window. Walking up onto the porch he thought more than likely his father went to sleep watching television. Charley had a habit of staying up late on occasion and after watching the news he'd watch an old movie. His mother, on the other hand, was not much of a night owl and usually turned in around ten o'clock.

He inserted his house key into the door, unlocked it, and entered, quietly closing the door behind him. He placed his travel bag in a small foyer walked down the short hall and made a right into the living room. Just as he thought, the T.V. was on and surprisingly he saw both his parents sitting on the couch. Tiptoeing across the hardwood floor near the fireplace he walked to a recliner adjacent to the couch. Unnoticed, he looked at the television screen and watched as Gary Cooper walked down the middle of the street in a western town. Not wanting to startle his folks he spoke in a regular tone of voice. "One of my favorites!"

Both his mother and father turned to greet their son but before they could utter a word Max announced in a joking fashion. "The prodigal son returns!"

His mother instantly got up, walked over, and hugged him. His father remained seated as he raised a bottle of beer in a toasting manner. "Welcome to the sunny south!"

Max looked at his watch. "What are you two doing up this late? It's after three o'clock."

His mother motioned at the television. "When you phoned us from Pennsylvania and said you'd be in about three in the morning your father and I decided to wait up. We watched the news, then two back-to-back Clint Eastwood movies and now we're in the middle of High Noon." Holding him out at arm's length, she complimented him. "You look great, son. How was your side trip to Lancaster?"

Max shook his father's hand and then seated himself in the recliner. "It was great to see Elizabeth."

Confused, Charley asked, "Correct me if I'm wrong but when Rich and I were in Gettysburg for the meeting with Brad Sykes and his father you told us later that night at dinner you and Elizabeth get together every Wednesday and Saturday. I assume she also went home for Spring break so why was it necessary for you to make the trip to Pennsylvania? Next week she'll be back at school just like you. What's the deal?"

"It would take over an hour to explain everything that has happened since you were in Pennsylvania. It's late and I'm beat. I'd like to hit the sack if it's all the same." Turning to his mother he asked, "If you could wake me about ten then over breakfast, I can bring you up to date."

With concern, his mother ran her hand down his arm. "Are you all right? I mean is everything okay?"

"I'm fine and I can assure you that you and Dad can sleep peacefully and not be concerned over anything. Now, if you don't mind, I'm going to stumble up the stairs, go to my room, get out of these clothes, and then crash and burn." Not waiting for a response, Max started for the stairs. "I'll see you both in about seven hours."

His mother, staring at her husband asked Max as he placed his foot on the first step. "What would you like for breakfast?"

On the third step, Max stopped and smiled back down at his mother. "Surprise me!"

At the top of the stairs, he walked down a hallway and entered the first room on the right. Staring at the familiar surroundings of his room, the room he had been sleeping in for the first eighteen years of his life, he stripped off his clothes, crawled beneath the cool sheets, and drifted off.

Max opened his eyes as he stared up into the face of his mother.

Pleasantly, she announced, "Ten o'clock on the dot. Breakfast will be on the table in ten minutes."

Swinging his legs over the side of the bed, Max yawned and replied, "Good, just enough time for a quick shower. I'll be down shortly."

Max entered the kitchen and surveyed the table his mother had set with scrambled eggs, toast, sausage links, and a large stack of golden brown buttermilk pancakes. His father, already seated at the table laid down the morning paper and pushed it to the side. "Let's eat!"

After pouring himself a cup of coffee from the pot on the kitchen counter, Max joined his father. His mother sat in between the two men in her life, lowered her head, and recited a short blessing. Finished, she passed a bowl of eggs to Max, while asking, "Sleep well?"

"Very well," said Max. "There's nothing like sleeping in your bed, in your own house."

Charley, buttering a piece of toast looked across the table at his son. "So, what's been going on since I was in Gettysburg?"

"Quite a bit has happened. There were a couple of things that happened before you and Rich came up that I was going to mention while at the meeting, but with the way things turned out, it wasn't necessary."

Charley laid down his knife and then gave his wife and son an odd look. "What are you talking about?"

"There are two different issues. The first is this." Reaching into his jeans pocket he removed the envelope, opened it, and took out the folded note, handing it across the table to his father. "I found this under my dorm room door. I guess it was about a week before the meeting."

Unfolding the note Charley read it, grimaced, and handed it to his wife as he spoke to Max. "It's obvious to me that Brad Sykes wrote this note…"

Before he could finish what he was saying, Max's mother chimed in as she read the note, "*This is far from over!*" Laying the sheet of paper down, she looked at Max. "This is very threatening! Why didn't you bring it up at the meeting?"

"Because it wasn't necessary and before you go off and start questioning my reasoning let me clue you into the second strange thing that happened… also before the meeting took place. The same week I received the note I was approached by two football players while at the gym locker room. From what they said to me they were most definitely on Brad's side of the Burger

Palace situation. If it hadn't been for my roommate, Scott, intervening, I think I would have come out on you know what end of the stick. And, like the note, I decided to keep it under wraps because of the way the meeting turned out."

"I don't understand," said his mother. "This note and those threatening football players indicate this Brad is even worse than he appears."

"I am well aware of that and I had every intention of bringing these two things up at the meeting. While sitting through the legal ordeal as it moved along I began to realize no matter what kind of defense Rich came up with we were losing. But then, toward the end of the meeting, Brad's father had a change of heart due to his son's untruthfulness. When he decided the lawsuit was to be dropped, I couldn't see any reason to throw any more logs on the fire. Brad's father's decision to let me off the hook was something I hadn't expected and to mention these two additional actions regarding his son may have rocked the boat. So, I kept the information to myself."

Max's mother took a drink of juice. "Then why are you mentioning it now…after the fact?"

"Well, I got to thinking, and based on the way Brad reacted when his father dropped the lawsuit I figured that what was written in the note might just be true. Brad refused to shake my hand at the meeting and the look on his face sent me a clear message despite the fact his father dropped all charges it wasn't over. I don't trust Brad. I have a very real feeling he still intends to get even with me…how or when, well your guess is as good as mine. The reason why I'm mentioning this now is because depending on what he has planned for the future, this information might just become important. I thought maybe while I'm home we could drop by and visit Rich, give him the note, and inform him about my confrontation with the football players. It might not be necessary, but I don't think it would do any harm to place these things in my file for possible use in the future if need be."

"I agree," said Charley. "I'll give Rich a call today and set up a meeting later in the week. Speaking of Brad, have you seen him around campus since the meeting?"

"Three times," admitted Max. "Twice he didn't even see me and the one time he did notice me was at a Starbucks downtown. He was with some friends of his and upon seeing me he made some snide remarks to those with him. I ignored him just like Rich suggested, and went ahead and ordered my coffee. Brad moved down the counter, got in my face, and said he hoped I have a good lawyer…because he does. After that, he just glared at me and then moved on. It's hard to tell what he's got rolling around in his mind but I can assure you he doesn't have my best interest at heart."

Charley reached for the maple syrup as he shrugged, "You said it might take an hour or so to explain everything that happened since I was up at school with you. I don't see what the big deal is. You've only been talking for ten minutes."

"That's just part one of what I wanted to talk to you about. The other thing that happened to me was after I got to Lancaster. It would seem my list of unsavory characters which includes, Brad Sykes and the two football players at the gym has increased. There are now three more people in my life who fall under the category of undesirables you don't want to cross paths with."

His mother sat back in her chair and exclaimed, "What on earth are you talking about? Are you saying you had a run-in with some people who are worse than Brad?"

"I'm not sure how bad these folks are. I managed to get away from them before they had an opportunity to get that close."

His mother sipped at her coffee and then spoke hopelessly, "I'm lost!"

Max went on to explain. "The three men I speak of were Mennonite. Only one of them spoke to me, his name is Simon Baumer. Later on, he and his two brothers, Thaddeus and Rupert, chased me but I escaped, I guess you could say in the nick of time."

Charley looked at Max's mother and laughed, "I don't mean to make light of what you describe as a close call but these three men sound like the chipmunks. I mean…come on, Simon, Thaddeus, and Rupert!"

Max quickly corrected his father. "I appreciate your attempt at humor but the chipmunks were Simon, Theodore, and Alvin. In the make-believe world of animals these three men would not be described as chipmunks but more along the lines of a pack of vicious wolves."

Max's mother tapped him on his arm and apologized. "We didn't mean to make fun of what you said, it's just kind of ironic …that's all. Please continue."

Smearing a pad of butter on a pancake, Max elaborated on his trip to Lancaster. "The first thing I'm going to do is answer Dad's question of 'What's the deal,' about going to Lancaster. A couple of weeks before

Spring break I received a note from Elizabeth explaining she had to go back to Lancaster because her father took a nasty fall in their barn and was seriously injured. Later, when we talked on the phone she told me she was not going to return to school until the coming fall semester, which meant we would not see one another for months. I came up with the idea of stopping by to see her in Lancaster on my way home for Spring break. When I left school this past Friday I planned on staying the night at a motel in Lancaster then the next day we were to meet secretly at a pond near her farm…"

Some forty minutes later Max finished up with all the details of his trip to Lancaster, "…The last time I saw her she was walking down a country road to her farm."

Max got up from the table and walked his egg and syrup-stained plate and utensils to the sink where he proceeded to rinse them off. His mother followed as she carried her plate which she placed in the sink and then leaned on the kitchen counter. "The last time you were home you dropped a bomb on your father and me while explaining you had met a Mennonite girl but that she was nothing more than a good friend. After you left and went back to school your father and I discussed your relationship with this Elizabeth and agreed that even though we knew very little about this girl she would probably be a better influence on you than a lot of girls you might hook up with while in college. Nonetheless, if I were in your shoes I think I'd take a step back and review what has happened to you since you met this girl. Think about it?"

She opened the dishwasher and started to load the interior rack with dishes while she continued to give her opinion. "When you first met Elizabeth it sounds like it was innocent enough. This eventually leads to you becoming friends with her and meeting her twice a week for lunch or dinner. But then, here comes the debacle at the Burger Palace. Correct me if I'm wrong but the very reason you clobbered Brad Sykes in the mouth was because of the lude comments he made about Elizabeth. This results in you getting tossed through a plate-glass window and losing your job, not to mention the possibility of being sued, which, thank God, did not prevail. Now, you show us this note indicating Brad is seeking revenge. And what about those two football players which you barely escaped from? None of these things would have happened to you if you had not met Elizabeth."

Handing his mother two plates, Max gave her a somewhat stern look. "Elizabeth and I have already discussed this. There was a point where she felt responsible for everything that happened before the meeting. I assured her none of this was her fault."

Charley walked to the sink and handed a dish to his wife. "I'm kind of on your mother's side on this issue. There is more to think about than just what went on before the meeting. What about what happened in Lancaster? You go to this farmers' market and run into this Simon character who just happens to be Mennonite. He refers to Elizabeth as his woman, and then he and his two brothers chase you through the parking lot after tossing your pie out into a field and then smashing your fish sandwich. You barely get away from them by the skin of your teeth. Then, when you meet Elizabeth at this pond she informs you Simon is courting her. There seems to be something here that doesn't add up, and that might just be you! Here you are, a nineteen-year-old freshman away from home for the first time in your life. You run into this, what you claim is a beautiful young Mennonite girl, and become good friends, but then strange things begin to happen.

"What doesn't seem to make sense here is that you, an average young man from South Carolina is trying to fit into a lifestyle different than you were raised in. From what you have told us she is very religious. I'm not saying in any way you are a heathen but think about it. We, your parents, know all about her but yet she tells you she cannot tell her parents about you. And what about Simon calling her his woman? Not being that familiar with Mennonite male-female courting relationships, maybe she is his woman. It was indeed a nice gesture for you to go out of your way to see her, but you had to meet her out in the middle of the woods somewhere where no one could see you together. Doesn't this all sound a little one-sided? Did you ever stop to think that maybe you're being played…as innocent as it may seem."

"I'll admit a lot of strange and unexpected things have happened to me during the short time I've been away at college but I can say with confidence Elizabeth is not, as you say, 'playing me!' There is something else about the Lancaster trip I have not discussed with you. The next thing I want to talk about is kind of heavy so I think we should go sit in the living room."

Max's mother closed the dishwasher and pushed the ON button while giving her son a deep look of concern. "Please don't tell me this is one of those moments when you're about to hear something and that you have to be sitting down. Please do not tell your father and me you have got this Mennonite girl pregnant!"

Max placed his hand on his mother's shoulder and shook his head in amazement. "You can both relax. You are not going to be grandparents. I just felt we might be more comfortable in the living room."

Seated in the recliner, Max faced his parents who were seated at either end of the couch. Crossing his legs he started the conversation. "What I am about to speak of, well, I was going to talk to your mother. It's just something I think a mother might understand better. But, the more I think about it the more I realize you'll just turn around and tell Dad about it anyways. I guess this is one of those kill-two-birds-with-one-stone moments. While I was visiting Elizabeth at this pond in Lancaster she shared something with me I never expected to hear from her lips. She told me when she was a young girl she asked her mother what it felt like to be in love. I'm not going to go into everything her mother said but the feelings she was told she would experience, she was now feeling…for me! In other words, I think she was trying to tell me she might be in love with me. You're probably not going to believe this but the little boy you raised has turned into a young man. What I'm saying is I explained to her I had some of the identical feelings for her she claimed she had for me. In short…the boy from South Carolina and the Mennonite girl from Pennsylvania might be in love. Since neither one of us has ever experienced this feeling before, we're not sure about all this."

Max's mother gave her husband a short look and then spoke to Max. "Son, there is a lot more to it than that."

"Yes, I agree," said Charley. "Did she tell you she loves you? Did you tell her you love her?"

"No, neither one of us said that because we're not sure how all this is supposed to work. But there is more to this than just the way we think we feel about one another. When I first got to the pond Elizabeth was not wearing her Prayer Kapp….that's a bonnet of sorts Mennonite women wear. She told me no self-respecting Mennonite woman would ever be caught dead out in public without their head covering. She explained to me she wanted me to see her as she is…a woman and not just a girl. In other words, she is stepping outside of one of the rules of her faith…for me! I've got to tell you, I felt quite honored that she would do that. Later on in our conversation, she held my hands, which we had never done before. Then, she kissed me. I kissed her back. What else was I supposed to do? Before I left to head back home I pointed out that if our feelings continued to grow, that at some point she may be faced with having to tell her folks about me."

Scooting forward on the couch Charley smiled at his son. "Max, the feeling for this girl you think you may be experiencing is nothing new. Since the beginning of time men and women have been falling in love. Your mother and I are well aware of the fact you are no longer our little boy but a young man. I can't tell you how many times we have talked about how when the time comes you would meet a wonderful girl that you would marry. Nothing would make us happier, but I've got to tell you this situation you find yourself in, well, you might want to tread lightly. Now, your mother and I know nothing of this Elizabeth other than what you have told us. I'm just saying you need to be careful. I mean…just suppose she does not return to school, that she tells you she has decided to marry this Simon. You could be setting yourself up for a big disappointment."

"I appreciate your concern, Dad," said Max, "but Elizabeth has told me she has no intention of hooking up with Simon Baumer. His courting of her was arranged between her father and Simon two weeks before she even went home. She told me she is not going to marry someone because of the way her community or her father feels. She wants to marry a man she loves. What's wrong with that?"

"There's nothing wrong with that," said his mother. "That's the way it's supposed to work, but you have to understand that the Mennonite culture, even regarding marriage may be quite different than the way we look at matrimony."

"We can sit here all morning and talk about this," said Charley, "but nothing we say here today will change anything. Time and chance happen to us all. As quickly as your relationship with this Elizabeth has blossomed, it could end just as rapidly. Who knows what the future holds? Years from now you may marry this girl, while on the other hand, she may wind up being nothing but a memory of your past. If I were you I'd concentrate on the things you can control in your life, like your education over the next four years. You must be careful, Son. Many a man and woman's life has been altered because of someone they meet in life and they wind up going in a completely different direction than what they planned. We've talked many times about how you want some time in the future to own your own financial business. That dream or goal hinges on your next four years at Gettysburg."

"I agree with your father," added Max's mother. Holding up the note she went on, "You have to be careful. You not only have the threat of Brad

Sykes hovering over your everyday activities but now we find that three strange men in Pennsylvania chase you through a parking lot. Does Elizabeth know about this and if she does how did she react?"

"Look," pointed out Max, "we're making this more complicated than it is. I found out while at the pond with Elizabeth that she was not aware Simon and his brothers followed me into the lot. She was only aware of what Simon said and did while I was at their tent buying a pie. When I told her how they chased me and how I narrowly escaped she was highly upset. She even suggested she should say something to her father or the elders in their community. I told her that was a bad idea as that would only lead to the exposure of our relationship. She agreed and told me not to worry because I would probably never see Simon and his brothers again."

Charley stood and signaled for a time-out. "Whether you believe it or not, Max, this entire situation is getting more complicated as the days pass by. I think what we need to do is contact Rich and set up a meeting. We'll take the note with us, tell him about your confrontation with the football players, and also mention what went on in Lancaster. At this point, there is nothing else we can do."

Picking up his cell phone from the coffee table, he punched in a number. "I'm going to give Rich a call right now."

Simon drank the last of his coffee and then pushed himself away from the large rectangular kitchen table. Patting his stomach he looked at Elizabeth's mother while complimenting her. "Clara, that was one good meal. As a man who is not blessed with a wife, I have to say home-cooked meals are few and far between for me. Your husband is a lucky man to have you for a wife." Lighting up a pipe, Simon threw the used matchstick on his dirty plate. "Speaking of your husband, I was just over to see him earlier today at the hospital. He tells me they are planning on sending him home next week."

Clara started to clear the table as she responded in a friendly tone, "Yes. that's what they tell us. He'll be restricted to bed rest for the first week or so then he can begin to move around the house on his crutches. My husband is not a man who enjoys or even welcomes sickness. I've seen him in the past in various stages of aches, pains, fevers, colds, and such and he never stops working. According to him, rest is rust. The doctors have told him it could be six months before he's back to normal. That being said, I want you to know how much my family appreciates you, your brothers, and some of the others who have been helping around the farm."

Turning to his brothers who were seated to his right Simon suggested, "Why don't you two head on back to our farm and make sure everything is locked down for the night? I'll be along in a couple of hours."

Thaddeus and Rupert stood, nodded at Clara and her children, then exited through the front door. Simon turned to Elizabeth and gave her a wide smile. "Do you think we could spend some time together out on the porch before I leave for the evening?"

Before Elizabeth could respond, her mother answered the question, "Why, of course. Lydia and Glenna can help me with the dishes. You and Simon go enjoy yourselves."

Elizabeth stood, smoothed her dress, and adjusted her bonnet, then with a feeling of reluctance started for the door. Simon, rising in politeness grabbed a shawl from the back of her chair. "It's a little chilly out this evening. You might want to throw this over yourself."

Opening the door for her, he gently draped the shawl over her shoulders and guided her out to the porch. Seated beside her on a long wooden bench, he looked out at the dark sky. "Spring is on the way. It's a busy time for me with all the new calves that will be born over at my place. I remember years ago when I was given my first calf by my father. That was over fifteen years ago and today from that one calf I have developed one of the largest dairy herds in the state. I still have that cow. Her name is Grace. My wife loved ol' Gracie. It's strange to think my wife has been in the ground now for twelve years and Grace is still alive. Of course, Gracie no longer produces milk. She just grazes out in the fields. I never thought one of my cows would outlive my wife."

Turning to Elizabeth he asked. "Let's see. You were just nine years old when I married Suzanna. She was the same age as you are…nineteen. She was a beautiful woman, and we had our entire lives in front of us. When she lost the baby and then passed on herself I thought I'd never be happy again. But time has passed, and the God Lord has blessed me with more than I could deserve. My cup surely overfloweth and I am blessed beyond measure. To tell you the truth. I've grown tired of being alone. I never thought my eyes would fall on another woman after Suzanna was gone, but now I find myself desiring you for my wife. I've been courting you now for over two weeks and I think things have gone well. Are you in agreement?"

Elizabeth didn't want to say anything that eventually might upset her father so she answered politely, "Simon, you have been quite kind to me and my family during this difficult time, but I must remind you that come August I'll be going back to college. When that time comes it will be difficult for you to continue this courtship. I've already explained to you I intend to finish up with my schooling before I consider marriage. Do you realize that will take three to four years?"

"We've talked about this before and I've told you I'll wait for you to graduate. I have even suggested we could marry and you can still attend college. I am a patient man and a woman like you is worth waiting for."

Elizabeth stood and walked to the porch railing. "There's something I want to ask you, Simon. It's about last Friday night at the market."

Simon puffed away at his pipe and blew a stream of tobacco smoke toward the porch ceiling. "Ask away!"

Leaning on the railing Elizabeth asked carefully, "Do you remember that boy who stopped by our tent and purchased a pie?"

"Yes, I do remember him. It was a blueberry pie he bought…wasn't it?"

Looking at Simon, Elizabeth remained quiet.

Simon removed the pipe from his mouth and raised his right hand in subtle frustration. "I do remember that boy. I thought he was disrespectful of you as a Mennonite woman. Did he not lay his hand over yours? You, as well as I know it is not permitted for an outsider to lay his hand on one of our women."

"This is true, but this rule also pertains to any man, even someone from our community who is not married to that woman. If you will recall you touched my shoulder and told that young man I was your woman…which I am not. Courting me does not give you the right to make that type of a claim."

Simon knocked the ashes from his pipe on the end of the bench, took a humbling breath, and then answered, "I do apologize for my incorrect choice of words. I should have said *our women* rather than *my women*. Please forgive me for my moment of weakness. I have told you I am a patient man and yet when I saw that young man's hand over yours I became impatient and spoke out of turn. I also apologize for laying my hand on your shoulder. I was just trying to make a point. I am sorry."

Turning the tables on Elizabeth, Simon probed, "For just a brief moment I got the strange feeling you knew the boy."

Elizabeth immediately lied as she spoke up. "Until that night at the tent, I've never laid eyes on him before. He was just a customer buying a pie…that's all."

Now, it was Elizabeth who was on the offensive. "There is something else that seems odd about that night at the market. Later on, when we were closing up for the night someone approached me and told me they had seen you and your two brothers chasing that very same boy through the parking lot and that he barely escaped and almost ran you over with his vehicle."

Doing some quick thinking, Simon answered, "First of all, whoever this person is who told you we chased this boy through the lot is mistaken. We did follow him because I was still not convinced he understood that you or any Mennonite woman should not be touched. We meant him no harm. I just wanted to speak to him about the situation and make sure he understood, and then I planned on apologizing for my actions back at the tent. Whoever suggested to you we chased this boy is an exaggeration of what happened. By the way…who is this person who talked with you?"

Lying, yet again, Elizabeth replied, "I'd rather not say. They did not want their name mentioned."

"That says a lot right there," said Simon. "If a person is going to accuse someone of something and they don't want to be involved as far as their name is concerned how serious can what they say be taken?"

"If what you say is true then please tell me why you had to throw that boy's pie out into the field and then smash his fish sandwich in the mud?"

Simon raised his voice slightly, "I know nothing about that. If someone, as you say said I threw this boy's pie out into the field and then smashed his dinner, I know nothing of it happening. Maybe one of my brothers tossed the pie. After we got in the lot we split up. I have no idea as to what they did."

Elizabeth, not satisfied with his answer, pushed as she asked another question. "This person told me you were nearly run over on Gravestone Road as this boy tried to drive away from the lot."

"Now that part is true and yet another example of why I feel that boy did not understand what I told him back at the tent. Tell me, Elizabeth why would he try and run me over?"

"I don't know as I was not there. Maybe we should just talk about something else."

"All right, but there is something else puzzling me about that night and it happened the next day."

Elizabeth was lost. "I don't understand what you're trying to say."

"I don't understand it either. Maybe it's nothing, but it is very strange. I remember when that boy tried to run me over. He was driving a green Jeep with out-of-state tags. I don't know what state he was from, I just know they were not Pennsylvania tags. On Saturday, the day after the market, Rupert was driving home from Manheim. Crossing the Landisville Road Bridge he sees this green Jeep parked down by the water. He didn't pay that much attention to the Jeep but did recognize it had out-of-state tags. I drove back to check it out but by that time the Jeep had moved on. Doesn't that seem strange to you?"

Laughing, Elizabeth ignored his suspicious question. "You are doing nothing but grasping at straws, Simon. That Jeep could have belonged to anyone and to say it is the same as the one that ran you off the road is ridiculous. It was probably just someone fishing in the creek." Moving toward the door, she continued, "You're right. It is chilly out tonight. I think I'm going to go back in."

Simon once again found himself apologizing. "I'm sorry. I guess our conversation didn't go that well tonight."

"It's all right, Simon. You better head home. Before you know it it'll be four in the morning and you'll have to be back over here to help with the milking. Good night. I'll see you tomorrow."

Two-hundred and forty-five miles to the north in Ithaca, New York, Brad Sykes guided his Corvette into the main parking lot of Buttermilk Falls State Park. Parking next to a late model Dodge Ram heavy-duty pickup he stepped out and walked toward a group of picnic tables situated next to the long sloping, frozen falls. It had snowed earlier that morning and there was a one-inch covering of fresh snow on the ground. Walking across the snow-covered grass he saw the person he was looking for. A young man about the same age as he sat on top of one of the wooden tables, his feet resting on the connected bench. As Brad approached, the young man, sporting crew-cut style hair, dressed in older jeans and a black leather jacket waved at Brad and addressed him at the same time. "Well, well, if it ain't 'ol Brad Sykes, recent Ithaca High School asshole, now turned college man. How the hell are ya!"

Brad returned the crude but friendly greeting while pointing at the young man. "Kip Griner, also an Ithaca High School asshole." Angling his thumb over his shoulder, he added, "I see you're still driving that big ass truck."

"Yep, and I see you're still toolin' around in that gas-guzzlin' Corvette."

Brad sat on the table next to Kip and thumped his friend on his arm. "I see you got my message from Hap over at the pool hall."

"Sure did, ol' Hap said you called him last night and told him you wanted to meet me here at the falls between ten and eleven." Looking at his watch Kip clarified. "It's 10:05 and I'm here. What's up?"

Brad looked over at the ice-covered falls, blew out a breath that vaporized in the cold New York air, and answered, "Need a favor."

Kip picked up a paper sack-covered bottle and handed it to Brad, suggesting, "Have a nip. It's cold as hell out here."

Brad slid the paper down slightly, unscrewed the top, and took a swallow of alcohol. "Whew…what am I drinking?"

Kip took a drink himself and answered. "Jack Daniels…Devil's Cut. This stuff can warm you up. So, what's this favor you need?"

Touching his bruised and discolored nose gently, Brad remarked, "As you can see I came out on the wrong end of a dispute."

"Heard all about it. Word on the street around town is some dude from South Carolina knocked you for a loop."

"Sucker pouched me is what he did. I never had a chance. For I knew it, it was lights out."

"I also heard your father was planning on suing your attacker."

"That was the plan. My father, myself, and our attorneys met with the student who hit me. He showed up for a meeting with his father and their attorney. After reviewing everything that happened our attorney said it was a slam dunk in our favor. The meeting went along quite well until the end when my father has a brain fart and decides to drop the lawsuit."

"So, you mean to tell me this guy just walked out of the meeting Scott Free?"

"That's exactly what happened and I was just left sitting there holding the bag. My father guaranteed this Max Miller, that's his name, that I would not retaliate in any way, but that's not the way I see it. I plan to get even, to settle the score. I want this Miller to feel the prolonged pain I've had to suffer. Aside from looking like death warmed over and not being able to play football for the last few games, I'm looked at as a big joke around campus. But here's my problem. I can't do anything to him myself. I have to have a solid alibi that I was nowhere near Miller when this accident happens. Understand?"

"I think I get where you're going with this. You need someone to make sure this so-called accident happens. What do you have in mind and when do you want this carried out?"

"I haven't decided just yet. First of all, I have to contact someone who can make this happen. I thought of you. That's why we're here today and that's the favor I need."

Kip took another short pull from the bottle and handed the alcohol back to Brad. "You and I go back a few years. We spent two years together in high school. Me, from the wrong side of the tracks, you were the wealthiest kid in Ithaca. It started as a strange friendship. Hell, most people didn't want anything to do with a loser like me and you, well you were out of everybody's league. Over our high school years, you bailed me out of trouble several times. If it wasn't for you backing me up, I'm not so sure I would have even graduated. I guess in a way I owe you something for always being there for me. What I'm saying is I can help you out with this favor, but I'm not the one who can pull it off. I know someone who might be able to arrange whatever you have in mind for this Miller character. The man's name is Bernie Anelo. He owns the State Street Pool Hall and a few other businesses here in Ithaca. He lives upstate over in Syracuse. He comes to Ithaca every two weeks to check on his holdings here. He always gives me a call before he comes to town. I always meet with him in the back room down at the pool hall. I've been working for him for about a year now. He depends on me to take care of things for him on occasion around here. We've become pretty close, and he has told me if I ever needed anything to let him know. If you want this favor of yours carried out, it has to be done professionally. Depending on what you want done it might cost you some money. It has been said Bernie is connected with some rather tough people in New York if you get my drift. He knows people who could get the job done. He was just here last week and will not return until the first week of April. If you want, I could talk to him then and see what he has to say."

Brad picked up the bottle and grinned deviously, "This sounds good, but I'll be back at school in April."

"That's not a problem. Leave me your number and I'll give you a call after Bernie and I talk. So, I guess you need to start thinking about how and when you want this Miller accident to happen. Bernie is a man who doesn't pussyfoot around when it comes to getting things done."

Brad got down from the table, closed the bottle, and nodded in the direction of their parked vehicles. "Kip, I say we go have some lunch. I'm buying!"

CHAPTER FIFTEEN

There it was, McPherson's Ridge. The high ground as it was referred to. Max stared down the gradual five-hundred-and-fifty-foot grass and weed-covered slope where the three-day Battle of Gettysburg had kicked off. Seated on a wood bench at the very top of the ridge he surveyed the valley below. It was there on July 1, 1863, when Confederate General, Henry Heth led a seven thousand-strong division up Chambersburg Pike where his men clashed with Union General John Buford's thirty-two hundred dismounted Dragoon Calvary. Outnumbered, Buford managed to stave off the Confederate attack for three and a half hours until Union Brigadier General John Reynolds arrived with infantry reinforcements. Despite the actions of additional Union troops on the field, the Confederate army won the day driving the Northern troops back to Devil's Den and Big Round Top. Over fifty thousand soldiers engaged in intense battle on that hot July day resulting in fifteen thousand killed, wounded, or missing.

In the distance to the south, the McPherson barn still stood. The, at one time ninety-five-acre farm where much of the fighting had taken place, was flanked on the west by Willoughby Run, the east by Pitzer Run, and at the very top of the ridge behind him, there was the three-story brick Lutheran Seminary with its famous white observatory tower where General Buford had watched the battle unfold on the ridge and valley below.

Max gazed at the surrounding fields and woods. It was mid-April, spring had arrived in Pennsylvania and the countryside was ablaze with scattered colors, yellow Forsythia bushes, lavender-colored Red Bud trees, and scattered yellow dandelions dotting the grass here and there. In five weeks, he would be headed back to South Carolina for three months of summer vacation. Since returning to college, things, at least as far as Elizabeth was concerned had not turned out the way he planned.

At the tail end of March, while heading back to Gettysburg from Spring break, he planned on meeting her at the pond for the second time. They had talked on the phone two days before his return trip when she informed him, she was down with influenza. The next week while at school she called him again and explained the sickness had infected her entire community. She was feeling better but busy taking care of neighbors and friends. Her father was now back home and slowly recovering from his accident. Max's suggestion that he could just drive over and see her at the pond, since she was less than two hours driving time away from school was squashed when Elizabeth told him they could not see each other until August when she returned to college. The Mennonite community she lived in was tight-knit and everyone knew everyone else's business. Everyone knew about the boy at the market who had purchased a pie and had rubbed Simon Baumer the wrong way which resulted in Simon nearly getting run over by the boy in his green Jeep. The fact that a green Jeep was seen parked by the Landisville Bridge the very next day had all the neighbors talking. At this point, there didn't seem to be any way for them to meet before she returned to school. It looked like the only communication they would have for the remainder of the school year and over summer vacation would be limited to phone calls twice a week on Wednesday and Saturday.

No sense in just sitting here thought Max. It was Sunday afternoon, he had no classes until Monday morning, the sun was shining, and the temperature was a pleasant sixty-nine degrees. According to the weather report earlier in the morning Southern Pennsylvania had seen its last snowfall and it was going to be a glorious day to get out and get some fresh air, maybe talk a walk.

He got to his feet and started down the long slope. He only traveled thirty yards when he came to an opening of a long fence line. His father had pointed out to him during his first trip to Gettysburg when he was seven that the battlefield was home to miles of fencing. Worm or snake fencing is what his father had called it. Five; six or even seven, eight-to-ten-foot lengths of split rails that intersected at right and left angles with other sections of split rail, forming a weaving line of fencing requiring no fence posts. It was quite ingenious.

He crossed a good two acres of low grass when he came to another fence line, climbed over, and continued another football field-length walk over low weeds and grass where he came to Chambersburg Pike. To his right sat Edward McPherson's old barn that had been purchased by the National Park Service back in 1904 as part of the battlefield restoration. The barn was originally built in the early 1800's, probably no later than 1820. At the time of the first day of the Battle of Gettysburg, a tenant farmer by the name of John Slentz was renting the barn from McPherson. During the battle the Union re-enforcements overran the farm and occupied the barn, resulting in a total loss of crops, equipment, and the structure itself. The Confederate army eventually swarmed the barn and ran the Union soldiers off leaving many of their wounded behind, many of whom lay in or near the barn for five days suffering in pain. Many a wounded man died for lack of immediate medical help.

McPherson sold the property in 1868 and it nearly burned to the ground in 1895. Later when the Park Service purchased the property, they refurbished the barn back to its original stature; a two-story Pennsylvania stone and painted white wood structure with a cantilevered forebay. The barn and the fields on the other side of Chambersburg Pike were now utilized by a local farmer who rented out horse stalls and grew corn.

As Max approached the barn from the backside, he noted three horses standing in an attached corralled area. He leaned on the fence and mouthed a clicking sound hoping that at least one of the horses would come visit him by the fence. The three horses gave him a subtle look but then went back to munching on a pile of tasty hay. He figured the horses were used to countless tourists trying to get their attention and probably didn't want anything to do with him. If his mother were with him, he didn't have any doubt that the horses would walk over for a visit. His mother had a way with horses. Ever since she was a little girl, she had always wanted to own one. After she married, his dad offered to buy his new wife a horse, but money was tight and besides, they had nowhere to keep the animal. It was years later when Max started grade school when his father surprised his mother, ironically on Mother's Day with a horse stabled at a local boarding farm outside of Summerville. How many times over the years had he, his father, and his mother driven out into the South Carolina countryside to Bailey's Boarding and Riding Stables for a leisurely afternoon of relaxing riding? His mathematical mind clicked in as he thought about all the horses that had been killed during the Civil War. Over one million horses had lost their lives while in service. He thought about some of the famous horses that had been in the war. Traveler, Robert E. Lee's favorite; Cincinnati, ridden by

Ulysses S, Grant; John Reynolds steed, Fancy and Joshua Chamberlain's horse, Charlemagne.

One of the six stall doors opened and a man chewing on a long weed and wearing coveralls led a tall grey horse out into the corral. He guided the horse to the pile of hay but the animal upon seeing Max slowly ambled over to the fence. Reaching up, Max caressed the long face as he stared at the big eyes of the friendly four-legged creature. The man gave Max a friendly wave and commented, "Nice day!"

Max continued to pat the horse's nose and replied, "Sure is."

Sitting on a bench next to the fence he watched as a truck, tour bus, and then three cars passed by on Chambersburg Pike, now a paved two-lane, heavily traveled local road that had not always been paved or even well-traveled. Back in 1863, Gettysburg was a quiet rural farming community. In those days the highway was just a one-lane dirt rutted road that daily probably didn't see much traffic. He laughed to himself when he thought of the word, *traffic!* Before the battle, the road was no doubt only traveled by an occasional horse-drawn buggy or lone rider. But, on July 1st, 1863, thousands of men marched in formation down the dirt road toward McPherson's Ridge. Who knows how many mounted horses or cannons had traveled the road that day?

He waited while two cars passed by then he ran across to a large field flanked by a grouping of trees known as Herbst Woods. Today and for many years it was called Reynolds Woods in honor of General John Reynolds, who while leading the Union Iron Brigade into the nearby woods was shot from his horse and died instantly on the battlefield. Forty yards up the road walking by a long section of fencing Max came to the massive monument in honor of Reynolds. The granite monument itself weighed four and a half tons, topped with a life-size bronze statue of General Reynolds sitting atop his horse. Reynolds was one of the highest-ranking generals to be killed during the war. Reynolds was from Lancaster, Pennsylvania, and had died within two hours of his home.

As Max looked back up the sloping ridge, he wondered what Heth's division thought as they marched up the road, Buford's Calvary entrenched behind low stone walls and fencing. It would be an uphill battle, but Heth held the numerical advantage of placing more men on the field.

Adjacent to the road, a good two hundred yards down Max crossed over and walked along another fence line, stopping at the eighth set of connected split rail. There it was, the tree stump that marked the area where Henry Heth had been shot. Despite being wounded at Gettysburg Heth survived the war, and years later while writing his memoirs mentioned the large oak tree on McPherson's Ridge where he had been shot, he thought, by a Union sharpshooter from McPherson's barn. In 1899 Heth returned to Gettysburg and pointed out the tree where he had been shot. Years passed, the tree was struck by lightning and badly damaged, so the Park Service had no choice but to cut the landmark tree down, leaving a low stump behind as the only indication that there had been a tree there. Over the years the stump itself had rotted and had dwindled to the low, circular remains of the famous tree.

He sat in the grass, laid back, and placed his hands behind his head while gazing up at the slowly moving clouds above. It reminded him of the times when as a young boy he would accompany his mother to the beach, and they would watch the cloud formations. His mother always saw images in the clouds, a frog, a caboose, a face, and yet he never seemed to see what she saw. He figured she just had a broader imagination than he.

Down by the fence line, a quarter mile away, he saw the Reynolds monument where he had just recently been. *Strange,* he thought. Two generals, one from either side of the conflict, both shot in the head on the same day at the same battle, John Reynolds died on the spot while Henry Heth not only survived the wound and the war but lived thirty-four years after the war came to an end.

As always, the mathematics of life came to mind. He was sure every soldier in the Civil War, whether an enlisted man, an officer, or a general knew going in there was a better-than-average chance of being wounded or worse, shot to death. It was mathematical. If your number came up, well then that was it! On July 1st, 1863, John Reynolds' number came up, while Henry Heth survived to live not just another day but over three decades. Mathematics was a strange phenomenon to try and figure out, especially in war.

He sat back up and crossed his legs Indian style and thought about a Civil War seminar his father had given three years in the past at a high school in Savannah. Civil War buffs from Georgia, Florida, North and South Carolina, and many other southern states were in attendance. When his father spoke about the war folks were always interested in listening to his in-depth and detailed descriptions of Civil War-related topics. He, himself had attended the seminar and was amazed at his father's vast knowledge of the generals who fought on both sides of the war. One of the topics his father had talked about was the number of generals who served during the war and the number who had been killed in battle. There were over one thousand generals who led soldiers during the war. There was a total of one thousand and eight, the Confederate army fielding four hundred and twenty-five generals while the Union army placed five hundred and eighty-three leaders on the field during the duration of the war. Seventy-three generals from the south had been shot and killed while the Union army suffered sixty-seven casualties when it came to their generals. This equated to roughly 14% of the generals being killed, the south losing 17% of their leaders, and the north losing about 11%.

In more modern times, even going back to World War I and II, the technology and the logistics of war decreased the number of generals killed in action to a minuscule level in comparison to the Civil War. The number of generals killed during the Civil War, even though high, was nothing compared to the level of death in the enlisted ranks. The mathematics regarding soldiers who died during the war was staggering. The number of men who fought in the war came in at 2.75 million, the South calling seven hundred and fifty thousand men to arms while the North fielded just over two million soldiers. The total number of deaths in the war was six hundred and twenty thousand, an average of five hundred and four men being killed daily, one in every five soldiers losing their lives.

Max watched what he thought was a family; a man, a woman, two young children, and a large black dog walking down the ridge when he decided to walk up the hill to the seminary and visit the museum.

The seminary no longer used the building for campus studies. It was now utilized as a tourist attraction, the three floors filled with interactive displays and Civil War artifacts housed in large glass cases. Approaching an information desk inside the main doors Max came face to face with an attractive young woman about his age he guessed. The girl smiled at him and brushed long locks of auburn hair from her face. "Good afternoon, sir. Can I help you?"

"Yes, I was wondering if I could get a ticket for the cupola tour."

The girl apologized, "I'm sorry, but the observatory is in the process of being repaired. We've had a lot of leaks this past winter. It's not scheduled to open for another month. You can visit the rest of the museum but not the tower. We're still in the off-season so if you want to tour the museum the tickets are discounted by 20%."

Max reached for his wallet and agreed, "That sounds like a good deal."

The girl took a ten from him, rang up the sale, and handed him back two ones and a ticket stub. "There…you're all set." Motioning to a counter display of brochures she pointed out, "If you'd like, the first row of brochures tells you all about the museum and what you can expect to see while here."

Holding up his ticket Max responded, "That won't be necessary. You see, I've been here before. When I was a youngster, my father brought me here to Gettysburg many times. He's a reenactor and on one of the days we spent here in the area, he brought me to this museum. We spent the afternoon looking at all the information and the displays. We took the observatory tour and he explained to me everything that took place on the first day of battle. Let's see…that would have been eleven years ago." Looking around the main floor, he went on, "The museum looks the same as it did back then but I'm sure I'll enjoy the time I spend here."

The girl squinted her eyes as if she were in deep thought then snapped her fingers as if a lightbulb in her head came on. "The whole time we've been talking I keep thinking I've seen you before. It just came to me. I've seen you several times over at the Gettysburg gym in the swimming pool complex."

Max placed the ticket in his pocket and nodded, "I'm a freshman at Gettysburg College and I do go to the swimming pool quite often….actually three to four times a week. Funny, I've never seen you there."

The girl laughed and replied, "I'm not what you would call all that noticeable. I don't hang out around the pool with other students. I'm pretty serious when it comes to swimming. I walk in, get in the pool, and swim five miles, then I leave."

"Five miles! I swim a mile when I go there and that wears me out."

The girl stuck out her hand. "My name is Kelly Waters, and I am also a freshman at the college. I'm also on the school swim team."

"Well then, that explains the distance you swim." Max shook her hand and introduced himself. "Max Miller from Summerville, South Carolina."

"Amazing! It would seem we have more in common than just swimming at the gym. I happen to be from South Carolina. I was born and raised in Walterboro. Do you know where that is?"

"Walterboro!" exclaimed Max. "Over the years my mother has spent a small fortune buying antiques and the like over there. It's one of her favorite places to go. I bet we go there at least five to six times a year. We usually make a day of it visiting all of the unique shops. My mother collects Nippon China, and she always manages to find a piece here and there. We always have lunch at a place called the Olde House Café out on Bells Highway. Do you know where that is?"

"Yes, I do know where that is. My family has dined there many a time. So, how long have you lived in Summerville?"

"All my life…to date, although we spend a lot of time over at a place called Fripp Island, south of Beaufort. My folks have a place over there."

Kelly, flabbergasted, couldn't believe what she was hearing. "I can't believe this. My folks have a place down on Edisto Island. Have you ever been?"

"Sure, lots of times. My father and I do quite a bit of fishing down that way. Some of the creeks we fish at are just below Edisto. Have you ever been over to Fripp?"

"No, I never have. I've heard it's a beautiful place. The closest we've ever been to Fripp would be Hunting Island State Park."

A couple walked in and approached the counter. Max backed away and gave her a subtle wave. "I better let you get back to work. Maybe we'll run into one another over at school."

Kelly waved back, "I hope so! It's nice to talk with someone from back home."

Three hours later, Max walked back down to the first floor of the museum. Passing the front counter, he noticed that another girl had taken over. Going to the counter he politely asked, "Where's Kelly?"

The girl, flipping through a brochure answered nonchalantly, "She left for the day. Is there anything I can help you with?"

"No, I just wanted to say goodbye. Thank you."

Out in the parking area behind the Seminary Building, Max walked to his Jeep and leaned on the hood, the Jeep reminding him of what Elizabeth had said about his vehicle; about how everyone in her community knew about the boy who had been at the market, had a disagreement with Simon Baumer and then almost ran him over in a green Jeep on Gravestone Road. The next day his Jeep was spotted near the Landisville Bridge, and it was thought it was the same one seen at the market. He and Elizabeth were the only ones who knew the truth; it was the same Jeep and everyone else was just guessing.

He took one last look down at McPherson's Ridge, started the vehicle, and pulled out, his last stop for the day in town. Leaving the Seminary behind he thought about some of the things his parents had warned him about. How he should be careful because in his relationship with Elizabeth, he might be setting himself up for a hard fall, that he might be being played or that maybe Elizabeth was Simon Baumer's woman. He didn't, not for a solidary second believe any of those things to be true. He knew his parents were just looking out for his best interest, but they had never met Elizabeth, never talked with her. He thought about something his father had told him years ago when he was in junior high and that a person should never come to a conclusion about someone else unless they have all of the information. He loved his parents dearly, but they did not have all the information about Elizabeth they needed to come to a viable conclusion. As far as he was concerned, she was as honest as the day was long. Making a right-hand turn from the battlefield, he figured he'd arrive at his destination in less than ten minutes.

Max parked the Jeep on the lot of one of the most popular eating establishments in town; Battlefield Pizza. Getting out he walked across the lot and entered the pizza parlor. Seven of the twelve circular tables were occupied, and a lone customer stood at the order counter. Standing next to the customer Max waited patiently when a young man wearing a flour-covered apron approached and asked, "What can we get for you, sir?"

"I'm not here to order anything," said Max, "but I would like to speak with the owner if he is in. I believe his name is Robert."

The boy wiped his hands with a small towel hanging from the apron and answered, "Yes, he's in his office. Can I tell him what this is about?"

"Yes, you can tell him a friend of Jim Steadman's is here to see him. My name is Max Miller."

"All right, Mr. Miller. I'll tell him you're here."

It wasn't even a minute when a short-haired, tall man dressed casually in khaki pants, a blue shirt, and a grey sweater vest came out from a door on the left, extended his hand, speaking with great excitement, "Max Miller…I'm Robert. Jim told me you might be dropping by to see me about employment. That was way back last year in November. I was expecting you to come see me, but when you didn't, I figured you just moved on to something else."

"I'm sorry," said Max. "It's just that I had a few things to get out of the way before I could get back to work. I guess you know what happened over at the Burger Palace a few months back. Jim told me he didn't want to let me go but he didn't have a choice. He said you two were friends and that you might be interested in hiring me."

Robert laughed and gestured at an empty table. "Better late than never. Care for a drink or something?"

Max politely declined, "No thank you, I'm fine."

Robert folded his arms across his chest and explained, "Jim and I go way back. We've been friends since we were five years old. Grew up right here in Gettysburg in the same neighborhood, attending the same high school. We went to different colleges but we both moved back here to town. Years passed and Jim became the manager over at the Palace and I opened this pizza joint. Been at it now for twenty-one years. Jim told me about what happened at the Palace and said you were the best employee he ever had. Jim's word is good enough for me so if you're still interested in working here, then you've got a job."

Max was beside himself. "That has to be the quickest job interview in history. Isn't there anything you'd like to ask me?"

"Yes, there are a few things I'd like to know. First of all…do you like pizza?"

"Who doesn't? I've always told my mother pizza is one of the essential food groups."

Robert stopped a passing waitress and instructed the young girl, "Would you be so kind as to go into my office and bring me a job application? They are on the small desk next to the banana plant."

As the girl walked off, Max inquired, "What else would you like to know about me?"

"Well, I'd like to hire you on as a delivery driver. How's that sound?"

"Sounds good."

"There are a few other things I'd like to ask you…like, do you own a vehicle?"

"Yes, I own a Jeep. It's not brand new but it runs like a top."

Robert asked the next question, "How well do you know Gettysburg?"

"I think I'm safe in saying I probably know Gettysburg better than any student at the college, that is except for those who live here. My father is a Civil War reenactor and he's been bringing me here every year for the past few years for the annual reenactment of the battle. I know all the main streets and quite a few of the secondary streets. I might have to familiarize myself with the outlying suburbs, but I don't see that as a problem. How far out do you deliver?"

"Five miles out. That's where we cap it. Something else I wanted to ask you. How flexible are you on hours you can work?"

"Monday through Friday I'm pretty tied up with classes over at school. Depending on the day most of my classes end around three to four o'clock. So, I can work any time after that during the week. As far as weekends are concerned, I can work any time you need me."

"So I take it you're interested then?"

"Yes, I am interested."

"You haven't asked me what the position pays."

"Never crossed my mind," said Max. "I figure you'll pay me what I'm worth."

"Here's the way it works. The position pays ten twenty-five an hour plus tips. Most deliveries will net a tip of two dollars, but it can be as high as five. It's kind of up to you. The more friendly you are the more people tend to tip. When it's all said and done you should be making about fifteen dollars an hour. I delivered pizzas down in Houston when I was in college. I found out most people just expect some dude to knock on their door and say, 'Here's your pizza.' I always added a little pizazz while talking to customers. Some weeks I made as much as twenty dollars an hour. That's more than you can make most places while in college."

The girl returned with the application and an ink pen which she placed on the table. Robert stood and spoke. "I've got some paperwork I need to attend to. After you get that app filled out you need to give it to Susan, she's my daytime manager. That's her over there by the counter. You'll need to give her your driver's license and your insurance card so she can make copies. She'll give you a schedule for this coming week. Hope you can start right away. I just lost two drivers. Glad to have you on board."

Back in his dorm room, he found Scott seated by the window reading. As soon as Max entered Scott laid down the book and greeted his room-mate, "Howdy there, Max. How did you make out at the pizza place?"

"They hired me on the spot. I start tomorrow night. I hope you like pizza."

"Of course I like pizza but what's that got to do with anything?"

"The manager told me at the end of the night more times than not they have a couple of pizzas that were made wrong so rather than throwing them out they give them to employees. It's just a perk of working there I guess."

Scott gave a thumb up and grinned, "Bring it on!" Getting up he walked over and sat on the edge of his bed. "Well, it looks like things are turning out well for you. You dodged the bullet on that lawsuit and now you get a new job."

Max sat on his bed and agreed. "Things are going well for me. It reminds me of something my father once told me when I was a freshman in high school. It seemed like nothing was going my way. I got cut from the baseball team, I got poison ivy and I had a cold all summer. The whole year was a bust for me. My father could see I was struggling day-in, day-out so he had a sit down with me. He told me, it's not so much that people have problems in their lives but how they react to them…what they do about them. You can either give up and say what's the use or you can deal with problems. That was almost five years ago when he gave me that advice and I didn't give it much thought until just recently here at school. The first problem I was faced with was that night at the Palace when Brad Sykes made those lude comments about Elizabeth. That was a problem for me and rather than walking away which is probably what I should have done I created a larger problem when I popped ol' Brad right on the kisser. My decision to club Brad resulted in a series of problems I caused by hitting him. I got thrown through a plate glass window and wound up going to the emergency room, not to mention the loss of my job. Then, on top of that, I'm notified that I might be sued by Brad's father. They patched me up at the hospital and after talking with my parents we contacted a lawyer and came up with a game plan to combat the lawsuit. As you well know I didn't get sued and here it is a few weeks later and I have a new job."

Scott, always upbeat agreed, "Like I said…things are looking up for you."

"Not everything. There is still the issue of Brad Sykes and the fact he feels this is not over. If I can get through the next five weeks without having to deal with whatever he has in mind, I might be out of the woods. I doubt if he is going to drive down to South Carolina over the summer to get his revenge."

"I think you're right. He'll probably just go back home for the summer like the rest of us. Who knows…when he comes back in August, he may have cooled his heels."

"Or, on the other hand," said Max, "he might wait until next year after school starts back up to even the score. He might be thinking that over the summer I'll forget about him and then when I return to school, and my guard is down then he'll strike."

Scott frowned. "Then what you're saying is Brad represents an ongoing problem that at present you can't do much about."

"That's precisely correct and that's not the only problem that's looming out there. Remember when I told you about my trip to see Elizabeth in Lancaster and how while at that market Simon Baumer and his two brothers chased me through the lot? Because of that and the fact my Jeep was seen parked in the Mennonite community now I can't drive over there to see her. I won't get to see her until August when she returns to school. And it also concerns me that this Simon Baumer is courting a girl who all but told me she loves me. I'm not all that confident this is all going to work out."

"And what do you mean…work out? Where do you see this relationship headed?"

"I don't know. I suppose we could still just remain friends, but after what happened at the pond and the things we said to each other our relationship has risen to a different and more serious level. Somewhere in the back of my mind, I keep thinking that maybe Elizabeth is fooling herself into thinking she could continue to have a relationship with someone outside her faith and her community. I just wish I knew what she was thinking. What does the future hold for a relationship between a boy from South Carolina and a Mennonite girl, who comes from such a different world?"

"If you're looking for advice from me regarding what females think I've got to tell you I don't have a clue. The female mind…how does it work and is it different than the way we as men think? This is something men have probably been trying to figure out since the beginning of time. Let me give you an example. I dated the same girl all four years in high school. We were one of those couples everyone in school said would get married in the future. We were, at least I thought, the perfect couple. We never talked about marriage because that seemed far off in the future. The first summer after we graduated things seemed all right until we were both set to go off to college, me to Hofstra and she down to Texas. I'll never forget the conversation we had about a week before we both left for school. She told me she thought we should step back from our relationship until this summer. She said she needed some space.

"This whole thing took me by surprise, and I didn't know how to answer her so I agreed. I talked with my grandfather about this sudden change of heart that she had and he sat me down and explained to me if I tried to figure out what was running through her mind it would drive me crazy. My grandfather is eighty-three and he claims after living for over eight decades he still couldn't figure out women. He went on to say since I was only nineteen years old, I didn't stand a prayer of understanding how women think. He said The Good Lord is in control of all things and no matter what we do or say will not change that.

"In short, he said that come the summer if Diane and I are meant to get back together, then so be it. If not, well then life goes on. So, you see both you and I share a similar problem. I'll just have to wait and so will you. Come next August, Elizabeth might not even return to school, she may decide to marry this Simon character or things may go back to the way they were before she left to go back home. At least you still get to talk with her twice a week over the phone. I don't know Elizabeth all that well. I only met her that one time when she came to tell you she had to leave school. She seemed nice. I hope things work out for you two." Standing, Scott announced, "I'm off to the gym for some weightlifting. I'm looking forward to some free pizza!"

Monday morning Max opened his eyes and looked at his alarm clock: 4:58. He tried to go back to sleep but found himself wide awake. *No sense in just laying here,* he thought. The school swimming complex opened at five in the morning. It was going to be a long day with four classes facing him, then it was off to his first day as a Battlefield Pizza delivery driver. A refreshing early morning swim sounded like a good idea. He grabbed his gym bag and threw on a pair of swim trunks, a towel, and his goggles. He was out the door by five-ten and would be in the water by five-thirty.

Max closed his locker, draped the towel around his neck, and headed for the pool. He was the only male in the locker room, and he wondered if there would be anybody else at the pool. He entered the pool area and scanned the eight-lane Olympic-sized pool. There was only a single swimmer in lane eight and no one seated around the perimeter. Throwing his towel over a plastic chair, he slipped the goggles over his head and climbed down the stainless-steel ladder into the cool water. At first, the water felt freezing, but he knew once he started his laps the temperature would be fine. He took a breath, submerged, and sank to the bottom, remained there for a few seconds, and then rose to the surface. Adjusting the goggles on his face he looked down at lane eight as the swimmer cut smoothly through the water, performed a swimmer's turn at the other end, and started back. The swimmer had what appeared to be a swimmer's cap on their head, so he assumed it was a female. Going under again, he let out a long breath, resurfaced, and began his first lap.

Twenty-seven minutes later he touched the edge of the pool. He checked the large clock over the steam sauna and noted he had turned in a better-than-average time for the level of swimmer he was. Normally he finished up his mile in the water in twenty-eight minutes. Getting out of the pool he draped the towel around his neck and headed for the sauna. Shutting the redwood door, he noticed the swimmer at the other end was still doing laps.

He only stayed in the hot sauna for twenty minutes. A quick shower, then breakfast and he would be at his eight o'clock calculous class. Sitting in a chair he watched as the female swimmer cut through the water like a hot knife through butter, the water calmly and slowly moving to her sides. He wished he could swim like that, rather than splashing erratic small waves in every direction.

The swimmer took two more laps then performed a smooth backstroke from one end of the pool to the other, stood up, and exited the water. Looking at the mysterious swimmer Max's assumption that it was a female was verified as a sleek, slender figure of a woman who stepped onto the edge of the pool and made her way to a small table and chair. She most definitely had a swimmer's physic, muscular shoulders and forearms then a V-cut torso, ending at her waist where she displayed strong muscle-toned legs. She removed her goggles and then her swim cap, placing them on the table as she shook out shoulder-length auburn hair. It was the hair that tipped him to the swimmer's identity; Kelly Waters!

Max made his way around the side of the pool and approaching her from behind he asked politely, "Excuse me, but is that you, Kelly?"

Kelly turned and flashing a wide smile, she responded, "Why, low and behold if it isn't Max Miller from the museum." From the looks of his wet trunks and matted-down hair, she realized he had been swimming. "Did you get your mile in? I didn't see you when you came in."

"Yes, I just finished. I saw you when I first got here. I watched you for a couple of laps before I entered the water. You looked pretty focused. I can tell you're an experienced swimmer and the way you made those turns…it was so smooth, effortless!"

Kelly pushed a chair out with her bare foot and offered, "Have a seat."

Sitting, Max asked, "Did you get your five in today?"

"Yes, I did. Took me just under eighty minutes."

"Five miles in eighty minutes. That's incredible! It takes me just under a half hour to knock out a single mile. Eighty minutes. Why that's sixteen minutes per mile. How long have you been swimming?"

Kelly dried her hair with a towel as she responded, "My mother started giving me swimming lessons when I was six months old. She still today, can outswim me. When she was in college, a couple of years before I was born, she tried out for the Olympic swim team. She missed the cut by three-tenths of a second and did not qualify. We have a pool at our house in Walterboro where she swims every day."

"I've thought about trying to swim maybe an extra quarter mile or so but by the time I finish up my mile, I don't seem to have the energy."

"How and when did you learn to swim?"

"I think I was about five or six years old. My father took me out to the ocean and told me I needed to learn how to swim. It took me about a month, but I finally caught on and now at least I think I can hold my own. If I find myself in a situation where I'm surrounded by water, I don't think I'll drown. That being said, I don't think I could ever be as good as you appear to be."

"It took me years to develop into the level of swimmer I am today. Tell you what. If you're interested, show up here next Wednesday at five a.m. and I can give you some pointers on proper breathing and how to work with the water. I bet we'll have you up to a mile and a half before you head back home for the summer."

Max thought for a moment and then replied, "All right then. This Wednesday I'll be here at five for my first extended swim lesson."

CHAPTER SIXTEEN

The next five weeks passed by quickly and before Max knew it, it was Friday, May 15th, the last day of his first year of college at Gettysburg. His last class of the day ended at three which gave him a couple hours to bike out to the battlefield, then he had to report for work at six. It was now 10:30 and he had just made his last delivery of the night, two large pepperoni to a house in a subdivision off Route 30. Pulling into Battlefield Pizza he entered the shop from the back door, dropped off the thermally insulated pizza carrier, and informed the night manager that he was off to South Carolina.

He stopped for gas, a hot coffee, and a chocolate-covered donut and started the beginning of his twelve-hour journey. He planned on driving straight through. He would have liked nothing better than to drop by the pond down from the Landisville Bridge to meet Elizabeth but considering what had happened that was now not possible. He didn't like the fact he was not going to get to see her until August. He thought about what he and Scott had discussed and knew his roommate was right. Come next August if he and Elizabeth were to pick up where they left off, well then, so be it.

Hour after hour passed as he drove through the night and early morning when he finally arrived at the Fripp Island Bridge. After swapping some pleasantries with the guard at the security building, he pulled to the right and entered the parking lot next to the Springtide Market. An ice-cold Coke sounded good. Walking up the twelve-foot-wide planked walkway he entered the market and looked at the familiar surroundings. How many times over the years had his mother sent him to the market for something she needed? Walking past the counter he saw the owner, Laurie, stocking some bottles of wine. Walking up behind her he stuck his index finger into her side and exclaimed, "Surprise!"

Startled, Laurie turned and upon seeing Max she stood up and gave him a hug followed by a peck on his cheek, then looked him up and down. "College hasn't changed you one bit. You look the same as you did before you left for the cold north. Your mom dropped by last week and told me you would be coming in today. I don't think your folks are here on the island right now."

Max walked to a nearby cooler withdrew a Coke, opened the bottle, and took a long swig. "I know. They won't be getting here until later this evening. We're planning on staying here for the next two weeks then it's back to Summerville."

Laurie leaned against a large upright glass cooler and asked, "What are your plans for the summer? I ask because I'm looking for some extra help around here. If you're interested, I could put you on the payroll for the next couple of months."

"No thanks," declined Max. "I know you could probably use the help and God knows I could use the money, but I plan on just relaxing. Ya know, walking on the beach, eating lots of seafood…just loafing around in the sunshine. I need to take advantage of this free time I have because before I know it'll be back off to Pennsylvania and another year of school. How much do I owe ya? I've got a hot shower waiting for me at the house and then a relaxing boat ride out into the ocean, maybe down Skull Inlet and then the marina. "

Laurie smiled, "Drink's on the house. Say hello to your parents for me."

Max headed for the door as he raised the Coke on high, "Will do!"

He pulled beneath the elevated house, walked up the wood steps, and unlocked the door. He no sooner entered the kitchen when he noticed an envelope with his name written on the front. At first, he was skeptical about opening the envelope as the last three envelopes he had recently opened had contained bad news. The envelope notifying him about the lawsuit meeting and then another envelope presumably from Brad Sykes informing him that, *this was far from over,* and yet a third envelope from Elizabeth explaining her quick and unexpected exit from school. Reluctantly he opened the envelope and read his mother's handwriting. *Welcome home to Fripp. We'll see you tonight at six. We have reservations at the Bonito Boathouse for dinner at seven.* He placed the note back on the counter climbed the steps to the second floor and a refreshing shower.

The shower over, he toweled himself dry and slipped into a pair of old jeans, a tattered Fripp Island cut-off sweatshirt, ball hat, and flip-flops. Next, he stopped at the refrigerator where his mother always kept a gallon of her homemade peach tea. Filling a thermos with the sweet concoction, he grabbed a power bar from the pantry, and out the door he went.

Down below the house toward the back of the open-air garage, he unplugged the family golf cart, climbed in, and started the machine. The red line on the electrical indicator displayed a full charge. Backing the cart out he headed down Tarpon, where he made a left on Bonito Drive, crossed the island canal, passed the Ocean View Golf Course, and a half mile later he parked the cart in the large, paved lot just down from the marina store. He grabbed his drink and a faded orange life jacket from the back of the cart and walked across the lot, skirting the Bonito Boathouse where there was a small series of floating deck walks leading to several anchored boats. Seven boats down there it sat; his father's fifteen-foot Edgewater Bowrider speed boat.

Max removed the custom heavy-duty boat cover, folded the blue tarp, and placed it in a storage compartment in the bow. Next, he unlocked the ignition switch, pressed the START button, and the thirty-horsepower JOHNSON TILL sprang to life. Placing the motor in the idle mode he stepped out of the boat and untied the line from the mooring. Kicking his lifejacket to the front of the boat he placed his tea in a beverage holder and double-checked to make sure he had everything he needed on board for an afternoon on the water. He had a life jacket, a first aid kit, an anchor, a set of wooden oars, and a South Carolina boat license which dangled in a plastic-protected holder on the steering column. Placing his sunglasses on his face he backed the boat out, cruised slowly through the marina, and then finally entered the Harbor River, where he made a right and headed east at half speed.

It wasn't long before he saw the back end of Sawgrass on his right, a group of around seventy houses nestled in tall pines. Sawgrass was an island on an island, the small community surrounded by the river and then salt marshes on the other three sides, a single road leading to the hidden habitat. On the other side of the river, he viewed what was commonly referred to as the backside of Fripp. Over the years, from time to time he and his father had ventured by boat out into the backside. It was home to countless poisonous snakes, alligators, and swarms of bothersome insects. It was not the most pleasant place for human beings to spend time. His father had stated there were probably areas in between the maze of small tributaries of brackish water where most people never stepped foot. The only reason to go back deep in the backside was to fish. Getting out of one's boat and walking around was considered foolish and somewhat dangerous.

At the northeastern edge of Fripp, he made a slow sweeping turn into Fripp Inland Inlet, passed beneath the Fripp Island Bridge, Hunting Island on his left. On the other side of the bridge, the waves started to act up as the tide was starting to come in. Passing the north end of the Ocean Point Golf Course he smiled as two black dolphins cut in front of the boat then circled and followed him for about thirty yards, then swam off. Making another right-hand turn around the Point as it was called, he was now faced with a three-and-a-half-mile stretch of open Atlantic Ocean water skirting Fripp's beach. Going out a quarter mile from the shore, he slowed the boat, put on his life jacket, and then opened the motor up full, the craft slicing through the choppy Atlantic. On his right, the beach appeared to be rather empty while on his left the ocean went on indefinitely and disappeared on the horizon where he noticed three commercial fishing boats bobbing on the waves. He sped past John Fripp Condos and eventually his parents' home near the end of Tarpon. It was here that he turned right into Skull Inlet and cut the motor to a crawl.

He slowly passed the turnaround at the end of Tarpon, then the Beach Club. When he came to Wardell's Landing, he swung the boat back around and headed back out toward the ocean, stopping at the confluence where the Atlantic and the inlet met. He cut the motor, dropped the anchor, and checked the time, almost 1:30. His mother's note had stated they had reservations at the boathouse at seven which meant he had three and a half good hours before he had to be back at the house to get ready for dinner with his parents. Removing his life jacket he placed it against the seat, then he opened the small compartment next to the dash and took out a bottle of suntan lotion, rubbing the white oily substance on his face and arms. Placing the sunglasses on his face, he took a long drink of tea and laid back, his head resting on the life jacket. Folding his hands across his chest he smiled as he felt the wonderful sun caress his face. Laying in the bottom of the boat he could feel the waves as they caused a gentle rocking motion. He closed his eyes as he put school, Brad Sykes, and Simon Baumer out of his mind. *This was the first day of his three-month vacation and he couldn't have been happier!*

The combination of the slight vibration and the low buzzing from his cell phone in his pocket brought him out of a light sleep. He checked his watch: 3:45. He had been sleeping for over two hours. He dug the phone from his pocket, wondering who could be calling. It was Saturday and Elizabeth was scheduled to call him at six, as always. It was too early for her to call. Maybe it was his mother calling to make sure he had arrived on Fripp. He couldn't imagine who else it might be.

Answering the phone, he was surprised to hear Elizabeth's friendly voice, "Hello Max! I hope you don't mind but I decided to call you a little earlier than usual. Ellen could not meet me later at six because she has to go into town with her husband. I hope this is okay."

Max sat in the boat seat and took a drink of his now warm tea and answered, "No apology needed. It's just as well. I'm supposed to meet my parents for dinner at seven. We're going to a place here on the island called the Boathouse for their Saturday night special, all-you-can-eat crab legs. We should talk now. How are things back up there in Lancaster?"

"The snow has all melted and the trees are blooming. My father is now able to walk with the aid of a cane. He managed to walk out to the barn this morning and help with the milking. The sooner he can get back to his daily routine here on the farm the better. My mother says he's driving her nuts what with him being inside all day long. Where are you now?"

"I'm on Fripp Island. Well, let me rephrase that. I'm not on land but I'm on the water. Right now, I'm sitting in my father's boat looking out at the ocean. I was just taking a short nap when you called. Where are you?"

"I'm out in our barn with Ellen. She's keeping an eye on the house while I call."

Max detected a slight trace of negativity in Elizabeth's voice. "Are you okay? You sound kind of down in the dumps. Is everything all right?"

"Everyone else around here seems to think everything is just ducky! My mother, my father, Simon Baumer the entire community think my marriage to Simon is a done deal, despite the fact I have not agreed to be his wife. The only person around here who knows I have no intention of marrying the man is Ellen. Why, just last night at the farmer's market a lot of the younger girls and quite a few of the married women in our community were saying how lucky I was because Simon had chosen me. All they can talk about is how wealthy he is and that he has the finest house in the community. They say I'll never want for anything when I become his wife. It's like everyone else's mind is going in one direction and mine is going the opposite. I keep thinking about how disappointed everyone is going to be when I return to college and the courtship comes to an end. I can just hear my father now, 'You turned down Eli Hoffman because he was a braggart and a loudmouth and now you turn down Simon Baumer, the most successful Mennonite farmer in the state.' The entire community, men and women alike will think I'm being too choosy or too good for any man in the community. If this happens it'll make things hard for my parents. As usual, Simon will be dropping by for supper tonight and I'll have to sit out on the porch with him as he tries to discuss our future together. It's already been three months since I left school and in all that time, I've only seen you once and because of what happened during that visit now I will not get to see you for another three months. I can't wait to get back to school and put all this behind me."

"I don't like the situation we find ourselves in any better than you," said Max, "but we'll just have to be patient."

"I know you're right but it's a lot harder for me to be patient than you. For the next three months, I'm confined to the limited activities of my community. The only freedom I can experience is when I walk down to the pond. You, on the other hand, have the entire world at your fingertips. You're seated in a boat on the ocean and looking forward to eating crab legs later tonight. I've never been in a boat, seen the ocean, or sunk my teeth into crab legs. I guess what I'm saying is I miss you and wish I were there with you."

"If I thought there was a chance for us to spend some time together, I'd leave tonight for Lancaster, even if it meant only seeing you for a short time.

I keep thinking about the things we talked about at the pond."

"Let's talk about something else. The more we talk about being together the more I realize that's not going to happen for the next three months. How is your swimming going? You told me a few weeks back you met another student at the pool who was on the swim team, and they were helping you to improve your distance."

Not wanting to reveal the student he had met was a female he skirted the issue, "I'm learning to control my breathing better and to swim through the pain when I become tired. I'm up to a mile and a quarter." Wanting to get off the subject of Kelly Waters, he added, "Some other good news. For the past few weeks, I haven't seen much of Brad Sykes. I reckon I don't have to worry about him until next year when school starts up and even then, he might just forget the whole thing."

"I hope so. Listen, I've got to go. Ellen just warned me that Simon and his two idiot brothers are walking toward the barn. We'll talk next Wednesday."

Before Max could even say goodbye Elizabeth cut the call off. Staring at his cell phone, Max looked out at the ocean and thought about how Simon Baumer, even though hundreds of miles away was indeed a pain in the ass. Pulling up the anchor, he decided to head back to the marina. He was looking forward to a great seafood dinner with his folks.

He didn't get back to the house until just before five. In a little over an hour, his parents would be pulling in. Grabbing a folding chair from the back porch he decided to sit out on the beach for the next hour and just relax. Locating a sandy flat section just beyond the stone retainer wall that backed up against the houses on the lower end of Tarpon, he dug his bare toes into the warm sand and watched as the water from the waves washed up onto the beach stopping two feet from where he was seated. He could tell from the sand line left by the previous waves that the tide was beginning the twice-daily process of retreating to the sea. He thought about a sermon the minister of the church where he and his parents attended had given the week before he left Summerville for his freshman year at Gettysburg. *All streams and rivers eventually flow to the ocean, but the ocean is never full, and the water returns to where it came from.* Having lived near the ocean for the first nineteen years of his life, Max never grew tired of the Atlantic. Mathematics, as always entered his thought process. The number of gallons of water in the sea could not be calculated just like the stars in the sky or the grains of sand on the beach. There were things in this world that even the mathematical mind could not comprehend.

His time on the beach passed rapidly as he watched occasional small flocks of pelicans fly over and numerous sandpipers scamper near the edge of the water searching for food. A seagull landed a few feet from him and after a few minutes of just standing there and staring at Max, the bird realized it was not going to be fed and flew off into the distance. He checked the time: 6:07. He needed to head back to the house. He was famished and looking forward to a great low-country meal at the Boathouse.

Max entered the kitchen from the back porch, where he saw his mother unpacking groceries. "Hello there, mother."

His mother immediately went to him and hugged him. "Your father and I noticed your Jeep in the garage. When we couldn't locate you here in the house, we figured you were down on the beach. I was just about to send your father to fetch you."

Max looked around the kitchen and inquired, "So where is the old man?"

"He went upstairs to shave and freshen up before we left for dinner. When he got home from the job he is currently working he didn't have time to get cleaned up so we just drove directly down here, stopped at Publix, picked up a few things and here we are! When did you get in?"

"I guess it was around noon or so. I took a shower and then a boat ride around the island. When will we be leaving?"

His mother put a gallon of milk in the refrigerator and answered as she looked at the clock on the kitchen wall. "Next twenty to twenty-five minutes. As soon as your father comes back down we're outta here."

"Sounds like a winner to me. I'm gonna throw on some more presentable clothes and then I'll be ready for endless crab legs!"

Minutes later Max found both his parents standing in the kitchen, his father nursing a cold beer, his mother wiping down the counter. Max did a little jig and joked, "I'm ready if you are!"

Charley finished his beer in two swallows and held up his car keys. "Bonito Boathouse…here we come!"

Driving down Tarpon, Charley asked, "I hear you took the boat out for a spin this afternoon. How did ol' Shiloh run?"

Max smiled at the mention of the family speedboat's name, after the famous Civil War battle, Shiloh. "Just like General Grant…she never gives up, just keeps plowing ahead."

His mother pointed a finger at Max and jokingly scolded both her son and husband. "Please, can we start Max's summer vacation off without mentioning some general battle of the Civil War? In case the two of you haven't noticed this is the twenty-first century, not the 1860's."

Charley, winking at Max in the rearview mirror stated with an air of comical authority, "I hereby conclude we immediately go into a state of armistice."

In the lot at the marina, Max's mother turned in the seat and spoke to her son. "What's new with Elizabeth? Is her father still on the mend?"

"I talked with her earlier today," explained Max, "and she seemed sad. I guess she's just tired of this charade she's playing with Simon Baumer but is also looking forward to August when we'll meet at school and things will get back to normal. She told me her father is improving by the day."

On the other side of the rustic doorway to the Boathouse, Charley approached a hostess's desk and presented a young girl with his amenity card. "My name is Mr. Miller, and we have a reservation for three this evening."

The girl glanced at the card and then opened a register book. "Just let me check. Ah…here it is." Grabbing three menus she signaled for another young lady standing by the door. "Would you please lead these nice folks to a table?"

The girl stepped forward, cradling the menus in her arms. "The downstairs booths are all occupied at the moment. It may be a few minutes before we have an available table or if you like we could seat you upstairs."

Max's mother answered the question with a wave of her hand. "Upstairs will be fine. I like the view up there and besides that eating crab legs at any level is a great joy."

They were seated at a window table on the upper level and were no sooner settled in when their waiter approached, "Good evening folks. My name is Elrod, and I will be your server this evening. Can I start you off with a beverage?"

Charley quickly answered, "I'll just have a tall draft."

Max's mother opted for a glass of white Zinfandel and Max ordered a tall sweet, iced tea with lemon. Before the server could turn to leave Charley spoke up. "We already know what we want to order if it will save you some time."

"Very well," said Elrod as he positioned his order pad and pen ready to write down their dinner request.

Charley stacked the three menus on the corner of their table and announced, "We are all having the all-you-can-eat crab legs. What sides come with that?"

"Cole slaw and island fries. Will that be everything?"

"Yes, I believe that'll do it."

When Elrod left the table, Max's mother gave him a stare but remained silent. Max knew that familiar look, which always indicated she wanted to ask him a question. Max crossed his legs and asked a simple question of his own. "Com'n…what's on your mind? Let's have it."

"I do have a question for you, but first I want to tell you all about my afternoon today which turned out to be quite interesting. I got a phone call late yesterday afternoon from Luther, the owner of the Washington Street Antique Shop in Walterboro, you know Luther. You've met him on several occasions when we went over there to shop. Anyway, he told me he had just come into possession of a Nippon tea set and thought I might be interested. He told me he had two different ladies who had been in and wanted to purchase the set. He told me he was holding it for me, but if I wasn't interested then he'd sell it to one of his other customers. I told him I was interested, and that I'd be over the next day, which was this morning. Your father had to work until around two o'clock, so I jumped in my car and headed over to Walterboro.

"I got there just after ten when the shop opened up. Luther had the Nippon items set back and when he brought them out, I just fell in love with the set. It's an eleven-piece set, a pitcher, five cups, and saucers. I checked the pieces out and they are 100% Nippon. He gave me a great price on the set and while he was wrapping the individual pieces up in paper, a woman and a beautiful young girl about your age were standing by listening to our conversation. I noticed the woman was holding two angel figurines. I told Luther to go ahead and wait on her, but the lady said she was fine, and they would wait. She asked me how long I had been collecting Nippon and I responded by telling her since high school. She told me she collected angels and had over two hundred in her house. She went on to tell me her grandmother had just died two months in the past and they were just getting around to going through her belongings. One of the things they found up in her attic was an old chest in which they found twenty-seven pieces of genuine Nippon.

"The next thing she said floored me. She said if I was interested, I could have them. I told her I was interested, and that I would give her a fair price. She refused, saying her grandmother would be pleased to know someone who cared for Nippon was getting them. So, I agreed to take the items off her hands. She said it would take a couple of days to get the set cleaned up and that she would bring it over to Luther's. We swapped names and phone numbers and that's where it started to get strange.

"When she found out my last name was Miller, and I was from Summerville she asked me if I had a son by the name of Max. You can imagine how off guard I was taken. When I confirmed I indeed had a son named Max, she turned to her daughter and they both laughed. The lady was Mrs. Waters and the young lady with her was Kelly Waters…her daughter who was a freshman this past year at Gettysburg. Kelly jumped in on the conversation explaining she had met you at the museum at the Seminary. A short time later you and she ran into one another at the pool. She said she was giving you some tips on your swimming. She knew everything about you; how you spend a lot of time over here at Fripp, how you're a math major and a Civil War buff. She said besides swimming together three days a week for the past few weeks you and she had ridden bikes out to the battlefield and had gone to lunch on two occasions."

Finished, she continued to stare at her son, while Max looked out at the river, his father staring at both his son and wife. Following a few moments of awkward silence Charley broke the ice while addressing his wife, "From the look on Max's face based on what you just said I think I'm the only one sitting at this table who is unaware of this new development."

Max gave his father a look of astonishment. "My friendship with Kelly Waters is hardly what I would call a *development!* I met her at the museum a few weeks ago and through a conversation we had we discovered that we are both from South Carolina. I found out she was on the school swim team and later on I ran into her at the pool. I was amazed that she swims five miles a day and I only manage one. She has been teaching me so I can increase my distance… and I have. I am now up to a mile and a quarter."

"That sounds innocent enough," said Charley, "but what does that have to do with a bike ride over to the battlefield and then lunch?"

"It's just the way things worked out. During our conversations at the museum, she found out I was a Civil War buff. During one of our many conversations at the pool, she said she had never been out to the battlefield. The only reasonable reply that seemed appropriate was to invite her to go. The next weekend we biked over there. She packed a picnic lunch which I had no idea she was going to do. Then, on another occasion, she thought it would be nice if we could have lunch together downtown sometime. I had no reason to refuse so I agreed. I know what both of you are thinking and you are way off base. She is just a friend…nothing more!"

Elrod interrupted their conversation when he returned with their drinks and told them their dinners would be out in about ten minutes. After he left, Charley spoke to Max. "That is the same thing you said about your relationship with Elizabeth…just friends and look where that has gone. You told your mother and me she all but said she loves you and you, in turn, told her you have some of the same feelings. You met Elizabeth last year right about November and here it is seven months later and both of you feel you may be in love. That's a pretty heavy result for a six-month friendship. Does Elizabeth know about this Kelly?"

"No, she does not. There didn't seem to be a reason to tell her."

"You felt there was no reason to tell anyone about this Kelly Waters."

Looking at both of his parents. Max pointed out, "I hate to say this, but it isn't anyone else's business. I'm nineteen years old and next month I'll turn twenty. I'm not your nine-or ten-year-old son any longer. Back in those days whenever I made a new friend at school or around the neighborhood when I got home, I would always tell you I had made a new friend, be they a boy or girl. I suppose I could have told you about Kelly, but the thought never entered my mind. My portfolio of friends is not that long to begin with. So, is this how it is? Every time I meet someone who I consider a friend of sorts I'm supposed to call my parents and inform them I now have a new friend."

"That's not the point," said Charley, "but this is! If you are in love with Elizabeth, don't you think you owe her at least some level of trust?"

"In this case no. We're not engaged, and I have not asked her to marry me. We are friends…very close friends and I don't see where telling her about Kelly is a matter to be concerned over."

"Let me ask you this, Son? Is this Kelly Waters attractive?"

Max objected. "What difference does that make?"

His mother spoke up. "Well, coming from a woman's viewpoint it does make a difference," Looking at her husband she described Kelly, "Slender, athletic, green eyes, long reddish-brown hair…quite the looker!"

"There ya go," said Charley. "How many boys your age have a friend that looks like what your mother just described? You say you met her at the museum. If Kelly had been a young man working there and he was on the swim team do you think you would have jumped at the opportunity to have him help you with your swimming?"

Max took a drink of tea and looked at his mother and then his father. "When you put it that way…I guess not."

"Exactly my point. Look, Son, your mother and I realize you are nineteen, soon to be twenty and I have no doubt there are plenty of good-looking women on campus. There is nothing wrong with testing the waters. What I'm saying is there are a lot of fish in the ocean and if you put too many of them in your boat…you could sink. Dating, courting or a friendship as you put it with a female can be a wonderful experience and yet on the other hand it can wind up reducing you to feeling like a fool depending on the outcome. Juggling more than one woman at a time is a difficult road to navigate."

Max's mother chimed in. "I agree with your father and even though you say this is none of our business we're just looking out for your best interests. After talking with Mrs. Waters and her daughter I tossed the thought around in my head that maybe you were kind of drifting away from Elizabeth and moving toward this Kelly. I've got to say that possibility made me feel better about you. I think your father would agree with me if you were dating a girl who was raised in what we consider the world of the normal rather than some religious community we would feel better about the direction you're headed."

Charley acknowledged, "I, for one have been somewhat skeptical about this relationship you have with this Mennonite girl, Elizabeth. I mean, where do you see this thing going? If you two are, as you feel, possibly in love then the relationship has to go to the next level, and I don't see that happening. We know of this girl, but only from what you have told us. We've never met her or even talked with her. You, on the other hand, have been kept a mystery to her parents and her community. What can the future possibly hold for two people from totally different lifestyles? It's like a homeless man on the street who is hungry. He passes a restaurant looks in the window and sees people dining. He wants to go in but knows he will never be served. It's kind of the same thing with you and Elizabeth. Now, or maybe even in the future, you may desire to marry her but her family and the community she lives in will not permit it. I see no positive result for you if you continue to walk that road. At this very moment, this Simon Baumer character is and has been courting her for weeks now with the approval of her parents. What are you going to do if she decides to marry this man?"

"She'll never marry him," said Max. "She told me so."

Max's mother interrupted. "I think this conversation is getting out of hand. We know this is your own business and I feel in the end you'll do the right thing…make the right decision. Let's not start your summer vacation with an argument. Now, my original question I wanted to ask you is this. Just as I was about to leave Luther's Mrs. Waters said she had an idea to run by me. She said she and her husband were throwing a barbeque over at their place on Edisto, Saturday two weeks from today. She said she was inviting a couple of their neighbors and that she was inviting our family as well. That way I could just pick up the Nippon at their barbeque. Your father wasn't aware of this until just now, but I'm sure he'll go."

"Of course, I'll go!" said Charley. "Barbeque and beer…count me in!"

Smiling at Max his mother asked her question, "Despite everything we have discussed this evening can we assume you will come along?"

"Yes, I'll go, but it won't change the way I feel about Elizabeth. Kelly and I are just good friends."

Charley clapped his hands once when he saw Elrod and a trailing waitress carrying their crab leg dinners. "Enough of all this talk. Let's eat!"

CHAPTER SEVENTEEN

Brad parked his Corvette across from the State Street Pool Hall and Grill climbed out, and placed a small handful of quarters in the parking meter. On the other side of the street, he surveyed the old building he had passed many a time over his years living in Ithaca. Today, May 30th was the first time he had ever stepped foot in the popular gathering spot for those who enjoyed a good game of pool or maybe even a card game. He had always heard the clientele who frequented the establishment were on the rough side. It was not a place he would normally go but following a call from his friend Kip, this is where they were to meet.

He pushed open the front door and entered a world quite different than what he was accustomed to. At first, he had to adjust his eyes, the lighting low except for a single hanging light centered over several pool tables. To his right, there was a long rustic bar with eight high-top stools. Behind the bar, there were shelves lined with various bottles of whiskey and assorted liquors. Three neon beer signs, one that was flickering hung above the shelving. A floating layer of barely seen cigarette smoke hung in the room like a misty fog. Of the eight pool tables three were occupied with groups of men. Across the back of the room, there were three old wooden tables, one occupied by four men amid a poker game. Brad approached the bar and asked the bartender, "I'm supposed to meet Kip Griner here at six. Is he here?"

The bartender, cleaning a glass with a wet towel motioned to a back room. "Yeah, he's here. He's in the back. He said he was expecting someone. That be you?"

Imitating the man's poor use of the English language, Brad responded, "That be me!"

"Just go through that door and you'll find him back there."

Brad walked across the old wood floor, passed through an arched door opening, and entered the back room, which housed four more pool tables and three tables. The room was empty except for Kip who was seated at a corner table, a cold drink in his hand. Upon seeing his friend, he held up the bottle and signaled him over. "Come on in Brad. Welcome to one of my favorite hangouts."

Pulling out a chair Brad seated himself and asked, "Where are the people we are supposed to meet?"

"They won't arrive here until six. It's a quarter of now. Relax, they'll be here. Would you like something to drink?"

"Well, maybe a ginger ale if they have one."

Kip signaled an older woman who appeared to be the sole waitress on duty. "Could you please bring my friend here a ginger ale?"

The woman didn't answer but responded with a nod of her head.

Kip took a drink while asking Brad. "One year of schooling down and three to go. Do you think you'll work for your father after you graduate?"

"That's the plan," said Brad. "My father, it seems, has my future all laid out for me. It's his intention after I have my business degree three years from now that I'll become a lower-level manager at one of his factories. Following a few years, he claims he'll move me up the corporate ladder, eventually to the point where I'll be able to take over the entire family business, but that's years down the road. How about you, Kip?"

"For now, I'll just stick with working for Bernie. He says I have a lot of potential and if I stay with him, I can make a better-than-average living."

The waitress returned and placed a tall glass of a clear sparking beverage in front of Brad, turned, and walked off without a word. She no sooner left the room when two men appeared in the open doorway, one taller than the other. The tall man wore a modern version of a brown leisure suit and had a gold chain hanging around his hairy neck. The shorter man was muscular and wore all black, pants, a shirt, and a leather jacket. The tall man held a mixed drink of some sort, the shorter man carrying a cup of coffee. Approaching the table, the tall man was the first to speak. "Which one of you is Kip Griner?"

Kip stood and offered his hand. "I'm Kip and this is my good friend Brad."

The tall man shook hands while the short man sat down and never even cracked a smile. The tall man introduced himself and his partner. "My name is Joseph, and my associate is Marvin. Let's get right to business. Mr. Anelo has sent us here as you Mr. Griner have requested the need for some assistance."

"The assistance you speak of is not required by me, but by Mr. Sykes here. So what is the process?"

"It's not that complicated. We need to know who, why, what, where, and when…in that order. Marvin will jot down some notes." Marvin withdrew a small pad and a pen from his shirt pocket while giving Kip and Brad a blank stare.

Kip motioned to Brad. "You're on the bubble."

"All right," said Brad. "The who is a fella about the same age as I. His name is Max Miller. He and I were at one time roommates in college this past year. He sucker-punched me at a restaurant causing me great discomfort. He broke my nose, the injury preventing me from playing football for the remainder of the year and I was viewed as a joke around campus. My father had every intention of pressing a lawsuit against Miller, but that did not pan out and Miller walked away free as a bird. I am not satisfied, and I desire that Miller pay dearly for hitting me without provocation. He lives in Summerville, South Carolina and his parents also own a summer property at a place called Fripp Island which is located down below a town called Beaufort, also in South Carolina." Handing Joseph, a folded piece of white paper, Brad explained, "I took the liberty of getting his home address from my father's files. I also have a photograph taken of Max and myself just after we both started school." Sliding the photo across the table. Brad went on, "That covers the who and why of the equation. Now, for the what! I need someone to inflict some suffering and painful blows on Max Miller."

Joseph looked directly into Brad's eyes and requested. "Suffering and painful blows. That's rather vague. You need to be more specific, Mr. Sykes."

"All right. Let's go with a broken nose, a broken arm, and a few busted ribs. I don't want him killed; I just want him to be roughed up some."

"A broken nose it is then," said Joseph. "Which arm do you want broken? Right or left?"

Brad thought and then answered. "He's right-handed so I guess the right arm."

"And the ribs," asked Joseph. Define a few?"

"Two or three will do."

"Now that that has been determined let's go over the where."

"Right now, he is in the process of a three-month vacation from school. The best place for this to take place would be around Summerville somewhere. I suppose it could take place at this Fripp Island but that happens to be a private island and if you're not a resident or a renter you can't get on the island."

Marvin was busy writing as Joseph asked his next question, "And now…the when?"

"I'm giving you a two-week window to accomplish my request. During two weeks in July, I am going to be on a fishing expedition with my father in Canada. The dates are from July 11th through the 25th. When this event takes place, I have no doubt Miller will try and implicate me as having something to do with his unfortunate injuries, so therefore this must be completed while I'm out of the country." Looking from Joseph to Marvin and back to Joseph, Brad stated, "I think that covers everything."

"Not quite," said Joseph. "There is the matter of the fee for the work requested. The price tag for this type of action will run you ten thousand… cash. Do you have the money with you now?"

Patting his jacket pocket Brad answered, "I have more than that with me. Do you want it right now?"

"Here's what we'll do," said Joseph. "Marvin will go to the men's room. Wait for about a minute and then you go in and give him the money. He'll come out and then a few minutes later you can return to the table."

"Will I get a receipt for my payment?"

Joseph laughed. "There are no receipts in this type of business. That would leave a paper trail the authorities could follow."

"How will I know the job has been completed?"

"You will get a short phone call three days following the Miller assignment. A voice will simply confirm…that your request has been successfully filled."

"If I could ask how do you plan on going about dealing with Miller?"

"It's better you don't know how we plan to go about the job. All you need to know is that we guarantee what you request will be carried out to your specifications. Are there any other questions?"

"No, I think you've answered everything I need to know."

"Good then. Let's get the money transaction over."

Marvin stood and walked to the restroom, Brad following a short while later. After they both returned to the table, Brad spoke, "Well I guess that ties everything up then…correct?"

Standing. Joseph acknowledged, "Indeed it does. In all likelihood, you will never see us again. You can rest assured we will carry out your wishes."

"I do have one other question and it probably has nothing to do with our transaction and that's just this. Marvin has not uttered a single word here at the table or in the restroom. I don't mean to come off rude. It just seems odd, that's all."

Joseph looked at Marvin and then Brad as he answered. "Marvin doesn't say much but what he does do he's quite good at. Simply put, he breaks bones. Come July, your Mr. Miller will meet up with Marvin. It will not be pleasant. Good day to you gentlemen!"

Kip and Brad sat in silence, watching as Joseph and his bone-breaking companion left the room. Finally, Kip spoke up, "Well it's done now. The wheels are in motion. All you have to do is wait for a phone call later in July and then I guess you'll be satisfied. How do you feel about all this?"

"I suppose there are a lot of people who would look at me as being kind of sadistic, but I'll not rest until I get my revenge."

Earlier in the day, hundreds of miles from the State Street Pool Hall and Grill Max guided his father's speedboat past Hunting Island and then St Helena Sound, the vast Atlantic Ocean on their right. Charley, seated in the back of the boat next to his wife checked his watch. "Ten after eleven. We told the Waters we'd dock around noon. It's only a thirty-mile ride over to Edisto. We're just about halfway. Looks like we're going to be a little early."

Max's mother, securing a crockpot of baked beans in a heat-insulated carrier between her feet, adjusted the sunglasses on her face. "I can't believe you two decided to make the trip by boat rather than our car."

Max gave his mother a thumbs up. "Where's your sense of adventure? It's a straight shot from Fripp over to Edisto. Dad and I have made this trip many times over the years when we go there to fish."

Turning to Charley, Max's mother brushed strains of hair away from her face due to the light ocean breeze. "I think you'll really like Mrs. Waters and her daughter. I don't know anything about Mr. Waters." She then asked Max. "Are you looking forward to seeing Kelly again?"

"Yes, I am," said Max, "but not for the reason you and Dad no doubt have rolling around in your heads. There'll be no hand-holding, no kissing, no lovey-dovey nonsense. Like I told you. We're just good friends. So, before we get there can we please just enjoy the day without you two trying to be matchmakers?"

Nearly ten minutes passed, and Max and his parents, sitting quietly while enjoying the ride past the Sound when Max pointed straight ahead for his mother's benefit. "See that coastline up ahead?" Without waiting for a response, Max kicked up the speed of the boat and announced, "We'll be there in less than five minutes."

A quarter mile out from Edisto Beach, Max made a slow turn to the left and headed for the south fork of the Edisto River that separated Edisto from Pine Island. A half mile up he made a right turn into a slip that led to a small marina that housed a fueling station and general store. Pulling into an empty spot, Max's mother saw Kelly running down the planked dock toward them. Kelly, dressed in bright white shorts, a pink top, and tan deck shoes waved excitedly, her semi-long auburn hair blowing across her face.

Charley, now standing bumped his son on his shoulder. "I know you said you were just friends with this girl, but I've got to say she is the best-looking friend you've ever had."

Max helped his mother out of the boat, then went about making the introductions, "Kelly, you as I have been informed have already met my mother. The gentleman standing in the back of the boat holding the twelve-pack of Coors is my father, Charley. Dad, this is Kelly Waters."

Charley stepped onto the dock, reached out, and shook Kelly's hand. "Nice to meet you, young lady."

After shaking both Max's parents' hands Kelly turned to Max and gave him a broad smile followed by a nonchalant hug and peck on his right cheek.

Backing away she remarked, "I'm so glad you came along. I can't wait to show you the island and spend some time together. Maybe we'll even get a swim in. If you will just follow me. Our golf cart is parked up by the store. It's only about a five-minute drive to our place."

Seated in the six-man cart, Kelly guided the island vehicle out a short drive and then made a right onto a paved road. Max, sitting next to her asked, "How long have your parents owned your place here on Edisto?"

"Let's see," said Kelly. "I think they bought our house here on the island when I was two years old. That would make it, I guess about seventeen years now. Over the years we spend more time over here than we do in Walterboro, especially during the summer months."

From the middle seat where Max's parents were seated, his father asked, "We, as a family, have never spent any time over here on Edisto, well that is except for when Max and I boat over here for a day of fishing. We've been to the marina and the store for drinks and snacks, but that's it. We've never been into the interior. How large is the island?"

Kelly made a left-hand turn as she responded, "I think it's around sixty-eight square miles and has a population of about twenty-three hundred. Of course, during the tourist season, the number of people on the island increases dramatically. It's not a gated community, but rather similar to a small rural county town. Everything you need is right here on the island. Well, that is except for a hospital."

Charley compared Edisto with Fripp Island, stating, "Sixty-eight square miles. That means that Edisto is ten times the size of Fripp which is just a tad over six square miles. We only have around four hundred regular residents and like Edisto the island population explodes during the summer."

Max's mother asked the next question. "What are you majoring in at school?"

"Sport's medicine. Being an athlete myself I understand how easy it is to become injured. Experts in the sport's medicine field are in high demand not only in colleges across the country but professional sports as well." Turning into a pine needle-covered driveway, Kelly pulled up in front of a glass-fronted A-frame surrounded by several tall pines. "Here we are," said Kelly. "Our little slice of heaven right here on earth!"

Charley's mother stepped out of the cart while admiring the home. "Why, it's just beautiful and the setting is perfect. I can see why you like it here so much."

Kelly motioned for them to follow. "Com'n, my parents and our other guests are out back."

They entered a backyard setting where the tall pines continued to dominate the landscape. A picnic table covered with a checkered cloth housed several covered dishes. A grill on the left of the yard was being tended by a man while Mrs. Waters was busy putting up three beach chairs. Two other couples were seated toward the back of the yard. Tapping her mother on the shoulder, Kelly announced, "Mother, the Millers are here!"

Mrs. Waters exclaimed, "Right on time. Good. We will be putting the dogs and burgers on in about an hour."

Max's mother held up her baked beans as she asked, "Where do you want this? The beans are still warm, but they may need to be heated up before we eat."

"Just put them on the table." Reaching for Charley's hand, Kelly's mother introduced herself, "Hello and welcome to Edisto, I'm Kelly's mother, Blanch. If you would like you can put your beer in that large blue cooler over by the table." She called to her husband who was the man at the grill. Blanch signaled the man over. "William, come on over and meet the Millers."

After introducing her husband to Max and his parents, they all walked to the back of the yard where two couples were seated beneath a large Southern Magnolia tree. "If I could get everyone's attention," said Blanch, "This is Charley and Kate Miller and their son, Max. Max was a freshman this past year at Gettysburg College and met Kelly while at school." Gesturing at the two couples she went on, "These wonderful people are our neighbors back in Walterboro. First, we have Dave and Audrey Meadows. They're newlyweds."

Dave stood and shook Charley's hand. "We're hardly newlyweds. We've been hitched for almost two years." Patting his wife's stomach, he explained, "We just recently found out that we are pregnant."

Kate shook Audrey's hand and congratulated the couple while Blanch introduced the other couple. "These other ol' coots are the Blanchetts; Archie and his wife June."

Archie, a man who was at least seventy shook Charley's hand while June stood and raised a beer she was holding as she announced, "And we *are not pregnant!*" Everyone laughed.

Kelly stepped close to her mother and asked, "How soon 'til we eat?"

"I imagine in about an hour to an hour and a half."

"If it's all right I'm going to give Max a golf cart tour of the island."

"Fine, just make sure you're back here in about an hour."

Taking Max by his right hand, Kelly led him around the side of the house. "Let's take a ride around the island."

Seated next to Kelly in the front Max asked, "Let me ask you something?"

Kelly pulled out onto the narrow street. "Go ahead…I'm all ears!"

"Back there at the dock when we first arrived. What was that hug and kiss all about?"

"It wasn't about anything. I mean, it wasn't that bad…was it?"

"I'm not saying it was bad, it was just unexpected."

"I didn't mean anything by it. It's just the way my mother raised me. She has always been touchy, and friendly when it comes to meeting people, so I guess I'm the same. If it bothered you, I'm sorry."

"No need for an apology. It just kind of took me off-guard. You see, it's not me. It's my parents. They have formed some sort of opinion that we are dating, and I assured them we are not. I told them we are just friends and there would be no hand-holding or kissing between you and me today and we no sooner pull in when you plant one on me. I'm sure on the way back to Fripp this evening I'll have some explaining to do."

"I'm sorry. I didn't mean to cause a rift in your family. If you'd like I could speak to your mother and set the record straight."

"No, that won't be necessary. It's not that big of a deal."

Max changed the subject. "Have you put any thought into what part of the country you'd like to work in after you graduate?"

"Not really. Graduation is three years down the line, and I have lots of time to think about my future." Making a right-hand turn, Kelly went on, "Between Walterboro and here on Edisto, well I've spent the first nineteen years of my life. I can't imagine living anywhere else, but I'll have to go where an opportunity comes up for me. Ideally, I'd like to live and work in a community near the ocean. My mother claims I have saltwater in my veins. I don't think I'd enjoy being inland, like in Gettysburg for instance. It's a nice community but it's a ten-to-twelve-hour drive to the ocean. It's a nice place to attend college but I could never live there. The ocean has always been medicinal for me. When we are here on the island if I'm feeling down, I can just jump in the ol' cart here and within minutes I'm on the beach right next to the water. Walking on the beach or just sitting in the sand looking out at the Atlantic always brings me such peace. So, what about you, Max? I know when we were at school you talked about someday owning your own financial business. Where in this great nation of ours would you like to work?"

"I haven't given it that much thought. I, like you, was raised near the water, the ocean. For the first eighteen years of my life, I depended on my parents to take me to the beach. Most of the time we went we would go down to Fripp. I remember the great summers I experienced on Fripp Island. I'd get up early in the morning and run down to the beach and frolic in the waves. Sometimes in the middle of the night as a boy of eight or nine, I'd sneak out of my room and venture out onto the deserted beach. I'd take a beach chair with me and sit a few yards from the water and wait until the tide eventually washed over my feet and if I waited long enough the incoming waves would grow to the point where they would knock me and the chair over. If my parents ever knew how I went down to the beach at two or three in the morning, why they'd skin me alive? What I'm saying is if I had my drouthers I'd like to work near the ocean maybe in Charleston or Beaufort and maybe even over in Savannah. Unlike you, I do like Gettysburg. I suppose it's because my father has been taking me there every year ever since I was seven for the annual reenactment. If it came right down to it I could live in Gettysburg, but I don't think that is going to happen. Three years from now when I graduate, I'll no doubt accept a lower financial position with a well-established firm. I'll learn the ropes and hopefully, let's say by the time I'm in my mid-thirties I'll have enough experience and money to start my own business."

Kelly pointed straight ahead as she announced, "Our first stop is going to be the beach, my favorite place on the island." Driving down a short access road she stopped the cart and turned the motor off, sat back, and viewed the Atlantic Ocean. "There is something I want to talk to you about. I was going to mention it when we were back at school, but I just couldn't seem to find the right time to bring the subject up. Now that we are away from Gettysburg, I feel this is a good time."

Max, not quite sure where she was going got out of the cart and did a deep knee bend and then walked a few paces out onto the sand, turned, and spoke, "I have no idea what this is about but like you say, I guess this is a good time."

Kelly got out and joined him as they walked toward the water's edge. "Okay, here it is. When we first met at the museum at the Seminary do you recall when I said I thought that I had seen you before?"

"Sure, I remember that. You said you thought you had seen me at the pool a couple of times."

"That's correct, but that was not the only time I had seen you around campus. I knew of you before we met that day at the museum. Like most students on campus, I had heard the story of how you, Max Miller, a mathematics student took out Brad Sykes with one punch. The word around school was that you did this to defend another student's honor, namely Elizabeth King. I never met Elizabeth or even talked with her, but I knew who she was. I'd see her around campus. She was easy to spot. She stuck out like a sore thumb what with the way she dresses. This did not bother me because a lot of students dress differently than most of us. There are students dressed in their traditional African attire or even Muslims. The way she dressed was none of my business. You would think that being a freshman myself I should have known her better, but the fact is there are two dorms for freshman females, dorm one and dorm two. Elizabeth was in number one I was in the other. She was not in any of my classes, so our paths just never crossed. I saw the two of you walking around campus and even downtown one time at a café. I overheard two girls talking about how you and Elizabeth were a couple. I didn't think anything about it and, once again, it was none of my business.

"Some of the people I knew said they supported you and that you had done the right thing by hitting Sykes. Once again…none of my business. I knew all about how you got thrown through a plate glass window, lost your job, and eventually sidestepped getting sued by Sykes' family. After we met. I thought about talking to you about the Brad Sykes incident and your relationship with Elizabeth but then I decided since you never mentioned either one, that I'd just let it go." Approaching the water, she stopped and gave Max a subtle stare.

Max kicked off his old sneakers and walked out into the shallow water. "So why are you bringing this up now?"

"I didn't mention any of this back In Gettysburg because I thought it might be a sore spot for you."

Bending down, Max picked up a small seashell and tossed it out into the water. "Hitting Brad Sykes, getting thrown through that window, losing my job, and surviving that lawsuit are all things I have tried to put behind me. Now, Elizabeth, well she's a different matter. Are you aware she had to leave school and go back home because her father had an accident?"

"Yes, I had heard that. She never did come back this year…did she?"

"No, she never did. In the past three months, I've only seen her one time and that was in secret in the woods near her family farm. I talk with her on the phone every Wednesday and Saturday. She claims she will be returning to school this coming August."

"Then you two are in a relationship?"

"I don't know how to answer that. We've only known one another since last November. During that time, we have become good friends, but there may be more to it than that. At first, we were just friends but when I met her near her farm, I guess it was about two months ago she all but told me she loved me. I guess I never realized it until that very moment I had similar feelings, which I told her. So, as it stands right now, we're not sure if we are in love or not, but I can tell you this. The way we feel about each other has gone way beyond the friendship stage. I've discussed all this with my parents, and they think I am setting myself up for a big fall. I understand what they are saying, and I guess anyone who views the relationship I have with Elizabeth would say it's rather one-sided. For instance, I have made my relationship with Elizabeth known to my parents, while on the other side of the coin she has kept her relationship with me a secret to her family. I know my parents may be right, but I just can't bring myself to admit that Elizabeth, as far as a future with her is concerned, is probably short-lived. We come from two different worlds. She is a Mennonite and has been raised with a different set of values and the way one should live their life than the world you and I come from."

Interested, Kelly asked, "So you don't see yourself marrying this Elizabeth?"

"Not really. How could it ever work out? She is not going to abandon her way of life, her family, and the Mennonite community she was raised in for some nineteen-year-old wet behind-the-ears South Carolina boy like me, and I'm sure as hell not going to move to Pennsylvania and become a Mennonite farmer pushing a plow around. It's not a win-win situation. If we were to marry down the road one of us would have to give up the world we come from. Besides that, she is presently being courted by an older wealthy Mennonite man who desires her to be his wife. She has told me she has no intentions of marrying this man, but the pressure being placed upon her to marry him makes me nervous. Her mother and her father, not to mention everyone in her community expect her to marry him."

Kelly kicked off her shoes and waded out into the water up to her knees. "If you are looking for advice from me, I'm sorry but you're out of luck. I, like you and Elizabeth, am nineteen. I've never been in love and have no idea what I would do if I found myself in the situation you find yourself in. Maybe I've seen too many movies with the proverbial fairytale ending where the man rushes to the woman and tells her how much he loves her regardless of the consequences."

"You're right," said Max. "The other day I was thinking that maybe I should just hop in my Jeep and drive up to her farm in Lancaster, Pennsylvania, knock on her door, barge in, and tell her parents the way I feel. But, this is not a movie, and the way I see it there is no fairytale ending to this. If I were to go to her parents and explain the way I feel about her, it would only result in making things more difficult for her. She has already explained to me if her father knew about our relationship, she would be yanked out of school, and possibly even shunned by her people. Besides the fact that I'm an outsider to their faith, I would not be accepted because I am already viewed by their community as a troublemaker of sorts."

"I don't understand," said Kelly. "If these people don't know who you are how could they label you as a troublemaker?"

"It's kind of crazy. They don't know who I am, but they know of me."

"How can that be?"

"When I traveled to Lancaster to see Elizabeth, I drove over there the night before we were to meet secretly. When I arrived there Friday night, I decided to go to a farmers market where she, her family, and other members of their community sell baked goods and other Mennonite products. She wasn't expecting me to show up there and when I did, we had to act like we didn't know each other. I was only at the tent for about five minutes if that. I purchased a pie from her and due to a misunderstanding with a Mennonite man who was working with her, I was chased by this man and his two brothers through the parking lot. They didn't catch me, but I think they had intentions of beating the hell out of me. I barely managed to escape and practically ran one of them over with my Jeep, which was witnessed by several people at the market. The next day I parked my Jeep next to a bridge near the woods where I was to meet Elizabeth. One of the men who had chased me the previous evening saw my Jeep but didn't put two and two together until the following day. Word of this strange boy in a Green Jeep, who happens to be me spread through the Mennonite community where Elizabeth lives like wildfire. Here's the kicker. The man that I had the misunderstanding with at the tent just happens to be the same man who is courting Elizabeth. So, you see if I were to drive over there to her farm, I would be recognized as the troublesome boy in the Green Jeep."

"The more you explain this relationship to me, the more I can understand why your parents are skeptical. Why, this sounds like one of the Amish novels you can get at the bookstore. I think you should just try and relax this summer and forget about what's going on in this community where she lives. Aside from talking to her twice weekly, there seems to be little you can do to make the cards fall in your favor. There are just some things in life you cannot control. At this point, you don't know if she is going to return to school or not. If she does go back to college and you two pick things up where they left off before she went back home, there are only two things that can happen. The feelings you two have for one another can either grow stronger or slowly fade. Nothing in life ever seems to be neutral. It's either good or bad, black or white, and so on and so on. You could spend the next two months of your summer vacation hoping for the best, but things might turn out for the worse. The only thing you can control is your own emotions. I say enjoy the next eight weeks and then whatever happens when you go back to school, well then so be it!"

Locating another seashell in the low water, Max tossed it out into the ocean as he agreed, "I think you're right. I should try and enjoy the next two months before I have to return to school."

Kelly walked out of the water and picked up her shoes. "There is one more thing I wanted to say about this. I want you to know I consider you a friend and I would never do anything to interfere with your relationship with Elizabeth, whether it be during this summer or when we return to school. If over the summer you ever feel you need someone to talk to, well, I'll be around."

Max helped his mother into their boat, turned, and took Kelly by her right hand. "Please thank your parents once again for their hospitality. It was nice to meet some of your neighbors and the barbeque was great. I think I'm going to go with what you said about trying to enjoy the next eight weeks before I have to go back to school. Who knows, maybe we can get together again before August."

"I think that would be nice," said Kelly.

Max backed the boat away from the dock, gave Kelly a subtle wave, and then turned the boat for home.

Charley seated in the back looked at his watch. "Eight o'clock. We should be back on Fripp before nine."

Minutes later, speeding past the St. Helena Sound Charley joined Max in the front of the boat. "That Kelly is quite the looker and intelligent as well. Whether your Elizabeth knows it or not she's got some stiff competition down here in South Carolina. Just sayin'."

CHAPTER EIGHTEEN

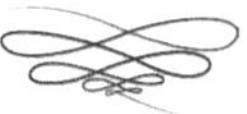

The Marsh Walk on Hunting Island was one of Max's favorite locations for crabbing. He parked his Jeep in the dirt lot adjacent to the Sea Island Parkway, grabbed his two crab cages and a cooler, and started the three-quarter mile trek across the marsh to the twenty-by-twenty-foot elevated railed deck overlooking the large tidal lagoon. It was a mid-July low country morning. The temperature was already in the mid-seventies and according to the weather report the forecast for the day would top out in the low nineties. With any luck, he'd catch his limit and be back at the house on Fripp before noon.

Walking down the winding dirt path he thought about the two women in his life. First, there was Elizabeth whom he had just talked to three days ago on Saturday. She was still putting up with Simon Baumer's attempt at courting her and counting the days until she returned to college. The other woman, Kelly, who he hadn't seen or talked with for well over a month seemed to be living up to her commitment of not interfering with his relationship with Elizabeth. He checked his watch: 7:10 in the morning. The sun was up, the skies were clear blue, and it looked like another great day of vacation lay ahead.

At the deck, he set the metal cages on the marred wood bench that lined the perimeter while placing his cooler on the old wood-planked flooring. Ten feet below the deck there were thousands of small fiddler crabs crawling back and forth across the inter-tidal mud flats next to the brackish water. A small flock of Saltmarsh Sparrows flew off to his right while two snow-white egrets stood motionless a few yards downstream, waiting for some small unsuspecting fish. Max opened the cooler and removed a small plastic bag containing bait, cut-up, fresh chicken parts. Opening both cages he secured the bait in each cage, then using a section of rope lowered the traps down into the murky water. Now, it was just a matter of time. Seated on a bench facing the east he positioned a pair of sunglasses on the bridge of his nose turned his face toward the bright sunlight and closed his eyes, thinking, it doesn't get any better than this!

Following the prescribed method of successful crabbing, which was checking your cages every fifteen minutes he pulled both traps up, found they were empty, and lowered them back down into the dark marsh water. He took a swig of water as his cell phone buzzed. He checked the time, not quite seven-thirty. Picking up the device he answered, "Hello."

"Hello yourself stranger, it's Kelly. I hope I haven't called you too early?"

"No, not at all. I'm just sitting out in the middle of a marsh doing some casual crabbing and soaking up some morning sun. Where are you?"

"Well, right now I'm in the process of loading up a bunch of birdhouses in the back of my car."

"What on earth on you doing with birdhouses? I didn't know you were interested in our feathered friends."

"I'm not all that interested in South Carolina's bird population; the bird domiciles happen to belong to my mother. She makes birdhouses in her spare time. Two years ago, for Christmas, I bought my father a book on woodworking. He never really took any interest in the projects suggested in the book, but my mother did. She decided to construct a birdhouse and it turned out pretty good, so she made another one. Who knew? Turns out, she's good at working with wood. She started selling them to neighbors and friends and someone suggested she get a booth at the City Market in Charleston and make her handy work available to the general public. So, last week she did! She acquired a booth for one month to test the waters. Last week she sold thirty-seven birdhouses. This past weekend she got a bad cold and couldn't go to the market, so she asked me if I'd watch the booth. I was wondering if you'd like to join me for a couple of days. We can catch up and have some good seafood for lunch and maybe even sell a birdhouse here and there."

Max thought and then answered, "I don't know how much help I'd be. My knowledge of birds and birdhouses is pretty limited. We have two feeders, but no actual birdhouses in our backyard in Summerville. My mother keeps the feeders filled up daily. She goes through a twenty-pound bag of bird food a week. Tell you what. I like the City Market. I haven't been there in quite some time. I think I'll take you up on your offer." Jokingly, he asked, "When do I start?"

"Tomorrow morning. The market opens up at nine-thirty. I'll have to be there about a half hour early to get unloaded and then set up the booth. I'm in Building Two, you can show up early and help me unload or you can just drop by later in the day."

"I'll be there at nine, and then later on lunch will be on me."

"Okay, sounds great! Gotta run. See you tomorrow morning in Charleston."

Max placed his phone back in his pocket and decided to check the cages again. The first was empty but the second rendered his first catch of the day. Checking to make sure the crab was not a female; he wrapped the live pincered shellfish in a damp paper towel and placed it in the cooler.

In just the first hour on the marsh deck, it seemed like the heat had risen ten to fifteen degrees. Drinking his second bottle of water he thought about his father who had just returned from his yearly trip to Gettysburg for the annual reenactment. This was the first time in the past twelve years he had not attended the popular Civil War activities in Gettysburg with his father. He felt bad for not tagging along on the traditional trip but going along with his father to Gettysburg just didn't have the same excitement it held in the past. His father told him he understood. After all, Max had just completed his first year of college at Gettysburg starting last August and extending through mid-May. Since attending school, he had biked or driven his Jeep over to the numerous Civil War battlefield locations every week. It wasn't so much he had grown tired of the battlefield but rather the thought of returning to the community where he had just spent eight months. The coming month of August was soon enough for him to return to Gettysburg, he didn't need to go over his summer vacation. It was now July 16th and his father had returned from his week of Civil War activities in Pennsylvania, ready to return to his everyday life of running Miller Construction Company.

By ten o'clock it was sweltering out on the marsh. Max stood and stretched as he checked the cages again. *Nothing!* During the last hour and a half, he managed to catch a total of four crabs. Lowering the cages back down he decided to spend another hour on the deck and then wrap things up. He had promised his mother that he would help her clean out the garage on Fripp. A voice from behind him was startling, "Good morning there!"

Looking up, he was face to face with a local park ranger. Returning the greeting Max spoke in a friendly tone, "Good morning to you as well. Looks like it's going to be a hot one today."

The ranger walked to the edge of the deck, removed her wide-brimmed hat, and looked down over the side. Seeing the two dangling ropes she asked, "Just the two traps?"

"Yes, Ma'am…just the two. I know the law. More than two cages and you then have to have a license."

"That's correct, son." Walking to the other end of the deck she wiped her forehead with a handkerchief. "Haven't I seen you here crabbing before?"

"You probably have. I normally come with my father. We haven't been over here to the Walk for let's see, I guess it was late last summer. You see, I've been away to college up north."

Not desiring any further conversation, the female officer placed the hat back over her short hair and bid him a good day. Watching her disappear up the path, he turned his attention back to the cages. He'd give it another hour and then it was back to Fripp.

Wednesday morning, he was on the road by six-thirty armed with an Egg McMuffin and a large orange juice. He was looking forward to a day at the market with Kelly. It was going to be a nice break from riding around Fripp in the family golf cart or walking on the beach. In just a little over a month and a half, he would be in his Jeep once again, the difference being that he would not be heading for a day in Charleston but making the twelve-hour trip back to Pennsylvania. Taking a bite of his breakfast sandwich he thought about how the summer was passing by way too quickly.

He pulled into a parking lot one block down from the market on Meeting Street, paid the attendant for the entire day, and then walked up the street. It was going to be another hot day, similar to his previous morning at the Marsh Walk. It was only a matter of a few minutes when he passed Building One and entered the second building. The long open-air structure was already bustling with vendors on both sides of the aisle stocking their goods and wares for the upcoming day of selling. It was the height of the tourists' season and Max knew from going to the market during the summer that it was going to be busy. Three-quarters of the way into the building he saw Kelly arranging several birdhouses on an eight-foot counter. Approaching, he raised his hands and spoke with an air of excitement, "How goes it this beautiful Charleston morning?"

Kelly wiped her brow. "I'm already sweating, and I've only been here for a half hour."

Inside the eight-by-ten kiosk, Max inquired, "Is there anything else you need to bring from your car?"

Inspecting the counter, Kelly placed her hands on her slim hips and replied, "No I think that's everything. I just have to get my register and credit card machine set up and we'll be ready, set, go."

Max looked out the open backside of the booth at the street and commented, "I can't believe how many people are out already walking around. So, tell me about your birdhouses?"

Seated in a folding chair, Kelly explained, "We have three different sizes. I guess to keep it simple you could call them small, medium, and then large. My mother constructs them from old skids she gets from various businesses. She then cuts the floor, roof, and sides from the skid boards, cuts the hole in the front then carefully places small shingles on the roof that she gets from a local hobby store. She then hand paints on both sides varied short, positive messages. She even has a few biblical verses on some of the houses. The small ones go for $29.95, the medium, ones $39.95, and the large ones for ten dollars more. The medium is the most popular. Our first week we took in just a little under thirteen hundred dollars. That's pretty good when you consider the booth rent for an entire month is only twelve hundred. It's pretty good money when you figure she has somewhere between five to seven dollars in each house. We only have about forty on hand right now so even though she is sick she's trying to make more out in our garage which has been turned into a small manufacturing area."

Max sat next to her, picked up one of the small houses, and silently read the painted message on the right side, *The sound of birds stops the noise in my mind!* Nodding in agreement he picked up another and read out loud, "Take someone under your wing!" Max grinned, "I might just have to buy one of these for my mother."

Kelly looked up and down the wide aisle as customers were already starting to file into the building. "The market doesn't officially open until nine-thirty, but if a customer wants to purchase before opening we are allowed to accommodate them. It doesn't get all that busy until around ten-thirty then it's crazy up to closing time." Smoothing out her long-flowered dress she crossed her legs and asked, "And how are things going with Elizabeth?"

Max hadn't planned on talking about Elizabeth, but Kelly's question seemed innocent enough. "Just talked with her this past Saturday. She still says she can't wait to get back to school to see me."

"And I can only assume you are equally enthused about seeing her again."

"I am excited about seeing her, but in the back of my mind, I really can't see our relationship going any further than two young people who think they may be in love with absolutely no chance of ever getting married. The worlds we come from are just too far apart. The more I think about our situation the more I realize it probably would be better if she married one of her kind."

"You mean like this Simon Baumer, you told me about."

"Possibly, but I don't think she'll marry Baumer because she loves the man. She may wind up marrying him due to the pressure being placed on her by her family and the community she lives in." Realizing he was rambling, he stopped himself. "Let's talk about something else. I'll have plenty of time to figure all that out when I go back to school."

Kelly snapped her fingers and started a new conversation. "Yesterday when my father got home from work, he told my mother he had won some sort of a raffle at his office. The winning prize is four passes to Fort Sumter right here in Charleston. He thought maybe this coming Sunday he'd take Mom and me over there on the excursion they offer. That left us with one available pass. Knowing how interested you are in the Civil War I suggested we invite you along. My father said it sounded like a great idea. So, what do you think? Would you like to go with us this Sunday?"

Max thought and then answered, "That sounds like a great way to spend a Sunday afternoon. Count me in! Have you ever been out there before?"

"No, no one in my family has ever gone out to the fort. I've always heard it's a nice trip."

"It is. I've been out there with my father three or four different times. On one occasion years ago, he conducted a one-day seminar on the history of Fort Sumter. The fort and Charleston itself hold a deep history when it comes to the war. Charleston was a hotbed of turmoil as South Carolina was the first state to secede from the Union. The Charleston Harbor and Fort Sumter were an extremely important seaport for the Confederacy. Before the war the United States had federal troops manning the fortress. This did not sit well with the citizens of Charleston, let alone the newly established Confederacy. The local authorities in Charleston quickly took over all Federal buildings in Charleston. The last bastion of strength to be held by the Federal government was Fort Sumter.

"Confederate Brigadier General P.G.T Beauregard sent a three-man emissary over to the fort demanding that Federal Major Robert Anderson and his troops surrender the fort and leave Charleston Harbor. Anderson refused and this resulted in a thirty-four-hour cannon bombardment of the fort. The first shots fired upon the fort were performed by cadets from the Citadel Military Academy which is still located right here in Charleston. Anderson and his men returned cannon fire, but the fort was not set up for the long artillery battle that ensued. Eventually, Anderson surrendered the fort over to the Confederacy and it was held by southern troops through the entire war until late February of '65 just before the war coming to an end." Realizing that he was going on and on, Max laughed, "I guess I better stop talking or there won't be anything left for the guides over at the fort to talk about."

Kelly was about to respond when she was interrupted by a female voice. "Excuse me but are you the birdhouse lady?"

Noticing a thirty-something-year-old woman and two young girls about ten to eleven years of age, Kelly stood and answered, "You must be referring to my mother. I'm the birdhouse lady's daughter…Kelly Waters. Nice to meet you."

The woman went on to introduce herself and the girls. "I'm Lori Tyler and these are my daughters, Liz, and Bethany. We're from Pennsylvania. The reason why I stopped by is because we have some close friends of ours who live in Binghamton, New York. Just last week they were down here in Charleston on vacation. On their way back home, they stopped in Pennsylvania to visit us. She showed me this lovely birdhouse she bought at the City Market here in Charleston. She knew I had been looking for a birdhouse and since we were going to be on vacation here in Charleston this week, she suggested we drop by and check out what you have to offer. I just fell in love with the one she purchased, and I see you have some here that are similar."

Kelly displayed the houses with a slight wave of her hand. "Yes, we have three different sizes. The prices are marked on each house."

The woman turned to her daughters and spoke, "Why don't you each pick one out, and then when we get home, we can hang them in our big tree out back."

The girls remained silent as they moved down the counter and started to examine the wood houses.

Curious, Max inquired, "You say you're from Pennsylvania. Whereabouts? The reason I ask is because Kelly and I just this past May finished our first year of College in Gettysburg."

The woman lit up as she answered, "My husband took the girls and me to Gettysburg for a long weekend last summer. It was quite enjoyable touring all the battle sites and going to the different museums. Gettysburg isn't that far from where we live over in Lancaster."

Now it was Max who seemed to become excited, "Lancaster! I have another friend who I met this past year who is from Lancaster. She's a Mennonite girl and she lives near East Petersburg. Her last name is King. I don't suppose you've heard of her family?"

"The name doesn't sound familiar. We live on the west side of Lancaster and besides that, we don't live near the Amish or Mennonite population. Have you ever been to Lancaster?"

"Just once. I stayed overnight near the East Petersburg exit. I was just there for a few hours. I did get to go to Roots Framers Market. Are you familiar with that?"

"Everyone in Lancaster knows about Roots. We go out there I'd say at least once a month. They always have such great produce, and we normally pick up a few dozen eggs. I also buy local honey there."

Tugging on her mother's sleeve one of her daughters held up a birdhouse while motioning at her sister who also displayed her choice. "We've picked out the two we like."

The woman opened her purse and asked, "How much for the two?"

Kelly gave her the price and taking the woman's card, she completed the transaction. The woman placed both houses on the counter and asked, "If you could just wrap these up for me and put them off to the side? I've still got some shopping to do. We'll be back in about an hour. Thank you!"

Max watched the woman, and her daughters walk off. "Well, that was easy. The market is not even officially open, and you've made a sale. If this keeps up, you're going to be out of stock in the next couple of days."

"I know. Over the past two days, my mother has made twelve new houses. I'll bring those along with me tomorrow."

Max placed two Styrofoam to-go boxes on the rear counter of the kiosk while looking out at the drizzling rain. "It doesn't look like it's going to be a very profitable day what with the overcast sky and the rain. It's now twelve-thirty and we haven't sold one birdhouse."

"That's okay," said Kelly. "Between Wednesday and Thursday, we sold thirty-five houses and since we opened for business last week we took in a little over three thousand dollars."

Max opened his box of lunch and did some quick math in his head. "When you consider the booth rent for the month is twelve hundred you and your mother have already made a sixteen-hundred-dollar profit minus the cost of the product."

Kelly added, "And we still have two weeks left on our contract for the booth." Surveying the counter, she pointed out, "We've only got thirteen houses left. I hope my mother can make enough to get me through tomorrow. Speaking of Saturday will you be joining me here at the market?"

"I'd love to, but I can't. I promised my father we would do some fishing tomorrow. Looks like you're on your own Saturday."

"Not really," said Kelly. "My mother is feeling much better and said she was coming tomorrow. You're still planning on coming with us on Sunday for the Fort Sumter trip…right?"

Max stabbed a piece of shrimp with a plastic fork and nodded, "Yep,

I'll be there. I'm looking forward to Sunday." Stuffing the bite of seafood in the side of his mouth he went on, "I love the seafood salad from Poogan's Porch. It's one of my favorite meals whenever I get an opportunity to come over here to Charleston."

Kelly opened her lunch and looked out at the wet street. "If this rain keeps up I think we'll probably blank out for the day."

The hours passed and the slow, steady light rain continued. Max loaded the last birdhouse on Kelly's cart and checked the time. "It's just after ten. Most of the other vendors have left. Are you sure you don't need any help loading up your car?"

"No, I'll be fine. Listen…drive safe and I'll see you on Sunday."

Doing some quick math, Max responded, "That's right, you said your father plans to leave on the one o'clock excursion over to the fort. I'll meet you and your family in front of the Fort Sumter Museum about twelve-thirty which means we'll be meeting up in about thirty-eight and a half hours from right now."

Kelly gave Max a sloppy salute and laughed, "See you then. Enjoy your day of fishing with your father."

Max watched as she walked out the end of the building and up the street in the rain. He walked out the other end of the building and started up the street in the opposite direction.

One block up he made a left and then a right where he had parked the Jeep on a side street. The rain was starting to pick up as he ventured down the dimly lit street. There was not a soul in sight, the unpleasant weather driving the tourists and locals into the nearby pubs and taverns. Just as he approached the Jeep he watched as a couple ran across the street and entered a brick-fronted building with a flashing red light: *Reds Bar and Grill.*

He extracted the keys from his pants pocket and was about to unlock the door when he was pushed from behind, his chest slamming against the driver's side window, his chin colliding with the upper door molding. Before he could react, he was jerked backward by his shirt collar and spun around. He managed a quick look at a man in a black ski mask when the man's gloved, clenched fist connected violently with his nose. His head was driven to the left from the force of the blow, as blood splattered across his left cheek and into his open mouth. His eyes began to glaze over, and he felt as if his knees were going to buckle. Another man, also in a black mask ordered the first man, "Get him down on the ground! We have to be out of here in the next few seconds!"

Max's legs were pulled out from beneath him causing him to slide down the side of the Jeep, Still dazed, he looked up into the covered faces, the only thing he could barely see were two sets of dark eyes. The second man stretched out his right arm and stepped on his hand while the first, shorter man produced a baseball bat that he savagely slammed down on his arm just below the elbow. Max could feel the nauseating crunch of breaking bones as he was pulled by his feet out into the street where the first man kicked him hard in the side four consecutive times. The second man ordered the first, "Get his keys…I'll get the wallet!"

The second man rifled through his pants pocket taking out Max's wallet, which he opened and removed the cash inside. Next, he threw the wallet in Max's face climbed in the Jeep, and started the vehicle. The other man kicked Max one last time and sarcastically remarked, "Have a nice day… pal!" He ran around the other side of the Jeep and hopped in the passenger side door. Max lay on his stomach in the middle of the street and watched the Jeep's taillights disappear up the street in the rain.

Slowly and painfully, he rolled over onto his back and stared up into the falling rain. He took a deep breath and winced from the pain emanating from his rib cage. He tried to move his right arm, but it just lay on the pavement like a broken rag doll. With his left hand, he reached up and touched his throbbing nose. The mixture of blood and rain ran down his throat as he coughed which caused even more pain from his rib area. Fearing that he might get run over by some non-focused tourist he decided to try and crawl out of the street to the curb a few feet away.

Mustering up all the strength he could he managed to crawl a few inches then collapsed back to the wet pavement. At this pathetic rate of forward movement, it would take him who knew how long to reach the curb. Suddenly a set of vehicle lights appeared at the end of the street. As the vehicle approached Max knew there was a possibility that he might get driven over. Painfully, he raised his left arm and tried to motion for the vehicle to stop. The lights flooded over him and then the car stopped two feet from where he lay. A couple, a young man and a woman, jumped out and ran to his side as the girl couldn't believe what she was seeing. "I can't believe it. Someone lying right in the street!"

The man kneeling on Max's right agreed, "I can't believe it myself. If you wouldn't have yelled at the last second, I'd have run over him!" Leaning down he spoke softly, "Are you okay mister?"

The woman on Max's left scolded the man. "What are you…stupid? It's plain to see this man is injured. Blood on his face and his arm. Com'n we have to get him out of the street."

Max objected as best he could, "No…don't try…to….move me. I think…I have …some busted…ribs. Call…an ambulance."

The girl removed a cell phone from her jean jacket and dialed 911. Within seconds she was speaking to someone, "We need an ambulance. An injured man is lying in the street. Where are we? That's a good question."

The man looked up and down the street and shrugged his shoulders, "Somewhere in Charleston."

With his left hand, Max signaled for the man to lean down close to him. "We are…one block down…from the…City Market…on a side street… just off…Meeting Street. Tell them…to look for…Reds…Bar and Grill." Exhausted from speaking Max watched as the man related the information to his female friend.

Both at his side, the girl explained, "They said they'd be here in about seven to eight minutes. Can we get you anything? Is there anything we can do?"

Max reluctantly took a deep breath and winced from the pain as he wiped at his eyes. "Do you…have anything…to clean…my face?"

"Yes," said the girl. "We have a box of tissues in the car. Be right back."

During the girl's short absence, the man asked Max. "What happened to you buddy?"

Max, finding it difficult to speak, waved off the man's question with his left hand.

The woman returned with the tissues and started to dab at his face. Suddenly, Max remembered as he pointed at the middle of the street. "My wallet…is in the street?"

The man turned and seeing the wallet answered, "Yeah. I see it. Just let me get it."

Seconds later he placed the wallet in Max's left hand.

Max, gaining control of his ability to speak in complete sentences spoke up, "They beat me, took my money and my Jeep."

The woman responded, "I'm so sorry. It's a good thing we happened by. I'd offer you something to drink but the only thing we have in our car is beer."

"That's all right. I'm not very thirsty." Turning his head to the side he spit blood and then coughed twice as he twisted his face in pain.

The woman wiped his face again. "They should be here anytime now. Just try and relax."

For the next couple of minutes, there was silence between Max and the concerned couple. A siren sounded in the distance and the man shook his head in confidence. "I bet that's them. You'll be on your way to the hospital before you know it."

Max closed his eyes while the rain continued to fall on his face. His mind was racing with so many thoughts. At this time of night Elizabeth was probably getting ready to turn in for the evening, Kelly was on her way back to Walterboro and his parents were more than likely sitting out on the deck of their Fripp Island home enjoying an evening drink. He had to call his parents and let them know what happened. Then he thought, *My cell phone! Did those two men take it?* Running his left hand down the side of his wet jeans he felt the square device in his pocket. The first chance he got he'd give them a call.

The siren grew louder but then faded to a slow drone and then stopped as the ambulance turned onto the street and stopped a few feet away, the red and blue flashing lights reflecting off the wet pavement. Two male paramedics appeared as they knelt on either side of him. The man on his left asked, "What's your name son?"

Max, now more relaxed since help had arrived, responded, "Max... Miller."

The other paramedics inquired, "Where are you from, Max?'

"Summerville."

"What happened to you?"

"I was mugged...robbed. Two men took my money and my Jeep."

"Looks like they beat on you a bit too."

"They did. I think my nose and my right arm might be broken. They kicked me four or maybe five times. My side hurts."

The second paramedic gently turned Max's head and shined a small surgical light in his eyes. "Here's the plan, Max. We're going to get you on a stretcher and then into the ambulance where we'll get you stabilized with some pain meds, then we'll be off to the hospital. We should be there in about ten minutes or so. We're going to take you to the ER, just so you know. You could experience some pain when we put you on the stretcher but as soon as we get you loaded up and administer some pain medicine, you'll won't feel a thing. Are you ready?"

Max gritted his teeth and remarked confidently, "Yeah…let's go!"

The pain from being lifted onto the stretcher caused his entire body to shake for a moment, but once he was on the stretcher he took a deep breath, winced from the nagging pain in his side, and then lied. "That wasn't all that bad."

Once inside the ambulance, he seemed to be more relaxed while the paramedic gave him a shot and then wiped his face with a cool alcohol-soaked cloth. "Just try and relax. By the time we get to the hospital, you should be out like a light. The next time you wake up you'll be in a comfortable room. Is there anyone you would like us to contact?"

"Yes, my parents. They are over on Fripp Island. It'll take them a couple of hours to get here."

The paramedic removed a cell from his jacket pocket and spoke, "Give me the number."

CHAPTER NINETEEN

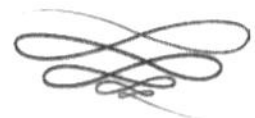

Max rolled his head to the right, opened his eyes, and stared at a six-foot row of bleary floor-to-ceiling gleaming white cabinets topped with a stainless steel countertop where there was a small plastic tray, some sort of bottle, a hypodermic needle, plastic gloves, and a package of small gauze bandages. Not completely coherent, he shook his head gently and squinted to get his eyes in focus. Looking straight ahead he discovered he was in an unusual bed covered with a sheet and a beige blanket. On the wall a few feet from the bottom of the bed there was a chalkboard with two names written in: Your nurses for the day: Julie and Barb. To the left, he saw a high metal stand that housed what appeared to be some sort of computer to which was attached three wires running to a receptacle in the wall, a tube attached to a suspended saline bag that was inserted into his left wrist. Finally, his mind was clear. He was in the hospital!

A door to the right of the monitor opened and a nurse entered. Seeing Max awake she smiled pleasantly. "Good morning, Mr. Miller. My name is Julie and I'm one of your attending nurses for the day. The night nurse told me they brought you in last evening." She approached the side of the bed, and with the aid of a digital thermometer took his temperature. "It's time to check your vitals."

She raised the bed slightly as she continued to speak. "We've been keeping tabs on you every hour on the hour. This is the first time I believe you've been awake since they brought you in." Checking a chart hanging on the wall she explained, "According to this, Doctor Wells will be coming in to see you sometime this morning. Oh yeah, your parents are here. I think they went down to the cafeteria for breakfast. They've been here all night. Your temp is good. Now give me your left arm and we'll get your current blood pressure." Placing the pressure cuff on his arm she began to pump, the cuff gradually getting tight on his upper arm. She released the pressure and read the numbers; "One twenty over eighty…perfect! How are you feeling?"

"Well, right now I'm not in any pain but I'm sure that's because of the drugs they gave me."

The nurse checked the monitor, and the saline bag then made some notes on his chart as she suggested. "There is a menu on your side table there if you want to order breakfast. Barb or I will be back to check on you in an hour. In the meantime, if you require anything just press the red button on the side of the bed. Try and get some rest."

Max watched as Julie exited the room, the door closing behind her, only to be opened again as his mother trailed by his father entered. His mother, seeing he was awake laid her coffee on a nightstand and walked to the edge of the bed while she spoke with great concern, "Max…how are you feeling?"

Before he could respond his father walked around to the other side of the bed shaking his head in amazement. "We got here right after midnight last night. They told us you had been found lying in the street in Charleston. We haven't been able to find out exactly what happened. So, what happened?"

Max was about to start his explanation of the previous night's attack when the door opened again, and two Charleston Police Officers entered. The officer in the lead apologized, "I'm sorry for the intrusion. Some officers were here last night to make out a report on your incident but you were out like a light. If you're up to speaking with us we'd like to get the information on what went down last evening."

Max moved slightly to his left to get more comfortable. "I was just about to tell my parents what happened. I'm glad you're here because now I won't have to repeat myself later on."

The other officer withdrew a pad and ink pen from his perfectly pressed uniform as he spoke, "We'll be taking some notes, and then based on what we find out we'll submit our report. Let's start with your full name."

"Max Miller."

"And where do you reside Mr. Miller?"

"We live in Summerville. By *we*, I mean not only myself but my parents."

"And I assume these folks are your parents?"

"That's correct," said Max's father as he introduced himself and the Mrs. "I'm Charley Miller and this is my wife, Kate."

The officer stood closer to the side of the bed and instructed, "Max, why don't you tell us what happened last evening."

"Well, everything happened so fast. I didn't have much time to take in a lot of detail. I had just left the City Market over on Meeting Street and as I was getting ready to unlock my Jeep I was pushed from behind. Then, I was pulled backward, spun around, and then I was hit in the face." With his left hand, he pointed at his bandaged nose. "I remember looking briefly at the man who hit me. He was short, I think muscular, and oh yeah, he was dressed in all black, including a black ski mask. He just hit me the one time. I felt like my nose exploded and I also felt like I was going to pass out. The next thing I know my legs are swept from beneath me and I'm on the ground next to my Jeep. When I hit the ground my focus, what there was of it was centered on my face which at the moment was throbbing. I remember the taste of blood in my mouth. The throbbing in my face was quickly replaced with the searing pain as the man who hit me went about breaking my right arm with, I believe it was a baseball bat. Next, the man kicked me in my right side three or four times, then they took my wallet and I guess my car keys because they drove off in the Jeep. Oh, and one other thing. The short man kicked me one last time before they hopped in the Jeep and drove off."

While the officer was busy jotting down information the first officer asked, "Aside from the fact both of your attackers were dressed in black, can you describe anything else about their appearance?"

"No, aside from the fact one was taller than the other, I have no idea of what they look like. Just two, I assume men dressed in black."

"Did they say anything to you during the attack?"

"Yes, they did. Well, let me rephrase that. The taller of the two did all of the talking. The one who was beating me never said a word. The first thing that was said happened just before I was pulled down to the street. He said something about getting me down on the ground because they had to be out of there in the next few seconds. After the first man broke my arm, I remember the other man saying, 'Get his keys…I'll get the wallet!' The last thing that was said was once again by the tall man. He threw my wallet toward my face and said, 'Have a nice day…pal!' Then they drove off up the street." Sarcastically Max smirked, "And that gentleman pretty well sums up my evening of adventure."

The officer closed the pad and placed the pen back in his uniform shirt pocket. "Sounds to me like one of two things happened. We've had quite a few carjackings this summer here in Charleston. The other possibility appears to be that they wanted cash."

The other officer interjected, "What my partner says is true but there seems to be something strange about this attack. If they just wanted your vehicle, then why would they bother breaking your arm and then kicking you? You were already on the ground. It seems like overkill to me. On the other hand, if they just wanted money, why would they take the time to apprehend your vehicle? It sounds like the two crimes are somehow related."

Charley added, "It does seem strange, doesn't it? It almost sounds too professional for a typical street mugging or carjacking."

The door suddenly opened and a man wearing a white smock was followed by Julie. Smiling, he introduced himself. "Good morning, everyone. I'm Doctor Wells." Looking at Max's parents and the officers, he suggested, "I can come back in a few minutes when the police are finished."

One of the officers offered, "No that's fine. We were just in the process of wrapping things up here." Handing Charley, a business card, the officer explained, "If your son happens to remember anything else please feel free to give us a call. We'll put out an APB on your vehicle. If your vehicle was stolen by a theft ring, then more than likely you'll never see it again. It will be taken out of state, used for parts, or repainted and sold at an auction to someone who has no idea the vehicle was stolen. If the incident, you went through was simply for the money we'll probably find your car on some side street or abandoned road out in the country. Either way, it's not pleasant. Thank you for your time and we hope you get to feeling better."

The officers filed out of the room and the nurse handed the doctor Max's chart. Sitting on a chair next to the bed the doctor stated professionally, "We gave you a quick going over last night when they brought you in. Based on what we discovered and the information you shared with the paramedics you have suffered damage to three areas of your body. I have seen many a broken nose over my years in practice. Yours is not the worst I've seen but it still appears pretty bad. Your right arm is broken, and you've probably received some damage to your rib cage. We won't know how serious these injuries are until we get a series of CAT scans and X-rays, which we will be getting from you later today. Once we have that vital information then we'll know what direction to go. Do you have any questions for me?"

"Yes, two. How long do you think I'll be here at the hospital and how long will it take me to heal up…ya know get back to normal?"

"Depending on the seriousness of your injuries it could be as long as three days, maybe four before you are released. At this time, I cannot give you an estimated time for a complete return to normalcy. We'll have to wait and see what the tests reveal. Before I leave is there anything else we can do for you at the moment?"

"As a matter of fact…there is. I haven't had anything to eat since yesterday for lunch. I was going to order but between visits with you and the police I haven't had the chance to call it in."

The doctor turned to the nurse and suggested, "If you'll just tell Julie here what you want she can get that ordered for you. Try and get some rest. We'll be conducting the tests this afternoon."

The doctor left the room as Julie picked up the hospital menu, asking, "And what did you want for breakfast?"

Charley stood and announced. "If it's all right with you, Max, I think your mother and I will head back over to Fripp, pack up, and then drive back to Summerville. That way it will be easier for us to visit. By the time we get back home tonight, it might be too late to drop by. We probably won't see you until tomorrow morning. Are you sure you'll be okay?"

"Look, I'll be fine. I'll eat my breakfast then I have to call Kelly and Elizabeth and let them know what happened."

Charley winked at his son and gave him a thumbs up, "I told you juggling more than one woman could be difficult."

Max waved off his father's attempt at wisdom. "Right now, Kelly and Elizabeth are the least of my problems."

He swallowed the last portion of his eggs, took a bite of toast, and washed it down with two long swigs of orange juice. Max checked the time on the wall clock: 10:15. He needed to get the phone calls he needed to make out of the way as the doctor had told him they would be taking him for tests sometime after twelve. Picking up his cell phone from the tray at the side of his bed he looked at the square device thankful his assailants had not commandeered his phone. Pulling up his contact list he punched in Kelly's name and waited. On the fifth ring, he heard her friendly voice, "Hello this is Kelly."

Max cleared his throat and then responded, "Hey Kelly…it's Max. I know you're at the market and I don't want to hold you up for long, but I have some bad news to share with you. After we parted ways last night, I was attacked by what the police are saying may have been two muggers who robbed me not only of the cash I was carrying but took my Jeep as well. They beat me up pretty bad and I am currently in the hospital. Looks like I'm going to be in here for a few days, so I won't be tagging along with you and your family tomorrow over to Fort Sumter."

Kelly's tone changed from her normally perky demeanor to one of great concern as she spewed out a series of questions, "Are you all right? Is there anything I can do? What hospital are you at? Can you have visitors?"

Max answered her questions in order. "This afternoon I have to undergo a series of tests to determine what action needs to be taken to put me back together. Right now, I'm feeling all right but that's probably due to the drugs they keep pumping into me. There isn't anything you can do or that I need. I'm at MUSC-Health University Medical Hospital here in Charleston. And, yes I can have visitors but it probably would be a good idea to hold off until this evening what with the tests and all."

Kelly followed up with two more questions. "What is your room number? When you say *beat up pretty bad,* what exactly does that mean?"

"My room number is 407 and my injuries at this point are a broken nose and right arm and they did some damage to my ribs. Please tell your father I appreciate the invite over to the fort. Try and sell a lot of birdhouses today and enjoy your trip tomorrow. Listen, I have to hang up. One of the nurses just came in. I guess I'll see you later this evening."

Julie picked up the digital thermometer and asked, "How was your breakfast?"

"Fine," said Max. "Time for another vitals check, huh?"

Julie approached the bed. "Hour on the hour!"

Minutes later, writing down some notes on his chart she reassured Max. "All in all, you seem to be holding up rather well. In a couple of hours, it'll be lunch and you get to savor another round of our wonderful hospital food."

Max realized she was joking about the quality of the food available. He laughed and commented, "Not exactly four stars is it!"

She placed the blood pressure cuff on his left arm and commented, "Let's get your blood pressure."

Julie no sooner left his room when Max decided to call Elizabeth. Picking up his cell phone he hesitated. Calling Kelly had been relatively easy, but not so with Elizabeth. As it stood right now and ever since she had gone back home, they had talked every Wednesday and Saturday like clockwork. But the thing was, she had always initiated the calls even though she, had no cell phone she had to use her friend, Ellen's phone. Elizabeth had given him Ellen's number in case he ever needed to call her aside from their scheduled weekly calls. He was beginning to think his father was right. A relationship with Kelly, someone from his world would be a lot easier to navigate. However, with Elizabeth, everything had to be kept a secret. He thought about not even contacting her and waiting until she called him later in the day but thought better of it. If Elizabeth found out he was in the hospital and hadn't called to tell her so, she would probably be upset. Punching in Elizabeth's name he listened to the low buzzing in his phone.

A female voice, a strange female voice answered as if she were hesitant, not expecting a call, "Hello…who is this?"

"This is Max…Max Miller…Elizabeth's friend from college. She gave me your number and said if I ever needed to contact her to just give you a call and then you would get hold of her to call me."

Ellen's voice took on a tone of excitement. "Max, I can't believe I'm getting to talk to you. Elizabeth has shared with me everything about the secret relationship you two have. We've talked about you so many times I feel as if I know you. I know you two talk every Wednesday and Saturday. That's right…today is Saturday. She'll be calling you around six o'clock tonight. Is there is a problem, why you are calling her?"

"Yes, there is a bit of a problem. She can call me at the regular time, but I might not be able to answer. I'm in the hospital down here in South Carolina. I have to go through a lot of tests today and I don't know when I'll be available to talk on the phone. I don't have the time to go into what happened right now, so when she calls if I don't answer tell her to leave a message."

"All right, I'll get your message to her. Listen, I'm in my kitchen and I see my husband coming up the walk. If he catches me on the phone, he'll want to know who I am talking to. It would be awkward. I'm hanging up now!"

Max stared at his phone which suddenly went dead. Tossing his cell on the bed he thought about how ridiculous all the secrecy about his relationship with Elizabeth was. Suddenly, his phone buzzed. Picking it up he thought, *That can't be Elizabeth!* Curious, he answered, "Hello."

"Max, it's Dad. Feeling any better?"

"No, about the same...what's up?"

"I contacted Rich Mathers about the attack. He'd like to come by with your mother and me tonight when we stop by for a visit. He has something important he'd like to go over with you. I don't have time to get into what it's about right now. It's too complicated to discuss over the phone. Did they schedule your tests yet?"

Max was about to answer when Julie and a white-clad hospital worker entered his room. Seeing he was on the phone, Julie approached the bed and whispered, "Time for your first test."

"Gotta go, Dad," said Max. "They just came for me. I guess I'll see you tonight."

Max laid his cell on the stand next to the bed and asked, "So how does all this work?"

"You don't have to do anything except enjoy the ride." Motioning at the attendant Julie explained, "This is Jerry. He is going to be wheeling you in your bed down to the next floor for some X-rays. You should be back here about one thirty or so, then you can order your lunch and then later this afternoon you'll be wheeled out of here for a CAT scan. They probably won't have the test results until late afternoon. Depending on how rapidly the results come back you may get to see Doctor Wells later today or he might wait until tomorrow morning. Anyway, things are moving right along. Are you ready for your short journey?

Max raised his left arm. "Lead the way!"

He was running across a vast weed-covered field. He was wearing his grey Confederate re-enactment uniform. His old canteen banged against his right leg as he approached a long line of fencing. There were soldiers from the Southern army on his right and left. The air was filled with smoke and the sound of both cannon and musket fire. Then he heard someone order, "Over the fence boys!

Quickly!" Climbing up the three rails he looked and in the distance, he saw the Union army entrenched behind a low stone wall. But rather than the traditional blue uniform the enemy was wearing black, including black ski masks. The soldier on his left fell from the fence, his face covered in blood. Four soldiers on his right were blown off the fence from the blast from a cannon. He, himself was thrown into the air as he landed on one of his dead comrades. He felt dizzy. He tried to get to his feet but then he discovered that his right arm was broken, and his face and rib areas were pulsing with extreme pain. Then, he screamed, "I'm not going to make it...I'm not going to make it!"

A soft hand on his left shoulder was shaking him gently. "Max...wake up. You're having a bad dream."

He suddenly opened his eyes and looked up into Julie's friendly face as he tried to sit up. "Get down Julie! You'll be shot!"

It was then that he felt a cool washcloth caress his forehead and right side of his face. Coming to his senses, he asked, "I was at Pickett's Charge in Gettysburg. I made it to the fence but that's where I was stopped. What time is it?"

"It's just after five. They brought you back from all your tests around one. You were so tired you decided you wanted to sleep rather than have lunch. I have to check your vitals and then you probably need to order your dinner. You also have three visitors waiting out in the hall to see you, your parents and another man. I told them they could come in as soon as I finished up. Are you okay now? Are you fully awake?"

"I'm fine...I guess it was just a bad dream. It seemed so real. I was lying in a field covered in blood. I was in the Civil War...at Gettysburg. As much as I dislike being here in the hospital this room is a much better place than lying next to that damn fence with all the screaming and bloodshed." Realizing he was rambling he held up his left arm and announced, "Let the vitals checking routine begin!"

Julie removed the blood pressure cuff from his arm as she asked, "Have you decided on what you want for dinner?"

"You must be reading my mind," said Max. "I have examined the menu and I think I'd like to have a go at that roast beef and mashed potatoes with a side of green beans. I think I'll add *Jello* and a piece of carrot cake for dessert. Iced tea will be fine."

She hung up his chart and gave him a thumbs up. "I'll get that dinner called in. It should be delivered from the kitchen in about an hour." Walking to the door, she asked, "Are you ready to accept your visitors?"

Max laid his head back on the pillow and confirmed, "Yes, yes I am."

She opened the door, signaled down the hall, and spoke in a jovial manner, "Okay, the patient awaits!"

His mother was the first in the room, followed by his father and then Rich brought up the rear. Charley and Rich took seats next to the large window that overlooked the hospital grounds below while Max's mother walked to the bed and placed her right hand on his shoulder. "How did all the tests go?"

"I think they went fine," said Max. "The doctor told me he will either have the results later this evening or possibly tomorrow morning." Turning his curious attention to Rich, Max spoke, "Dad informed me you were coming along this evening and you had something important to talk about. So, what's up?"

Rich looked at Charley and Kate in wonder, shook his head in amazement, and then replied, "Your father told me all about the attack, and I, for one cannot believe you haven't mentioned one thing about Brad Sykes. I mean, think about it. It seems strange to me the first thought that should have entered your mind after getting punched directly in the nose would have been centered on Brad. Have you forgotten that you broke his nose eight months ago and just barely dodged getting sued? Have you forgotten that letter he left beneath your dorm room door stating, *This is far from over!* Have you forgotten his negative reaction at the end of the meeting when his father announced he was dropping the lawsuit? We all agreed it was quite obvious he was out for revenge. Have you not considered that Brad Sykes might be behind this attack?"

Max stared out the window in wonder and then answered, "Actually I haven't given Brad Sykes a thought since, during, or after the attack, well that is until just now when you mentioned him. We talked about how down the road somewhere in the future Brad would try to get his revenge. When nothing occurred during the remainder of the school year, I figured I would be safe this summer. Do you think Brad Sykes would travel down here to Charleston, watch me for a few days until his opportunity came along, and then strike? That just doesn't seem very realistic."

"It does seem unrealistic," said Rich, "but not impossible! Think back to the attack. Could one of the two men have been Brad?"

Max tried to form a mental picture of the two assailants. He looked directly at Rich and stated, "The man who did all of the talking could not have been Brad. He was too tall and on the slender side. I heard his voice very distinctly. His voice was much deeper than Brad's. Now the other man, who never mentioned a single word and inflicted all of the physical damage to me could have been Brad. He was short, and muscular; and had one of those solid fireplug frames similar to what Brad has. Aside from that, it's hard to say. The only feature I saw was the man's eyes and at that, with it being nighttime and rainy they just appeared as dark."

"Let me ask you this," said Rich. "Did the man who broke your nose, and your arm and then kicked the hell out of you seem angry during the attack?"

"No, he didn't display any signs of anger. He was very controlled as if he knew exactly what he wanted to do. The other man gave all the orders and actually, looking back it seemed rather professional for just a couple of muggers or car thieves. I don't think the short man was Brad because his every move was orchestrated by the other man. That action doesn't sound like the Brad Sykes I know. Brad doesn't like to follow orders and likes to do things his way. If he did bring the other man along with him, how it all happened doesn't make sense. I don't think Brad was there."

"How about this then," said Charley. "Do you think there is the possibility Brad could have paid someone else to do his dirty work?"

Rich answered immediately. "That thought has crossed my mind as well. Seeing how he acted at the meeting with his father after the lawsuit was dropped I wouldn't put it past him. He could have paid those men to drive down here, stake you out, and then strike when the opportunity availed itself."

"Excuse me," said Kate, "but this all seems so unreal. Why would this Brad Sykes go to all the trouble to pay someone to do his dirty work as you say?"

"You've never met this boy," explained Charley. Gesturing at Rich and Max, he went on to say, "The three of us have. This is a spoiled, wealthy kid who always seems to run right on the edge of the cliff. According to what we discovered before the meeting with his father and his attorneys, Brad Sykes has a history of getting into trouble because of his attitude toward others. His father has always been there to bail him out. Brad has access to unlimited funds or at least enough to pull off something like what happened to Max. This is just the type of underhandedness I think he is capable of. He gets the satisfaction of getting his revenge and short of paying someone else to do the deed, he is uninvolved."

Kate got a look of frustration on her face as she inquired, "During my life as a mother I have asked both my husband and my son a lot of questions, but I never thought a time would come when I would ask this. When you say Brad could have paid to have Max beaten, what would something like that cost?"

Rich was quick with a response. "If he hired some local friends from up where he's from he could have gotten by with paying them a couple of grand. If this was done by professionals, they wouldn't touch a job like this for less than ten to fifteen thousand and that's chump change to a rich kid like Sykes."

Max held up his left hand to ask a question. "Let's just assume for the moment that Brad was involved, whether it be his presence during the attack or his hiring someone to exact his revenge. How would we, or can we even prove any of this?"

Rich agreed, "Short of someone coming forward and admitting Brad was present during the attack or that he paid someone to assault you, there is nothing we can do that will amount to anything. I think the first thing we need to do is find out where Brad Sykes was on Friday, July 18th. I'm going to send my detective friend up to Ithaca, New York where Brad lives. With any luck, he might be able to find out Brad's whereabouts at the time of the attack. To be honest with you without any solid proof you might just have to move on and forget the whole matter."

Their conversation was interrupted when Doctor Wells entered the room and smiled as he looked at Max's visitors. "The last time I was here your parents were here with the police. Now, I see they have returned but this time with another friend of yours I assume."

Max made the introduction. "Doctor Wells, this is Rich Mathers, a close friend of our family. Rich works for a law firm here in Charleston."

Shaking Rich's hand the doctor commented, "It's always wise to know a good attorney." Turning to Max he held up a chart he was carrying. "The test results are in, and things are not as bad as we had anticipated. That doesn't mean you're out of the woods because there are several procedures, we need to perform to get you put back together."

Placing the chart on the side table the doctor took a seat next to the bed. "First of all, let's talk about your broken nose." Pointing at his nose he went on to explain. "The tests show that the bones and the cartilage in your nose have been displaced. This can be corrected by a simple procedure that can be performed right here in your room. The nose is a very sensitive area of the body so you will be under when we reposition the interior. It'll take around six to eight weeks for your nose to heal up. For the first few weeks, you'll be on pain medicine, and you'll have to see an ear, nose, and throat specialist that I'll be recommending. When we release you from the hospital, probably two days from now your nose will be bandaged. This bandage will have to be changed daily and can only be removed permanently when the ENT gives you the go-ahead. You can expect the area around your nose and eyes to be discolored for seven to ten days. Even after the six-to-eight-week healing time frame, you must be careful for the next six months or so to not bump your nose or expose it to anything other than normal activity."

The doctor motioned at the chart as he went on, "Now, let's talk about your right arm. There was never any doubt your arm was broken. The X-rays display very clearly that you broke the two main bones in your right forearm. Let me explain." Using himself as a model the doctor pointed at his upper arm. "There are three main bones in the arm. The first and the largest is located in your upper arm. It is called the Humerus bone and is attached to your shoulder socket. From there it runs down and connects with the two main bones in your forearm, the Ulna, and the Radius. The Ulna runs from the elbow down to the tip of your little finger and the Radius goes from the elbow down to the thumb. In your case, both the Ulna and the Radius have been broken. This requires surgery and is normally done on an outpatient basis but since you're already at the hospital we'll perform the surgery here. Repositioning your nose is a simple process and will not take that long, so later tomorrow we'll get in your arm, and using metal plates and screws we'll put your arm back together. Just like the nose, your arm will take around six to eight weeks to heal. During this time your arm will be in a cast supported by an arm sling. Once again, even after your arm is healed up you have to take precautions for the next six months to ensure the arm does not get reinjured."

He pointed at Max's rib cage while holding up three fingers, "Third, we have to repair your ribs that were injured. You have one fractured rib and two bruised ribs. Not that bad. Unless the ribs are severely broken there is no actual surgery required. In your case, the three injured ribs will heal on their own. This is done by following four steps: ice packs, prescribed medications, rest, and most importantly, avoiding a lot of activity. It should take about three to six weeks for the ribs to heal. All of this being said you should be released the day after tomorrow. Any questions?"

Max raised his left hand and spoke. "I do have one major concern and that's just this. I am scheduled to return to college in Pennsylvania in six weeks. With my injuries will that be possible?"

"Yes, I think so. Your nose and your arm will be well on their way to being healed by that time. Your ribs should be healed up by then. However, that being said you still need to be careful what activities you become involved in for the next six months or so. If you take a fall or a hit you could reinjure your nose, arm, or ribs. So, you should be able to return to school... but carefully. I don't see you as having a lot of problems when it comes to healing up. Young people tend to mend more rapidly than us older folks." Standing, the doctor grabbed the chart and started for the door. "With that, I'll leave you to your visitors. See you early tomorrow morning."

It seemed to Max like the door to his room was a revolving door as when Doctor Wells left, the door wasn't even completely shut when in walked Kelly. Upon seeing her both Max's parents became excited, his mother jumping up and giving her a friendly hug. "Kelly! Thank you so much for dropping by." Anxious for Max to spend time with Kelly, Max's mother turned to Charley and Rich and motioned for them to get to their feet, "Gentlemen, I think we should give Max some alone time with Kelly."

Kelly seemed embarrassed. "Don't run off on my account."

Max agreed, "Yeah, what the hell. You don't have to leave."

Charley held up his hand, objecting to Max's remark. "No, your mother is right. You've seen enough of our ugly mugs for the day."

Max's mother hesitated at the door while Charley and Rich filed out. "I'll be back in the morning to spend part of the day with you before and after your surgery. Your father won't be coming along until later in the evening. He has a job he needs to finish up tomorrow."

The door was almost shut when Julie entered carrying his dinner. Displaying a tray with three covered dishes she announced, "Roast beef with all the fixin's."

Kelly apologized, "If I knew it was dinner time I could have waited to come by later."

Max removed the plastic covers from his dinner as he inspected the meal. "Doesn't look that bad." Picking up a fork he asked, "I hope you don't mind if I eat in front of you?"

"No, go right ahead." Seating herself in a chair by the wall Kelly looked around the room. "I can't remember the last time I was in a hospital as a patient or even to visit someone. So, tell me, how did the tests turn out?"

Cutting into the beef, Mas responded, "My nose and right arm are broken just like they figured. They are scheduling two surgeries tomorrow. My ribs have to heal up on their own. According to the doctor I should be released the day after tomorrow. It looks like for the rest of the summer I have to take it easy. I guess I'll be spending a lot of time sitting on the beach. The doctor also said that I could return to school but any extra activities outside of attending my classes are to be very limited."

Kelly squinted her face in a twisted frown, and remarked sarcastically, "We'll, I guess that puts the ol' kibosh on swimming together."

Combining a forkful of green beans with mashed potatoes Max responded, "Even after the cast is removed I may not be able to swim for another six months. I won't be doing any bike riding shortly either. If I happened to have a mishap while riding, I could reinjure my nose, arm, or ribs again. Aside from going to classes, the only other exercise I'll get to experience is walking."

Kelly shrugged. "I'll miss our swimming time together. I could walk around campus with you, but like I've said all along. I don't want to do anything to interfere with your relationship with Elizabeth. By the way, does she know you're here at the hospital?"

"I called her friend, Ellen who told me she would be in contact with Elizabeth and would let her know. Today is Saturday, one of the two days each week we get to talk." Looking at the clock on the wall, Max bit into a buttered roll and remarked, "Normally she calls me around six o'clock. It's five thirty now, so I should be hearing from her in the next half hour."

Kelly smiled at Max. "I have to leave in about twenty minutes, which is just as well. You certainly don't want me hanging around while you're talking to her. Besides, I have to get back home. We only have three birdhouses left and two weeks left on our booth contract. My mother has got me, my father, and two neighbor ladies working like crazy trying to get more houses built before Monday. We canceled the trip over to Fort Sumter. Turns out the tickets are good for the summer, so we can just go later. Who knows, maybe you'll be healed up enough to tag along."

"That would be nice," said Max, "but right now it's hard to imagine getting back to any sense of normalcy."

The time passed quickly while Max went about devouring his dinner in between varied topics he and Kelly shared: the next month and a half of vacation that remained until they returned to school, his upcoming surgeries, his recovery time, and the fact that his Jeep was gone. Checking the time Kelly stood and gestured at the door. "Well, I've got to run along. You'll no doubt be out of this place by the next time we meet up. I hope we can get together and spend some time before all of our vacation is gone. Call me after you get out of here and you're settled in at home. If there is anything you need, or I can do just give me a buzz." Leaning over she gave him a quick peck on the cheek and gave him a wink. "Everything is going to work out."

She no sooner left the room when his cell phone rang. Picking up the device he answered, "Hello!"

The sound of Elizabeth's soft voice was a comfort to him. "Hello... Max. I've only got about ten minutes as Ellen has to get back home. There are so many questions I have for you and so little time. Ellen told me you called and said you were in the hospital. What happened to you?"

"I was attacked by two men in Charleston Friday night. They took my Jeep and the money from my wallet. In the process, they broke my nose and my right arm and gave me a good kicking in the ribs. I have two surgeries scheduled for tomorrow. I should be released the day after tomorrow. The doctor tells me it will be six to eight weeks before I'm healed up and even then I have to take it easy for six months. I'll be able to return to school come August but aside from attending classes any other activity will have to be confined to walking around campus."

"Do they have any idea of who did this to you?"

"No, none at all. The police claim it could have just been a carjacking or a robbery. I was just in the wrong place at the wrong time."

There was a prolonged moment of silence when Max asked, "Did you hear what I said?"

"Yes, I heard. Have you considered that this could have been at the hands of Brad Sykes? When you mentioned your nose got broken Brad was the first thought that entered my mind."

"Don't feel bad. That's the same thing our family attorney said. We talked about it and agreed that as much as Brad dislikes me would he go to the lengths to travel down here to Charleston to get his revenge. That being said, the possibility of Brad being behind the attack has not been completely ruled out just yet. My attorney is sending a detective up to Ithaca, New

York where Brad lives to see if he can find out where Brad was on the evening of the attack. I think it's a dead end, but it can't hurt to check it out. Listen, enough talk of me and my problems. We'll both be back at school in six weeks and our relationship can return to what it was before. We can meet at the fountain, take walks downtown, and eat at some of the cafes we have grown to love. Are you looking forward to going back to Gettysburg?"

"Are you kidding? Of course, I am. I can't wait until I'm back on campus far away from Simon Baumer and his constant courting. You would think by this time he would get the message that I have no intention of marrying up with him. Just last night we had a conversation where he questioned why I even wanted to return to college. He had more than enough money to support me for the rest of my life and I didn't need to be concerned about having a nursing career. Like I said before. The man is used to getting his way and will not accept anything other than what he wants.

"Last night before I turned in for bed I had a long talk with my mother. I told her in confidence that I had no intention of marrying Simon because I did not love the man. She told me being a woman that she understood and said there were several Mennonite women in the community who had married because of family arrangements or due to the opinion of the community. She told me that sooner or later, I was going to have to tell my father how I felt. She also said the word around the community is that I would eventually accept Simon's proposal. It was the opinion of many that I would be a fool to not accept him as my husband. Sometimes I wish I were not Mennonite. The world I live in has some very specific borders that cannot be crossed. Come August, I'll be glad to be back at school. When my father discovers I am not going to marry Baumer he will be highly disappointed. After all of the time Simon has invested in courting me, I imagine he will be upset beyond description. An eligible man, a wealthy man, a man who any other available Mennonite woman would gladly marry is going to be turned down by me…Amos King's daughter. There's a lot of pressure on me. At times I feel like just giving up, but then I realize a decision to marry Simon would be a commitment I would regret for the rest of my life. Why does life have to be so complicated Max? Look, I have to go. My time is up. I'll call you next Wednesday."

Max, glad that the negative conversation about Baumer was at an end agreed, "I'll be out of the hospital by then. I'll either be at our home in Summerville or possibly down on Fripp. One last thing, hang in there,

August is just around the corner." The phone went dead and Max pitched it on the bed between his covered legs. Laying back he looked up into the ceiling and thought, *Maybe my father is right! What possible future could there ever be between myself and a Mennonite girl? Am I just spinning my wheels?*

Brad Sykes sat on a large rock overlooking a vast lake that disappeared in the distant Northern Canadian wilderness. Taking a long pull on a cigarette that hung from his lips, the silence of the evening was broken when his cell rang. Scooping up the phone he answered, "Brad Sykes here!"

The strange voice on the calling end was low and monotone, "Mr. Sykes…your request has been completed."

Just like that! The call was over. Brad smiled to himself and flicked the remaining cigarette out into the crystal-clear water.

CHAPTER TWENTY

Max, walking out of a Truckstop diner north of Richmond, Virginia followed his father across the dirt lot where they arrived at his Jeep. Charley flipped the keys to Max and asked, "Are you up to driving some? We're just a little under four hours out from Gettysburg."

Catching the keys in his left hand, Max grinned, "That sounds like a good idea. The most I've driven the past few weeks has been over to Fripp which amounts to an hour and a half driving time. I think I can get us to Gettysburg. If I get tired, well then you can jump back in the driver's seat."

He lowered himself down gently into the seat and remarked as he frowned slightly. "Even though the doctor said my ribs are 90% back to normal I still feel some pain if I move the wrong way. I guess it's just going to take some time." Reaching across his body with his left hand he inserted the ignition key and the engine sprang to life. "I can't tell you how happy I am they found my Jeep, what was it, two days after I was released from the hospital. Just like the officer said, if it wasn't a carjacking they'd find my vehicle abandoned somewhere."

Charley added, "And that somewhere turned out to be a field outside of Mt. Pleasant."

Max pulled out of the lot onto an access road that led to 95 North. Cruising along at seventy-five miles per hour he slightly raised his right arm which was still in a cast supported by a sling. "There are several things that still puzzle me about the attack. I can understand them hitting me once to eliminate me from preventing them from taking my wallet and the Jeep but why was it necessary to break my arm and then kick the hell out of me? I mean, think about it. They used a baseball bat on my arm. Doesn't that sound like overkill to you? Thinking back it seems to me like they knew exactly what they wanted to do. Like it was already planned out."

Charley agreed, "What you're saying is planned out by Brad Sykes."

"I guess that is what I'm saying, but when Rich's detective friend found out that Brad was with his father in Northern Canada from July sixteenth through the twenty-fifth, that proves he was not in Charleston or even in the country on July eighteenth, the evening of the attack."

"But let's not forget that he didn't have to be in Charleston if he ordered or had someone else do the deed."

"Even if that happens to be true we can't prove it. We can't prove Brad was responsible for the threatening note I found beneath my dorm room door. We can't just simply say we feel based upon Brad's caustic attitude at the meeting that he is responsible for the attack. I've had six weeks since the attack to think all this over and I'm ready to move on and put the incident behind me. For all we know maybe it was just a couple of muggers after some cash, meaning that Brad may have had nothing to do with any of it."

Charley gazed out at the passing Virginia countryside as he continued the conversation. "I've thought about that myself and that very thought could be good news or bad."

"What do you mean?" asked Max.

"Okay, here it is. If Brad is behind the attack oddly you can now breathe easy knowing that he got his so-called revenge and you can move on with your life without having to look over your shoulder for the moment when he'll strike. That's the good news. Here's the bad. Let's suppose the attack was some local Charleston muggers who have absolutely nothing to do with Brad. Do you think for a moment Brad will be satisfied because someone else broke your nose and your arm? Gettysburg is a small college and we already know how fast news travels around campus. In his mind, I can't imagine your current injuries replacing his ill feelings of revenge toward you. What I'm saying is there is a possibility you may still in the future have to deal with whatever Brad Sykes has in mind."

"And," added Max, "for the next few months I'm not going to be in tip-top condition. If Brad decides to strike out at me before I'm completely healed I could reinjure myself."

Charley changed the topic. "This is your second year at school. Your sophomore year. I recall my second year of college. Things went more smoothly than my freshman year. I now knew my way around, most of the professors, and what I could expect. College, especially my second year became my home away from home."

"I think I know what you mean," said Max, "but this year may not be that relaxing and casual. Last year after Elizabeth had to go home because of her father's accident and I was kind of left, well I guess you could say… alone. Shortly after she left I met Kelly and even though we were just friends she kind of filled the void of not having Elizabeth around. Even though Kelly has stated she intends to do nothing to interfere with my relationship with Elizabeth, the fact remains I am still going to be friends with her, despite my feelings toward Elizabeth. Do you think Elizabeth will have a problem with my friendship with Kelly? I mean why would she?"

"Why would she?" repeated Charley. "Elizabeth may be a Mennonite woman, but don't forget *she is a woman!* I have seen firsthand the way Kelly acts when she is around you. A peck on the cheek, a subtle hug, and occasional hand-holding. If a stranger saw you two together I'm sure they could rapidly form an opinion that you are a couple. If Kelly, as innocent as it may seem, does these things on campus and Elizabeth sees or hears about it, she may take it the wrong way. We already know she is being courted by this Simon Baumer character and that as far as a Mennonite farmer goes he has a lot to offer her as her husband. There is a lot of pressure on her to marry Baumer. If she senses you have a level of interest in Kelly, she might jump ship, drop out of school, go back to Lancaster, and become Simon Baumer's wife."

"And no one in her family or the community she lives in will ever know of me. If Elizabeth and I make it through another year at school and we still feel as if we are in love with one another, something has got to give. I have kept nothing about my relationship with her from you and Mom and yet I have remained a secret from her family. If, by some miracle, I were to marry her, why that wouldn't take place for at least another three years when I graduate from college? I don't feel like being someone's secret for the next couple of years."

"Sounds to me like you've got an upcoming decision to make later this school year. Are you going to go all in with Elizabeth and will she agree to inform her family about you, or are you going to throw in the towel and go in the direction of Kelly? I already told you juggling more than one woman could be tricky."

"You make it sound like I'm deceiving both of these girls. I have been upfront with Kelly and told her the way I feel about Elizabeth and she has told me she understands. After school starts I have every intention of telling

Elizabeth about my friendship with Kelly. Why, I might even invite Kelly along to lunch sometime with Elizabeth and me."

"Take my advice," warned Charley. "You do not want to go down that path. That would be like driving a truckload of dynamite down a rut-filled road. If you take them to dinner at the same time you'll find yourself on the end of a short fuse and when it blows up it won't be pleasant."

Max pulled up in front of the local Enterprise, shut the engine down, sat back, and carefully stretched. "Well, I made it. I think I'll just grab a shower then unpack and get my room set up. I won't be rooming this year with Scott. He doesn't get in until tomorrow. He told me he is joining one of the campus fraternities. According to what Elizabeth said the last time we talked she is also arriving on campus today. We plan to meet at the fountain like we did last year and then walk downtown for a bite later this evening. We have a lot of catching up to do. Have you decided on whether you're going to drive to Harrisburg and grab a flight or are you going to drive back down to Summerville?"

"I think I'm going to fly back. I have to get up early tomorrow. I'm starting a new strip mall job in Beaufort. If I drive back, I'll be tired as hell come the morning."

Waving goodbye to his father who drove off up the street in a late model rental, Max hopped back in his Jeep but didn't feel like going back to campus. His classes didn't start until two days down the road. Despite his numerous injuries he was excited about his return to Gettysburg; his home away from home. Since he had nothing pressing on his open schedule he decided to grab a large fountain drink at the gas station across the street then he would drive over to the battlefield and spend the afternoon relaxing in the warm August sun. He wasn't supposed to meet with Elizabeth at the fountain until six. That meant he had nearly six hours before he had to head back to his room, shower, and then hook up with her for a much-antici-pated dinner.

He parked his Jeep in the paved lot off Emmitsburg Road, walked across the road, and entered the site of the final battle at Gettysburg, known as Pickett's Charge. Sitting on a wooden bench situated a few feet behind a long, low stone wall he looked across the vast field at Spangler's Woods three-quarters of a mile in the distance. It was there on July 3rd, 1863, where Robert E, Lee amassed approximately fifteen thousand Confederate troops on Seminary Ridge for a massive frontal attack on the Federal position where he now sat peacefully, along with a few other scattered battlefield visitors. Back then on that hot July afternoon six thousand, five hundred Union troops defended the wall. The Federals were outnumbered two to one, but they had the advantage of the wall for protection whereas the Confederates had to march across the open field directly into the Union line.

He carefully lowered himself and sat next to the wall on the grass and peered out over the stone barrier, past the Emmitsburg fence, and across the sprawling openness to the woods. What a frightening sight it must have been for the Union men at the wall as they took in the enemy nearly a mile off in the distance. When the Confederate regiments stepped out of the shelter of the tree line and formed up fifteen thousand strong in a long grey line over a mile and a half in length there must have been many a prayer that was said by the boys in blue.

But, by this time the nerves of the Union troops had been shattered following a one-hundred-and-fifty cannon non-stop bombardment lasting nearly an hour. Max's mathematical mind clicked in as he thought about that final day of battle in Gettysburg. It was a hot day; it was said to be 87. The Union forces had at least an equal amount of cannon positioned behind the stone wall and they aggressively returned fire, both sides doing little damage. The order was given by General James Longstreet for the Confederate lines to move out. The cannon fire had all but stopped now, the Union troops awaited the thousands of Southern men marching in their direction. When the southern troops walked past the lengthy line of cannons manned by the artillery crews they quickly increased their marching technique to the quick-step, a rapid form of marching, almost a slow run. This allowed the Confederates to cover eighty-five yards a minute. Under long-range Union artillery fire which blew gaping holes in their line, they approached the Emmitsburg Road fence in seven minutes.

Looking out at the fence which was a mere one hundred and ninety-five yards away he tried to imagine what it must have been like as the

Confederates clamored over the fence and now faced thousands of aimed Union muskets. Civil War muskets were good for around two hundred yards, but they were extremely inaccurate. The first volley from the Union men behind the wall was not all that effective but as the Southern troops continued forward the dead and wounded began to pile up.

The results of the attack were devastating, the South lost over six thousand men that day suffering 20% casualties while the North only lost fifteen hundred soldiers representing a 23% loss. Lee escaped with 40% of his army decimated, and admitting the failure of the assault on July 3rd was entirely his fault. Despite these great losses of men and equipment, the Confederate Army fought for what they believed in for two more bloody years until their surrender at Appomattox Courthouse in Virginia in '65.

His attention on the field that spread out before him, Max's concentration was interrupted by a familiar voice, "Howdy there…youngin'."

Max turned his head and smiled when he saw 'ol man McCulhay towering over him. Struggling to his feet supporting his body with his left hand on the stone wall, Max grinned, "Kellem! I was wondering if I'd ever run into you again out here on the battlefield."

Kellem shook Max's left hand as he stared at his cast-protected right arm suspended by the sling. "I'd ask how your summer went but from the looks of that arm, I'd say…not so good. When did that happen?"

Sitting on the stone wall Max gently raised his right arm and answered, "This happened back six weeks ago in Charleston. I was attacked by two men who robbed me of my money and my Jeep. In the process they not only broke my arm but my nose as well and then they kicked the hell out of me resulting in me suffering three bruised ribs. My nose is on the mend and my ribs are practically healed up, but the arm is going to take a few more weeks. I'm scheduled to see a local doctor in two weeks to see if they can remove the cast. Even then I'll have to take it easy for the next few months to allow complete healing. Needless to say, my second year of school will be getting off to a much different start than what I imagined it would. So, how have you been?"

Kellem removed his knapsack from his back, laid it on the bench, and looked out across the vast field. "Same 'ol…same 'ol. Work on the farm, hike over here to the battlefield daily, and thank the Good Lord for each day. You know what the Lord says, '*This is the day that the Lord has made, let us rejoice and be glad in it.*' I can think of no better way to enjoy the day than to spend time out here in these peaceful hills and fields." Sitting on the bench he opened the knapsack as he went on, "And, as always, I bring my lunch with me." Unwrapping a sandwich, he held it up, asking, "Hope you don't mind, but if I don't eat I get cranky!"

Before Max could respond, Kellem held up a bright red apple and spoke, "The first time we met up on Little Round Top, if I recall I gave you a banana. You'll have to settle for an apple this visit." Offering the fruit to Max he nodded as if to say. *Here..take it!*

Max took the apple with his left hand while admiring the round, red fruit. He polished it on his shirt as he remarked, "I think this is the brightest red apple I've ever seen. Where did you get it?"

Kellem took a bite from his sandwich and answered, "They're called Red Delicious and we got them right out of our orchard on the farm. My great, great-grandfather planted forty-two apple trees decades ago right on the edge of our property. Our family has always had apples. Over the years between rough weather and occasional insect attacks, we've lost some of the trees. We're down to seventeen still standing. This year we experienced a bumper crop. Harvested nearly twenty-five bushels."

Max bit into the fruit and wiped some juice from the side of his mouth. "I think this is the juiciest and the sweetest apple I've ever tasted…thanks!"

Kellem looked in the direction of the distant Little Round Top. "Have you been back up there since we met?"

"No, I haven't. How about you?"

"Yep, I've been back up there quite a few times since we talked on that famous hillside. That was one of the most pleasant battlefield conversations I've had with visitors over the years. Sitting there listening to you go on and on about Joshua Chamberlain and the 20th Maine and the unrelenting assaults of the Confederates I have to say it was quite entertaining. Back around the end of April, I was over at the farmer's market in downtown Gettysburg. Ran into a friend of mine who has a granddaughter who attends college here in town. She works part-time at Battlefield Pizza and told her grandfather they hired a new delivery driver by the name of Max. I got to thinking and was wondering if that was you?"

"Well, you can stop wondering because it was indeed me. I have to drop by and see the owner in the next couple of days. I told him when I left for the summer that when I came back to school I had intentions of returning to work for him. He told me he would be glad to have me back."

Gesturing at his injured arm, Max rolled his eyes. "I'm not so sure what with the way my arm is that I'll be able to deliver pizzas for the next few weeks, maybe even months. I might have to find some other type of work until I'm completely back to normal. Hell, maybe I won't be able to work at all until after the first of the year."

Rubbing his right hand over his rough, low-cut beard, Kellem squinted at Max and then pointed his bony index finger at him. "'Tell ta what. I might just have some work you could do for me on the farm. Ever mow grass with a riding mower?"

"Sure, plenty of times. We have an acre and a half in Summerville. When I was in high school that was one of my bi-weekly chores."

"Well, there ya go. Me and my brothers, we got seven acres around our house and the barn. Needs to be cut every other week up through about the end of October. All you'd have to do is put gas in the ol' John Deer, drop your butt in the seat, put the dang thing in gear, lower the blades, and off you go. How much did they pay you at that pizza joint?"

"With tips, it came out to be somewhere between twelve to fifteen dollars an hour."

"I'll pay you twelve an hour to mow my grass. Now, you may be thinking that it won't take all that long to mow seven acres therefore you won't make much money, but I have another similar job. We also have another John Deer piece of equipment. It's larger than the riding mover but smaller than a regular tractor. We use it to cut in and around the seventy-three acres of Christmas trees we grow. That in itself is a full-time job. Why I bet you could make more working for me than you could delivering pizzas. I see this as a great opportunity for you to make some money and besides, you'd be doing me a big favor. I just lost two of my workers, one of whom happened to be my mowerman. Whadda ya think?"

"The way you explain the job, you make it sound like a no-brainer. I don't have to drive around town looking for an address, hop in and out of my vehicle, or carry pizza boxes which after a while can get quite heavy. All I have to do is sit on the mower and steer it here and there. When do you want me to start?"

"How about next week?" Removing a pencil and a small pad of paper from his knapsack, Kellem wrote down his number and handed it to Max. "Give me a call this coming Monday and we'll set up a rotating schedule that will evolve around your classes."

Max tucked the slip of paper in his shirt pocket and moved on to the next topic. "When I was home this last summer I told my father about our conversation about that young Confederate ghost soldier your grandfather saw standing by the fence at your farm back in 1938. When I told him the ghost soldier appeared again by the fence thirty-one years later and was seen by you and fit the description right down to his canteen, my father was amazed but not surprised. He once again confirmed there are a lot of ghost stories and appearances in and around the Gettysburg battlefield. I don't suppose the Confederate ghost has made another appearance since we last talked?"

"Nope, but then again it's not like I go out by the fence daily and wait for him to show up. For all I know he could have walked up to the fence several times over the years and either I wasn't home or wasn't paying any attention. Like you said. It's just one of those things that's hard to explain. Who knows! When you start mowing over at the farm if you keep an eye out maybe he'll drop by."

Max laughed, "Well I hope he doesn't appear until after my arm is healed, because when and if I have an opportunity to see this ghost soldier I'll probably fall right off the mower."

Kellem joined in on the laughter, stood, and strapped on his knapsack. "Gotta start to head back home. Remember, give me a call in the next few days and we'll get you set up."

Max watched as the old man walked down the road as he thought, *For an old codger he sure has a lot of spunk.*

Leaning on the wall for support Max pushed himself to his feet. Time to head back to my new dorm room.

Back on campus, he parked his Jeep one block from where he roomed the previous year. Climbing the steps to Bell Hall he entered a large comfortable reception room where there was a young man seated at a desk near the back wall. Approaching the desk Max addressed the studious-looking youth, "My name is Miller and I'm checking in for my sophomore year. I received a letter informing me I was rooming here at Bell Hall."

The young man flipped through a chart on the desk and finally replied, "Let's see; Maiser, Malloy, and yet here you are…Miller. That would be Maxwell Miller…correct?"

"That's correct but everyone calls me Max."

"All right then, Max. If you'll just show me your college ID card, we'll get you set up."

Max opened his wallet and laid his ID on the desk. The young man scanned the card and placed a mark next to Max's computer-printed name. "My name is Luther. I'm a senior and the Bell Hall scribe this year. You'll be staying on the third floor with the other sophomores. Juniors are on the second and seniors occupy the first floor. Here is your room key. That will be room 317. Here is a list of house rules. Pretty standard. Monday through Friday you must be in the dorm by eleven at night unless you have a work pass. Saturday and Sunday there is no room curfew, no females allowed in the room, no loud music or noise after eleven, and a bunch of other rules you can read at your convenience. We did have you scheduled to share a room with another sophomore but he transferred to another school, so for now you'll have the room to yourself. Welcome to Bell Hall and we wish you a wonderful year here on campus."

Max picked up his suitcase, walked to an open elevator door, entered, and pushed the button for the third floor. His room was to the left near the end of the hall. The door was unlocked. Entering, Max took in his new surroundings for the upcoming school year. It was much the same as last year, two single beds, two small desks with a chair each, two dressers, two closets, a small refrigerator, and one bath. Not faced with which bed he desired seeing as how he had the room to himself, he dropped his suitcase on the bed next to the window and checked the time: 3:15. Plenty of time for a shower and then maybe a short nap before he met with Elizabeth at the fountain at six. Turning on the showerhead he stripped off his clothes and stepped into the stream of hot water.

At five-thirty his alarm sounded bringing him out of a light sleep. Sitting on the edge of the bed he ran his fingers through his short hair, got up, and went to the bath where he splashed cold water across his face. Donning a pair of khaki shorts, a Fripp Island t-shirt, a ball hat, and old flip-flops he was out the door, down the elevator and on his way to the fountain three blocks away. It was a typical mid-August Pennsylvania summer day. The heat was stifling and the slightest movement caused one to break out in sweat.

The fountain was in full working order. He sat on a bench and watched as the water cascaded down over the three concrete tiers into a circular pond below. There were only two other students seated around the centerpiece of the college. Most of the student body would not be showing up until tomorrow. He checked his watch: 5:57. Elizabeth was always on time and her unblemished record of punctuality continued as he saw her making her way down the sidewalk thirty yards away. Her ever-present limp was still with her, but hardly noticeable as Max recalled how she said that it was a lot worse during the winter months. She looked the same as the last time they had met, long, dark blue dress buttoned up to the neck, high-top shoes, and of course, her starched white bonnet. As she got closer, he stood and gave her a friendly wave. She stopped just a few feet from where he stood and folded her hands in front of her as she spoke softly, "Max!"

Max held out his hands and answered in a joking fashion, "In the flesh!"

She slowly moved forward, raised her arms, and hugged him as she placed her head on his chest and whispered, "I have waited all summer for this very moment."

He caressed her back with his left hand, wondering if they would kiss. *Would it be appropriate?* After a few seconds they released, but then Elizabeth reached out and took his left hand in her right as she looked him up and down. "You look better than I thought you would. If it wasn't for that cast and the sling who would know you got the tar kicked out of you."

"Let's sit," said Max. "We have so much to talk about."

Seated next to him, Elizabeth stared at his bare legs and then asked, "I didn't even realize you ever wore shorts."

"Normally I don't but with this August heat, I thought I'd just throw a pair on. I hope this does not offend you."

"No, not at all. It's just that we as Mennonites never wear shorts. The men always wear their standard work clothes and a Mennonite woman would never expose her legs to anyone other than her husband."

She gently reached up and asked, "Can I touch your nose? It doesn't look like it has been broken."

"Yes, you can touch it but be careful. It's still kind of on the sensitive side."

She reached up and softly ran her fingertips over the left side of his nose. "It appears to be normal."

"Well if you would have seen me the morning after it got broken you would have most assuredly recognized that it was broken. They had to place the bones and the interior of my nose back in place."

"And your ribs. How are they?"

"Much better. There was a time when if I took a deep breath or moved the wrong way it sent a wave of intense pain through my body." Holding up his right arm he explained, "My arm is the last thing that needs to heal up. I have to see a doctor later this month to see if they want to remove the cast. All in all, I won't be doing any swimming or bike riding until maybe after the first of the year. Any physical activity I get will come from walking." Desiring to get off the subject of his injuries, he waved his left hand. "Enough about me! How are things going with you? Are you glad to be back at school?"

Elizabeth responded much differently than what he expected. "The night before I left to come back here I slept like a baby with the anticipation, after waiting for months, to see you again. But the next morning my excitement about leaving for my second year of college was squashed when my father explained to me Simon Baumer had requested that he, rather than my father drive me to Gettysburg. I tried to object but my father was having none of it. He was convinced that I would marry Baumer since the man had courted me all through the summer. My mother remained silent as most Mennonite women do when it comes to a major decision made by the man of the house. I had little to say about the matter. I had no money and no car. I was dependent on the support of my family, mainly my father who was determined that I should marry and Simon Baumer, at least in his eyes was the man. If I wanted to return to school, I had to go along with what my father said. So, the ride over here from Lancaster was not that pleasant what with Simon constantly talking about our future together as man and wife. He just can't accept the fact that I have no intention of marrying him, or anyone for that matter until at least three years from now when I graduate college."

"Hold on here a minute," interrupted Max. "Didn't you say in your faith when a young man courts a woman that they are not to be left alone for any great length of time?"

"I did say that, but in this case, that particular rule of the community is being bent by my father. Normally, a girl my age is being courted by a young man probably close to her age, maybe a little older. Simon Baumer does not fit into that category for two reasons, First of all, Simon is an older man, ten years my elder so he is viewed as more mature and responsible, and secondly, the man is filthy rich. You'd be surprised how having a lot of money can influence decision-makers or bend the rules. In short, my father trusts Baumer. I mean it's not like the man has never been with a woman before. He was married at one time and then his wife passed away."

Holding her hands up in frustration, she went on, "Anyway, for an hour and a half I had to sit in his black Cadillac during the drive over here and listen to him go on and on about our future together. I can see why he is successful. He will not accept no as an answer. Every time I come up with an objection about his plans for us, he quickly allows my thoughts to roll off his back and then he comes at me in a different direction. For instance, when I tell him that I am not going to marry until I get out of school in three years, he says he will wait until that time for us to wed but then adds if school is that important to me we can go ahead and marry now or later this year and I can still go ahead and complete my education. He told me he had informed my father if I agreed to marry him he would pay for the remainder of my schooling. He even stated he would buy me a car of my choosing and he would even purchase a house here in Gettysburg where we could live while I'm attending school. According to him, he can drive back and forth to Lancaster a few times a week because he has plenty of help to run the farm and his business interests. I feel as if I'm alone in this situation with nowhere to turn."

Somewhat confused, Max looked deep into Elizabeth's eyes as if he were trying to understand. "Listen, we've known each other now for almost a year and during that time I have learned quite a bit about your faith...the Mennonite faith; how you were raised, and some of your beliefs. Now, I'm not sure how it works in your world, but out here in mine when a young man or woman reaches the age of eighteen they are considered a young adult, capable, according to the law of making their own decisions without any objections that at least would hold up from their parents. We're old enough to vote and at one time before they changed the law, old enough to drink and smoke. As an adult of nineteen years of age, as a Mennonite woman are you considered an adult free to make your own choices?"

"Like so many things," said Elizabeth, "as a Mennonite woman, my life as a female is quite different than females in your world. As long as I live beneath my father's roof regardless of my age I am considered a child and the responsibility of my father. As a Mennonite girl, I was raised to eventually become a wife. The skills I have are centered around working on a farm and being subservient to a husband. Here I am nineteen years of age still considered a child by my parents and yet a young girl in our community who might only be sixteen, but who is married would be referred to as an adult.

"In the Mennonite community, women are always cared for and under strict guidelines from their fathers, and then when they marry that responsibility falls to the new husband. As a Mennonite woman, in the eyes of your world we no doubt lead a very mundane life. But we as Mennonites look at it as a simple way of living. I can't tell you how many times over the summer I thought about approaching my mother and father and telling them about our relationship, but then quickly erased that thought from my head. If I were to do that I would be yanked out of school and I would probably never see you again unless you came to the farmer's market or we continued to meet at the pond."

"And what would happen if you refused to leave school?"

"If I did that then I would become an outcast not only in my own home but in the community. I cannot afford to go to school on my own. Like I said I have no money, no car, no skills which would allow me to survive in your world. The truth is, the only way our relationship can continue is if you remain a secret. I know that honesty is the best policy but in my case, if I were to be honest with my parents, that would be the end of our relationship.

"As long as we're talking about how difficult things may be for us this coming year there is something I need to tell you. Before Simon left to drive back home he told me he plans to drive over here every two weeks to spend some time with me. This, by the way, has been approved by my father. When he comes for a visit he will no doubt take me out for dinner or lunch. People from school will see us together. Some might think that he is my father or an older brother. My point is that we were known last year as a couple and that will continue this year. If Simon Baumer sees us together and catches wind that we are a couple it's going to get ugly and fast. If he sees you or your green Jeep he'll remember that night at Roots. If you'll recall he acted very negatively to you just touching my hand. Can you imagine how he'll react if he discovers we are seeing one another? Last year we had no reason to be careful about what we did or where we went. But this year is getting off to a rough start what with your concern over Brad Sykes's revenge and then when you pile Simon Baumer on top of that, we'll always have to be looking over our shoulder."

Max stood and held up his left hand. "This initial meeting with you is rapidly turning out to be frustrating. There is nothing we can do today that is going to prevent what might happen tomorrow or even the next day, week, or month. Let's just try to enjoy the time we have together and let the chips fall where they may."

Elizabeth stood, reached out, and took his left hand as hers. "I agree and so does the Good Lord who tells us not to worry over the future. We are not guaranteed the next minute or even the next hour. He only gives us twenty-four hours at a time, so I say let's enjoy the rest of this glorious day by walking downtown and relaxing over a good meal. The Lord tells us that there will be problems in the world but not to fear because He has conquered the world. Let's not allow the Brad Sykes and the Simon Baumers of this world to steal our joy."

"That's some of the best advice I've heard in some time," said Max. "What say we go to that Italian restaurant we went to after we first met."

Vannuccis Italian Restaurant was filled, and Max and Elizabeth were seated at a table just inside the front door. Despite how busy the eating establishment seemed to be their spaghetti dinners were brought out just fifteen minutes after they were seated. Max was just pouring some of their famous meat sauce on his noodles when a voice from behind him caught his attention. "Max! I see you made it back okay. I was concerned what with your arm and all."

Before Max could respond, Kelly introduced herself and the tall young man at her side. "Max, this is Rudy. He's the captain of our swim team. Rudy, this is Max Miller and this lovely young lady with him must surely be Elizabeth." Walking around the table she extended her hand to Elizabeth as she went on talking, "Hello, my name is Kelly. Max talks about you constantly. I feel like I know you. You're even more beautiful than Max described. You're a lucky girl to have a fellah like Max at your side." Tugging on Rudy's sleeve she suggested, "Come on. Let's let these two enjoy their meal. We just finished up. See you guys around campus. Have a nice evening."

With that, they turned, exited the door, walked by the front window, and disappeared down the street. Elizabeth, reaching for the bowl of sauce, inquired, "How do you know...this Kelly? Was she in one of your classes last year?"

"No, actually I didn't even know she attended school here until we met I guess it was about a month or so before school ended this past May. I met her at one of the battlefield museums and we got to talking and it turns out she lives in a town called Walterboro which is about an hour away from where I live. I found out she was on the swim team and then later on I ran into her at the school pool. Towards the end of the school year, she was helping me with my swimming; technique, breathing, and stuff like that. Over the summer her parents invited my family to a cookout at their beach house. We sort of became friends seeing as how we are both going to school here in Gettysburg and both from South Carolina."

Pouring sauce over her noodles, Elizabeth asked, "She and that Rudy. Are they a couple?"

Since Kelly had never mentioned Rudy before, Max simply replied, "I don't know. I've never seen him around campus." Scooping up a forkful of spaghetti, Max suggested, "We better come on and eat before this gets cold!"

CHAPTER TWENTY-ONE

Max circled the last tree in the first row, pulled out onto the long dirt road that ran parallel to Chambersburg Pike, placed the John Deer 3720 in neutral, raised the rear trailing mover blades, then put the small tractor in gear as the forty-four-horsepower engine propelled the machine down the lane toward the main entrance to the McCulhay's farm. He looked out the open window at the fall color of the leaves on the opposite side of the road and pumped his right arm which was resting on the window frame twice. It was late October and he had much to be joyful about. The Pennsylvania countryside was ablaze with red, yellow, and bright orange leaves. His right arm was now free of the cast and sling he had brandished for nearly three months. His nose and ribs were back to what he felt was normal, but the doctor had informed him his arm, despite the fact it was cast free would be sore and achy for the next couple of months.

It had been two months since he returned to school. He felt like his body was not in the physical condition it had been the previous year. Since there was no swimming or bike riding allowed because of his recent injuries, any exercise he got was the result of walking around campus, downtown, or hiking out to the battlefield. He didn't even have the opportunity to jump in and out of his Jeep while delivering pizzas. Before and after his classes and on the weekends he now spent his time sitting on McCulhay's mowers cutting the grass around their farm and out in the acres of trees.

His relationship with Elizabeth seemed to be going along fine despite the fact Simon Baumer dropped by every two weeks to spend time with her and continue his seemingly unending courtship. In his heart, he knew, at least according to Elizabeth that she had no desire to marry Baumer. Following one of his visits, she always seemed to be down in the dumps for a few days but then recovered to her normally jovial self and remained that way until the next unwelcome visit from the millionaire Mennonite farmer.

Max realized she was under a lot of pressure from not only her father but the community where she was raised to marry Baumer. Just recently she had told Max she wished she could just be honest with her father and tell him she had no interest in Simon Baumer but did have strong feelings for a boy she had met at school. This level of honesty, even though it seemed like the right thing to do would only lead to her father yanking her out of school and returning her to their farm where his chances of never seeing her again were quite evident. So, for the time being, he and Elizabeth were willing to let things go along as they were, hoping eventually Baumer would give up the idea of Elizabeth being his wife.

He steered the tractor to the right, drove for ten yards, and then stopped next to a large utility barn where they kept all the equipment for caring for the thousands of trees. Shutting down the tractor, he opened the cab door and jumped down, then walked to the barn and was about to open the double doors when he was vigorously shoved from behind. The front and left side of his face slammed into the left door and before he could react he was spun around and punched violently in the stomach. Doubling over in pain, through glassy eyes and a bloody nose he looked up into the bearded and surly face of none other than Simon Baumer, his two ominous-looking brothers, Rupert and Thaddeus standing off to the side, their fists clenched in anger.

Max tried to catch his breath and then spoke up, "Simon Baumer. I figured you'd show up sooner or later." Standing, he reached up and wiped blood from beneath his nose. Half smiling at the large man he asked sarcastically, "What brings you over here to our neck of the woods?"

Baumer placed his large calloused hands on his hips, glared at Max, spit a stream of dark tobacco juice off to the side, and then answered, "Been coming over here every couple weeks to see Elizabeth King. Been courting her all summer and I intend to make her my wife and you need to step out of the picture. Do you understand?"

Wiping more blood from the side of his face Max looked at Rupert and Thaddeus and then back to Baumer. "What makes you think she wants to marry you? I don't know all that much about marriage but I do know it takes two people who agree to spend the rest of their lives with one another. I don't believe Elizabeth would agree with what you propose..."

Before Max could finish what he was trying to say Baumer reached out with his right hand and roughly forced Max back, his head banging against the wooden barn door. Jamming the index finger of his left hand into Max's chest, Baumer moved close and spoke in a degrading manner, "I know who you are…Miller! I remember you from that night you came to the farmers market to see Elizabeth. I knew right off you were trouble. You were lucky that night when you sped away in that Green Jeep which by the way was seen near the Landisville Bridge the next day. You've been seeing Elizabeth right under her father's nose. And that's not all! Ran into a friend of yours yesterday. Name of Brad Sykes I believe it was. Said he roomed with you last year and that you broke his nose because of some insignificant comment he made about Elizabeth. Said you and she were considered a couple. Said the relationship between you two has continued this year. I knew ever since I started to court Elizabeth that something was going on. Now, it has become clear. You have stepped into her world of being a Mennonite and you've interfered with how she is supposed to live her life. You have no business trying to have an affair with a Mennonite woman, especially Elizabeth King, who is my woman and who will become my wife! You've crossed the line and my brothers are here to make sure this nonsense between you and Elizabeth stops today."

For some strange reason which Max at the moment could not figure out, he was not the least bit intimidated by Baumer and his brothers. "What about Elizabeth? Don't you think she has a say in all this?"

"Maybe out here in your world, a woman might have a say, but Elizabeth comes from a different way of life. A life where she was raised to be a Mennonite wife to a Mennonite man, and in this case that man happens to be me!"

Baumer increased the pressure on his chest as he explained, "You'll never see her again. After talking with this Brad friend of yours I visited Elizabeth's father and explained what was going on over here. He was not a happy man. He drove over here this morning, pulled Elizabeth out of school, and took her back home where she belongs.

"One other thing, before we go we intend to leave you with a message you will not soon forget." Drawing back his left hand he punched Max in his gut, then pulled his head up, getting in Max's face. "I imagine after the beating you're going to get we won't be seeing you over in Lancaster County…ever!" Another hard gut punch sent Max sliding down the barn door to the ground where he doubled up in pain. This was followed by a kick that glanced off his right leg."

Turning to his brothers, Simon ordered, "Boys...get over here and get your licks in. We don't want to kill him. We just want him to get our message!"

One of the barn doors opened slowly and there stood ol' man MuCulhay, a double barreled shotgun leveled at Simon's head. Holding the gun in his right hand he puffed away on his pipe with the left. "Now, what's all this?"

Baumer, out of respect for the gun aimed at his face became humble but was not intimidated. "This isn't any of your business mister."

Leaning against the barn siding, Kellem flashed an evil grin. "Oh, but I beg to differ with you, my friend. You see, you and those two clowns with you are on my property and it appears you are in the process of beating the hell out of one of my employees. So, you see, this is my business." Stepping forward, Kellem sharply ordered Simon, "Get over there with those other two idiots."

Baumer didn't move a muscle but remained where he was standing in defiance.

Kellem aimed the shotgun to the left of Simon and pulled the trigger, the loud gunshot blast echoing in the nearby woods. Kellem moved closer and jammed the gun against Simon's broad chest. "I've got one more shell in here. If I have to ask you again to move and you don't you'll get it right in the legs and then you can crawl over there to your friends."

Simon slowly backed up and stood a few feet away from his brothers. Pointing at the gun he spoke in confidence. "Like the man says. He only has one more shell in that gun. He can't get us all."

Kellem smiled as he raised the shotgun above his head and pulled off the second round, reached into the back of his jeans, and produced a black, semi-automatic Beretta that he waved at the trio of men standing before him. "This little character right here holds seven rounds and I'm sure I can get them all off before you move an inch. So, if I were you I wouldn't try anything stupid. Comprendo? Excuse me...I forgot. You don't appear to be of Spanish descent. Let me rephrase myself. Understand?"

Turning back to Max, Kellem asked, "You all right, Son?"

Max slowly stood and leaned against the barn. "Yes, I think I'll be fine."

Puffing on his pipe Kellem looked up and down at the threesome standing before him. "Looks like you fellas bit off more than you can chew."

Simon gave Kellem a look of disgust and asked, "Do you have any idea who I am?"

Removing the pipe from his mouth Kellem replied, "No, I don't know who you are and I don't much give a crap."

Baumer puffed out his chest and standing very erect, he explained, "My name is Simon Baumer and I happen to own the largest farm in Lancaster County. I swing a lot of weight over there. Maybe it is you who has bitten off more than can be chewed, as you say."

"Well, Mr. Simon Baumer you might just be a big deal over in Lancaster County, but whether you realize it or not you happen to be in Adams County and Gettysburg happens to be the county seat. You happen to be playing in my backyard right now where I have lived for over eighty years. I know the mayor and the chief of police and I am also seated on the city council, so don't go thinking you're anything remotely close to a big deal in these parts. Now I don't know what this is all about and I don't much care. Here's the way this is going to go. You three Lancaster County buffoons are going to turn and walk back up the road, climb in that ugly-ass Cadillac of yours, and drive your asses back over to where you came from. I'm going to count to five and if you're not moving then I'm going to start shooting. Now…git!"

Simon signaled for his brothers to move but hesitated before he followed as he spoke directly to Max. "Miller! If you know what's good for you you'll stay away from Lancaster County. If you try to see Elizabeth you'll have to deal with me."

Rupert and Thaddeus walked up the dirt road quickly but Simon lagged, walking slowly as if he were silently saying, *I decided to leave!*

Max walked over and stood next to Kellem as they watched Simon and his brothers walk up the road and then climb in their long black car, but not before Baumer turned and gave Kellem and Max a vigorous middle finger.

Kellem grinned at Max and puffed on his pipe while nodding up the lane. "If that man is the example of how the Mennonite clan lives over there in Lancaster County, well I guess I'm glad I live here. I thought those people were supposed to be non-violent."

Max looked at the blood on his hand and asked, "Is there someplace where I can wash this blood from my hands and face?"

"Sure, let's walk up to the main house. You can get cleaned up in the downstairs bath." Looking at Max's nose, Kellem with concern asked, "Do you think you'll be needing a bandage of some sort? Your nose looks pretty bad. Do you think it got broken again?"

Gently touching his nose and moving in slowly from side to side, Max confirmed, "No I don't think it's broke. When I hit the barn door the side of my face took most of the impact. He kicked my right leg but didn't manage to get near my ribs. I think I'm going to come out of this without any additional injuries."

Walking up the gravel road Max gave Kellem a gentle nudge on his shoulder. "Thanks for bailing me out back there. Who knows what would have happened if you wouldn't have intervened?"

Kellem banged his pipe on his leg knocking ashes to the ground. "Maybe after you get cleaned up you can tell me what that was all about."

"That's the least I can do since it happened on your farm."

Ten minutes later Max walked down the hallway from the bath into the farmhouse kitchen, where he saw Kellem seated at an old antique table. Kellem grinned and exclaimed, "Well you don't look any the worse. What say we grab a couple of cold ones and go sit out back by the fence? I always enjoy sitting out there, especially this time of year what with all the fall color." He walked across the kitchen and opened a large refrigerator. "I assume you drink an occasional beer?"

"I don't drink that much but after what happened, I think I deserve a cold beer."

Handing Max a bottle, Kellem grabbed his own and motioned toward the door. "Well, let's head on out to the fence."

They walked across the mowed yard by two bird feeders and a small fountain that served as a bird bath. Arriving at the corner of the property the split rail fencing took a right angle and ran up the right side of the yard, around the main barn, and then up a gravel road.

Kellem pointed at three large cut tree stumps, "Have a seat."

Seated on one of the stumps Max took a swallow of beer and then gazed past the fence at the gradual hill that ended thirty yards in a tree line. "About what happened earlier," said Max. "The whole situation started so simple and innocent but has recently turned into somewhat of a problem. I'll try and give you the short version because a lot has happened since I first met Elizabeth King. If I get too detailed why we could be out here until midnight."

Kellem shrugged off Max's attempt to shorten his story. "You're doing all the talking. I'm just here to listen."

"It all started my Freshman year…last year. I decided to attend a school football game. Thinking back, if I hadn't gone to the game that evening, none of what I'm about to explain would have ever happened. So, anyway, there I am sitting in the stands next to this strangely dressed young woman…let me say….a beautiful young woman. As it runs out she was a Mennonite from Lancaster…a freshman just like me. During the game, she accidentally spilled hot chocolate all over me, which led to an awkward conversation. I ended up asking her out for dinner and she refused.

"Later in the week, we run into one another and she informs me she has reconsidered my dinner request. So, we went and things just kind of developed from there. We'd go for walks and occasional lunch or dinner and became the best of friends, despite the fact we come from two different lifestyles, mine being a down south country boy and she comes from a strict, religious by-the-book Mennonite way of life."

Kellem waiting for an opportunity to speak, asked, "So you were quite interested in this young woman?"

"Yes, but only from the standpoint of being great friends. I enjoyed her companionship so much. Every time we went somewhere together, she was always experiencing something new: a food she had never tasted before, the way things work out here in the world away from how she was raised. A few weeks later I'm working the late shift at Burger Palace when in walks my roommate, this pain in the ass sports jock from New York. He and three of his pals order and then seat themselves in the dining area. While I'm delivering their orders this Brad character, who was, by the way drunk, throws his food at me and then makes some rude comments about this Mennonite girl, this Elizabeth King. I had enough, blew a gasket, and punched him right on the nose, knocking him out. One of his friends throws me through a plate glass window which results in my going to the hospital. Brad's father, who happens to be a wealthy alumni of Gettysburg College decides to sue me, which for the life of me doesn't pan out. I walk away free as a bird except for the fact that Brad vows to get even with me at some point in the future."

Taking another drink of beer Max went on, "Then, just before spring break Elizabeth has to go back home to Lancaster because her father took a nasty fall in their barn. Later when I talked with her on the phone she told me she needed to take the rest of the year off and would not return here to school until the new semester kicks off…almost six months. Before I went back home for spring break I decided to drive over to Lancaster and spend some time with her. This had to be accomplished in secret as her family knows nothing of me. If her father found out she was seeing a boy like me, not of the Mennonite faith, he would then take her out of school permanently, and I may never get to see her again. I went to a farmers market they have over there where some of the families in her community sell baked goods and the like. That was the first time I met Simon Baumer, the big ugly cuss who accosted me back there at the barn. While I was purchasing a pie from Elizabeth, I placed my hand over hers, which this Baumer saw. His reaction was anything but friendly. He stated that she was his woman and I had no right to touch one of their women. I then made the decision it would be best if I left, which I did, but Baumer and his two brothers followed me out to the parking lot. I managed to barely escape and at the time didn't have an idea what they had in mind but based on the way I just got whooped up on I'd say they were out to teach me a lesson.

"The next day, as planned I met Elizabeth at a pond out in the woods a mile or so away from their farm. It was there at that pond where she all but told me she was in love with me and I responded by telling her I felt the same way about her. I finally headed down to South Carolina to spend the summer with my parents and Elizabeth and I continued to speak on the phone a couple of times each week. Much to both my despair and Elizabeth's, Simon Baumer went to her father and got permission to court his daughter. Elizabeth has no more intention of marrying Baumer than the man on the moon but is leery of telling her folks about me because then that would upset the apple cart."

"And this apple cart you speak of," said Kellem, "is the relationship you and this Elizabeth have."

"Yes, she would like nothing better than to tell her father about her feelings for me but if she did she feels our relationship would come to an abrupt halt. Then, on top of all that I met another girl at school before I went home for the summer. Her name is Kelly Waters and I guess the reason we hit it off so well is the fact that she and I are both from South Carolina."

"So a second woman enters the picture."

"Yes and no. It was different with Kelly. Don't get me wrong, she's a looker, but our relationship is based on friendship. I have shared with her the way I feel about Elizabeth. My parents and myself were invited over to a cookout at a summer place they own and I even helped Kelly out for a few days with a business her mother has. That's how I wound up getting my nose, right arm and ribs busted up. One evening while I was leaving the market where Kelly was selling her mother's crafts I got jumped and got the hell beat out of me, plus my Jeep was stolen. Initially, my father and I along with our attorney felt that the attack had been at the hands of Brad Sykes, but that was ruled out because he wasn't even in the country when I was attacked. We even considered it could have been Simon Baumer who attacked me in Charleston, but that didn't make any sense because, at that point, the man aside from seeing me at the market in Lancaster didn't know who I was or I was even seeing Elizabeth, the girl he was actively courting.

"Eventually August rolled around and Elizabeth and I returned to school, both of us excited about rekindling our miles-apart relationship to once again being able to spend time together. She had told me many a time over the summer during our phone conversations that once she returned to school Baumer would more than likely become discouraged and put this idea of their future marriage behind them both. But not so! He not only got permission from Elizabeth's father to drive her back to school but set it up so he could drive over here from Lancaster every two weeks to see her. It seemed to us like there was no escaping this Baumer.

"One thing leads to another and Baumer, via information from my old nemesis Brad Sykes finds out about Elizabeth and me, and tells her father about how he has been deceived by his daughter which leads to him driving over this morning so I'm told and pulls her out of school and back to the farm she goes. Baumer then, along with his two brothers decides to drive over here and teach me a lesson to stay away from his future wife. Well, you know the rest of the story from there. You showed up with your shotgun and that pistol and ran the three of them off. As things stand right now…I don't know what I'm going to do. Any suggestions?"

Kellem put his beer on a tree stump and responded with surprise, "If you're seeking advice on women you're barking up the wrong tree as it has been often said. My brothers and I, all of us are over eighty years of age and not one of us has ever been married. Don't get me wrong. I've had my share of women especially when I was a younger man, when I was in the Navy. I never spent enough time with a particular woman to get that involved to where I even considered marriage.

"As time went on I guess I just couldn't see the need to marry. My brothers and I have always enjoyed the life of being bachelors. I can honestly say I have never been in love with a woman. The closest I've ever been to loving anything or anybody was a dog we had on the farm here. He was just a young pup, probably a year or so old at the time. We started to feed him and he just sort of stayed on. We named him Moses and he was with us for I guess it was for about seventeen years. I loved ol' Moses and when he died it tore me up inside something awful. He passed on fifteen years ago and every time I think of him I start to tear up. If your feelings for this Elizabeth are anything close to the way I felt about Moses then I say you've got a decision to make.

"You can just let this whole thing go, in which case she might not have any other choice but to marry this Simon Baumer or you can drive over to her farm in Lancaster, walk right up to their front door, bang on it, and then talk to her father. Tell him the way you feel about his daughter and that you intend to marry her. What's the worst thing that could happen? He could kick you off his property and tell you to stay away from his daughter, in which case you'll survive and move on with your life but at least you'll always know you gave it a try. If you don't go over there it might be something you'll regret for the rest of your life…the not knowing. The way I see it. You have nothing to lose."

Max shot Kellem a stern look. "You do remember that Baumer warned me to stay away from Elizabeth and Lancaster County. I'd hate to run across him and his brothers again, I might not be so lucky next time."

"This is true, but the question is just this, what are you willing to do to save your relationship with Elizabeth? Does she mean enough to you to forgo the ramifications of the possibility of facing Simon Baumer? If the answer to that question is yes then I say you need to get your butt over there and try to straighten this out. If the answer is no, then I think you should just move on and put all this behind you. Chalk it up as a bad experience."

Max gazed off into the trees beyond the fence. "I guess I've got some thinking to do and not a lot of time to do it. It's time for me to crap or get off the pot." Looking toward the farmhouse he asked, "I haven't seen your brothers this week. Did they go somewhere?"

"Yes, they both went down to Florida. I drove them over to Harrisburg two days ago where they caught a flight down to Jacksonville. They'll be staying with my sister Rose who lives with her husband in St. Augustine. My older brother, Joseph may decide to stay with her permanently. He's eighty-five and he doesn't get around like he used to. He's getting to the point where he needs a lot of help which my sister who is in her early seventies is willing to do. So, it looks like from here on out it'll just be me and my other brother Seth running this place. Where does the time go? It just seems, like it was yesterday, that the three of us were wild youngins running out in the woods and fields that surround this farm. I imagine the day will come when someone is going to have to decide for me."

Pointing his beer bottle at Max, Kellem stated with conviction, "Enjoy your youth, Max. The years rush by and before you know it you're an old man like me. If I was you I'd marry up with that Mennonite gal and have a bunch of kids. You don't want to wind up like me. Eighty-three years old and alone. I've got more money than I know what to do with but looking back over my life if I had to do it over again I'd find me a nice gal and then raise a family."

Max got up, walked to the fence, and looked out at the dazzling fall leaves at the top of the slight ridge. Turning around, he faced Kellem and asked, "Isn't it somewhere along here where you saw that ghost soldier?"

Nodding up the fence line Kellem responded, "Two sections up, about twenty feet to your right…that's where I saw him." Getting to his feet he walked down the fence line stopping in the middle of an eight-foot span. "It was right here where I saw that soldier. The same place where my father saw him as well."

"Correct me if I'm wrong but didn't you say the sightings were thirty-some years apart?"

"Thirty-one years to be exact. My father saw that soldier back in 1938 and then I saw him thirty-one years later in 1969."

"And you're positive it was the same soldier?"

"Well, I can't say for sure because I didn't see the boy in '38. I only saw the soldier in '69. But, that doesn't make any difference. The description of the soldier my father saw and the one I saw matched perfectly, young Confederate soldier, probably between eighteen, nineteen, maybe twenty years old, dressed in a ragged Confederate grey uniform, musket held in his right hand, wounded in his upper right arm and lower left leg. And, oh yeah. He had this old wooden canteen suspended by an old section of rope. That is the same way the soldier I saw standing right on the other side of this fence looked like. He not only appeared the same but acted in the same manner when approached. My father said the boy turned and limped off back up into the woods right up there. When I approached the boy, he limped off in the same way and disappeared in those trees."

"Didn't you tell me you tried to follow him?"

"I did, but when I got on the other side of the fence the strangest feeling came over me."

"What kind of a feeling was it?"

"It's hard to describe the way I felt. All I know is that it was strong enough to make me climb back over to this side."

"And you say in the last four to five decades the soldier has not reappeared?"

"Not that I know of."

Max sat his beer on the ground and climbed up and over the fence and stood on the other side. "It feels the same over here as it did on your side. I don't understand."

"It was just that one time when I saw the boy when I felt strange standing on that side. Hell, I've been up in those woods a zillion times walking around up there. Where you are standing right now happens to be part of the battlefield. This fence line marks the end of the park property."

"Do a lot of battlefield visitors walk down here to the fence?"

"Not really. We don't get many sightseers out this way. That part of the battlefield was remote as far as any serious fighting was concerned. It has been said during the three-day battle that the Confederate army had encampments about a mile or so beyond those trees."

Max took the last swig of his beer, handed the empty bottle to Kellem, and then pointed at his Jeep parked next to the main barn. "I best be getting back to campus. I have three classes tomorrow and then it's the weekend. I've got some thinking to do. If I decide to drive over to Lancaster I'll let you know."

CHAPTER TWENTY-TWO

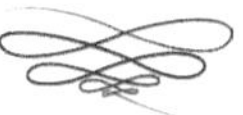

It was the last Saturday in October and Max found himself cruising down Route 30 just twenty miles from Lancaster County. He had left Gettysburg at ten-thirty in the morning, stopped for breakfast and gas, and figured he'd arrive at the King's farm somewhere between twelve-thirty and one in the afternoon. He had gone over and over in his mind what he was going to say to Elizabeth's father and maybe even her mother depending on who he got to talk to and that's if her parents would even speak with him. He had stopped by the McCulhay farm and spoke with Kellem before he hit the road just as he promised the old man. Kellem told him he thought he was doing the right thing regardless of how things turned out. He also explained to him that depending on what happened Max could depend on him for support, whatever that may be.

Max thought about contacting his parents and telling them about what he was up to but knew they would object, reminding him that they felt the relationship would not work out, which for the moment seemed to be true. He was not sure how Elizabeth was going to react when he showed up at her front door. Would she welcome him or would she buckle under the pressure from her parents, community, and Simon Baumer? If she was not willing to back up what he had to say, he was quite sure her father would send him packing. There didn't seem to be all that much sense in trying to figure out how Elizabeth or her parents would react to his surprise visit. He had a rehearsed spiel that he planned on unleashing on Mr. and Mrs. King, but depending on what they said or did could very easily change his verbal plan.

Arriving at the East Petersburg Exit he pulled off, drove past the motel where he had spent the only other night he had stayed in the Lancaster area, and stopped at a small market-gas station. He was now within ten miles of the farm and the sensation of nervousness was starting to wrap around his head. He thought a cup of hot steaming coffee might help to calm his nerves. What he needed was a shot of whiskey, but the idea of showing up at the King's farm with alcohol on his breath was quickly ruled out.

Coffee in hand, he retraced the same route he had taken on his previous journey to Roots Farmer's Market. Within minutes he found himself driving through East Petersburg, where he took a left on Landisville Road, the final leg of his journey to the King farm. He passed, what he thought was Simon Baumer's enormous farm on the right and wondered if the man was nearby. He erased the thought from his mind, the very idea that he would run into Baumer was not in his plan for the day.

Passing several farms he finally saw the mailbox at the end of a dirt lane that read: King. Pulling into the dirt lane he stopped his Jeep and thought is this a wise thing to do? I can still turn around, drive back to Gettysburg, and just try to forget this entire situation. But then he recalled what Kellem had said about how he felt he was doing the right thing and no matter how it turned out at least he had tried to rectify the problem. Pressing down on the accelerator he spoke out loud to himself, "Here we go!"

The farm sat back from at the end of the lane about a hundred yards from the main road. Keeping the Jeep's speed at five miles an hour he slowly passed a fence on the right and a large grove of trees on the left. The main two-story white farmhouse sat directly ahead of him and to the right, there was a massive white barn where a large bull inside of an attached pen munched at a pile of fresh hay. He wondered if that was the bull Elizabeth had told him about who stepped on her foot when she was a little girl, causing her to limp at times. To the left of the house, there were several outbuildings, a chicken coup, a sheep pen, and an equipment structure. The farm looked organized, neat as a pin with red Geraniums and Yellow Daisies planted along the front of the porch.

The porch itself was simplistic. A wooden swing attached to the porch ceiling, an old decorative milk container, and three hanging ferns. Parking his Jeep a few yards from the house he climbed out and watched as five chickens ran around the side of the porch. Climbing the three wood steps that led up to the porch he noticed a black cat curled up on an old tattered towel at the corner of the swing The cat, upon seeing him raised its head, gazed at him for a second, and then returned to its peaceful sleep. Positioning himself squarely in front of the front door, he smoothed his shirt and ran his fingers through his hair. He took a deep breath and thought, *It's now or never!*

He knocked on the door five consecutive times, then waited. He thought about just turning and running back to his Jeep and speeding off but it was too late now as the door opened and there directly standing in front of him was an older, heavier version of Elizabeth. The woman, probably in her mid-forties was dressed much the same way he had seen Elizabeth numerous times, dark blue, buttoned up to the neck dress, white bonnet on her head, laced up high top shoes. She also had an apron wrapped around her waist, flour smeared across the white lace fabric. Max could see where Elizabeth got her good looks as he gazed at the woman's face, rosy cheeks, green eyes, and blond hair.

The woman smiled at him and politely spoke as she folded her hands in front of her. "Good afternoon...Sir."

Max smiled back and responded, "Can I assume that you are Mrs. King...Elizabeth's mother?"

The woman's face took on a hopeless smile as she looked beyond Max toward his Green Jeep. Looking back to him she supposed, "And you must be Mr. Miller."

"Yes, I am Max Miller. I went to school with your daughter over in Gettysburg."

"I am well aware of that Mr. Miller. Why have you come to our farm today?"

"Well I wanted to see Elizabeth but more than that I wanted to speak to you and your husband. I feel your family has the wrong idea about the relationship your daughter and I have. I was hoping if I came over that I could, I guess, set the record straight. Whatever you and your husband have heard or been told I can assure you that Elizabeth is innocent of any wrongdoing." Not allowing Mrs. King to respond, Max inquired, "Is your husband around today?"

"Yes, he is. At the moment he is out in the field behind the barn with some neighbors putting up some new fencing."

Looking in the direction of the barn Max asked, "Could I possibly see him for a few minutes? I have some things to say to both of you that I feel are very important."

Sternly, Mrs. King replied, "With everything that has happened I don't think my husband would be interested in talking to you, but I'll send one of my sons to fetch him. That's all I can do." Turning, she summoned one of two young boys who were seated at a kitchen table, "Nathan…go down behind the barn and tell your father he has a visitor here to see him. Go on…do it now!"

The young boy stood and answered politely, "Yes Ma'am." Running past Max he jumped down the porch steps and bolted across the yard to the barn."

Max, out of curiosity asked Mrs. King, "I noticed you didn't tell the boy to let your father know who I am."

"That's because I do not want any trouble in my house today. Those neighbors I spoke of who are down there with my husband happen to be the Baumer's. I don't need Simon Baumer stomping up here to the house and making any trouble."

Max tried his best to smile. "I can assure you, Mrs. King if Simon Baumer comes up here there will be no trouble from me."

Rolling her eyes she remarked, "It is not you I am concerned over. My concern is centered on Mr. Baumer."

Gesturing at Max's Jeep, she went on, "I've seen you before. You were at Roots a while back. You purchased a blueberry pie from my daughter and you upset Mr. Baumer. People say you sped out of the parking lot that night."

"You're correct in what you say. I was at the market and I did buy a pie. You're also correct when you say I sped out of the parking lot, but that is not the complete truth and that's one of the things I'd like to clear up."

Crossing her arms across her chest, Mrs. King asked her next question, "People also say that the same Jeep…your Jeep was seen parked down by the Landisville Bridge the next afternoon."

"That is true. I did park my Jeep down there. I met Elizabeth at a pond somewhere around there and then I went home for the summer."

"So then you are the mysterious boy in the Green Jeep?"

"Well, I guess if you want to put it that way…then yes, I am."

Looking toward the barn, Mrs. King nodded, "Here comes Amos now. Thank God, Simon is not with him."

Mr. King displayed what Max thought was the perfect farmer. Muddy galoshes, heavy denim, worn work overalls, brown shirt, gloves, and a straw hat, bearded and weathered face. Walking briskly he stopped when he saw

Max's Jeep at which point his head slumped, then he made his way to the bottom of the porch and stared up at Max. Removing his gloves he tucked them in his coveralls and spit on the ground, then wiped his mouth. "If you own that Jeep then I'll call you Max Miller."

Walking down the steps Max extended his right hand and replied. "I am Max Miller. It's nice to finally meet you, sir."

Refusing to shake Max's hand Mr. King explained, "You'll have to excuse me Miller for not being all that friendly, but the truth is you're not welcome here on my farm. If you came to take Elizabeth back to school or to see her I'm afraid neither one of those things is going to happen. It looks like you not only wasted time coming over here but a tank of gas as well. You might as well just get back in your vehicle and drive back to Gettysburg. You are never going to see Elizabeth again…ever!"

Just then, walking around the side of the house Elizabeth appeared carrying two buckets of water. Upon seeing Max, she instantly set the buckets on the ground ran to his side and hugged him as she exclaimed, "Max…I can't believe you came!" Turning to her parents she spoke, "Mama, Papa… this is Max, the boy I was telling you about."

Amos was blunt and to the point. "We've already met. Mr. Miller was just about to leave. Elizabeth…come over here and stand beside your mother."

Reaching down she took Max's hand and stood her ground. Max released his grip and suggested, "I think you better do what your father says."

Taking a step toward Mr. King Max humbly stated, "Mr. King, if I could just have a few moments with you I think I have some information that will solve our differences. In all the time I have known Elizabeth she has always told me how strict she was raised and that you as her father are brutally honest and quite religious. Now, I am not the most religious man on the face of the planet but I do know that in the Bible somewhere it states that the truth will set you free. If you are religious and honest then I think you would want to know the truth…the absolute truth, not someone's version of the truth or the partial truth…but the genuine truth.

"If, after hearing me out it is still your decision that I am never to see your daughter again, I will abide by your wishes and never bother you, your family, or Elizabeth. I did come here today in hopes of seeing Elizabeth but mainly I came to see you, Mr. King. I want you to know Elizabeth is entirely innocent of any wrongdoing in our relationship. If anything she has displayed her true Mennonite upbringing and if I never get to see her again, well then…so be it. My father has always instilled in me that if you decide without considering all of the facts then you are but a fool."

"Are you calling me a fool, Miller?"

"No, I'm just asking you to hear me out and then I'll be on my way. But, when I leave I want to know in my heart that Elizabeth is not going to suffer for something that has been misconstrued. Do you want the truth, Mr. King?"

Elizabeth looked at her mother and then stepped close to her father. "Papa…I'm asking you to please hear what Max has to say. If, even after hearing the truth you are still of a mind to turn him away then I too will abide by your wishes."

Looking at his daughter Amos spoke firmly. "You know it is my wish that you and Simon should marry up. If after hearing what Mr. Miller has to say and I still send him away, then you will agree to marry Simon?"

Elizabeth gave Max a look that plainly said, *What else can I do?* and then answered her father. "Yes, I will agree to marry Simon Baumer but only after you hear Max out."

Removing his straw hat from his head Amos wiped his brow with a handkerchief and then relented, "All right, that seems fair. I will listen to what Mr. Miller has to say but I'm not saying I'll change my mind." Looking at his wife he ordered, "Clara, I want you to take Elizabeth into the kitchen while Mr. Miller and I go into the parlor. We are not to be disturbed. We shouldn't be all that long and then Mr. Miller can be on his way, I can get back to my fencing and also tell Baumer that there is going to be an upcoming marriage between him and my daughter. If you'll follow me, Mr. Miller."

Max watched as Amos kicked off his muddy boots and then trailed Amos into the kitchen and then an adjoining room where there was an old-looking Lazy Boy recliner, a side table, three wooden chairs, a long table, a fireplace, and a bookshelf. Amos seated himself in the recliner and offered Max one of the uncomfortable chairs. "Please have a seat, Mr. Miller."

Max tried to make himself comfortable but the stiff back chair offered little in the way of comfort. Placing his feet squarely on the wood slat floor he folded his hands on his lap as he looked across the room at Amos who opened a wooden box and removed a pipe and a pouch of tobacco. Holding up the pipe, Amos asked, "Do you smoke Mr. Miller?"

"No, never have," said Max. "Never had the desire."

Removing a pinch of tobacco from the pouch Amos tamped it down into the bowl of the pipe and asked his next question, "Are you a drinking man?"

Max, realizing that Mr. King was trying to read his character responded, "If you are referring to alcohol I would not refer to myself as a drinking man. Do I have an occasional drink…yes."

Adding another small amount of tobacco to the pipe, Amos struck a match on the edge of the side table, placed the pipe between his lips, held the match to the bowl, and began to puff, small clouds of the aromatic tobacco wafted into the still air of the room. Shaking the match until it was no longer burning he placed it in a small lid that served as an ashtray and took three short draws on the pipe, then remarked, "One of my neighbors up the road makes what we call Pennsylvania moonshine. Every year in January I purchase a jug from him. It lasts the entire year as I only indulge with one swig on Saturday afternoons." Smiling at Max, he added, "I guess we all have our little crutches in life we cling to. What do you want out of this life, Miller?"

Max replied with confidence, "Well, first of all, I want to get my college degree in financing, and then after I graduate I'll no doubt have to work for a financial firm somewhere and eventually I'll open my own business. I want to marry a nice girl, own a home, and raise a family. If I can accomplish those four things then I'll consider myself as successful."

Puffing away on his pipe Amos asked, "Do you know the Lord…son?"

"If you're asking me if I believe in God, well yes I do. I was raised Methodist."

Amos continued with his questions, "What do your parents do for a living?"

"My father owns a construction company and my mother is a homemaker."

"Where do you call home?"

"Summerville, South Carolina, down near Charleston."

"That's down by the ocean…correct?"

"Yes…it is. This past summer my father and I did quite a bit of fishing in the Atlantic." Max decided to ask a question of his own. "Do you enjoy fishing, Mr. King?"

"Yes, I do go on occasion. Never catch much of anything but I find it very relaxing." Laying the pipe in the makeshift ashtray Amos rubbed his beard and stated flatly, "Let's get down to business Mr. Miller. Let's hear what you have to say."

"I agree. That's why I came. I met your daughter quite by accident last year when I was a freshman at Gettysburg College. I went to a school football game and sat next to Elizabeth. I noticed right off how differently she was dressed than the other female students on campus. But that is not what drew my attention to her. It was her wholesomeness that seemed to overwhelm me. I guess I stared at her too long and I became embarrassed.

"You see, Mr. King I am not what you would call a ladies man. Here I was nineteen years old and I had never been on a date short of my high school prom. Later on during the game Elizabeth accidentally spilled a cup of hot chocolate all over me. She was so upset and kept apologizing and I kept telling her that it wasn't anything to worry over. She continued to ask me if there was anything she could do and for some reason, that I still haven't quite figured out, I asked her to go to dinner with me. This was awkward for me as I had never asked a girl out on a date in my life. I guess you could say I was sailing in uncharted waters. You and Mrs. King must have done a good job raising your daughter because she refused me immediately.

"I realized that I had crossed some sort of line, became even more embarrassed, said goodbye, and left the game, realizing what a fool I had made of myself and that I would more than likely never see her again. Later in the week, we ran into one another between classes and she introduced herself and said she had prayed about my dinner request and decided if she ran into me again she would be willing to go. I have to tell you, Mr. King, at that point I was rather confused. So, it all ended with the both of us agreeing that we would go some time.

"A few days later we went to dinner and despite the different ways in which we were raised we shared so many interesting things. We talked about her life growing up on a farm and I talked about swimming and fishing in the ocean and we went on and on. Things just kind of went from there. We would go to an occasional dinner or lunch or for a walk or sometimes we'd just sit and talk about whatever came to our minds. In short, we became the best of friends. I told my parents all about Elizabeth but Elizabeth said that as far as her family was concerned our friendship would have to remain a secret because as a Mennonite young woman, having any sort of a relationship with a boy outside of her faith would be frowned upon."

Making himself more comfortable in the chair Max rested his left ankle on his right knee and continued talking as he looked across the room at Amos, who while listening never changed his expression one time, but kept puffing away on his pipe. "Things went along smoothly for Elizabeth and me until I think it was around February when you took a fall out in your barn. Elizabeth had to come back home to help out because of your injuries and during a phone conversation I had with her on her friend Ellen's phone she told me it looked like she was not coming back to school until next August which meant we would not see each other for six months.

"A few weeks later spring break rolled in and I was going to go home to South Carolina for about two weeks and spend time with my parents. I suggested to Elizabeth that I might drive over to Lancaster on my way home and spend a couple of hours with her. She said we would have to meet in secret at a pond out past the Landisville Bridge. I arrived in town the night before and decided to go to the Roots Farmer's Market where Elizabeth told me she would be. She told me there was no sense in going over there because she would be working in a tent and probably not be able to get away. Well, I went anyway, located your tent, and low and behold there she was. She was surprised, to say the least, to see me. Of course, since no one knew we were friends I had to act like a stranger who was interested in buying a pie. That was the first time I met Simon Buamer and what a scary man he was. I put my hand over top of Elizabeth's in a friendly manner which Baumer saw and he went off saying that Elizabeth was his woman and how I had no right to touch any Mennonite woman. I figured it would be for the best to purchase my pie and then move on.

"As I'm leaving the market I discover that Baumer and his two brothers, I believe their names are Rupert and Thaddeus are following me and do not appear to be all that friendly. Thinking they meant me harm, I put a fish dinner that I had purchased and my pie on the hood of a car and ducked into a field. I couldn't believe what happened next. Simon seemed so angry as he stomped my dinner into the ground with his boot and then tossed my pie out into the field. I barely got back to my Jeep and escaped before they could get to me. I've got to tell you, Mr. King, I don't think Simon Buamer is the man that you want your daughter to marry. I mean who in the world would smash someone's dinner and then destroy a perfectly good pie? I think the man has anger problems."

"Come now," said Amos. "Have you never lost your temper? From time to time I think we all do."

"Well, Mr. King, normally I don't lose my temper. But last year while I was working at a burger place in Gettysburg I did lose my temper. I wouldn't mention it but it had to do with your daughter."

Taking the pipe from his mouth Amos seemed surprised. "You lost your temper with my Elizabeth?"

"No, she wasn't even present when this happened. My roommate and some of his friends dropped by for a late-night snack. They had all been drinking and quite frankly were out of hand. Brad, my roommate made some rude and unsavory comments about Elizabeth. At first, I just walked away but he wouldn't let up so I hit him right in the face…knocked him out I did. One of his friends wound up tossing me through a plate glass window. Later on, when Elizabeth found out what I had done, even though I had done it for her honor she insisted that what I had done was wrong. So, once again, you have done a good job of instilling your beliefs in your daughter."

Waving his hands slightly in the air, Max continued, "I'm sorry. I'm getting off the point. Getting back to my previous visit to Lancaster. The next day after escaping from the wrath of the Baumers I met Elizabeth at a pond out in the woods down from the Landisville Bridge. This, what I thought was going to just be a meeting of two friends turned out much different than what I expected. Elizabeth was there at the pond waiting for me but she had let her hair down and was not wearing her bonnet. She said this was not permitted out in public but wanted me to see the real person that she was. As time passed she told me she was pretty sure she was in love with me and I told her that I felt the same about her. We held hands, kissed, talked for the next hour and then I left for South Carolina knowing we would not see one another for months. We continued to talk on the phone over the summer.

"One of the topics happened to be that Simon Baumer was courting her. You may not be aware of this but Elizabeth never had any intention of marrying Simon. She was afraid to tell you because she thought you would take her out of school. Plus she would never get to see me again. Here's my point, out on the porch when Elizabeth said she would abide by your wishes and marry Baumer if you would just hear me out, well that took more courage than I think I could ever muster. To think she loves me that much that she would go through years of suffering rather than have you think poorly of me. What I'm saying is that Elizabeth King, your daughter, is a woman of vast wisdom. Once again, I say you have done a great job of raising your daughter."

"Let me ask you this, Mr. Miller. Have you been intimate with my daughter?"

"That's a hard question to answer Mr. King. Some people would describe intimacy as holding hands, kissing, and hugging. All of those things we have done. There are no doubt others who would describe intimacy as a sexual act that your daughter and I have never engaged in. To be honest the thought never crossed my mind. You see, Mr. King I'm not so sure I'd even know what to do. I've never been with a woman."

Holding up his index finger Amos added, "And my daughter has never been with a man and that's the way it should be."

Nodding, Max spoke up, "We can agree on that then."

A few seconds of silence followed as if Amos were thinking when Max spoke up again, "There is one last part to this story, Mr. King and that's just this. When Elizabeth and I returned to school this last August we were well aware of the fact our sophomore year was going to be much different than our freshman year. The previous year we looked at our relationship as based on a friendship but this year we were two young people who were in love. I guess most folks would view that as a good thing but in our case we found ourselves in a love relationship that could not possibly go anywhere. We talked about this to great lengths. If we were to marry I told her I had no intention of becoming a member of the Mennonite faith. I mean, come Mr. King, can you envision me as a farmer?"

Amos smiled at Max's humorous statement while shaking his head as if to silently say, no.

"The other side of the coin," said Max, "was not any brighter. Elizabeth said she was not prepared to leave her community and how she had been raised. So, what were we to do? Two young people who were in love, but with no hope of ever spending our lives together. It was very frustrating plus we were faced with Simon Baumer driving over to Gettysburg every two weeks to spend time with Elizabeth and continue his courtship. There was little I could do and well, Elizabeth had to just simply play along with Baumer's courtship if she wanted to continue her schooling."

Max stood, and for effect walked across the room to a window for his final performance. Looking out the window he turned back and leaned on the sill. "Then the crap hit the fan as my father likes to say. Brad Sykes, the boy who I hit in the face, who ever since our encounter has vowed to get even with me runs into Simon on one of his visits and tells him that Elizabeth and I are a couple and had been for almost a year. It must have been right after that when Baumer came to you and passed on the information he received from Brad. I guess that very day you drove over to Gettysburg and brought Elizabeth back here to her home. Of course, I had no idea any of this happened at the time."

Walking to the center of the room Max faced Amos. "The very next day I was working on a tree farm there in Gettysburg completely unaware of what had taken place. The day was at an end and I was in the process of putting a tractor in the barn when I was shoved up against the barn, face first. Then, I'm spun around and punched in the stomach. While I'm trying to catch my breath and wiping blood from my face there stands none other than Simon Baumer, his two brothers standing close by. Baumer proceeds to tell me in no uncertain terms that Elizabeth is his woman she is going to marry him and that I need to step out of the picture. I tried to explain to him that Elizabeth had no intention of marrying him but he wasn't having any of that. He punched me two more times in my stomach which sent me sliding down the side of the barn. Then, while I'm lying on the ground, unable to defend myself, Baumer kicks me in the leg and orders his two brothers. These were the words he said; 'Come on boys. Get over here and get your licks in. We don't want to kill him, we just want to teach him a lesson.' Can you honestly in your heart, Mr. King desire that your wonderful daughter marry a man who would not only smash another man's meal and toss a pie out into a field let alone toss me into the side of a barn, hit me three times and then kick me when I'm down. In regards to me he used the word, *kill!*"

Returning to the chair, Max sat and finished his story. "Thank God, the owner of the farm intervened with his shotgun and ran Baumer and his brothers off. Simon Baumer, the man you want for your daughter's husband turned as he was leaving and flipped us the bird."

The look of confusion on Amos' face deserved further explanation which Max supplied quickly. "He made an obscene gesture with his middle finger."

Understanding, Amos shook his head, raised his thick eyebrows, and spoke, "I am well aware that Simon can have a temper but these things you have brought to my attention are disheartening to me as a father and as a fellow Mennonite. If the elders were to hear of this they would be appalled."

Max breathed a sigh of relief. "That's it, Mr. King. I've said what I came to say and I thank you for your time, sir."

Mr. King laid his pipe on the table while speaking, "Earlier out on the porch you said something about the truth setting you free. You quoted some scripture from the Bible. You said you were not sure where that verse in the Bible was located but that it was in there somewhere." Opening a small drawer on the front of the side table, Amos removed a Bible and confirmed, "The verse you quoted is actually from John 8:32 where it is written, *You will know the truth and the truth will set you free.*" Tossing the Bible across the short expanse that separated them Amos warned, "Catch!"

Max reacted quickly catching the holy book in his hands.

Amos smiled and asked, "You read the Good Book much?"

Max stared at the Bible in his hands. "Not regularly. I suppose while at church over the years our pastor has covered most of it. I take it you read this quite often."

"Every evening after supper. I've read the Bible cover to cover many times over my life. There is an answer in that book for any problem we as people may face. You also asked me out on the porch if I wanted to know the truth...and I do. According to you, Mr. Miller you claim to have revealed to me the truth. Let's see if that is true. Are you willing in front of me, a man of God to place your hands on that Bible and swear to me before our God that you have spoken the truth?"

Max didn't even hesitate but placed the Bible on his lap and placed both his hands over the worn cover. "I swear before God and you Mr. King that every word I've spoken to you this day is the truth. I added nothing and I left nothing out. I have told you the absolute truth."

Amos got up from his chair as he remarked, "Good!"

Walking across the room he reached for the Bible which Max returned. Taking the well-read book he proceeded to the parlor door, opened and spoke to his wife, "Clara, come into the parlor and bring Elizabeth with you."

Mother and daughter entered the room while Amos placed one of the wooden chairs next to his chair. He directed his wife to sit beside him and then spoke to Elizabeth. "Take a seat next to Mr. Miller."

After everyone was seated Amos sat back in his recliner and looked to his wife and then to his daughter, "Mr. Miller and I had quite the conversation. I believe, Clara, that you and I before today did not have all the complete information regarding our daughter's relationship with Mr.

Miller here, who has sworn on the Bible that what he has revealed to me is the truth, and I have no other choice but to belief this young man. Without getting into a long-winded explanation, of what we discussed, I am releasing you Elizabeth, if it is your desire, from any further attempt on Simon Baumer's part to continue his courtship. I do not believe he is the man you should marry. I intend to contact the elders about some of his recent behavior toward Mr. Miller."

The words spoken by Mr. King seemed to take the air out of Elizabeth as she let out a deep breath almost as if she were releasing the frustration that had built up inside her.

Amos continued to speak as he looked at Max. "Now that that matter has been put to rest let's discuss what the future holds for my daughter. You say, Mr. Miller, you and my daughter are in love. Are you prepared to marry her at this time or shortly?"

Max thought before he responded and then replied. "Yes I do want to marry Elizabeth but I am not prepared to do so at this moment."

"If you were to ask my daughter to marry you when would this event take place?"

"Not for at least three years. We, both of us have to complete our college years and then we can marry sometime after that. Elizabeth can complete her schooling over the next three years and well, during the summers can continue to live here at her home."

"You make things sound so easy, Mr. Miller. Let me ask my daughter. Elizabeth, are you of the mind to marry Mr. Miller should he ask you?"

"Yes, father…I am."

"If you choose to marry this young man, a man who is not of our faith you must be prepared to enter his world and leave ours. The world outside of this farm, or our community, can be and often is a cruel place. In our community, everyone believes in God Almighty. Not so, out there in the world. You will be faced with many non-believers and those who could care less because you love the Lord. You have no transportation and you cannot operate an automobile, you have no money to speak of and no skills other than working on a farm that would be of value out there. Here, in our community, you are of great value to everyone who lives here. Out there, there will be many who will not consider you of any value. You will have to make your way.

"My decision in this matter is just this. Your decision is my decision. If you choose to be with Mr. Miller…so be it. But, by making that decision you must leave today with him. Mr. Miller's idea of you attending school for the next three years and still living here and then marrying him down the road would never work. Our community is tight-knit and everyone knows everyone else's business. This could never be kept a secret, nor do your mother or I choose to do so. After you leave with Mr. Miller we will have to go to the elders and explain that you decided to leave our faith. Everything your mother and I have is tied up on this farm. Your older sister who is married lives just up the road. We still have small children to raise. If we tell the elders we gave you our blessing we would then be shunned and it would be almost impossible for us to live here. So, understand this is your decision. We have paid for your second year of college and I have no intention of receiving a refund for the remainder of this year. So if you choose you can continue your education. We cannot support your last two years of college as you will no longer be of our faith. If it is your choice to go with Mr. Miller then you must give me your decision in the next minute. Are you prepared to make that commitment?"

Elizabeth looked at Max and then reached over and took his hand in hers as she asked, "Max…can we make it?"

Squeezing her hand gently, Max confirmed, "We'll be just fine."

"All right then," said Amos. "Elizabeth, you need to pack whatever is yours, place it in Mr. Mlller's vehicle, and then be on your way."

Elizabeth's mother stood and held her hand out to her daughter. "Come, I will help you to pack."

Elizabeth followed her mother out of the room while Amos banged his pipe on the side of the ashtray emptying the ashes. Mr. King looked at Max and stated, "You do realize that my daughter is now your responsibility. When she leaves with you she will not be able to return here, at last not that easily. When the community learns that this was her decision they'll turn their back on her. That may seem very unfair, but this is the way our faith works, and she is choosing to turn her back on the community. This does not mean that she is not a good person. She is just making a choice that is quite rare in our faith. You're a young man and taking the responsibility of caring for her is a large task for such a young man as yourself."

"Let me ask you this, Mr. King? Normally a Mennonite girl of the same age as your daughter would marry a Mennonite boy about my age, give or take. Would it not be just as hard for a young Mennonite man to marry as it is for me?"

"That's an interesting question, Mr. Miller and the answer is no, it would not be as hard as what you are going to face. In a Mennonite community, everyone looks out for everyone else, especially a newly married young couple. The husband is indeed directly responsible for his wife's well-being but he has the support of the entire community if need be. I do not know your parents but I assume they will support you and Elizabeth in your relationship and eventual marriage, but wherever you choose to live will all your neighbors be there for you if need be? You do not have to answer that question because I already know the answer. The answer in almost every case is no. We, as Mennonites, are not without sin, but because we choose to not be a part of the world in which we live; a broken, fractured world where most people are out for themselves we strive to live a less sinful life. The majority of people in your world are too busy worrying about their own needs to be concerned about their neighbors. You may look at your world much differently than what I have just described, but that's just the way I see things. That is none of my concern now. Elizabeth has made her choice. I am only releasing her to you because I believe you are a strong young man. Even though it may seem to you that we are abandoning our daughter, we will pray not only for her but for you as well. It's in God's hands now."

Opening his wallet Amos removed a one hundred dollar bill and smiled. "I don't carry that much money on me as a general rule but I do keep this hundred-dollar bill in my billfold as a reminder. You see, Mr. Miller money is important to everyone. No matter whether you're a Mennonite like me or a Methodist like you; Catholic, Jewish, Hindu, or even a non-believer… one has to have *some money.* It's one of the few things about your world that I agree with. We all need money to survive. My farm is larger than most of the farms in our community, that is except for Simon Baumer's place. I have no desire to have the level of wealth that Simon possesses, but I do want to make sure I have enough money so that when I pass on, my family will survive for years to come. You say that you are in college to get a degree in finance. I can only assume that even at your young age you understand how money works. I was wondering if you could explain to me how this stock market works?"

"When you say *works,* are you interested in how the market operates or are you interested in becoming an investor in the market?"

"I have a fair amount of money I have placed in a local bank over the years. Every month when I receive a statement from them I read that I'm only receiving around 1% return on my money. About two months ago I was installing some kitchen cabinets in a home in an upscale part of the city. The owner of the home happens to own a local car dealership and is quite wealthy. Over lunch, he explained to me that if I took some of the money I have in the bank and invested it in the market I could yield 6% to 8% rather than the paltry amount the bank is paying me."

"What this man told you is true. I've been investing in the market ever since I was ten years old when my father bought me some shares in a company called Walmart. Still today, I own shares in Walmart and many other companies I have chosen to invest in. The first thing I would do if I were you rather than just jumping into the market would be to go to a bookstore or even the library and get a book on investing in the market…"

For the next forty minutes, Max talked about some of the stocks he owned, how to buy and sell, stock splits, and how to keep a reserve fund in the bank for emergencies.

Their in-depth conversation was interrupted when Mrs. King knocked on the door and informed them that Elizabeth was packed and ready to go.

Amos motioned for Max to follow as they walked from the parlor into the kitchen where Elizabeth stood next to two old suitcases and a large wooden chest.

Smiling at her father she spoke softly, "I've packed everything I own Papa. I'm ready to leave with Max."

Clara wiped a tear from the side of her cheek as she stated, "Well then, let's get you loaded up."

Both Elizabeth and her mother grabbed a suitcase each while Amos spoke to Max, "If you would be so kind, Mr. Miller. Would you grab one end of that hope chest and we'll get it in your vehicle."

Max had his back to the door as he stepped out onto the porch but he could see the look of surprise on Amos' face. Turning his head he saw Rupert leaning against the porch railing, his brother, Thaddeus seated on the swing, a long weed dangling from his mouth. Simon stood at the bottom of the steps while cleaning mud from the bottom of his boots with a stick. Staring at Max and then at Amos, Simon asked angrily, "What's going on? Where are you going, Elizabeth?"

Amos put his end of the trunk down first and Max followed as he moved next to Elizabeth. Amos descended the steps and confronted Simon as he gestured at Max. "Simon, I think you know Mr. Miller here.

He visited us this afternoon and we had the most interesting conversation. According to Max, he has met you on two occasions, once at the farmers' market and then over in Gettysburg at his place of employment. Based on what he said I have been informed that both times were quite unpleasant. A couple of things you need to be made aware of. First off, I intend to go to the elders regarding your behavior toward Mr. Miller and second I have released my daughter from receiving any further courting activities on your part. In short, she is leaving with Mr. Miller who is not only taking her back to school but plans to marry her within the next three years or so."

Simon who was taller than Amos moved close to him and spoke in a degrading manner, "Amos, I have no regard for the elders. I moved past their rulings a long time ago."

Amos motioned for Max to pick up the trunk as they started down the steps. Walking past Simon, Amos explained, "Your disregard for the leaders of our faith is disturbing but at the moment not my concern. My daughter, on the other hand, is of great concern to me. What a fool I have been for thinking you would be a proper husband for Elizabeth."

Reaching into his pocket Max hit his key fob and the back of the Jeep slowly opened. The heavy trunk was no sooner in the back when Baumer stepped forward and grabbed Max by his shirt collar, snarling in his face. "I told you Miller not to come over here to Lancaster County. Your shotgun-carrying farmer friend is not around to save you now." In the next second, the back of Simon's large right hand slapped Max as he yelled into his face, "You have done nothing but interfere with our way of life. You are nothing but trouble." He drew back his hand to strike Max a second time but was prevented from doing so by a hard, swift hit with a broom that knocked him to the side as he released his grip on Max.

Rubbing his right shoulder he stared at Elizabeth's mother who held the broom inches from Simon's face. Stepping closer she ordered Baumer. "Back away from this young man. I just knew if you came up to the house there would be trouble."

Giving Mr. King a stern look, Simon spoke in an overbearing tone, "Amos…control your wife!"

Taking the broom from his wife Amos stepped in front of Simon and ordered in a calm, even voice, "Mr. Baumer…you may be considered a big deal here in our community but right now you happen to be on my property…my farm, and I'm telling you and your brothers to go on home now before I beat the living daylights out of you with this broom!"

Simon seemed at a loss for words, then turned and spoke to his brothers. "Com'n, let's get off Mr. King's farm. It's obvious he and his family are partial to outsiders rather than those of their community."

The King family and Max watched as Simon and his brothers walked down past the barn and then seconds later sped off up the lane in their Cadillac.

Max wiped a small trickle of blood from the side of his mouth while addressing Mrs. King. "Like I promised, if Baumer came up here I would cause you no trouble."

Removing a handkerchief from his pocket Amos handed it to Max and apologized, "I'm sorry you had to experience Simon Baumer's wrath while on my property."

Dabbing at the blood, Max smiled. "It's all right." Looking at Elizabeth he suggested, "Well, I guess we better be on our way."

Elizabeth gave her mother and then her father a hug before walking to the Jeep. Hesitating before climbing in she asked her mother, "I'll come back to see you. I'm not sure when. Maybe I'll bring you a grandchild years from now."

Clara did not answer but looked to her husband for an answer. Mr. King seemed sad as he answered, "You will always be our daughter and despite everything that has happened here today there is going to be a lot of talk around our community. Perhaps, in the future, you may be able to return for a visit. We'll see."

Max climbed in the driver's seat next to Elizabeth started the Jeep and slowly drove down the lane. At the end of the lane, he stopped before turning onto the road. Leaning toward Elizabeth he took her hand and spoke softly, "A lot has happened in the last hour or so. Once we turn down this road there is no turning back. Are you sure this is what you want? It won't be easy but together you and I will make it. I promise you."

Elizabeth stared up the road and smiled. "Down that road, there is a whole new life awaiting me." Loosening her bonnet she removed it from her head and shook out her long blond hair. "Next stop…Gettysburg!"

CHAPTER TWENTY-THREE

Max, seated on one of four wooden benches spaced evenly around the school fountain looked at the gray, overcast sky. Rain was on the way. In a few days, November would be upon them and rather than rain, the cold upcoming temperatures would result in snow. It was amazing to him how he had adapted to the cold weather of Pennsylvania since he had first arrived in Gettysburg his freshman year. Several things had changed since then. He recalled how his father had said his second year at school would go much smoother. *If only his father and his mother knew!*

It had been less than twenty-four hours since he had brought Elizabeth back to school. Sooner or later he was going to have to get together with his parents and tell them about his decision to marry her. His parents already thought that their relationship was short-lived. He wondered how support- ive his folks were going to be when he explained to them how his plans had somewhat changed. Here he was, a twenty-year-old young man who was now responsible for a girl who was only nineteen years of age herself. Things were moving a little faster than what he was accustomed to. Normally, when making a decision he could take a few days or depending on the situ- ation, a few weeks to decide what path he wanted to travel.

While at the King's farm, things turned out much differently than what he had envisioned. He had simply driven over to Lancaster County to set the record straight. He had never in his wildest imagination thought he would be bringing Elizabeth back to school with a promise to her father that they would marry within the next three years or so. There were so many thoughts spinning around inside his head. He needed to talk with someone and since his parents were not readily available at the moment, he decided to go over to the McCulhay farm and discuss his plans with Kellem. After all, Kellem had said he would be there to support him.

It was 1:10 on a Sunday afternoon. Free of any classes for the day he decided to take Elizabeth along over to Kellem's place. He felt strangely different as he sat there on the bench waiting for her like he had done several times. Last year he had waited for a girl that he was friends with, this year he had waited for a girl he was in love with, and now, since his visit to the King farm he found himself waiting for a girl he was going to marry. For some reason, he felt much older than twenty and then realized that this feeling was just his imagination. Looking down the rounded sidewalk he saw Elizabeth as she made her way up the path on the opposite side of the fountain. Bundled up in a warm winter coat she limped around to his side of the circular pond where Max offered her a seat next to him. Looking up at the sky she announced, "My father told me back in August we were in for a hard winter."

"That's all right," said Max. "The sooner winter gets here the sooner next spring will be upon us."

She took his left hand in her right and asked, "Are we still going over to the McCulhay farm today?"

"Yep, I think you'll like Kellem. He, like your father, is a farmer, a tree farmer. His farm reminds me a lot of your father's place. He doesn't have any livestock or chicken coops or many of the things you are used to back in Lancaster but he does have thousands of trees he grows. He is easy to talk with and looks at things in a very simple way. His advice is sound." Looking at his watch, he went on, "I told him we'd be by between two-thirty and three o'clock so we better get moving."

When they turned from Chambersburg Pike onto McCulhays' lane Elizabeth agreed with Max's comparison of Kellem's farm and her father's back home. "This place does remind me of home and look at all the trees. What does he do with them?"

"Most of them are sold as Christmas trees. I've been working on Kellem's place here for the past two months keeping his grass mowed and the weeds out in the fields low. Last week he told me with winter setting in the grass would no longer need to be cut until next spring. The weeds out in the fields have started to slow down what with the colder temperatures setting in. He told me next week I'll be helping him out with the actual trees. Trucks from Michigan, Virginia as well as right here in Pennsylvania will be rolling in here soon for loads of trees that they will sell for Christmas. He said we would really be busy up through the end of November and then things would start to taper off."

As they stopped next to the two-story farmhouse, Elizabeth glanced around the property. "This does remind me of back home."

Kellem who was seated in a rocking chair on the wrap-around porch stood as they parked. Meeting them at the bottom of the porch steps he greeted his guests. "Welcome friends!"

Elizabeth stepped out of the Jeep and was introduced by Max. "Kellem, this is Elizabeth King, the girl I've been telling you about. Elizabeth, this is Kellem McCulhay, the owner of this farm and I must say, a dear friend."

Kellem admired Elizabeth dressed in her usual Mennonite garb. "So this is Elizabeth. You're every bit as lovely as Max described you. I can see why he drove over to Lancaster to see you, and I might add, despite the warning of Simon Baumer not to come." Extending his right hand, he added, "This boy right here thinks the world of you. I, for one, after meeting this Baumer character cannot believe Max was able to bring you back to Gettysburg."

Elizabeth shook Kellem's hand. "I can't believe it myself. My father, who is very set in his ways, released me to Max. We're to be married in the next few years."

Looking at Max in utter amazement Kellem slapped his knee and exclaimed, "Well, I'll be if that don't beat all! Ol' Max here drives over to simply talk with your father and winds up bringing his future wife back. That's pretty amazing. Come on inside. I don't know if you two have had lunch yet, but I do have a freshly baked apple pie I bought this weekend. What say we each have a slice while you tell me all about your trip."

Max guided Elizabeth up the porch steps while Kellem reached for the door. "I don't know if Max warned you or not about the condition of my home. My brothers and I are not the best housekeepers in the world so you'll have to forgive us for the untidy manner in which we live."

Inside the small foyer, there was barely room to walk as both side walls were crammed with coats and sweaters, the floor jam-packed with shoes and boots. Next, they entered a large what appeared to be a dining area. The walls were lined with various hutches of size and color, stuffed with knick-knacks that were in no logical order. Two of the three pictures that hung on the wall were crooked, the other had a crack in the glass. A large antique table with several different types of chairs was piled high with boxes and scattered newspapers. Pointing toward the next room Kellem remarked, "We'll be having our pie in the kitchen."

Elizabeth stood in the doorframe that led to the kitchen and stared at the unorganized conglomeration of pots, pans, and dishes stacked in the sink and on the counter. At the far end of the room, there was a stack of cardboard boxes from the floor to the ceiling, the ceiling itself sagging over the refrigerator from a previous water leak. The walls were decorated with the most hideous wallpaper Elizabeth had ever laid her eyes on, the wall covering ripped and peeling here and there. Pulling out a chair at an old-fashioned metal kitchen table, Kellem offered. "Please have a seat while I get that pie."

At a loss for words, Elizabeth looked around the cluttered kitchen. The home where she had been raised was mopped and cleaned daily, not a dust ball to be found. Max shrugged at her indicating that it was nothing to worry over. Setting a delicious-looking deep dish pie on the table, Kellem drove a hunting knife down into the center of the desert, the handle wavering back and forth. Looking at Elizabeth, he asked, "And what would you two like to drink? I have milk, fresh brewed iced tea, and coffee that I just recently put on."

Elizabeth was quick to answer, "Coffee...black!"

Kellem smiled. "Ah, a woman after my own heart. And how about you Max?"

Staring at the knife in the middle of the pie Max answered, "Milk will be just fine for me."

Kellem placed a gallon of milk on the table, opened a cabinet took down a bright red coffee cup, blew out any dust that had accumulated, rinsed out the cup, and set it on the table as he poured hot coffee. "There ya go, darlin'." He then sat at one end of the table and looked from Max to Elizabeth who were sitting across from one another. Addressing Elizabeth, he tried to explain, "Once again I apologize for the condition of my home but you see we haven't had a woman's touch in this house for let's see I guess it'd be forty-some years. Our sister, Rose left the farm right after she turned eighteen when she married a truck driver from Florida. After all these years they still live down there and are happily married. My mother always kept the house neat but after she passed on my brothers and I, the three bachelors, as we like to call ourselves never could seem to get into a regular cleaning routine. We do run a mop or broom around here occasionally, like this morning when Max called me and told me he was bringing you by. I mopped the kitchen floor and wiped down the table and chairs. I was going to try and tackle all those dirty dishes but I just didn't have the time."

Max sat back in his chair and raised his right hand. "Speaking of brooms, if it hadn't been for Elizabeth's mother over in Lancaster I might not be sitting here this afternoon."

"That's right," said Elizabeth. "While we were getting ready to leave the farm Simon Buamer shows up and strongly objects to what is taking place. He slapped Max and was going to strike him again but then my mother whacked him with her porch broom and sent him and his brothers on the run. I, for one, think we have heard and seen the last of Simon Baumer."

Raising his cup of coffee in a toasting fashion, Kellem agreed, "Well, let's hope so!" Taking a drink, he asked, "You say you two have agreed to get married. Max, did you ask for her hand right there at the farm?"

Kellem's question brought a sudden look of doubt to Max's face. "Now that you mention it, no! I never asked Elizabeth to marry me. I just simply told her father that I had a desire to marry his daughter."

The next question came, "Did Elizabeth say she wanted to marry you?"

Elizabeth answered instantly, "When asked by my father if I would accept a marriage proposal from Max I replied, with a yes!"

"So, in all both of you committed to Elizabeth's father that you would marry one another but you never really asked Elizabeth and she didn't accept."

Elizabeth held her hand to her lips, almost as if she were embarrassed while Max chimed in. "Come to think of it, I never did ask her to marry me nor did she accept. I guess we just assumed that we would get married. I guess you would have had to be there to understand how everything went down."

Kellem pulled the pie tin close to him. "Well, I have no doubt the two of you will marry but I think at some point, that you, Max, need to ask this young lady properly…"

Elizabeth interrupted, "Max does not have to ask me what I already know, nor do I have to accept what I already know is in his heart. We will marry…we just don't know exactly when."

"And," said Max, "that's one of the future things we wanted to talk to you about. We know down the road we will be husband and wife, but there are several obstacles we must face first."

Cutting the pie into even sections, Kellem asked, "Like what?"

"For one thing, we've got to go to my parents and tell them about our plans. Right now, as it stands they don't have the slightest idea we plan to wed. I'm kind of figuring on maybe this Thanksgiving, or even better this Christmas of me and Elizabeth driving down to Summerville and dropping this good news on my folks."

"Good news for you," remarked Kellem, "but how do you think your parents are going to react? If they are footing the bill for your college education I'll bet you a dime to a dollar they are expecting you to complete all four years here at Gettysburg and then you'll have your degree in financing. But, like you said, you probably won't be getting hitched until after both of you graduate."

"Graduation! That, right there is yet another hurdle we have to jump," said Max. "This current year is not a problem. Elizabeth's father has agreed to not ask for a refund for his daughter's second year at school, so up until this coming May when school ends for the year, things will go along as usual. I'll stay in my dorm, Elizabeth in hers, we'll attend our classes and continue as friends in the eyes of the student body. We intend to keep our future marriage a secret in and around campus so I would appreciate it if this conversation does not leave this room."

Kellem ran the thumb and index finger of his right hand over his lips as if he were sealing them. "Mum is the word! So, when the school year ends why does that become a problem for you?"

"Normally, I would go down home to South Carolina for the summer and Elizabeth would return to her farm in Lancaster County, but since her father released her to marry me and essentially leave her faith and step out into a world the Mennonites are mostly opposed to she is no longer welcome back in her community. What this boils down to is Elizabeth would have to live with me and my parents over the summer until school starts next August, which presents us with another hurdle. Her father has no intention of paying for her schooling for her junior and senior years.

"This presents a major problem for us. The yearly tuition at Gettysburg is a little over fifty-six thousand dollars and that does not include things like buying your books and living expenses. When you throw those items into the pot the cost of being a student here in Gettysburg is close to seventy thousand. That means that we have to come up with one hundred and forty thousand dollars for Elizabeth to complete all four years of college. Over the years I've done a fair job of saving money and I have enough currently to get her through her junior year but after that, I'd be tapped out. I suppose we could take out a loan for the remaining seventy thousand but I don't think we want a bank loan hanging over our heads for years to come."

Kellem seemed disturbed, "Are you saying Elizabeth may not be able to attend the last two years of college?"

"That is a very distinct possibility, but she may not have to have four years of schooling to accomplish what she wants."

"I don't quite understand," said Kellem.

Elizabeth sipped at her coffee as she tried to explain her situation. "If I were to attend all four years of college I would then have my Bachelor's degree in nursing. My original plan was after I got my degree I would return to my community and be of service to my people, but now that I have been turned out that's not going to happen. As it turns out I can get an Associate's degree in just two years which would qualify me for a job at any nursing home in the state."

"And," added Max, "that type of position would pay somewhere in the area of forty-two thousand dollars a year. That's not too bad when you consider I'll still be in school for two more years. Between my working here or wherever I wind up working over the next couple of years combined with her salary, we could save some serious money. We don't plan on starting like most young married couples who walk out of a church with little or nothing in the bank. Over the next three years, we could save a nice little nest egg."

Sliding a slice of pie on a plate across the table to Elizabeth, Kellem remarked, "Whether you realize it or not you've got quite a smart young man there sitting across from you. I think, in the long run, you two will fare just fine. Like I always say, people don't plan to fail, but they often do... fail to plan!"

When everyone had a slice of pie in front of them, Kellem asked Elizabeth to bless the food. After she bowed her head and said a short prayer of thanksgiving, Kellem held up a finger and announced, "I said I would support Max in any way I could which includes anything that involves you Elizabeth. Sitting here listening to your plans and all of the hurdles, as you call them that you have to negotiate I have a plan rolling around in my head that might help you young folks out. Here it is! There just so happens to be a summer house attached to the main farmhouse here. It has never been used for anything other than storage ever since our mother passed away. It has two bedrooms upstairs, a kitchen, a bath, and a small living room down. If we started to work on getting that place cleaned up I bet we could have it livable in a few months."

Max looked at Elizabeth and then at Kellem. "What exactly are you saying?"

"What I'm saying is just this. Looking down the road to next year when school starts in August, you, Max, will be returning for your junior year and I assume that Elizabeth will return also, but she will not be attending school. Why should you two have to pay rent for an apartment for her to live in when I have a house right here on the farm where she could live? Come to think of it if we got to work on the place why she could move out of her dorm later this year and live here? Now, if all this works out there is a strict stipulation that you will have to follow and that's just this: You, Max, could not live there. I will not allow two people to live in sin on my farm. You'd have to remain at your dorm except when you come by to spend some time together."

Max was astonished at Kellem's offer. "That sounds like a great idea but at some point after we return from Summerville she'll probably be getting a job at one of the local nursing homes. We've already decided that she needs to learn how to drive a car, get her driver's license, and then via my Jeep drive back and forth to work. I don't need my Jeep to get around campus. I can walk to most places that I need to go. Another question I have, if we get this summer house cleaned up and livable and Elizabeth decides to live here, besides keeping the attached living quarters clean would there be anything else she would be responsible for?"

Kellem stuck a fork in his slice of pie. "Well, let's talk about that. Tell ya what, how about if I were to hire Elizabeth to work on the farm on a part-time basis? If she moves in later this year or early next year she could not only keep the summer house clean but this place as well. If, she has a mind to, why she could cook and iron? And next spring we have to put our garden in. There are lots of things she could help us out with around this place. I'd pay her twelve dollars an hour just like I pay you. You already told me you two wanted to save some money up before you got married. With you both making twelve dollars an hour that figures out to be twenty-four dollars an hour between the both of you. Now, you can work all the hours you want but when you consider you both are still in school you might only be able to give me thirty hours each a week. I'm not sure what that adds up to but I think that would be a good way for you to start saving, plus Elizabeth has a nice place to live, and I might add, similar to the farm she was raised on."

Doing some quick math in his head, Max responded, "Let's see, if we both were to give you thirty hours at twelve per that would equate to sixty hours which means that we would garner about seven hundred and twenty dollars a week or two thousand eight hundred and eighty dollars per month. I think that's pretty good for two young folks just starting." Looking at Elizabeth, Max asked, "What do you think? How does all this sound to you? Would you like to live and work here on Kellem's farm?"

Elizabeth folded her hands neatly on the table. "I feel Kellem's offer is a blessing. When I left my father's farm in your vehicle I left a place where I had lived for the first nineteen years of my life. A way of life I had grown accustomed to. And now, I find myself in a position that I chose to place myself in where I can never return there. I'm going to miss living on that farm. One of the things my father pointed out to me was that I had no skills other than working on a farm that I could put to use out here in the world and now you're telling me I could live here on this farm, that I can clean, cook, iron and plant a garden. These are things I was raised to be able to do and do well as a Mennonite wife. If we could arrange for me to live here that would make me very happy as long as Max is okay with this arrangement."

"If you'd be happy living here, then I'm okay with Kellem's offer."

Kellem chewed on a bite of pie and asked Elizabeth, "You say you can cook and I have no doubt that you can. My brothers and I cook on occasion, but to be honest, most of what we eat aside from vegetables from our garden is microwaved, so when you say cooking, what exactly do you mean?"

Elizabeth cut into her pie as she answered, "You name the meat, I can prepare it. Beef, lamb, chicken, turkey, pork, fish. I can bake, fry, broil, smoke, or panfry whatever you want. I can bake bread, pies, cookies, and cakes. I know how to make casseroles out of just about anything as well as all kinds of soups. My father always said that I put a great breakfast on the table and whoever I married, well that was going to be one lucky man. And before you ask about my cleaning skills. Why that's just second nature to me. You give me a couple of days and I'll have this place so clean you could eat off the floors. As far as helping out with your garden, there is not a vegetable that can be grown in Pennsylvania I have not grown back home. My father taught me how to plant and raise corn. Some of the best corn in our community came from our farm. I also noticed you have a small apple orchard. We have fruit trees on our farm and I know all about the care of fruit trees and harvesting the fruit. There isn't that much that takes place on a farm that I am not capable of doing."

Slapping the palm of his hand on the table, Kellem explained, "Well, by golly…you're hired! When do you want to start?"

Elizabeth slapped the table as well. "I can start tomorrow if that's okay. The sooner we get the summer house cleaned up the sooner I can move in."

Kellem agreed. "Let's finish up our pie then we'll take a look at your new home."

Max and Elizabeth followed Kellem as they walked around the back of the house where they came to an attached section that ran half the distance of the main house. It was fronted by three concrete steps with a wrought iron railing that was loose. On each side of the faded wood door, there were windows covered with bent, mangled Venetian blinds. The second floor had two windows in the front and one on either side. The guttering on the left side of the house was badly dented and the downspout was missing.

Reaching for a ring of keys from his coveralls Kellem sorted through the assortment of dangling keys while he spoke, "I haven't been in here since last May when I was looking for something. That was almost six months back and I haven't been in here since, so it's hard to say what we'll find inside." Locating the proper key he inserted it and turned the doorknob, opened the door, and stepped back. "After you."

Max stepped into the semi-darkness of the first room while knocking several cobwebs out of the way. Stubbing his foot on something he stopped and ordered the others, "Hold on, I just bumped my foot into something."

Suddenly, the room was filled with dim light when Kellem reached up and flipped on a light switch. Making his way to a window, he commented, "Probably just a box that fell over. Let's get these windows open and get some fresh air in this place. I'll get the one on this side if you'll get the other one."

Elizabeth remained standing just inside the door as she gazed at piles of boxes filled with old clothes, shoes, and plastic bags stuffed with who knew what.

Kellem walked past two folded chairs and an old patio set while motioning toward the rear of the summer house. "The kitchen is right over here. It has a complete set of pots, pans, utensils and about everything else one needs to run a kitchen."

Elizabeth watched as a mouse appeared between two boxes and then scooted across the wood floor. Picking up a box she dropped it on the unsuspecting creature. The noise captured both Max and Kellem's attention. Kicking the box to the side Elizabeth bent down, picked up the tiny rodent by its lifeless tail, and stated. "Back home we had field mice all around the farm. We also had several barn cats that kept the rodent population under control, but on occasion, one would get into our house. My mother or I would swat it with a shovel, broom or whatever was handy at the time and then toss the dead or groggy mouse outside to the cats." Opening the door she tossed the rodent outside and asked, "I don't suppose you have any resident cats on the premises?"

"No," said Kellem, "but it might not be a bad idea to get a couple."

Max shook his head in amazement at how Elizabeth had handled the mouse. "I can't believe how calm you were. Most females would have jumped up on a chair screaming all the while."

Elizabeth walked into the kitchen. "Well, I guess you just never met a farm girl before."

The kitchen was a repeat performance of the first room, with cobwebs, dust balls scattered across the floor, and the kitchen countertop cluttered with boxes, and overflowing bags of clothes. Standing next to the refrigerator Kellem nodded in agreement to what Max and Elizabeth must have been thinking. "I told you the place needed a lot of work. Come on let's go on up to the second floor. I don't think there is as much junk up there for the simple reason that my brother and I don't have the energy to haul much up the steps."

Just like Kellem had stated, the upstairs was free of boxes and discarded knickknacks and the like. The hardware floors were old and creaky, the thick dust on the windows allowing only a pale amount of light in the house. Flipping on a light switch, Kellem pointed out, "Like I said, not as much junk up here but it sure needs a good cleaning before it can be used as living quarters." Sitting on the side of one of the beds a small cloud of dust filtered up into the air. Waving the dust from his face, he shrugged, "I guess we'll have to get some new linens up here."

Max touched one of the walls where there was evidence of a previous water leak, as he noted, "Guess we'll have some patching up to do as well." Sitting on the other bed he looked at Elizabeth, "It does need a lot of work. What do you think?"

Elizabeth sat next to Max and held his hand. "I couldn't possibly move in here the way it sits right now, but I do see potential in this house. This is going to take more than a couple of weeks. We might not be able to make the place livable until next spring. It's just going to take a lot of elbow grease and time. I say we get started tomorrow."

"Sounds good to me," said Kellem, "All you need to do is the work. I'll supply you with whatever you need to get the job done, mops, buckets, cleaning supplies…whatever. Starting tomorrow you're on the payroll. You can come and go as you please and I'll always be around here somewhere for anything you may need." Standing, he started for the steps. "Let's go back down to the main house and make some plans for this project."

Two hours later, Max pulled the Jeep into the parking lot of a local Kentucky Fried Chicken and suggested, "That pie at Kellem's was good and the only thing I had for breakfast was a banana and I skipped lunch. I'm starving and I have a hankerin' for fried chicken. Have you ever had Kentucky Fried?"

Elizabeth frowned. "Fried chicken from a fast food place…never! How good could it be?"

Parking the Jeep in the lot, Max stated, "How about if we let mathematics answer that question? Kentucky Fried Chicken officially started back in 1952 which means as a company they have been in business now for sixty-five years. Currently, they have over twenty thousand locations in over one hundred and forty countries. Over one hundred and eighty-five million people view one of their ads every week and they and their affiliates serve over twelve million customers a week. I was reading that just this last year their annual sales were somewhere around twenty-three billion. In the fast food industry, the math states very clearly that a lot of people like their chicken. I think it's the best there is. Fried chicken is one of my favorite meals. Kentucky Fried is even better than my mother's. You'll be seeing her next month or thereabouts, so don't mention that I think Kentucky Fried is better than hers! A mother never wants to hear that her cooking is not as good as fast food."

Proudly, Elizabeth sat up. "I bet this Kentucky Fried Chicken is not nearly as good as mine!"

"Maybe…maybe not," said Max with a smile. "Is your fried chicken that good?"

"The best! But for now, you'll just have to take my word for it. Here's what we'll do. The first meal I prepare at Kellems will be fried chicken. We'll let your taste buds be the judge and after you taste *my fried chicken* I'll remind you of this very conversation."

CHAPTER TWENTY-FOUR

Max learned his ten-speed Schwinn against a tall tree next to the road, climbed a small rocky knoll, and sat on a large boulder while looking out across the vast field spread out before him. Today was the first time since returning from his summer vacation that he had visited the battlefield. Taking in a deep breath of crisp fall air he stared at the dense trees to the east and south, the leaves creating a patchwork of brilliant red, yellow, and orange. At the northern edge of the nineteen-acre field sat yet another battlefield site: the Peach Orchard. The connecting field he was in was called the Wheatfield and was known as one of the bloodiest battles in American history. Over twenty thousand Union and Confederate troops fought back and forth for nearly four hours on the second day of the Battle of Gettysburg. Despite the intense heat of that July day control of the field had switched hands six times, over six thousand men losing their lives that afternoon. The very knoll where he was now seated had been the site of intense fighting back then. He and his father had come to the Wheatfield many times and still to this day, Max was amazed at the tenacity of both armies.

He pulled a long weed out of the nearby grass, stuck it between his lips, leaned back, and gazed up at the blue sky dotted with occasional white puffy clouds. His day had gone quite well. He breezed through his two morning classes, only to find out his one o'clock class had been canceled. Elizabeth had a seminar to attend so he had the day to himself. He thought about driving over to the battlefield but opted for his bike, which his doctor had strongly suggested that he stay away from until after the first of the year. Defying the doctor's orders he hopped on the bike and carefully pedaled over to the Wheatfield. Opening a knapsack he had brought along he took out a bottle of water and a peanut butter power bar. He had a lot of thinking to do.

Since Simon Baumer and his brothers had approached him at McCulhay's farm only four days had passed. During that time he, thanks to Kellem had escaped certain injury from the Baumers, had driven over to Lancaster in hopes of talking with Elizabeth's parents, somehow had convinced Mr. King to not only stop Baumer's courtship of his daughter but had released her to him. Yesterday he had spent the afternoon at Kellem's farm discussing their future and now today he found himself relaxing at the Wheatfield.

At some point, the pace of the way things were unfolding had to slow down. Gazing at a large cloud passing overhead, he realized that his moment of relaxation had arrived. There were quite a few things to be concerned over, but nothing pressing at the moment. His thoughts of being alone in the Wheatfield were quickly erased when he noticed a green-clad park guide leading a group of eight battlefield visitors out from behind a small clump of trees in the distance near the west end of the field. Single file, the line of visitors followed the guide along a path that skirted the battlefield site. Their short walk was halted when the guide stopped at a monument nestled in a small grouping of trees. Even though the monument was too far off to read, Max knew what the stone and brass structure represented. He and his father had walked down there many times.

The last time he had visited the Irish Brigade monument was eight months in the past when last spring he had spent an afternoon at the park, one of his stops that day, the Wheatfield. Even though the park guide and his guests were a fair distance off Max could see the guide pointing and waving his arms while he explained how the Union Irish Brigade had been involved during the battle. Five minutes passed and the guide led the group along the western edge of the field, the tour over. Turning his attention back to the field Max decided before leaving for the day he'd hike around the field. Laying in the soft grass next to the boulder he closed his eyes and thought about how he was going to explain to his parents about the upcoming marriage in three years.

"Howdy there!" The strange voice caused Max to open his eyes and he sat up quickly, turned, and saw the park guide standing a few feet away. The guide, realizing he had startled Max apologized, "I'm sorry…didn't mean to give you a scare."

Max sat on the boulder and replied, "That's all right. I was just day-dreaming." Motioning at the monument at the bottom of the field Max asked, "Was that you I saw down there with those tourists?"

The guide removed a pack of cigarettes from his coat pocket and ignored his question, but introduced himself, "My name is Les. I'm a guide here at the park. Haven't I seen you before on the battlefield?"

"You probably have. I visit the battlefield quite often. My father and I are reenactors and I'm also a student at Gettysburg College. I find it very peaceful out here in these historic fields. Why, you could have seen me almost anywhere: Devil's Den, Little Round Top, The Railroad Cut. I get around to all the sites quite a few times in the year."

Placing a cigarette between his lips Les produced a lighter, lit his smoke, and drew in the first shot of nicotine. "Ever run into ol' man McCulhay during your visits?"

Amazed, Max sat up straight and answered. "If you mean Kellem McCulhay, I sure have. I've seen him on two different occasions. He's quite the character. It's funny you should mention Kellem. I was just at his farm yesterday. I work for him, helping him out around his farm."

Les agreed. "Kellem is indeed quite the character. I can't tell you how many times while I'm giving a tour Ol' Kellem wanders by. Once in a while I'll call him over and introduce him to my visitors. He's kind of a fixture around these parts. He never says too much, just asks folks where they are from, welcomes them to Gettysburg, and then moves on. I told him a couple of times he would make a great tour guide." Taking another drag on his smoke Les looked out across the field while asking, "Since you have visited all of our battlefield sites which one is your favorite?"

Max stood and stretched, "That's a hard question to answer as each location has its own story to tell like right here at the Wheatfield." Pointing to the south end of the field, Max elaborated, "On July 2nd, 1863 Confederate General George Anderson led his Georgia brigade through those woods down there and attacked Union General Regis de Trobriand's Union regiments who were positioned behind that stone wall. The fighting was brutal and went on and on until both sides ran out of ammunition. Anderson's men jumped over the wall and the Union troops were on the run but then General David Birney ordered a bayonet charge which drove the Confederates back until Union reinforcements arrived."

Max motioned at the surrounding, boulder-strewn knoll as he continued with his rundown of the battle, "Later in the battle, a South Carolina brigade led by General Joseph B. Kershaw crossed the Rose farm and attacked the Union position on this knoll, right here! The South Carolinians drove the Union forces off the knoll, but this was short-lived as the Union Irish Brigade mounted an attack and drove the Confederates back. Back and forth it went for hours. There were over twenty thousand men involved in the battle for this field and the casualties in the end resulted in a 30% loss of life. That equates to one out of every three soldiers involved killed, wounded, or captured. Amongst those killed here at the Wheatfield two were generals, Southern Brigadier General Paul Semmes and Northern Brigadier General Samuel Zook. Semmes was shot in the leg and removed from the battlefield. The surgeons did all they could but they could not stop the infection and Semmes died on July 10th eight days later. Zook was shot in the abdomen, but the efforts of the surgeons failed and he died shortly after midnight on July 3rd."

Standing on one of the boulders Max displayed the surrounding knoll while explaining, "There was a lot of bloodshed right here on and around this knoll. Every time I come here I can just envision soldiers on both sides hiding behind some of these very boulders as they leveled their muskets at the enemy. Many of those men died right here where we now stand. All in all the battle of the Wheatfield is called by many; the harvest of blood! The meaning was that there was so much carnage here on this field that the spilled blood contrasted with the golden wheat. It must have been a horrible sight."

Les pointed his cigarette at Max and complimented him, "Short of a few details I couldn't have explained what happened here any better. Ever consider being a park guide?"

"As much as I like talking about The Civil War the thought never crossed my mind. I would like to ask you a question, but before I ask, I want to apologize right up front because what I'm about to ask may offend you, and believe me, that is not my intention."

Les stubbed out his cigarette butt on one of the boulders and shredded the remaining tobacco-filled paper to the ground. "It's rather hard to accept an apology from someone when you have no idea what they are talking about, so go ahead and fire away and we'll see where this lands."

"Well," said Max, "I was wondering. As a man of color, how do you feel about the Civil War?"

"My answer to you is just this, you are not the first person out here on the battlefield who has asked me that very question. Before I give you an answer let me give you a prelude to my life before moving here to Gettysburg. I was born and raised in Baltimore, Maryland. I lived in the ghetto there for the first eighteen years of my life with my two older brothers and my mother. My father abandoned the four of us when I was just three so I can't recall that much about the man. My mother was the salt of the earth, a more religious woman you'd be hard-pressed to find. She read the Bible every day and made me and my brothers attend church weekly. My mother had what I call deep wisdom, which she claimed came from the Bible. Over the years she tried her best to instill her religious and moral values in her three sons. We were extremely poor, but somehow we always managed to get by. My mother dearly loved all three of us but always said I was the only one who paid her much attention.

"According to her, my two older brothers had ears that did not hear and eyes that did not see, hence as they grew older they were constantly in trouble with the law. I, unlike my brothers, did not take to the streets and all the trouble that awaited one there. I studied hard in school, determined to graduate from high school and then move from the ghetto. I became obsessed with baseball and practiced all the time. I played on a little league team and then in high school. Turned out I was better than average. My baseball skills netted me a scholarship to the University of Maryland where I not only met my future wife but received my degree in business. We married, I got a job with a major insurance company, and got transferred here to their Gettysburg office as a claims adjuster. These days I can say without a doubt that I have been blessed. I have a wonderful wife and a great job, I own my own home in a nice neighborhood and I have two lovely daughters. So, as a man of color, I am living the American dream."

Les placed his booted foot on one of the boulders and went on to explain, "During my school years in Baltimore, I can't exactly pinpoint when but we studied the Civil War and of course, slavery. I always discussed with my mother what I was taught in school and I remember her telling me we had ancestors who were slaves. This was appalling to me as a young boy. To think I had ancestors in my family who had suffered the degradation and cruelty of slavery was shocking to me. When I became a tour guide here in Gettysburg I looked at slavery in a much different light than I did as a small boy from the ghetto. There are some people of my color who still today blame a person like you, a white person for what happened over a century and a half ago to their ancestors. I think that is way out of line. Slavery, as it was during the Civil War ended over one hundred and fifty years ago, but many of my people still want to cast blame on your people. Now, I'm not saying all white people are good nor am I saying the same of my people. Here's the way I see things. The Emancipation Proclamation was passed by Lincoln back on September 22, 1862, freeing 3.5 million African Americans from slavery."

Les looked up at the sky with an attitude of hopelessness and continued, "Here's what gets me! Especially up here in the north. Some of my people continue to argue with white folks from the north over the past issue of slavery. It doesn't make any sense to me today, in the past, or in the future. Do these people not realize that it was the North who stood up and stated very loudly that slavery was wrong, that it had to be abolished, that the slaves in the South had to be set free? The southern states at that time did not appreciate ol' Abraham Lincoln putting together an army to invade the south to free the slaves, so we wind up with the Civil War.

"Some of the numbers regarding the Civil War are staggering, over ten thousand battles over four years with six hundred and twenty thousand soldiers losing their lives. Now, out of these ten thousand battles Gettysburg ranks right at the top as the bloodiest conflict that took place with over fifty thousand dead during the three-day campaign. Let's break that down and look at what happened right here at the Wheatfield. In four hours six thousand men breathed their last, even though the slaves had previously been freed. So why, nearly ten months after the slaves had been freed were the two armies still at each other's throats? The typical Confederate soldier was a dirt farmer who didn't own or was even interested in having slaves. They were fighting for their rights. They did not want Lincoln and those in the north telling them what they could and could not do. The typical soldiers from the north were of the same ilk, farmers, shopkeepers, and the like. Out of the six hundred and twenty thousand men who died in the Civil War probably at least half if not more fought for the North and 99% of those boys were white and they died fighting a war to free my people. I am not glad there was a Civil War but I am glad it resulted in my people being set free. Does that answer your question?"

"Yes, it does and it makes perfect sense although many people don't see it that way."

Les reached for Max's hand. "Listen, I have to report back to the main tour center. I'm told I have a bus load coming in here from Florida and that they will be here at the Wheatfield in about an hour. That means I will be telling forty-two passengers and a bus driver all about what went on here at the Wheatfield. I hope we run into one another again sometime. It has been my pleasure to talk with you."

"Same to you," said Max as he shook Les's hand and watched him walk away.

Max picked up his knapsack and slung it over his right shoulder. He grabbed his water and started down the two-foot-wide cut path through the three-inch grass and weeds that covered the field. Halfway across the field, he took a right at an intersecting path that led to a tree line on the southern edge of the Wheatfield. A few yards out from the trees there sat the stone wall where the Confederates had the Union boys on the run. Directly in front of the low stone barrier, there was a stone-mounted metal marker that explained what went on in this section of the battlefield. Max read the inscribed metal words that were pretty much along the same lines as he had explained to Les about what happened at the wall. There was a framed, plexiglass-covered picture depicting the bayonet charge that had taken place. Sitting on the wall he dropped his knapsack to the ground and wedged his water down between two stones.

He thought about the bayonet charge and it reminded him of his senior year in high school when his father had given a seminar over in Beaufort. The seminar was about Civil War weaponry and as usual, his knowledgeable father gave the audience a detailed and interesting rundown on weapons utilized during the war, one of those items being the bayonet. Max had attended and as usual, was amazed at his father's delivery of Civil War facts. Sitting off to the side in the first row he watched as his father walked out onto the elevated stage and took a seat in a lone wooden chair centered on the stage. When his father went to a speaking engagement he always reminded him of some sort of superhero. During the day he was this hard-working construction worker who by the end of the day was usually covered in mud and dirt, but whenever he gave a seminar he somehow changed his appearance into what appeared to be a college professor. His father had what he called stage presence and all eyes were on him as he crossed the stage. Smiling, he remembered almost word for word what his father had talked about that day.

"Good morning ladies and gentlemen. My name is Charles Miller. My friends call me Charley and my close friends refer to me as Chuck. I have been asked to speak to you today about Civil War weaponry. Nearly three-quarters of a million men lost their lives during the war between the states…" For the next three hours, his father talked about the cannons used by both the Confederacy and the Union, the twelve-pounder Napoleon, the twelve and twenty-four-pounder Howitzer, up to one hundred and fifty pounders.

After a lunch break at noon, the group returned an hour later for the afternoon segment which was centered on the typical Civil War soldier and his musket. The stage looked very different as his father had decided to use several props for the afternoon talk, an eight by ten U-shaped ten-foot high wooden structure complete with an old hanging mattress. His father strolled out onto the stage as he carried his authentic 1862 Enfield Civil War rifle and bayonet, around his waist was strapped a genuine Civil War equipment belt complete with cartridge box, cap box, and bayonet scabbard. He went on to explain that he had purchased the rifle, bayonet, and belt at an auction years in the past and stated that the gun was still in working order. For the next ten minutes, he went into great detail about the Civil War soldier and his musket.

Sitting in the grass, his back against the stone wall, Max reviewed in his mind what his father had shared with the group that day. "There were two types of muskets that were used during the war, the Springfield and the Enfield. Both of these rifles were loaded and fired following the same procedure. Now, most of the soldiers in the Confederate infantry were farmers and were used to living in the great outdoors, living off the land, hunting, and the like, so it was only natural they would bring their guns with them when they enlisted in the southern army. The Union also had young and old men alike who were farmers who joined the ranks, but many of the soldiers in the north came from large cities and were not accustomed to handling a firearm. Because of this, raw recruits were drilled for hours on end in the procedure of loading and firing their musket. The South, as well drilled their troops for the simple reason that other than being a sniper the in-line infantry soldier had to acquire patience and speed when in battle."

His father held up his Enfield and went on, "Depending on who you talk to there are eight, nine, or ten steps involved when loading and firing a Civil War musket. The reason why there seems to be some confusion on the exact amount of steps required is because some soldiers were so proficient at the process that in some cases they could perform two steps at a time. Myself, well I have gone through the process thousands of times and for me, the ten-step rule seems to be the best. That being said, at this time I am now going to demonstrate those steps. The first step may or may not be used depending on whether the soldier is kneeling standing…lying down or charging across a field. For now, let's assume that I am in the midst of battle and I'm behind a stone wall, in which case the first step comes into play… the stock of the musket must be placed on the ground. This will allow the powder to flow easily down the barrel."

Going down on his knee his father placed the stock on the stage floor and continued, "The next step is to reach in your cartridge box and remove a paper-wrapped cartridge, tear it open with your teeth, and pour the powder down the barrel, making sure you do not drop the minie ball, because the next required step is to place the ball into the barrel. It should fit snugly but not tight. The next steps are three fluid movements: withdraw your ramrod from the holder beneath the barrel, place the ramrod in the barrel, and push the ball down onto the powder. The ball itself has a cone-shaped head which must face the front end of the barrel so the flat end when rammed down will be next to the powder. Withdraw the ramrod and more than likely you will not place it back in its holder because, in the next passing seconds, you will be repeating the process. Pick up the musket and cock the hammer back, reach into your cap box and remove a percussion cap and place it on the nipple where the hammer will make contact. You then check to see if the hammer is back, aim, and then fire. Immediately you repeat the process. A well-trained soldier in the Civil War could load and fire his weapon three times in a minute…sixty seconds."

His father motioned for Max to come up onto the stage and explained, "My son, Max, who is here with me today is going to assist me in a live demonstration to see if I can accomplish what was expected of the Civil War soldier. I will be performing the step-by-step process I just explained to you. I will repeat the process three consecutive times while Max keeps a stopwatch. I will be firing into that mattress and of course, I will be using blanks, so be warned. Prepare yourself for three loud gunshots in the next minute or so. I will be performing this demonstration from the kneeling position."

Charley turned to Max and spoke, "Whenever you're ready!"

Max looked out at the audience who seemed to be on the edge of their seats, looked at his father, pressed the start button on the stopwatch, and shouted, "Go!"

His father reached into his cartridge box, withdrew a paper-wrapped cartridge, ripped the top off with his teeth, and poured the powder down the vertical barrel. His father resembled a machine as he went through the entire process and fired the Enfield, then repeated the movements a second time, and then fired again. When the third shot rang out and reverberated through the auditorium, Max stopped the watch, walked over, and joined his father. Smiling at his father he announced proudly to those in attendance, "Fifty-seven seconds…three seconds less than a well-trained soldier." This was followed by a standing ovation lasting for nearly thirty seconds when Max's father raised his hand for silence.

When the crowd silenced he emphasized, "Despite my performance, I can assure you I am not better than a well-trained soldier in the Civil War for the simple reason that I performed in a relaxed environment. During the heat of battle, in most cases, the Civil War soldier had to load and fire his weapon under what can only be described as a stressful situation. A fellow soldier next to you could be lying there, bleeding to death, screaming in pain from a fatal bullet from the enemy, bullets could be whizzing by your head, then there was the noise of cannon fire and the smoke-filled nauseating air. And then there is that moment when the enemy mounts a charge, hundreds of men running directly at you. Do you stand your ground or run?" Reaching into his scabbard Max's father withdrew his bayonet, "Hence…the bayonet!"

He held up the pointed metal weapon and stated, "The bayonet is twenty-six and a quarter inches long and the blade itself measures twenty-two and a half inches. This is referred to as a socket bayonet." Demonstrating he continued, "The round socket at the end of the bayonet is slipped over the barrel of the musket and then snapped in place. The bayonet was rarely used in combat but was considered frightening to soldiers in both armies. From reading many authentic documents and letters written during the war most soldiers, if they had to die preferred to be shot rather than run through with a two-foot blade of sharp steel. Even in close combat, the bayonet was rarely used. Many soldiers preferred to attach their bayonets before a battle even if the enemy was on the opposite side of a field. As the enemy drew closer the amount of time a soldier had to reload and fire was cut significantly so the bayonet was their last line of defense unless they decided to turn and run which many a soldier did. The most famous bayonet charge took place at Gettysburg at Little Round Top where Joshua Chamberlain and his men completely out of ammunition routed the Confederates who still had ammo. His actions that day earned him the Medal of Honor."

He removed the bayonet from his musket and waved the pointed object at the crowd. "The amount of men killed by the bayonet in the war was less than 1%. The bayonet had many other uses, it could be used for stirring beans or bacon in a pan, it could be used for cutting meat, it could be used as a tent stake or even as a candle holder."

Max looked into the trees behind him where General Birney had organized a bayonet charge that at least for that moment turned the tide of the Battle of the Wheatfield. Looking across the field toward the rocky knoll he noticed two vehicles had pulled in while the adults watched as five small children ran to the knoll and began to climb over the boulders. One of the women began to take pictures of the children at play while one of the men scanned the field with a set of binoculars. When the binoculars came to the stone wall, the man hesitated. Max, thinking that the man had spotted him seated on the wall waved at the man, who, in turn, raised his right arm and waved back. Max smiled as he thought about how time had a way of curing everything, Here, he and a stranger were exchanging pleasantries while over one hundred and fifty years in the past strangers in the same field killed one another. *Time to move on,* he thought. Picking up his knapsack and bottle of water he walked along the wall in the direction of the north end of the field.

His thoughts turned to the week ahead, starting tomorrow when he and Elizabeth following their classes, would be going out to Kellem's farm, Max helping with tree shipments, and Elizabeth beginning the daunting task of cleaning up the summer house. As discussed at Kellem's kitchen table, he would supply Elizabeth with whatever she required to get the job done. Elizabeth estimated that it could take well into December or possibly after the first of the year before the two-bedroom quarters would be fit for habitation.

He thought about his parents once again and what their reaction would be when he sprang the news of the future wedding on his folks. It was the first week of November and Christmas break was six and a half weeks away. He had plenty of time to figure out how to announce his intentions to his mother and father. As always he tried to weave the world of mathematics into every situation he encountered. The math of this particular situation was rather simple. He had a little over six weeks before he would be speaking with them, the future marriage was at least three years down the road, and he and Elizabeth were both going to be working and saving as much money as they could.

Passing the north edge of the field he made his way down the cut path that led to the Irish Brigade Monument. Standing in front of what he had always heard was one of the most visited monuments on the battlefield Max thought about the Irish and how over two hundred thousand Irish immigrants had served during the war. Since the bulk of the Irish resided in the north the Irish that were represented in the Union army were much larger than the Irish who fought with the South. The Irish were proud people and proud of their new home…America. They did not want to be viewed as cowards so many an Irish lad signed on.

Walking up the path that led back to the knoll, Max thought about the Mennonites and their attitude toward the war. Like today they were pacifists and did not agree to any type of conflict or fighting. It must have been difficult to be Mennonite in those days because even though they opposed slavery they also opposed the very war that could put an end to slavery.

Back at his bike he climbed on and pedaled down the road leading back to town. He felt tired as the bike ride and his hike around the Wheatfield had worn him out. A warm meal at one of his favorite café's sounded good and then he would just relax for the rest of the day. Tomorrow it was back to his classes and then he and Elizabeth would be off to Kellem's.

CHAPTER TWENTY-FIVE

Thursday, November 19th three weeks had passed since his relaxing afternoon at the Wheatfield. Stabbing the bottom of a skid loaded with Christmas trees Max maneuvered the forklift down the dirt road, stopped at the rear of a forty-foot refrigerator semi, and raised the skid to the bed of the truck, where the driver waited with a heavy-duty hand jack. *Two more skid loads* thought Max, *and this truck is out of here.*

Max parked the lift next to the road and climbed down, removed his work gloves and ball hat, wiped his brow with the back of his hand, and took a long refreshing swig of cold water. Kellem, knocking dirt from his coveralls with a straw hat took a bottle of water from the cooler on the back of the lift and commented, "We have one more truck scheduled today. Should be rolling in here in the next hour and then we'll call it a day." Unscrewing the top, he took a drink and looked up at the sun while running his fingers through his thinning hair. "Still planning on taking Elizabeth down to Summerville over Christmas vacation?"

Sitting on the ground next to the front tire, Max answered, "Yep, that's the plan. I've been running over in my mind for the past three weeks how I'm going to approach my folks about this upcoming marriage. I've come up with several different ways to tell them about the plans Elizabeth and I share, but I have concluded that it would just be better to be upfront, ya know, tell them the way things are."

"Being honest is always the best path to take in any situation," said Kellem. "I hope it all works out for you two. Speaking of Elizabeth, she has, over the past three weeks made some serious progress on getting the summer house in order. When I first met her when you brought her out here to the farm, she appeared to be just the way you had previously described her to be, plain, quite religious, at times, even on the quiet side. Over the past weeks, I have come to know her quite well. Beneath her strict, by-the-book Mennonite dress attire and her simple way of looking at life, I find her to be very refreshing in the way she approaches things. She is extremely organized and a harder worker you'd be hard to find. During the past three weeks, she has carried numerous boxes of items, aside from the kitchen utensils and cookware out to the barn where she has sorted through every box and categorized everything to where I can see what I have, what I want to keep, give away, or pitch. She has done a marvelous job. The few times in the past when I have entered the summer house and taken a look at all the junk my brothers and I have accumulated, I always just throw my hands in the air, not having any idea as to how to approach getting the place cleaned up. Before she got started today she told me she would be taking the last few loads out to the barn. Tomorrow, I plan on sorting through everything and making some decisions. There will be a few things I'll keep, but for the most, I'd say between throwing stuff out or donating items to our local Goodwill, I'll be rid of a lot of junk that has cluttered the summer house for years."

"As long as we're talking about getting rid of stuff," said Max, "Elizabeth was telling me on the way over here earlier she might bring the idea up to you of having a yard sale out by the main road. Why give a lot of your stuff away when you could probably make a few hundred dollars and also make some people happy by getting a good bargain on something you no longer want?"

Kellem looked out at the main road and then back to Max. "That sounds like a great idea. Besides the summer house, the main house is packed with old stuff my brothers and I have no use for. I bet we could move a lot of items if we had a yard sale."

A Home Depot rental truck lumbered down the road and stopped short of where they were seated. Max placed his hat back on his head and remarked, "I thought the next truck was not supposed to be here for an hour?"

Kellem responded by shaking his head. "That's not the truck I'm expecting. Just probably a local who wants a tree."

The truck was pulled to the side of the road into a small dirt clearing when two younger men climbed out, the driver, tall and slender was well dressed in khaki pants, a button-down shirt topped with a burgundy colored sweatshirt embossed with some sort of insignia. The passenger was shorter, sporting fashionable jeans and an identical sweatshirt. Upon close examination of the second youth, Max lowered his head and spoke in a low tone to Kellem. "I know the passenger. That's Brad Sykes."

Surprised, Kellem remarked, "You mean that guy you punched in the nose last year?"

"The one and only!"

Brad walked across the grass and stopped directly in front of Max and Kellem. "Well, if it isn't my old roommate, Max Miller. How the hell are ya?"

Max, not wanting any trouble, answered, "Fine…and you Brad?"

Sticking out his chest and standing as erect as he could Brad responded in a bragging tone, "Things couldn't be better for me! I'm playing varsity football and I've been accepted by the largest and most prestigious fraternity on campus, Phi Delta Theta." Pulling on the edges of the sweatshirt he gave Max a cocky grin. "Phi Delta is the same fraternity my father attended while he was at school here in Gettysburg. He was the president of his fraternity his senior year." Thumping his companion on his shoulder Brad proudly stated, "Not just any ol' male student can get into Phi Delta. I don't imagine you're in a fraternity…are you?"

"No," said Max sarcastically, "I'm not. I've made my new home over at Bell Hall with several, I guess you could say young men who are not as fortunate as you happen to be."

Brad blew off Max's attempt to insult him, removed a pack of cigarettes from his jeans, and addressed Kellem. "You don't mind If I smoke…do you?"

Kellem, realizing what a smartass Brad Sykes was raised his right hand. "Go right ahead. It's a free country."

There was a moment of awkward silence when Brad spoke up as he gestured at their rental truck. "We've been given the task of driving over here to purchase two Christmas trees for our frat house. We're going to need an eight-footer and the other one can be six feet. That sounds like something you would have lying around here somewhere?"

Kellem pointed at a large corral of cut trees that were leaning up against some fencing. "Right over there. Anything you want from four feet up to nine. Pick out what you want and we'll get you loaded."

Brad, trying to express his superiority asked, "What type of trees do you raise here on this… so-called farm?"

Kellem gave Max a slight wink, then answered, "We have Frasier Fir, Douglas Fir, and Spruce. You can get the six in the Frasier Fir or Douglas but if you're looking for a eight-footer we only have the Douglas Spruce. The eight-footers are at the back of the lot. Take your time…look around."

Brad gave Max a smart assed glare as he and his companion walked over to the corral. Watching them walk off Kellem remarked. "I can see why you punched that idiot. He's pretty full of himself…isn't he? He's arrogant…smug!"

"Yeah, he is that…he is that indeed! I think he still has it in for me."

"Do you think he'll give us any trouble?"

"No, I don't, at least not here in your presence. He's too smart for that."

"Well, let's just wait and see what happens."

Fifteen minutes later Brad and his friend walked back across the road to where Max and Kellem waited. Reaching for his wallet, Brad stated, "We found the two trees we are interested in. A six-foot Frasier and an eight-foot spruce. How much do we owe you?"

Kellem glanced over at the two trees they had leaned against the outside of the corral. "Frasier's are eight dollars per foot and the spruce are nine dollars per."

While Kellem was busy adding up the figures in his head, Max quickly answered the mathematical question. "That'll be one hundred and twenty dollars."

Opening the wallet Brad peeled off six twenties which he handed to Kellem. "There ya go. We'll need those loaded up…pronto!"

Taking the money, Kellem gestured toward the corral. "Pull your truck over to the fence and we'll get those trees bundled up for you. We'll also cut about an inch off the bottoms so they will be ready to accept water once you place them in a base."

Another ten minutes passed when Max and Kellem loaded the six-footer last. Walking around the side of the truck Kellem thanked Brad for the purchase and wished him and his friend a happy holiday.

Brad turned to climb up into the truck when he hesitated, snapped his fingers, and turned back while speaking to Max. "Didn't I hear that you were attacked this past summer down in, I believe, it was Charleston? Heard you suffered a broken nose and arm and you got some ribs kicked in. That true?"

Max gave Kellem a look and then answered, "Yes, I was attacked."

"Normally I would feel bad if that happened to someone, especially someone I know, but in your case I say…It couldn't have happened to a nicer person considering that you broke my nose last year, preventing me from playing football. Can't say as I feel all that much compassion for you Miller."

"Your lack of compassion," said Max, "is of no surprise to me. What does surprise me is you seem to know all about the attack. The only other person on campus who knows about the attack is Elizabeth and I'm quite sure she didn't discuss it with you."

"Whatever are you saying, Miller? Are you accusing me of somehow being involved in your South Carolina injuries? I'll have you know that I was in Canada on a two-week fishing trip in July with my father when you were attacked."

"I'm not accusing you of anything," said Max. "It just strikes me as strange that you know so much about the attack."

Brad took two steps and was inches from Max's face as he raised his voice in anger. "You better watch your step, Miller. You might not be so lucky in the future. If you'll recall last year when you, your father, and that fancy lawyer from South Carolina faced off against my father and his attorneys. You dodged the bullet that day and walked out of there free as a bird. If my father had not had a change of heart you would have been toast, but for whatever reason you were allowed to get off the hook. If you so much as indicate to anyone that I am responsible for the attack you suffered in Charleston, I'll go to my father. Since he knows I was with him in Canada at the time of the attack and couldn't possibly have had any involvement in the incident he'll have you once again in front of his lawyers and this time you won't get off so easy. So, my advice to you is to keep your mouth shut!"

Kellem, upset with how Brad was conducting himself was about to speak but Max held up his hand for silence.

Brad gave Kellem a head-to-toe look of disgust and then turned to climb in the truck but then stopped and turned back to Max again. "By the way, Miller. I ran into someone the other day you may know. An odd sort of character by the name of Simon Baumer. I went downtown with some of my friends to grab a bite when we walked into this small café, and who do I see sitting there, none other than your gal pal, Elizabeth? She was there with an older gentleman. The way he was dressed I figured he was Amish, Mennonite, or whatever the hell Elizabeth is. At first, I thought it might have been her father, but then I realized he was not old enough, so I guessed maybe an older brother.

"After we were seated I decided to be social so I got up and approached their table. I said hello to Elizabeth and explained to this man that last year I was a roommate of the boy who was dating Elizabeth. I went on to say that everyone on campus knew you and she were a couple and the relationship had continued into this year as well. This man, who was with Elizabeth stood, grabbed my arm, and said that was impossible because he was in the process of courting Elizabeth and they were planning on getting married." Flashing Max an evil grin Brad laughed. "You can only imagine how embarrassed I was. I apologized to Elizabeth for bringing up the subject. She just sat there in silence, probably embarrassed herself. I mean, think about it. Here she is with a man who is courting her and the subject of her two-year affair with you pops up. I could see things were getting awkward so I excused myself and started to walk off, when this man who I must say was quite scary led me off to the side by the front door and told me his name was Simon Baumer. Then he asked me what your name was. I didn't have much of a choice so I told him your name, Max Miller. He asked me where he could contact you as he wanted to speak to you about him and Elizabeth. I explained to him that I was not sure where you were living on campus but I did know you worked over here at McCulhay's farm. He said he was going to drop by and visit you. He seemed pretty upset over you and Elizabeth. I can't imagine being on the opposite end of a conversation with a pissed-off man like Baumer. Did he drop by to see you?"

Max thought for a second and then answered, "Yes, he did."

Thumping his friend on the shoulder Brad flashed Max a sly grin and asked, "And how did that work out for you?"

Kellem had enough as he took a step toward Brad. "Baumer did drop by to see Max. He had these two dumbass brothers with him. They made a few comments and tried to throw their weight around, but I guess they weren't counting on running into me. I ran the three of them off...sent them back over to Lancaster County with their tails between their legs. I don't imagine we'll be seeing them any time soon."

Brad, not intimidated by Kellem also took a step forward, the space between them barely a foot. Looking directly into Kellem's eyes, Brad in disbelief, stated rudely, "You're trying to tell me an old fart like you ran Baumer, and you say his brothers off. I, for one find that hard to believe!"

"Believe it!" said Kellem. "You see when you're staring down the barrel end of a twelve-gage shotgun, the individual holding the gun, in this case, me….has the upper hand and their words tend to be rather weighty."

Brad gave his friend a look as if to say, *watch this!* "If you're trying to intimidate me, old man, forget it! Three things, I'm smarter than you and I'm younger than you and I don't see a shotgun nearby so don't get to thinking you can just run me off that easily."

"Well, you know what they say? Two out of three isn't bad. You're correct on two accounts. You are younger than me and I don't have my shotgun with me at the moment, but if you think you're smarter than me you're even dumber than I thought. You're nothing but some idiot-rich kid who doesn't know his ass from a hole in the ground. I know all about you and what went down at the Burger Palace between you and Max last year. I think you got exactly what you deserved."

Brad moved closer and Kellem, who much to Brad's delight backed away, but then drew up the edge of his work shirt revealing the revolver stuck in his belt. "I wouldn't get too cocky there son!"

Brad froze as he stared at the partially concealed weapon, then spoke. "Are you threatening me?"

"No, not at all. I'm just saying that you have your trees and you've paid me so now you need to get the hell off my property!"

Holding his hands out in confusion, Brad smirked, "Is this any way to treat a paying customer?"

Kellem placed his right hand on the butt end of the revolver, and suggested strongly, "Get your ass out of here…now!"

"I intend to inform my father about what went on here today. He swings a lot of weight at the college. I'm sure the college will not be pleased with one of their locals, meaning you, pulling a gun on two students who simply wanted to purchase some trees."

"You tell your father whatever you want. That doesn't mean a tinker's damn to me. Your father might still after all these years be a big deal on campus, but beyond the campus grounds, he doesn't mean shit around these parts. I've lived right here in Gettysburg for over eighty years and I know every farmer for miles around not to mention most of the business owners and local political figures. If you start to stir up any crap here in this town or even this county, you're life as you know is going to get very uncomfortable. If you so much as lay a finger on Max or Elizabeth who both happen to work for me, or if you destroy anything I own, believe me… you'll regret it! Now, git!"

Brad gave Kellem and Max a prolonged stare and then spoke to his companion, "Com'n, let's get the hell off this pathetic farm!"

Max and Kellem stood and watched as the rental truck turned around in the clearing then sped up the dirt road leaving a trail of dust behind. Placing his arm around Max, Kellem joked, "You might just be more trouble than you're worth! You are by far the best employee I've ever had. You're always on time, you do what I ask and never complain about a thing, but you seem to have more baggage than anyone that's ever worked for me. First, Simon Baumer and his brothers come over here to beat the hell out of you, and now this Brad Sykes, who still has it in for you shows up. It's almost as if you're traveling around with a target on your back."

Walking down the road toward the equipment shed, Max responded, "I can't argue with you there, but there is a difference between Baumer and Sykes. Even though they both have money, Baumer I feel will forget about Elizabeth and move on. Now, Brad Sykes is a different animal. He is only wealthy due to his father's success. His father has probably moved on regarding his son getting popped in the mouth, but Brad is still holding onto his ill feelings toward me."

They arrived at the shed as Max pointed at the main road as a semi-turned down the lane. "I think the truck you spoke of has arrived."

Kellem rubbed his hands together and looked at his watch. "We should have him loaded up by four o'clock and then what say I take you and Elizabeth uptown for dinner."

Three-quarters of an hour later Max was loading the last of three skids on the back of the truck when he noticed a black, late-model sedan pull into the clearing. In white lettering, the advertisement on the side of the vehicle boldly stated *THE GETTYSBURG TIMES*. Two well-dressed gentlemen stepped out of the car and looked around. Kellem, who was standing a few yards to the left of the clearing approached the two and offered his hand. "Howdy there, what can we do for ya?"

The man who had been driving introduced himself, "My name is Clark Slocum and I'm a reporter with The Gettysburg Times. This other gentleman is Jim Powers and he is an investigative reporter for The Pittsburgh Post Dispatch. We're looking for a Kellem McCulhay. Would he happen to be in the vicinity today?"

Kellem grinned and shook Slocum's hand, answering, "I'm Kellem McCulhay. Welcome to my farm." Gesturing at the surrounding fields of trees, Kellem remarked, "There's not much of a secret to what we do around here so I can't even imagine why an investigative reporter would want to speak with me. Why the visit?"

The Pittsburgh reporter stepped forward and answered the question, "I think I can answer that best because the reason why we are here is partially because of me. I've been here to the Gettysburg Battlefield I'd say ten to twelve times over the years. The first time I was here was with my parents thirty years ago in 1987. It was the week when they always celebrate the anniversary of the three days of battle. I was only ten years old at the time but I remember how excited I was to be here. On July 2nd of that year I was with my parents in a field out beyond the fence that borders your property from the battlefield. There I was running around in my little union outfit with my fake sword and rifle. I remember running down toward your fence when I saw what I thought was a southern reenactor.

"During the course of the day I had my picture taken with many a reenactor. This reenactor was a boy about nineteen maybe twenty. He was dressed in Confederate grey, carried a musket and appeared to be bleeding. Being a kid I was curious so I approached this boy. He instantly turned and limped off into the woods beyond your farm and then as if by magic…he disappeared just like that! I couldn't believe it. I was going to mention it to my parents but since I had a habit of stretching the truth I figured they would not believe me. So, to escape having my father yell at me I kept what I had seen to myself. Like I said., I have come here to the battlefield many a time, usually on July 2nd and I always return to your fence where I saw that soldier. I never saw him again and I have never discussed with anyone what I saw here when I was ten, but I have never forgotten that moment.

"Then, earlier this year. I guess it was at the end of September I was at a conference for news reporters held in Cleveland Ohio. I met a fella in the bar one evening and we got to talking and for some reason the Battle of Gettysburg came up. He went on to tell me he had visited the battlefield a few years ago in 2010 and had seen what he thought was a reenactor by this fence. When he approached this what he described as a young Confederate soldier, the young boy turned and limped off into a wooded area and just simply disappeared. The way he described the young soldier reminded me of the youth I had seen back in 1987, twenty-three years before when I had seen what I had always thought was *my soldier!* One of the things the man I was talking with recalled about the soldier he had seen was that he was carrying this old wooden canteen suspended over his shoulder by an old frayed looking rope. There was no doubt about it. The soldier I had seen when I was ten had the same type of canteen suspended by a rope. It had to be the same youth. This strange coincidence got me to thinking and I thought this would make a great human interest story. So, I contacted Clark here and explained I wanted to drive into town and come by the farm and meet you and see if you could shed any light on the matter. And so…here we are! I was wondering if you could spare us maybe twenty or thirty minutes to see if you could add anything of significance to what I saw as a young boy and what the man from Cleveland witnessed?"

Kellem looked down at the ground, shook his head, and then looked at the two reporters but remained silent. His reaction caused Slocum to remark, "From the way you responded to Jim's question either you do have information on these strange instances or you have been asked about this before and you're tired of talking about it."

"Over the years I've had people from time to time who drop by the farm and ask me about the strange appearance of the young Confederate. I always tell them that it's just one of many ghost stories people talk about here on the Gettysburg Battlefield. Now, that being said there is a lot more to the story than just that young soldier who seems to pop up on July 2nd from time to time. Tell you what. If you can hang around for another ten minutes or so until we get this truck loaded, we can go up to the house, drink some iced tea and I'll tell you what I know to be true."

Shaking Kellem's hand, Jim smiled. "Deal!"

Seated at an old picnic table in a screened-in porch on the side of the house, the two reporters watched as Kellem entered the porch holding a pitcher of iced tea and five unmatched drinking glasses. Elizabeth followed carrying a tray that contained a small bowl of sugar cubes, a plate of sliced lemon and a larger plate of store bought cookies. Placing the plastic pitcher in the center of the table, Kellem stacked the glasses next to the pitcher and offered, "Help yourself gentlemen. Fresh brewed this morning."

Elizabeth placed the items she was carrying next to the pitcher and sat next to Max who was sitting directly across from the two men. No one reached for the tea so Max decided to get the ball rolling as he took the pitcher, filled his glass, and then slid the plastic container across the table to Slocum, who, in turn, filled his glass and picked up one of the cookies as he stated with a wide smile, "Fig Newtons! I can't tell you the last time I had one of these."

Kellem stuffed one of the fig cookies into his mouth and agreed, "They're my favorite, I pick up a package every week at the grocery."

Elizabeth slid the cookie plate toward Powers, but he refused and added, "I've always been an Oreo man myself." Before anyone could react to his comical response, he continued while addressing Kellem. "Before you were saying that there is more to this potential ghost story than just the appearance of the Confederate youth."

"That's correct," said Kellem. "But before I get into that let me give you some background into my relatives because that relates to these sightings. One of my great grandfathers, William McCulhay emigrated to America from Ireland back in 1847, smack dab in the middle of the Potato Famine, which I'm sure you are familiar with. The famine lasted five years starting in '45 and ending in 1850 resulting in the deaths of between seven hundred thousand and one million Irish. The year 1847 was known as black '47 as the famine was at its worst that particular year. In '47 over one hundred thousand Irish emigrated either to Canada or here in America. William sold everything he had and booked passage on a ship sailing for New York. He, his wife, Sarah, his two sons, Joseph and Jonathan, and his daughter, six-month-old Mary Kate were on their way to the land of milk and honey."

Shaking his head in disgust, Kellem went on to explain, "Not so! The ship he booked passage on was like many a ship that sailed from Ireland in those days. Coffin ships they called them. The captain and his crew stuffed as many Irish as they could down in the hull of the ships. The living conditions were deplorable and during the forty-three-day voyage across the Atlantic one out of every five Irish died from lack of proper nutrition, dehydration, or disease. Passengers died daily and the crew had no other choice but to toss the dead over the side for the safety of those who were still living. It had been said that sharks swam next to the ships as they, from instinct knew that dead bodies would be placed in the sea daily." Wiping a tear from his eye, Kellem sadly added, "I always tear up when I think about the horrid fact that little Mary Kate died and never saw the shores of America. How horrible it must have been for William and Sarah to give their precious daughter up to the sea."

Kellem apologized, wiped his face with a handkerchief, cleared his throat, and then continued with the story. "Despite the horror of that trip across the big water William and his family arrived in New York City in the fall of 1847. There were already a great number of Irish in the city, who were established and they tucked my father and his family in until they were on their feet. William found work, saved his money, and then in the spring of 1849 he made the decision that New York was not where he wanted to raise a family. Purchasing a buckboard he packed up his wife and sons and they headed out across New York State and then down into Pennsylvania. When they arrived here in Gettysburg William looked at the surrounding countryside and said, '*This is the American dream and this is where I will raise my family.*'"

Taking another Fig Newton, Kellem explained, "Gettysburg, back in 1849 was much different than it is today where the population is around ten thousand. Back then, there were maybe two hundred residents, that, most of whom were farmers. As far as an actual town was concerned there was probably just a smattering of buildings, a general store, a livery stable, maybe a blacksmith shop, and so on. William and his family were accepted into the small local population with open arms as William was a bit of a preacher. He was always reading and quoting the Bible so he was given the task of preaching each Sunday at a small church that had been constructed. Even though William was a very religious man he was known as quite the wheeler-dealer. And I say this is a good way. He was always willing to give neighbors a helping hand, solid advice, or even an occasional loan. Due to his good nature, he was blessed with many favors from friends and neighbors, and by the time 1852 rolled around he had accumulated five hundred and twenty-seven acres of prime farmland, which resulted in William becoming the most prosperous farmer in Adams County. He had vast fields of corn and tobacco, and herds of cattle and sheep. He had peach and apple orchards and large vegetable gardens."

Motioning out at the yard Kellem went on, "This house right here was not in existence back then. William did own this property but it was an insignificant part of his acreage. The original McCulhay farm was located about a mile southeast of here out by the Emmitsburg Road. This area right here was on the very edge of his property holdings and was utilized as a dumping ground of sorts, which many farms back then had. Down there at the far edge of the fence, which you can't see from here there is a slight depression that's about six yards wide. At one time there was a thirty-yard-long and twelve-foot-deep gully that ran through there. This is where William would drag trees that were blown down or boulders that were out in the fields or anything else he had no use for. You can barely see the outline of that gully now but it plays a major role in the story I am about to share."

Kellem refilled his glass of tea and continued, "The years went by and William and his family continued to prosper, and by 1860 Gettysburg had grown to a rural farming community. Then in 1861, the Civil War broke out but news of the war did little to affect the residents of Gettysburg or the State of Pennsylvania for that matter. Many a Pennsylvanian joined up with the Union army and some of those who enlisted were from Gettysburg, one of them being William's oldest son, Jonathan. His younger son, Joseph met a young woman from Harrisburg and they moved to Philadelphia. For the first two years of the war, there was little to no fighting that took place on Pennsylvania soil as most of the fighting took place in the south, mostly Virginia. This all changed in June of '63 when Robert E Lee led an army of seventy thousand strong up into Pennsylvania where he ran headlong into General George Meade and his army of ninety thousand. The stage was set for a battle of Biblical proportions between the two armies and the hills and valleys around the peaceful town of Gettysburg was the unfortunate host. History tells us that for three straight days in early July, the two armies fought back and forth in what has been termed the most brutal and costly battle of the war.

"On July first, second, and third in 1863 over fifty thousand men became casualties within a few miles of where we now sit. Lee pulled what remained of his army out of Gettysburg on July 4th, Independence Day, and Union General Meade did likewise in the next few days leaving a swath of devastation behind. Many a home and farm burned to the ground, fields of crops trampled or destroyed by thousands of men and horses, local livestock had been butchered and the surrounding landscape scarred for years to come. Those who lived here in Gettysburg were left with the daunting task of getting back to what was considered normal. I imagine many families who lived here back then were probably of the opinion that their town would never be the same.

"The first few days following the three-day battle the surrounding fields and hills were strewn with dead soldiers and horses. The number of dead left behind was astounding. Eight thousand soldiers and three thousand horses. The people in town and on the local farms had to do something as the soldiers and horses lay rotting in the hot July sun. Nature took over as wolves and wild pigs came out of the woods, tearing the flesh from the bodies, crows pecking out eyes, and on and on. Out there in the fields, it was nothing short of hell. The good people of Gettysburg in their wagons and buckboards went out into the fields and gathered up all the Union soldiers and horses, disposed of the horses, and gave the soldiers a proper burial."

Confused, Max held up his hand as he interrupted the story, "Wait a minute! You said they gathered up all the Union soldiers. Were there not Confederate dead on the field?"

"There were plenty of dead Confederates out there in the fields but the compassion of the Gettysburg residents only went so far. There was such an intense feeling of bitterness amongst the people who lived here because Lee had brought his army to their town and by doing so had destroyed their way of life that they decided to leave the Confederates to rot in the sun. William McCulhay did not share that opinion with his neighbors and friends. Hitching two mules up to one of his hay wagons he ventured out onto his five-hundred-acre property, all of which had been ground that had seen fighting during the three days of the conflict. He discovered thirty-three dead Confederates. It took him three trips but he eventually got all of the dead Confederates over here to his *dumping ground!* He took any valuables he could locate from the soldiers which was next to nothing as the dead had been pilfered by other soldiers or Gettysburg residents. William did find several muskets, canteens, and cartridge boxes which he placed out in his barn. He then lined the thirty-three soldiers up shoulder to shoulder down in that twelve-foot-deep gully, covered them with lime, and then six feet of dirt and rocks.

"After the crude, but necessary burial he spent the next two days clearing his acreage of seven cannons that had been destroyed and a fence that he had constructed along the Emmitsburg Road. He hauled the damaged cannons back to this area where he placed the metal components over there in the trees at the end of the gully. Any wooden parts of the cannons he placed in the gully over top of the graves of the soldiers. The final item he cleared from his land was the fence along the Emmitsburg Road that had been blown to hell and back from cannon fire. That fence, still today remains one of the most famous battlefield fences in history. Many a Confederate on July 2nd, 1863 lost their life when they approached that fence on the third day of battle. If you have or if you ever do see a film or read a book about PIckett's Charge you'll hear about that fence. During that day, the fence was destroyed and William found scattered sections of broken posts and rails lying everywhere. He gathered up all the sections he could find and returned them to this area and placed them over the graves as he planned to burn the wood cannon parts and the broken fencing."

Max and Elizabeth sat quietly as they listened to Kellem, the two reporters jotting down notes of the history of the farm. Standing, Kellem walked to the screening and looked out at the filled-in gully, thirty yards in the distance. "Story has it that William waited for about a week before the burning was to take place, but his actions got waylaid as the winds picked up and prevented him from having the planned bonfire. Gettysburg already had enough problems without burning down the surrounding woods due to the high winds. A week later the winds finally calmed down but then the rain set in and it rained on and off for the next two weeks, soaking the wood so that it would be nearly impossible to burn until it dried out.

"In mid-August, nearly a month after the burial, on a Saturday William decided the conditions were good for the bonfire. He lit the wood, the fire eventually ignited and he was glad that he was finally going to be rid of the cannon parts and the old fencing. Then, a few minutes into the fire…he heard it! Muffled voices. At first, he cocked his head not sure what he was hearing but then it was obvious that it indeed was voices. He could hear shouts and screams and distinct words, *Forward! This way Boys! Over here!* This was followed by three gunshots and then more screaming. He looked in every direction in the distance for those who were creating the mysterious voices. There was not a soul in sight. The fire died down and William did not attempt to relight the bonfire. When he discovered that the voices and gunfire were coming from beneath the fire, well it scared the *you-know-what* out of him. He jumped in his wagon, drove back to the farmhouse, and never returned to this area again."

Clark, following a few seconds of silence asked, "Are those dead soldiers still buried out there in the gully?"

"No, they are not," said Kellem, "but I'll get to that in a few moments because there are a lot of other things that happened before they were exhumed."

"I also have a question," said Powers. "Who else knew about the buried soldiers other than William?"

"William," said Kellem, "was not sure if he had done the correct thing by burying those men on his land so he decided to keep what he had done to himself, that is except for his wife, Sarah. When he got home that afternoon he told her about the burial and the voices and gunshots coming from beneath the fire. She was not the least bit upset because her husband had buried the soldiers, but was upset because he had not prayed over them in doing so. William argued that he couldn't pray for an enemy army that had invaded their town, and more importantly, an army that was in support of slavery. He thought that the Good Lord would deal with each soldier he had placed down in that gully. His wife, who was quite superstitious went on to say it wasn't any wonder there were screams and voices and whatnot. Because of the way they had been buried, they were restless souls crying out for justice. William and Sarah finally agreed the soldiers buried out in the gully would remain a family secret, only known to the two of them."

Powers asked a second question. "Did anyone else ever hear the voices?"

"Yes, over the years on several occasions when folks happened to be in the field out behind the gully the voices were heard. William was approached several times about the strange voices coming from his property. He downplayed the entire situation by saying that it was just another Gettysburg ghost story. Eventually, everyone in town knew about the strange voices and gunshots, but it was viewed just the way William explained it. Just another ghost story!"

Powers probed deeper. "You already told us the bodies were eventually exhumed, but what happened before that? Was the secret of the thirty-three buried Confederates ever made known to anyone other than William's wife?"

"The secret was kept between Sarah and William for the next three decades. Then Sarah passed away from a fever at the age of seventy-one in 1893. Jonathan, their oldest, survived the war and returned home in '64. William and Jonathan continued to run the farm until 1899 when William got extremely ill and on his deathbed bed told Jonathan about the thirty-three soldiers buried in the gully. Shortly before he took his last breath he told Jonathan that he needed to keep the secret in the family and only share it with his wife and oldest son, whose name happened to be Charles."

Clark spoke up, "If I'm following this correctly then Charles was your great-grandfather."

"That's correct and he married a woman by the name of Loren. They had two sons, the oldest being Lucas, my grandfather who was now running the McCulhay farm. In 1935 he was approached by the Gettysburg National Military Park Foundation with an offer he could hardly refuse. They wanted to purchase four hundred and fifty acres of farmland the McCulhay's had owned for nearly ninety years. My grandfather not only sold the acreage they were interested in but the farmhouse as well. The McCulhay land holdings were now the seventy-seven acres that surround this house.

"In the spring of '36 Lucas and my father, Robert, who was his oldest son built this farmhouse. The next year, '37, Charles and Lucas decided to see if they could reconstruct the old fencing that had been thrown in the gully. Many of the rails and posts had rotted but there was enough of the fencing left to piecemeal together a forty-foot section of the original Emmitsburg Road fencing. The fence that you see right out there that runs down the back of our property is that very fence and it borders our property from the National Battlefield. The next thing they tackled was to see if they could salvage enough components from the piles of metal and wood cannon parts to construct an actual Civil War cannon. Out of the seven damaged cannons that were originally taken from the field of battle by William; Lucas, and Robert were able to build three cannons, which they placed behind the fencing facing the battlefield, and as you can see they still stand today."

Slocum refilled his tea and asked, "As the years passed did the addition of the fencing and the three cannons spark any interest of battlefield visitors?"

Kellem, who returned to the table took another fig cookie. "Not at first but eventually over the next few years visitors walking the battlefield out behind our farm noticed the fencing and the cannons and just assumed they were part of the military park. They climbed over the fencing, the children climbed on the cannons and all this despite they were on our property. My father placed NO TRESPASSING and PRIVATE RESIDENCE signs on the fencing. This cut down on most of the invaders as my father referred to them but still, occasional people came onto our property.

"In the fall of '37, my grandfather died peacefully in his sleep. My father became so upset with people stepping onto our property that he considered taking down the fencing and removing the cannons, but then after talking with a number of the curious visitors he discovered that they were not approaching the farm because of the fencing or the cannons but to hear the mysterious voices they had been told about."

Powers inquired, "So after all that time had passed the voices were still haunting the farm?"

"Yes, they were, but for the most part, believe it or not, I had grown accustomed to the Confederate screams and shouts. But then, in 1938 my father was coming out of the barn, and he saw what appeared to be this young Confederate re-enactor, nineteen, maybe twenty years of age, filthy grey uniform. The boy was carrying a musket and was bleeding from his right leg. He also had this wood canteen, suspended by old rope. It just so happened that the date was July 2nd and the annual Civil War re-enactment was in full swing. My father, being social approached the boy who turned and limped off toward the woods, but disappeared just before entering the trees."

Jim Powers was beside himself. "How you describe this young soldier sounds identical to the boy I saw out there by your fence when I was ten. It also matches the description of the boy the man I met In Cleveland claims he saw when he was here. This story is even more amazing than what I had anticipated."

"Well, you just keep taking notes because there is much more to tell. Years passed and we still heard the voices from time to time and for some reason, there was a spike in battlefield visitors who wanted to see if they could hear the voices. There were always tourists driving down our lane or walking up to the fence, walking across our yard, and on and on. My father became tired of telling people they were trespassing and having to tell people they had to remove themselves from our farm. It got to the point where he realized the only way to stop people from coming to the farm would be to eliminate the voices. He figured if he got rid of the bodies then the voices would go away.

"Since 1863, when William buried the soldiers in the gully there were only a handful of family members who knew about the mass grave of Confederates. At the time my father decided to rid himself of the bodies, only he and my mother knew of the bodies in the gully. I remember the evening after supper when my mother and my father sat myself and my siblings down in our living room and they told us about the bodies that William McCulhay had buried in the gully. I was ten at the time and my father made us swear that we would not mention this to anyone because it was a family secret…but soon it would not be.

"The first thing my father did was contact a lawyer friend of his. He wanted to make sure that by not making known to the public the fact that there were thirty-three Confederate soldiers buried on our property he would not get into any legal trouble. After my father explained the entire story to his lawyer, the lawyer said that he had to do some research and that he would get back to my father the next day.

"The following day they met and the lawyer explained to my father that from what he was able to find out, besides the fact the burial had taken place over a century and a half ago, it had taken place during the time of war and that William McCulhay had done the humane thing. At that point, my father decided to contact the Mayor of Gettysburg and get the ball rolling to exhume the bodies. After hearing the story the mayor contacted the Gettysburg National Park Service about the Confederates buried out there in the gully. The park service contacted the state who in turn contacted the federal government and the cat was out of the bag as they say. What my father and his lawyer thought was going to be a simple process turned out to be national news.

THIRTY-THREE CONFEDERATE SOLDIERS WERE FOUND BURIED ON GETTYSBURG FARM!

"Within a week of contacting the Mayor, the Feds showed up here at the farm with official documents allowing them to investigate the burial. The following week a military archeological expert and an assisting crew rolled onto the farm prepared to exhume the bodies. What started as the removal and replacement of the bodies turned into a three-ring circus. All of the major television networks were here not to mention countless reporters from across the country. The Gettysburg Times ran an article on the possible exhumation and it seemed like everyone in town or who read the local paper drove over here to witness the operation. It got so bad that they had to call in the state police to keep the public at bay. It took an entire week of around-the-clock professional digging to exhume the bodies, which were transferred over to the Gettysburg Military Cemetery where the Confederates were laid to rest.

"A special two-foot-high walled burial plot was constructed and the Battlefield Society wanted it to be named the McCulhay Massacre, but my father refused them to use our family name, so the marker at the plot simply stated that the thirty-three soldiers buried there had been found at a local farm. Well, people aren't stupid, and it didn't take long before everyone who lived here or came to the battlefield to realize that it indeed was our farm."

Slocum continued to take notes as he asked, "So, can we assume over the years you were plagued with countless visitors?"

"We were…we were indeed! They came to see where the gully was and where the Confederates had originally been buried. They also came for two other reasons, to hear the voices and see the young Confederate that showed up on July 2nd from time to time."

Powers interjected, "So then that means there were other sightings than the three we are aware of?"

"I suppose so, but no one ever said they had talked with anyone who had seen the boy. They had only heard that he had made an occasional appearance."

Powers fired off yet another question, "After the bodies were reburied over at the military cemetery did the voices go away?"

"Yes, they did…but not for long. If I remember correctly about six months passed with no voices but then they started up again. Why…who knows? My father speculated that when they exhumed the bodies they could have possibly left behind small particles of bone or muscle tissue that had been absorbed into the ground, hence, parts of the soldiers could still be down there. So yes, the voices can still be heard from time to time, but it's not as often as it used to be."

Closing his writing pad Powers finished off his tea. "Well now, that's quite the ending to the story?"

Kellem smiled at the two reporters. "That's not the end…there's more! The year was 1969 and my father had long since passed on, my mother moved to Florida to live with our sister. My brothers and I, the three bachelors were now running the farm. I remember that day. Even though what happened that day occurred nearly five decades ago it remains clear as a bell. I was walking from the house over to the barn when I happened to look out at the fence line. Believe it or not, there standing by the third section from the end stood this young what appeared to be a reenactor. Normally this would not have surprised me as it was July 2nd and the reenactment of the Battle of Gettysburg was in full swing. There were reenactors everywhere in town and throughout the surrounding fields and famous battlefield sites. But this was just not another reenactor. It was a young boy, maybe nineteen, twenty, a year or so older. He was wearing an old tattered Confederate uniform and he was carrying a musket. He was bleeding and he had slung over his shoulder a wooden, rope-suspended canteen. The boy fit the exact description as the reenactor my father had told me he had seen at the fence thirty years prior. I just froze as I stared at the youth, who was leaning on the top rail of the fence. Slowly, I started to walk across the backyard in his direction. At first, he just stared back at me, but then he turned and limped back toward the woods at the top of the rise. Amazed at what I was seeing and experiencing I ran to the fence hopped over and followed the boy, but then he disappeared just before he arrived at the tree line. I thought about walking up to the woods but thought better of it as a strange feeling flooded over my body, almost as if I shouldn't be where I was. I can't really explain the way I felt, but once I climbed back over the fence into my yard the feeling was gone…and so was the boy.

"Up until today, I thought the only two sightings there had ever been were witnessed by my father back in 1938 and then the sighting I experienced in '69. You, Mr. Powers, explained to me earlier in our conversation that you saw the same boy in 1987 and this reporter you met in Cleveland saw what could have been the same boy years later in 2010. And that, gentlemen is where we are at this moment. That's my story. I've added nothing to it or taken anything away from what happened. Take from this what you will. Believe what you will."

Both Powers and Slocum sat quietly when Jim finally broke the silence. "That's a rather amazing ending to an incredible story. You have given me much more information than I thought I would get by coming to see you here today." Closing his writing pad, he went on, "I think I have more than enough information here to create an interesting article that people will enjoy reading."

"Here, here!" said Clark as he placed his writing pad in his suitcoat pocket. "But here is the question. I do not doubt that Jim will run an article in The Pittsburgh Post Dispatch as I intend to do so here at the Times, but how will the article affect you and your farm?"

Not sure how to answer, Kellem replied, "In what way?"

"I think I can best answer that," said Powers. "An article about this story written in a paper in Pittsburgh will no doubt be read by thousands of people, but their reaction to the article will have little effect on the day-to-day operation of your farm, primarily because the distance between here and Pittsburgh is over three and a half hours and the average person is not going to drive over here because of some ghost story, no matter how compelling.

"On the other hand, if the Gettysburg Times runs a similar article here thousands of local folks will read what is written, and because they are ten, fifteen, or even thirty minutes distance from here they are more likely to visit your farm. This article could result in your farm becoming a zoo with every Tom, Dick, and Harry in the area driving over here to see this mysterious gully, the fence where the ghost soldier appeared, or to hear the strange voices. Eventually, the newness of the article will wear off but for a few weeks or even months after the article becomes public you can expect a constant flow of curiosity seekers."

Kellem waved off the possibility of a great number of locals invading his privacy. "If it gets too bad I'll just run them off. So, what's next?"

Powers stood as he answered, "I head on back to the Steel City, type up a report, and present it to my editor. He'll then decide if it's printworthy. If he gives it the go then I'll contact you with a run date. You should hear something from me in three to four days."

Slocum also stood and agreed. "I also will have to get with my editor but he already knows I'm over here interviewing you. I have no doubt he'll put the okay on running the article because unlike Pittsburgh this is local news from right here in our community. I will also call you before the article runs in the paper."

Powers reached for Kellem's hand. "If there is nothing else I guess we'll be on our way then. We thank you for your time and the historical information regarding your family."

Slocum nodded at Max and Elizabeth and followed Powers out the screen door where they climbed in the sedan and drove off up the lane.

Kellem turned to Max and Elizabeth and clapped his hands once. "Well that was interesting…wasn't it? Listen, it's still early and I promised you two dinner uptown. What say we get crackin'? I've got something I want to talk with you kids about on the way to town. It's about next week when Thanksgiving rolls around."

Pulling out of the lane onto Chambersburg Pike, Max asked Kellem, "Now, what's all this about Thanksgiving?"

Kellem, sitting in the front passenger seat turned sideways so he could talk to both Max and Elizabeth. "I was wondering what you two have planned for Thanksgiving. I know that you, Elizabeth cannot go back to Lancaster to your father's farm and you, Max are not planning on going down to Summerville. What kind of plans do you have for turkey day?"

Max looked in the rearview mirror at Elizabeth and shrugged. "We haven't discussed what we plan on doing. I imagine we'll probably eat somewhere in town."

"That's the same thing my brother and I will be doing, Golden Corral as always. I'm up for an old-fashioned Pennsylvania Thanksgiving feast and we can have it at the farm." It'll just be my brother, myself, and of course you two, but there's a catch. My brother and I are not much on cooking, so if you're interested, Elizabeth you can cook the meal for us. What say?"

Elizabeth's face lit up with excitement. "Are you kidding! Of course… I'll cook. Why, ever since I've been three years old I've been helping my mother in her kitchen. One of the things I miss most about not being able to go back home is that I'll never be able to cook a meal in a farm kitchen. But now you tell me I can prepare a Thanksgiving feast at your place. It would be my pleasure to prepare the meal. What would we have for the meal?"

Kellem winked at Max as he answered Elizabeth's question, "You're the cook…you plan the menu. Tell you what. When you come by tomorrow for work why don't you bring a list of things that you'll require? Later in the week, we'll go to the grocery and I'll spring for everything."

Holding her head with her hands Elizabeth grinned, "My head is just spinning. We'll have a turkey and maybe a ham. I'll whip up some of my mother's chicken and dumplings. We'll also have corn, glazed carrots, and a green bean casserole. I'll bake a couple of pies, throw a cake together and there will be deviled eggs and a relish tray. I can hardly wait to get started."

Max stopped for a stop sign and made a right toward town as he exclaimed. "With all this talk about food…I'm starving!"

CHAPTER TWENTY-SIX

Max crossed the Pennsylvania-Maryland border and laid on the horn shouting, "Maryland!"

Elizabeth, in the passenger seat, gave him a strange look, asking, "What was that all about?"

Max gestured at the passing countryside and drum-rolled the steering wheel. "It's a family habit, well, at least for my father it is. Ever since I was a youngster and even today whenever my father crosses from one state to another he honks the horn and yells out the name of the state. It's just something I grew up with and that I always do when crossing state lines."

Elizabeth agreed and placed a stick of gum in her mouth. "I know exactly what you mean. As a little girl back in Lancaster whenever my father and I would head out to our barn for early morning milking, when we would finish up, which was normally around five o'clock, on the way back to the house he would always give our barn bell two tugs, the loud clanging announcing that milking was done for the day. It was a habit he performed daily. The few times when my father was sick and I had to do the milking myself, like my father, when I finished I rang that bell."

Max continued with the crossing state borders conversation as he passed two semis. "Didn't you tell me you have never been out of the state of Pennsylvania?"

"Yes, and until I started to attend school back in Gettysburg, I never left Lancaster County."

"So then this is a first for you?"

Elizabeth looked at a large field where a herd of cows were lazily grazing. "I guess so."

Passing another truck, Max adjusted the Jeep's heater. "This week should be very exciting for you. You are going to experience a lot of things for the first time. Later today you'll be crossing over into three other states: Virginia, North and then South Carolina. And, after we get to Summerville my mother might run you over to Georgia"

Curious, Elizabeth asked, "Why would she take me to Georgia?"

"One again, habit," said Max. "Down Route 95 South about an hour or so from Summerville, just across the state line of South Carolina there is a store called Peach World. It's one of my mother's favorite places to go. If it can be made from peaches Peach World has it. They have the best peach pies and all sorts of breads and candies made from peaches. And, oh yeah, they have these peach slushies there that are to die for. I always get a large when I go."

"Slushy," remarked Elizabeth. "I don't believe I've ever had one."

"Well then, that will be yet another first for you this coming week. You have quite a few firsts awaiting you when we get to Summerville. You're going to get to see the ocean for the first time in your life, and you're going to have lobster that you've told me you've never tasted. Why, my father might even take you out on the ocean in his boat. This is going to be a very exciting week for you."

"I suppose, but there is one first I'm not looking forward to that might not only be awkward but makes me nervous."

"Whatever would that be?"

"Meeting your parents for the first time has got me on edge. What if they don't like me? What if I'm not accepted by your family?"

Max waved off her concerns. "Why would anyone not like you? Believe me, my parents will accept you with open arms. You're the best thing that ever happened to me."

"Your parents might not feel the same way. They don't even know I'm coming for Christmas."

"Look," said Max, "I could have told them I was bringing you along, but I thought it would be better if you were a surprise, so I simply told them I was bringing a surprise for Christmas."

"You don't think they know you're bringing me along?"

"No, how could they? You're going to be a complete surprise to both of them."

"That's what has me so nervous. I'm not just some friend from school you're bringing home for the holiday. I'm not even a girlfriend that you're bringing along. I am the girl you are going to marry. Talk about a first. I bet your parents have never had to deal with that before!"

Max reached across the seat and placed his right hand on her shoulder. "Don't worry. I think I know my parents quite well and I think they'll accept you into our family as one of their own."

"I hope so. Seeing as how my parents and my community back up there in Lancaster have all but disowned me, right now you and Kellem are all the family I have. This morning before we left I prayed to God He would see to it that your family would welcome me."

"Everything is going to work out fine. I understand your nervousness because I had some of the same uneasy feelings when I drove over to Lancaster to face your parents, mainly your father. Your mother was very easy to converse with but your father was a tough nut to crack. I knew if I told him anything but the truth he'd see right through it. Thinking back I still find it hard to believe he released you from his strict beliefs. Do you think you'll ever go back to the farm for a visit?"

"I'd like to go back some time, maybe after we're married…maybe after we have a child in the future. Having a grandchild might soften the way my father feels about me." Pointing up the highway, she asked, "What time will we be getting into Summerville?"

"Right around six and that's if we don't run into any traffic jams or construction. When I talked with my mother last evening and told her I would be arriving this evening around six she said she was going to prepare dinner at the house because after the twelve-hour drive, I'd probably be too tired to go out to eat. By the time we get in it'll be dark."

Yawning, Elizabeth closed her eyes as she adjusted the seat to a more comfortable position. "I think I might try and rest for a bit."

"Okay," said Max, "but be warned. Within the next hour, we'll be crossing over into Virginia and I'll be honking the horn again and shouting, 'Virginia!'"

Out of respect for Elizabeth who was still sleeping peacefully, Max refrained from laying on the horn and announcing Virginia when they crossed the state line. Stopping for gas in Southern Virginia, he woke her up and suggested they grab something to eat as they were not quite halfway to their destination.

On the road once again, Elizabeth handed a deli sandwich to Max, then unwrapped a ham and cheese sandwich she had selected at the gas station. Taking a small bite, she held up the sandwich and remarked with a broad smile, "Another first! I've never eaten anything while in my father's car. It was strictly forbidden."

Max sipped at a large Coke and reached for his sandwich. "Speaking of eating, I think the Thanksgiving meal you prepared at Kellem's was out of this world. I've never had a turkey cooked in a bag like that. You have got to explain the process to my mother, and the stuffing was the best I've ever had and my mother's is pretty good."

Elizabeth took a swig of apple juice and asked, "So I guess those two reporters we talked with at Kellem's farm are both going to run articles about this Civil War ghost business on his farm and about that fence?"

"Yeah they are, but they both decided to wait until next year and run the article the first week of July during the annual reenactment. That way, there will already be an influx of battlefield visitors in town and it may not seem that unusual for people to be snooping around. I don't feel that many people will come looking for the ghost soldier or strange voices from the gully or the fence. I could be wrong but I think for the most part it'll go right in one ear and out the other as far as most folks are concerned."

"How do you feel about the story Kellem told those men? Do you believe any of it to be true?"

"Hey, you sat right next to me during the entire conversation. You have to admit his story was very compelling….and believable, so yes, I do believe what he told us to be the truth, especially when you consider the ghost soldier was seen on four different occasions by four different individuals who described the young soldier down to the last detail as the others had witnessed him to be. How can you dispute what four different people claim to have seen over eighty years and the fact that the soldier never seems to age? It's hard to believe, but how do you go about disproving what they saw? I, for one, cannot explain any of it, and since I was not there to see what they saw how can I say it is not true? How do you feel about it?"

"I can answer that question without even taking time to think about it. I was raised as a Mennonite to believe in the Bible and its teachings. The Bible tells us there is a spiritual realm that cannot be seen by the human eye. This realm consists of God and his angels and Satan and his fallen angels or demons. Aside from this spiritual realm, I do not believe ghosts are roaming around the face of the earth."

"Well, you would know the Bible far better than I, so tell me, does the Bible even mention ghosts?"

"The Bible does not describe ghosts the way most people nowadays do. The term, *ghost* is mentioned in the Bible a few times. Here are a couple of examples. Do you know the story in the Bible where Jesus walked on water?"

"Of course, doesn't everyone?"

"Not everyone, but most people have heard this amazing story. The disciples were in a boat when a strong storm blew in. They look out across the raging waves and what do they see…walking on the water…a ghost! Jesus told them, *'Do not be afraid…it is I!'* Once they recognized Jesus they realized they had not seen a ghost as first thought. Another example of the word ghost happened when Jesus was crucified on the cross. Toward the end of this horrible ordeal, he gave up the ghost which is a way of saying he died. Then, there is also the Holy Ghost whom everyone always talks about. The Holy Ghost is the Spirit of God. I remember many years ago when I was a young girl I attended a prayer meeting at one of the homes in our community. The topic of ghosts came up and the conclusion was that these so-called ghosts are in all actuality demons sent by Satan to deceive those of us who are still living so that we can communicate with the dead. This can draw us away from God.

"All in all, based upon what I was taught and what I heard Kellem speak of, well, it can be rather confusing and as you say, hard to explain. There are a great number of things in life I do not understand, things which cannot be explained. Whenever I feel this way I always revert to a scripture I learned as a young girl, God's ways are not our ways and our thoughts are not His thoughts. As sure as the heavens are higher than the earth so are His thoughts and ways higher than ours. Does that answer your question?"

"It does, but now I am more confused than ever. You've given me a lot to think about."

Laying down her sandwich Elizabeth suggested, "I have an idea. For the remainder of the trip let's not talk about ghosts and whether they exist or not. Let's talk about the great week we have in front of us. I can't wait to see the ocean!"

They exited left from South Carolina Route 26 and then Max made another immediate left onto Route 78 and pointed up the two-lane paved road. "We'll be at the house in less than five minutes. I don't know about you, but I'm starved."

Elizabeth adjusted the visor mirror so she could see herself. She brushed bangs of hair away from her face and straightened her starched white bonnet. "I do hope your parents won't be shocked when they see me in my plain clothes. Maybe I should have worn something more appropriate for our first meeting."

"This initial meeting with my parents is going to be a lot different than when I first met your folks. Your parents had heard of me but knew little about our relationship. My parents, on the other hand, know everything about our relationship, well that is except for the fact we plan on getting hitched. So I don't think your plain dress attire is going to shock them. When we walk in and I introduce you you're going to look exactly as I have described you to be. Their surprise will not stem from the fact you're dressed plainly but that you're standing in their house. They are finally going to meet you after hearing all about you for the past year and a half. Believe me, if I didn't think this was going to be okay I would have never placed you in a position of embarrassment. Ten minutes from now you're going to be laughing right along with my parents."

Two miles down the road Max made a right into a stone pillared entranceway boldly stating the name of a subdivision, Goose Creek. Making a left and then going around a long sweeping curve passing several homes, he pulled into a driveway, stopped the Jeep, turned off the ignition, and gestured at the two-story stone-fronted home. "Here we are. Home sweet home!"

Getting out, he opened the rear door and grabbed the two suitcases they had brought along. Elizabeth remained seated in the passenger seat as she stared at the front porch with its two white wicker rockers and matching end table. Approaching the passenger side door Max tapped on the window and joked. "You can't meet my parents sitting out here in the Jeep. Let's go meet Mr. and Mrs. Miller."

Elizabeth stepped out smoothed her long black dress and took a deep breath. "I'm afraid I'm just having some last-second jitters."

"To be honest, I kind of feel the same way," said Max, "but together we can get through this."

Elizabeth raised her eyes toward the black sky and stated, "I need to say a short prayer." With that, she slightly raised her hands and stared into the darkness above. "Your power is made perfect in my weakness, therefor I will boast all the more gladly about my weakness for then Your power will come upon me and then when I am weak it is then that I am strong!" Smiling broadly at Max she took her suitcase from his hand and started for the porch. "Come on, let's do this. What are you waiting for?"

Max, amazed at the last-second transformation in her general makeup, followed her up the short steps, stopped and opened the door, stuck his head inside, and hollered, "Hello, is there anybody in here?"

From the kitchen, Max heard his mother's familiar voice, "He's here!"

In the next couple of seconds, she appeared in the hallway, a mixing bowl in one hand and a large spoon in the other. The smile on her face quickly vanished when she saw Elizabeth standing next to Max.

Before Max could utter a word of explanation his father fell in line behind his wife as he stared at his son and this strange girl.

Finally, his mother broke the awkward silence. "With all we have heard about you, then you surely would be Elizabeth King?"

Max responded, "Elizabeth, this is my mother and father, Kate and Charles. Mom, Dad, I'd like you to meet Elizabeth King. She's the surprise I told you I was bringing."

Trying to recover from the shock of seeing Elizabeth, Charley reached for the bag Elizabeth was holding. "Welcome to our home. Here, let me just take your suitcase."

Max, to lighten the moment, reached out and shook his father's hand. "It's been a long day. We drove straight through. We're both tired and starving! Will Elizabeth be staying in the guestroom?"

Kate agreed as she sat down the bowl and spoon on a nearby small table. "Yes, I think that would be best. After we eat I'll have to get up there and put down some fresh sheets and run the vacuum."

Elizabeth spoke up. "Please, do not go to any trouble because I am here."

"Nonsense," said Kate, "It'll only take but a few minutes."

Charley handed Elizabeth's suitcase to Max. "Why don't you show Elizabeth up to her room?"

Kate agreed, "Yes, I'm sure Elizabeth would like to freshen up a bit before dinner."

Elizabeth nodded. "It would be nice if I could straighten myself around some. It has been a long day."

Max started down a hallway as he suggested, "Com'n Elizabeth, I'll show you to your room."

Following Max up a staircase she trailed him down an upstairs hallway to a door at the end of the hall. Opening the door, Max flipped on a wall switch, the room instantly flooded with light. Walking across the room, he placed her suitcase on the bed as he displayed the room. "I hope you'll be comfortable up here. This has always been our guestroom. I can't remember the last time anyone used it. The bathroom is just down the hall. My room is at the other end of the house. If there is anything you need just let me or my mother know and we'll see to it."

Elizabeth sat on the edge of the bed as she looked around the cozy room. Matching cherry dresser and nightstand, three framed seashore pictures hanging on the walls, and a wooden table lamp with a lace shade. Nodding at the light purple walls she commented. "Lavender…my favorite color."

Max, at the door, remarked, "I'm just going to drop my suitcase off at my room and then head downstairs. How long do you think It'll be before you freshen up?"

She removed her bonnet, shook down her hair, and ran her fingers through the blond locks. "I shouldn't be more than ten minutes or so. Let me ask you something. How do you think my first meeting with your parents went?"

"I think it went about the way I figured it would. My parents were expecting a surprise, but I don't think they were expecting you. I feel they acted pretty normal when meeting someone for the first time."

Elizabeth rolled her eyes. "You can't tell me that you did not notice a moment of awkwardness from your mother?"

"Yes there was a brief moment of awkwardness when she seemed to be at a loss for what to say, but I still think that was just the surprise of seeing you."

"You don't think the way I was dressed or the way I looked was a shock to her or your father?"

"I'm not sure. I mean it's not like I didn't explain to them before how you dress or what you believe in. They already know those things. We've talked before about the fact that both of my parents feel our relationship is short-lived. I mean up until you walked in with me you were just a girl in school I was dating. Now…you're here!"

"I feel like I should say something when I go back down…something that will put your parents at ease."

"My parents will be fine and there is no reason for you to feel as if you have to say something. Once we are gathered around the table with a plate of food in front of us we'll all be laughing and joking and having a great evening. I say we just let things work themselves out. I'll see you downstairs in a few minutes."

Kate, at the stove, stirred a simmering pot. Using a large wooden spoon she scooped out a small portion of stew and took it to her lips, and twisting her face, commented, "Way too hot." Turning down the heat, she turned to her husband. "I think we screwed up, well, not you but me. I didn't do a very good job of welcoming Miss King to our home. I need to apologize to her when she comes down."

"I don't think that's a good idea," said Charles. "I think we should say something to Max first. He knows her much better than we do. Why rock the boat if it's not necessary? Let's wait and see how dinner goes."

Max bounded down the stairs and then into the kitchen, interrupting his parents' conversation. "Boy, it sure is good to be home. When we left Gettysburg this morning it was thirty-seven degrees. When we pulled in here it felt like it was in the low seventies. I don't think I'll ever get used to the cold winter weather up in Pennsylvania."

Charley looked at Max and commented. "Didn't take you long to freshen up."

Walking to the kitchen counter Max plucked a small section of cheese from a snack tray and answered, "Just splashed some water on my face and I'm good to go! Elizabeth should be down in about ten minutes."

Joking, Charley gave his wife a nod. "Better get used to it, Son, I mean if you're going to be around a woman. They always seem to take a lot longer to get themselves ready."

Kate poked her husband with the mixing spoon, and ordered him, "Would you please get the iced tea and the lemonade out of the fridge and put them on the table out on the porch." Addressing Max, she went on, "I thought it would be nice, considering the warmer-than-usual temperature if we could eat out there."

Max grinned and took another piece of cheese. "I don't care where we eat, as long as *we do eat!*"

Charley closed the refrigerator door, placed the two pitchers on the counter, and looked at his wife, and then at Max. "Son, there is something your mother and I have been talking over. We feel we may have failed to welcome your friend from college to our home. We think we may owe her an apology."

Max looked at his parents. "It looks like you two had the same conversation down here Elizabeth and I had up in the guestroom. We both agreed there was a moment of brief awkwardness but decided to let it slide and just have a nice dinner. There is no need for an apology. We both realize that she was quite a surprise. She was very concerned on the way down here that she might not be accepted by you. I assured her she would be. So, let's just have a nice dinner and hopefully you'll get to know one another. Let's just let things work themselves out. Okay?"

"Okay," said Charley as he walked out onto the porch.

Surveying the various bowls and plates of food his mother had prepared Max complimented her, "Everything looks delicious. I miss your cooking."

For the next few minutes, Max and his father walked back and forth from the kitchen to the porch while carting napkins, plates, silverware, drinking glasses, and varied bowls and platters of food, all the while Kate continued to stir the pot on the stove. Everything situated on the picnic table on the porch, Max and Charley stood off to the side discussing the family business and how things were going. Suddenly their conversation was interrupted when Elizabeth appeared at the end of the downstairs hall as she announced her entry. "What smells so good down here?"

Max and Charley stared in silence at Elizabeth while Kate was once again at a loss for words. There stood Elizabeth: adorned in a bright white and yellow sundress, her feet strapped into fashionable sandals, her hair tied back in a ponytail. The shock of seeing her in anything but plain clothes caused a stunning sense of silence from the others in the kitchen.

Finally, Max went to her and held out his hands in amazement. "I didn't realize you owned any other clothes other than what you normally wear."

Elizabeth spun in a tight circle and displayed her new clothes as she confessed. "The other day when you were at class and I was working over at Kellem's I had him run me over town to Walmart where I picked up a couple of outfits. What do you think? Do I look like a normal girl?"

Kate, who was practically in tears went to Elizabeth and hugged her as she held her out at arms-length and looked her up and down. "You look simply marvelous. I, for one, am so glad you have come for Christmas."

Elizabeth shot Max a casual glance and he returned her look of relief with a wink.

Leading Elizabeth across the kitchen to the stove Kate answered her previous question. "Stew is what you are smelling." Picking up the wooden spoon she scooped out a small portion and suggested, "Try a taste and tell me what you think."

Elizabeth sipped at the concoction and then smiled as she licked her lips. "That is good! What is it called?"

"Frogmore Stew."

"I've never heard of it before."

"Unless you are from South Carolina or have visited the state you probably wouldn't have heard of it. It's a local staple around these parts. It's comfort food and quite hearty."

Elizabeth handed back the spoon and inquired, "What's in there?"

"Six ingredients: Old Bay seasoning, new potatoes, smoked sausage cut into two-inch pieces, corn on the cob, cut to three-inch sections, shrimp and a small amount of salt."

"The consistency of your stew reminds me of some of the stews my mother back home used to make. She always said if you can't eat it without a fork then it's not stew!"

Kate turned to Charley and Max, and remarked, "This is one smart girl we have here!"

Putting on a pair of oven mitts, Kate carefully picked up the pot and spoke to Max. "If you'll open the door to the porch this is the last item that goes on the table."

Kate placed the stew in the middle of the table, surveyed the spread, and nodded in approval. "Let's all be seated. I think we can now eat."

After everyone took their place Charley extended his hand to his wife and spoke softly, "If everyone would join hands then we can say grace."

Holding Max's hand Elizabeth smiled. She felt welcomed.

The blessing over, Max's father reached for a platter of crab cakes and handed them to Elizabeth. "Let's get started while everything is still hot."

Elizabeth took one of the crab cakes as she asked, "What am I about to eat?"

Kate placed a portion of stew on her plate. "That, my young lady is a crab cake and we also have peel-and-eat shrimp, bread sticks, of course, the stew, and this." Holding up a bowl she explained. "This is mac and cheese and not just any ol' mac and cheese. This is from a place called Steamers which is on the way to Fripp Island over in Beaufort County. I picked up a few pounds of it last week when we were over there. It happens to be Max's favorite. He claims it's the best, not only in Beaufort Country but possibly the entire state."

Charley cut into a crab cake and spoke to Elizabeth, "We understand you are taking nursing up there at Gettysburg."

Swallowing a small bite of mac and cheese. Elizabeth covered her mouth and then answered, "That is correct. My original plan was to attend four years of college which would allow me to receive my bachelor's degree in nursing. After graduating I planned on going back home to Lancaster where I would get a job position at one of the local hospitals. I've always held an interest in helping those who are elderly or sick. Just recently, my plans changed because I will not be able to afford college tuition for my junior and senior years. This forced me to graduate at the end of this school year with an associate degree."

Kate frowned and inquired, "I'm so sorry to hear that. Was your scholarship not for the entire four years?"

"I never had a scholarship. My father was paying for my education but has decided not to pay for my last two years."

Charley chimed in, "It seems sad your father could not afford to send you to school the last two years."

Elizabeth took a long sip of lemonade and replied, "He has more than enough money for my last two years. He had decided he is no longer going to foot the bill."

Kate looked at Max and asked the next question. "So, when next May comes around and you graduate with your associate degree, I assume you'll be moving back to Lancaster to pursue your nursing career?"

"No, I will not be returning home. I'd like nothing better but I can no longer go home."

Charley, who had been listening, asked, "Why on earth not?"

"Because my parents sort of disowned me."

Confused, Kate probed, "Then if you cannot go back home after you are finished with your schooling where will you go?"

"I've already looked into that and it turns out that with an associate degree, I can get a job at the hospital or one of the local nursing facilities in Gettysburg earning somewhere around forty thousand a year. I don't think that's too bad for a Pennsylvania farm girl."

Charley ran his fork through his bowl of stew while asking, "It's probably none of our business, but I'm wondering after all the years of being raised beneath your parents' roof that you would be disowned?"

Elizabeth hesitated in her answer when Max spoke up. "I think I can best answer that. It was because of me that she was turned out by her family. I have told you all along during our relationship that Elizabeth's parents did not even know I existed. If her parents found out she was involved with someone outside of her faith, then her father would pull her out of school and she would have to return to Lancaster. Well, that's exactly what happened! Her parents recently did find out about our relationship but were fed the wrong information. This resulted in her father pulling her out of school. I just couldn't sit by and simply let this happen so I drove over to her farm to confront her parents and set the record straight. I told her father that I wanted to marry his daughter and Elizabeth stated she wanted to marry me, so after a lengthy conversation he decided Elizabeth was free to make her own decision. By making the decision she wanted to marry me, someone outside of the Mennonite faith, she was in a sense renouncing her faith. Hence, she cannot return to her home."

Kate looked at Charley in confusion and then asked Max. "Let me get this straight. You and Elizabeth concocted this marriage story to prevent her father from yanking her from school, which didn't work out anyway because he is now refusing to pay for her last two years."

"That question can only be answered by saying yes *and no!* Yes, my plan did backfire because now Elizabeth's schooling has been cut short. The marriage portion as you call it was not a story. It happens to be the truth. Elizabeth and I are planning on getting married."

Kate dropped a piece of shrimp she was about to pop into her mouth. "You can't be serious. What do you mean…married?"

Charley answered his wife's question. "It's not that hard to figure out Kate. Hundreds of thousands of people do it every year. Ya know, walk down the aisle, say I do, buy a house, put a white picket fence around it, and raise a family….like we did."

"That's not what I mean…Charles!" Smiling pleasantly at Elizabeth, Kate explained, "My confusion is not centered on you but in my son. We had assumed he was going to complete his four years of college, then acquire a job with a financial firm and at some point open his own accounting business. We always figured at some point down the road after he graduated he would marry." Looking directly at Max, his mother asked, "You are going to complete college…correct?"

Max held up his hands in defense. "Look, this is starting to get out of hand. I only said we were going to get married…I didn't say when the marriage was to take place. First of all, I have every intention of completing my four years at college. Elizabeth and I are not planning on tying the knot until after I graduate which equates to the fact we probably won't get married for at least three years from now."

Elizabeth cleared her throat to get everyone's attention. "I know this issue is a family matter and I at this point am not a family member but I would like to interject something. If I thought for even a second my love for your son was going to cause problems within his family I would have never agreed to marry Max. Ever since my family disowned me, which was weeks ago, Max and I have discussed how and when we were going to tell you about our future marriage. When Max invited me for Christmas we thought that would be the best time. We talked about how we were going to tell you on the way down here earlier today. We knew it might be awkward, but agreed that together we could get through this. I have prayed to God about our relationship and I am confident as long as we keep our love for one another pure that the Good Lord will bless us. I learned a long time ago not to be overly concerned about what people think of me, but to remember that God knows what's on my heart. So, there you have it. Case closed as they say!"

Kate looked across the table at Charles as she shrugged and then turned to Elizabeth. "My husband and I have always trusted Max to do the right thing. Sitting here listening to you speak I feel he has made a wise choice in choosing you as his future wife."

Charley smiled at his wife approvingly and then asked, "What kind of plans if any have you made regarding your future together?"

Max was quick with his reply. "Last week we opened a checking and savings account for Elizabeth and for the past two weeks, she had been studying for her driver's license test. Currently, we are both working for Kellem on his farm. He is paying us twelve dollars an hour each, so together we are saving some money."

Probing, Kate asked, "Who is this Kellem?"

Max supplied the answer, "Kellem McCulhay in this old codger who I met on Little Round Top. He owns a farm that sits right on the edge of the battlefield in Gettysburg. We stuck up a conversation and wound up being friends. Long story short. He hired Elizabeth and I to work on his farm."

Charley chimed in on the conversation, "This relationship you two share has turned out to be much different than what Kate and I thought it would. Over the past year or so as Max has kept us up to date on the way you feel about one another, we always thought based upon the fact you come from two very different ways of being raised that the relationship was short-lived and could never lead to a marriage. We knew Max was never going to convert to your faith, Elizabeth, and become a Mennonite farmer and we also knew you would not leave your faith for him, but it's apparent that's what happened. I have another question for you two. When the end of this school year arrives and Elizabeth leaves with her associate degree what will take place? For instance, Max would normally head down here for the summer and you would go back to your farm in Lancaster. But, seeing as you cannot go back Elizabeth, what are your plans for the summer?"

Max, once again was quick with a response. "Depending on whether Elizabeth gets a job or not she may spend the summer with us here in Summerville. If she does acquire a job at the hospital in Gettysburg or one of the local nursing homes then she'll remain in Gettysburg and I'll come home for the summer."

"That's right," added, Elizabeth, "and Kellem has offered to allow me to stay at a summer house he has on the farm at no charge."

Charles took a large bite of stew and remarked, "It sounds to me like you two have thought this thing through. We just want you to know we will support you two in whatever you decide to do."

"That's right," chimed in Kate, "and now I think we should talk about all the wonderful things we'll do over the holiday while you're home. That reminds me. This year your father and I thought it would be nice to spend Christmas over at Fripp Island, but that was before we knew we would be having a guest. Maybe we should reconsider."

"Nonsense," said Elizabeth. "Don't change your family plans because I'm here. I'd like to see this Fripp Island. Max has told me so much about it I feel I've been there. I would love to see it. I assume I'll be able to see the ocean there?"

Charley clapped his hands. "Then Fripp Island for Christmas it is! We'll get up early tomorrow, have breakfast, pack, and head on over to Beaufort County. Why, before noon rolls around tomorrow, Elizabeth you'll be dipping your toes in the Atlantic!"

CHAPTER TWENTY-SEVEN

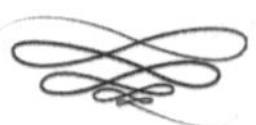

Charles guided the family car across the Beaufort River on Route 21 South, pulling into a gas station on Ladies Island. Hopping out of the car he pointed at the station and shrugged, "Gotta use the restroom. Fill 'er up, Max!"

Kate, climbing out of the car stretched and then spoke to Elizabeth who was standing next to her. "I think I'm going to use the ladies' room as well."

Elizabeth looked at Max who was removing the nozzle from the pump and stated, "I think I better go too."

Max unscrewed the gas cap inserted the nozzle and watched as the spinning numbers on the pump gauge began to add up to the unknown total. He hadn't even pumped in two dollars' worth when his cell phone signaled an incoming call. Digging the phone out of his jacket pocket, he wondered who could be calling him as he answered, "Hello."

A familiar voice instantly identified the caller. "Max. it's Kellem. Seeing as how you're on Christmas vacation I debated with myself whether I should call you or not but then decided to be on the safe side that I should."

Noticing a sense of urgency in Kellem's voice, Max replied, "What's up? Is there something wrong?"

"I guess you could say that. Last night somebody burned my barn down."

"What do you mean…burned your barn down?"

"Last night around midnight I got up to get me a glass of cold milk, I looked out the window and the barn was in flames."

"How bad is it?"

"Burned to the ground…lost everything in there; my car, my mowers, and some other equipment. There's nothing left but a pile of rubble and charred car and equipment frames. It's a total loss. By the time the fire company arrived, it was too late so they decided to let it burn out."

"Were any of the trees on the farm destroyed?"

"Nope, just the barn."

"You said *somebody* burned down the barn. How do you know that? Did you see them?"

"No, I imagine they were long gone by the time I noticed the fire."

"How do you know it was burned by someone?"

"An arson investigator dropped by this morning. He said that from the evidence he discovered the fire was deliberately set. He also said whoever set the fire was far from a professional arsonist. He could tell exactly where the fire started and what was used to ignite the blaze. According to him, it was very amateur…but still effective."

"Who on earth would want to burn down your barn?"

"That's the same thing the police asked me. I told them I didn't have any enemies except for two recent run-ins with two very different and unsavory characters; Simon Baumer and that other asshole, Brad Sykes."

"Do you think Baumer or Sykes would burn down your barn?"

"You tell me, Max. They were both on my property recently. Baumer tried to beat the crap out of you and that Sykes idiot all but threatened me."

Max turned to see if his parents or Elizabeth were in earshot then turned back to the pump and in a lowered tone asked Kellem, "Did you tell the police about the incidents with Baumer and Sykes?"

"I did," said Kellem. "They said they might pay Baumer and Sykes a visit and ask them some questions. I just wanted to call you and warn you and Elizabeth to be careful. This might just be the beginning of something bigger."

The pump made a thudding noise indicating the tank was full. Removing the nozzle Max noticed his parents as they approached. "I've got to go Kellem. Keep me posted on what happens."

"If anything else develops," said Kellem, "I'll give you a call. Have a nice Christmas."

Placing the nozzle back in the pump, Max spoke to his father. "Car's filled up and ready to go!"

Elizabeth was now standing next to Max's mother as Kate pointed at a building adjacent to the station. "That's Steamers right over there."

Remembering, Elizabeth climbed in the backseat as she stated, "Isn't that the place that has the great mac and cheese?"

Kate, in the front, confirmed, "Indeed it is, and not only that, Steamers is one of our favorite restaurants in the area. We'll probably grab lunch or dinner there later this week."

Back out on the two-lane road, Charley pointed down the highway. "In about twenty minutes we'll be on Fripp."

Kate turned sideways in the front seat so she could speak to everyone. "It's three days until Christmas. That means we have lots of leisurely time to spend over the next couple of days. Is there anything in particular you kids would like to do?"

Max looked out at the familiar sights he had seen hundreds of times over the years while answering, "One of the things I wanted to do is spend some time fishing with Dad. It's been quite a long time since he and I went out in the boat."

"I think some alone time with your father is an excellent idea," said Kate. "Tell you what! Why don't you and your father plan on doing that tomorrow and Elizabeth and I will have a girl's day out." Without waiting for confirmation on the upcoming local fishing expedition, Kate laid out her plan. "After breakfast in the morning, you two boys can head out to the ocean and Elizabeth and I will drive on over to Savannah. And, oh yeah I want to stop by Peach World and pick up a few items."

Joining in on the conversation, Elizabeth exclaimed, "Peach World! I know all about this Peach World. Max told me all about it. I'm looking forward to one of those peach slushies. What is this Savannah you spoke of?"

Kate was quick with her response. "Savannah is a city just over the Georgia State Line." Gesturing at Charley and Max, she explained, "We must have gone there hundreds of times over the years. There is a lot of history about the town and I think we might even take one of the tours they offer and then there are numerous gift shops and antique stores we can browse around in."

As they passed through the tiny community of Frogmore Max's mind was far from his upcoming day of fishing with his father. He was concerned over the fact there was a possibility that either Simon Baumer or Brad Sykes set Kellem's barn on fire. Having had unpleasant dealings with both Simon and Brad he didn't put it past either one of them to burn down that barn. He wasn't sure if he was going to share this latest bad news with his parents or not but he was going to say something to Elizabeth. For the next fifteen miles, Charley and Max sat in silence while Kate and Elizabeth talked non-stop about the planned trip to Savannah.

When they approached the Harbor River Max pointed to his left at a building situated next to a marsh that bordered the slow-moving water. "That's Johnson Creek right there. Another one of our favorite eating places over this way. If you'll look further out you can see the ocean."

Excited, Elizabeth sat up as erect as she could and looked beyond the restaurant and in the distance saw the Atlantic. Frowning, she remarked, "It doesn't look nearly as big as what you described it to be."

Max laughed. "That's because you can only see a small portion of it from here. In a few minutes when we get to Fripp you'll have a much better view."

Driving across the three-mile section of the parkway that passed over Hunting Island Elizabeth gazed in amazement at the thick trees and foliage that lined the road. "It looks like pictures of the jungle I have seen in books."

Charley had to brake as a deer appeared out of nowhere and scampered across the road.

Elizabeth pointed at the antlered creature and remarked, "Max told me there were a lot of deer down this way. We had deer on our farm back in Lancaster. They were pretty skittish and would run off at the slightest sound. Max has told me that the deer on Fripp are very tame."

Kate gestured up the road. "We'll be crossing the Fripp Island Bridge in the next couple of minutes."

Elizabeth read a sign in a clearing on her right that advertised: Marsh walk. Pointing at the clearing she asked, "What's the Marsh walk?"

"That is one of the places we'll go this week," said Max. "It's a trail that leads out into the marsh to a dock where you can just sit and relax and watch the sunset or do some bird watching or crabbing. I usually go there at least once every time I'm on Fripp."

Elizabeth gazed through the trees at the vast marsh as she remarked, "It would seem there are a lot of interesting things to do down here."

"There is," said Max, "and unfortunately in the short time we'll be spending on the island we won't have an opportunity to do them all, but you will get to see the ocean." Breaking out of the tree line, he pointed to the left. "As we cross the Fripp Island Bridge if you'll look out there you'll see the ocean."

Craning her neck to get a better look, Elizabeth commented, "You were right. It does look a lot bigger than back there when we saw it before."

Several seagulls landed on the bridge railing causing Elizabeth to laugh. "Look at all the birds!"

"Well, if you like birds," said Kate, "there are hundreds of species on the island."

Seconds later Charley guided their vehicle to the guard shack, spoke briefly to the uniformed guard, and was signaled through. They drove no more than a few yards when they had to stop for three deer who slowly walked across the road. Three golf carts in a row coming in the opposite direction passed by as the drivers and passengers waved. Elizabeth tapped Max on his shoulder. "Those three cars were so tiny. What kind of cars are they?"

Max laughed as he answered, "They are what we call golf carts. It's the best way to get around the island. The speed limit is only fifteen miles an hour and the island itself is only six square miles so having a car on Fripp is not a necessity."

Kate chimed in, "We have a golf cart. In the next couple of days, we'll all cruise around the island in the cart. We can drive over to the marina or out to Ocean Point in the morning and see the dolphins frolic in Fripp Islet."

At the intersection of Tarpon Boulevard and Bonito Road Charley announced, "We'll be at the house in about two minutes. It's almost at the end of the island."

They drove by several spacious homes flanking both sides of the road causing Elizabeth to comment in wonder. "The homes are so beautiful and large, but let me ask. There doesn't seem to be many people around."

Kate was quick with an answer, "It's the off-season right now and will remain that way until about May when folks from all over the country will spend a week or two here on Fripp."

Elizabeth smiled as she observed six deer lying in the front yard beneath some palmetto trees of a two-story Cape Cod designed home.

Charley made a left into a driveway, pulled the car beneath their elevated house, and honked the horn once. "We're here!"

When they stepped out of the car, Charley spoke to Max and Elizabeth, "Why don't you two go on down to the beach? Kate and I can take care of getting everything inside."

Max agreed as he took Elizabeth's hand and led her through the pillared garage and up a set of wood steps.

On the landing, Elizabeth stopped dead in her tracks as she stared out at the Atlantic Ocean. Placing her hand on her chest she spoke softly. "Oh my!" She looked to the left, to the right, and then straight out onto the distant horizon where the water seemed to intersect with the sky. "You were right when you said the ocean was big." Pointing to the southwest she continued to speak, "Are those boats I see out there?"

"Yes," said Max. "They're fishing boats. Shrimpers can stay out there for two to three days catching shrimp." A small flock of Pelicans flew above in formation as they glided on the ocean breeze.

Pointing at the birds, Elizabeth remarked, "I guess your mother was right when she spoke of all the species of birds here on the island." Elizabeth stepped closer to the railing and asked, "Can we go down to the water?"

"Sure, but I don't think we'll be able to walk on the beach, at least here because the tide is in and the waves will be right up against the stone sea barrier. It would be too dangerous, especially for someone who has never walked on the beach. Later on, we can drive the golf cart back down Tarpon to a beach access where we can get onto the beach, but for now, we can walk across the deck out to the steps and sit while enjoying the view." Talking her by the hand, he suggested, "Shall we?"

Grasping his hand, she replied, "We shall!"

They stopped three steps from the bottom where the waves were splashing against the bottom step. "We can sit here for a while. The waves won't come up this high."

Elizabeth looked to her left and inquired. "Is that a part of the ocean?"

"No, that's Skull Inlet which borders this end of the island. The beach curves around this end of the island and extends in the opposite direction for just over three miles to Ocean Point at Fripp Inlet which we crossed when we went across the bridge. Angling his thumb over his shoulder Max continued, "The Harbor River runs from Fripp Inlet over to Skull which hems in the backside of the island with water."

A stiff ocean breeze blew Elizabeth's hair in every direction. Smiling she remarked with a wide grin. "The breeze feels wonderful. I can't imagine living here and seeing this every day."

Max sat down and Elizabeth followed as he took both her hands in his. "I've something to tell you and we might as well get it out of the way."

Before she could reply Max went on, "When we were back there getting gas earlier I received a call from Kellem. Last night someone burned down his barn."

A look of deep concern instantly covered Elizabeth's face. "How bad was it?"

"It was a complete loss. Burned to the ground. Kellem said he lost everything that was in there. An arson investigator said it was evident the fire was set on purpose."

Placing her hand over her mouth, she exclaimed, "Who would do such a thing? Kellem is such a good man, why he wouldn't hurt a fly."

"Kellem," said Max, "while talking to the police told them about how Simon Baumer came to the farm previously and beat on me. He told them he ran Baumer and his two brothers off at gunpoint. He also explained how Brad Sykes and one of his college chums were also at the farm recently and Brad all but threatened him. The police, from what Kellem said might ask both Baumer and Brad some questions about the fire."

Almost as if she had taken offense, Elizabeth remarked sharply, "Simon Baumer could not have set that fire!"

Somewhat shocked, Max asked, "Why do you say that? You saw how violent he was toward me when I was at your farm. He even hit me. He attacked me on Kellem's farm as well. What makes you think Baumer wouldn't stoop to burning down Kellem's barn?"

"Because I know the man and everything about him. Don't forget… he courted me for three straight months over this past summer. He was convinced I was going to be his wife. He confided in me. He opened up to me and told me everything about his past life and his plans for the future. I know him inside out. Now, I think we can both agree he is on the rough side when it comes to holding his temper, but I happen to know he is deeply religious. I'm not saying he's perfect…no one is! There is no way he would burn down another farmer's barn. I say this because years ago he lost two barns in an electrical storm. He lost quite a bit of equipment and even some cattle. As a farmer himself, he understands how the loss of a barn can affect an operation. He might be short-tempered but he is still a Mennonite and I am convinced beyond any doubt he has moved on with his life and could care less about our relationship. There are any number of eligible female Mennonite women who would gladly marry up with Simon Baumer. Simon did not burn that barn.

"Now, Brad Sykes is a different story. He is an immature young man who has and still holds a grudge against you for the incident at Burger Palace your freshman year. I wouldn't put anything past him. I think the police will be wasting their time by talking to Simon. He has nothing to gain by burning Kellem's barn. Brad, on the other hand in my opinion is a dangerous person. I'm not saying he is guilty of burning down that barn but between him and Simon, Brad is the one I would focus on if I were the police."

Jim Sullivan, of the Manheim Township Department, made a right-hand turn onto Landisville Road while speaking to Detective Luther Vanderway of the Gettysburg Police Department. "We'll be at the Baumer farm in less than five minutes. I've lived here in East Petersburg all my life to date and I know Simon quite well. He owns two businesses here in town and owns the largest farm in Lancaster County, maybe the state. I for one cannot believe he would be involved in a barn burning over in Adams County or for that matter anywhere. He is well thought of by the members of his Mennonite community and throughout the county. As far as I know, he's never had any trouble with the law. He can be short and rude with people but that isn't a crime."

After passing three massive white two-story barns and a large herd of cattle Jim pulled his car up in front of a creek stone two-story home surrounded by a covered porch. Two German Shepherds lounged peacefully on a rug at the end of the front porch. Getting out Jim pointed out to Luther. "Don't worry about the dogs they're harmless." The two canines raised their large heads as the duo approached but then went back to their morning of leisure. They were not even up the porch steps when out the front door stepped Simon himself. Recognizing his longtime friend, Simon reached for Jim's hand. "Jim, what brings you out this way?"

Jim shook the large man's hand and responded, "I wish I could say this is a social call but it's strictly business."

Turning to Luther Jim made the introduction, "Simon, this is Detective Luther Vandeway of the Gettysburg Police. If you have a few minutes he'd like to ask you some questions."

Simon looked Vanderway up and down and frowned as he asked,

"Why would the Gettysburg Police have any interest in coming to my farm let alone want to speak with me?"

"If we could just sit for a spell Detective Vanderway can explain the reason for his visit."

Not feeling all that cordial about having the police at his home, Simon sat on the top step and offered, "Have a seat!"

Jim joined him, but Vanderway remained standing. Following a moment of awkward silence Luther placed his right foot on the bottom step and spoke. "Mr. Baumer, I'd like to ask you some questions about a barn fire that took place two days ago over in Gettysburg."

Confused, Simon gave Luther a stern look. "Why would you have any questions for me about a fire in Gettysburg?"

"You were in Gettysburg recently. Is this not correct?"

"Yes, I was. Over the summer I was courting a young Mennonite woman by the name of Elizabeth King. Her father's farm is just up the road a couple miles from here. I was convinced she would become my wife and she gave me no reason to figure otherwise. Later, after she went back to school in Gettysburg I drove over to see if there was anything she needed plus I wanted to see her. While I'm there I run into this college lad who informs me his roommate has and is still having an affair with my Elizabeth. You can imagine how I felt. Based upon the fact Mr. King had approved of my courting his daughter I was sure he was not aware of his daughter's involvement with this young college man. I contacted Mr. King and that very same day he drove over to Gettysburg and removed her from the school and brought her back here to their farm. I decided to get in touch with this young man and set him straight. No self-respecting Mennonite woman would ever consider having a relationship with someone outside of our faith."

Vanderway gave Simon a casual smile and asked, "And this young man's name is Maxwell Miller...correct?"

"Yes, he's the young man who was seeing Elizabeth."

"According to Kellem McCulhay, the owner of the barn that was burned, he states you and your two brothers confronted Mr. Miller while he was working on his farm."

"That is also correct but what does that have to do with this McCulhay's barn?"

Vanderway took three steps out in front of the porch, kicked a small rock into the nearby mowed grass, turned, and placed his hands on his hips while addressing Baumer. "Motive, Mr. Baumer…that's what! McCulhay told us he was present when you talked with Miller at his farm. He claims you attacked Miller."

"Two things," said Simon. "First, attack is the wrong definition as to what happened. Secondly, McCulhay wasn't present when I had, what I call a disagreement with Miller. Sure, I'll admit I slapped him around some but that can hardly be defined as an attack!"

"McCulhay claims you hit Miller and knocked him to the ground."

"How would he know that? He didn't enter into our conversation until after Miller and I disagreed about Elizabeth. Have you talked any of this over with Miller?"

"No, we have not. At the moment he is out of the state, but Miller did speak with McCulhay at great lengths about another situation where you two bumped heads. We have been informed you contacted Elizabeth's father about her relationship with Mr. Miller. Shortly after that, and after your confrontation with Miller at the McCulhay farm Miller drives over here to see Elizabeth's parents to try and straighten out some of what you told Mr. King. Apparently, after speaking with Elizabeth's folks they decided to allow her to make her own decision and she chose Miller over you. When she and Miller were in the process of leaving the farm you show up and attack Miller again!"

"Once again detective, it was hardly an attack. True, I did hit the young man but you do not understand why. Elizabeth was going against everything our Mennonite community stands for. She was going to marry outside of our faith. I was not about to allow that to happen, but it did. I've moved on from my obsession with courting Elizabeth King. I have no reason to burn down McCulhay's barn. If anything, you should be questioning him about how me and my brothers were treated while on his farm. That old man fired a shotgun a few feet from our heads and then ran us off with a revolver he had."

Vanderway held up his right hand. "McCulhay claims you threatened both him and Miller."

Simon stood and waved his hand in front of him. "I've had about enough of this nonsense. Has this Miller pressed charges against me?"

"No, he has not."

"Has this McCulhay pressed any charges against me?"

"No."

"Then I can assume you are grasping at straws. Am I considered a suspect in this barn burning?"

"No, you are merely a person of interest."

"Well, since you put it that way, then I have no interest in continuing this conversation." Turning to Sullivan, Simon continued, "Jim…you and I have been friends for a long time. You're always welcome here on my farm. As for you, Mr. Vanderway. I think you should now leave and head back across the Susquehanna River to your county. Good day, gentlemen!" With that, Simon turned, walked up the steps, and entered his house without another word.

Jim spoke as he looked at Vanderway. "That didn't go all that well… did it? Do you want to drive up the road to Amos King's place?"

"No, I don't believe that will be necessary. If you'll just drive me back to the station I think I'll head on home."

Walking to their car Jim asked, "Are there any other persons of interest?"

"Yes, there is a young man who at one time roomed with this Miller at school. He and Miller didn't exactly see eye to eye on things and were involved in a physical dispute last year. This young man, a fella by the name of Brad Sykes was also at the McCulhay farm where he recently had a run-in with both Miller and McCulhay. Currently, he is up in New York State on Christmas break. He'll return to school next week at which point we'll have a sit down with him."

Kate flipped on her right turn signal and pointed at a mobile home-shaped clapboard building just off the highway. "Here we are…exit 58. I haven't been over here for a couple of months. If you enjoy peaches I think you'll like this place."

Exiting Route 95, she guided the car down Route 87 for a few yards then got off and parked in a dirt lot adjacent to the unique store which was topped with a huge billboard advertising: PEACH WORLD.

Getting out, Elizabeth commented as she looked at six other cars situated on the lot. "Looks like they are really busy."

As they crossed the lot Kate pointed out, "They are always busy. They have a great reputation and since they are just off the highway it's easy for people to pull off and shop." Opening the screen door, she smiled, "Com'n, let's go on in."

Inside, Elizabeth stepped to the side as she took in the interior of the building, a large rack to her left containing various bottles of peach wines and sodas. A long counter ran the distance of the structure where there were displays of peach bread, peach salsa, and assorted candies which you could sample. Along the front window, there were jars of peaches, jams and jellies, peach pies, and other assorted peach food novelties. Reaching for a sample plate of pralines Kate suggested, "Here, try one of these. They're wonderful."

Elizabeth reached for one of the candied treats while Kate spoke to the counter girl, "I would like a pound of these and two peach pies to start with. How is your peach bread today?"

Elizabeth chewed on one of the sweet pralines as she wandered down the aisle, sampling a small piece of peach bread and then a handful of pecans. Ten minutes later, seated once again in the car, Kate held up a peach slushie while offering a toast to Elizabeth who was holding a slushie of her own. Taking a long drink Elizabeth smiled. "Max was right. These are delicious!"

Back on Route 95, Kate pointed at a large green road sign that read; Savannah 51 Miles. "We should be in Savannah in forty-five minutes or so. We'll grab lunch and then do some sightseeing and maybe some shopping." Passing a slow-moving truck Kate went on, "Speaking of food, on the way back home this evening we need to stop at Publix Grocery and pick up everything we'll need for our Christmas dinner."

"I'm glad we're talking about Christmas dinner." said Elizabeth, "because I want to ask you something. Would you mind terribly if I help you prepare the meal?" Before Kate could respond, Elizabeth explained, "Ever since I was a little girl I have always helped my mother in the kitchen, whether it be breakfast, lunch, or dinner. I just wouldn't feel right sitting at the dinner table enjoying a good meal I had nothing to do with as far as preparation goes."

Kate reached across the seat and patted Elizabeth's left hand. "You must have read my mind. I was going to ask you if you wanted to help. To be honest with you…I'm going to need you at my side. Max told me last night about the wonderful Thanksgiving meal you prepared at Kellem's farm. He told me about how you cooked the turkey in a bag and it was the best he ever tasted. I have heard about cooking a turkey in a bag but have never attempted it. When we hit the grocery later today you can help me pick out whatever we need."

Elizabeth, sitting up in excitement asked, "What else are we going to have aside from turkey?"

"Well, I was thinking of two meats. We can pick up one of those pre-sliced honey-baked hams. Of course, we'll have corn, glazed carrots and even a green bean casserole. Then, there will be hot rolls, mashed potatoes, and stuffing which Max also claims is the best he's ever had. I'm thinking of deviled eggs, and both a vegetable platter and cheese tray, maybe with some sliced sausage. Of course, we'll have the peach pies and I may bake a chocolate cake. How does all that sound?"

"It all sounds so wonderful. I'm getting hungry just sitting here talking about all the food we plan to have. Would you mind if I make something on my own?"

"Of course not. What do you have in mind?"

"Let's see. I'd like to bake a shoofly pie and along with showing you how to cook the bag turkey, I'd like to make sage stuffing. I think I'll also whip up a huge batch of ham and dumplings."

Kate smiled broadly and stated, "Now it's me who is getting hungry. Let's grab some lunch!"

A quarter mile out from Fripp Island east of Ocean Point, the Miller family fishing boat bobbed in the low waves as Max's line grew tight. Gripping his pole, he spoke to his father who was at the front of the boat. "Think I've got a bite!"

Charley grinned and replied, "Glad someone's having some luck. We've been out here for two hours, and so far we haven't caught a thing."

Max pulled the pole toward his chest and began the process of reeling in what he hoped was his first catch of the day. Seconds later a seven-pound seabass lay in the bottom of the boat. Removing the hook Max placed the fish in their cooler and joked with his father. "That's one to nothing. You better get serious if you intend to beat me today."

Charley smiled. "I see you haven't lost your touch when it comes to fishing."

Max opened a small cooler and grabbed some bait which he proceeded to attach to his lure. Casting his line back out into the ocean he took on a serious tone. "Dad, there's something I need to share with you. I wasn't going to say anything to you and Mom about it but the more I think about it I realize that I should."

Charley gave his son an understanding look. "Sounds serious."

"It might not be anything to worry over, but then again it might. On the way down here the other day when we stopped and gassed up I received a call from Kellem McCulhay, the farmer Elizabeth and I work for. He told me his barn burned down and an arson investigator stated that it was set on fire by someone who didn't know what they were doing. In other words, it was not a professional job. He told the police when asked if he had any idea who might have set the fire that he recently had run-ins with two people at two different times, Simon Baumer and Brad Sykes. Basically what happened is that Kellem ran both of them off at gunpoint."

"Hold on a minute," said Charley. "You're going to have to back up some because I'm lost."

"A couple of weeks ago Simon stopped by the farm to let me know in no uncertain terms he intended to marry up with Elizabeth. Things got out of hand and he started to get physical with me. Fortunately, Kellem was nearby and ran Simon and his two brothers off with his shotgun and a revolver he had. Simon didn't take too well at being run off and there is that possibility he returned later and lit the fire. The police said they were going to question Baumer about the barn."

"How does Brad Sykes fit into this?"

"Some time later Brad and one of his fraternity brothers stopped by the farm to purchase a couple of Christmas trees. Brad started a conversation about how he heard about my getting attacked down in Charleston. I told him it seemed odd that he knew so much about the attack as I had not shared the situation with anyone on campus other than Elizabeth. Brad took offense and said if I so much as even suggested he was responsible for the incident down in Charleston he would contact his father and I might not get off as easy as the first time his father intervened. The police are going to question Brad about the barn burning as well as Baumer. When, and if the police do contact Brad about the fire at McCulhay's farm I'm afraid Brad will contact his father and we might be facing yet another lawsuit. I thought maybe we might want to contact Rich in case we have to face Brad's father and his lawyers again."

"If the police do not mention your name while questioning Sykes then why would he involve his father?"

"He knows I was there when he was at the farm and that we argued. He also knows I was present when he threatened Kellem. He'll just assume I had something to do with the police questioning him. If he contacts his father about the situation then that could lead to trouble!"

Charley reeled in his line and looked up at the darkening sky. "I guess it wouldn't hurt to contact Rich and let him know what's going on. If you'll recall he did a bang-up job when we faced Sykes' father and his lawyers.

"All right, here's what I think we should do. When we get back to the house I'll call Rich and see what he thinks we should do with this information. Starting the engine, Charley checked the dark sky again. "We better head in. It looks like there's a storm brewing."

CHAPTER TWENTY-EIGHT

Sam Phillips, Dean of Gettysburg College, pushed the blinking button on his inter-office phone and spoke softly into the device to his secretary. "Yes, Phyllis…what is it?"

"You have a call from Detective Luther Vanderway of the Gettysburg Police on the line. Do you want me to put him through?"

"Yes, I'll speak to him." Another button instantly flashed and Sam pressed it, picked up, and spoke. "Luther…we haven't talked since last summer at the Policeman's ball here in town. What can I do for you?"

"I wish I was calling to schedule a golf game but I'm afraid my call is of a business nature. We need to question one of your students about a case we're currently working on. I thought I'd give you a call first before we proceed."

"I see and what is the student's name?"

"Bradley Sykes. I assume you know who he is?"

"Yes, quite well. Brad is Harmon Sykes' son. Harmon attended college here over twenty-some years ago and now his son attends. Can I ask what the questioning is regarding?"

"No, and that's why I'm calling you. The case is still open for investigation. I am well aware of who Harmon Sykes is and that he has over the years been a powerful and generous alumni of the college. We realize his son, Brad is of age and is an adult but I thought it might be best if you contact his father first. We are planning on questioning Sykes tomorrow. I would ask that aside from contacting his father you keep this under your hat."

"All right, here's what I'll do. Harmon Sykes is a close friend of mine. I'll call him later this morning and then I'll let you know how he reacted. I know Harmon well and I can almost say for sure he will not allow his son to be questioned without him being present. I'm not sure how he'll react, especially without knowing what the incident is about, but if I had to take a stab at what Harmon will do I'd say he'll either fly down here or give you a call and try to find out what's going on."

"Sounds good. I'll wait for your call. Let's get together for lunch after the first of the year."

"Count me in," said Sam. "I'll call you later today after I contact Sykes."

Sam, no sooner hung up when he rifled through his rolodex in search of Harmon Sykes' number. Locating the number, he picked up the phone, dialed, and then waited when on the fourth ring the familiar voice answered, "Hello."

Phillips responded, "Harmon…it's Sam down here in Gettysburg."

"Sam, how in the hell are you? How's the weather down your way?"

"Typical Pennsylvania winter…cold and wet. How are things up there in Ithaca?"

"We've had a hard winter up this way. Lots of snow and ice." Hesitating, Harmon remarked, "What's on your mind? I'm sure you didn't call me to discuss the weather."

"I called you to discuss a situation that involves your son, Brad. I just received a call from Detective Vanderway of the Gettysburg Police who plans on asking your son some questions tomorrow about a case they are working on. He wouldn't tell me what the case is about but I got the feeling your son may be suspected of some sort of involvement. I thought I'd give you a call and let you know what's going on. I'm sorry, but that's all I know at the moment."

"Have you or anyone else there at school talked with Brad about this?"

"No, I just got off the phone with the police. I thought it would be best to call you."

"Do you have this Vanderway's number?"

"Yes, I do."

"And you say the police are going to question my son tomorrow. Did they give you a time frame when the questioning would take place? And another thing, did they say where the questioning would take place?"

"They did not give me an exact time or location, only that the questioning would take place tomorrow."

"Give me Vanderway's number. I'm going to give him a call and see if I can get clarification on their intentions."

Detective Vanderway was just getting out of his car at police headquarters when his cell phone buzzed. Taking the phone to his ear, he answered, "Vanderway here."

"Detective Vanderway…my name is Harmon Sykes. I'm Brad Sykes' father. I'd like to ask you some questions about the interest your department has in my son."

Leaning against a police cruiser Vanderway responded, "Dean Phillips told me he was going to contact you and more than likely I could expect a call. To answer your question, just let me say the Gettysburg Police are working on a current case and we feel your son may be involved or may be able to answer some questions we have."

"If you would be so kind can you tell me exactly what the case is about?"

"Despite the fact your son is of age and an adult, I am not obligated to give you that information, but since you have taken the time to contact me combined with the fact that you are close friends with Dean Phillips, I'll give you a brief run-down. On December 21st there was a barn fire here in Gettysburg. The local arson investigator states the fire was set. The owner of the property where the barn was situated claims your son and one of his frat buddies were on the property a few days before the fire. According to the owner he and your son, Brad had words and the owner asked your son to leave. Days later the barn is burned to the ground. We thought maybe your son could shed some light on the incident."

"Are you insinuating my son had anything to do with the fire?"

"No, your son presently is not a suspect but he is a person of interest. We'd just like to ask him some questions."

"Are there any other persons of interest or is it just my son you wish to question?"

"There is one other person of interest who we have already spoken to."

"Does this person know my son?"

"I have no idea. Look, I can't discuss all of the ins and outs of the case over the phone. We are going to question your son tomorrow."

"A couple of things, Detective," said Harmon. "I am going to contact an attorney; Michael Dolstrum located right there in Gettysburg. I will also be flying into Harrisburg later today. I will then drive over to Gettysburg and meet with my son and Dolstrum. I would prefer when you question

Brad that it not be conducted at police headquarters. I am going to arrange with Dean Phillips that the questioning takes place at his office. Would this be acceptable?"

"Yes, I think we can swing that. Let's say ten o'clock."

"Well then, until tomorrow morning. Thank you for your cooperation, Detective."

Brad Sykes, perched on a bar stool at one of the local college hangouts in Gettysburg, stubbed out his cigarette in a bent metal ashtray while taking the last swallow from a bottled beer. About to signal the bartender for a second beer, Brad's cell phone buzzed. Picking up his phone, he answered, "Yeah!"

"Yeah…what the hell kind of way is that to answer a phone? This is your father!"

Surprised, Brad responded, "Dad…what's up?"

"In using your vernacular, I'll ask you the same…what's up with you? I just got off the phone with the Gettysburg Police. They are planning on questioning you tomorrow about a barn that was burned there in the area. Do you know anything about this fire?"

"No, I don't. Well, wait. I did hear something on the news about a barn that burned down, but why would the police want to question me?"

"The reason for the questioning is because you happen to be a person of interest. From talking with Detective Vanderway, I was left with a very distinct feeling the police feel you may have been somehow involved."

"That's insane! Why would I want to burn down someone's barn?"

"The police have informed me the man who owns the property where the barn was located stated you were on his property a couple of days before this fire. Is this true?"

"The news said that Kellem McCulhay's barn burned down. I was there a few days before the fire. I was sent there by my fraternity to purchase two Christmas trees, which I did."

"Vanderway states this McCulhay and you had words or some sort of disagreement while you were on the property. Is this correct?"

"Like I said, I went there to buy two trees. Max Miller was there with this McCulhay. I guess he works for the man. Miller started to accuse me of somehow being involved when he was attacked down in Charleston. I told him that was impossible because at the time I was with you up in Canada on a fishing trip. I also told him if he persisted with his accusations I would contact you and he might not get off as easy as the first time he met you. Look, Father, if anyone should be upset about what went on at that farm it should be me. Ol' man McCulhay ran me off his place at gunpoint!'

"Do you mean to tell me this man drew a gun on you?"

"Not exactly. He had this revolver tucked in his pants which he displayed as he ordered me off the property. But, despite that, I did not burn down McCulhay's barn."

"Look," said Harmon, "we can talk over the phone for the next hour and wind up accomplishing nothing. I will be flying into Harrisburg on my private plane later this afternoon. I'll then rent a car and head your way. I intend to contact Michael Dolstrum, the attorney who represented us before when we met Miller, his father, and their attorney. I'll give you a call when I get close to Gettysburg. The three of us will have dinner somewhere there in town and we'll put together a plan for this meeting with the police. In the meantime…stay out of trouble!"

Before Brad could respond his father ended the call. Staring at his phone, he signaled the bartender. "I need another beer and a shot of Jack!"

Elizabeth looked through the rear window as she enthusiastically remarked. "Goodbye Fripp Island. Hope to see you again soon!"

She turned in her seat and spoke to Max. "The week here on the island with your folks was wonderful and all the time before I got here I was thinking I might not be accepted by your family. After spending the day with your mother over in Savannah and helping her prepare our Christmas dinner, not to mention going fishing with you and your father I feel like I am part of your family."

"I know my parents quite well and believe me…from the way they reacted you have been accepted. My mother told me she likes you and that I could have not chosen a better girl to marry. My father didn't say much and he can be a man of few words. I can tell you this. If he didn't like you he would have told me. All in all, you a now a member of the Miller clan and our future marriage, even though special will be a family event. You are already connected with my parents."

Brushing hair away from her face Elizabeth gestured up the road. "When do you think we'll get to Gettysburg?"

"It'll be nearly twelve hours. We'll be getting back on campus a day earlier than most students."

"I like the idea of getting back a day before classes start. It gives you a day to get acclimated to college life again. Speaking of Gettysburg have you heard anything more from Kellem about the fire?"

"He called me this morning while I was down in the garage packing the car. What with saying goodbye to my folks and all I thought I'd wait until we were on the road to update you. He said the police contacted him and said they talked to Simon Baumer at his farm and things didn't go that well."

"That doesn't surprise me," said Elizabeth. "I cannot imagine Baumer being that excited about the police approaching him on his farm. I can't see him being cooperative with the police. And, like I said all along, Simon could not have and would not have burned down Kellem's barn. As rude and short-tempered as he can be burning down someone's barn is not something he would consider. I still think Brad is a much stronger candidate as the culprit. Are the police going to question him as well?"

"Yes, Kellem said he got a call from a detective who said they were going to question Brad at the Dean's office this morning at ten o'clock. He also told Kellem that Brad's father and an attorney representing their family would be present. That means unless the police have some solid proof Brad set the fire he'll probably walk away from this without any repercussions."

"You sound like you agree with me; that Brad and not Simon set the fire."

"It doesn't make any difference what I think. Brad or Simon, either one of them could be responsible for the fire, and then on the other hand maybe they weren't. But when you take the time to think about it, who else would have a reason to set the fire? Kellem ran both of them off his farm. I was there on both occasions and I've got to tell you; Simon Baumer and Brad Sykes were equally upset about how they were run off. As far as I'm concerned I feel Brad is still out to get even with me for popping him on the nose. I wouldn't put it past him to take his revenge out on Kellem."

Sticking her head in his office door a secretary announced, "Dean Phillips. Detectives Vanderway and Parks have arrived. Do you want them in here or in the conference room?"

"Show them to the conference room Phyliss and tell them I'll be right in." Looking at his watch he explained, "There will be three other gentlemen showing up shortly. When they arrive please send them in."

Sam made his way down a short hall and then entered a door on his right. The room was sparsely furnished with a long table and eight surrounding cushioned chairs, a small chandelier centered on the ceiling. Three pictures of the college hung on the paneled walls. Seated at the far end of the table sat Detective Vanderway and another man Sam had never met. Vanderway stood as Sam approached and extended his right hand. "Sam, it's good to see you. This is Detective Parks….Frank Parks to be exact. He just recently transferred here from Chambersburg. He's working this case with me."

Parks shook Sam's hand as he checked the time. "Nice to finally meet you, Dean Phillips. I've heard a lot of nice things about you. Don't mean to be out of line but it's now five after ten. It was our understanding the questioning was to start at ten. I hope Harmon Sykes hasn't changed his mind about our meeting."

"Not to worry, Detective. I've known Harmon for many years and if he says he'll be here then you can count on it. They're probably just running a little late."

Vanderway, who didn't seem concerned turned to his partner. "It'll be all right, Frank. I'm sure Sam is correct. They'll be here."

Just then, the door opened and Sam's secretary announced, "The other parties have arrived."

Sam gestured at the secretary. "Show them in please."

Stepping to the side she extended her hand and the three new arrivals entered; first Harmon, followed by Dolstrum, and then Brad. Harmon and Dolstrum were dressed in expensive three-piece suits while Brad wore a blue sports coat emblemed with his fraternity. Khaki pants, a blue shirt, a red tie, and cordovan loafers rounded out his dress attire. Sam immediately went about making introductions. "Detectives Vanderway and Parks, this is Harmon Sykes, his son Brad, and a local attorney Michael Dolstrum, of Dolstrum, Eichman and Dunn." While everyone was shaking hands, that is except for Brad who slumped down in a chair at the table, Sam addressed the secretary, "Would you please bring in the coffee and water?"

The secretary turned and exited the room while answering, "Certainly, Dean Phillips."

Taking a seat toward the middle of the table Sam gestured at those who were not yet seated, "If everyone would grab a seat, I think then we can begin."

Mr. Sykes and Dolstrum seated themselves, the attorney opening a briefcase and extracting a tape recorder, a notepad, and a pen. "I hope no one has any objections to my recording this meeting?"

Parks appeared to be disturbed as Vanderway spoke up, "No objections here."

Sam folded his hands on the table and addressed the entire group. "Since this meeting is taking place here at my office I'll start by saying I am simply present today because the police contacted me and explained that Harmon requested the questioning take place here on campus. There is no protocol on how this meeting is to be conducted and if there are no questions then I'll turn the floor over to Detective Vanderway."

Placing a legal pad in front of him, Vanderway cleared his throat and started, "We originally contacted Dean Phillips yesterday informing him we were going to be questioning one of his students here at school, namely, Brad Sykes. So let us begin. Let me ask this young man who is here with us this morning." Addressing Brad, Vanderway asked pleasantly, "Are you Brad Sykes?"

Brad, thinking the question was ridiculous answered smartly, "Yes, I am indeed Brad Sykes. Did you think my father would bring along an imposter?"

Harmon immediately corrected his son. "Brad…just answer the man's questions. There is no reason for any unnecessary conversation."

Brad gave his father a deadpan stare and then slumped down in his chair with a look of boredom on his face.

Parks moved uncomfortably in his chair while Vanderway continued, "On December 21st of this year a barn owned by Kellem McCulhay, one of our local farmers burned to the ground, resulting in a loss of not only the building but the contents as well. The County Arson Investigator states the fire was set on purpose, meaning that it was not an accident."

Dolstrum spoke up, "And what proof other than this investigator's opinion do we have?"

"Glad you asked counselor." Reaching inside his briefcase Vanderway withdrew an official-looking document. "I have with me here the investigation report complete with where in the barn the fire started and the accelerants used. According to the investigator the job, if one wants to refer to it in that matter was very unprofessional, but still quite effective."

Dolstrum politely inquired, "May I see the document?"

"Better than that," said Vanderway. "I have a copy for your records."

Dolstrum scanned the document and only commented on one section. "I see here where it states gasoline was used to start the fire. Did the owner of the property keep gasoline in the barn?"

"According to McCulhay…no."

Dolstrum slid the document over in front of Mr. Sykes while Vanderway continued with his next statement. "It is our understanding based on what McCulhay said that Brad and a friend of his from his fraternity dropped by the farm earlier the same week of the fire."

Dolstrum answered with instant confidence, "My client, Brad Skyes, was indeed at McCulhay's farm on December 18th, he and one of his fraternity brothers, Howard Fields went to the farm to purchase two Christmas trees. McCulhay had a young man there who was working for him. This young man just happens to be Maxwell Miller, the same student who punched my client in the face over a year ago."

Detective Parks jumped in on the conversation, "I'm glad you brought up Miller, Mr. Dolstrum. Your client, Brad, and this Miller had a conversation that started quite friendly but then turned ugly. Brad told Miller he had heard Max had gotten attacked over the summer while down in Charleston, South Carolina. Brad even went as far as to list Max's injuries. Miller told Brad it seemed odd he knew so much about the attack as he hadn't told anyone on campus other than his girlfriend about the attack. Your client, Brad flies off the hook and proceeds to tell Miller that if he even suggests he was somehow involved in the South Carolina attack he will contact his father and that Miller might not get off as easy as the first time they met. The conversation seemed to end when Brad there tells Miller to keep his mouth shut!"

Dolstrum smiled at Parks as he asked calmly, "And Miller told you about this conversation?"

"No, he did not," answered Vanderway. "At this time we have not spoken to Mr. Miller. He has not returned from Christmas break yet. The conversation between Brad and Miller was told to us by Kellem McCulhay who was present during the entire time Brad was at the farm."

Harmon was about to say something when Vanderway held up his hand as he was not finished speaking. "McCulhay states that Brad began to get back into the truck they had driven when he stopped and began a new topic. Brad addressed Miller, saying that he ran into someone he might know. The name of this person is Simon Baumer which strikes me as very strange because this Baumer is also a person of interest. Do you know this Simon Baumer?"

"Now hold on for a sec," said Dolstrum, "We have no idea who this Simon Buamer is." Looking at Harmon he asked, "Do you know this Simon character?"

Harmon shrugged, turned, and asked his son. "Do you know this man...this Simon Baumer?"

"No, not really. I only met him one time and that was for a few brief seconds. I didn't mention him to you or Mr. Dolstrum because it was just a chance meeting and besides that, my meeting this Baumer has nothing to do with some man's barn burning down."

"That may or may not be true," said Parks. "Why don't you tell us about your conversation with Baumer?"

Brad, realizing he should have said something to his father and his attorney about Baumer tried his best to explain. "I told Miller I met Simon Baumer at a restaurant in downtown Gettysburg. I told him Baumer was an odd sort of looking man dressed in all black. He happened to be with a young Mennonite woman who just happens to be Miller's girl. Trying to be social I go over to their table, and thinking Baumer was the girl's father based on their age difference I explained that during my freshman year, I roomed with another student who at the time was dating Elizabeth King. That's the girl who was with Baumer, and that as far as I knew they were still seeing one another. The man, at that point, said that was impossible. He had been courting Elizabeth over the entire summer and they planned on getting married. You can imagine how I felt.

"Before I could graciously walk away from their table, the man stood and guided me off to the side where he introduced himself. Looking back, he was a rather scary-looking individual. He told me that he was Simon Baumer and he wanted to know the name of the student who was seeing Elizabeth. At the time I didn't think I had a choice so I told him, Max Miller. He then went on and asked me where Miller could be contacted. I told him I wasn't sure exactly where he lived on campus but that he worked on a local farm for a man by the name of McCulhay. Baumer said he was going to visit this Miller and set things straight. He seemed quite pissed. I told Miller I couldn't imagine being on the opposite end of that conversation with this Baumer.

"So, I asked Miller if Baumer had dropped by to see him. Miller told me he had so I asked him how that worked out. It was then that this McCulhay got involved in the conversation that up until that point seemed civil. He answered the question stating Simon Baumer and his two brothers did drop by, started to throw their weight around, and were run off by him. A couple of other things were said and then he displayed this revolver he had tucked in his pants. He ordered us off the property which we quickly abided by seeing as how he had a gun. We left and I have never returned to his farm, therefore leaving it an impossibility that I burned down his damn barn!"

Parks withdrew some papers from his jacket pocket and unfolded them while stating, "That's very interesting but your story especially, the ending does not jive with what McCulhay told us. It seems as if you have left out some very interesting parts of what was said and done that led to him displaying his revolver."

"Like what, Detective," asked Dolstrum. "Brad's story matches up with everything he told me and his father."

Laying the sheets of paper flat on the table, Parks flipped to a third page where he pointed about halfway down Kellem's statement. "McCulhay states here that after he explained that he ran off Baumer and his brothers Brad stepped forward toward McCulhay and said he found it hard to believe an old fart like Kellem could run off Baumer and his brothers. It was then that McCulhay explained that he ran the Baumer's off with his twelve gauge shotgun. Then, Brad here says he is not the least bit intimidated and steps even closer to McCulhay at which point Kellem displays a revolver tucked in his pants. There were some other things mentioned about how Brad was going to contact his father and then McCulhay said you were nothing but a stupid rich kid who didn't know your ass from a hole in the ground. Shortly after that, he ordered you to get off his farm and you responded by saying, 'Let's get off this pathetic farm!' Three days later the barn is burned to the ground."

"Listen," said Harmon, "this is all very enlightening but it doesn't add up to squat! Not one thing has been brought up this morning that indicates or proves my son took out this McCulhay's barn. If anything, my son is the victim here. First of all, he got punched in the face a year and a half ago by this Max Miller. Then, Miller all but accuses him of being involved in this attack that took place down in South Carolina, which is impossible as my son was with me in Canada. Then, while purchasing two Christmas trees he gets into somewhat of an argument with Miller and this McCulhay which results in my son being ordered to leave this farm under the threat of being shot. You, gentlemen, have produced not one shred of evidence that my son is responsible for this barn burning!"

Vanderway produced an envelope from his suitcoat pocket and stated firmly, "We have one more piece to this potential puzzle and when you snap it in place it seems to form a pattern." Holding up the envelope for all to see Vanderway went on, "If you will notice the front of the envelope has a typewritten name on it, namely Miller!"

Opening the envelope he continued, "Inside we have an eight by eleven standard piece of typing paper. Centered on the page in bold typewritten letters is a message that reads: THIS IS FAR FROM OVER! This strange note was discovered beneath Max Miller's dorm room door shortly after his confrontation with your son, Brad, at the Burger Palace last year. If this message was generated by your son and if it means what I think it does, it indicates your son may be out for revenge towards Miller."

Placing the typewritten sheet back inside the envelope Vanderway slid it down the table in Dolstrum's direction. "There you go. Look it over. The message is rather simple and to the point." Extracting another envelope from his jacket he slid it down the table. "We also brought along a photo-copy of the envelope and the contents for your records."

Dolstrum opened the original envelope and unfolded the note. Examining the message he tossed it on the table as if were nothing followed by a snide comment. "This proves nothing! It could have been typed by any number of people, including Miller himself. Does this Miller own a type-writer?"

Vanderway answered sarcastically, "I have no idea. Does Brad Sykes own a typewriter?"

Dolstrum laughed sarcastically and then spoke, "We can banter back and forth all day but it remains that you have nothing solid linking Brad to the barn fire."

"And another thing," chimed in Harmon, "If this note was discovered as you say shortly after the Burger Palace incident then why did Miller's attorney not bring it up at the meeting when we were considering suing Miller? If it was that important why did they not bring it up?"

Parks jumped in, "We asked Miller's attorney the same question. He states that Max had the note with him during the lawsuit meeting and at that time had kept it to himself. According to Miller's attorney, who made this note available to us, Max had every intention of bringing up the note but when Mr. Sykes surprisingly dropped the suit Max thought, '*Why rock the boat.*' The note at that time was not needed."

Harmon sat up straight in his chair and asked both detectives, "If the note was not considered important then why is it now important?"

"Because," said Parks, "back then it was simply a typewritten threat and not backed up with any action or retaliation toward Miller. But now, a year later Max is mysteriously attacked and the man he worked for has his barn burned to the ground. I see what could be a pattern of retaliation here."

"Pardon me, Detectives, but from where I'm sitting that seems pretty thin."

Dolstrum spoke up, "I agree with Mr. Sykes. Nothing you have said or presented us with this morning holds much water if any at all. That being said if there are no other questions then I say we wrap this up and go our separate ways."

"I do have one other question," said Vanderway. "Where were you Brad on December 18?"

Looking hopelessly at his father and then at Dolstrum, Brad raised his hands in frustration and then replied, "You have got to be kidding me! That was nearly two weeks ago. You can't expect me to be that detailed about what I did or exactly where I was fourteen days in the past."

"So, you're saying you cannot give us an answer to the question?"

"Sure I can answer that. I was probably on campus, maybe at football practice, and then I had classes every day. I probably had breakfast, lunch, and dinner that day also. I probably even took a dump at some point. How much detail do you require?"

Harmon held up his hand for his son to stop talking. "I think that's enough, Brad. I think our detective friends here get the picture. If there is nothing else then can we assume the meeting is concluded?"

Looking at Parks, Vanderway acknowledged, "I don't think we have any other questions at this time. This meeting may be over but our investigation will continue. We may want to question your son again."

Dolstrum turned off the recorder and placed his pad in his briefcase. "Just be careful about what you say. This is a small community and if the word leaks out that my client is in any way mentioned as a suspect, we will bring lawsuits against the city, this McCulhay, and maybe even Max Miller." Turning to Sam Phillips, he went on, "Sam, you and I have been friends for nearly twenty-five years but if I hear of anything negative coming from this office regarding Brad Sykes I will not hesitate to sue the college... just saying. Friends are one thing, but business is business."

Sam shot Brad's father a look of concern that Harmon gently shook off as not necessary. Vanderway stood and gestured to his partner, "I think we'll just take leave then. In the next couple of days, we intend to contact Max Miller and ask him some questions about what went on at the farm."

Sarcastically Brad asked, "Will Miller be required to be questioned here at the Dean's office as I was?"

"Probably not," said Parks, "Miller is not a person of interest as far as the fire goes."

Vanderway started for the door as he addressed the group, "Gentlemen, I hope no further questioning will be necessary but if we do have any other questions we'll be in touch. Good day!"

Parks followed Vanderway out the door and stared at Brad but remained silent.

Dolstrum stood as he picked up his briefcase. "I guess then we'll be on our way as well."

Sam also stood and held his right hand out to Harmon. "If we could just step into my office for a few moments there is something I'd like to say."

Brad gave the Dean a stern look and asked, "Does that mean me as well?"

"Yes Brad, it does because what I have to say involves you." Starting for the door Sam gestured, "Gentlemen...if you will."

Not even two minutes passed when Sam seated behind his office desk, finished his cup of coffee setting the empty mug on a nearby credenza. Brad, seated in a chair by the window was not all that comfortable being in the Dean's office. Harmon and Dolstrum were seated next to one another across from the desk. There was a moment of awkward silence in the room that Dolstrum broke as he asked the Dean, "So, Sam, as an impartial observer what did you make of our little meeting with the police?"

"You must be reading my mind, Michael, because that is exactly what I wanted to speak to you about. During the meeting, I was an impartial observer as you state, and despite the fact no proof surfaced that indicates Brad was involved in the barn fire the police brought up some very interesting points. My impartially in this matter changed toward the end of the meeting. Michael, you mentioned the college may be sued depending on how we handle this situation. It was disturbing to me when you said, 'Friends are one thing, but business is business!'

"This potential situation with Brad will be handled by this office and the school as any other student-related incident would be handled. I, in no way, will suppress actions that the school is obligated to take just because of who Brad is; namely your son Harmon. I cannot and will not allow the integrity of this institution to be altered in any way because you have supported the college financially. I also cannot allow the fact that the three of us have been friends for twenty-five years to influence what I think must be done."

Harmon spoke up as if he had been scolded. "Sam, as Brad's father it is my duty to protect him and make sure his rights are not tampered with and as far as Michael here is concerned, as an attorney at law he is obligated to do what is right for his client, Brad."

Sam, seeing that Harmon was getting upset, folded his hands on top of his desk and went on to explain, "These things you bring up are true and both of you must understand that as Dean of this college, I must look out for its best interest. When I consider the long-standing friendship the three of us have shared this situation with Brad saddens me. Twenty-five years ago both of you were freshmen here at Gettysburg, I was in my third year as a professor. You both sat in my business administration class for four years. Not even a few months after having you both in my class I realized the two of you were headed for bright futures. We have, all three of us come a long way since those days.

"Harmon, here, without a doubt probably the wealthiest and most successful student to ever graduate from this institution, and you Michael; a better attorney one would be hard to find. Back then, who would have thought I would rise to the position of Dean of this college? Those facts are the positive parts of what I want to say. The negative point I want to bring up, Harmon, is your son. When you attended school here you were the model student; and quarterback of our football team, leading us to four consecutive championship seasons, a feat that has never and probably never will be duplicated on our gridiron. You were president of the student council and held other prestigious positions here at school. A more popular student I don't think we have ever had here. And you, Michael. Such brilliance I have never seen before in a young man."

Michael interrupted Sam's long dissertation. "Sam…get to the point. I don't see where anything that has to do with our past or current friendship has to do with Harmon's son, Brad?"

"Then let me get right to the point," said Sam. "This college was here a long time before the three of us attended and it will be here long after we are all dead and buried in the ground. This town, Gettysburg, has always been supportive of this school and I as Dean am obligated along with the president of this college to uphold a certain and very distinct level of integrity that the town itself expects. Brad here, it would seem has a habit of surrounding himself with a laundry list of behavior that is not consistent with what we expect from our students. Last year, he and three other football players were arrested for public intoxication, destroying property, and disorderly conduct. Brad spent the night in our local jail. We have three different complaints about his behavior at college functions, namely parties where Brad inappropriately touched female students. Earlier this year Brad and some of his frat buddies were reported as throwing eggs and tomatoes at statues over at the battlefield. Now, there is this possibility that he somehow was responsible for attacking another student down in South Carolina and we now have this barn fire controversy he seems to be right in the middle of. I think the most disturbing thing brought up at our meeting this morning was the threatening note found in Miller's room. In short, Harmon, your son does not measure up to the adage about the proverbial apple not falling far from the tree. Your son, it would appear is nothing like you, Harmon. For this reason, I feel it would be in the best interest of the school, your son, and yourself if he transferred to another institution of learning."

Brad sat up in his chair and spoke to his father, "What is he trying to say? Am I being kicked out of this school…am I being expelled from Gettysburg?"

Sam, rather than Harmon answered the question, "No, we are not kicking you out or expelling you Brad. We, the school, are strongly suggesting you transfer to another school."

"But why?" objected Brad. "I have done nothing wrong, at least that deserves being expunged from this college. I don't understand." Looking at his father and then at Dolstrum, he waited for an answer.

Michael spoke up in Brad's defense, "I have to agree with Brad on this. He can't be expected to leave school because of the Burger Palace incident. He never raised a hand to Miller but yet he was punched in the face and prevented from playing football for the remainder of the year. He was practically accused by Miller of attacking him down in South Carolina which is impossible as Brad was out of the country at the time with his father. So far, the police have not come out and stated that they feel Brad set the barn fire, but that they may want to question him again. This mysterious threatening note doesn't prove a thing. There is no proof Brad typed that message. I'm sorry Sam, but I think what you are suggesting is over the top and very unfair."

"My office is not a courtroom Michael so don't think you can sway me with some bullshit reverse phycology. As far as Brad is concerned you have conveniently left out very important parts of this entire situation. For instance, you forget to mention, Brad that night at the Burger Palace had too much to drink and even though he never raised a hand toward Miller he threw food at him, and then Miller was tossed through a plate glass window and wound up losing his job there. Miller went to the hospital and Brad here spent the night in jail.

"I can't speak that much about this South Carolina business or even about the recent fire at the McCulhay farm, but there is one thing I am sure of; Brad and three of his frat buddies were caught over at the battlefield throwing tomatoes and eggs at statues. They were reported, picked up by the police, and taken downtown. They were only held for about an hour when they were released and told they would be contacted at a later date. Turns out that the Gettysburg Battlefield, being a national park is on Federal land, and the statues that they bombed happen to be government property. Once the police figured out that Brad and his friends had committed a federal crime by defacing property on federal land our local police decided to call the Feds and let them handle the situation. Sure enough, two weeks later the president of the college got a surprise visit from two Federal agents here at the president's office. Since the crime at hand involved students from this college they came to us first before contacting the students involved so that we would be in the loop. They explained to us that defacing property on federal land results in a ninety-day prison sentence and a minimum fine of five hundred dollars. We asked the agents if we as a college could keep this in-house and handle the problem ourselves and avoid any negative publicity. They agreed if the college paid the fine and whatever the cost was of cleaning up the statues they would walk away from any further investigations regarding the students.

"Brad and the other fraternity brothers who were involved were called to my office and were told about the deal we had worked with the Feds. We also told them that it was only because of the generosity of Brad's father in the past with his financial support of the school that we were letting them off. We also told them if they got into any further trouble here at the school or in or around the community that they would all be thrown out of this institution. They agreed and went on their way."

Visually upset, Harmon asked, "Why was I not contacted about this federal business."

"Like I said. We decided to handle this in-house. As long as the boys agreed to behave themselves we decided to move on and not involve any of the parents. After all, these boys were all of age and capable of making important decisions about their futures."

Harmon shook his head and gave Michael a glance asking, "Michael, I value your opinion. What do you think about this?"

"Well, I was just sitting here thinking about a particular class Sam taught us in his classroom when we were seniors. The class was all about knowing when to cut your losses when in business. When to take a step back so that you could later once again move forward and in the long run be better off. Harmon, this may be one of those situations. Thanks to Sam your son and the boys got off easy. What I'm saying is that they dodged the bullet. The Feds are not people you want to mess with. If you want my opinion…here it is. It's your decision but if I were you I'd transfer Brad to another school and move on. I think it would be best not only for the school and yourself Harmon but Brad as well. Let him get a fresh start somewhere else. You asked me and that's my answer."

Harmon stared at Michael for a second, then at his son, and finally at Sam before speaking. "Sam, I think Michael here is correct. I thought that it would be great for my son to attend the college where I received my degree. But so far that has not panned out. It's time for me to cut my losses and move on. Brad will transfer to another school."

Brad, in a rage, stood and clenched his fists, his face red as a beet. "Father, you cannot be serious. You cannot allow these men to kick me out of this school! I won't have it..I just won't do it!"

Sam reiterated, "Brad, you're not being kicked out, you're just transferring to another college."

"That's bullshit and you and everyone else in the room know it!" Pointing at his father Brad continued in a loud voice, "I am no longer your little boy, Father. In case you have not noticed I am almost twenty-one years of age and can make any decision I want and there is nothing you can do about that!"

Harmon gave his son an odd smile. "Listen to yourself, Son. How long do you think you'd survive here in college without the support of myself and your mother? Without us to support you, why you wouldn't make it one semester? You have no job and the only money you do have comes from my pockets. You don't even own that Corvette you drive around in. The car is in my name and I make all the payments. Now, why don't you use your head and sit down and listen? You have a decision to make. You can go with my plan of transferring to another school where you can finish your education and still come out as a success down the road or you can go off on your own and be a failure. Here's your choice. I'm going to be parked in front of your frat house an hour from now. You can go back to your room pack your belongings and meet me there. We'll drive to Harrisburg, fly back home on the family jet, and next week we'll come up with a new plan for your future. If when I arrive in front of the frat house you are not there ready to go…well then; you're on your own. It's your decision."

Brad stood, gave Sam the finger, and stormed out of the office.

Lowering his head in shame, Harmon apologized. "I'm sorry, Sam. I did not raise my son that way." Shaking his head in disgust he went on, "Every man who has the privilege of having a son always desires that his son turn out better than himself. It appears that Brad, my son, is not better. I'm so sorry."

Michael spoke up. "Harmon, do you think Brad will go back to Ithaca with you?"

"I think he will. He knows where his bread is buttered. If he is as smart as I think he is, then an hour from now he'll be standing in front of his frat house ready to go back to Ithaca."

Harmon stood as he addressed Michael. "Well, I guess I best get you back to your office." Turning back to Sam, he reached for the Dean's hand. "Despite all of this I hope we can remain friends."

Shaking Harmon's hand, Sam acknowledged, "We'll always be friends, Harmon, regardless of what happens."

Harmon turned to leave, hesitated, and then spoke, "One last thing, Sam. I'm sure there will be some paperwork that has to be completed as far as my son's transfer is concerned. I would ask that the paperwork simply state he has decided to transfer to another school. That there will be no mention of anything he has done or has thought to have done."

Sam smiled, "Consider it done Harmon."

CHAPTER TWENTY-NINE

Max made a left onto the lane leading to Kellem's Farm and instantly recognized that the familiar barn across the road from the old farmhouse was gone. As he drove closer to the house the absence of the barn brought a sense of sadness to his thought process. Parking his Jeep at the side of the house, he got out and slipped on a pair of heavy-duty work gloves. Crossing the dirt road, the odor of burned wood and metal hung in the air. Kellem, who was pushing a wheelbarrow of assorted scorched metal objects, stopped when he saw Max. Wiping his brow with a rag he waved.

Max stopped short of the grass that bordered the road, reached out, and shook Kellem's gloved hand. Looking at the charred remains of the barn, he commented, "It's hard to believe your barn is gone."

Kellem sat on a nearby tree stump, opened a cooler, and removed two cold bottles of water, offering one to Max. "It's a total loss." Pointing at some burnt metal frames that looked like charred skeletons he explained, "That's what's left of my car, two tractors, and my riding mover. Thank God, I've got good insurance. The problem is, they won't make good on my claim until the investigation is closed."

Max took a swig of water and asked, "Are you going to put up a new barn?"

"Sure am, but I think I'm going to go with one of those new metal jobs I've seen advertised on television." Looking Max over from head to toe, Kellem smiled, "I see you came prepared to get dirty."

"Wouldn't have it any other way," said Max. "Last night after I got in and phoned you, you said you could use some help. My classes don't start until tomorrow afternoon so here I am. Elizabeth wanted to come along today but she has three classes. She did tell me to let you know she is coming over later this evening and plans on making us dinner."

Kellem removed his gloves and looked up at the dreary sky. "Looking forward to that. I imagine by this evening we'll be plain tuckered out and ready for a good meal. You sure got a good one there in Elizabeth. You should consider yourself one lucky man. Let's see, by the time you graduate in what, two years you'll be twenty-two years old. I can't imagine you putting off marrying her too long after that. If I'd met someone like Elizabeth when I was a young wiper snapper I would have married up and by now I'd probably have a passel of grandchildren. But, I guess that was never in the cards for me, or my two brothers." Talking another gulp of water, Kellem grinned, "And here I sit...an eighty-year-old bachelor."

Looking at the destroyed remains of the barn, Max inquired, "Do you have anyone else coming by to give us a hand today?"

"Yes, as a matter of fact, my regular crew which amounts to six men is scheduled to report for work at nine o'clock. Even if the barn had not burned they would still be here on the farm working. I usually keep the boys around until after the New Year and then I lay them off until March when I call them back for spring planting."

"Listen, I hope you don't mind," said Max, "but I got a call yesterday from the Gettysburg Police. They said they'd like to ask me some questions about what went on at the farm days before the fire regarding both Simon Baumer and Brad Sykes. I told them I was coming over here to give you a hand with the cleanup and they asked me if it would be all right if they talked with me here. I agreed. I hope that's okay?"

"Sure, why not! What better place to interview you than the scene of the crime? What time did they say they'd be by?"

"A Detective Vanderway said he and another detective would be here about ten. He said they'd be here for maybe an hour. Said they just have a few questions."

Kellem looked at his watch. "Well then, that gives us two good hours before the law shows up. Let me just dump this load over there by the house and then I'll show you what needs to be done."

Max was pitching some charred barn siding in the back of a pickup truck when he noticed a late model, dark-colored sedan pulling up next to the house. Thumping Kellem on his shoulder he remarked while pointing, "Bet that's the detectives."

"It is," said Kellem. "That's the same car they drove over here right after the fire. Com'n, let's go on up to the house. They can ask their questions out on the screened-in porch. I'll put a pot of coffee on."

Kellem approached the car as he reached out to shake Vanderway's hand. "Detectives Vanderway and Parks… I'd like you to meet Max Miller."

Max, wiping his hands on his jeans nodded, shook both men's extended hands, and started for the house. "I think I'll wash up a bit before we get started."

Kellem gestured toward the porch and suggested, "I thought we could just sit out here." Opening the screen door he addressed both men, "If you'll have a seat I'm going to make some coffee."

"Please, don't go to any trouble on our account," said Parks. "We've already had breakfast which included an entire pot of coffee. If I drink another cup, I'll float away."

Vanderway slapped his partner on his back as he nodded in agreement.

Both men seated themselves at the picnic table while Kellem announced, "I'm still going to make that coffee. I could use a cup."

Max dried his hands with a paper towel, exited the downstairs bath, and entered the country kitchen where he found Kellem busy at the counter. Pouring water into the coffeemaker Kellem nodded toward the porch, "Why don't you go on out and get started with the detectives? I'll be out with the coffee in a few minutes."

"You don't want me to wait for you?"

"No, you go ahead. They already questioned me right after the fire. They came here today to ask you questions…not me."

Realizing Kellem was correct, Max walked out onto the porch and took a seat in a plastic chair near the screen door. Crossing his left leg over his right knee he held out his hands, "Ready when you are gentlemen!"

Parks removed an envelope from his suitcoat pocket and then extracted three sheets of paper which he placed on the table. "This is the statement we took from Mr. McCulhay shortly after the fire. We wanted to drop by and spend some time with you, not so much to ask you questions but to verify what Kellem passed on to us. We know you were present when both Simon

Baumer and Brad Sykes were here at the farm. We don't doubt anything Mr. McCulhay told us, but we wanted to get your first-hand version and see if we can learn anything new that may assist us in this case."

"Very well," said Max. "How do you want to proceed?"

"Let's do this," said Vanderway. "Rather than read to you what Kellem told us why don't you start by telling us about the farm visits of both Baumer and Sykes."

Max rubbed his hands together and started, "I can't remember the date when Baumer and his two brothers showed up here, but I can tell you it was around the end of October, about a month or so before Brad dropped by. I was just coming out of a tool shed up by the main road when I was approached by Baumer and his brothers…"

For the next half hour Max explained everything in detail that happened during Simon and Brad's visits to the farm to the best of his memory, finally finishing up, "The last thing Brad said was, 'Let's get off this pathetic farm,' and then he and his friend drove off." Reclining in his chair, Max shrugged, "And that's everything in a nutshell."

Parks folded the three sheets of paper containing Kellem's statement as he remarked, "Your version of what happened pretty much aligns with what Mr. McCulhay here told us. The one thing I feel we did learn today that we were rather vague on was the relationship you and this Elizabeth had, and I guess still have, and how it caused Simon Baumer to fly off the handle."

Vanderway jumped in on the conversation. "Not to defend this Baumer character, but it's very easy to see why he felt or feels the way he does about your relationship with a girl that he was courting and planning or marrying. According to you, he attacked you twice, once at the King farm and then right here out by the main road. Combine that with the fact that Kellem here fired a shotgun, not at Baumer and his brothers but near them and then displayed his handgun and ordered them off the property didn't sit well with Simon Baumer. When I went over to Lancaster County to talk with him I contacted the Manheim Township Police first and the sheriff went with me to Baumer's farm. Before we even arrived at the farm this sheriff told me Simon Baumer is the wealthiest Mennonite farmer in the state and is used to getting things his way. We, at this point, have no proof Baumer set the fire, but we have not eliminated him as a suspect. I talked with the Manhiem Sheriff before I left Lancaster County and he said he'd keep his ear to the ground and if hears anything suspicious he'd give me a call."

"So," said Max, "for now I guess that leaves the spotlight of suspicion on Brad Sykes."

Parks chimed in, "You would think so, but after we questioned Brad in the presence of his father and their attorney, just like in Baumer's case we have no real proof Brad set the fire either. During the questioning, Brad was very rude and quite frankly bored with the fact he had to even be there at the Dean's office answering our questions."

Vanderway added, "Myself, well I think Sykes appeared to be more nervous than Baumer when questioned. They both have the motive to set the fire, but it seems to me Baumer is too smart to go down that road. Brad Sykes doesn't strike me as all that intelligent. I think he is riding on the coattails of his father and I say this because of a call I received from Dean Phillips a couple of hours after we questioned Sykes. It's kind of a good news-bad news scenario. Good news for you Max and bad news for us as the police."

"I'm afraid I don't know what you mean?" said Max. "How is a call to you, the police good news for me?"

"It's good news for you because you no longer have to be leery of any retaliation from Brad Sykes. Believe it or not, he has decided to transfer out of Gettysburg College and go back with his father to Ithaca, New York to another school somewhere else."

Max, in confusion, stated, "I can't believe he would just up and leave school, especially the school where his father attended."

"Dean Phillips told us Brad's father didn't give his son much of a choice. The college, at the request of the Dean, suggested strongly that Brad consider transferring out. Initially, Brad objected and stormed out of the Dean's office. But, in the end, it didn't make any difference. Brad Sykes, at least at this point in his life could not survive without his father's support. So, the good news is that with Sykes being back up in New York State any threat he previously represented has all but been eliminated from your life. The bad news is that now with Brad not being here in this area it makes it more difficult to ask him any further questions or even keep an eye on him. We have contacted the Police Department up in Ithaca and have made them aware of the situation regarding the barn fire. They said they'd keep an eye out and notify us if they hear of anything that might point to Sykes as the culprit. In the meantime, I'm afraid that's all we can do for now."

"Let me get this straight," said Kellem. "Unless the Sheriff over in Lancaster County or the police up in this Ithaca, New York come up with something, this case is all but over."

"Looks that way," said Parks. "We've pretty must exhausted every option we have on our end."

Snapping his fingers, Max suggested, "What about this friend of Brad's, this Howard Fields who accompanied him here to the farm? Maybe he knows something?"

Parks placed the envelope back inside his jacket pocket. "We did talk with Fields, later on in the day after we questioned Brad. In short, Fields said he didn't care that much for Sykes. He only came to the farm with Brad because he was told to do so by some senior members of the frat house. Fields told us that after they left the farm Brad was cursing up a storm but other than that never indicated he had intentions of getting any revenge. Fields did go on to say Sykes was not very popular with most of the students in the fraternity. Aside from that, talking with Fields turned out to be another dead end."

Max stood and stretched, "Well, I guess that's it then for your questions today?"

Vanderway stood. "It is..it is indeed." Turning to Kellem he apologized, "I'm sorry about the loss of your barn. If we have any additional questions or if we hear anything you'll be the first to know."

Kellem and Max watched as the two detectives walked out of the porch, climbed in their car, and drove off. Kellem clapped his hands once and gestured toward the woods beyond the fence that bordered his property. "I've got an idea. I think the boys have a pretty good handle on the cleanup. Let's say we go for a hike out on the battlefield. I haven't been on a hike for the last two weeks. I miss my walks. What do you say?"

"That sounds like a great idea. I haven't been to the battlefield since before Thanksgiving. Just let me freshen up a bit more and then we can leave."

Enthused, Kellem started for the kitchen. "I'll get my knapsack. I'm going to whip us up a couple of sandwiches, grab two bananas and some water and we'll be on our way."

"While you're getting our lunch together, I'm going to go out to my Jeep and get a pair of walking shoes I have. I can't walk around the battlefield in these work boots. I'm also going to give Elizabeth a call."

Minutes later, Max was lacing up his shoes when Kellem entered the porch. Slinging his knapsack over his shoulder, he suggested, "Let's head out to the fence and then we can decide our destination for the afternoon."

While crossing the yard Max pointed at the grassy slope on the battlefield side of the old fence. "I've got a great destination in mind. How about General Lee's Headquarters?"

"Sounds good," said Kellem. "That's about two and a half miles from here. There and back will be five miles. That's a pretty good jaunt." Climbing over the fence Kellem pointed to the west. "General Lee…here we come!"

Max climbed over the fence and inquired. "Isn't this fence section right here where that Confederate ghost appeared?"

Kellem tapped the marred top rail with his right hand as he replied, "Yep, it was right here. This is the rail he was leaning on. Stood right about where you are."

Max looked off into the nearby woods at the top of the slope and took two steps away from the fence. "Didn't you tell me when you started to approach this soldier that he limped off into the woods and when you hopped over the fence to follow him you felt strange?"

"Yes, it was very strange. I really can't explain the way I felt but that feeling caused me to jump back over the fence into the backyard where, by the way, I no longer felt the strange sensation."

Scratching his head, Max asked, "And how do you feel now? Do you feel strange?"

"No, I feel perfectly normal."

"Why do you think that is?"

"The difference in the way I felt then and the way I feel now may have something to do with the fact that the ghost soldier is not here at the moment."

"This is all very strange," said Max. "Where do you think the soldier went after he walked into the woods?"

"Who knows where a ghost goes," said Kellem, "but if I had to guess I'd say he would head over to the area where Lee had his headquarters as that was where the bulk of the Confederate Army was camped. Since we are headed in that direction why we might be taking the same or similar route the ghost took."

Max stopped at the edge of the woods and looked back down at Kellem's farm. "I can't believe we're having this conversation."

"I can understand that. You didn't see this ghost soldier…I did!" Stepping into the tree line Kellem supported himself with the help of a large elm. "About fifty yards we'll be out of these trees where we'll come to a large field. My great-grandfather at one time had tobacco planted there. Now, it's part of the battlefield and surprisingly an area of the national park where a lot of tourists don't visit. The reason being that this surrounding area didn't see much fighting, at least that we know of."

Following Kellem through the dense trees Max inquired, "Do you think all these trees were here back in 1863?"

Kellem stopped next to a massive oak and touched the side of the thick trunk. "Probably not. Remember that was over a hundred and fifty years ago. Large trees, like this oak were probably here, but many of these trees were not. It's strange how nature works. The ground, meaning hills, mountains, and even the slope we just climbed remains the same no matter how much time passes, but the vegetation eventually dies off and is replaced with new growth. What I'm saying is these woods were here back then but probably looked different than they appear today."

Five minutes later they emerged from the trees and there before them was a vast weed-covered field. Resting his right foot on a small boulder at the edge of the trees Max looked across the expanse to yet another line of trees a football field's length in the distance. "My father and I over the years have walked every inch of the surrounding battlefield sites and yet, I can't seem to remember ever being here."

Starting across the field, Kellem spread his hands out at arms' length, displaying the wide field. "I have, as well been to every nook, corner, and cranny of the battlefield which encompasses 9.3 square miles equaling over 5900 acres. I can tell you every square foot of ground the battlefield covers is considered hallowed ground, but not every section of it is considered worthy of visiting. Like this field, there are no markers or statues…why? Because, during the three days of battle no major confrontations took place right here. This is not Culp's Hill or Little Round Top or any number of other known documented conflicts between the two armies back in July of 1863, so, therefore, this field and the surrounding acreage does not represent much interest to battlefield visitors."

Kellem kicked his way through knee-high weeds and continued, "There could have been fighting here in this unknown area but on a much smaller scale. For instance, let's just say a handful of Confederates got separated from their regiment and were trying to find their way back to the main camp. They could have run into a small group of Union soldiers who may have been lost as well. Remember this was foreign ground to both armies. Both of these groups could have been wandering around and wound up in each other's faces. Hence a small skirmish erupted, men may have been killed right here in this field and yet, that particular fighting moment was never documented. I have no doubt there were several small fights between a few soldiers here and there. This is probably one of those areas, a section of the battlefield where we don't know what happened. Who knows, maybe deserters on both sides escaped the battle as they fled across this field off into the Pennsylvania wilderness."

Max bent down, pulled a long weed from the ground, and stuck it in the side of his mouth as he spoke. "I imagine that even today there are countless descendants of those who fought here on both sides who can say that one of their past relatives fought and died in the Civil War at Gettysburg."

Kellem turned around and started to walk backward, facing Max. "That's exactly my point. There are a lot of folks around in this country who can say one of their ancestors died right here at Gettysburg, maybe at the battle of the Peach Orchard or the Wheatfield which is more specific than just saying they died here. Many a man no doubt died in fields just like this one or in these trees up ahead and their descendants will never know. All they know is that 'ol Joe or Pappy Jake died at Gettysburg. That's sad."

They walked in silence for the next twenty yards when they entered the second tree line, Max kicking at the fallen leaves that covered the forest floor. Looking up at the towering trees he smiled. "Most of the leaves for this year have fallen."

At his side, Kellem agreed, "Yep, fall is my favorite time of the year, but now wintertime is upon us. With all the rain we had this past year the fall colors of the leaves were outstanding."

Max, continuing through the trees added, "For late December the temperature is warmer than usual."

Kellem agreed, "It's been an easy winter so far. They say we're not going to get much snow until late January."

"Speaking of January," said Max, "in two days it'll be January and the new year will be here. Where does the time go?"

"That shouldn't be something a fella your age should ask. You've got your whole life ahead of ya. Now, a man who has been around for eight decades can easily ask that question. I'm still in pretty good health but in the next few years my exit on the highway of life will no doubt be coming up."

Max laughed, "You're too ornery to die ya ol' coot! I bet you'll be out here walking around these fields when you're in your nineties."

A deer scampered out from behind a stand of tall bushes, stopped, stared at Max and Kellem then bolted off into the woods to their left. "This is one of the few areas of the battlefield where one can see any deer," said Kellem. "I suppose that's because very few tourists come to this area. For generations my past family hunted in these surrounding fields and woods, well, up until we sold most of the acreage, we owned to the National Park Service.

"After this land was under their jurisdiction hunting was not allowed. Just on the other side of these woods, there is an old deer path that has been there for decades. It's more than a path. These days it's a dirt service road utilized by the park service. I've seen them out here on their ATVs. I talked with two park workers one time when I was out here walking. Their mission that day was to cut up a downed tree and clean up the remains of a deer that had died. Then, of course, there is maintenance to the surrounding fields. They have to be mowed every other month to keep the vegetation from taking over the area."

Max picked up a small section of bark that had fallen from a tree, examined it, and then threw it to the side as he changed the subject. "Sounds to me like the case of your barn burning is rapidly coming to a close."

"I think you're right in what you say," said Kellem. "I also think we have seen the last of Baumer and Sykes. I can move on without any fear of further retaliation from Simon Baumer and you and Elizabeth can concentrate on your schooling. What do you think will happen to those two idiots?"

"Baumer has more than enough money to erase the pain of being rejected by Elizabeth. He'll move on with his life, and probably find another lady to marry. Like you said, we'll probably never see him again. Now Brad is a different animal. His father will no doubt see to it he is enrolled in another college somewhere. Maybe even closer to home where he can keep a close eye on his son. Brad, unfortunately, unless he receives some sort of magical wakeup call, will continue to be a wise ass. I think, in the long run, he'll still wind up being a success. His father does not seem like the kind of man who would sit by and allow his son to fail. But fail or succeed, like Baumer, we'll probably never cross paths with him again in our lifetime."

Kellem stepped out of the trees and acknowledged, "Thank God for that!"

A few feet out into the next field, just like Kellem had stated, there was a service road, which was little more than two adjacent tire tracks with grass growing in the small median. Stepping onto the makeshift road, Max grinned. "Just like you said, here's the old deer path." Looking to the west the rough road went up a slight rise and then disappeared into some trees. "I assume we're heading west to get to Lee's Headquarters…correct?"

"That would be correct," said Kellem.

Max looked to the east and inquired with interest, "How far does the road go in that direction?"

"There's a farm owned by one of my neighbors, Sam Bledsoe, about a mile down the road. The National Park Battlefield ends about a half mile or so down that way; then you're on Bledsoe's land. He has a stream-fed lake there the deer like to frequent. Bledsoe puts out salt licks and keeps the lake clean as a whistle. He won't allow any hunting on his property, so the deer know instinctively they are safe at the lake." Removing one of the waters from his knapsack, Kellem took a swig and offered, "Care for a water?"

Max waved off the offer, "No…not thirsty."

Kellem pointed the bottle of water west and stated, "Let's get moving then. It's another mile and a half down the road to our destination. We'll be there before you know it. But before we get there there's something really interesting, I'd like to show you. It's about a half mile down the road."

They stopped at the top of a hill and Kellem pointed at a large elm tree and exclaimed. "There it be!"

Max, duplicating Kellem's choice of slang asked, "There what be?"

Walking to the tree that sat off the road five yards Kellem reached out and touched the base and then pointed about halfway up into the bare branches. "If you look up there real closely you can see where a branch was sawed off and then they put tar over the exposed cut to keep the tree from getting diseased. This is kind of a famous tree out here on the battlefield."

"And what makes this particular tree so famous?"

"I guess it was back about three years ago, a year before you started school here in town, there was a small group of bird watchers right here in this area. One of their group happened to be looking at this tree with a set of binoculars when they spotted something unusual. They all walk over to the tree and sure enough there encased in one of the branches is a rifle. One of them climbed up there and tried to detach the gun from the branch but the rifle itself had become part of the tree. They reported it to the park service who came out here with a Civil War artifact expert and sure enough, the rifle was an authentic Civil War musket. After much deliberation, they decided that the gun could not be separated from the branch without damaging the rifle, so they cut the branch down with the rifle intact."

Interested, Max asked, "And what did they do with this combination branch and rifle?"

"They have it on display down at the main museum in town. The reason for the musket being found in the tree is a mystery but experts figure it probably belonged to a sniper, Confederate or Union, they could not determine. They figured that when you consider the tree was at the top of this hill it was probably a sniper's nest. The sniper got shot, fell out of the tree and his musket got caught on a branch over the last one hundred and fifty-some years and became part of the tree itself. Pretty amazing when you think about it."

"That is amazing," agreed Max, "and it fits right in with what you were saying about any number of small, what most people would consider insignificant, conflicts between the two armies. For instance, look at what might have happened here at the tree. A possible sniper gets shot out of the tree, falls to the ground dead, or is taken back to a field hospital where he may or may not have survived. His musket is left behind and remains in the tree for over one hundred and fifty years until it is discovered. That sniper was probably killed while in this tree and his descendants will never know how he died."

"And even if this sniper did get medical attention and survived," pointed out Kellem, "he no doubt had no opportunity to come back out here for his musket. He probably figured that when he fell, his gun fell as well. Anybody could have picked up a discarded musket at the side of the road, but we know that's not what happened. The musket remained in the tree all those years until it was recently discovered." Starting down the road Kellem looked up at the darkening sky. "We better get moving. Looks like it could rain later this afternoon. We might get wet."

Kellem stood at the top of a rise and pointed down below where there sat a small farmhouse fronted by a fenced-in yard. To the left across another small grassy area, there was a utility barn. Chambersburg Pike ran right next to the house and across the street there was a small, paved parking area. An American flag fluttered in the gentle breeze at the front of the two-story stone house. Max took in the view and commented, "Not one car in the parking lot."

"This is the off-season right now," said Kellem. "Things won't pick up on the battlefield sites until next spring. Let's go on down. There are some picnic tables next to the parking lot. We can sit there and enjoy our lunch in peace. The place looked pretty deserted."

Walking down the grassy slope and in front of the house Max asked, "Ever been inside?"

"In all the times I've been over here, I never have. How about you?"

"The house is only open for tours on special occasions. One year when my father was here for a reenactment he brought me along, I was only ten at the time, but I remember that he managed to arrange a tour for himself and a few other Civil War historians. Of course, I got to go along. The house itself sits on four acres and at the time of the battle was owned by Mary Thompson who was 60 years old. She remained in the house during the three-day battle. Lee chose her house as his headquarters because it was centrally located in the middle of his lines. It also provided him with an excellent view of the surrounding countryside as the house sits at the top of Seminary Ridge. While staying there Lee only utilized half of the downstairs spending the time he was in the house in the main living room and bedroom. It has been said he spent very little time inside the house. Supposedly, he took his meals there and of course, slept there. Most of his time was spent riding around the outskirts of the battlefield giving orders to his troops. The house is also the place where he berated General Jeb Stuart for not supplying him with the movements of the Union army."

On the other side of the Chambersburg Pike Kellem removed his knapsack and sat down at the first of four picnic tables. Max sat on the opposite side and noticed a utility ATV stop in front of the house. Two park service workers got out and started to remove some paint buckets from the rear of the all-terrain vehicle. Unwrapping a sandwich that Kellem shoved across the table, Max remarked, "Looks like the park service is doing a little touch-up at General Lee's Headquarters."

Kellem agreed, "There's a lot of work involved in taking care of nearly six thousand acres; structures, statues, markers, the roads, and then there's the thousands of trees. Let me ask you something?"

Max swallowed a bite of ham, cheese, and rye bread and then answered, "Go right ahead."

"You've told me several times that you are a mathematics major, that numbers are a big part of your life. When we first met up on Little Round Top you explained the entire battle as related to numbers. When you think of numbers in a major battle in a war normally one would think of hundreds, thousands, or even hundreds of thousands, but I want to ask you about a single person who represents just one soldier. The soldier I speak of is General Stonewall Jackson. Do you think if he had been here at Gettysburg the outcome of the three days would have been different?"

Max laid down the sandwich and answered the question with great conviction. "That is something we'll never know as Jackson was killed on May 10th, 1863, just two months short of the battle here at Gettysburg. If he would not have been killed, he would have been here with Lee and the Confederate army. Stonewall Jackson was Lee's right-hand man while General James Longstreet was Lee's left. Lee had many an outstanding general in his army, but Jackson and Longstreet were the two men he always confided in. Jackson and Longstreet had two very different ways of leading their troops. Jackson, who was quite religious, was brutal on the battlefield. It was not enough for him to defeat the enemy in battle, but to kill every last Union soldier there was. Like the first battle of Manassas, Jackson not only defeated the Federal troops but chased them halfway back to Washington, totally demoralizing them. He would order his men to attack and continue to attack retreating troops until it became too dark to fight. Longstreet, on the other hand, was much more conservative in his approach to battle… more of a tactical leader while Jackson was relentlessly in the enemies' face."

"I don't know much about ol' Stonewall," said Kellem, "because he was not here at Gettysburg, but my interest in the man stems from a conversation I heard earlier this year while hiking over near Plum Run. Three men were having a conversation about Jackson and the difference he would have made if he had been here. They walked off before I could hear how the conversation went so, I have always wondered what difference he would have made. I mean, think about it. What difference could one man make in the epic three-day battle that took place in and on these surrounding fields?"

"I can answer that," said Max. "The difference he, this one man could have made, would have altered not only the outcome of the entire three-day conflict here at Gettysburg but the remainder of the war and more than likely history to some extent."

"In what way?" asked Kellem.

"Well let's take a look at the way the first day of battle ended. Lee and his overwhelming numbers drove the federal troops back to Big and Little Round Top. Lee gave an order to one of his staff members to ride out and locate General Ewell and to tell him that, *if at all possible,* drive those people, meaning the Union troops off those hills. This was an order that was not followed by Ewell because Lee's orders had been misunderstood. If Lee's orders had been to drive the enemy off those hills at all costs, Ewell would have more than likely done so, but because of Lee's statement, *if at all possible,* that left Ewell the power to make a decision. His decision was that it was not necessary to do so, hence following the first day of battle even though the Confederate Army had been successful and driven the Union Army back, the Yankees still held the high ground. Now, here is where Jackson would have come into play. Stonewall would not even have to receive the order to drive the Union Army off the hills, he would have just gone ahead and proceeded to do so. He would have continued to press the Union troops, not only driving them from the hills but probably halfway back to Carlisle. If this had happened then the roles on the second day of battle would have been reversed with Lee holding the high ground and General Meade who was in command of the Union forces attacking Lee on the fortified high ground rather than Lee having to do so, which we know turned out to be devastating to the Confederates."

"So, what you're saying is that Jackson could have been a pivotal decision-maker here at Gettysburg."

"Precisely!" said Max. "And now that we have talked about what might have happened let's talk about what did happen. Since General Jackson was not present, that left Lee to depend on General Longstreet who had a much different opinion of what should be done at the end of the first day of battle.

"Longstreet knew since the Union Army held the high ground and were reinforced it would be foolish to attack them as things stood. He suggested to Lee they redeploy and move toward Washington as there were no Northern troops between the Confederate Army and the capital of the Union. If they made this move then Meade would have to follow them and then they could fight the Union Army on the ground of their choosing and if they could get close enough to the capitol Lincoln might just call off the war, which in essence would be a victory for the south. But Lee refused to retreat in the face of the enemy, stating he had never left the field of battle in the hands of his adversaries. No, they would stay and fight. Longstreet strongly disagreed with Lee's decision but his great respect for the commanding general was too great to continue to argue his point. This decision by Lee turned out to be costly and his entire army was nearly destroyed over the next two days of battle."

Kellem started to peel one of the bananas. "I guess we'll never know what might have been if Stonewall Jackson would have been here, will we?"

Looking at General Lee's Headquarters, Max agreed, "No, we never will."

CHAPTER THIRTY

Dean Phillips stood erect at the outdoor elevated podium and gestured at the six hundred and ninety-two seated graduating students while addressing not only the graduates but the many guests in attendance, "I proudly give you this year's graduating class of Gettysburg College."

The students seated in neat rows of white folding chairs stood and cheered as they tossed their graduation caps into the late May spring air. Max held on to his cap in doubt of not being able to locate it after the momentary celebration. Pushing his way through the crowd of jubilant students, he replaced the cap squarely on his head, clutched his diploma in his right hand, and began the search for his parents, Elizabeth and Kellem. Emerging from the rows of chairs, many that had been accidentally pushed over, he saw Elizabeth waving at him while standing next to his parents and Kellem beneath three large oak trees.

He crossed a paved walkway where he was met by Elizabeth who ran up to him, giving him a congratulatory hug. "I'm so proud of you. After four years of study, you now have your degree. Come on, your parents want to get some pictures."

Charles was the first to speak as Max approached, "Ah, my son, the mathematics wizard has finally graduated from college." He gestured at Max's mother and stated proudly, "Your son is now a young man."

Kate hugged Max as she wiped a tear from her eye. "Where does the time go? It seems like just yesterday we were bringing you home from the hospital."

Charley slapped his son on the back, and laughed, "Good grief, Kate, that was twenty-two years ago."

Max, displaying his mathematical mind added, "Or, approximately eight thousand, thirty days."

Kellem approached and extended his right hand. "Congrats, Max. You've got your whole life ahead of you and I wish you all the luck in the world."

Kate handed her cell phone to Kellem and asked, "Would you please get some photos of our family under these trees?"

"Of course," said Kellem. "You get yourselves situated and I'll take a few."

Max stood next to his father while Kate gently took Elizabeth by her right arm and softly stated, "Com'n, you're in these pictures."

"No, that would not be right," objected Elizabeth. "This is a special occasion for your family and your family only."

"Nonsense," said Kate, "you're my future daughter-in-law, my son's soon-to-be wife. You are already part of this family."

After three family photos, Kate suggested, "I would also like to get photographs of Max with his father and then one with me and of course a picture of Max and Elizabeth."

Max posed next to his father and gestured at Kellem. "We also need to get a picture of me and Elizabeth with Kellem."

The requested pictures complete, Charley patted his stomach. "I don't know about the rest of you…but I'm starving. I've made reservations for all of us at Dobbins which offers the best steak in Gettysburg. I say we head on over as our reservations are for eleven. I'm looking forward to a great lunch."

Kellem started across the grass and stated, "I'll meet you there. A big steak, baked potato, and a salad sound wonderful."

Seated at an antique wooden table in the rustic dining room at Dobbins, Charley raised his glass of Chardonnay and suggested a toast. "Here's to my son, Max, a graduate of Gettysburg College who is now in possession of a four-year degree in finance, which I am more than confident will lead to a highly successful future."

Kellem also raised his crystal wine glass and added, "And let's not forget that part of his amazing future sits right here at this table." Turning to Elizabeth, he complimented her, "They say that behind every man there is a good woman, and you are indeed that."

Kate raised her glass, "Here, here!"

Max took a drink of wine as he addressed Kellem, "Strange, you would say that, after all, you've never been married, never had a good woman at your side, and yet you are quite successful."

Kellem took a short sip. "Just lucky, I guess!"

Their waitress approached the table with a basket of hot rolls and a small plate of butter and announced, "Your lunch will be out in about twenty minutes. I apologize for the delay in your meals but with it being graduation day we are extremely busy."

Charley reassured the girl as he nodded at Max. "That's quite all right, we understand. One of those graduates happens to be my son here."

The waitress smiled at Max while she laid the rolls on the table. "Congratulations, and if there is anything else you need just let me know. How is the wine?"

Elizabeth fingered the side of her glass and answered, "I think the wine tastes wonderful." Taking a short nip she smiled, "This is the first time I've ever had wine or for that matter alcohol of any sort."

Max placed his glass on the table and explained, "And it will probably be a long time before you indulge again, at least when you're with me as I don't drink that much. Most people who drink spill more in a year than I drink."

"Speak for yourself," said Kellem. "I have a glass of red wine every night before I turn in. My doctor said it's good for me…just the one glass nightly." Taking a sip he addressed Max's parents, "Charles, Kate, I have to say that you have done one hell of a job in raising your son. And, I must add that Max has made a wise choice in Elizabeth as his soon-to-be wife. For a young couple who is in their early twenties, when they marry, they'll be off to a much better start than most young married couples. I've known these two for the last four years now and I think they make a great team. I've had many a conversation with these two about saving money and planning for the future and I think they are well ahead of the game."

Elizabeth, buttering a roll pointed her knife at Kellem as she agreed, "I have been employed at The Lutheran Retirement Village for almost two years now. Just recently I received a pay raise and have managed to save about twenty-five thousand a year."

Kate seemed amazed. "How on earth did you manage to save that much money?"

"Easy," smiled Elizabeth. "My living expenses are practically nothing what with living rent-free on Kellem's farm. I have no grocery bills as he purchases all the food for the farm, and I prepare it for meals." Laying her roll to the side, she continued, "For me, I'm not sure if Max and I are going to have a much better start than most young married couples because I am not that familiar with marriages outside of the Mennonite faith. When a young couple gets married in the faith that I was raised in, the Mennonite community makes sure they have everything they need to get off as you say to a good start. In most cases, the young man's father will provide the new couple with a small farm complete with a house and barn. Livestock is provided by the community as well as any equipment to run the farm. Since I am no longer a Mennonite, I have learned that in this new world that I have chosen to enter it is up to a young married couple to make their way and I think Max and I are doing so."

Max opened a pad of butter as he chimed in, "I couldn't agree more with Elizabeth. I remember back when I was just ten years old on my birthday that year, Dad gave me a stock certificate worth five hundred dollars of Home Depot stock along with a book about how to not only invest in the market but how to buy and sell stocks. I read that book until the front cover came off and over the next eight years up until I moved away from home to attend college right here in town, I amassed just over forty thousand dollars in my account. During my four years here at school, I have added another nine thousand to that total leaving me with just a tad bit over fifty thousand in my investment portfolio. I don't think that's too bad for a twenty-two-year-old South Carolina boy."

Splitting open a roll, he continued, "When you combine that with what Elizabeth has managed to save our pre-marriage nest egg comes in at about one hundred thousand. I think that's pretty good for a young couple." Slathering butter on one half of the roll, Max went on, "I've got some news to share with everyone this morning. No one at this table other than Elizabeth is aware of what I'm about to say, but we are both very excited about an opportunity that has landed in our laps."

"More good news," said Kellem. "Bring it on!"

Max pushed the half roll to the side and then spoke, "It was just about two years ago right after Kellem's barn burnt to the ground when I started working part-time in between my classes for Williamson's Financial Service in downtown Gettysburg. Sam Williamson, who if I'm correct, is the same age as Kellem here offered me a job at his business, saying that he needed a helping hand. I remember the day he contacted me. I had just got back from my last class of the day when there sat this strange old fellow waiting for me in the dorm lobby. He said that a close friend of his, who he never mentioned by name, found out that he was looking for some help at his office and this unknown person suggested that Sam talk with me. The long and short of our conversation was that I took him up on his offer to work in his office on a part-time basis during the week usually on Saturday.

"When I later discovered that Kellem here and Sam Williamson grew up together right here in town and that they had remained lifelong friends it didn't take any great feat of detective work to find out that the unknown person who suggested me as a great part-time employee turned out to be Kellem. I've worked for Sam now for a little over two years and last year he offered me a full-time position which was somewhat difficult for me to handle considering I still had classes my senior year to contend with. But when you consider all the experience I was gaining in the field that I was going to college for I figured I was just simply jump-starting my future career. Sam Williamson has been in the financial business for over sixty years and working with him closely I have to this point gained more experience in the field than most young men and women my age."

Max held up both hands in an apologetic gesture for rambling on as he explained. "Last Wednesday when we were finished up for the day Sam asked me to have a cup of coffee with him up the street at his favorite café. Over coffee and a cheese Danish he explained to me that he is going to retire and has been considering retirement for the past year. He told me that at eighty-four he was getting to the point where dealing with facts and figures was becoming quite the task. He also told me that over the past five decades, he had made more money than he would ever be able to logically spend at his age and that it was time to throw in the towel.

"I told him I appreciated the fact that he had employed me over the past two years and that I was going to miss working with him. I went on to ask him if he had any interested parties in purchasing his business. He said two national financial chains were interested but that he would much rather sell the business to a private firm or individual. He took a long drink of coffee and then asked me if I was interested in purchasing the business. To say the least, I was at a loss for words and quite frankly could not believe what I had just heard.

"My silence was no surprise to Sam. He went on to say that when he was just out of college and looking for work, he was offered a full-time position where his office is located now. That was Blackwell Bookkeeping and Taxes. He worked for Blackwell for about ten years when old man Blackwell sold him the business. Since Blackwell had given him an opportunity way back when, Sam thought that he would at least give me a first chance at taking over the reins of his business. I was still at a loss as to what I should say so he went on to point out that he knew how my mind worked, that at that very moment I was starting to do the math of owning the business... which I was. I asked him what he was selling the business for and what the terms of the sale would be. He told me flat out that he was going to sell the business for two hundred and fifty thousand dollars."

Max's father spoke up, "Why that's a quarter of a million!"

Kate agreed, "That's right and a quarter of a million dollars sounds like a lot more than two hundred and fifty thousand!"

Max smiled at his mother and confirmed, "It's the same amount no matter how you phrase it."

Kellem jumped in on the conversation, "Can you afford that kind of money and if you can what are the terms of the sale?"

Max, who had taken a bite of his roll, swallowed and then answered, "20% down and then 20% of my monthly income until the full amount is paid off."

Kate was trying to calculate what 20% of a quarter of a million was when Max cleared up the equation. "That's fifty thousand dollars right up front."

Charley confirmed, "Fifty thousand dollars... isn't that the amount you have managed to save to date?"

"Exactly, and now I'm going to put that money to work."

"Isn't that kind of risky, not having anything to fall back on?"

Elizabeth answered, "He, or I should we still have fifty thousand dollars in my savings."

Kate shrugged, "But that's your money."

"I don't look at it that way," said Elizabeth, "Whatever I have and whatever Max has goes into our future marriage. Like Kellem said... Max and I are a team."

"Look," said Max, "we can sit here all afternoon and discuss the pros and cons, the upside and the possible downside of buying this business but I have done the math and it works out. The business as it sits right now brings in about three hundred thousand a year, which equates to a monthly income of twenty-five thousand a month. My 20% monthly payment to Sam will be approximately five thousand. Then on top of that, I've the rent on the building which is one thousand seven hundred and fifty and my school loan is just five hundred. Throw in a couple of hundred for utilities and you come up with a fixed monthly output of seventy-five hundred and that leaves Elizabeth and I with a cash flow of seventeen thousand, five hundred dollars per month. That equals a yearly income of right around two hundred thousand a year and that doesn't even include Elizabeth's income."

"Two hundred thousand a year," said Charley. "That's more than what I make in a year, and it took me years of hard work to get to that level," Raising his glass he made another toast. "I think Kate and I raised a pretty smart son if I do say so myself!"

Kellem placed his glass back on the table and asked, "So when is this marriage we've been hearing about for the past couple of years going to take place?"

Max looked at Elizabeth and replied, "I think I'll let Elizabeth answer that question."

Elizabeth immediately spoke up. "When Max and I decided we would marry we agreed that we would wait at least until we both graduated from college. I have been out of school now for two years and Max just received his four-year diploma. We've been seeing one another now for four years. We've been talking recently, and we have decided that we will have a June wedding…this June...next month."

Kate was beside herself. "Next month…in June! That's just around the corner. It's May the 16th right now. June will be upon us in two weeks. That doesn't leave much time. There is a lot of planning that has to go into a wedding!"

Max grinned at his father as he addressed his mother. "Calm down, Mom. We've set the date for June 20th…the first day of summer. That gives us about five weeks to get everything set up."

Elizabeth placed her right hand on Kate's shoulder. "We've agreed on a simplistic wedding. Max suggested that we marry on Fripp Island. He told me that they conduct weddings there all the time right on the beach. I think that sounds just wonderful. Don't you?"

Kate agreed, "A wedding on the beach at Fripp does sound wonderful.

I've seen many weddings take place there and I've been to two weddings on the beach as a guest. Five weeks is not as long as you think. There's still planning that has to be done, like flowers and music, and then someone has to take photographs. Invitations have to be sent out and we have to contact a minister…and then there's the wedding gown."

Max seemed to have an answer for everything his mother had mentioned. "We can order flowers and have them delivered to the house the day before and keep them at the house until just before the ceremony. We don't need any live music. We can have taped music. We can get one of the guests to take pictures. We only need a few with the family as we are not interested in one of those full-blown wedding albums. Dad, you can get Pastor Mullins from the church in Beaufort to come out to the island."

"My wedding gown will not be a problem," said Elizabeth. "I have my mother's gown that she gave me years ago which my sister also was married in. As far as the wedding party is concerned, I've asked my best friend Ellen back in Lancaster to be my matron of honor. Her husband doesn't like the idea of her going all the way to South Carolina to my wedding especially because I turned his proposal of marriage down years ago. Ellen happens to be a strong-willed woman and demands that he drive her to Philadelphia where she will catch a flight down to Charleston. Max and I will pick her up at the airport, then after the wedding, we'll make sure she gets a flight back home."

Charley asked, "And who have you chosen Max, for your best man?"

Raising his glass in a toasting fashion Max spoke across the table to Kellem. "I was hoping that you would do me the honor of being my best man."

Kellem hoisted his glass and responded with a wide smile. "You can count on me to be there on that beach…tuxedo and all. Hell, I can't remember the last time I was even at a wedding let alone in one."

Kate downed a long drink of wine and then took a deep breath. "I'm sorry that I seem so worried about everything, but this is my only son's wedding. I just want everything to be perfect." Placing her right hand over her mouth she exclaimed, "And what about the weather? What if it rains? The house on Fripp is not big enough to conduct a wedding when you consider all the guests we'll have there."

"I've considered that," said Max, "If we have bad weather then we can have the wedding at the island community center. They have a chapel there and a large gathering area where we can have the reception."

Charley took his wife's hand and confirmed, "It would seem that our son here has thought this entire process through and has an answer for everything that might arise." Raising his glass once again, he stated, "Here's to my son and his wonderful bride-to-be!"

Kellem put his glass down and seemed somewhat dejected.

"Max, picking up on his odd behavior asked, "Kellem…is there something wrong?"

The old man shrugged and replied, "Well sort of, but …not really."

Max frowned. "That makes no sense at all. What gives?"

"I as well had some good news to share with the group today but with the announcement of your marriage and especially the fact that you are buying your own business it kind of squashed what I had to say."

"I don't understand," said Max. "How could our upcoming marriage and my new business affect what you have to say?"

Kellem stammered. "Well, you see, I too… am considering retiring. I'm getting too old to be tossing Christmas trees around and besides that keeping up the property is becoming too much for me. Just like Sam Williamson I too am eighty-four years old, and I guess what I'm saying is that I am also ready to throw in the towel."

Max, still confused, probed, "I still don't see what your retirement has to do with my marriage or my going into business for myself."

"There's more to it than just retiring. I'm going to be moving down to Florida to live with my sister and my one surviving brother. That means I'll have to sell the farm. I was going to ask you Max if you would be interested in buying the place but since you invested everything you've saved over the past years into your own financial business, I don't think that's even possible…that is, even if you were interested."

Charley spoke up. "I've never seen your farm, but Max has told me all about its seventy-six acres of Christmas trees and then another seven acres where the house and barn are located. How much are you asking for the property?"

Kellem raised his eyebrows as he answered softly. "Eight hundred and fifty thousand. It's a turnkey business. I'm selling not only the tree farm but the house, the barn, and…everything, well that is except for a few antiques that my sister would like to have."

"Eight hundred and fifty thousand!" said Kate. "Why that makes a quarter on a million sound rather small in comparison." Looking at Max she inquired with curiosity. "If you were not buying this financial business, would you consider, or even at that, could you afford to buy Kellem's farm?"

"Eight hundred and fifty thousand is a big number," said Max. "If I were not purchasing Williamson's business, I think Elizabeth and I could have swung buying Kellem's farm, but that would probably involve taking out a bank loan which I prefer not to do at this time in my life. I suppose we could have bought the farm despite buying the business, but I don't want to bite off more than we can chew. Does that make sense?"

Everyone at the table nodded in agreement as Max continued, "Elizabeth and I have in the past talked about the fact that if Kellem ever decided to sell the farm we would consider buying the place. Of course, that was before I decided on this new business venture. Elizabeth has always told me how much she enjoys living on the farm, taking care of the cleaning and odd jobs, and making meals there. She has always said that the place kind of reminds her of her father's place back in Lancaster but on a smaller scale."

Kellem smiled at Elizabeth. "I never knew you felt that way about the farm."

Elizabeth confirmed, "Oh yes…yes indeed. If I ever had a place like your farm I'd plant a large vegetable garden, probably put up a chicken coup, maybe have a few cows and maybe a horse. I mean that's the way I grew up…on a farm. You know what they say, 'You can take the girl off the farm, but you can't take the farm out of the girl. I guess I'll always be a farm girl at heart."

Leaning forward Kellem placed both his hands flat on the table. "I've got a crazy idea. First of all, I have two interested parties in the tree farm but not the seven acres that the house and barn are situated on. I can easily sell the seventy-six-acre tree farm for four hundred and fifty thousand. That leaves the seven-acre property which I would sell for the remaining four hundred thousand. Here's my idea, I like you kids quite a bit and if you're interested, I'll sell you the house, the barn, and the seven acres for three hundred and fifty thousand. It's only money and I've made a great deal of it over the years. But that's just part of my proposal. Would you kids consider renting the property, for let's say a thousand a month? We could set up a lease with an option to buy."

"As good as I am with numbers," admitted Max, "I am not that familiar with real estate terminology. How would it work if we decided to go down that path?"

"Well, first of all, I would require no down payment. Every month when you send me a payment, in this case one thousand dollars, I will earmark 25% of that payment to be set aside as a future portion of your down payment. What this amounts to is that for every one thousand you pay me I will set aside two hundred and fifty as a down payment that could be applied to a future loan if down the road you decide to buy the place. I would set up the lease, for let's say three years. I think that's enough time for you two kids to decide if you want to buy."

Max's mind was working quickly as he calculated, "So let me get this straight, a thousand a month for three years means that we would be paying you thirty-six thousand and you would be willing to set aside three thousand each year which equates to nine thousand accumulated for a down payment at that time based upon a loan that we would get."

"I believe those numbers are correct," said Kellem.

Max had more questions, "Could we make double payments from time to time and can we pay off the entire amount before the three-year time rent limit ends?"

"Yes, you can do all those things according to your future financial position."

Max looked across the table at Elizabeth and asked, "What do you think about this?"

"It's only a thousand dollars a month," said Elizabeth, "and that wouldn't even have to come out of the income of your new business. I could easily pay that amount out of my weekly income. Of course, that's just my opinion, but all in all, I would love to live on the farm. When you think about it, I already am and have been living there for the past two years or so. I think Kellem's farm would make a great home for us as a newly married couple."

Max raised his glass. "It would seem that the wonderful events of this day warrant one toast after another. Kellem...you have a deal."

Kellem agreed, "Okay then! I was not planning on moving until early July so that gives us plenty of time to fill out an agreement. Besides that, I've got a wedding to attend down on this Fripp Island I've heard so much about."

Amos King entered Baumer's Hardware Store in East Petersburg and walked up to the sales counter where an older man named Henry, the manager was busy opening a case of light bulbs. Recognizing Amos as a familiar customer, Henry laid down his utility knife and greeted the local farmer, "Well, hello there Mr. King. What brings you to town?"

Amos was about to reply when Simon Baumer walked out of an office behind the counter and noticed Amos.

Smiling broadly, Simon welcomed his neighbor. "Well, I'll be if it isn't ol' Amos King from up the road. It's been what, about three weeks since we talked over at the farmer's market. What can we do for you?"

Wiping his brow with a handkerchief Amos remarked, "It's hotter than Hades out there." He then held up a well-used, bent barn latch and explained, "I'm in the process of replacing my barn doors. I need two sets of barn door hardware and latches…black if you have them."

Simon turned to the manager, suggesting, "You can just go on with what you were doing Henry. I'll take care of Mr. King." Simon pointed toward the back of the store. "I think I have just what you need. Just got some barn hardware in a few weeks back and I'm pretty sure we have what you want in that black."

At the next to the last row of metal shelving, Simon pointed at some bins that contained barn hardware. He selected a black barn hinge and handed it to Amos. "Is this what you had in mind?"

Amos flipped the hinge over in his hand and inspecting the metal device, he replied, "Yes these will be just fine. How about the handles?"

Simon grabbed two different-style black barn handles and held them up. "We have two kinds" square and oblong. Which would you prefer?"

"I think the square one will do."

Simon grabbed a retail bag from a nearby hook. "And how many of the hinges do you require?"

"Well, I have two doors with six hinges which means I'll need twelve altogether. As far as the handles are concerned, I'll need four."

Counting the number of hinges that he placed in the bag Simon frowned. "It looks like we're going to be short four hinges. I have all four of the handles. I can order you the other hinges. It'll be about a week before they come in."

"That's all right," said Amos. "Why don't you ring me up for the whole lot at least that way I can get one of the doors up now and then after the remaining hinges arrive I'll put up the other."

Simon handed the bag to Amos and smiled, "On the house!"

"What do you mean, on the house?"

"What I'm saying is that there will be no charge."

Amos objected, "I cannot allow you to do that. I'm not a charity case. I have more than enough money to purchase the needs for my farm."

"My decision to give these items to you at no charge has nothing to do with whether you can afford them or not. It's the least I can do for you. It's my way of apologizing."

"Apologize…apologize for what?"

"For making a complete jackass of myself at your farm that day when Elizabeth was leaving with that Miller boy."

"Good Lord, Simon. That was almost three years ago. That's water under the bridge."

"That may be but I still need to make things right. I had no right to hit that young man. It's just that I was so in love with your daughter and was convinced beyond any doubt that she would be my wife…and there she was leaving…forever! I just couldn't believe it. I just lost my head."

Amos placed his right hand on Simon's shoulder in friendship. "I too thought that Elizabeth and you would marry. It was a complete surprise when Miller showed up at my farm and requested to talk with me. After listening to that young man, I thought that he was a good person, unlike many of the people we find who live outside of our faith. He said that he loved Elizabeth and that at some point down the road, he would like to marry her. When I questioned my daughter, she agreed and said that she wanted to marry Miller. After considering everything that was said I gave her a choice, marry Miller and leave our faith, never to return, or stay in the faith and tell the young man goodbye. She chose Miller and as you know has left the Mennonite faith…for good. It was her choice. As you are well aware Simon, the Good Lord gives us free will and will not interfere with decisions we make. It was my daughter's choice, not mine or my wife's. We continue to live here in the Mennonite community and have said goodbye to our daughter three years ago. End of story!"

Simon pushed the bag toward Amos's chest. "Just the same I want you to have this barn hardware…at no charge…please."

"I'll not argue with you, Simon. If that is your wish, then so be it."

Placing the four handles in another bag, Simon asked, "Speaking of Elizabeth have you and the wife heard from your daughter lately?"

"For the longest time…no, but then last week we got a visit from Ellen Stoltz, or I should say, Ellen Hoffman. If you'll recall she married Eli Hoffman a few years back. Anyway, Ellen and Elizabeth have been friends since they were little, and I guess they still are. Ellen said that she and Elizabeth stay in touch weekly by phone and that Elizabeth wanted to speak with my wife and me. It was around noon when Ellen dropped by, and she said that Elizabeth was going to call her on her cell phone at twelve-thirty and that she was to hand the phone over to her mother first and then to put me on. I asked Ellen why after all this time was my daughter calling me now. She went on to say that Elizabeth and Max were going to get married this June, which is just around the corner.

"So, there we were in the sitting room drinking iced tea and swapping pleasantries when her phone buzzed. She answered the phone and after listening to whoever was on the other end, handed the phone to my wife. My wife says, 'Hello,' and then a few seconds later tells me that it's Elizabeth. After listening for about a minute, my wife speaks into the phone and says, 'I'd love to come but that's up to your father.' She then hands the phone to me and says, 'Your daughter would like to speak with you.' The conversation didn't last all that long. Elizabeth explained to me that she was getting married on June 20th in South Carolina and was inviting me and the wife to her wedding. I reminded her of what I told her when she decided to leave our faith and go with Miller…that down the road there would be ramifications. I told her that she would always be my daughter by blood, but that was where our relationship ended. She was not welcome back on the farm and the wife and I had no interest in attending her wedding and then I ended the call…didn't even thank her for the call or say goodbye. Simon, life can be hard at times."

"I've never had a daughter," said Simon, "but I imagine it must have been quite difficult to turn down your daughter like that?"

"It was, but what it comes right down to is that there is a fine line between family and our Mennonite beliefs. I can't say that my heart has not been broken."

Simon shook his head in apparent sadness. "Elizabeth broke my heart when she left that day with Miller. Just out of curiosity did Ellen say anything else about Elizabeth?"

"Not directly to me and that's because I left the house and went out to the barn following the call from Elizabeth. Later that afternoon when I went back to the house my wife told me that Ellen hung around for a few minutes after I left. She told my wife that Elizabeth was getting married on a beach on an island in South Carolina called Fripp. She said that it was going to be a very simple wedding with herself as the matron of honor and some old farmer by the name of Kellem who happens to be good friends with Max. Turns out this Kellem owns a farm and Elizabeth has been living there for the past two years. Ellen also said that Miller was considering buying a business in Gettysburg. All in all, she said that Elizabeth said things were going quite well for them."

Amos held up the bag of hardware. "Thank you for the barn door parts. Is there any paperwork we need to do, or can I be on my way?"

"No, you go right ahead Amos. All we have to do is subtract what I gave you from our inventory which has nothing to do with you. Maybe I'll see you at the farmer's market next weekend?"

Hesitating at the door Amos gave Simon a casual wave as he replied, "Probably will."

Simon approached the sales counter while speaking to his manager. "Henry, I'm going to be out of town on business the next two days or so. I'm confident that you can keep this place afloat during my absence. If there are any problems, you have my cell number."

CHAPTER THIRTY-ONE

Brad Sykes sat behind his office desk as he stared at the picturesque view of Cayuca Lake three stories below. Enjoying an expensive Havana cigar his moment of leisure was interrupted by a soft knock followed by his secretary opening the door. Popping her head in she informed her boss, "Mr. Sykes…you have a visitor. His name is Simon Baumer. Are you available to speak with him? He says it's quite important that he see you."

Brad held up his right hand for her to stop speaking as he thought, *Simon Baumer! I remember him. What on earth could he want to speak to me about?* Extinguishing his cigar in an expensive glass ashtray, he waved some lingering smoke away from his face and replied, "Yes, show Mr. Baumer in. I'll speak with him."

Seconds later the secretary ushered Baumer into the office closing the door behind her. Simon Baumer looked the same as the first and only other time Brad had met the man; scary, tall, with an unkempt bearded face and piercing eyes. Dressed in all black, he held a black-banded straw hat in his right hand. Hesitating as he looked around the plush office he finally spoke, "Brad Sykes…do you recall when we met before?"

Brad acknowledged, "I do…it was in Gettysburg at a café, which you will have to forgive me the name. What brings you up to Ithaca?"

"I have something I wish to speak with you about. Do you mind if I sit?"

"No, go right ahead. Would you like a drink?"

"No thank you. I'm fine."

"Well, if you don't mind then I'm going to have one."

Simon remained silent as Brad got up from the desk and walked to a small liquor cabinet, opened it, and removed a bottle of Bourbon. Pouring himself a generous portion he opened a small refrigerator, extracted three ice cubes from the tiny freezer, and plunked them into his drink. Seated again behind the desk he held up the glass, took a short nip, and commented, "I normally knock back a stiff drink in the afternoon while here at the office."

Simon glanced at an antique clock on a nearby credenza and remarked, "It's only ten o'clock in the morning. A little early for a drink…don't you think?"

Brad took another swallow, then set the drink down and agreed, "Yes, it is far too early for a drink, but I remember the only other time we met. I thought you were quite frightening in your appearance back then and I feel the same way now. You sir…are a scary man! I just thought a good drink would calm my nerves."

"Has it?"

"I'm now quite sure yet as you haven't told me why you've come to see me."

Reassuring Brad, Simon smiled. "Relax, Mr. Sykes…I'll not harm you. The truth of the matter is that I have recently received some information you may find very interesting."

Brad sat forward and folded his hands on the top of the desk. "Please… continue."

Simon placed his hat on the corner of the desk while explaining, "I recently found out Elizabeth King and Max Miller are getting married next month which is just a few weeks away."

"And why do you think this information would be of interest to me? I only attended school at Gettysburg for two years and during that time Miller and the King girl were a couple. Everyone on campus knew about their relationship and I suppose that was because it was so odd. Miller was one of us. Ya know, a good ol' American college student, and Elizabeth, well she was like you…a Mennonite."

Simon gave Brad a frown and stated, "You make it sound like being Mennonite is a bad thing."

"That's not what I meant. Elizabeth King was just so different from most of the other students. The way she dressed, the way she kept to herself. It just seemed odd that she and Miller hooked up…that's all. It's no surprise to me they are getting married…and to tell you the truth I could care less. If you came to Ithaca to give me the news about their upcoming wedding, I'm afraid my lack of concern means you made a long trip for nothing."

"There's more to it than that," said Simon. "Yesterday I drove over to Gettysburg to see if I could find out where you live. I got there early in the morning, so I decided to grab some breakfast. While at this café I was in the process of eating when in walks these two-strapping-looking young men who were wearing Gettysburg school jackets. After they ordered I walked over and asked if they were students. Turned out they were. They were football players who were attending summer classes for extra credit. I asked if I could join them. They seemed hesitant but agreed. I asked them if they knew you. They both knew who you were and said they had played football with you there at school."

Brad, not knowing where the conversation was leading, asked, "Did you ask them their names?"

"No, I did not, nor did they ask mine. I asked them if they knew where you lived and they told me…Ithaca, New York and they also said you were working for your father. One of the boys asked me why I was interested in you because the fact was you had left school toward the end of your sophomore year. The other boy laughed and said that the word around school right after you left was that you had decided to attend a school closer to your home, but the scuttlebutt around campus was that you had been tossed out of the school mainly because of a barn fire on Kellem McCulhay's farm."

Shaking his head in wonder Brad retorted, "Part of what you say is true and parts are just speculation. I did leave school toward the end of my second year at Gettysburg. The reason why I left had nothing to do with my desire to attend school closer to my home. The Dean, following an interview with me conducted by two detectives from the Gettysburg police regarding the fire at McCulhay's farm, suggested quite strongly I consider transferring to another school. I disagreed with their request but my father, who was in attendance during the interview decided it would be best if I came back here to Ithaca with him. In essence, I was kicked out of school."

"So, then you were a suspect regarding the barn fire?"

"Not in so many words. They said I was a person of interest."

"But they never charged you with anything?"

"Of course not. They had no proof!"

"Then why the expulsion from school?"

"The fire at McCulhay's was the proverbial straw that broke the camel's back as they say. There was bad blood between Miller and me that started back in our freshman year. I got into a verbal confrontation with him at a place where he worked, and he wound up sucker-punching me. I had extensive damage to my nose that prevented me from playing football for the rest of the year. I was the laughingstock of the school and most of the other players on the football team. As a football player, I was in incredible shape while Miller was known as a mathematics geek around campus. He took me out with one punch. That was quite embarrassing for me as well as for my father who, as an alumni has contributed millions of dollars to the college over the years. Much to my delight my father decided to sue Miller, but during a precursor meeting to going to court my father up and changed his mind and let Miller walk away Scott free. I vowed to myself I would get even with Miller."

"So, you burned down his friend Kellem McCulhay's barn?"

"No, I did not burn down that barn, but I did get even."

"How?"

"That's in the past and I see no reason to discuss that with you. The bad feelings between Miller and myself and a few other mischievous deeds I was involved in combined with the possibility that I set the fire caused the school to suggest I transfer out."

"Let me ask you this?' said Simon, "If you would have not been a person of interest in the barn fire would you have completed your education at Gettysburg?"

"Most definitely!"

"Well then, the way I see this is you have every reason to be upset with not only Kellem McCulhay but this Miller as well. If they would have not suggested to the police that you could have been responsible, then you could have remained at Gettysburg."

"My frustration with McCulhay was short-lived…"

Simon interrupted Brad, "So that means you did not burn down the man's barn."

"I already told you that was not my doing and as far as Miller is concerned I no longer hold any feeling of seeking revenge toward him." Holding out his hands displaying the lavish office and the magnificent view of the sprawling lake, Brad elaborated, "I've turned over a new leaf since leaving Gettysburg. My father, who happens to swing a lot of weight in this town and also knows the board members at Ithaca College was able to get me enrolled for my junior and senior years at their school. I decided to study my butt off and stopped playing football as I realized it was a waste of time as I was never going to go pro. I met a girl in my senior year at school who was studying for her law degree. We just got engaged two months back. I'm in the process of having a large lake house built a couple of miles up the coastline. My father owns a great number of businesses in and around the state and he turned this business, Sykes Uniforms and Cleaning Supplies over to me. If I do well, then about two years from now, he states that he will assign me to a business with even more responsibility. In short, I've got plenty of money and a great future ahead of me, so why would I be concerned over Miller, his soon-to-be wife, or even this McCulhay character?"

"This changes things…somewhat," said Simon. "When I came up here to see you, I had intentions of traveling a particular road and thought maybe you'd be interested in tagging along, but it looks like I'm on my own."

Brad took another sip of Bourbon and remarked, "I don't have any idea what you are talking about."

"From what you have told me," pointed out Simon, "you have buried the hatchet. I, on the other hand, still have an ax to grind with both Miller and this Kellem McCulhay. Like I told you before. I courted Elizabeth King for six months and was confident beyond any doubt that we would marry. Max Miller destroyed my plans with the King girl. I happen to be quite successful and when I set out with a plan, I always succeed…without fail! Miller interfered with my marriage plans with Elizabeth and I can't let that slide without some sort of satisfaction. Then there's this Kellem McCulhay who stuck his nose in where it did not belong. Do you recall one of the last things I said to you the first time we met?"

"Vaguely. If I remember correctly, you asked me where you could contact Max Miller. I was not sure where he was staying on campus."

"That is correct and then you went on to tell me you thought he worked for McCulhay at his farm."

"Yes, and now I remember the last thing you said. You were going to go to McCulhay's farm and explain to Miller the way things were between you and the King girl."

"That is precisely right and I did go to McCulhay's to confront Miller. I took my two brothers along with me to the farm. We found Miller there and after a brief conversation with him regarding my courtship of Elizabeth King and our future marriage he was not all that receptive to what I had said. This led to me slapping him around a bit, which I did not enjoy but I wanted him to understand he was interfering with the Mennonite faith, and it appeared words alone were not getting through to him. Just when I thought I had the upper hand McCulhay shows up, fires a shotgun at me and my brothers, and then displays a handgun which he threatens us with as he orders us off his property and explains to me that we need to get back across the Susquehanna River over to Lancaster County and never return to Adams County. I have to tell you I have never in my life had a gun fired at me or been threatened by a person with a gun. Furthermore, I have never been talked down to the way McCulhay talked to me. I deserve some pay-back!"

Brad nodded in agreement, "Then it was you who burned that barn down!"

Simon gave Brad a stern look and responded, "We can sit here all day long and debate over who did or did not burn down that barn and it doesn't make a difference. Either way, McCulhay got what was coming to him, but it's not enough as far as I'm concerned. Both he and this Miller need to suffer because of what they have done to me."

"That may be, Mr. Baumer, but you have to understand I am no longer interested in gaining any sort of payback from either McCulhay or Miller. I've moved on with my life and have no desire to join you in your search for payback."

"I understand, but I have a question for you."

"Go right ahead…ask away."

"You said earlier you had gotten revenge on Miller, and that you didn't want to discuss it. My question is this, after you inflicted this revenge on Miller did you gain any satisfaction?"

"That's two different questions, Mr. Baumer, and I'll answer both. First, I did not inflict the revenge on Miller and secondly, I did get satisfaction."

"I'm afraid I don't understand."

"Let me put it to you this way. The secret to getting successful revenge on someone is to have it done without the slightest shred of evidence that you were involved, which is exactly what I was able to accomplish."

Simon shook his head in confusion and spoke matter-of-factly, "I have always considered myself a man who is reasonably intelligent, but I still do not get what you are telling me."

"All right, let me go at this in another way. I'm probably going out on a limb by telling you this, but I don't have any other way to explain it. It just so happens that I know someone who knows someone. In other words, there are people, who for a price can accomplish things for an individual they do not want to be directly involved with. You inform these folks what it is you want done, you pay their fee, and go your way, and no one will ever know you were even involved."

Simon remained silent after Brad was finished speaking as if he were in deep thought but then finally responded, "Do you or are you still in touch with these people?"

"Yes and no. I never met the people who carried out my request or who made the decision to act. I only met the go-between person who just happens to be a close friend of mine."

"This friend of yours…does he live close by?"

"Yes, he lives here in Ithaca. I can't tell you the address because I do not know where in town he lives. We went to high school together and quite frankly raised a lot of hell as young boys. He spends a great deal of time at a local pool hall here in town. Since I have returned to town we usually get together at least once or twice a month and have a few drinks. I have not seen him for almost three months now as I am trying to create a new circle of friends what with my new way of life."

"Then you could, if you had to, get in touch with this person?"

"Yes, I could. It would be just a matter of a phone call."

"Do you think these people would talk with me?"

"The only person that may talk with you would be my friend. You would never meet or talk with the decision makers or those who carry out the request."

"Can you, or will you contact this friend of yours on my behalf?"

"I could do that, but I won't, because then I am involved. Tell you what I'll do, and I do this only because you came all this way to see me. I will supply you with my friend's cell number. I cannot guarantee he will talk with you, and if he does, I also cannot guarantee he will pass your information onto the people he works for."

"That's fair. If you'll give me the gentleman's number, I'll give him a call, and depending on how he reacts I'll go from there."

"Okay then." Withdrawing a gold-plated ink pen from an oak pen holder, Brad jotted down the number and handed it across the table to Simon. "There you go. Good luck!"

Simon read the number silently to himself, folded the note, and stuck it in his shirt pocket. Standing, he smiled. "Thank you, Mr. Sykes. The long drive up here from Lancaster may turn out to be worth it after all."

"One last thing before you go," said Brad. "I think it would be in our best interest if we never cross paths again."

"I understand what you're saying, I was never here, and this meeting never took place."

"I like the way you think Mr. Baumer."

Getting up Simon walked to the door but then turned back facing Brad. "This friend of yours. He'll know we met. Other than the people he will have to talk to can he keep his mouth shut?"

"My friend, who you may wind up talking to falls into the category of a bit unsavory, but the one thing he is not is untrustworthy."

Simon nodded at the closed door and asked, "What about your secretary? She knows I'm here and as you may well know from my appearance, I am not a man whose appearance is easily forgotten."

"I'll take care of that. She is well-paid and has no reason to talk about your visit. After you leave, I'll tell her you were here on business and leave it at that. Good luck to you, Baumer. We'll never talk again."

Removing the note from his pocket Simon held it up. "Thanks for the information."

The door closed, Brad finished off his drink in three long swallows, walked over, and looked down at the glistening lake as he thought, *I wonder what Baumer has in mind for Miller and ol' man McCulhay?*

The State Street Pool Hall and Grill sat just down the street from the fire station just like Kip had informed him over the phone. Parking his car Simon climbed out and looked up and down the street. In many ways, Ithaca reminded him of Lancaster. He hadn't been to that many medium-sized towns and the ones he had been to always had the same things, just under different names. There were always barber shops, laundromats, restaurants, and other varied businesses that every community needed. Waiting for a local police cruiser to pass by he started across the street.

Hesitating at the front door he noticed all the neon beer and liquor signs situated in the windows. He had never been into a drinking establishment and before he even opened the door, he knew his Mennonite appearance would turn some heads. Opening the door, he stepped in, stopped, and looked around at the pool tables, the bar, the jukebox, and a dart board hanging on the wall. There were two men playing pool and three perched on bar stools. A baldheaded bartender wiping down the bar top noticed Simon, leaned over, and said something to two of the patrons, which caused all three to turn and stare in Simon's direction. Not to be intimidated Simon walked up to the bar, removed his hat, and politely inquired, "I'm here to see a young man by the name of Kip. He told me he would be here. Is he?"

The bartender answered the question. "Yeah, he's in the back. Can't miss him. He's the only one in the backroom right now. Care for a drink?"

"No, I'm here on business."

Simon nodded at the three men, then made his way across the room and walked through a wide-arched opening where he saw a young man about the same age as Brad seated at a corner table. Kip, noticing Simon, signaled him over to his table. Simon approached and watched as Kip placed the four of diamonds beneath the five of spades, flipped another card over from a small stack in his hand, examined the seven lines of playing cards spread out before him, cursed, and threw the cards in his hand to the side. Looking up at Simon, he inquired, "Ever play solitaire, Mr. Baumer?"

Simon looked at the scattered cards and then replied, "If you mean cards…no, never. It's against my faith."

Taking a swig from a bottle of beer, Kip asked a second question, "Is drinking also against your faith?"

"For the most part yes, but as a Mennonite I have an occasional drink."

Gesturing at a chair Kip offered, "Take a seat….would you care for one of your occasional drinks now?"

"No, I'm here to talk business."

Kip leaned back and balanced the back legs of his chair against the wall, crossed his arms, and gave Simon a serious look. "Before you called me earlier, I received a call from Brad. He told me to expect a call from you and that I should prepare myself to talk with a very unusual character which you appear to be. He told me you had some business to talk over with me. He wasn't sure exactly what you had in mind but did say it had to do with two men, a Max Miller and then a man by the name of Kellem McCulhay. He said you were a very wealthy farmer, and you could no doubt pay for any services rendered."

"I am wealthy and your fee whatever it may be will not be a problem for me."

The front legs of the chair banged back down to the floor as Kip sat forward and took another drink. "When Brad called, he told me in no way other than the call did he want to be involved. He is and has been a good friend of mine since high school, so this conversation is just between you and me. Whether or not I take it to the people I work for depends on what your request is. But before we even get into that I want you to be aware we have already been involved with Max Miller in the past from a request from Brad. I'm not sure how my superiors will view additional action toward Miller. Depending on what you want accomplished, this McCulhay may be discussed but Miller might be off the table."

"Two things," said Simon. "At this point, you have no idea what it is I want accomplished and I have no idea what your fee will be. Let me just say this. Without even knowing what this will cost me I am willing to double whatever your fee will be if Miller is included in my request."

"That's pretty ballsy, making a statement like that," said Kip. "I think what you have said will go a long way when I go to my people. Now, what is it you want done, let me be very clear, I need names, a date, a location, and the actions that you require. There can be no secrets. We need to know everything right up front if we are to be involved."

"Agreed," said Simon. "This is what I want done…"

Stopping in front of what appeared to be a colonial two-story brick building connected to a block of similar brick structures, Max pointed at the gold-plated sign over the off-red door: WILLIAMSON FINANCIAL SERVICES. "Here it is…620 Carlisle Street…our new business. Sam is going to meet us here today. I give him the check for fifty grand, and he turns over the keys and all the records of the business."

Elizabeth looked up the street and remarked, "Just one block down from the town square. You're right in the middle of everything. Looks like a great location."

Max gestured, "Shall we go in?"

They walked through a small foyer complete with two antique coat racks and a hammered metal umbrella holder then entered the main room. Elizabeth stopped in the center of the room and turned in a complete circle. "This is so comfortable looking. It reminds you of someone's living room rather than a business office." She glanced around the interior, original dark hardwood floors polished to a high luster; a circular Pittsburgh Pirates throw rug centered in the front half of the office. To the left, there was a long, dark green leather couch in between two older walnut end tables upon which there was a neat stack of magazines. On the opposite side of the room, there were two black leather chairs, an antique floor lamp, and a coffee table. In the far corner of the room, there was a small table that housed a coffeemaker, napkins, and cups, along with a basket of sugar and cream packets. A crystal chandelier was suspended from the twelve-foot ceiling and the surrounding walls were decorated with framed photographs of professional sports teams from Pittsburgh: the Pirates, the Penguins, and the Steelers. A walnut desk sat near the back of the room fronted by two wooden chairs padded with green leather. Sitting on the couch Elizabeth commented, "Very cozy. I like your office. Is there just one room?"

Max joined her on the couch while answering, "No, there are two other rooms, a back office where we keep our filing cabinets and our main computer and then there is the restroom, and we also have a large walk-in closet where we keep supplies."

Their conversation was interrupted when Sam walked out of the back office and spoke, "I thought I heard someone come in."

Instantly Max stood and introduced Elizabeth, "Sam, this is Elizabeth, the girl I've told you so much about these past two years."

Sam extended his hand. "Nice to finally get to meet you, Elizabeth. I'm Sam Williamson. What do you think of the place?"

Elizabeth shook Sam's hand and complimented him, "I was telling Max that the office seems so comfortable. I imagine your clients feel right at home when they come in."

Snapping his fingers Max reached into his shirt pocket. "Before I forget here's the check for the down payment."

Sam unfolded the check, examined it, and then angled his thumb back over his shoulder. "The office keys are lying by the computer. There are two sets. I've gone through all the files and have made sure everything is up to date. Speaking of that I have sent out letters to all of our clients to inform them I am retiring and that you are taking over the business. The transition should not be that difficult as you have worked closely with all of our clients for the past two years. For the first few months after I leave, please feel free to call me at any time with any problems you encounter. If there is nothing else or any questions you have, I'm planning on taking you two uptown for a nice lunch." Smiling at Elizabeth Sam winked. "I can't wait to hear all about this wedding that's just around the corner."

CHAPTER THIRTY-TWO

Charley put a tall glass of orange juice next to a plate of bacon and eggs, placed his hand on Max's shoulder, and proudly announced, "Today is the day my son takes a wife."

Max stabbed a slice of bacon and added, "And speaking of my soon-to-be bride where is she? She has always been an early riser. I was looking forward to having breakfast together this morning."

"She is down at the community center with your mother and Ellen. There is a lot of work that goes into preparing the bride for her special day; her hair has to be done, then there's her nails and the dress has to be perfect. Besides that, the groom, meaning you, is not permitted to see his bride until she walks down the aisle or in this case, the beach. It's considered bad luck if you see her beforehand."

Max looked at the kitchen clock and frowned, "The wedding is not scheduled until one o'clock. It's now eight. What am I going to do for the next five hours?"

"It's more like three hours," said Charley, "I would strongly suggest that by around eleven you shower up and then get into your tux."

"That still leaves a lot of time for just waiting around. By the way… where is Kellem?"

"He got up before sunrise and went out to the beach. I told him to be back here at the house by nine. I figure the three of us can hop in the golf cart and we can show Kellem the island."

Elizabeth, dressed in a grey sweat suit sat in a cushioned chair as she stared out one of the side windows of the community center. At the moment she was surrounded by three professionals who were busily working on the bride's appearance. A hair stylist clipped here and there as she fashioned Elizabeth's blond hair, a makeup artist applied blush and eyeliner to her face while a lady from a solon in Beaufort worked on her nails. Ellen and Kate were busy making last-minute alterations to the gown. A snack tray of crackers and assorted sliced meats and cheeses, along with a pitcher of iced tea on a small, cloth-covered circular table was centered in the room.

The hairdresser held a mirror in front of Elizabeth and asked, "What do you think? Are the bangs the right length or do you want them a little shorter?"

Inspecting her blond hair in the mirror, Elizabeth replied, "I think my hair and the bangs look really good." Switching to another topic she remarked, "On the television this morning they said we are to get some rain later this afternoon. I hope it holds off until after the ceremony on the beach."

The stylist made some minor adjustments with a can of hair spray and a brush as she replied, "Since the wedding is going to start at one o'clock I think you'll be fine. According to what I heard the rain is not even supposed to hit Beaufort and the surrounding area which includes Fripp until about two. By that time, you'll officially be Mrs. Miller and you'll be back here for the reception." Standing in front of Elizabeth the stylist held out her hands and smiled in approval of her work. "Your hair looks stunning! You're going to be a lovely bride. Your future husband is going to be a very lucky man."

Thirty minutes later Elizabeth and Ellen sat together in a small dressing room. Ellen checked the time on a wall clock and reached over and took Elizabeth's hand. "It's just past eleven. In a little less than two hours you'll be standing on the beach and soon after that moment, you'll be married. I'm so excited for you. I want to thank you for not only inviting me to your wedding but allowing me to be your matron of honor."

Elizabeth took both of Ellen's hands in hers and smiled at her best friend. "The time since we were little girls on the farm has passed by quickly."

"I know," said Ellen, "It seems like just yesterday we were running through the fields surrounding the farms we grew up on. Back in those days who would have ever thought we would be married women someday? That was the furthest thing from our minds."

"Time has a way of changing everything," said Elizabeth. "The years went by, and I turned down Eli's proposal of a courtship, then later he winds up marrying you. I was leery of your marriage to Eli, but you have told me on several occasions that he is a changed man…no doubt because of the strong-willed woman you are."

"I too, had great concerns about the courtship that Simon Baumer proposed to you. I knew all along you had no intention of marrying the man, but I was also aware of the pressure of not only your family but the community for you to marry. And now look! In a couple of hours, you'll be married to the man you love…Max. It's a shame your parents are not going to be here to witness your wedding, but I understand how your parents must feel, especially your father. There are times, believe it or not, when I wished I would have made the decision to leave the Mennonite faith, but I don't think I would have had the strength to do so. You have called me a strong-willed woman, but I have to say the strength you have displayed in your decision to leave the faith and marry Max took a lot of courage. This morning during my prayer time I asked God to forgive me for my thoughts which were centered on the fact that tomorrow afternoon I'll be on a plane back to Lancaster County and my life as a Mennonite wife and you'll be on your way to a life that will be much more exciting than what I have to look forward to."

Elizabeth placed her right hand on Ellen's cheek, assuring her best friend. "Your life is going to be just fine…because you're a good person… the best person I know."

Max straightened his bowtie and adjusted his cummerbund, then turned to face Kellem. "How does your monkey suit fit?"

Kellem pulled at the tight collar and replied, "I never in my life had to wear one of these contraptions before. I'd just as soon be in my old dirty coveralls, but that would not be appropriate for a wedding, now, would it?"

"I suppose not," said Max. Checking the time, he suggested, "It's twelve-thirty, I guess we better head downstairs. My father said he wanted the three of us to have a short nip of whiskey out on the porch before we go down to the beach."

Kellem grinned, "I'm in!"

Charley held up the full bottle of whiskey when he saw Max and Kellem emerge from the kitchen. "It's about time. I was afraid I was going to have to get started by myself."

Charley poured a small measure of the light brown liquor into three glasses, set the bottle down, and raised his glass. "Here's to my son, Max, on his wedding day."

Max and Kellem each took a glass and quickly downed the alcohol. Kellem made a slight face but then grinned, "That tastes like another, but I think I'll hold off until the reception."

Opening the screen door Charley gestured at the wooden walkway. "Shall we gentlemen?"

They were no sooner out the door when Charley spoke to Kellem. "It's your job to get Max down to the beach. I have to go back to the house and meet the girls when they arrive as I am walking the bride out and then giving her away. See ya in a few!"

Max stepped from the bottom step onto the sand and looked at the wide beach. "Thank God the tide is out."

As they crossed the sand, he and Kellem took in the guests that were in attendance: Pastor Mullins, the Neiboks, Max's grandparents on his mother's side, Kate's sister and her family, Rich, his attorney, all four of Charley's employees and their families, assorted neighbors and friends from Summerville and Fripp Island; over fifty people in all. A white plastic, flower-covered arbor was positioned out a few yards from white folding chairs supplied by the community center. The pastor smiled as Max and Kellem approached. Stopping just in front of the pastor Max held out his hands. "We're here…now what?"

Pastor Mullins motioned with his hand. "I need you, Max on my left and then Kellem can stand to your left. Then, it's just a matter of waiting for your bride to walk down those steps and out here to the beach. After that, by the powers given me by the State of South Carolina, we'll get you and your lady hooked up…as they say."

Kellem asked Max, "You nervous?"

Max winked at his friend and answered, "A little, I guess. How about you?"

"Me! Why would I be nervous? You're the one getting hitched."

The low voices of the guests and the gentle sound of the waves were interrupted when the taped music began the wedding march. Bumping Max on his elbow, Kellem nodded toward the walkway as arm in arm Charley guided Elizabeth toward the steps. The guests stood and turned toward the walkway as they waited for the bride to step onto the beach. Ellen, and then Kate, adorned in a light blue summer dress followed at a distance, not wanting to take away from Elizabeth's arrival.

Max leaned toward Kellem and whispered, "I met her four years ago at a football game and here we are getting married."

Kellem smiled. "Life is good!"

Elizabeth stepped gently onto the sand, looked at Max, and gave him a wide smile. Walking between the rows of chairs and standing guests she looked to her right and left. She did not recognize one person but smiled at them as if she had known them for years. Three feet from the pastor Charley positioned Elizabeth in front of Max and then backed off to join Kate who had taken a seat in the front row. Max could not take his eyes off Elizabeth, the off-white taffeta and lace wedding gown fit her perfectly. A simple strand of pearls hung at her neck and her hair was topped with a flowered Tiera.

The pastor opened his well-used Bible and spoke to Max and Elizabeth. "If you would please join hands we can begin." Looking directly at the couple he then looked out at the guests and announced, "We are gathered here today…"

Nine minutes later the service ended with the pastor's final words as he raised his hand above Max and Elizabeth. "I now pronounce you man and wife." Nodding at Max, he continued, "You may now kiss the bride!"

The onlookers stood and applauded during the extended kiss when the bride and groom turned and faced the guests. Looking into Max's eyes, Elizabeth stated softly, "After four years …we made it."

"That we did!" beamed Max. A roll of thunder far out at sea sounded. Looking out into the vast ocean Max suggested, "We better get off the beach. It could be raining in a few minutes." Turning to Pastor Mullins, Max shook the minister's hand. "Thank you and we'll see you at the reception. Do you know where it is?"

"Yes, I've been there many times."

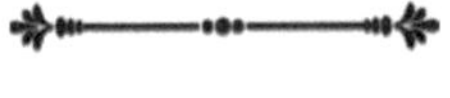

By the time Max and Elizabeth arrived at the community center, the festivities were in full swing. People were milling around, snacking on peel and eat shrimp, finger sandwiches, and Hors D' oeuvres while holding varied drinks in their hands. When the newly married couple was announced they received a short applause, then they made their way to the main table where Ellen and Kellem joined them. Following a few moments, Charley announced that dinner was catered by Johnson Creek and would be served buffet style out in the hall. Kellem stood and gave a toast and then blessed the meal. For the next hour, everyone relaxed while eating, Max and Elizabeth visited each table talking with guests easy listening music playing in the background. Finally, the DJ announced that the bride would have the first dance with Charley and then there was the mother-son dance and then Elizabeth and Max took the floor for their dance. After that, there was the cutting of the cake and then open dancing.

Kellem was just cutting into a large piece of cake when his cell rang. Excusing himself from the table he walked out into the hall which at the moment was deserted. He answered his phone, "Hello."

"Kellem…it's Sam Williamson…how was the wedding?"

"The wedding went fine. Right now, we're at the reception. I was just about to eat some cake. I'll tell Max and Elizabeth you called."

"There's more to this call than any concerns I may have about their wedding. I'm afraid there's some bad news."

"And I was having such a great day," said Kellem. "Let's have it!"

"I don't know how to put this, so I'm just going to go ahead and do the best I can. The business that Max recently purchased from me…well, someone broke in and destroyed the office!"

Looking around to make sure no one was listening, Kellem asked, "What do you mean destroyed?"

Fifteen minutes passed when Max looked out a window at the pouring rain and then asked Elizabeth, "Do you know where Kellem went?"

Elizabeth looked over the crowd and then replied, "No I don't. He excused himself from the table a while back and has not returned. I think he had a phone call."

Max also glanced at the people who were standing here and there, dancing and talking. "It seems like a long time for a phone call."

"It'll be all right," said Elizabeth. "Maybe he stepped outside to smoke his pipe."

Just then, Kellem appeared in the doorway to the hall as he made his way through those dancing. Elizabeth, pointing with a forkful of cake, remarked, "There he is."

Seated again at the table Kellem tucked a napkin in his starched shirt and picked up a fork and spoke to Elizabeth. "Had a phone call."

Elizabeth asked, "Is everything okay?"

"Yes…nothing to worry about. Now, let me get my teeth into this cake."

Charley pulled up his sleeve and looked at his watch, yawned, and then commented to his wife. "It's almost seven. Looks like just about everyone has left. It's been a long day and I'm ready to head back to the house."

Kate gestured while boxing up the last of the cake. "I agree, besides that these new shoes I purchased are killing my feet." Turning to Max and Elizabeth she asked, "How do you two feel, after all, it's your wedding?"

Elizabeth answered the question as she let out a long sigh. "I'm beat! I never imagined getting married could be so exhausting. I too am ready to head back to the house and just prop up my feet and relax."

Kellem bowed in front of Elizabeth and announced in a poor rendition of an English accent, "Your golf cart awaits, Madam!"

Max laughed. "Have you ever even driven a golf cart?"

"No, but how hard can it be? Turn the key, step on the gas, and down the road you go. Com'n. The sooner we get to the house the sooner we can all relax."

Ellen, who was cleaning off one of the tables suggested. "I can just ride with Max's parents if it's all right."

Taking his bride by the hand, Max exclaimed, "Well then, it's back to the house."

The newlyweds entered through the kitchen hand in hand where they found Charley, Ellen, Kate, and Kellem sitting on the screened-in back porch overlooking the ocean. Kellem, seeing the newlyweds first, stood and raised his drink, "And here they are…the Millers!"

Max, wearing jeans, a button-down yellow shirt, and deck shoes guided Elizabeth who was once again wearing the grey sweatsuit out to the porch. Looking out at the steady rain, she remarked, "I was looking forward to watching the sunset, but this rainy weather has put an end to that. Anyway, it's nice to be back here at the house. I am much more comfortable in what I'm wearing now than the wedding dress."

Seated on a wicker rocker Max commented while displaying his bright shirt and old jeans. "Me too!"

Kate crossed her legs and asked, "So what are your plans for the next two days? You stated earlier in the week that you were going to wait until Tuesday to go off on your honeymoon."

"Well, first of all," said Max, "Tomorrow morning Elizabeth and I have to run Ellen over to the Charleston Airport for her flight back to Philadelphia. Her flight is for 9:10 and she has to be there two hours ahead of time so that means we'll have to pull out of here no later than six. We'll hang around the airport and make sure she gets off okay, and then we plan on spending the day doing some light shopping in Charleston. We'll spend Sunday and Monday at the Summerville house and then on Tuesday we'll drive down to Florida where we board passage on a cruise ship for the Bahamas. Two weeks later we return, spend a couple of days with you guys, and then it's off to Gettysburg and back to the real world."

"What about you, Kellem?" asked Charley. "You're welcome to stay as long as you want but I know you want to get back and get ready for your move down to Florida."

"I hate to leave because it's so nice here, but I think I'll pull out tomorrow when these kids head over to Charleston."

Max, who had been looking at Kellem, thought for a moment and then spoke, "Kellem, you and I have known one another now for four years and we have worked together for two. Over that time, we have talked about many things and I think I know you quite well. I could be wrong, but I thought I just saw something in your eyes that does not reflect a moment of relaxation. Is there something wrong?"

"Well, I'll be," said Kellem. "I always thought I was rather good at shielding my thoughts, but I guess I wear them on my face. There is something wrong and I'm not sure this is the place or the time to bring it up, but as they say, the horse is out of the barn. I was going to wait and discuss this later or maybe even after your honeymoon, but the more I think about it the more I realize that you would want me to be right up front with you. Besides that, if you found out I knew about this and did not say something to you I think you'd be upset."

Kate, who was refilling her beverage, asked, "Whatever are we talking about?"

Kellem finished off his drink in two swallows and then spoke, "Okay, here it is. As you are probably all aware I received a call at the reception. I took the call out in the hall out of respect for Max and Elizabeth. The call was from Sam Williamson. He started by saying he hoped the wedding went well, but then got into the real reason for the call…the bad news."

Concerned, Max asked, "Is Sam all right? What about his family…are they okay?"

Kellem held up his hand. "Sam and his family are fine. This has nothing to do with them. He went on to tell me that your new business was broken into and the office was completely trashed…I mean destroyed."

"I don't understand," said Max. "Who would want to destroy the office?"

"I'm afraid at this point we do not know the answer to that. But before we even go down that road let me explain everything to you as Sam told it to me. The break-in must have occurred sometime last night. Early this morning about six thirty, Victor, the man who runs the tattoo shop above your business decided to go to work early as he had some painting he wanted to get done. Parking out back, like he always does, he noticed the back door to your business wide open with broken glass lying in the entrance. Sam told me you would know who this Victor is."

"Of course, I know who Victor is…Victor Sanchez. He's owned the tattoo parlor for over twelve years according to what Sam told me when I first started working there. Over the past two years of working for Sam, I bet Victor has been in our office once or twice a week. Every other Wednesday he brings us donuts and coffee. We even do his taxes. Victor, in my opinion, is as honest as the day is long. Whatever Sam told you that Victor said, well you can be assured it's true. So, what else did Sam say?"

"Between the open door and the broken glass, Victor decided to investigate. He sticks his head in the open door and yells in, 'Is there anybody in here?' No answer. Thinking it's odd that the door is open, and no one is around he goes back to his car and gets a flashlight, goes back, and ventures down the hall until he comes to the restroom. The door was open, the vanity had been ripped from the wall and broken to pieces, and the toilet had been pulled away from the wall and smashed to bits, almost like someone had taken a sledgehammer to it. The mirror was broken, there were several holes punched in the walls and there was spray paint everywhere, the walls, the ceiling, and the floors.

"He then continued down the hall where he came to the supply room, which was in much the same deplorable condition as the restroom. The shelves were torn down and broken in several pieces, the supplies were scattered everywhere and once again the room was full of holes that had been made in the walls and there was more spray paint."

Appalled, Kate sat up straight in her chair and stated, "Who in their right mind would do such a thing?"

Kellem held up his hand. "There's more. Victor entered the main office and then the back room. The furniture had been slashed with some sort of knife, both of the desks were smashed, and the drawers were dumped and then broken and tossed about. The two lamps were broken, the overhead lights were smashed and in keeping with the other rooms there were numerous holes in the walls and spray paint."

Charley looked at Max and then spoke, "Sounds like a pure case of vandalism to me."

Ellen jumped in on the conversation. "Maybe they were robbers looking for money or something of value."

Kellem stood and walked to the screened-in railing of the porch and looked out at the ocean. "Vandalism, robbery…those very things ran through my mind as Sam was telling me what he had seen. You see, Sam told Victor to call the police and that he was driving over to the office. By the time Sam arrived the police were there."

Kate asked, "What did the police think?"

"The same as almost anyone would think. It was a case of vandals or thieves. But then, while Sam was looking over all the damage, he noticed something the police had overlooked. Both computers were missing, not smashed, or thrown on the floor, but missing. The fireproof filing cabinets which there were four had been broken into and were tipped on their sides. If it had been vandalism the paperwork in the cabinets would have been strewn everywhere. Whoever was responsible for the break-in not only took the computers but all the paperwork as well. This very fact led Sam to believe that the criminals were not your common vandals or small-time crooks."

"Kellem brings up a valid point," said Max. "First of all, why would they take both computers?"

Kate, trying her best to understand, took a stab at answering her son's question. "Maybe it could be that the thieves wanted to try and sell the computers."

Chiming in, Charley added his two cents. "No, that doesn't make any sense, at least not in today's world. Years ago, thieves may have stolen computers, but nowadays everyone and their brother owns a computer. Aside from the fact that stolen computers can be sold so they can be refurbished and sold as used units is becoming a thing of the past. Brand new computers in this day and age have become very affordable, so why would most people desire a used one?"

Max stood and signaled for everyone to stop talking. "This is getting us nowhere. We can sit around here all night and try to figure out why it happened or who is responsible and all we'll wind up doing is creating more confusion. The only thing I can honestly say at this moment is this untimely incident changes everything. I don't mean to seem rude, but Elizabeth and I have a lot to talk about. We're going to take a walk on the beach and think this thing through. By the time we return, we'll inform you what we plan to do."

Elizabeth joined him at his side and spoke softly. "I think Max is right. We need to discuss what happened."

Watching Max and Elizabeth open the screen door and walk out onto the walkway, Kate poured herself another drink. "This is not the way I pictured those two spending the evening of their wedding."

Hand in hand Max and Elizabeth walked down the beach while Max kicked at a broken shell and then spoke. "We have some decisions to make and now that we are married, I want us to make them together. Tomorrow we still need to get Ellen to the airport and see her off. That fact does not change. What happens after that is what we need to discuss. I know you are looking forward to our cruise and the honeymoon, but with our business being temporarily destroyed maybe we should cancel until a later date."

"I was thinking the same thing," said Elizabeth. "We can go on a honeymoon anytime in the future. I feel right now getting the business back up and running is much more important. Besides, how could we even begin to enjoy our planned getaway with this current problem hanging over our heads?"

"Okay then, we agree the honeymoon is off for now. Do we still spend a couple of days down here or should we head back and get to work?"

"I'm going to leave that up to you," said Elizabeth, "but if you decide to go back to Gettysburg after we get Ellen off on her flight, I'm good with that."

Max guided Elizabeth down the beach and suggested, "We don't have to make that decision right now. We'll sleep on it tonight and make our decision in the morning."

Elizabeth ventured out to the edge of the water as Max continued their conversation. "You spent quite a bit of time with Ellen before the wedding and I'm sure you talked about several things. I have a question for you. I know you had her go to your folk's farm and invite them to the wedding. Besides telling your parents we were getting married; did she discuss anything else with them?"

"Since she was with my parents for over half an hour, she told me she let them know we were doing fine; about how you were buying a business and we were going to be purchasing a house. Why do you ask?"

"If you've told me once you've told me several times; about how close-knit the Mennonite community you lived in was. Do you think there is that possibility the information Ellen gave to your parents could have become known by Simon Baumer?"

"I can't say for sure, but it could have. Ellen told me she informed Eli, her husband, about the same things she told my parents. He could have run into Baumer or maybe even my father who may have had a chance conversation with Simon. Who knows?" Stopping, Elizabeth gave Max a strange look. "Are you trying to say that Simon Baumer could be responsible for the destruction of your office?"

"I'm just thinking ahead to the moment when we get back to Gettysburg when the police may ask me if I have any reason to believe anyone would ransack the office. I can think of no one other than Simon Baumer and maybe even Brad Sykes who would do this…and I say this for a partic-ular reason. Sam told Kellem that not only had the computers been taken but all of the paperwork from the file cabinets as well. This is not the work of vandals but more along the lines of someone who wants to hurt my business. Aside from my customers having their information exposed, what other reason would there be to take these things? Sykes and Baumer are the only two people I can think of who may fall into that category. Remember Kellem's barn fire? Both Sykes and Baumer were persons of interest, but no charges were brought against either because the police had no real proof either one was guilty. Both or one of them may still be harboring ill feelings toward me."

"I understand what you're saying, but I think that's a bit of a stretch. It's been over two years since that barn burning and the same amount of time since you've seen or talked with Sykes and Baumer. Ellen told me Simon had moved on with his life and as far as she knows has never men-tioned you or me. Why now, after two years, would he strike out at you? Another thing. Brad Sykes left school two years past and is probably up in New York State working for his father. If you decide to mention Sykes and Baumer as potential suspects all you may wind up accomplishing is stirring the pot which could ultimately backfire on you. In this case, if they are not guilty and have truly moved on leaving their ill feelings toward you behind them, if the police decide to question them you may wind up rekindling their anger."

"I hadn't thought of that, but there could be some truth to what you say. In the next day or so if we decide to head on back to Gettysburg, we'll have plenty of time to decide what we are going to do and what we may tell the police." Stopping, Max looked up at the darkening sky. "We better start back." Taking both Elizabeth's hands in his he looked out at the ocean and then spoke, "I want to say something to you. It's an apology."

"What could you possibly have to apologize for?"

"This is your wedding day, a day which is supposed to be filled with happiness and joy, and now look at what has happened…a situation that has put a damper on your special day."

Elizabeth squeezed his hands and looked into his face. "I did not marry you just for this day. We have a lifetime of days, weeks, months, years, and decades ahead of us. One of the things the minister said was for better or for worse. I know right now it may seem like we're getting off to a rough start but let me share something with you my grandfather told me when he was on his deathbed when I was a little girl. He said you can either fill your head with your problems or God's presence. I never forgot that. Believe me, I've tried both, and keeping your mind on His presence rather than your problems is a much more peaceful way to live your life. Everything is going to work out just fine."

Simon Baumer sat on his front porch watching the sunset in the west when his cell phone buzzed. Picking it up, he answered, "Simon Baumer."

A strange voice on the other end responded, "Mr. Baumer, the first part of your request has been completed." The phone then went silent as the caller ended the message. Simon removed a cigar from his coat pocket, lit up, and sat back as a broad smile came to his face.

CHAPTER THIRTY-THREE

Max crossed the Susquehanna River at Harrisburg and checked the time: 9:15. Yawning, he drum-rolled the steering wheel while looking out at the river. "It was just over twelve hours ago when we saw Ellen off in Charleston. I imagine she's home by now. We'll be pulling into Kellem's place at about ten. Since he left early this morning he's probably already at the farm. He told me he was not planning on leaving for Florida for another two weeks. Sam is planning on meeting me at the office at seven tomorrow morning. He said he'd have the police there to answer any questions I might have. Kellem asked me last night if it would be all right if he came along. Are you planning on going?"

"No, I think I'll just hang out at the farm," said Elizabeth. "I have two weeks of vacation time on my hands since we canceled our honeymoon. I want to get a head start on getting the entire house cleaned so that when we move from the summer house to the main house everything is neat. The barn needs swept out and the garden I planted needs weeding. Don't worry about me. I've got plenty to do to keep busy."

At 6:45 the next morning Max pulled into a parking space in the alley behind his office. Sipping at a hot coffee he had purchased at the gas station he always frequented, he looked at the backdoor of the building and spoke to Kellem. "I can't tell you how many times over the past two years I have walked through that door arriving for work or taking out the trash to the dumpster?"

Kellem stared at the door, now secured with a padlock and heavy chain, the door itself crisscrossed with bright yellow crime scene tape. Another car pulled in.

Looking over at the driver Max noticed that it was Victor, who smiled at him, got out, and walked to Max's open window.

"Good morning, Max. I'm sorry about what happened to your business. Sam called me last night and told me you and he were meeting the police here this morning. He said it might be a good idea if I was present since I was the first one on the scene."

"Nice to meet you," said Kellem. "How's the tattoo business?"

Victor grinned. "Couldn't be better. Are you in the market for a tat?"

Rolling up his sleeve Kellem displayed an American Eagle tattoo as he explained, "Nope, got mine some sixty years ago when I was serving in the Navy, but thanks just the same." Gesturing at the chained door Kellem remarked, "Guess we'll have to wait until someone shows up with the key."

Victor started to back away as he announced, "I think I'm going to go up the street and pick up a dozen donuts and some coffee."

Kellem reached into his pocket. "Need some money?"

"Nope, this is on me. Be back in a few."

Max stepped out of the Jeep, leaned against the brick wall of the building, and made a sarcastic remark. "Nothing like a glazed donut and a cup of coffee while one is wading through the destruction of their business."

Kellem reassured his friend. "When we get in there it might not be as bad as Sam made out."

A white Cadillac pulled in next to Max's Jeep and Sam hopped out holding a key in his right hand. "Sorry, I wasn't here when you arrived. Let's go on in. The police should be arriving in a few minutes."

Sam opened the door and stepped to the side. "Go on, but be careful. There's crap all over the floor. We left everything the way it was found. Before you go in I have to warn you…it's a mess!"

Max was the first through the door when he stopped and held out his hands. "It's so dark in here. I can't see a thing."

Kellem came to the rescue producing a small flashlight from his pocket.

Sam, who also was wielding a light shined it down the hall revealing broken sections of drywall, busted shelving, toilet paper, and assorted office supplies scattered about. "Wait here," said Sam. "I'll go on in and pull all the blinds up so some sunlight can get in."

Kellem bumped Max on his shoulder. "Looks like the police are here."

Two suited men stepped out of a car and approached Kellem and Max who had stepped back out of the building. The man in the lead stuck out his hand as he addressed both men. "Good morning gentlemen…Detectives Vanderway and Parks. Remember, we talked with you, what was it…two years or so back right after that barn burnt down."

"That's right," confirmed Kellem, "and to this day that crime remains unsolved. Hope we have better luck with this mess."

The hallway was suddenly flooded with the early morning sun when Kellem stepped back inside. "I guess we can go on in."

Wading through the assorted broken and strewn articles across the floor, Max shook his head in wonder, "Boy, somebody did a job on the place." Running his fingers down the wall he went on, "Randomly spray painting the walls seems immature."

They passed the supply room, and everything was just the way Sam reported it. Sticking his head into the small room, Max lowered his head as he kicked at some broken shelving. "Why would anyone do such a thing…. holes punched in the walls spray paint everywhere? Whoever did this must have been very angry."

Vanderway, standing directly behind him added, "Not necessarily. If this was done by vandals, they were probably laughing and having the time of their life."

Max backed out of the room and continued up the hall to the main room and the back office. Surveying the broken desks, slashed furniture, shattered lights, damaged walls, and paper that had been tossed everywhere, he picked up a binder and a calendar and placed them under his right arm. Looking around the main room, he moved some broken drywall out of the way and sat on the floor with his back to the wall. "It's going to take a small army and a lot of elbow grease to get this place back in order."

Kellem sat next to Max placed his right arm around Max's shoulder and reassured him, "Well for what it's worth you can count on me to give a helping hand. I've got all the tools we'll need and I can always call in my crew to help out. We can get everything you need from Lowes. Since I own a farm I have a contractor's discount we can use to purchase drywall, paint, and whatever else we'll need."

Max spoke to the detectives "I assume you have questions for me?"

"That we do," said Vanderway. "At this point, we have not one clue as to who may be responsible for this destruction. So, here's the million-dollar question. Do you have any idea or any reason why or who would want to destroy your business?"

Max thought about answering Vanderway's question with the idea that had been and still was floating around inside his brain, but responded with a simplistic, "No!"

Surprised at Max's answer, Kellem spoke up, "Well, this might not be any of my business. I mean I don't have a dog in this fight aside from Max being a close friend of mine, but I have to say I have my thoughts on who might be responsible for this catastrophe. The same two individuals who both Max and I thought could have been responsible for the burning of my barn, Simon Baumer and Brad Sykes."

Detective Parks, who had remained silent since entering the building, asked Max. "Do you concur with what Mr. McCulhay has stated?"

"Actually…I do, but the reason why I did not bring up their names is that I might just be making things worse than they already are. If I point out that Baumer or Sykes could have been responsible for all this, I'm quite sure you will question them. That's all well and fine but if it turns out they are not guilty or that we can't prove their involvement, the anger these two men had for me in the past may flare up." Displaying the surrounding destruction, Max explained, "I've got enough problems with just getting this place back up and running. I certainly don't need one or both of those men traveling the road of personal revenge again. It's been two years since I have heard from either one and I don't want to get involved in their lives."

Vanderway took a small pad and an ink pen from his pocket and made a note. "This is very interesting. The two people of interest in the barn burning turn out to be the same persons of interest in the destruction of your office. Does that not strike anyone else as a wee bit odd?"

Parks agreed, "I think it's more than odd. We've only been here for a few minutes and already we're beginning to connect the dots."

Max frowned, "Does this mean you intend on questioning Sykes and Baumer, because to be honest with you I'd just as soon not go down that road."

"I hate to say this, Mr. Miller, but we as the police have to follow up on whatever information we receive. This very well may be your business, but we just can't shove what happened here under the carpet. If we do not pursue any lead, even the slightest lead, it could be our ass. This has already been in the newspaper, not to mention all of your clients and the neighboring businesses who have been affected. We can't at this time just simply say, 'Oh well, let's move on and forget about this.' People expect us to do our job and the public in general will expect some sort of explanation as to why this happened.

"Now, down the road a few weeks, we at that point could report that we have no evidence that points at anyone, but right now that is out of the question. When we report back to our superior and inform him the two men who were persons of interest in that barn fire, which by the way is still an open case, are the same two mentioned as possible suspects in this case, I can guarantee you, Sykes and Baumer will be contacted and questioned. It very well could turn out the same as when we questioned them before resulting in a dead end, but they need to be questioned. I might just be grasping at straws here but I feel what happened here at your office may be what I would label as delayed retaliation or revenge which reveals a pattern. I can understand how you want to move on with your business and your life minus any further potential trouble from Sykes and Baumer, but we still need to look into their possible involvement."

Vanderway walked to the window and looked out at the street. Turning back, he addressed everyone in the room. "There is no question about this. Sykes and Baumer have to be questioned. But they could be approached in a way that does not include you Max or even you Kellem. We could simply state that since the barn burning case is still open and this current case involves the same persons of interest, we had no choice but to interrogate them."

Max was skeptical and replied, "I'm not so sure Sykes and Baumer would buy into that philosophy. These are not stupid people we are dealing with. I can only assume Sykes after leaving Gettysburg College went on to graduate with a degree in business and well, Simon Baumer no doubt has more money than all of us combined. He did not climb to the level of success he enjoys because he is stupid. I think they'll see right through your plan, but if you must speak to them, well then so be it."

"Well, if you want my two cents," said Kellem, "I think the police should go ahead with their investigation and speak with both Sykes and Baumer. Look at it this way. If we feel one of these people is responsible for this mess but are unable to prove it they have already done their damage. They would be foolish to add on additional retaliation, especially if they know by the police questioning them, they are under the microscope of the law."

The conversation was interrupted when Victor walked into the room, a box of donuts in one hand and a tray holding hot coffee in the other. Noticing the detectives, he placed the box and the tray on a small chair that somehow had managed to escape being damaged. "Good morning, gentlemen. My name is Victor. I own the tattoo parlor above. Sam asked me to drop by this morning in case you have any questions for me. To be honest I don't have anything to add other than what I already told the officers who responded right after I discovered the break-in."

"I do have a question," said Vanderway. "Looking around, is everything pretty much the same way as when you first walked in?"

Victor opened the box, removed a donut, and looked around. "Yes, I'd say so."

"So then, the computers were not here when you showed up."

"That's correct."

"And the file cabinets in the other room were knocked over on their side."

"Correct also."

Sam jumped in on the conversation. "When Victor called me, I drove right over and I noticed that all of the files…the paperwork stored in the cabinets had been taken as well."

"It seems odd to me," stated Parks, "if this was done by vandals that they would take the computers and all that paperwork. That fact alone tends to make me think someone is out to affect your business Mr. Miller… in a negative way. If I may ask, what type of information was stored in the computers and the file cabinets?"

"Look," said Max. "I just recently bought this business from Sam and before that, I was employed here for a little over two years. Over that time frame, I have worked closely with all of the clients listed on those computers and whose information was in those filing cabinets. Sam, on the other hand, ran this business for over the past half-century, so I think he is more qualified than I to tell you what vital information has been stolen."

Max gestured at Sam to continue, as the previous owner cleared his throat and then began to speak, "There are currently seventy-four clients on the records, some as new as just a few months old while others have been on the books for decades. Some of the owners of the businesses listed are some of my best friends and it saddens me to think their information has been compromised. The type of information we're talking about here varies from one client to the next but overall creates a serious problem for each one of them. I'll get back to that in a moment.

"The information that was stolen, depending on the client, includes their name, address, and contact phone number. In some cases, we're talking about social security numbers, credit card information, bank statements, tax information, how much money they earned, and even a list of their employees and other important private information. I have not discussed this with Max as of yet, but I would strongly suggest over the next few days he not only send a letter to each one of his clients explaining this stolen information problem, but he phone each client and explain the steps they need to take to protect their business and their employees. Believe it or not, the damage that surrounds us here in this office could pale compared to the potential damage if this information falls into the wrong hands."

Vanderway made a note on his pad and then addressed everyone in the room. "All the more reason for us to question Sykes and Baumer." Walking over to one of the file cabinets, he bent down and ran his fingers across a section just below the lock that was badly marred. "Look here," he noted. "Someone drilled into the secure lock to break into the cabinet. This was not done by a group of vandals. Whoever did this, well they knew what they were doing. It could be that the vandalism that was done is a diversion of why the perpetrators broke in. They wanted the information on the computers and in the cabinets. In other words, they could hope to gain identity theft via bank accounts, credit cards, tax information, and so on."

Getting up, Max walked over and examined both cabinets. "If what you say is true well then that eliminates Baumer and Sykes as potential suspects."

"Not necessarily. The combination of all the vandalism and the theft of the computers and the files could be an attempt to hamper your business. I mean, look at this place. You're not going to be conducting business here until you get this place back in shape. I'm no expert on how long it takes to repair this type of damage, but I imagine it'll take a few weeks. The entire time that your business is closed you're losing money every day, then there is the sad fact you could lose some of your valued customers. If I was one of your customers, in this case, I would understand and would not take my business elsewhere, but that's just me. Some of your clients may feel differently."

Max looked out the front window as he asked, "So when do you think you'll get around to questioning Baumer and Sykes?"

"We'll probably get that underway in the next few days. Right now, I think we're done here and if you don't have any other questions we'll head back to the office and talk with our superior to get the ball rolling." Handing Max one of his business cards, Vanderway suggested, "If you think of anything else or have any more questions, please feel free to give us a call. We'll notify you before we question Baumer and Sykes. Good day, gentlemen and I wish you speed, Mr. Miller, in getting your business back on its feet."

After the detectives vacated the office Victor extracted another donut from the box and held up his coffee. "I'm afraid I must leave also. I have two appointments this morning. I'll check in with you later as I would like to give you a hand in getting this cleaned up. I probably won't be free until after one o'clock. Talk with you then."

"It would seem that everyone is leaving," said Sam. "I too am going to head back home where I am going to create a form letter for all of your customers." After I get it set up, I'll run off copies and then I'll give you a call, Max. Each letter we send out must be personalized to each client. We can mail out the letters from my home and all the home calls to your customers can be made from there as well. Your clients must hear directly from you so they can be assured you have the situation under control. If necessary, I will also talk with some of the older, long-standing clients. When do you think you'll be ready to start cleaning this place out?"

Max picked up a section of broken drywall and answered, "I can see no reason why we shouldn't get started immediately. You in, Kellem?"

Bending down and picking up some broken baseboard Kellem grinned. "I wore these old jeans for just that reason. I say let's get started!"

"Good," said Sam. "When I get home, I'm going to call and have an industrial-size dumpster delivered out back for all the trash. I'll call you when I have the letters ready."

Max removed his cell from his pocket while speaking to Kellem who was dragging a large section of broken drywall down the hall. "I'm just going to give Elizabeth a call and tell her we've decided to stay here for a few hours to clear this place out. While you're out back will you bring in the push broom and trash bags we brought along?"

"Sure, and while I'm at it I'm going to walk up the street to Ace Hardware and purchase a shovel and a regular house broom. It's almost nine o'clock right now. I say we work until noon, grab some lunch uptown, then come back and put a few more hours in."

Max walked out of the restroom and dried his hands by rubbing them together. Joining Kellem at a window table, he remarked, "For just the two of us I think we got quite a bit done so far. We hauled all of the damaged furniture, shelving, and drywall out to the rear lot."

"And," added Kellem, "we managed to save quite a bit of the office supplies. When we get back, all there is to do is shovel out all the small debris and then sweep. Tomorrow we can begin to tear out the rest of the drywall, take down the damaged blinds, and toss out the broken toilet and vanity.

"Later on, you're going to require a good electrician and a plumber. I've never hung drywall so we're going to need a good drywall man in here. We can put up new shelving and do any painting that needs to be done. Have you put any thought into what it's going to set you back to get this place remodeled?"

"The thought has crossed my mind but It's hard to calculate the eventual cost because I'm not sure about all I'll need. If I had to take a wild stab, I'd say it's going to be thousands…maybe ten thousand…maybe more! I always knew someday I'd own my own business and along with ownership comes the expenses of operating. Two things, I never in my mind imagined I would own a business this shortly after graduating from college, and secondly, who would have thought that the business would be ransacked? When I purchased this business weeks ago, I was confident I could make it work. First of all, I am familiar with all of the clients, and I've worked with all of them. I am an educated individual who understands the ins and outs of running this type of business but yet I find myself amid a colossal catastrophe. I feel like I no more than got out of the starting blocks and I've fallen on my face. You saw the office. Does it look like I'm winning this race?"

Kellem sat in silence not quite sure what to say. Finally, he spoke; "Are you up for a little advice?"

Max smiled. "I guess I did come off a bit negative…didn't I?"

"Yeah, you did, but that's just a natural reaction. Take it from me. I've been around the block…meaning life, quite a few times and I can tell you from over eighty years of experience from time to time you're going to get knocked down. That's a given. This office destruction without a doubt has knocked you off your feet, but here's the thing! Are you going to get up?"

Biting into an egg salad sandwich, Max stared back at Kellem but remained silent.

"Look," said Kellem. "I think we can say you got punched right in the face, your nose got bloodied and right now you're not seeing that. You have some doubts about how to go about correcting this situation. You're on the mat in the center of the ring, flat on your back. You, and only you can decide if you're going to get up and when and if you do get back up what is your plan going to be. It's your decision and no one else can make it for you. Whoever perpetrated this disaster upon you, whether it be Brad Sykes, Simon Buamer, or whoever is probably having a good laugh.

"The way I see this is if you stand up and get to work all they will have accomplished is a short-lived intermission in your business. You have a lot of support surrounding you. You have a great wife in Elizabeth, and I am sure your parents will help you in any way they can. You not only have Sam and Victor in your corner but me as well. I am prepared to waive your rent payment for let's say three or four months to help you defray the expenses of getting the supplies you need to get the business back online. I do not doubt your ability to see this tragedy through. I have faith in you, and I know the others as well. So, what's it going to be?"

Max pushed his sandwich to the side, sat back, and flashed a wide grin across the table. "I'm going to miss you when you're gone. You always know the right thing to do or say. I can only hope that by the time, and that's if I make it to your age, I will have acquired the level of wisdom you seem to possess. My answer to you is *yes!* I am going to get up and fight and as soon as we finish up with our lunch we're going to walk back down the street to the office and tackle that monster."

Elizabeth, wearing an old pair of faded overalls over top of one of her favorite work t-shirts pulled a small section of weeds from the dirt with her gloved right hand. Tossing the weeds in a bucket, she sat in the garden dirt and wiped her brow with a handkerchief while staring up at the bright after-noon sun. For late June it was hotter than normal. There was not the slight-est hint of a breeze in the air and the nearby trees thirty yards out from the fence were perfectly still, not a single leaf moving even the least bit. Staring up at the blazing sun she imagined that it was just as hot over in Lancaster County on her father's farm. She often thought about her parents, and this was one of those moments. Would her father ever forgive her for leaving the Mennonite faith, would she and Max ever be welcomed at the farm where she was raised? Would her mother and father ever accept her future children despite the fact they were born outside of their beliefs? Bowing her head she said a short prayer, "That's all in your hands, Lord. Your will be done."

Back on her knees she moved down the row of vegetables and started to reach for more weeds when she was startled by a muffled voice. She looked in the direction of the fence where she thought the voice came from but saw no one. Turning, she looked at the barn and then the house; no one. Think-ing it was her imagination she went back to her weed-pulling. Seconds later she again heard the indistinguishable voice.

Standing, she stared at the fence line where she was sure the sound of the voice came from, but there was no one there. She quickly checked the barn and then the house again. No one. Removing her gloves, she dried her sweaty hands on her coveralls and walked to the edge of the garden all the while looking at the fence and beyond. The first time she heard the voice she automatically wrote it off as her imagination, but the second time she heard it, she knew it was real. She wasn't sure what the voice had said, just that she had heard it.

Walking across the yard she stopped at the fence that bordered the farm property from the battlefield and looked off into the trees at the top of the slight rise. It was the height of the tourist season and there were battlefield visitors scattered around the surrounding fields. Maybe she had heard a voice that had come from the trees, but that did not seem possible as the voice had been too loud to come from that distance.

Leaning on the fence she thought about what both Max and Kellem had talked about from time to time. Those restless dead Confederates that had at one time been sloppily buried over one hundred and fifty years in the past where a gully at the end of the fence line had at one time been located. But all those bodies had been exhumed by the government and properly buried in the Gettysburg Battlefield National Park. The thought that she may have heard one of the many ghost voices that from time to time could be heard from the area of the fence was rapidly erased from her mind.

She turned from the fence but then noticed a man and a woman with two small children emerge from the tree line at the top of the slope. The small boy and what appeared to possibly be his sister ran down the slope toward the cannons and the fence much to the disapproval of the woman, who shouted for them to stop! The young girl started to stop and heed her mother's warning but when she saw her brother continue, she ran after him. Elizabeth watched as the boy approached the fence, ducked in between the wood rails quickly, and started to climb on one of the cannons. The woman, out of breath reached the fence and sternly ordered the boy, "Mitchell! Get off that cannon and get back over here…now!" The boy reluctantly obeyed the woman as Elizabeth looked on without a word.

Finally, the woman apologized. "I am so sorry. I guess they did not notice the no trespassing or private property signs. I do apologize. They are just so excited about being out here on the battlefield, especially Mitchell. He just loves all the cannons."

"No harm done," said Elizabeth. "I don't imagine the boy could damage a cannon."

By this time, the man who had walked down the slope also apologized. "We're sorry for the invasion of our children onto your property."

Elizabeth smiled at the couple. "It's quite all right. They're just trying to have some fun."

The woman reached across the top of the fence and extended her right hand. "My name is Stella Wilson, and this is my husband, Stan. These two little monsters are our son and daughter…Mitchell and Molly."

Taking the woman's hand Elizabeth responded, "Elizabeth Miller. My husband and I live here on this farm."

Stan, touching the private property sign, inquired, "So I take it the three cannons are not part of the battlefield exhibits?"

"That's correct," stated Elisabeth. "According to what the owner of the property tells us these three cannons are the result of seven destroyed cannons that were used here during the Battle of Gettysburg. From all of the parts that were found in the surrounding area, the previous owner of the farm was able to construct these three." Tapping the top rail of the fence, she went on, "And parts of this fence, most of it, I am told is the actual fencing that was out by the Chambersburg Pike back some one hundred and fifty years ago during the three-day battle."

"Very interesting," said Stan. "Mitchell here, over the past year has shown quite a bit of interest in the Civil War and plans on turning in a paper next year for school on what he did over the summer. I hate to ask but do you think we could get a picture of him and his sister with you by one of the cannons."

Being gracious, Elizabeth replied. "Of course…come on over children."

Following three quick photos, Stan ordered his family, "I think we have taken enough of this nice lady's time. Let's get back up the hill. It's a long walk back to the car."

Elizabeth watched the family of four walk back up the slope, confident that the mystery of the voice she had heard had been solved. The laughter of the children from the trees had no doubt been carried down into her backyard. "Ghost voices….how ridiculous!"

CHAPTER THIRTY-FOUR

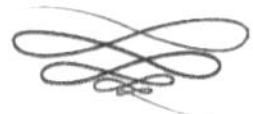

Kellem, walking out of the backroom displayed himself while speaking to Max. "I think I got more paint on myself than I did the walls."

Max, in the process of painting the baseboards in the main room, looked up and upon seeing the old man, laughed: off-white semi-gloss paint in his hair, streaked on the right side of his face and both arms, his coveralls spotted here and there with the thick white substance. "You look like you were in a paint war. I hope you won!"

Holding up a brush, Kellem grinned, "I did…just finished the second coat. I think that'll do the trick, but we'll have to wait for it to dry before I tackle the hallway. Where is Elizabeth?"

"She's out back painting the baseboards for the supply room and the rest of the trim work." Taking a break Max sat by the newly installed front door and looked around the office. "When we walked in here a week and a half ago if you would have told me we'd be this far along I wouldn't have believed it."

Joining him, Kellem asked, "Heard from any of your clients?"

"After we mailed out the letters, I followed up with phone calls and so far, everyone seems to understand the situation we are facing. As of today, I have not received any news about any of my clients taking their business elsewhere. Sam has been a big help and if not for many of my clients being longtime friends of his, I may have lost a lot of business."

The conversation was interrupted when Elizabeth. who was covered with more paint than Kellem, walked in and announced, "Between the two of us we must be wearing at least a gallon."

Elizabeth laid her brush on a paint-stained rag on the floor, stretched, and then looked at Max. "I don't know about anyone else but I'm ready for lunch."

"Sounds good to me," said Max. Just as he was about to get up his phone buzzed. Digging the device from his pocket he answered, "Hello."

Not paying him any attention Elizabeth walked to the newly remodeled bathroom to get cleaned up while Kellem slipped out the backdoor for a pre-lunch smoke with his pipe.

Minutes later Elizabeth and Kellem walked side by side into the main room where they found Max securing the lid back on a gallon of paint. Looking at the duo he held up a small hammer in his hands and explained, "The call I just received was quite interesting. It was Detective Vanderway. He was calling me from a gas station in Elmira, New York which happens to be on the way to Ithaca, where our dear friend Brad Sykes currently resides. According to Vanderway, they contacted the police in Ithaca and a detective up there is going to accompany Vanderway to the place where Sykes is employed. Vanderway told me he was planning on meeting the detective in Ithaca at police headquarters, discussing the case there, and then the two of them will pay Brad a visit around two o'clock."

Kellem, placing his pipe back inside his coveralls asked, "Did Vanderway say anything about questioning Baumer?"

"No, he didn't mention Baumer, and I didn't have a chance to ask him that question. I'm sure they'll get around to Baumer, but apparently, right now they are focusing on Sykes."

"Enough with all this talk about Sykes and Baumer," said Elizabeth. "I'm famished. Let's head up the street and grab a bite. In the next ten minutes, I plan to be enjoying some lunch."

Detective Vanderway made a right turn from State Street as he remembered the address he was looking for: 120 E. Clinton. He hadn't even traveled the length of a football field when he arrived at his destination; The Ithaca Police Department. The building was a brick structure on the left flanked on both sides with ample parking, and the right parking area was filled with police cruisers and other public official vehicles. Pulling into a visitor's spot on the left side of the building, Vanderway got out, straightened his tie adjusted his sports coat, and walked to the main double glass door entrance. Hesitating inside to get his bearings he saw an elevated desk that was signed: INFORMATION.

He no sooner stood in front of the desk when a female officer smiled and spoke, "Good afternoon, sir. What can we do for you?"

The Detective responded, "My name is Detective Vanderway. I'm with the Gettysburg, Pennsylvania Police Department and I have a one o'clock appointment with Detective Martinson."

She scanned the desk and then replied. "I have a note right here from the Detective. He said he is expecting you and that I should let him know when you arrive. If you just walk down the hall on the left his office is the third door on the right. I'll give him a call and tell him you're on the way."

Giving the officer a sloppy, but casual salute Vanderway thanked her and started down the corridor while checking the time on his watch. He was fifteen minutes early.

Coming to the third door he noticed a small rectangular metal sign centered on the door that read, Det. Martinson. He knocked twice then opened the door and entered, closing the door behind himself. A man wearing a grey suit was just hanging up the phone.

Standing, the man introduced himself, "Detective Martinson…you must be Vanderway."

Vanderway walked to the desk and extended his right hand. "Nice to meet you, Detective."

Martinson gestured at a wooden chair. "Please, have a seat. Would you care for coffee, maybe a bottle of water?"

"No thanks…I had breakfast on the road which included three cups."

Taking his seat, Martinson inquired, "How was your trip? Did you have any trouble locating our department?"

"No trouble at all. Your directions were right on the money. I was going to fly up but when I found out it was just under a four-and-a-half-hour drive, I hopped in my car and drove up. I've never been to this part of New York State before. It's quite beautiful."

"I like it here. I was born and raised in the area. Graduating from Ithaca College, I met my wife while on vacation in Virginia quite a few years back and now I find myself trying my best to keep the peace here in town. Speaking of the peace how are things down in Gettysburg?"

"For the most part, there is not a lot of crime in Gettysburg and the surrounding area, but we do have an occasional mishap, which is why I am here today."

"Speaking of that," said Martinson. "After we talked on the phone yesterday, I did a little checking on Brad Sykes. First of all, let me say he comes from a very powerful and well-liked family. Harmon Sykes, his father is not only the wealthiest man in Ithaca, but one of the richest in the state which is saying quite a bit when you consider how much wealth there is in New York City itself. If Harmon were to run for mayor of this city, he would win hands down. He has contributed generously to our local charities and at one time sat on our city council. He owns several businesses not only here in town but throughout the state.

"Now, when it comes to his son Brad, one would think the apple does not fall far from the tree, but in Brad Sykes' case, the boy has fallen a great distance from the trunk. He is not anywhere the man his father is. When he was growing up as a young lad his parents always made sure he had the best education money could buy so he always attended exclusive, private schools. Needless to say, Brad was always a problem for his parents. I can't tell you how many schools he got booted out of because of his rebellious behavior. That boy was in one scrape after another, but his father always bailed him out. Finally, with no other choice, Harmon decided his son would complete his last two years of high school here at Ithaca High. He graduated and went on to college and according to you attended Gettysburg for his freshman and sophomore years."

"That's correct," said Vanderway. "I met Brad and his father, Harmon, during an investigation we had regarding a barn fire that we felt Brad may have been involved with, but we had no real proof, so we had to pass on Brad as a person of interest. The college as it turns out grew tired of his antics while at school and suggested he transfer out, which I think was just a polite way of kicking him out of school. That was two years ago and the last we ever heard about Brad Sykes. Now, with this new case of the destruction of a business that happens to be owned by a student, he bumped heads with the college, that and some other interesting facts have led us to shine the light of suspicion once again on Sykes. So, we decided he should be questioned, so here I am. What do we know if anything about Brad Sykes today?"

"We did a little snooping around and Brad Sykes has cleaned up his act. He completed his education here at Ithaca College and is now employed by his father running a chemical and cleaning supply business here in town. The word around town is he met a girl while in school. She happens to be from a wealthy family from down in Elmira. Brad currently is engaged to this girl, and they plan to wed later this year. It is said they are building a large lakefront home a few miles up the coast of Cayuga Lake. So, for right now Brad Sykes seems to be the model citizen, at least around these parts."

"Okay," said Vanderway. "How, when, and where are we going to question Sykes?"

Standing, Martinson took his sports jacket from a wood coat rack and slipped it over his broad shoulders. "I thought you and I could just drive over to his place of business and pop in. It's only about a twenty-minute drive. We have not contacted him so his reaction to our little visit should prove to be interesting. Come on I'll drive and you can fill me in with all the ins and outs of this case."

After leaving the downtown section they drove up Rt. 34, the lake spread out to their left. Vanderway admired the crystal-clear water while remarking, "That is a beautiful lake. How large is it?"

Martinson, gazing out at the passing expanse of water elaborated, "I think the lake is around sixty-six square miles and I know it's the longest lake in the Finger Lakes Region. Cayuga Lake is one of the perks of living in this part of the state. I own a small powerboat and I spend a lot of time on the lake fishing. I can't tell you how many picnics my family has had along the shoreline." Changing the subject, Martinson pointed to a road sign coming up on their left. "We're almost there. We take a left up ahead, drive down that road which runs perpendicular to the lake, then in about a quarter mile we'll be at Sykes Chemical and Cleaning Supply."

"How do you think Sykes will react to our visit?"

"I don't have any idea. I've only seen him one time since he's been back and that was right after he returned here to town. He got a speeding ticket on the other side of town. When he came into the office to pay the fine, I saw him as he was leaving. He simply nodded at me and moved on. Other than that, I see him from time to time cruising around town in the Corvette he owns. I've never spoken to the young man. I've met his father and have spoken to him on several different occasions around town; golf outings, charity events, stuff like that. Brad Sykes probably doesn't even know I exist. You no doubt know the boy better than I. You said you questioned him before. How do you think he'll react?"

"I only met him one time and that was two years ago. I recall him as being very smug and impolite. His father, Harmon, was there and one of our local attorneys was also representing him. He was not the most cooperative young man I've ever met. But that was then. You tell me he has cleaned up his act so he may very well turn out to be completely different than what I remember. But even so, the fact that he is not expecting us could take him off-guard. If he does have anything to hide it might show in his mannerisms or the way, he answers our questions."

Pulling up in front of a brick and glass three-story structure situated next to the lake, Martinson got out and admired the building. "Doesn't look much like what you would think a chemical and cleaning supply business would look like…does it?"

Vanderway agreed and followed Martinson to the main entrance as he listened to the Detective explain. "This is their main office. They also own a large warehouse about a mile down the road." Opening the door, Martinson gestured, "After you!"

The interior of the building was impressive, wood floors polished to a high luster, expensive flock-painted walls, extravagant and very modernistic lighting, the entire right side of the spacious room adorned with a floor-to-ceiling glass case housing examples of the many products the company offered. The back wall was glassed-in, a backdrop of the lake creating a feeling of warmth and comfort. An older woman was seated behind a long black desk. Upon seeing the two new arrivals she stood and welcomed their visitors. "Good afternoon, Gentlemen…what can we do for you?"

Martinson approached the desk while Vanderway admired the vast product display in the glass case. Martinson spoke professionally. "We are here to see a Mr. Brad Sykes. Is he available?"

The woman walked to the side of the desk as she replied, "Yes, I believe he is in at the moment. Do you have an appointment with Mr. Sykes?"

"No, we do not, but I believe he'll have time to see us." Moving his sports coat to the side he displayed his police badge attached to his belt as he went on, "Detective Martinson with the Ithaca Police."

Vanderway remained quiet while joining Martinson and flashed his open wallet which housed his badge.

The woman placed her right hand over her heart and softly replied, "Oh my! Is there a problem?"

Martinson ignored the woman's concern. "Why don't you just give your Mr. Sykes a ring and tell him we'd like to see him."

The woman straightened her short hair and raised her chin in pride as she responded, "Just let me give him a call."

Seated once again at her desk she pressed a button on the intercom system and after a few seconds spoke, "Mr. Sykes…the Ithaca Police are down here in the lobby. They would like to have a few moments with you?"

Listening intently, the woman replied, "Yes…I'll tell them." She then released the button, sat back, and spoke with what little authority she had at the moment. "He said to give him a minute or so then you can head up to the third floor. You can take the elevator over there in the corner or the stairs on the left."

"I hate elevators," said Martinson, "We'll take the stairs. By the time we get up there that will give your boss his minute."

Following Martinson up the stairwell, on the second floor, Vanderway remarked, "I wonder why Sykes needed a minute or so. What do you think he's hiding?"

"Probably nothing," said Martinson. "I think he's just giving himself some time, however short it may be, so he can collect his thoughts. Think about it. You're sitting there in your office and out of the blue the local police are here to see you. If he has something to hide he's in the process of doing that right now…if he can. If he doesn't have anything to hide he is probably wondering why we are here to see him. He doesn't know who I am so my appearance may not be a big deal as far as he may be concerned, but you, on the other hand, are a different matter. Do you think he'll remember you from when you questioned him two years ago?"

"I think he will. It was a rather intense hour or so with his head on the chopping block. He was nervous, rude, uncooperative, cocky, and quite frankly not interested in being there. I got the feeling he thought he was better than me. Right now, he is expecting someone from the Ithaca Police to walk into his office, not someone from the Gettysburg Police. He may be preparing himself to receive you, but I'm sure he'll be somewhat shocked to see me once again in his life."

On the third-floor landing to the left, there was a set of large oak double doors that were closed. Vanderway sarcastically remarked, "Well that figures. You would think that most executives expecting someone to come to their office would have the door open and that they would be waiting to greet you with a friendly handshake. That closed door means Brad Sykes still thinks he is better than most people."

"I'm not even going to knock," said Martinson. "Let's just go on in!"

Pushing open the door on the right Martinson entered, Vanderway on his heels. Brad sat behind his oversized desk as he watched the two men enter. Standing, he welcomed them as he spoke in wonder. "Good afternoon, gentlemen. And what do I owe the presence of the Ithaca Police here in my office to this day?" It was then that he noticed Detective Vanderway and the smile on his face faded but then he quickly recovered, reaching for Martinson's hand. "Brad Sykes…and you are?"

Shaking Brad's hand, Martinson made the introductions, "Detectives Martinson and Vanderway. We've never met before, but I think you and Detective Vanderway are familiar with one another."

Brad nodded at Vanderway but sat back down refusing to shake his hand. "Yes, I remember the Detective from Gettysburg. That was what… two years ago…right?"

Vanderway answered, "Thereabouts!"

Brad gestured at two black leather chairs situated in front of the desk as he offered, "Please be seated."

Both Detectives sat while Brad continued to speak, "I can only assume since Detective Vanderway is in our presence that you have come to speak to me about an issue in Gettysburg…otherwise why would he be here?"

"Very astute, Mr. Sykes," said Martinson. "I think I'll let Detective Vanderway explain his reason for being here." Nodding at Vanderway, Martinson sat back while removing a small pad and pen from his coat.

"Before I begin," said Vanderway, "let's take a little stroll down memory lane. I assume you remember the name…Max Miller?"

Brad threw up his hands and remarked smartly, "Here we go…Max Miller! I have not seen him or heard anything about him for the past two years. Look, it's no secret Max and I had our differences. We roomed together our freshman year, but we were never really that close. You know the story, Detective. I made what some folks would say is a crude remark about Miller's girlfriend and he popped me on the nose, my father had intentions of suing Miller but backed off. Everyone knew I was not happy with my father's decision, and I made it known around campus that I was going to get my revenge, which by the way never really happened.

"Sometime later, the next year I ran into Miller on that tree farm, and we had words again. It was right after that when the McCulhay barn burned down. I very quickly became a person of interest and you and another detective questioned me. You had no proof of my involvement, but because of that and some other minor incidents at school, I was asked to leave Gettysburg College…which I did.

"To tell you the truth I was glad when I got back home here and finished my education at Ithaca College. My past days while attending school in Gettysburg are what a lot of people would say are blemished and they are certainly entitled to their opinion. But that's all in the past. Since returning here to theca I have turned over a new leaf. I graduated, received my degree in business and here I am today working for my father. The Brad Sykes you see seated before you today gentlemen is nothing like the Brad who attended school down in Pennsylvania. Why, I have even met a girl in school who I happen to be engaged to and we plan to wed later this year, so why you are here to see me remains a mystery." Sitting back as if he were proud of his new life, Brad stared at both Detectives as he waited for a reply.

Vanderway gave Martinson a look indicating he was not impressed with Brad's rundown of his current life. Leaning forward he emphasized, "Mr. Sykes, it is all well and fine that you have turned over a new leaf as you say, but you are still a person of interest regarding a crime recently committed back down in Gettysburg."

Brad, gesturing in doubt, responded, "I have no earthly idea as to what you speak of. Please, enlighten me!"

"Shortly after Miller's graduation, he purchased a local business there in town. Then, a few weeks later someone broke in and destroyed the business, stealing two computers and some important paperwork which has caused a lot of concern in our community."

"Well, that's unfortunate," remarked Brad, "but what does any of that have to do with me? I could care less about Max Miller, his business, or his life. I've moved on and I have no hard feelings toward him whatsoever. Let me set the record straight gentlemen. I did not, two years in the past, burn down McCulhay's barn nor am I in any way involved in the destruction of this new business he has acquired. Your concern over me as a person of interest in this recent crime is nothing more than an exercise in futility. You're grasping at straws by coming here to question me in hopes of apprehending your culprit. I know nothing of this crime."

"That may be," interjected Martinson, "but we still have questions for you." Positioning his pen over the pad he went on, "Can you account for your whereabouts on Friday, June the nineteenth?"

Brad displayed a cunning smile and stated in a firm tone, "You know what, Detective. I don't think I'm going to answer any of your questions without the presence of my attorney and my father."

Martinson confirmed, "You do realize that by not cooperating with us, the police, we can haul you out of here right now and take you down to police headquarters where the questioning can and will continue!"

Brad remained steadfast in his demeanor. "You must think I just hopped off the back of a turnip truck, Detective! If I have learned anything from my father over the years it is how the world works, especially the law. I am well aware that you can take me downtown, but let it be known that before I leave this office all it will take is one phone call to my lawyer, and by the time we arrive at police headquarters or shortly thereafter he or one of his staff will be there to represent me. I don't imagine you'll have me there for more than ten to fifteen minutes and I'll be walking out the door leaving you two looking like the fools you are. Considering who my father is and the weight he swings in this town do you think you can come to my place of employment, one of his many businesses, and intimidate me?"

Feeling as if he were in control, Brad stood and walked to the window as he lit up a cigar, looked out at the lake then turned and addressed both men. "You can question me, but that is not going to transpire until some-time tomorrow. When you leave which I have a feeling will be in the next few minutes you can just go on back to your headquarters and wait for a call from my attorney, which you will receive within the next few hours. At that time he will explain to you where he, my father and of course myself will meet with you. I can guarantee you it will not be at police headquarters or even one of my father's businesses. It will be at a neutral location, where I feel comfortable. Then, in the presence of my lawyer, you can ask your questions."

Vanderway, a bit shocked, looked at Martinson not quite sure how to respond. Martinson looked back and shrugged and also remained silent.

Brad grinned at their discomfort. "Strike out...did we gentlemen? It's not as bad as it may seem. This may work out in your favor. Tomorrow you can not only ask your questions but believe it or not I may have some information that may solve this crime committed against Miller. That's all I'm going to say for now. But know this, tomorrow when we meet the in-formation, I have to share with you may or may not be relevant, but I think it will be something you will be quite interested in. Until then gentlemen."

Walking to the closed door, Brad opened it and suggested, "I believe that's all the talking I am prepared to do today. If you don't mind gentlemen, I have things I must attend to, one of them being contacting my attorney. Good day!"

Martinson stopped on the second-floor landing and apologized to Vanderway. "Looks like we just lost the first round."

"That may be," said Vanderway, "but the fight has just begun. Looks like I'm going to spend the night here in town. Where would you suggest?"

"Well, if you want to stay close to the police department you could get a room at the Ithaca Hotel. It's right downtown in the center of everything. I can call the office and have them book you a room."

"Sounds good," said Vanderway. "I assume you'll call me when you hear from Sykes' attorney?"

"Better than that. After we get you checked in, you and I can have a nice dinner at the hotel and then maybe a couple of drinks at the bar. That should eat up a few hours and by that time maybe we'll get the call."

"After being in the unpleasant presence of Brad Sykes dinner and a few drinks sounds quite relaxing."

Three hours later, following dinner and conversation, the two detectives were perched on bar stools at the Ithaca Hotel bar nursing their second round of drinks. Martinson was just about to take a sip of his scotch and water when his cell phone buzzed. Holding up an index finger he stated, "Have to take this call. With any luck it might be Sykes' attorney." Answering the phone, he spoke professionally, "Martinson here." After a short pause, he spoke again, "I see…nine o'clock tomorrow morning…we'll be here."

Placing his phone on the bar next to his drink he confirmed. "That was none other than Melvin Smithe, the highest-paid and most powerful attorney in the city. They say that if you're sitting on his side of the table more than likely you'll come out on the winning side of things. I've seen him in action in court. He's quite good. He, Harmon Sykes, and of course, his son Brad will meet with us, believe it or not right here at the hotel in a large suite at the top of the building. Harmon is half-owner of the Hotel and suggested we meet here."

"So", asked Vanderway, "what's our plan?"

Martinson looked at his watch, took a drink, and replied, "It's still early. We've got plenty of time to talk before tomorrow morning. Let's lay out our plan."

Martinson checked the time and took the last swig of his third drink. "It's just after eleven. My wife is probably wondering where in the hell I'm at. I'm going to head home and get a good night's rest. I'll meet you here in the lobby at seven-thirty. That'll give us over an hour to have breakfast, then we'll head up to the top and meet Brad, Harmon, and Mr. Smthe. Have a good night. I'll see you in the morning."

Stepping into the elevator Martinson pushed the tenth-floor button and the door closed. Standing near the back of the moving cubical, Vanderway remarked as he patted his stomach. "I think I overdid it at that breakfast buffet. I feel like I put on an extra ten pounds. I think it was all those pancakes I choked down my gullet."

Martinson watched as the blinking numbers indicated that they had just passed the fourth floor. "I always eat a big breakfast. It's the most important meal of the day and besides that, after I get to the office depending on what the day brings, I might not have any time for lunch, at times… dinner."

The elevator came to a slow halt and the automatic, stainless-steel door slid open. Martinson stepped out and placed his hands on his hips. "Are you ready for this?"

"I think so," said Vanderway. "It's not like I'm going to be walking into a room of strangers. I've met and talked with Brad and his father before. Now this attorney…Mr. Smithe is a different matter. If he's as good as you say we might have a difficult time."

Looking at a set of doors labeled Suite One, Martinson started down a marble-tiled floor. "Smithe said we were to meet in Suite Three."

Vanderway followed Martinson down a wide corridor and stated, "It's going to be interesting to hear what information Brad Sykes has for us. Personally. I think he's full of bull crap. Otherwise, why would he require an attorney?"

At Suite Three, Martinson took a deep breath and suggested, "Shall we!"

Rather than just barging in, Martinson knocked on the oak door and waited. The door was opened by none other than the well-dressed Harmon Sykes who welcomed the new arrivals. "Gentlemen, please come in!"

Vanderway trailed Martinson through a spacious foyer and across a dining area to a lavish living room complete with two white couches on either side of a fourteen by twenty foot black and white oriental rug. A matching white chair was positioned at the far end of the rug in front of a large plate glass window that offered a spectacular view of the city. Decorative paintings and potted plants were tastefully placed around the room. Brad, in a light beige suit, was seated on the couch on the right and a man dressed in a dark blue pinstriped double-breasted suit sat comfortably in the chair with his right leg crossed over his left. He wore a blue and yellow power tie and his feet were encased in black, Italian leather wing tips.

Looking at the Rolex on his wrist he stood and remarked, "Right on time, Detectives. I admire punctual people." Reaching for Martinson's hand he went on, "Melvin Smithe, I believe we have met on a few occasions, probably in court."

Martinson shook the attorney's hand and introduced Vanderway, who likewise shook hands.

Smithe motioned at the empty couch on the left and suggested, "Please be seated."

He then sat back in his chair while Harmon joined his son on the opposite couch. "I believe everyone else knows one another. Detective Vanderway here and one of his associates questioned my son two years ago while he was attending college in Gettysburg. My son, Brad, met Detective Martinson for the first time yesterday at his place of employment." Motioning at a glass-topped table on the far wall on the right, he explained, "We have coffee, water, and an assortment of bagels and donuts for anyone who desires a beverage or a bite." No one responded or moved so Harmon went on, "Well then I think we can get started. My son informs me you visited him yesterday in regard to a business owned by Maxwell Miller in Gettysburg that was recently broken into and destroyed. He informed me that you were quite concerned over the break-in and destruction and the fact that some computers and important paperwork were stolen. My son felt when you started to question him that he needed not only myself but legal representation present. With that, I think I'll turn this meeting over to our attorney."

Smithe reached over and took a manila folder from a glass end table and opened it, extracting a calendar. Clearing his throat he began as he opened the calendar. "I believe the only question you asked my client before you left, which he did not answer was his whereabouts on Friday, June the nineteenth. We, at this time, are prepared to give you that information." Standing, he walked over and handed the calendar to Martinson, then returned to his chair. "You will see the calendar is for this year and that June is displayed. If you take notice you can see where Brad noted that on Thursday, June eighteenth through Sunday the twenty-first the name, Merchants. The Merchants happen to be the parents of Alicia Merchant, the young lady Brad happens to be engaged. Alicia and her parents arrived here in Ithaca late Thursday evening for the beginning of a weekend with the Sykes family. Friday morning, the day of your so-called break-in, Brad's mother, Alicia, and her mother were off to a day of shopping and making wedding plans for this coming fall. Brad, his father along with his future father-in-law went to the Ithaca Country Club for breakfast and then eighteen holes of golf, then lunch and then another round of golf.

"Next, they spent about an hour or so in the club's sauna and then retired to the bar for drinks. The evening ended with a lakeside bar-be-que at the Sykes' residence, followed by an evening of pleasant conversation. What they did Saturday and Sunday is insignificant as the day in question is Friday and where Brad was at that time. I think the calendar and my explanation of the activities he was involved in are self-explanatory. My client could not have possibly been in two places at the same time. Since he left Gettysburg two years ago, he has never one time returned. If necessary, we can within the next few days, supply you with verification in the form of people who not only saw Brad but in some instances were actually with him on the nineteenth."

Smiling confidently, Smithe remarked while reaching over and turning on a recorder. "This portion of our meeting will be recorded and for a very specific reason. Any planned questions that you have may be altered or not even asked after the information my client is prepared to give you. The information you are about to receive is what I would call a game changer and will completely exonerate Brad from any involvement with this Gettysburg break-in and theft. After hearing what my client has to say we must have a verbal agreement that he will be immediately eliminated as a person of interest…understood?"

Martinson answered in astonishment. "You cannot expect Detective Vanderway and myself to agree to something like that without knowing what the information is."

Smithe agreed. "I did not say you had to commit before hearing the information…but afterwords."

Martinson turned to Vanderway, asking, "What do you think, Detective?"

Looking Brad square in the eye, Vanderway answered, "Let's hear what the boy has to say."

Smithe smiled at Brad and suggested, "Tell them your story, Brad… don't add anything or leave anything out."

Brad looked at Martinson but then gave Vanderway a hard stare while speaking to the Detective. "First of all, Detective, I do not appreciate being addressed as *boy!* For the remainder of this meeting, you can refer to me as Brad, Mr. Sykes or if you do not want to use my name you can address me as a young man." Feeling as if he had established the way things were going to go, he smiled boldly and continued, "Let me start with a continuation of how you started yesterday's meeting by suggesting we take a stroll down memory lane.

"During the questioning I went through two years ago, the name of Simon Baumer was brought up and how I had met him at a café there in Gettysburg. When I think back to when I first met the man I have to say I was more than intimidated. I was quite frankly shaking in my boots. Simon Baumer is one scary man. There he stood, right in front of me, a large muscular man dressed in all black with his unkempt beard and piercing eyes. I know he is of the Mennonite faith and that as a people they detest violence, but I thought that at any moment he was going to beat me over the head with a Bible. When he told me he was going to visit Max Miler and set things straight I've got to tell you I did not envy Miller. During my questioning at the dean's office, you mentioned that Simon Buamer was a person of interest. I think I have pretty much established that I did not burn old man McCulhay's barn to the ground. Now, Simon Baumer, why

I wouldn't put it past him to burn down that barn."

Vanderway interjected, "This is all very interesting but I for one do not see what any of this has to do with the recent destruction of Miller's business."

Brad held up his hand and calmly stated, "Patience, Detective, patience. I was just getting to that. You see, unfortunately, I had the unpleasant experience of meeting Baumer for a second time in my life and it was just as unsettling as the first time we met. It was back about two months ago when Baumer showed up at my office right here in Ithaca. Detective Vanderway, sat in the very chair Bumer sat in while at my office. We talked for maybe I guess it was about a half hour. It wasn't all that long but I have to say I was just as leery of the man as the first time we met. I told him this and he assured me he was not here in Ithaca to do me any harm. It was only after that that I began to feel a bit relaxed with this scary man sitting in my office.

"It was then that he informed me why he was visiting me. I cannot repeat verbatim every word he used but I'll try to be as accurate as I can. He went on to explain to me he had driven up from Lancaster to see me because he was planning on getting revenge on both Max Miller and Kellem McCulhay and he wanted to know if I was interested in joining him. I immediately explained to him that I was no longer of a mind to get revenge on either of the two men he mentioned. I explained to him that I had cleaned up my act, was engaged to get married, and was working for my father. I made it clear to him that in no way was I interested in joining him in his plans of retaliation."

Brad hesitated in his rundown on Baumer's visit which gave Martinson a chance to speak. "Why would this Baumer character still after, what… two years, be interested in getting revenge on this Miller and this other person…McCulhay?"

Brad turned his next comment to Martinson, explaining, "Vanderway is very familiar with why Baumer could still be seeking revenge. There are some facts about the past you are not familiar with. Simon Baumer is a wealthy Mennonite farmer and he was in the process of courting a young Mennonite woman by the name of Elizabeth King in hopes of marrying up with her. Little did he realize Max Miller and Elizabeth had been seeing one another, unbeknownst to her Mennonite community. Turns out, Elizabeth King chose Max Miller, a man outside of her faith, over Simon Baumer. This was quite upsetting to the powerful Mennonite farmer and since the

King girl decided to marry Miller, Baumer, feeling that his future wife was taken from him is set on getting even with the man who stole his woman. I don't know how or even when we spoke what he had in mind for Miller, just that he had some sort of a plan of revenge."

Interested, Vanderway spoke up, "How did Baumer react to your refusal to aid him in his plan?"

Brad sat forward on the couch and stated firmly, "He was quite disappointed and I for one do not believe Simon Baumer enjoys being told no. During his visit to my office, I was on edge and very uncomfortable. You would think that sitting there in my own office I would hold the upper hand but Baumer has a way about him that can be very discomforting, I apologized to him saying I was sorry he had driven up from Lancaster to see me and now it seemed as if the trip was for nothing. He thought for a moment and then asked me if there was anyone I knew who might be able to help him out as he had been depending on me to join him in his plan. He said I was more familiar with the way the world outside of the Mennonite faith worked than he was and he was not sure how to proceed.

"Disappointing Simon Baumer and getting on his wrong side is something I don't think anyone would welcome so I appeased the man by giving him the phone number of someone I know. I went on to tell him I was not even sure this person would talk with him. I wrote down the number and gave it to him. He thanked me and I told him I thought it was best if he didn't contact me ever again. Thank God, he went on his way. Never heard from the man again."

"If I am understanding you correctly," probed Vanderway, "you supplied Baumer with a contact, according to you someone you know, whom he could talk with. This almost, no, it sounds like you gave Simon Baumer the number of an individual who could assist him with his plan against Miller. I'm afraid we are going to have to have the name of this person he contacted."

Brad was about to speak when Smithe interrupted, "That is not going to happen, Detective. My client agreed to meet with you here this morning to supply you with information he may have regarding the destruction of Miller's business, which he has done. We are not going to divulge the name of the contact for two reasons. First, the contact was at one time a good friend of Brad's. This friend, so I'm told, often runs in the wrong circles. Brad, since returning to Ithaca has made great efforts to change his life and he has done so, therefore he no longer associates with this person. If he were to tell you the name, Brad could then be facing retaliation.

"The second reason for not revealing the name is because, simply put, we are not required to give up the name. My client gave a man a phone number...that's all. We, at this point, do not know if Simon Baumer made the call or if he is even guilty of destroying Miller's business. Let me make something clear to you gentlemen. Detective Martinson knows of my successful legal profession well. I have a 95% success rate when it comes to the cases I accept. I rarely lose. If you should continue to press my client with further pressure to gain the name of this mystery person, I will sue both the Ithaca Police and the Gettysburg Police departments. You, gentlemen, will not stand a chance. I'll sue you for defamation of character and several other items I am sure I can come up with. Now, if I were you I'd switch gears immediately and place my focus on this Baumer. My client has already told you this intimidating Mennonite farmer came to see him and told him straight out he was seeking revenge on Miller. Do you have any other questions for Brad at this time?"

Martinson looked to Vanderway for the answer, who replied, "Yes, I do. Do you know if Baumer called this mystery person?"

Brad smirked, but answered, "My attorney already answered that question. I have no idea if he made the call."

"Have you seen or talked with Baumer since the meeting at your office?"

"Haven't seen hide nor hair of the man or heard from him and I hope I never do."

Vanderway stood, nodding at Brad and his father then spoke to Smithe. "It was nice to meet you, Melvin."

Gesturing at Martinson, Vanderway started for the door.

Martinson followed but then hesitated as he turned and addressed the attorney. "Don't underestimate me, Smithe. I happen to be very good at what I do. Within a few days, I'll know the identity of this mysterious person. I know every lowlife in this town and the surrounding county; everyone who as you state runs in the wrong circles. When I discover who this individual is we'll question them. I'll even mention that Brad here told us he gave their number to this Baumer character. We'll get to the bottom of this past friend of yours, Brad, and here's something to think about. You needn't be concerned about us bothering you again. What your attorney said may just be true. When this person finds out you more or less told us about them, well then maybe you need to be concerned about retaliation from this person. Good day to you gentlemen!"

Outside in the wide hallway, Martinson apologized to Vanderway. "That's two strikes against us. First, we struck out at Brad's place of business and now it appears that at least for the moment, we have struck out back there in the presence of Brad's attorney."

Vanderway pushed the down button on the elevator pad and responded with a smile. "There is no need to apologize. This might just work out yet. If what Brad Sykes told us is true then it looks like Simon Baumer may be our man."

"Are you going to question this Baumer when you get back to Gettysburg?"

"Without a doubt, but I think I'm going to wait a few days to see what you can find out about this so-called past friend of Brad's. I think right now I have enough information to question Baumer as a possible suspect, but if there is more information out there we can discover it might make our case even stronger."

"All right then. I'll start to put out some feelers around town and see what we come up with. As soon as I learn anything I'll give you a call."

The two detectives had no more than stepped out of the suite when Smithe stood, walked to the large window, and looked out over the city. "Make no mistake about it. Detective Martinson wasn't blowing smoke up our asses when he said he was good at what he does. I've heard that once he gets on the scent, he doesn't let up. What I'm saying is within the next couple of days Martinson will uncover the name and the whereabouts of this so-called friend of yours, Brad. When we first met and talked about this situation you told me you did not want to divulge the person's name, but now that is not possible. You need to tell your father and me who this person is and where they can be located…like right now…today!"

Brad joined Smithe by the window as he objected, "I'd just as soon not do that. If this person finds out that the police are questioning them because of something I said this could lead to trouble for me. You see, it's just not my old friend, it's the people he works for. I'd just as soon not ruffle their feathers."

"Their feathers are going to be ruffled whether you reveal the name to us or not. If Martinson talks with this person before we do, that presents us, or I should say you with the possibility of being indirectly tied in with this business down in Gettysburg. Giving that phone number to Baumer was not the smartest thing you could have done. You should have just left him to walk."

"Look, you never met this man Mr. Smithe. He's very intimidating and I just wanted him out of my office."

"If you are willing to take the chance of being implicated in this Gettysburg crime, that's up to you. Your father hired me to protect you and that's all I'm trying to do here. If you do not want to give me the name, you're opening yourself up for additional problems. As it stands right now, you're off the hook, but the minute Martinson discovers who this person is, well that could change everything. So what's it going to be?"

Brad looked at his father who simply shrugged in agreement with Smithe. Walking to the refreshments Brad poured a cup of coffee, added cream and sugar, and then asked, "If I give you the name then what will happen?"

"We have to contact this person immediately before the police find him. You or your father cannot in any way contact this person. Right now you stand an excellent chance of walking away from this situation, so why muck up the works by getting involved? All you have to do is supply me with the name and their location and I'll contact them."

Harmon, who had remained quiet for the last few minutes, finally spoke, "But won't that result in the same reaction as in being contacted by the police?"

"No, it will not," pointed out Smithe. "but when Martinson approaches this person it will be done negatively. Martinson will want to know about their past relationship with Brad, if they knew Simon Baumer, and if they called them or met with them. Martinson will be digging for any vital information he can get. When I approach this person, it will be done as a gesture of help. I'll explain how the police came to see you Brad and that the police know Simon Baumer was given their phone number. I'll strongly suggest that it would be best if they leave town for a few months until this thing blows over."

"That sounds just peachy but what guarantee do we have that my friend will leave? He and or Baumer could try and throw me under the bus."

"Not if we give them some incentive."

"What do you mean…incentive?"

"Cold hard cash. You know what they say…money talks!"

"So, what you're saying is that we offer this person money to leave for a few months. How much money?"

"I don't think you'll get them to leave for anything less than ten thousand, maybe twenty, or it could go as high as thirty grand," said Smithe.

"And what if this person still refuses to leave…what then? Do we offer them even more money?"

"No, I would cap the amount I'll willing to give them at thirty grand. If they are not acceptable to our offer, then there are other ways to make this person unresponsive to the police."

Brad looked at his father, then asked Smithe, "I'm afraid I don't understand what you're saying."

"You do not need to understand anything beyond offering them the cash. Let me just say that at times, even in the legal profession an occasional underhanded act is necessary. Don't ask me to explain any further. If it comes to that I will discuss it with your father. You don't need to know anything about that sort of thing. Hopefully, this friend of yours will take our cash offer and hide out for a few months. So, once again Brad, what's it going to be?"

Brad thought for a moment and then responded, "I'd rather offer them the cash than go down this other road you speak of." Looking at Harmon, Brad asked his father, "What do you think?"

Harmon didn't even hesitate. "I agree with you. The cash we have plenty of. In considering what you have salted away, I'd say the amount Mr. Smithe is suggesting is a small price to pay for putting one's self at ease."

Brad stood. "That's it then. The name is Kip Griner. I went to high school with him and up until a few months back we were close, but I have gone to great efforts to avoid associating with him. He normally hangs out at the State Street Pool Hall. He's there every day. You can always find him in the back room at a corner table. It's what he calls his office. If he is not there you can leave a message for him and he'll more than likely contact you."

"Good then," said Smithe. "You need to get to your bank and be back here no later than one o'clock with the cash. I'll drop by this pool hall this evening and make him our offer and with any luck by tomorrow morning he'll be on the road to parts unknown and Martinson will be left holding an empty bag."

Brad walked to the door and stated, "Well then, I'm off to the bank."

CHAPTER THIRTY-FIVE

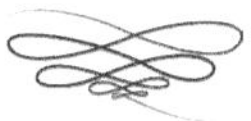

Brad, enjoying a late morning breakfast sandwich and a large orange juice stared out his office window at the lake when his intercom buzzed. Pushing the reception button, he answered, "Yes, Noreen…what is it?"

"I have your father on line one."

Laying down the sandwich, Brad responded, "Put him through."

Two seconds later his father's voice sounded, "Good morning, Son."

"Hey, Dad. Any news from our attorney yet?"

"Yes, that's why I'm calling. He called right after you left the house this morning with some good news. He went to the pool hall last evening around seven but was told Griner was not there and not expected until around eleven. So Smithe went back home and then returned to the hall just before eleven o'clock. This time he was successful, Griner was there. Smithe did not go into great detail about what was discussed but told me we could now relax. Smithe laid it on thick and believe it or not Griner accepted his proposal of leaving town for four months. Kip wouldn't do it for ten but when Smithe offered him twenty grand, he agreed to leave.

"Right now, Kip Griner is on his way to parts unknown. We are not quite out of the woods yet as when Martinson discovers Griner has suddenly up and left town, he's going to be upset and could suspect us of somehow being involved with his sudden exit from town. If Martinson pays you another visit just simply say you know nothing about Griner and let him know if he wants to speak to you any further then he is to contact our attorney. In short, Detective Martinson will hit a dead end and that should just about put an end to this Miller business."

Brad asked, "So I guess this means Vanderway will go ahead and question Baumer."

"I suppose so, but that's none of our concern. If Simon Baumer is responsible for the destruction of Miller's business he'll have his hands too full with his problems to be concerned over you. Smithe did mention the possibility that Baumer might try and involve you, but said he wouldn't have a leg to stand on. If Baumer tries to contact you again at your office inform your secretary to tell him you are not available. Likewise, if he tries to phone you…. the same thing; you're not available. I have a very distinct feeling Baumer is going to be questioned in the next couple of days and if what he suggested to you about his plans for revenge turns out to be the destruction of Miller's business, then you'll want to distance yourself from this man."

"Not a problem for me," said Brad. "I hope I never see him again."

Ending the call, Brad sat back in his swivel chair and relaxed. He had succeeded in throwing Simon Baumer under the bus by supplying Kip Griner's name and location to Smithe. As far as he was concerned he had played his cards perfectly. He had thrown any suspicion that the police had on Baumer, distracting the police from concentrating on him. Through his attorney, he had thrown Martinson a curve he would not be able to hit, at least for the next four months. By that time, if Baumer was guilty of orchestrating the crime against Miller, he only had one concern that only he and Griner knew of and that was the phone call he had made to Kip, explaining that Baumer might be giving him a call. If the evidence of that call was revealed, then he might have a problem and become at least partially involved. He needed to find out where Kip went so he could inform him if he was questioned in the future about Baumer the call between the two of them must be kept secret. It was the only hurdle he had not jumped and if enough time passed then it might not be an issue."

Max was in the process of directing two men where he wanted the new office furniture placed when Detective Vanderway appeared in the hallway. "Morning, Max!" Walking into the main room he gazed around at the newly painted walls and baseboards. "This doesn't look anything like the first time I was here which was what? Two, two and a half weeks back. You and whoever has been assisting you have done an incredible job getting the place back in order. When do you think you'll open the doors for business?"

"We could be open in a week," said Max, "but I'm going to say two weeks to be on the safe side. I still have to purchase two new computers and I have ordered two security file cabinets. It's going to take some time to get all the required information downloaded and then there are some loose ends we need to take care of. I want to make sure when we open we can offer the level of customer service our customers have grown accustomed to."

Sitting in one of two available chairs, Vandeway noticed a cooler by the door. Wiping his brow with a handkerchief he asked, "I don't suppose you have something cold in there to drink, do you?"

Max lifted the lid and inspected the contents. "We have sodas and water. What's your poison?"

"Water will be fine." Taking the cold bottle from Max, Vanderway commented in satisfaction, "It's hotter than hades out there. The last time I checked it was ninety-seven degrees outside. You must have a good air-conditioning system. It feels really good in here."

"I imagine you didn't drop by to update me on the current heat wave we're experiencing?"

"You're right," said Vanderway. "I wanted to bring you up to speed with the progress we are making in questioning Sykes and Buamer. I returned from Ithaca two days ago. I did not contact you as soon as I got back as I was waiting to hear from the detective I met with up there. He is following up on a lead Brad Sykes gave us."

"I could be off base here but that sounds like Sykes is off the hook."

"After questioning Sykes, we concluded that the only way he could have been involved was to hire someone to destroy your business. Other than that he could not have even been here in town on the day of the crime. His lawyer presented us with proof that showed from June 18 up through the 21st he was with his family and the family of some girl he is engaged to. Sykes also told us that believe it or not Simon drove up to Ithaca to visit him. According to Brad, Baumer explained to him he wanted to get revenge on both you and McCulhay. He wanted to know if Brad was interested in joining him in his plans. Brad told Baumer he was not interested but did give him the number of someone he could talk with.

"Detective Martinson, the detective I met with, tried to locate this individual but they mysteriously left town before he could question them. Right now it looks like it's going to be difficult to pin anything on Sykes, so tomorrow, I'm driving over to Lancaster County, meeting up with the local

Sheriff's department, and then we'll have a go at Baumer. If you'll recall the last time we questioned him we came away with nothing. This time, however, we possess a lot more vital information than what we had before, information I'm sure Baumer does not know we have. It's going to be interesting to see his reaction when we bring these things up. Based on what Sykes revealed to us we know Baumer was planning revenge on you. Now all we have to do is prove he went ahead with his plans. He's going to have a tough time talking his way out of this." Standing, Vanderway motioned with the water bottle. "I'm going to give the authorities over in Lancaster a call. I'll drive over there in the morning and we'll get in Baumer's face and see what happens. I'll give you a call tomorrow evening to update you on how things went."

Max ushered Vanderway to the back door and wished him luck on the upcoming Lancaster trip. Watching the detective drive up the alley Max decided to call it a day. He needed to get over to the farm and clean up for Kellem's last dinner in town as the next day he was flying down to Florida. He was happy for the old geezer but he was also flooded with a sense of sadness. Not having Kellem around was going to be hard on not only him but Elizabeth as well. After he was gone the farm would never be the same. Locking the back door Max thought that life had to move on and even though Kellem's life was winding down he and Elizabeth were just starting their life together as a young married couple.

Seated at a table at the Pike Restaurant and Tap House, Max and Kellem waited for Elizabeth who was still making her dinner selections at the buffet. Max unwrapped his utensils while speaking. "Aside from having breakfast with you tomorrow on the way to the airport, I guess this will be one of the last two meals we'll share."

Kellem rolled his eyes. "I know I'm over eighty years old but don't write me off just yet. If I'm welcome I plan on making an occasional trip back up this way to visit you and Elizabeth."

Elizabeth joined them at their table and seated herself as Max filled her in on the brief conversation she had missed. "Kellem here was just saying he might come back to Gettysburg now and then for a visit, that's if he's welcome."

"If you're welcome," exclaimed Elizabeth. "Come on, Kellem, you know you're welcome here at the farm anytime. If I had my druthers I'd just as soon you stay here at the farm with us…until the Good Lord calls you home. You could continue to live in the main or the summer house… your choice. I'd do all the cooking and cleaning. You wouldn't have to lift a finger."

"I appreciate the offer, but my sister needs my help with our brother, He's gotten to the point where he can't do much on his own. I suppose one of these days I may wind up traveling the same road of oldness."

Elizabeth raised her glass of water in a toasting fashion. "May that never be!"

Joining her in the toast, Kellem clinked her glass with his and added, "Well, not at least shortly. You're not going to get rid of me that easily. I'll be back to see you in a few months and you folks might even consider a trip to visit me down in Florida."

Max raised his glass. "Then it's a deal! It's not a permanent goodbye, it's see you later!"

Vanderway walked through the door of the Manheim Township Police Department and following a short conversation with the desk sergeant was directed to Jim Sullivan's office. Entering the room at the end of a short hallway, Vanderway greeted the Manheim Township Sheriff. "Good morning, Jim. Bet you thought you'd never see me again."

Jim stood and extended his right hand. "You're right on that. What was it? Two, three years back when we drove out to pay Simon Baumer a visit about that barn fire. After you called me yesterday and informed me you were driving over to question him again, about yet another crime I started to roll around in my mind how our previous visit turned out…not so good. Did you ever find out who was responsible for that fire?"

"No, we never did, but as an officer of the law, you know as well as I that things that seem to be buried have a way of eventually working themselves to the surface. We have an eyewitness who claims that Baumer talked with him about getting revenge against not only Max Miller but Kellem McCulhay as well. When we approach Baumer this time, I feel we'll be better prepared."

Jim closed a Venetian blind on the window as the morning sun was flooding his office. "I know we talked last night over the phone about the possibility of Baumer's involvement in the destruction of Miller's business, but I think we should go over it again before we approach Simon."

"All right," said Vanderway. "On June 19 of this year, someone broke into Max Millers' place of business…"

Ten minutes passed when Vanderway finished up. "The investigation, at this point is centered on the fact that Brad Sykes informed us when we went to question him that Simon Baumer approached him with plans for revenge. Now, whether that is true or not, we'll just have to wait and see how Baumer reacts to our visit."

Sullivan asked, "Do you believe everything this Brad Sykes told you?"

"Normally I'd say no, but in this case, I believe what he has told us. That does not mean he is not holding something back. He's not completely out of the woods just yet. The spotlight may not be directly on him right now, but depending on what we find out when we speak to Baumer this could very well backfire on Sykes."

Standing, Jim suggested, "Let's head out to Baumer's and see what we can come up with."

Traveling south on the main street of East Petersburg, Sullivan pulled into a gas station and pointed at a long one-story structure across the street. "That's Baumer's Hardware right over there. I just happen to know the vehicle he drives. That black Cadillac parked on the side of the building belongs to him. The parking lot looks full. I say we park here and walk over. Maybe, just maybe we can ruin Simon's day."

Sullivan approached the front door and read a note that had been taped to the glass. *We are in the process of taking inventory. Sorry for any inconvenience this may cause. Come in. We are open for business.*

Inside the front door, they hesitated as they viewed a few customers milling around and several blue apron-clad workers who were busy tallying items on the shelves with handheld inventory calculators. Addressing one of the workers, Sullivan inquired, "Boss in today?"

The young girl gave the two men a strange look and responded by pointing at a door just to the right of the sales counter. "If you are referring to Mr. Baumer, yes I believe he is in. I saw him go into his office about five minutes ago. Would you like me to get him for you?"

"No," said Sullivan, "We'll just go on back…and thank you."

As they passed a long row of packaged nuts, bolts, and screws, Vanderway asked, "You still friends with Baumer?"

"Yeah, I guess you could say that. It's not that we're that close. It's just that we've known one another for quite a few years now. The last time I saw him was over at the farmer's market a couple of months back." Stopping at the office door, Jim reassured Vanderway, "Look, if you're concerned about whether I'll do my job in regards to a so-called friend of mine…don't be. I'm sworn to uphold the law just like you. If it turns out Baumer is guilty I'll be standing right next to you if we have to haul the man in." Reaching for the doorknob, Jim nodded, "Now, let's go on in."

Inside a ten-by-twelve, extremely cluttered office Vanderway and Sullivan stared at what could only be described as a room full of disorganization and confusion. The right side of the room was lined with warped shelving stacked high with product manuals and cleaning supplies. The wall on the opposite side of the room was covered with floor-to-ceiling cardboard boxes labeled in black magic marker: register tape, customer bags, office supplies, and on and on. The blades of a fan centered in the ceiling turned slowly, and only two of three bulbs in the light fixture were in working order. Seated behind a desk covered with various reports and printouts sat Simon Baumer, the wall behind him stacked with even more cardboard boxes. Seeing the two men, Baumer smiled when he saw his friend Sullivan but then frowned when he noticed Vanderway. Pushing a coffee cup and a large ledger to the side Simon sat back in his swivel chair and propped his booted feet on the desk. "Jim Sullivan, what can I do for you? Paint, hardware, lumber. Whatever you need I either have it or can order it."

Sullivan reached across the desk shook Simon's large, calloused hand and explained, "You do remember Detective Vanderway from Gettysburg?"

Simon, not the least bit cordial replied, "Yes I remember the Detective from when you brought him out to my farm, I guess it was a couple of years back about some barn fire over in his neck of the woods. I cannot say I enjoyed his visit then and I'm not that excited about seeing him here at my place of business now. I told you when you were both at my farm before that you, Jim, are always welcome there, Detective Vanderway…not so much! The same goes for my place of business. So, my question is, what in the hell do you want, Vanderway?"

Vanderway glared back at Simon and remarked, "Since this is Sheriff Sullivan's stomping grounds, I think I'll let him answer that question."

Jim sat on the edge of the desk, loosened his tie, and then spoke, "It would seem there has been, yet another crime committed over in Gettysburg where the two main persons of interest happen to be the same two we questioned about that barn fire, which by the way to this day has never been solved. I, or I guess you could say we, find that quite interesting. Don't you?"

"No, I do not find that interesting at all. In case you haven't noticed I am in the middle of my yearly inventory and I don't have time for any of this nonsense. I had nothing to do with that barn fire and I know nothing about this other crime that was committed in Gettysburg you speak of. How could I possibly be a person of interest regarding a crime in a city I have not been to in over two years?"

Vanderway spoke up, "Simple. The crime we speak of was the destruction of Max Miller's new business. Someone thrashed the place and stole two computers and some personal information about Miller's customers. When we started to investigate we found out the only two people Miller could think of who have it out for him are you and Brad Sykes. We have already questioned Sykes and he has been all but cleared of any suspicion."

Sullivan casually searched Baumer's face for any sign of surprise or frustration but Simon displayed no signs of breaking down or panic.

Running his hand through his rough beard Simon nodded at Sullivan and shrugged, "I assume you have questions for me, so go ahead and ask, but I have to say I don't have much time to waste talking about something I know nothing of."

Vanderway leaned against a stack of cardboard boxes and asked his first question. "Let's start by first finding out where you were on Friday, June nineteenth of this year." Raising his eyebrows and pursing his lips Vanderway waited for an answer.

Giving the Detective a sour look, Simon opened his desk drawer and removed a daily planner which he laid on the desk. Opening the well-used binder he flipped pages until he came to June. Clearing his throat he tapped a notation that was marked for the second and third week of June. "According to my records, I was in Philadelphia for a livestock convention starting on the fourteenth and running through the twentieth. I couldn't have possibly been in Gettysburg as I was in Philly." Tossing the planner across the table, Simon added, "Read it for yourself, Detective!"

Vanderway read the planner and tossed it back on the desk. "This only proves you were not present during the crime…it does not mean you were not involved."

Smirking, Simon retorted, "Tell me, Detective, how can a person be involved in something if they were not there?"

"I can answer your question but first we have to back up some. I'm not going to ask you if you remember who Brad Sykes is because we know you recently paid him a visit at his place of business up in Ithaca, New York."

Sullivan studied Simon's face closely for any weakness or doubt in his demeanor.

Simon, not showing any signs of facial or body movement that would indicate he was nervous, calmly answered, "I did drive up to Ithaca to see Mr. Sykes on business. You see, I not only use cleaning supplies here at my business but on my farm as well. I also sell cleaning supplies here at the store. My current vendor raised his prices significantly, which I did not appreciate so I thought I'd find a new outlet, a new cleaning supply vendor. I found Sykes Cleaning Supplies in one of my vendor catalogs, liked what I saw, and decided to drive up and see if I could work a deal with Sykes' company. So, yes I was in Ithaca and I did talk with Brad Sykes. I don't see how any of that leads you to believe I am involved in this recent crime in Gettysburg."

"We'll get to that in a minute as I have some other questions. Sykes told us you just unexpectedly dropped by with no previous phone call or correspondence. He said you just drove up and dropped in out of the blue. You just showed up. I am not a businessman, but I do know that just dropping in on someone is not the normal way business is done."

Simon waved off Vanderway's version of the way he thought business should be handled as he laughed. "What may be considered in your world as normal may not be the way we as Mennonites conduct our business affairs. I like to meet a man face to face, not using emails or phone conversations. I find it a more honest way to conduct business."

Vanderway looked down at his feet and shook his head in disbelief. "It's apparent that someone, either you or Mr. Sykes is lying. Your versions of the meeting at his place of business do not coincide."

Baumer shrugged in wonder, "And how is that, Detective?"

"Brad Sykes never mentioned any conversation about your desire to purchase cleaning supplies from his company. He claims the reason you visited him was that you still sought revenge against Max Miller and Kellem

MaCulhay and you wanted to know if he wanted to throw in with your plans."

Amused, Simon picked up a half-smoked cigar laying on the side of a can lid utilized as an ashtray, opened the desk drawer and removed a lighter, lit up the used stogie, and remarked, "Where do you come up with these crazy accusations? Two years ago you suspected me of setting MaCulhay's barn on fire and now you're all but accusing me of being involved in this Miller's business being destroyed. Why now, especially since I have not been to Gettysburg or seen either Kellem McCulhay or Max Miller in over two years would you even consider that I am seeking revenge on either of these men?"

"In the police business, we call it motive, Mr. Baumer, the very reason why someone is motivated to commit a crime. In your case the motive is obvious. You spent a great deal of time courting Elizabeth King, hoping she would become your wife, but that didn't pan out so well for you as she chose Max Miller as her husband. We know you assaulted him two times, at the King farm right here in Lancaster County and then over in Adams County at Kellem McCulhay's place. We also know McCulhay ran you off his property at gunpoint. It's a well-known fact you don't care for Miller or McCulhay. Even though the barn fire at McCulhay's place is two years in the past, your name is still on file as a person of interest. I could be wrong here but I see a pattern of revenge regarding both Miller and McCulhay that you always seem to be right in the middle of."

Simon grinned and responded, "I am not that familiar with the way the law works in your world Detective, but I do know that until you can prove my guilt, then you are just treading water."

"You make it sound like treading water is a bad thing, Mr. Baumer. In your vernacular, because I am treading water on this current case I'm working on you seem to think that I am not going anywhere. Someone, either you or Brad Sykes is lying and as long as I stay above the surface, the truth will eventually float to the top. For now, there does not appear to be much I can do but we do have a lead we are following up on and that's just this. Sykes told us, despite the fact he was not interested in teaming up with you that he gave you a contact who might be able to assist you.

"At this point, we have not identified this contact but sooner or later we'll discover the person Brad Sykes put you in contact with. Their story, however it turns out will either coincide with your version of the meeting you had with Sykes or with what Sykes told us. And with that, I'll just say good day to you Mr. Baumer. I can guarantee you that our paths will cross again, days, weeks maybe months from now, but we will talk again." Without another word, Vanderway walked out the door leaving Jim Sullivan alone with Simon.

Jim looked at Simon with doubt and stated clearly, "All I can say at this point is I hope you haven't bit off more than you can chew." Hesitating at the door, Jim turned back and continued, "If it turns out you are guilty of this crime in any way, shape, or form I will not be able to bail you out. I'll have to do my job. Hope it doesn't come to that!"

Sullivan no sooner left the office when Simon buried his head in his hands as he leaned forward over his desk. Taking a deep breath he opened a drawer and removed a bottle of Bourbon and a glass. Filling the glass to the brim he downed the alcohol then refilled the glass and took another short swig. Just then his cell phone buzzed. Picking up the device he answered, "Simon Buamer."

The voice on the other end seemed surprised, "I got you on the first try. I thought it would be more difficult to get in touch with you."

Not recognizing the strange voice, Simon inquired, "Who is this?"

There was a moment of silence, then the voice replied. "It's Kip...Kip Griner. We need to talk."

Simon amazed that Griner had called him, let out a sarcastic laugh followed by a harsh statement, "Well, speak of the devil. Two detectives just left my office after questioning me about the destruction of Miller's business. And guess what? Part of our conversation was about you. The police at this point do not know who you are, only that I was put in contact with you. How could this possibly happen?

"When we last talked you guaranteed me your people would carry out my request against Miller and in no way would I even be suspected. So, tell me Griner why are the police questioning me? This was supposed to be completed without any problems on my end. I have half a mind to drive up there and beat the living hell out of you!"

"Come now, Mr. Baumer, do you think you can intimidate me, a man who is well connected with a group of very powerful people? Don't be foolish! Look, you can't blame me or the people I work with for the interest the police have in you. We kept our end of the agreement. We arranged to destroy Miller's business as you requested and we still intend to carry out your wishes of revenge on this McCulhay character next week as planned. The reason why you were questioned by the police was not sparked by anyone on our end but by none other than Brad Sykes, who was recently questioned by the police about the Miller situation.

"A lawyer who represents the Sykes family came to see me about a week ago. He explained to me that Brad told the police he had given you my number as someone who might be able to assist you. Sykes did not divulge my name to them but no doubt felt that eventually, the Ithaca Police would discover that this unknown person was me. This lawyer offered me a substantial amount of cash to disappear for the next few months. This incentive was no doubt funded by the Sykes family. The problem for Sykes is that after he gave you my number he went ahead and called me to let me know you might contact me. If the police find out about that call well then that ties him into all this.

"What I'm telling you is Brad Sykes threw you under the bus by informing the police that you came to him for his assistance against Miller. He also pitched me as well under the same bus when he revealed my name to his attorney. I can only avoid the authorities for so long and eventually, they'll locate me and then, you know what will hit the fan, but I have a solution to solve both your problem and mine. We simply eliminate Brad Sykes from the equation."

Simon stared at the far wall of his office and then asked, "What exactly do you mean when you say, eliminate?"

Kip, not desiring to be all that definitive over the phone, replied, "Let's just say that Sykes, after it's all said and done, will not be a problem for either you or me. If we work this correctly why after Brad is gone he could wind up taking the fall for not only the revenge against Miller and McCulhay but that barn fire as well and eventually you and I just go on our merry way."

"By saying gone are you implying that his life will come to an end? Because if that's what you mean I can have no part in anything like that."

"If that's what has to be done, you will in no way be involved. Actually, the less you know the better. When this goes down I have a feeling the police will question you, but not to fret. Before we make this move you will be contacted on the date it is to take place. In this way, you can make sure that you have a rock-solid alibi. Make sure on that day you are nowhere near Ithaca. Spend the day somewhere where a lot of people will remember your presence. After the deed is done you will also be contacted and that will be the end of it…and Brad Sykes."

"There is nothing I need to do on my end?"

"Not a thing. You just go on about your daily business and wait to be contacted. One more question before we end this call. Do you want us to go ahead with your plans for this McCulhay?"

"No, I think that would just stir the pot even more. Things need to simmer down around here and that would just make things worse. So let's just forget about McCulhay."

"You do realize," said Kip, "that we cannot issue you a refund because of the fact that we only accomplished half of your request that you have now canceled?"

"That's understandable. Maybe you could put that money toward the elimination of Sykes."

"Well, that's it then Mr. Baumer. The next time you hear from me will be a call informing you about the date of Brad Sykes' last day on earth. Good day to you, Simon."

CHAPTER THIRTY-SIX

A knock at the front door caused Elizabeth to turn from the simmering pot she was stirring. Wiping her hands on the apron she wore; she made her way across the kitchen and through the living room where she opened the door. There with a wide grin stood Detective Vanderway. Returning his smile Elizabeth placed her hands on her slim hips and asked pleasantly, "Why, Detective, what brings you out to the country?"

Vanderway leaned against one of the porch posts as he replied, "It's nice to see you, Elizabeth, but I came out to see your husband. Is Max around somewhere?"

"He is…he's out in the barn staining an old table and chairs we just purchased. I can call him if you'd like."

"No that's all right. I'll just head out to the barn if that's okay."

"That would be fine but before you walk out there, I'm going to ask a favor."

In agreement with whatever she had in mind, Vanderway nodded.

Folding her hands Elizabeth pointed a finger at the Detective and remarked, "Stay right where you are. I was just about to take some fresh brewed iced tea out to Max. Would you be so kind and deliver a refreshing drink to him?"

"More than happy," said Vanderway. "I don't suppose you could muster up a cold glass for me also…would you?"

"You must have been reading my mind. Be right back with those teas."

Beyond the fence line at the edge of the farm property Vanderway's attention was suddenly drawn to the far edge of the fencing where he thought he heard a muffled voice as if someone were giving a command, but seeing no one, turned back as Elizabeth stepped out onto the porch holding two tall glasses of tea which she handed to him. Vanderway, taking the teas gestured with his head toward the fencing. "I swear I just heard someone out there, but there doesn't seem to be anyone around."

The possibility of Vanderway hearing a strange voice was waved off as Elizabeth joked, "Probably just some ol' Civil War ghost! I'm sure you've heard the stories around town about how that fence out there is haunted."

Vanderway, looking at the fence remarked, "I did hear about voices not only out by the fence but around your property, but that was a few years back. I haven't heard anything recently, well except for the voice I thought I just heard. Tell me, you and Max have lived here for a spell now. Are you two of the opinion that the fence or the farm is haunted?"

Elizabeth frowned. "Speaking for myself, I have never bought into that ghost business around here. Now if you were to ask Max you'd get an entirely different story. He is convinced Civil War ghosts are here on the farm. He has never actually seen one but, like you and some others claim he has heard strange voices. I think it's just a bunch of nonsense."

Vanderway took a sip of tea and replied, "I agree with you. I have never believed in ghosts myself but that voice sure was strange. With that, I'm off to the barn."

Walking to the edge of the porch Elizabeth offered, "Depending on how long you're here you're welcome to stay for dinner this evening, Detective."

"Love to, but I'm afraid after I talk with Max, I have to drive over to Lancaster County and pay your ol' nemesis, Simon Baumer a visit."

"Sounds serious!"

"It could be. We're not sure just yet. Turns out Brad Sykes was killed in a car explosion yesterday. I just have a few questions for Max and then I'll be on my way."

Elizabeth placed her left hand over her mouth as she softly exclaimed, "Oh my! I'm sure you're aware, Detective, that Brad was not one of my favorite people in life or Max's as far as things go, but it saddens me to think he is no longer in this life. I'll say some prayers for his family."

"That's good. We could all use some prayer these days. Listen, I have to speak with Max about all this. I'm sure after I leave he'll fill you in on all the details we currently have." Turning, Vanderway made his way across the yard and then down the dirt drive toward the barn.

Elizabeth watched the Detective until he turned the corner and disappeared. Looking at the tree line beyond the fence she thought about Brad Sykes and Simon Baumer; two individuals that over the past few years she and Max had grown to dislike as they both had caused Max to constantly look over their shoulders not quite ever sure of what the day would bring, and now one of them was dead. Killed in a car explosion is what Vanderway had said. Well, that was none of her concern at the moment. With all the enemies Brad had made while in college well then just maybe he got what he deserved.

Catching herself in a moment that bordered on hatred for Sykes and Baumer, she raised her eyes to the sky and said a short but meaningful prayer, *Dear Lord, please forgive me for having ill feelings toward Brad and Simon.*

Vanderway no sooner rounded the corner of the metal barn with its gray siding and green corrugated roof when he heard a familiar song coming from the barn. It was an old song, one he remembered from his youthful days, Credence Clearwater Revival's *Born on the Bayou.* Entering through the large sliding open doors he saw Max seated in a folding chair at the far end of the lengthy barn. Walking across the concrete floor, Vanderway considered yelling to get Max's attention but then thought better of it.

Walking over to a small radio he pushed the off button which caused Max to turn instantly when the music stopped. Seeing Vanderway standing there with the teas held in his outstretched hands Max immediately stood and laid a two-inch staining brush on a rag on a nearby table. "Detective Vanderway! I see you've been up to the house. I was expecting my wife to bring me a drink, certainly not the local law enforcement." Unfolding another chair, he offered. "Have a seat. What brings you out this way?"

Vanderway crossed the floor, handed Max a tea, and then seated himself. "I'm afraid I have some bad news to share with you."

Max sat back down and took a quick swallow as he waited for the Detective to continue.

Vanderway placed his tea on the table, grimaced, and then spoke, "I guess there's no gentle way or appropriate means to tell you this, but Brad Sykes was killed yesterday at his place of business during a car explosion."

Max took on a manner of concern as he replied in utter surprise, "That's horrible! I mean you are well aware of the fact that Brad and I were not the best of friends, but still to die in a horrible accident like that, well it's just unbelievable!"

Vanderway shook his head and responded, "It was not an accident. The car was rigged to explode. What I'm saying is Brad Sykes was flat-out murdered. There wasn't much left of that young man, an arm, an ear, and some other assorted body parts. We know it was Brad as they discovered his wallet that somehow survived the detonation. Between the wallet and dental records, he was identified. His Corvette was blown to smithereens."

Max trying his best to take in what he was hearing asked in wonder, "And you say this happened at his place of business?"

"Yes. I was just there about a week back. Detective Martinson and myself, well we sat in Brad's office and discussed at great lengths the destruction of your business. It always amazes me how things can change from one day to the next. One day you're sitting in a man's office having a conversation and then days later the same man dies in a horrible car explosion. According to his secretary, who was injured by flying glass from the front windows of the business, Brad had just left for the day. The next thing she knows the glass front of the building explodes and glass and car parts are flying everywhere. She was hit by a lobby chair and knocked out. That's about all she can remember about the blast."

"How do they know the car was rigged to explode, that Brad was murdered? Maybe the car just malfunctioned."

"The crime scene investigators found parts of what they have identified as a sophisticated car bomb. It was a professional hit."

"Who would want to kill Brad Sykes? I mean, we both know he had many an enemy in college and around town here but what could he have been involved with that would render him being murdered?"

"These are some of the same questions the Ithaca Police are asking. Well, at this point it goes beyond the police. Harmon Sykes, Brad's father, aside from grieving the death of his only son, is pushing the local authorities to get to the bottom of this quickly. Sykes swings a lot of weight in Ithaca and he's got a lot of friends in high places which means the death of his son will get a lot more attention than the average citizen in those parts, which brings us to you!"

"Me! Come on, Detective. You can't possibly even suspect me of somehow being involved in Brad's death."

"Involved yes, responsible…no!"

"How could I possibly be involved, as you state in Brad Sykes's death?"

"Perhaps, I should have worded your involvement more casually as in your *possible involvement.* Let me explain. I had a long phone conversation with Detective Martinson last evening about Brad Sykes' death and after tossing around varied reasons for his demise we came to the possible conclusion that it may have something to do with our recent visit when we spoke with him."

Interested, Max inquired, "In what way?"

"Believe it or not both Detective Martinson and I feel the same way about this situation and that's just this. If you would not have mentioned Brad Sykes and Simon Baumer as possible suspects in the destruction of your business we would have probably never questioned them. What I'm saying is there is a better than average chance that if we would have not questioned Sykes he would still be walking around on the face of the earth."

Max gave Vanderway a hard look. "Pardon me, Detective but I think that's stretching things a bit. How could my mention of his name as a possible suspect lead to his being murdered? I must be missing something here."

Vanderway sat back, crossed his legs, and explained, "Detective Martinson asked me after we talked with Sykes in Ithaca if I believed what Brad told us. I told him that knowing Sykes well from when he attended college in Gettysburg, that normally I would not put much stock in what he says. But after questioning Sykes and finding out that he had turned, according to him, over a new leaf and no longer held ill feelings for either you or Kellem McCulhay my opinion of him has changed. He received his business degree in college, was successfully running one of his father's businesses, and was engaged to a prominent young lady from Elmira, New York.

"The fact that Baumer admitted himself he traveled to Ithaca to meet with Sykes matches with what Brad told us except for the reason for the visit. Brad claims Baumer told him he was seeking revenge against you and McCulhay, but Baumer said he went there on business, that he wanted to secure Sykes Cleaning Supply as a new vendor for his hardware business. Someone is lying and I am leaning toward Simon Baumer as the culprit. Brad told us he turned down Baumer's request to join him in his plans for revenge but did supply Baumer with someone he could talk with. That doesn't add up in my book.

"If it is true that Buamer went there seeking help in getting revenge on you only to be informed by Sykes he was not interested, then why would Sykes give Baumer someone whom he could talk with? Furthermore…talk about what? Let me ask you, Max. If you went to someone seeking information or assistance to get something done and that individual refused, but gave you the number of someone who could help you would you not assume the person you were told to contact would be able to help you? This sounds rather suspicious to me. If Sykes was not willing to assist Baumer but did give him a number to call then the individual had to be someone who knew about revenge…how it could be handled or what could be done, maybe even for a price be able to carry out Baumer's wishes."

"Do we know who this person is…this individual who Sykes supposedly put Baumer in contact with?"

"Originally no. Sykes would not divulge the name to us as he claimed this person was a friend of his, but that he had more or less broken off his friendship with this person because he was trying to turn his life around. He also said if this person was ever questioned by the police and found out Brad had revealed his name to the authorities, it might not go well for Sykes. As it turns out Ithaca is not that much larger than Gettysburg, hence everyone knows everyone else's business. Martinson did some checking around and the name he came up with was Kip Griner, who conveniently skipped town before he could be questioned. Griner as it turns was close with Sykes when in high school and their relationship continued until Brad moved back to Ithaca. Griner has always been known as sort of an undesirable citizen. Martinson claims Griner is employed by a man who owns some businesses in Ithaca and it is thought that he is connected with organized crime out of New York City. It is also a known fact that Griner is a liaison with these people with one of their illegal activities and that's just this, for a price, these people will carry out something an individual wants done but does not want to be involved with themselves."

"And these people get away with this sort of thing?"

Taking a drink Vanderway smirked, "Come now, Max, you can't be that stupid to believe these types of things do not happen in the world in which we all live?"

"I guess what you say is true. I just don't like to think about such things. So, where does this leave us? Are you and this detective from Ithaca convinced this Griner character arranged to have my business destroyed?"

"Right now, we are not convinced of anything. It's more along the lines of speculation. If Brad Sykes did supply Baumer with Griner's number that tends to lead us in the direction of believing Sykes was familiar with Griner's contacts and what they are capable of. Otherwise, why would he put Baumer in contact with Griner?"

Before Max could respond Vanderway answered his question, "If he did give Baumer, Griner's number then he had to be aware of what Griner and the people he works for are capable of."

"So, what you're inferring is that Griner arranged to have my business destroyed at Baumer's request."

"Possibly, that and then some. It could be that Sykes previously used Griner to not only burn down your friend Kellem's barn but also had you attacked down in Charleston. Think about it. Brad Sykes was in Canada when you were attacked in South Carolina and Baumer was at a livestock convention when your business was being ransacked. Perfect alibies in both cases. They get their revenge but yet walk away free as a bird."

"But can you prove any of this?"

"That's the main problem we're faced with. With Sykes dead who we can no longer question and with Griner on the run who knows where that leaves us with just Simon Baumer. If we cannot talk with Brad Sykes or Kip Griner and if we can't come up with something that ties Baumer in then eventually, he'll be off the hook."

"Despite everything you've told me this morning is there anything Elizabeth and I should do or be on the lookout for?" Not waiting for Vanderway to respond, Max continued, "And another thing, how about Kellem? As you are well aware he has moved down to Florida to live with his sister. I believe you said Baumer was seeking revenge not only against me but against Kellem as well. Do I need to contact him and make him aware of a possible threat?"

Vanderway took another drink as he answered, "Let me answer your second question first. I think it would be wise to contact McCulhay and let him know about what's happened and what was said during the meeting between Sykes and Baumer. There is probably little he can do other than be careful and keep his eyes peeled for anything out of the ordinary.

"As far as your first question goes you and Elizabeth need to be watchful also. You no longer have to face any threats from Brad Sykes but his father Harmon may come into play. Remember, he is well aware of the past discord between you and his son. I can guarantee you Harmon will leave no stone unturned until he gets an answer as to why Brad was killed. Add to that the fact that Kip Griner, who is associated with organized crime is out there running around somewhere. Simon Baumer who is at least at this point only a person of interest is reported to have revenge on his mind when it comes to you. You and your wife must be vigilant until we get to the bottom of all this. I'm just saying…be careful."

"Correct me if I'm wrong, but did you not recently question Baumer about the destruction of my business, and according to you that didn't go very well? How do you think he'll react to now again being questioned but this time about Brad Sykes' death?"

"In the next couple of hours, we'll know. I'm going to be driving over to Lancaster County. The sheriff over there at my request is going to have Baumer drop by his office to answer some questions. Baumer, who does not seem to care for me much is not aware I am to be present during the questioning, otherwise, I don't think he'll agree to the meeting. Sheriff Sullivan told me he intends to turn the screws on Baumer and try to get to the bottom of all this. I have a very distinct feeling that Baumer will try and dump all the blame on Brad Sykes, who because he can no longer defend himself is an easy target. We'll see!"

Standing, Vanderway finished off his tea and then gestured toward the open barn doors. "I best be on my way. Our meeting is scheduled for eleven this morning." Touching the edge of one of the stained chairs, the Detective remarked, "Nice job on the chairs. I'll let you know how things turn out. See ya around!"

Baumer, entering the sheriff's office found Jim Sullivan seated at his cluttered desk. Jim glanced at the wall clock: 11:05. Standing, he offered Simon a seat. "I was beginning to wonder if you were going to show."

Simon seated himself across from the desk and responded, "You know me better than that Jim. If I say I'm going to be somewhere then I'll be there." Looking around the office Simon continued, "My reason for arriving a few minutes late is because I do not relish the idea of coming to the local police department. I'd rather not spend any more time here than I need to. I've got a lot to accomplish today and spending a great amount of time talking to the police is not one of them. How long do you think we'll be?"

Jim picked up his desk phone as he answered, "That depends." Speaking into the mouth of the phone Jim stated nonchalantly, "All right!"

Simon reacted to the short call and asked, "What was that about?"

"It's nothing to be concerned over. There are a couple of others that I have invited to join us."

In the next second Vanderway entered the office trailed by two large, uniformed officers. The officers seated themselves on either side of the door while Vanderway took a chair at the far end of the desk on Simon's left.

Simon shoved back his chair and stood in defiance as he glared at first Sullivan and then Vanderway. "If I would have known Detective Vanderway was going to be here I would never have agreed to come today, but you already know that, Jim."

Jim folded his hands on the desktop and smiled. "Take it easy Simon and sit back down. If you are thinking about leaving us the two officers by the door will not allow that to happen. At present you are not under arrest; you're just here to answer some questions we have. That being said, if you want to make a scene and try to leave you will then be arrested for not co-operating with the police, which we have every right to do. So, do yourself a favor and sit."

Simon turned and gave the officers the once over, then sat back down while speaking to Vanderway. "I do not like you, Detective and I do not like the way this whatever it is, is being handled."

Vanderway responded, "Well for what it's worth I'm not that fond of you either, Mr. Baumer!"

Frustrated, Simon spoke directly to Sullivan. "I have to say this little trick of yours doesn't sit well with me. Depending on how things go here today our friendship may be in danger of coming to an end. What could you possibly ask me that we have not already covered? I did not burn down McCulhay's barn nor was I in any way responsible for the destruction of Miller's business. What else could there be to discuss?"

Vanderway answered the question sternly, "Murder…for one thing!"

Simon, who knew that eventually he would be questioned about Brad's death was well prepared to act as if he knew nothing about Brad's demise. "Murder! Whatever are you talking about?"

Vanderway moved close to the desk and explained, "Yesterday…Brad Sykes was killed in a car explosion at his place of business!"

Acting the part, Simon hesitated for effect and then asked as if he were confused, "And you think he was murdered?"

"Definitely," said Vanderway. "The police found evidence of a car bomb that had been professionally attached to the car. There was not much left of Sykes to speak of. He probably never knew what hit him."

Simon continued his charade and remarked with a tone of concern. "I can't hardly believe what you're saying. It was just recently, as you are well aware, that I paid Sykes a visit to his office. To think that now he is no longer alive, well, that's just hard to imagine. Who would want to murder a young man like Brad Sykes?"

Vanderway shot Sullivan a quick look and then spoke sternly to Baumer. "We were hoping you could answer that very question for us."

Acting as if he were amazed, Simon retorted, "How could I possibly answer a question like that? Remember I'm not of the same world you live in and as a Mennonite, we do not murder people, as the people in your world do. We are a peace-loving people."

"Really," said Vanderway. "You're going to sit there and tell us how peace-loving you are. Was it not you who hit Max Miller several times while at McCulhay's farm and then again at Amos King's place?"

Objecting, Simon quickly answered, "We've already been over those two instances and those situations are not a reflection of the way I live my life as a Mennonite. Both of those acts were nothing but an extremely emotional time for me as a Mennonite. Do you have any idea what it is like to court a young woman who you plan to wed and then have her stolen away from you, especially someone who is not of the faith? I'll admit right now, and I have admitted it was wrong of me to lash out at Miller. But I can assure you I have moved on with my life. I hold no ill feelings toward Miller or even McCulhay as I once did."

Simon took a deep breath and continued the falsehood of his knowledge of Brad Sykes' death as he stared up at the ceiling.

Sullivan, who noticed this odd behavior spoke, "Simon, I just saw something in your facial expression that indicates you have more to say." Standing, Jim walked to a water cooler, removed a small paper cup from a holder, and poured himself a drink. Downing the cold water, he turned and faced Baumer. "If you know anything, even the slightest detail about Sykes' death, we need to know about it right now. If you remain silent and eventually, we find out what you are keeping from us it may not go well for you."

Banking on Sullivan's past friendship, Simon looked at Jim trying to play on his feelings. "I have always trusted you, Jim. But not so much in Detective Vanderway here. If I tell you what I know I need some sort of guarantee that I can walk away from this. Deal?"

"As a longtime friend of yours, I will try to do everything in my power to help you, but you have to realize this now has gone far beyond a barn burning and destroying a business office. We're talking murder and there is only so much I can do. As an officer of the law, I am obligated to do my sworn duty."

Jim aimed his next comment at Vanderway. "How do you feel about what Mr. Baumer here is offering us?"

"Well, like you Jim, there is only so much I can do. Before I can commit to any sort of deal, I'll have to hear what he has to say, then we'll see."

Simon, playing his part to the hilt hesitated as if he were thinking and then responded, "All right, I'll tell you what I know and I guess I'll just have to trust the legal system you both represent. Could I get a cup of water?"

Jim, who was still standing by the cooler acknowledged, "Of course!"

Handing Simon the water Jim stood next to his desk and leaned against the wall, crossing his arms. "Let's hear what you've got, Simon."

"Okay, but before we get into who I think murdered Sykes let's back up some. That barn fire at McCulhay's place two years back was not my doing. Lord knows I had every reason to burn that old man's barn down because of the way he mistreated me, pulling a gun on me and all. I wanted desperately to get even with McCulhay, but I guess I had one of those turn-the-other-cheek moments and decided to just move on. I always figured Brad Sykes burned down that barn, but was never sure until I went to see him in Ithaca. As I have stated before when we talked at my place of business, I went to see him about acquiring him as a new vendor for cleaning supplies for my store. I did not call him beforehand, I just drove up there."

Tossing the now empty water cup into a nearby trash container, Simon went on, "We were not even five minutes into a business conversation when Brad changed the subject and I have to say, looking back he took me by complete surprise. He explained to me that his revenge for Miller and Mc-Culhay was still on his mind and a priority. He was not sure exactly what he was going to do but asked me if I wanted to team up with him as he figured that I still held some contempt for Miller and McCulhay. I immediately told him I had moved on and was not interested in being involved with his revenge plans. He went on to say the only involvement he required from me was my checkbook, explaining he simply wanted me to fund half of the money required to complete his plan. Other than that, I would be in no other way involved. To say the least, I was a bit confused and that's exactly what I told him.

"He told me that unlike the world I live in as a Mennonite, in his world there are people who for a fee will accomplish anything an individual desires to be done. He went on to explain to me that he had a friend right there in Ithaca who was connected to some powerful people in New York, who through this friend of his had done some work for him in the past. I guess the look of confusion on my face prompted him to explain further, which Brad did. He told me through these people he arranged to have McCulhay's barn burnt to the ground. He also utilized these people to get even with Miller in the past. He did not reveal to me what he had in store for Miller and McCulhay but said it would cost up to twenty grand for the work to be done. He said all he was asking for was half of the fee and then through these people would take care of the rest. Needless to say, I was appalled and refused to be involved in whatever plans he had. We talked for a few more minutes and then I decided to leave, telling him I didn't think I wanted anything to do with him, let alone having him as one of my vendors.

"The last thing Sykes said to me was that based upon what he revealed to me about his plans for revenge he thought it would be best if we didn't meet again…ever! He told me these people from New York if ever exposed because of something I passed on, that it may not go well for me. Then, I left. Time passed and then I received a visit from you fellas at my hardware store where you questioned me about the destruction of Miller's business. It was at that moment when I realized Brad Sykes had no doubt followed up with his plans to have these New York people carry out his revenge against Miller." Looking directly at Vanderway Simon pointed out, "With all that being said I am going to answer a question you must have on your mind. Why did I not explain all this to you when you were in my office? The very thought that these people, at least according to Sykes might confront me if I said anything about their involvement kept me from mentioning any of this. I wasn't quite sure what to do. Imagine me, a Mennonite farmer, getting involved in the ways of your world, a world I was taught to stay away from and here I am right in the middle of all this."

Vanderway was about to reply when Simon held up his hands for silence. "Hold on, Detective, because there is more, I have to say. You no sooner left my office that day when I received a strange phone call from someone by the name of Kip Griner. He proceeded to tell me he and Brad had worked closely together regarding Miller. It didn't take any great amount of intelligence or imagination to realize I was talking with the contact that Brad said he had. Griner went on to explain to me the people he worked for were quite upset because the Ithaca Police were looking to question him about the Miller business. He told me he had to leave town to avoid talking with the police and more than likely it would be some time before he could return to Ithaca. When I finally had an opportunity to speak, I told this Griner I had just been questioned by the police. He said that did not surprise him and that Brad Sykes had thrown not only him and his people under the bus but me as well and for that reason his people were going to eliminate Sykes from the equation. I told him I did not understand what he meant, and he said it was better if I didn't know. He then told me we would never speak again and then the call ended." Holding up both hands Simon smiled, "And now I am finished!"

Relaxing in the chair as if an invisible weight had been lifted from his large frame, Simon folded his hands in humbleness and stated softly, "And there you have it. That is all I know. Is that enough information for you to consider working a deal for me?"

Sullivan looked to Vanderway for a response. The Gettysburg Detective was quick with an answer. "Even though that was a very enlightening story there remains the process of further investigation and fact-checking that needs to be done to substantiate your claims about what happened."

Surprised and somewhat shocked Simon retorted, "Are you disputing what I have said as the truth?"

Vanderway waved off Simon's caustic response. "I have no intention of disputing what you have told us. It's just that we have to verify your statement. You see, Mr. Baumer, I've been a detective for nearly twenty-two years now, and over that time I have heard many eyewitness reports or statements about what happened in any number of criminal situations. Some are true down to the last word while others are pure fabrication. At times, people can add this or that to their story or they can leave out important facts. We'll consider what you have told us. We'll take what you have said, dump it into the hopper of investigation, shake it around, and see what comes out the bottom…hopefully the truth."

"Do you mean to tell me after I have told you what I know that I do not have a deal with the police?"

"I'm not sure what kind of a deal you're searching for," said Vanderway. "Whether you realize it or not you already have a deal of sorts with us…the police. Unless you have anything else to say, you'll be walking out of here in the next few minutes. You will not be cuffed, arrested, or carted off to jail. You're free to go. What better deal could a man ask for than that?"

"Well, for one thing," stated Simon, "I would like to be assured that I will not be hounded by the police as I have been as of late. Can you give me at least that assurance?"

Sullivan answered, "That depends on how the investigation pans out. This may be the last time we speak, or we may contact you again. Let me explain something to you, Simon. Your concern over being hounded as you say by we, the police should be the least of your concerns. There are currently two other entities lurking out there in the world you may have to worry about."

Simon gave Sullivan an odd look as he inquired, "What could be worse than having the police interested in you as a person of interest in a murder case?"

Interjecting, Vanderway explained, "Dealing with us is the least of problems you may be facing. As the police we will do everything by the book, but not so others that you may have to deal with." Seeing Baumer was still confused, Vanderway continued, "The two entities Jim speaks of are Kip Griner and the people he works for and then there is Harmon Sykes…Brad Sykes' father. These people in New York and Harmon Sykes have deep pockets and therefore are quite powerful. I imagine you fashion yourself, a Mennonite farmer, as being wealthy, but Griner's people and Mr. Sykes could buy your farm a thousand times over. Think about what has happened as of late. Brad Sykes lost his life in a car explosion that was a professional hit and according to you carried out by Griner's people. If it turns out to be true Brad Sykes was eliminated because he led the police in the direction of these New York folks that is something you need to consider as dangerous…dangerous for you, Simon. They know Brad talked with the police and now he is dead and they will find out you have talked with us, so the question is…are you next?"

Simon looked at Sullivan, and asked, "What do you think Jim? Do you think these New York people would consider, me, a farmer, a threat to those activities?"

"We can't say for sure, but I would not think if I were you that they consider you harmless."

"How could they possibly know about this meeting and what's said? Do you intend to contact them?"

"No, we will not talk with these people and more than likely the New York police will not either. These people are very powerful and possess an uncanny ability to find out things. What I'm saying is they'll know about this meeting, and they could come calling."

Simon gave Vanderway an uncomfortable stare and then asked, "What of this Harmon Sykes…Brad's father? Just because he is wealthy does not mean he is dangerous!"

Vanderway shook his head as if indicating that Baumer knew not of what he spoke. "Mr. Baumer, I have in the past sat in a meeting with Harmon Sykes and I can assure you this is a man who you do not want to get on the wrong side of. Sykes is just as dangerous as these folks from New York; he just approaches problems differently. The New York people will do whatever is necessary to protect themselves from being exposed, while Mr. Sykes will also do whatever is required but he will come at you legally and because he has more money than the man on the moon, he can manipulate the powers to be with his checkbook. In the world I live in, money talks and can convince people to look the other way or change their opinion in favor of what Sykes desires. He is every bit, if not more dangerous than these New York people. If I were you, I'd stay close to your farm until we get all this sorted out. Be careful of strangers who may enter your life. They can smile in your face and stab you in the back at the same time and you'll never see it coming."

Simon stood and spoke to Sullivan while ignoring Vanderway. "Is there anything else for me today?"

Sullivan looked to Vanderway for a response. The Gettysburg Detective gave an affirmative nod at which point Simon walked to the door, gave the two officers present a dirty stare, and exited the office.

Simon pulled his Cadillac out of the parking lot and smiled to himself as he made a left on Manheim Pike. He thought he had done an excellent job of bamboozling the police. As far as he was concerned he had successfully planted in the minds of Sullivan and Vanderway that Brad Sykes was responsible for McCulhay's barn fire when the truth was that he and his two brothers had torched the place. It appeared that now Sykes would take the fall for that little incident. He had also, in his mind convinced the police that Sykes through contacting Griner had arranged to have Miller's business sacked when, in fact, he, Simon had made the call to Griner to arrange the revenge on Miller. Sykes would no doubt be blamed for this crime as well. It seemed like a no-brainer. Sykes was not around to defend himself and as long as Kip Griner did not talk with the police then ol' Simon Baumer was in the clear. Passing a long cornfield Simon had only two concerns, Griner's New York people and Harmon Sykes. He felt like so far he had dodged the bullet, but needed to get back to the business of running his farm and business. He needed to get back to being a Mennonite farmer. The world that Max Miller, Brad Sykes, and Kellem McCulhay lived in was just way too complicated for his taste.

Max, drying his hands walked out of the downstairs bath as the aroma of chicken and dumplings filled every corner of the country kitchen. Elizabeth, who was placing a plate of freshly baked bread on the kitchen table motioned to her husband. "Have a seat, dinner will be up in the next few minutes."

Pulling out a chair Max complimented his wife's cooking. "It smells wonderful in here…it always does when you're at the stove."

Speaking to Max with her back turned, she asked, "How did things go with Detective Vanderway? He told me about what happened to Brad Sykes, but aside from saying he had gotten blown up in a car explosion, didn't go into much detail. He said you would probably fill me in later."

"I will, but let's wait for all that after we eat. What happened to Brad is not what I would call great dinner conversation."

Elizabeth placed a large bowl of steaming chicken and dumplings in the center of the table, stirred the tasty concoction, and then sat opposite Max. "I have something much more pleasant for us to discuss." She beamed as she pushed locks of hair from her face. "I went to the doctor yesterday as I have not been feeling well for the past few mornings. I figured I was catching a summer cold but after examining me he gave me his diagnosis. I'm pregnant!"

Max, who was reaching for a pitcher of iced tea sat the pitcher back down as if he couldn't believe what he was hearing. "Pregnant…really! Is it a boy or a girl?"

"It's too early to tell right now. We probably won't know for a month or so. Do you want a son or a daughter?"

"It doesn't make a difference to me. Right after dinner, I'm going to call my parents. They'll be so excited, especially my mother. She has always said she cannot wait to be a grandmother."

"Well, when you call her let her know that next March, actually early March she'll officially be a grandmother and you'll be a father of a little Miller baby, be it a boy or a girl. I think I will also phone my parents in Lancaster and tell them the good news, not that it'll make any difference, but as my parents, they have a right to know. Maybe the birth of this baby will soften how they feel about me." Folding her hands, she bowed her head and softly suggested, "Why don't you bless our food for we are truly blessed!"

CHAPTER THIRTY-SEVEN

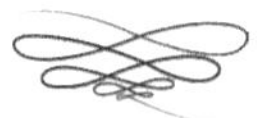

Max pushed his forty-two-inch cut John Deer riding mower out of the barn, checked the oil, and then topped off the tank with gas from a five-gallon plastic container he kept just inside the door. Gazing around the seven-acre property he thought about what a great day it was turning out to be. July 2nd, the second of three days of the 159th reenactment of the Battle of Gettysburg. Screwing the top back on he placed the fuel container inside the barn and noted the thermometer mounted on the edge of the door. Eighty-three degrees, two degrees hotter than the eighty-one-degree temperature in and around Gettysburg back on July 2nd, 1863. Over a century and a half in the past many a soldier in both the Union and Confederate armies had awoken that morning, not realizing this would be the last day of their lives. They, no doubt, had a light breakfast, packed up their gear, and marched off to meet the enemy, not knowing what the day held in store. For many, it was to be the last meal they would ever enjoy.

He climbed on the mower, pushed in the clutch, pulled out the choke, and turned the key, the seventeen-and-a-half horsepower engine sprang to life. Placing the mover in the forward position, the lawn-cutting machine rolled across the gravel road to the very edge of the two-acre grass-covered area behind the old farmhouse. Max engaged the blades, and the mover took on a deeper sound as he guided the machine past the back porch, a neat forty-two-inch swath of cut grass now behind him. Making a right at the fence he looked at the slight indentation beyond the fence where Kellem had explained there at one time had been a deep gully where his fourth-generation great-grandfather had buried thirty-three Confederate soldiers. According to Kellem, this was the very beginning of the occasionally heard, strange voices.

He made another right turn at the fencing, and he was now mowing the fence line that separated his property from the national battlefield. Maneuvering his way around the three evenly spaced cannons facing the battlefield he continued down the fence where he came to the third section from the end where Kellem and his father had seen what Kellem referred to as a Confederate ghost soldier. Kellem saw the soldier some thirty-one years after his father had seen the same soldier standing by the fence. Passing the section of fencing Max glanced off into the tree line at the top of the rise where both Kellem and his father said the soldier had vanished.

Distant cannon fire from the reenactment of Little Round Top interrupted his thought process about the ghost soldier as he made another right and followed the fence line to the barn where he made yet another right and began his second trip around the spacious yard. It was reenactment week in Gettysburg, and he had been hearing the distant cannon fire since ten o'clock that morning. From previous reenactments, Max knew the sound of cannons would continue for the next few hours.

Reenactment week in Gettysburg was the busiest week of the year for the town; thousands of Northern and Southern reenactors from all across the country flooded into town and the surrounding fields to reenact the three days of battle. It was indeed a busy time for anyone who owned a restaurant, one of the museums or gift shops. Every room at the local motels was spoken for. Other than that, most of the residents considered reenactment week a pain in the backside. It was hard to get around town and their normal lives were dramatically affected by the influx of Civil War enthusiasts in their blue or gray uniforms marching up and down the streets, riding horses, some hitched to wagons. He had decided to take the week off because the number of local customers who would come to town would be few and far between. He needed a break anyway. There were a lot of things he wanted to get done around the farm and reenactment week was the perfect time to stay at home away from all the activities in and around town.

Passing the house, a second time he looked at his watch: 4:15. He figured as always it would take just over an hour to mow the back section. Watching a helicopter fly over he thought about the past year and how peaceful things had been. It was two years past when Brad Sykes had been killed in that car explosion. His father Harmon had paid him a visit at his office two weeks after Brad's death. He had been warned by Vanderway that Brad's father may seek him out. The short meeting with Harmon Sykes turned out to be quite pleasant. Sykes explained that he was well aware of the past bad blood between Max and his son but felt his son had turned the corner and was traveling in the direction of becoming an upstanding resident in Ithaca. The meeting only lasted for twenty minutes and after discovering that Max could not supply him with any information that would lead to those who killed his son, Harmon thanked him for his time and went on his way. Two years had gone by, and Max hadn't heard from Harmon Sykes since.

The last time he had talked with Detective Vanderway had been two months in the past when the detective dropped by his office to explain the case of Brad Sykes' death was still open, but he doubted if they would ever uncover the truth of what happened. Detective Martinson from Ithaca phoned Vanderway and explained they had exhausted their efforts to locate Kip Griner. They had contacted Kip's employer, Bernie Anelo, who claimed Griner had simply up and left town and as far as Brad Sykes' death was concerned, he knew nothing about it. Martinson said Griner, more than likely was living in New York City using an alias and would no doubt never return to Ithaca. Any suspicions regarding Simon Baumer had been dropped as they had no proof, he even contacted Griner about the destruction of Max's business. If the people Griner worked for took Brad out it would never be proven without Griner's testimony. All in all, it was over, and everyone needed to get back to their lives and move on.

Max passed the third cannon and thought about how fortunate he was for a twenty-four-year-old college graduate. Here he was, barely out of school for three years and he not only owned a home but had his own business which was doing better than he had anticipated. He was married to Elizabeth, a better wife he could not have wished for. She was solid as a rock when it came to her attitude about life. He had been quite concerned about her fitting into the world outside of the Mennonite faith she had been raised in. He had not only been blessed with a wonderful wife but twin daughters, Hanna and Audrey, who were now two years of age. Life at the moment was good. Even Elizabeth's parents had softened their stance about their daughter leaving their faith. Amos King had driven Elizabeth's mother and her best friend Ellen over to the farm to spend the first week with Elizabeth helping out with the new twins. His mother, Kate, was beside herself over the birth of the twins and she and Charley had driven up to Gettysburg to spend two weeks with mother and daughters. Kellem had visited them weeks before the births and vowed to return this coming fall. All the troubles he had experienced since arriving in Gettysburg his freshman year, which included Brad Sykes, Simon Baumer, his attack in Charleston, and the destruction of his business seem to fade away as he felt the warm sun on his face combined with the wonderful smell of freshly cut grass.

He guided the mower to the side of the barn, shut the machine down, climbed off, and walked to a picnic table situated on an old ten by twelve cracked concrete slab. Opening a thermos, he took three long swigs of ice water, then grabbed a bag of charcoal and dumped the appropriate amount into his smoker grill. Applying an even portion of charcoal lighter fluid over the black briquettes, using a fire starter he ignited the charcoal, several flames leaping up a few inches but then receding to a low bed of fire. Placing the charcoal and the lighter fluid back on the table he looked to the west where another barrage of cannon fire sounded. Sitting at the table he surveyed the grass he had just cut and thought, *two acres down and five to go.*

About to take another drink of water his arm became frozen as he held the thermos just inches from his lips. He couldn't believe what he was seeing. There at the third section of fence stood a southern reenactor. The make-believe soldier appeared to be a young boy, eighteen, nineteen, maybe twenty years of age. The young boy was staring directly at him. He was attired in what looked like an authentic Confederate uniform, although the uniform had seen better days. He held an Enfield rifle in his right hand. Moving slightly to his right the boy stumbled but then steadied himself by holding onto the fence.

Thinking the young man needed some help or directions Max got up slowly and started across the grass. Raising his right hand in a friendly gesture, he waved and addressed the soldier. "Howdy there! My name is Maxwell Miller. This is my place."

The boy, who remained silent backed away from the fence but kept hold of the top rail as if he were afraid to fall.

Max, now just a few feet from the lad smiled as he asked, "And you are?"

The boy remained silent, looking back over his shoulder and then at the farmhouse and then back to Max as if he were afraid. Max, now standing on the opposite side of the fence no more than three feet from the boy, extended his left hand. "What's your name?"

The boy refused his hand but softly replied, "Samuel Pritchard. My friends call me Sam."

Max followed suit, and replied, "My friends call me Max!"

In the next few seconds, Max quickly took in the boy's appearance: standard, grimy Confederate gray forage cap, army issue faded shell gray shirt and trousers, the shirt missing three of its buttons and ripped just below the boy's right armpit. The fabric was torn just above his right elbow surrounded by what appeared to be a large patch of fresh dried blood. The right sleeve was tattered and three inches shorter than the left. The pant legs were both shredded at their edges and overall, the uniform looked filthy. His sockless feet were encased in a pair of well-worn heavy-duty black, scuffed ankle-high shoes. All of the standard Confederate equipment a soldier required was present: a three-inch wide, well-used belt which contained his cartridge box and cap pouch, scabbard, and bayonet. Tucked in the belt, much to Max's surprise was a Confederate fighting knife, in this case, an Arkansas toothpick, a dangerous weapon when it came to hand-to-hand combat. A marred wooden canteen supported by a frayed rope was draped over the boy's right shoulder and hung at his left. This resembled the same canteen Kellem and his father had stated that the ghost soldier possessed. Suddenly, Max realized he might be standing across the fence from that very same ghost. If not that, then this had to be the most realistic attired and equipped reenactor Max had ever encountered over his years of reenacting. The youth looked exhausted; the right side of his haggard face smeared with dirt. The most astounding thing about the boy was the blood slowly oozing from his lower left leg. *How could a reenactor possibly get wounded? Maybe he had fallen on a rock or a sharp object.*

When it appeared, the boy was not going to speak Max asked what he thought was the next logical question. "Where're you from?"

The boy shifted his weight from his left leg to the right as he winced in pain, but then answered, "Small town down in Alabama called Five Points."

Max probed, "What regiment are you with?"

The boy spoke up with a sense of pride, "Forty-Seven Alabama Law's brigade Hood's division…Longstreet's Corp."

Recognizing the famous Confederate names, Max remarked, "Now there's some good men!"

Somewhat astonished, Sam asked, "You know these men?"

"No, I've never met them, I've just heard of them."

When the boy's next question or comment did not come, Max inquired, "You look plumb worn out. Is there something I can get for you? Maybe some water. It's awfully hot out here today."

The boy's face seemed to light up as he answered, "If I could just get some water, I think I'll be fine."

Max angled his thumb over his shoulder and explained, "Just so happens I have a thermos full of ice water over there on that picnic table. Why don't you come on over the fence and get your fill?"

"That sounds right inviting but you're a Yank. You might not be in the Union army but you're still a Yankee. Never met one yet I could trust."

Max grinned and explained, "Just because I live up here in the north does not mean I'm a Yank. The truth be known I am a Southern sympathizer. I was born and raised near Charleston, South Carolina in a town called Summerville. My folks still live there. One of these days I might move back."

Sam looked back up the rise and out across the yard past the farmhouse and softly asked, "You don't think any Yanks will come by? What about these cannons?"

"No Yankees will come by, not today. I've been out here working all day and so far you're the only soldier north or south who has dropped by. I think you'll be safe on my farm. I guarantee it! These cannons have been abandoned."

The boy took another look around, then agreed, "All right, but just long enough to get that water, and then I'll have to be on my way. Somehow, I've got to get back to my regiment." With that, the boy bent down and stepped in between the middle and top rails of the fence. Using his rifle as a makeshift cane he slowly limped across the yard constantly looking to his right and left for the enemy.

On the patio, Max gestured at the wood table and suggested, "Sit down and relax." The boy sat down slowly and leaned his rifle, in reach, at the end of the table. Max poured cold water into the plastic thermos top and offered it to the boy.

Sam took the cup, sipped carefully, and was satisfied with the taste then gulped down the rest, some of the cool water running down his sweaty chin and neck.

Smiling at Max, Sam asked politely, "Could I have another?"

Max responded, "Sure, you can drink it all and I have more in the house. We can even fill your canteen up for you."

Sam downed the second cup of water and handed the cup back to Max as the sound of cannon fire sounded in the distance. Looking in the direction of the booming noise, Sam tried to stand but stumbled as he spoke, "I best be off. I've got to get back to my regiment." Standing by the table he took a deep breath and stared off into the trees at the top of the rise. Grabbing his rifle he smiled at Max and said, "Thank you for your kindness and the water. I need to go." Turning, he took one step and went down on his left knee.

Max took him by his right arm and helped him to his feet and then back to the table. "You're not going to get very far on that leg. Listen, I've got an idea. My wife is a trained nurse. She could clean and bandage your wound. It wouldn't even take but a few minutes then you can be on your way back to your regiment."

Sam rubbed his right hand across his dirty face, thought for a moment, and then replied, "I wouldn't want to be a bother to you folks. I only came for the water. I don't want to be of any trouble for you and your wife."

Waving off Sam's concern Max assured the boy. "It won't be a problem. Just let me go up to the house and get the wife and we'll have you patched up in no time. You just stay put."

Max jogged across the gravel road and the grass to the back porch, opened the screen door, and yelled, "Elizabeth…we've got a situation out here by the barn!"

Elizabeth, who was busy in the kitchen walked quickly into the small dining area, wiping her hands on her apron. With a look of concern, she asked, "Is there something wrong?"

"Yes and no. I mean it's not anything to get upset over. A reenactor wandered onto our property. He's pretty exhausted but more than that he's got an open wound in his left leg. I don't think it's all that serious but the wound does have to be cleaned out, medicated, and then bandaged. You'll probably need some warm soapy water, a washcloth, some clean towels, peroxide, antiseptic, gauze, or some sort of bandage. No need to hurry, but don't dally. I don't want him to run off before we get him patched up."

Elizabeth stepped out onto the porch and looked toward the barn. "Is that him sitting there at the table?" Turning she nodded at the twins who were fast asleep in a playpen on the porch. "I think we have everything we'll need. The twins should be fine here on the porch, but if they start acting up while I'm working on your Civil War patient you might have to attend to the girls." Walking back in the doorway she spoke over her shoulder. "Go on back out there. It'll take me a couple of minutes to gather the things I need. I'll be along shortly."

Max walked back to the patio and spoke with confidence to Sam. "My wife will be here in a few minutes. She said she could get you bandaged up." Flipping up the top of the smoker grill Max asked, "You hungry?"

Sam shook his head in dismay. "It's been almost twenty-four hours since I last ate."

"Well, you're in luck then, Sam. Before you showed up, I was just about to cook up some dogs and burgers."

In amazement, Sam gave Max a strange look and then stated, "You Yankees eat dog?"

Laughing, Max explained, "No, we do not eat dogs. They're called hot dogs. They are a type of beef. You have had beef before?"

"Not since I've been in the army. Back home in Alabama my mother used to cook us up a beef steak once in a great while and we had beef stew when we could afford it."

Max opened up a nearby cooler held up a hot dog and a hamburger patty and identified each one. "Hot dog…hamburger. Same beef, just shaped a little bit different than those beef steaks you've had in the past."

Sam stared at the dog and burger in confusion. "You northern folks sure have some funny ways about you and some strange names for some of your food."

Max laughed again as he placed several dogs and burgers on the grill while causing Sam to comment. "That's one of the strangest cooking fires I've ever seen. Do all Yankees cook like that?"

Stirring the hot coals around a bit Max answered, "Only if you're cooking outside."

The food conversation was interrupted as Elizabeth approached, introducing herself. "Hello there…my name is Elizabeth and I'm Max's wife. He tells me you have a wound that needs to be cleaned and bandaged."

Displaying his Southern upbringing Sam made an effort to stand in the presence of a lady, but the pain in his leg prevented him from doing so.

Elizabeth laid the medical items she had brought along with her on the table as she gestured for him to stay seated. "There is no need for you to get up on my behalf." Placing her hands on her slim hips she inquired, "Now, about this wound. Where exactly is it?"

Sam touched his upper right arm where the dried blood stain was and answered. "I've got two wounds. Got stuck in my arm with a bayonet and then got shot by a Yankee in my lower left leg."

Looking at Max in confusion Elizabeth asked her next question. "Which wound is giving you the most pain?"

"That would be my leg. The wound in my arm seems to have stopped bleeding but my leg feels like it's getting worse, and the bleeding won't stop."

Moving around the table Elizabeth suggested. "Well then, let's take a look at that leg first. If you could, would you please roll up your pant leg and stretch your leg across the bench there and we'll have a look see."

Max, flipping the burgers and moving the hotdogs to a new position on the grill was amazed at the way Elizabeth had instantly taken control of Sam's problem.

She examined the leg wound two inches below the knee and offered a quick diagnosis. "Looks like the bullet passed right through the edge of your leg. It took a small section of your muscle tissue and skin with it, but aside from that doesn't look that serious. It appears the heat of the bullet itself cauterized the top half of the wound but the bottom where the bullet passed through is still bleeding. The first thing I'm going to do is clean up the wound and the skin around the area then we'll dab some peroxide on and in a couple of minutes the bleeding should come to a halt."

As Elizabeth went about dabbing at the wound with a warm washcloth Max casually asked. "Seen much action since you joined up?"

"Not at first," said Sam. "The 47th was formed down home in Alabama in late May of '62. I guess that'd be about a year or so back. I was only seventeen when I joined up with my two friends, Billy, and Chester. The first week of training involved marching and learning the different bugle calls and drum signals. Then in early June, we were sent up to Virginia where we continued to drill for the next two months. During that time, we, all of us as recruits got to thinking that we'd never see a Yank. Then it happened. In early August we went into battle at a place called Cedar Mountain. I along with most of the others were scared to death. Being in actual battle is a lot different than training. Now we had to do what we were trained for. The company I was with was placed behind a fence near some woods and about an hour into the fighting were ordered to fire across a field at the advancing Yankees. I fired my rifle; I think it was six or seven times and to this day I have no idea if I hit one of those Yanks. Before they got all that close to our fortified position the cannons, we had on their left busted up their ranks and we were ordered to charge which we reluctantly did, but the Yanks ran off and we won the day. I remember me, Billy, and Chester along with the rest of the Forty-seventh tossing our hats in the air and yelling at the retreating boys in blue. We had been victorious our first time out.

"Then, toward the end of August, we found ourselves in Manassas which everyone was calling Bull Run. The battle at Cedar Mountain seemed like child's play compared to what went on there. The number of soldiers fighting there was far greater than our first encounter. My regiment didn't see any action during the battle as we were held in reserve. I never even fired my rifle. Then, following hour after hour of fighting word got back to us the Confederate army had run the Union army off and once again, we were the victors. I was beginning to think our army could not be defeated."

Elizabeth held up the small bottle of peroxide as she spoke up. "I've cleaned the wound and now I'm going to apply some of this. It's going to sting some, maybe even burn a little but that's good…that means it's working. Ready?"

Sam looked at Max and then nodded at Elizabeth, at which point she poured a small amount of the clear liquid on another washcloth and pressed it to the open wound. Sam braced himself and let out a low moan followed by a low hissing. Wiping a tear from his right eye he remarked, "It does burn."

Placing the bottle back on the table Elizabeth assured the boy. "The burning sensation will pass in the next few seconds and then I'm going to clean the wound a second time, let it dry, and then I'll apply some of this antiseptic ointment on and around the wound."

Max, thinking it best to distract Sam from what Elizabeth was doing continued their conversation, "So where did you go following Bull Run?"

Sam turned his attention to Max. "It wasn't but a day or so later when we battled the Yanks at a place called Chantilly. It was more or less like the battle at Cedar Mountain except the outcome was neutral. Both armies fought there but no one walked away with a victory. I guess it was about two weeks later in mid-September when we marched into Maryland at a place called Sharpsburg. We faced off against the Yanks on September 17th and as long as I'll live, I'll never forget that day. My regiment and quite a few others wound up in this cornfield. I believe it was called Miller's field." Addressing Max, Sam asked, "Didn't you say your last name was Miller?"

"Yes, I did," said Max.

Wondering, Sam spoke again, "This Miller in Sharpsburg. He a relative of yours?"

"No, I don't think he is."

"Well, anyway there we are in this cornfield. It was total confusion as cannons from both sides were firing into the field. The standing corn was soaked with the blood of soldiers from both armies. A blast near me knocked me off my feet and when I got up I saw four men from my regiment who were blown to pieces. I turned and here comes this Yankee soldier charging right at me. his bayonet pointed at my stomach. I had just enough time to raise my rifle and get a shot off. Shot him right in the liver and he went down like a sack of potatoes. I felt bad as I had never shot a man before. I walked over to him and noticed he was no older than I was. He had this look on his face as if he knew it was his time. Another cannon blast lifted me off my feet and when I hit the ground I blacked out. When I woke up there was no one around so I crawled out of the field into the woods where I stayed put until some boys from a Texas regiment wandered by. I joined up with them and eventually, we got back behind our line of defense. Later on, that day I spent a few hours bringing up ordnance for the cannons. Hours passed and we finally withdrew. The word around our regiment was that the Yanks had licked us, but we had given them a run for their money. I'll never forget that boy's face…the one I killed in that cornfield."

Elizabeth, just finishing up wrapping a three-inch section of gauze around Sam's leg, remarked while securing the bandage with medical tape. "There you go. Now let's see that arm."

Sam removed his filthy shirt, placed it to the side, and apologized, "Sorry Ma'am if I don't smell like roses but I haven't bathed in nearly two weeks."

Elizabeth stared at the boy's dirt and sweat-covered chest and arms. Ignoring the strong body odor, she inspected a two-inch cut just above the elbow. "The bleeding has stopped but we still need to clean out the wound and follow the same process as we did with your leg. We should be finished up in about ten minutes or so."

Max, flipping the dogs and burgers asked, "So where did they send you after Sharpsburg?"

Sam cleared his throat as he took another drink of water. "Aside from a couple of small skirmishes it was pretty boring and then we wintered up at Fredericksburg, Virginia. With winter setting in we all felt the fighting would die down until the spring. Not so! The Union army decided to cross the Rappahannock River and stage a massive attack in early December. First, they ransacked the town of Fredericksburg, all of the good southern citizens fleeing their homes and businesses. Then they advanced on us. We were well fortified at the top of a long rise called Marye's Heights behind a four-foot-high stone wall. We had nearly three thousand men from Georgia manning that wall. Up the long rise, those Yanks came, row after row of brigades, regiments, and divisions. My regiment along with other Alabama regiments and some boys from your state, South Carolina were positioned just behind those manning the wall. Our duty was to load one rifle after the next and hand them to the men on the wall. It went on for hours. I couldn't believe how those Yanks just kept coming and how we just kept killing them. It seemed so senseless. They never even got close to the wall and eventually, they withdrew and once again we were the victors. I felt sick to my stomach and that boy I had killed back there in that cornfield in Sharpsburg seemed like such a small thing compared to the men I had loaded rifles for who were killing one after another of the enemy. That day I promised myself I would do whatever it took to survive the war and get back home…something most of those Yanks climbing Marye's Heights now would never be able to do."

Elizabeth applied a portion of the peroxide on the cut and Sam's reaction was somewhat less noticeable.

Continuing with action he had seen Sam spoke up, "Before we knew it the New Year rolled around, and most of us couldn't believe the war had not ended. Spring came and then summer and the Forty-seventh didn't see much action, that is until General Lee decided to move the army up north here to Pennsylvania. We started our long journey on June 3rd and marched every day during that month. We marched in the heat, sometimes in the rain, each day our goal of reaching Pennsylvania one day closer. When you spend hour after hour, day in, day out marching you have a lot of time to think and of course talk with those on your right or left. None of us were sure why we were heading for Pennsylvania but the word in and amongst the ranks was Lee could no longer sustain the army in Virginia. But, in Pennsylvania, a state that has been all but untouched by the ravages of the war, there were lush farmlands and orchards and plenty of livestock. Another reason for the invasion of the north was because it was thought if our army could get close enough to Washington and threaten the capital then maybe, just maybe Lincoln would call an end to the war. The general population in the north is dissatisfied with the way the war is going and it's costing a fortune to support the Union army. Yet, another reason for heading up here to Pennsylvania is if we can gain a major victory in the north then maybe France or England will join the Confederacy in our efforts to win the war."

Elizabeth, with an opportunity to speak taped off the gauze bandage on Sam's arm and remarked, "There you go, you're all set." Holding up two small white pills she suggested, "Take these with water, and in about thirty minutes or so the pain should be gone."

Looking at the pills in the palm of her hand Sam replied, "What are these?"

In amazement, Elizabeth stared at Max and then answered, "Just some simple aspirin."

Sam, still staring at the pills remarked in wonder. "You people up here in the north have many things we do not have in the south."

"Then what do you take for pain?"

"In the army, they use morphine or chloroform and at times just plain ol' whiskey."

Not understanding how backwards and misinformed Sam was she stood and scooped up the medical supplies as she announced. "I'll just be heading back up to the house." Looking at Max who was flipping the burgers she explained, "Looks like we'll be eating in a few minutes. I'll be back in a jiffy with baked beans, potato salad, and fresh lemonade."

Sam watched Elizabeth walk back to the house when he held up the pills and asked Max. "So, what do I do with these again?"

Max placed his hand to his mouth and explained, "Just place them in your mouth and then take a few swigs of water."

Swallowing the pills, Sam rubbed his lower leg. "I'm thankful your wife got the bleeding stopped."

Max inspected the hot dogs and asked, "When did you arrive here in Pennsylvania?"

Sam was quick with an answer. "The last day in June we finally stopped near a town called New Guilford. I think it's around twenty-five miles or so from here. We arrived there late in the evening and didn't have an opportunity for any type of supper. So, most of us ate some green apples from a nearby orchard and then we turned in for a good night's rest, which turned out to be short-lived. We were rousted out of our bedrolls at two in the morning and told we were pulling out on a forced march to Gettysburg. We were on the road by three and we marched all night long and into the morning, arriving here at Gettysburg somewhere between two and three in the heat of the day. We no sooner arrived than we were told to form up for battle. We couldn't believe it! We had no supper the previous evening and then no breakfast. We were exhausted and hungry and our canteens were empty from the long march. We no sooner formed up when some of our regiments went to the right and began to engage the Yanks in an area where there were all these giant boulders."

Max, realizing exactly what Sam was talking about added, "I know where that is, it's called Devil's Den."

"If that's what it's called then someone named it correctly because it looked like hell over there. Soldiers from both sides lay wounded or dead on and in between those blood-stained rocks. The rest of our regiment, the 47th, the 15th, and the 4th Alabama along with two Texas regiments were ordered to sweep across this short valley to where the Union army had established a line of defense. Despite intense cannon fire, we drove those boys back and even took some of their cannons. We then found ourselves at the bottom of a long sloping hill backed up by another higher hill."

Confirming what Sam was describing Max remarked, "The small hill is called Little Round Top and the larger hill is known as Big Round Top."

Sam shook his head, "Well, I wouldn't know about that but since you live in these parts I reckon, you'd know. The word was passed through the ranks we were to take the smaller hill. It was said the left flank of the entire Union army was positioned at the top of the hill and if we could swing around and get behind them then we could attack the main body from behind and not only win the day but possibly the war. Up that hill, we went. The going was slow as we made our way up, stepping over small boulders and logs. Cannon fire on our right was taking out groups of men here and there and the air was filled with smoke. Finally, after what seemed like a half-hour's climb, we saw the Union boys tucked in behind logs and rocks up the hill about eighty yards. We advanced a few more yards, stopped, and then received a hellish barrage of rifle fire from up above. We fired back and reloaded. Back and forth we went loading, firing, and reloading, soldiers on both sides dropping like flies. Then we were given the order to withdraw back down the hill thirty yards or so where we reformed and up the hill we went again. This second attempt got us about twenty yards closer than the first attack. Back and forth we swapped lead and then we backed off again. We repeated this process several times. I can't remember how many times we attacked but with each attack, we gained ground and crept closer. Each attack became more difficult than the previous as there were Confederate dead and wounded everywhere. On the next to the last assault our regiment got mixed with the Fifteenth and we came within fifteen yards of the Twentieth Maine, the left flank of the Union army. They hit us with a round of galling fire, which we returned and then charged before they could reload. We breached their defensive position, and the hand-to-hand fighting was brutal. I got knocked to the side by a soldier who had been shot and when I tried to get to my feet two others landed on top of me. I did get to my feet but was knocked back down by a well-aimed rifle butt that slammed into my shoulder. Before I could react all of our boys who were still standing were retreating again back down the hill. Much to my surprise, and the rest of us who had survived we were told to form up again for yet another attack. Our captain told us the Yanks could not stave off another attack and they had to be low or out of ammunition. I loaded my rifle and lined up next to Billy and Chester. The command to advance was given and up the hill, we went again, hopefully for the last time. Not a shot came from up above, but then we heard someone from above give the order…CHARGE! The Yanks took us off-guard as they staged a bayonet charge. Those boys in blue, it seemed like hundreds were racing down the hill each one brandishing the much-feared bayonet. Any soldier, whether from the north or south would be quick to tell you they would rather be shot than run through with a bayonet."

Max, well aware of the famous bayonet charge staged by Union Colonel Joshua Chamberland was eager to hear Sam's version. "And then what happened?"

"I think most of us got one shot off, but they were on us before we had a chance to reload. They had the advantage of running downhill and about the only thing we could do was run. Billy tripped over a log and a Union soldier stabbed him in his leg and was about to stab him again when Chester jumped on the soldier and hit him in the head with a rock. They were wrestling around, and I tried to pull Chester off so we could escape and that's when I was stabbed in the arm with a bayonet. The soldier who stabbed me tripped and Chester yelled at me, 'Run!' Down the hill we went. Since we were in no position to outfight the Yanks, we would outrun them.

"Hopping over boulders, dead and wounded men we ran down the hill and across the valley, many a Yank on our tail yelling and screaming at us. When we got to that Devil's place you talked about with the large boulders we cut to the left while many in our regiment went to the right. We must have run for twenty or thirty minutes when we, finally out of breath, stopped in a cornfield up there above that rise beyond your fence. Me and Chester were tired, hot, and thirsty. I had just bent over to catch my breath when five Union soldiers appeared right in front of us in the corn. It all happened so quickly. Chester was shot in the throat, and I knew he was dead before he hit the ground. I wasn't going to fight it out with those five Yanks, and I turned and ran but only got a few yards when I felt a bullet rip through my lower left leg. I knew I had to stay on my feet because they would finish me off. A few more yards and I stumbled and rolled to the side.

"It was only by the grace of God those Yanks ran right by me. They never saw me. They no sooner passed me by when I got up and started through the field in the opposite direction. After a short while, I came to the top of that rise right up there where I saw your farm. I figured if I could just get some water and rest for a bit then I would try to get back to my regiment. I walked down to the fence, you saw me, and well…here I am. Got that water and bandaged up as well. Can't thank you and your wife enough."

Elizabeth carrying a tray with two bowls and a glass pitcher approached the table while announcing. "All right gentlemen. I have with me baked beans, potato salad, and homemade lemonade."

Smiling, Sam remarked, "I haven't had any lemonade since I joined the army. My mother used to make it all the time back home. She'd always use plenty of sugar. Said that was the only way to make good lemonade."

Elizabeth placed the tray on the table and then poured a full measure of the light yellow drink into a cup and handed it to Sam. "Your mother and mine must have been cut from the same bolt of cloth when it comes to lemonade. She always used lots of sugar and that's the way I like to make it."

Max, placing the meat on a platter asked Sam, "What do you think you'd like to eat…dog or burger?"

Finishing a long swig of the sweet beverage Sam responded, "I'm not sure. I've never had either."

Max placed the tray on the table, stabbed a burger and a hotdog, and placed one of each in what Sam viewed as strange-looking bread. Max, noticing the odd look on Sam's face explained, "These are call buns. They're probably different than what you're used to." Pointing at ketchup and mustard bottles, he further explained, "The condiments are right there."

Sam stared at the bright red and yellow plastic containers and repeated, "Con…di…ments?"

Talking to Sam as if he were a Confederate soldier from 1863 rather than a reenactor, Max went on, "They are flavors that can be put on the meat to make it taste even better. The red one is kind of like a tomato taste and the yellow is sort of spicy. When you were back home in Alabama did your mother not have gravy or something like that for the meat?"

"Sure," said Sam. "She made gravy with about every meal we had."

Elizabeth, who couldn't quite understand why Max was speaking to the young boy in the manner he was joined in on the weird conversation. "You shouldn't feel odd because you've never had a hot dog before. I didn't enjoy my first hot dog until my freshman year at college. I met Max at a football game and that's when I had my first dog."

Cocking his head, Sam asked, "Football game?"

Max, realizing the young man was not going to understand many of the things that were said, answered, "It's not important. What is important though is that we bless this meal, and then that we get ta eatin'."

He then nodded toward Elizabeth to say grace, but then Sam spoke up, "Would you folks mind if I said the blessing? It's the least I can do after all you've done for me."

Folding her hands reverently Elizabeth responded, "Why of course."

Bowing his head Sam folded his hands and then began. *"He who dwells in the shelter of the highest will rest in the shadow of the Almighty for I will say of the Lord…"* Sam stopped speaking and looked toward the sky as he smiled.

Thinking the blessing was over Max reached for the baked beans but was stopped when Elizabeth continued praying, *"He is my refuge, my fortress, my God in whom I trust, surely He will save you from the fowler's snare and the deadly pestilence. He will cover you with his feathers and beneath His wings you will find refuse...."*

Elizabeth stopped praying and looked across the table at Sam who picked up where she had left off, *"His salvation shall be your shield and your rampart. You shall not fear the terror of night nor the arrows that fly by day, not the pestilence that stalks in the darkness, nor the plague that destroys the midday..."*

Sam stopped and nodded at Elizabeth as if she knew what to say next, which she did, *"A thousand may fall at your side, ten thousand at your right hand, but it will not come near you..."*

Back and forth they went Sam: *"You will only see it with your eyes and see the punishment of the wicked..."*

Elizabeth: *"If you make the Most High your dwelling, even the Lord, who is my refuse then no harm will befall you, no disaster will come near to your tent..."*

Looking directly at Max, Sam continued as if the next part of the prayer was meant solely for Max, *"For He will command His angels concerning you to guard you in all your ways, they will lift you in their hands so you will not strike your foot against a stone..."*

Elizabeth seemed like she was on a roll, *"You will tread upon the lion and the cobra; you will trample the great lion and the serpent..."*

"Because He loves me, says the Lord," said Sam, *"I will rescue him; I will protect him, for he acknowledges My name..."*

Elizabeth added, *"He will call upon me and I will answer Him. I will be with him in trouble..."* Elizabeth stood and raised her hands toward Heaven and then addressed Sam, "An finally."

Sam finished the long prayer; *"I will deliver him and honor him. With long life, I will satisfy him and show him my salvation...Amen!"*

Elizabeth added an 'Amen' of her own and then smiled at Max who at the moment seemed to be lost as he stated, "I guess that was a blessing of the food, but I'm not sure."

Sam quickly cleared up Max's bewilderment. "That was Psalm 91."

Chiming in, Elizabeth explained, "It's one of my favorite prayers. It's a prayer of acknowledgment that reminds us that the Lord is always at our side and that he will protect us."

Sam added to what Elizabeth said, "That God's angels will protect us. My mother used to and still does to this day say this prayer morning, noon, and night. Over the years I heard her pray it so much that eventually I had it memorized and I too say it daily."

Elizabeth reached for the lemonade. "My father made me memorize Psalm 91 explaining it was a prayer of protection."

Max shrugged as if he understood what his wife and this strange young boy were saying while passing a paper plate that contained a hot dog and a burger across the table to Sam. "Help yourself to some beans and some of that potato salad."

His plate full of food, Sam watched as Max took a bite of a hotdog, then duplicated the process, taking a small bite himself. Chewing. he had a look of doubt on his face, but then he swallowed and grinned, "This is good!" This was followed by Sam taking a bite of the potato salad which he swallowed and spoke again, "I've never seen potatoes made this way, but they taste wonderful."

Pleased that Sam was enjoying the food, Max asked, "What do you plan on doing after the war?"

"Well, if I survive which I plan on doing, the first thing I'll do is go back home to Five Points. It'll be good to get back home. I've got a girl back there waiting for me. She's the same age as me. Her name is Rose, and we've known each other since I guess we were three years old. She lives just down the road from our place. When we were seven, I asked her to marry me and we both just laughed. Ten years later when I was seventeen, I asked her to marry me and this time she answered, 'Yes.' But there was a condition. I was just about to join up with the Confederacy and she told me in no uncertain terms she would only marry me when I returned from the war. She had no intention of marrying up with me before I joined up because if I was killed during the war then she would wind up a widow. The day I left for the army I told her I would return and that's why I have to do everything possible to survive and get back home."

Interested, Max asked, "When you say everything possible what exactly does that mean? Does that include the possibility of desertion?"

Sam hesitated while taking a forkful of beans as he objected strongly. "There is no way I would ever desert the army. If I did that, I would never be able to go back home. I would be disgraced. Besides, I've seen firsthand what they do to deserters. They either get hanged or shot by a firing squad. If I am to be shot to death I'd rather it be the enemy than those from the same army I fight with. So no, I'll never desert!"

"Okay, I get that, but other than desertion what does everything possible men?"

Drinking some lemonade Sam responded, "What it means is shaving a little off around the edge of battle. Many of the men in my regiment and I'm sure others may run a bit slower than we are ordered to, or we may charge a little slower than ordered. That boy I killed at Sharpsburg is a good example. When I woke up the morning of the battle, I had no plans to kill another person but when that young Yank came at me with that bayonet I knew it was either him or me. I do not doubt if I hadn't shot him, he would have tried to kill me and because I killed him rather than him killing me, well that was just one step closer to getting me back home. At that moment I realized I had to do whatever was possible to survive. I don't wake up every morning with the thought in mind that I'm going to kill Yanks but that during the day I will do whatever it takes to survive and return home to Rose."

Laying down the burger he had taken a bite of Sam reached into his shirt pocket and removed a folded piece of paper while speaking, "I got me a letter here from Rose that she sent me last year. I keep it right here in my pocket close to my heart and whenever I go into battle or start to feel down, I take it out and read it and I remember why it is I have got to get back home."

He unfolded the letter and handed it across the table to Max. "You can read it if you'd like."

Max kindly refused, "I wouldn't think of reading that letter. What's in there is between you and Rose."

"It's all right," said Sam. "All she has written about is what's going on back in Five Points and how she misses me. Go on…you can read it."

Taking the letter, the first thing Max noticed was the date, October 2, 1862. Reading the date, he remarked, "This letter is dated 1862."

"That it is," said Sam. "It was written by Rose's hand ten months ago. I didn't receive it until the week of Christmas last December."

"So if I'm correct then," said Max, "You've had this letter with you for about seven months."

Sam took another bite out of his burger and responded, "Yes, I guess so."

Max looked at Elizabeth wondering if she was thinking the same things he was, then he spoke again to Sam. "It just seems odd. The letter itself seems much older like it was written a long time ago. The paper seems worn and fragile."

"That's because I've had it here in my shirt every day since I received it. It's been through rain and heat, plus the fact that I read it every day."

Max read the short letter and noticed it was signed, *All my love, Rose.*

He folded the letter handed it back to Sam and spoke with sincerity, "Your Rose sounds like a nice girl and she has lovely handwriting."

Elizabeth who at the moment felt out of the loop asked politely, "If I could ask if it's not too personal what does the letter say?"

Max gestured at Sam and replied, "I think I'll let Sam explain what was written."

Sam placed the letter back inside his shirt pocket and then answered, "Rose writes that first of all, she misses me terribly. She goes on to say she hopes the war will end soon. The Yankees burned down two farms just up the road from her place. When the Yanks came to Rose's place, they took their horses and livestock, all of the canned fruits and vegetables they had put up, but did not destroy the farm. She writes the local preacher dropped by to see how they were getting along. She finishes up by saying her sister who happens to live in Atlanta just had a new baby. She ended the letter telling me I needed to be careful and not get killed so when I get home we can marry."

Max changed the subject as he could see that Elizabeth was getting emotional as she wiped a tear from her eye. "That canteen you have there. Could I take a look at it?"

Sam nodded and handed the canteen across the table.

"This is a genuine Civil War canteen," said Max. "Do you have any idea how hard these are to find? This one looks like it was made with oak, probably sealed with beeswax. It has traditional metal bands with wood plugs. Normally they come with a cloth strap, but I see you have used some rope for your strap."

"When I joined up they issued me the standard tinned iron canteen with a grey cloth cover but I lost it at the battle at Sharpsburg. Later on, that day I took this one here from a dead Yankee. I figured he had no more use for it and I did. If you turn it to the other side, you can see where I carved my name in the wood."

Max turned the canteen over and there ruggedly carved was the name. *S. Pritchard 47th Alabama.* Admiring the canteen, Max inquired. "Why the rope and not the cloth strap?"

"After a few months, the strap wore through. I found this old rope in an abandoned barn down in Virginia, so I just made my strap."

Handing the canteen back to Sam Max asked another question, "I don't suppose you have any ammunition on you?"

"I do. When we left New Guiford I had sixty rounds in my cartridge box and an extra twelve in my cap pouch. I think I still have around twenty rounds left."

"Would it be possible for me to see one?"

Sam opened his cartridge box, removed a round, and handed it to Max.

Max was instantly amazed as he examined the cartridge while speaking. "This is an actual Civil War minie ball, about 1 oz. in weight, a half inch in diameter, the three standard rings with a coned top. This is the real thing....a 59 caliber minie ball!"

Sam, giving Max an odd look stated matter of fact. "Of course, it's real. Wouldn't do much good if it wasn't."

Max asked, "Do you think I could keep this?"

"Why not," said Sam. "After all you've done for me."

Looking off to the west Sam slowly stood as he announced, "It would seem the cannon fire had stopped. It's getting late in the day…only about three hours of light left. I reckon they've stopped fighting for the day." Testing his left leg, he smiled at Elizabeth. "Whatever you did to my leg it seems to be much better. I had best be off now. I have to try and find my regiment. I'm not sure what direction to go."

Elizabeth handed him a small bottle of aspirin as she explained, "If the pain starts to come back just do like you did before…with water."

Sam put the bottle in his pants pocket, walked around the table, and reached for Max's hand. Nodding at Elizabeth he smiled broadly. "Thanks for your hospitality. I may never look at a Yankee the same way again after meeting you. I thank you for the water, for bandaging me up, and for the vittles. I'll say a prayer for you tonight that no soldiers, north or south come to your farm and cause you any trouble." Shaking Max's hand firmly he tipped his hat to Elizabeth, turned, and started across the yard where he slipped through the old fence. He hesitated and waved. At the top of the rise near the trees he stopped and turned back and raised his rifle on high as if to say goodbye one last time then he stepped into the trees.

Elizabeth began to clean up the table while commenting, "Well if that wasn't one of the strangest conversations I've ever had with another person."

Max, checking to see if the fire had cooled down enough to dump the coals, added, "That it was… indeed." He walked to the edge of the patio and stared off into the trees as he spoke over his shoulder. "Do you love me?"

Elizabeth, taken by surprise answered as if she were dumbfounded, "Where did that come from? I would have thought that was settled and understood a few years back. Of course, I love you."

Max placed his right foot on the bench and inquired. "If you truly love me then I can assume you trust me as well."

"What's gotten into you this evening? What's with this trust issue all of a sudden?"

"Because you may have to display a level of trust in me tomorrow that you cannot even imagine."

"Whatever are you talking of?"

"I can't fully explain that to you at this moment, but I can tell you it has to do with that boy…Sam Pritchard. But before I try to explain what I think may be happening I need proof and the only way I can get that is if I go to town to the Hall of Records and take a look at their archives. If I happen to find what I'm looking for then when I get home, we'll have a lot to talk over. If I don't find the proof, I need then we'll just have to say us meeting Sam Pritchard was nothing but a strange experience. If I leave now, I can be back in about two hours. Will you be all right here by yourself?"

Giving her husband a look of *Are you kidding me,* she explained, "I'll be fine. I'll bathe the girls and then I'll put them down for the night. Then, I'll relax with a cup of coffee and work on my quilt. If you're going to go you had better leave now. It'll be dark in a couple of hours."

CHAPTER THIRTY-EIGHT

It was just after nine o'clock when Max walked in the screen door and yelled, "Elizabeth...I'm back!"

Elizabeth, seated on the couch, answered, "In here in the living room."

Max, leaning on the doorframe held up his cell phone. "I found what I was looking for. It's unbelievable!"

Pushing an unfinished quilt to the side, Elizabeth patted a seat cushion, inviting him to sit. "Come, sit with me, and tell me what it is you have found."

Max walked across the room and stated, "I will, but first I have to download a picture from my phone onto my computer which will create an eight-by-ten document. It will be easier to explain my discovery with the aid of the hard copy of the picture. It should only take me a few minutes. You better put some coffee on because we have a lot to talk about."

Minutes later Max strolled back into the living room where he found Elizabeth arranging a pot of coffee, two mugs, and a plate of homemade oatmeal-raison cookies on a small coffee table. She sat, smoothed her dress, and straightened her bangs. "I'm all ready to hear about your trip to town."

Max sat next to her, laid a sheet of copy paper on the table in front of her, and announced, "Here it is!"

Elizabeth stared at the rows of printed information and not realizing what she was looking at picked up the paper and examined it closely. "What am I looking at?"

"That, my dear wife, is a copy of one of the sections from the archives that lists those in the Confederate army who died here at the Battle of Gettysburg. The names are listed in alphabetical order, and you happen to be looking at a page that lists some of those whose last names start with the letter P. If you will, please read the sixth name down."

Elizabeth ran her index finger down to the sixth name and read it out loud, "Samuel Pritchard." Giving her husband a quizzical look, she shrugged. "And?"

Max remarked in confidence, "That's our Sam...Sam Pritchard!"

"You mean that young boy I just bandaged up?"

"Exactly!"

Elizabeth apologized, "I'm sorry I'm not as enthused about this as you. When I was out there you never mentioned his last name. You just referred to him as Sam. And while I'm thinking of it, how could that young man who was with us be listed as a Confederate soldier who died, what...over a hundred and fifty years in the past? You told me he was a reenactor. I'm not understanding what your point is here."

Tapping the paper, Max explained, "That young boy who you patched up, in all actually may not be a reenactor."

"If not a reenactor...then who?"

Max poured himself a cup of hot coffee and gave Elizabeth a look that indicated he was not sure of what he was saying. "I know you're going to think I'm off my rocker here, but that young man who was out in our backyard may not be a reenactor...but the ghost soldier Kellem told me about. His father saw the ghost soldier standing by the fence back in 1938 and then thirty years later, Kellem himself sees the same young Confederate soldier standing at the same section of fencing. In both cases when approached the soldier limped off onto the trees and vanished. Do you recall when those two newspaper reporters, one from Pittsburgh and the other from right here in town came to visit us here at the farm and they talked about how one of them had seen the same soldier back when he was ten years old while visiting the battlefield, not to mention that sighting happened right out there by the fence and then the other reporter said he ran into a man who claimed to have seen the same thing. That's four different appearances at four different times at the same location. The soldier never ages and looks the same in every one of the sightings. That boy, Sam, who sat right out there at our picnic table matched the description down to the smallest detail. You just can't sluff something like that off as a mere coincidence. I'm pretty sure that we, you, and I just shared a meal with a ghost!"

Undaunted, Elizabeth picked up a cookie and remarked, "We've already had this ghost discussion before, and I told you back then that I do not believe in ghosts and despite this piece of paper you have shown me I still do not believe in their existence." Taking a bite of oatmeal raisin she continued, "What makes you so sure the Sam Pritchard listed here is the same as the one who sat in our backyard?"

"It's obvious…read the entire description the archive states."

She ran her finger across the printed name and information and read out loud. "Pvt. Samuel Pritchard…47th Alabama…Five Points, Alabama… Died July 3rd, 1863, near the Emmittsburg Fence, Pickett's Charge."

Before Elizabeth could react Max interjected, "What more proof do we need? That boy told me his name was Samuel Pritchard and more than that he explained to me he comes from a town in Alabama called Five Points. He not only informed me he is with the 47th Alabama regiment, but his name and his regiment were crudely scratched into the side of his canteen."

"Could there not have been more than one Sam Pritchard in the 47th Alabama?"

"I doubt that very seriously," said Max, "There is a possibility there could have been another soldier with the same name in the army, but in the same regiment and from the same town…well that seems highly unlikely."

"I'll tell you what seems unlikely," said Elizabeth, "and that's just this. The record of this soldier's death, this Sam Pritchard was compiled what, let's do the math, that would be about one hundred and fifty-six years ago. From what you have told me about the Battle of Gettysburg it sounds like it was a very chaotic time with all the dead and wounded there were. I am sure record keeping back in those days was not as sophisticated as it is now. How can you be fully confident in records that are over a century and a half old?"

"I realize these records are over one hundred and fifty years old but it's all I have to go on. Given the fact that identification of those who died in the battle at Gettysburg was conducted in a far less sophisticated procedure than what would be utilized today you have to understand that burying the dead after the three days of battle was a horrific task. Burial teams were sent out onto the battlefields on July 4th and over the next few days thousands of soldiers, north and south, were found. Most of these soldiers were buried right where they had died or at least close to where they had fallen.

"This was done for two main reasons. First, there was still a war going on and the Union army and the local citizens could not be sure Lee would not attack again in the next few days and the second reason was even more of a threat. With thousands of decaying dead soldiers and over three thousand dead horses scattered around the fields in the July heat, it would become a health hazard. Many of the dead in both armies were buried in shallow graves no more than ten to twelve inches deep. A week following the three-day battle heavy rains came and washed away the top layer of dirt covering these bodies exposing legs and arms. Between the birds pecking at the decomposing bodies and wild hogs digging the corpses up and tearing them apart it was indeed a grisly time in and around Gettysburg.

"I guess about two months passed when Lincoln pushed for a national cemetery in Gettysburg where the dead could be buried. It was decided this would be done but only Union soldiers were to be reburied there. The dead Confederates would lay in their shallow, makeshift field graves. Years later many Southern states demanded that their dead be transferred back down south, which eventually they were, buried at various cemeteries throughout the South. Despite all of this, what seems like mishandling of the dead there was a system of identifying those who were buried and this was based on what could be found on the dead. There were no official dog tags for soldiers in those days but there were other methods soldiers adopted so they could identify those who were killed,"

Collecting his thoughts, he took a drink of coffee and then continued, "Soldiers on both sides of the war went into battle after battle with more than just the fear of being killed. The thought they could be killed and not identified was disheartening. No one wants to die and be *unknown!* Civil War soldiers were very innovative and used several different techniques in case they were killed and needed to be identified. The most popular method was that soldiers would write their rank, name, regiment, and hometown on a small piece of paper, and then with the use of a pin they would attach this makeshift name tag on the inside of their hat, sleeves, or trousers. An-other method used is they would engrave their name into the soft lead of their belt buckles."

Elizabeth swallowed the last bite of her cookie, followed by a sip of coffee as she commented, "This is all very interesting and quite education-al, but I still do not see how any of this historical information proves the boy who sat out back in our yard is the same soldier listed here. I am most definitely not convinced the boy I patched up is a ghost. I am convinced he is simply a reenactor. I have seen you dressed up in your Confederate reen-actor get up and aside from the fact he looked more realistic than you, it's the same thing. He is a reenactor…not a ghost." Sitting forward to make her next point she remarked, "That boy could not possibly be a ghost. He spoke to me, and I cleaned his wounds and touched his skin. He bleeds real blood and he even shed a tear when I applied that peroxide. Can you feel a ghost's skin? Can a ghost bleed? Can a ghost shed tears?"

Looking at Max she waited for a response which he answered awkwardly, "I cannot answer these questions. I do not know any more about ghosts than you."

Elizabeth, thinking she was slowly winning the friendly debate, pointed out, "The fact the boy was stabbed in his arm by a bayonet and shot in his keg proves that he is not a ghost."

Max rebutted her statement and emphasized, "The fact he *was stabbed* and *shot* proves that he *is not* a reenactor. I've been going to reenactments with my father ever since I was twelve years old. I have participated in nearly thirty reenactments over the years, and I can state firsthand that it is impossible to get stabbed or shot at one of these events. Live ammunition is never used, and bayonets are prohibited on the battlefield. I can guarantee you that the boy did not receive those wounds at a reenactment.

"Do you recall when he removed his shirt so you could see to his arm? He apologized to you for the way he smelled from his body odor. He told you he hadn't bathed for two weeks. No self-respecting modern-day reenactor would go for two weeks without bathing. That way of thinking goes beyond the world of reenacting and enters into the world of stupidity. I have over the years been in many a reenactment and I have never gone one day without bathing. The uniforms we wear are made of heavy wool and even if worn during the cooler months during a fall reenactment after a day of running around fields, charging, retreating, or whatever is called for it can be quite exhausting and after sweating all day, believe me, one needs a bath or a shower. Not bathing for two weeks is inconsistent for a reenactor."

Raising his coffee cup to make his next observation he went on, "And another thing…what about that canteen he had? You may not realize this, but that canteen was an actual wooden Civil War canteen, not a knockoff or a remanufactured replica, but the real McCoy! I should know because my father has one at home in a glass case along with some other Civil War relics he has purchased over the years. Those canteens are hard to come by and I know he paid a pretty penny for the one he has. He would never even think of taking that canteen into a reenactment. It's far too fragile and may fall apart. In short, what I'm saying is no reenactor would ever take an authentic item like that canteen to a reenactment. That boy, Sam Pritchard, even scratched his name, and his regiment along with the date 1862 into the wood. If that canteen is authentic and I believe it is then why would a reenactor scratch up the side of a valuable collector's item with his name, date, and regiment? That doesn't make sense!"

Elizabeth realizing her thoughts of changing Max's opinion of Sam Pricthard was rapidly being erased sat quietly while her husband continued to offer even more proof that Sam was indeed a ghost and not a reenactor.

"And another thing you probably did not notice that I did. Sam was not wearing any socks, which was common amongst many a Confederate soldier. Many of them did not even have shoes, but they went into battle. A reenactor would never go into a two or three day reenactment without socks on their feet. As realistic as reenactors try to appear they still want to have some level of comfort. And while we are on the subject of feet that boy was wearing a pair of Brogans…authentic Civil War-issued shoes; heavy, ankle-high black shoes. My father also has a pair of those he bought at an auction. A reenactor would never consider wearing anything that is a collector's item. It was easy to see that the shoes the boy had on had seen hundreds of miles. Shoes that a reenactor would wear are replicas of the original Brogans and are only worn a few times a year, hence they are in better condition. While we are on the subject of being authentic what about that bullet he gave me? That was a genuine 1862-'63 Civil War minie ball. He said he started the day with sixty rounds and had an additional twelve in his cap box. When he arrived at our farm, he still had twenty rounds on him. Why would a reenactor have live ammunition at an event where live rounds are not permitted? I could go on and on. What about that old letter he had from Rose? It was dated October 1862. How can you explain all these things?"

"I can't explain any of them," said Elizabeth, "but let me just say that if you were a lawyer giving your final summation at a trial to determine whether this Sam Pritchard was a reenactor or a ghost and I was a juror I would be impressed with all the proof you bring forth, but I still would not concede that the boy is a ghost. It's just too unbelievable!"

Elizabeth reached across the couch and gently patted Max's hand as she spoke in a non-threatening manner, "We can sit here all night long and go back and forth about this issue and I feel the result would be as it sits right now. I believe Sam Pritchard is a reenactor, probably a reenactor that should be awarded an Academy Award for his performance and you feel that he is not a reenactor…but a ghost. At least, can we agree on that?"

Max smiled. "Yes, we can agree on that."

She went on as she tapped the paper. "Let's just say for the moment that I agree with you. I don't, but let's just say I do for the sake of arguing. If this young man listed here who died on July 3rd, 1863 is the same boy who sat in our backyard and ate a hot dog then that is pretty amazing and unexplainable. And if that is true, what difference does it make? This ghost soldier appeared here at the farm back in 1938, then was seen again some thirty years later. This ghost was also seen at some point by that reporter when he was ten years old and the other reporter claims he talked with a man who also saw this ghost. So what we are saying is this Sam Pritchard has been here before on several occasions, none of which can be explained. My point here is what difference does any of this make? If we tell others about the experience we had today, some will believe us and some will not. In the long run, it will turn out to be just another unexplainable ghost story. Again, what difference will it make?"

"You bring up an interesting point," said Max. "I thought about what a difference any of this makes on my way back from the Hall of Records and about halfway home it hit me! There is a difference and it happened today in our backyard. Today was the fifth appearance of Sam Pritchard we know of. In all the other appearances he never crossed over the fence into the yard. Today…he did! Before today, he never communicated with anyone. Today he did! He talked with us, ate with us, you bandaged him up. All those things make this appearance different than the others. The question is, why did he come into the yard and speak with us? He claims it was just for the water, but I think it goes far beyond that. I think he was looking for something…something he needs that over the years he has not been able to find."

Elizabeth frowned in confusion. "Like what?"

Max picked up the paper and answered, "Well, I've been thinking about that also. According to this list, Samuel Pritchard of the 47th Alabama died one hundred and fifty-six years ago on July 3rd, 1863 during Pickett's Charge near the Emmittsburg Fence. Tomorrow is July 3rd and the one hundred and fifty-sixth reenactment will take place right here at Gettysburg at the site of the actual battle.

"There will be thousands of reenactors participating. But more than that I believe something else is going to happen tomorrow. I'm getting the strange feeling that out there on the other side of that fence, it's not 2019, but 1863. I say this because of something Kellem told me about his encounter with this strange soldier. He said when the soldier limped off up the slope that he jumped over the fence to follow him but got the strangest feeling, as if he were not supposed to be there, so back over the fence he came.

"I think what happened is this, Kellem, when he followed the soldier over the fence found himself unknowingly in 1863. If it is true then out there on the other side of the fence, tomorrow July 3rd, 1863, Sam Pritchard will line up with fifteen thousand other Confederate men and march across that one-mile-wide field. They will have no idea that they will be annihilated, butchered. Most of them will never make it to the stone wall that the Union troops will be crouching behind. Many of the southern boys will die at the Emmittsburg Fence from either well-aimed muskets or from devastating cannon fire. One of those who will die tomorrow according to this paper is Sam Pritchard."

Gently shaking the paper in the air, Max went on, "I might be way out in the left field here but what if on July 3rd, 1863, when Sam Pritchard was killed in battle at the Emmittsburg Fence, that fence may have been the last thing he saw on the face of this earth. And as he lay there dying on the battlefield while staring at that fence, he probably realized he was never going to get back home…to ever see Rose again. Maybe that's why he keeps returning to our fence on July 2nd. Think about this, Kellem told me that the fence in our yard his great-great-grandfather constructed…the posts, and the rails are sections of the actual fence that was out there during the battle over a hundred and fifty years ago. It has always been thought that was the cause of the strange voices that are occasionally heard. I think Sam keeps returning to the fence in hopes of surviving and eventually going back to Alabama to be with this Rose."

"If you were writing a book," commented Elizabeth, "in the world of fiction you might have a bestseller on your hands but in the real world, most folks are not going to swallow that story. First of all, if Sam, this ghost soldier keeps returning to the fence in hopes of surviving the war and then returning to Rose, then why in the past did he never come into the yard before, like he did with you? Why, on this visit did he cross over the fence from 1863 into our world of 2019?"

Max sat back and crossed his arms. "I think he came into the yard because he has always been looking for something and maybe he feels that I can give it to him!"

In amazement, Elizabeth responded, "Really, and what pray tell would that be?"

"I think he is searching for a way to get back to Rose and just like all the other ghosts that have been seen over the years around Gettysburg which are referred to as the *restless dead*, he cannot cross over from his life to eternity, so he keeps returning to the fence where he took his last earthly breath."

"And what is it that you can give him and how could you possibly accomplish that unbelievable feat?"

"Look, I know this must be hard for you to understand, and believe me, it's just as hard for me to try and explain what I think may be going on. I believe that what I can give him is a way back to Rose and I can try to accomplish that by saving his life, preventing him from being killed tomorrow at Pickett's Charge."

Widening her eyes Elizabeth gave her husband a long stare of doubt. "If I was confused before, now I am even more befuddled. Sam Pritchard died over a century and a half ago. How can you save him…tomorrow?"

Max held his head in his hands as he tried to elaborate. "I think this is becoming more complex than what it is. Okay, let me explain. I believe that on the other side of that fence somewhere out there on the battlefield it is 1863, not 2019. Tomorrow is July 3rd, and on that date in 1863 Lee ordered an attack on the Union forces which round up being called Pickett's Charge. If Sam Pritchard is out there, he nor any other soldier in the Confederate army has a clue what is going to happen tomorrow. Now, here is how I can help. I already know what is going to happen, and in most cases, if you know what's going to happen before it does you can avoid, at times catastrophic results. For instance, let's say you live in Florida, and you are warned that a potential hurricane is going to rip through your community. You already know what's going to happen and if you leave the area before the storm hits you may just be saving not only your life but your family's as well. It's the same kind of situation here. I know what's going to happen tomorrow and if I can steer him away from the Emmittsburg Fence during the battle, then he will survive the day, and maybe, just maybe he'll survive the remainder of the war and return to Rose."

"Once again," said Elizabeth, "this sounds like a wonderful novel of fiction, but in the real world I do not see or can imagine how this could be accomplished."

"Do you remember when we first came back to the house after Sam went his way and I told you that you may have to trust me more than you ever have before? Well, here is what I meant. For me to save this young man, first I must find him. I have a plan in mind for doing just that, and even though I thought I would sleep on my thoughts tonight and then make a decision in the morning I am going to go through with my plan… which is just this. Tomorrow morning following a hearty breakfast, I plan on decking myself out in my full Confederate regalia…my reenactment uniform, and then leaving before the crack of dawn, I will cross over the fence and venture out into the battlefield. I know that it will be dark, but I know those fields like the back of my hand. I know where General Lee had his headquarters and surrounding this area is where his army was camped. It is in this vicinity where the 47th Alabama will be encamped. When I get on the other side of the fence and near Lee's headquarters, I will find one of two things. I may find that the encampment will be filled with reenactors and I may even locate Sam Pritchard, at which time we'll have a good laugh. On the other hand, I may find myself actually in 1863, and if I can locate Sam then, somehow I will have to convince him before the coming battle that he needs to listen to me and go where I lead him, so that he can not only survive the day, but possibly the remainder of the war and then return to Five Points and Rose. What do you think?"

Squinting her eyes at him as if she were about to say something that was based on wisdom, she replied, "I will not tell you what I think, but I will tell you what I know. When you get on the other side of the fence out on the national battlefield park, eventually daylight will descend on the land and all you are going to be able to find or experience is a large group of reenactors, just like there always is here this time of year. You may even find this Sam Pritchard and like you said you'll both have a good laugh. Later in the day, tomorrow you'll return to the farm and confirm everything I'm saying now. But there is also something else I know, or at least I think, because I don't know exactly how God works. If it were possible for you to go back in time, in this case over one hundred and fifty-six years and as you say, save this young man's life I think that would be wrong."

Max not completely understanding where Elizabeth was heading interjected, "How could it possibly be wrong to save another person's life?"

"I'm not quite sure but I feel that you would be going against the law of God, that you would be playing God."

Max looked at his wife in astonishment, then asked, "Whatever are you talking about? How could I, a person who is far less religious than you even consider going against the law of God, as you say…playing God?"

Elizabeth could see that Max was on the verge of getting upset. She moved closer to him and apologized, "I did not mean to ruffle your feathers, but I think you're being pretty unrealistic about this situation. Let me explain what I mean."

Tapping the paper she added, "This, what I think may be considered an official document, states very clearly in black and white that Pvt. Samuel Pritchard from Five Points, Alabama, a member of the 47th Alabama Regiment died on July 3rd, 1863, near the Emmittsburg Fence during Pickett's Charge. Whether you or I choose to believe it or not it was God's will that Sam would take his final breath on that day, at that time. In other words, it was *his time.* The Lord tells us in the Bible that we can live to be seventy to eighty years of age if we have the strength. Ol' Sam Prichard was what… maybe twenty years old when his number as we say *came up.*

"Just sitting here thinking about his death back in 1863 kind of makes one sad. Here, you and I sit, both in our early twenties…married, with two lovely daughters, you own your own business and we have our place. Sam Pritchard never got to experience any of those things. He died at that fence during a Civil War battle that took place over a century and a half in the past. It was God's will that Sam and many other a soldier die on that day and that's just part of life and something that we all have to accept. Now, listen to me. I do not feel you are looking at this realistically or even mathematically. You're always saying that a mathematical computation cannot be broken or proven wrong. The mathematics you are suggesting do not add up."

Max. who was normally the one explaining math to others found himself on the receiving end of a mathematical problem as he replied, "Please…go on."
"Since you asked, well then, let's just suppose for a moment that you could go back in time and save this young soldier. If by doing so, he winds up surviving the war he then returns home to Alabama and marries this Rose. They have children, which results in grandchildren and great-grandchildren and on and on. Because you saved this boy generations of people were created that I guess you could say were never intended to be here. Then, there's the opposite side of the coin. If he, as it stands right now is dead and does not return to Alabama and marry Rose another mathematical figure comes into play. Rose, being a young woman, no doubt mourned the loss of her loved one, meaning Sam. She may have become an old maid and never married or she may have married another young man and from their mar-

riage there was and is now a generation of people, who knows where in the country that stemmed from their marriage. What this adds up to is that if you save that boy and he winds up marrying Rose there will be people here who are not supposed to be and what is to happen to those who were meant to be here from her actual marriage to this other young man?"

Max sat in silence amazed at Elizabeth's mathematical theory and was about to speak when she continued, "And here's something else you may not have considered. If this Sam Pritchard, survives this Pickett's Charge he may in the future before the war ends kill another soldier that was not intended. By saving this young man, you may just be altering hundreds, maybe thousands of lives between 1863 and the present today 2019. Think about that!"

Max shook his head in wonder and then smiled at his wife. "Why did I not think of these things? How could I have missed that? Considering what you have pointed out, now I have to do some rethinking." Standing, he stretched and took a final swig of coffee. "It's almost ten-thirty. I better hit the sack if I'm planning on going out to the battlefield before daylight."

"Then, you're still planning on going in the morning?"

"Yes, but I may be making this journey for a different reason than saving Sam's life. There are still a great number of unanswered questions surrounding this ghost soldier or reenactor or whatever he is."

Elizabeth picked up the coffee pot and plate of leftover cookies and suggested, "You go ahead and head on up. I need to straighten up a little bit down here and then I'll check in on the girls. You need to get a good night's rest."

CHAPTER THIRTY-NINE

The twins were sleeping peacefully on a pallet of soft blankets that Elizabeth had arranged on the living room floor. Busy at the stove, she stirred a skillet of scrambled eggs, then slid them onto a plate which she placed on the kitchen table when she noticed Max standing in the doorway dressed in his old tattered, faded gray Confederate reenactment uniform. Snapping to attention he clicked his heels which was more of a low thud due to the worn imitation Brogans on his feet. He gave his wife a stylish salute and stated, "All present and accounted for!"

Elizabeth smiled at her husband and waved a spatula in his direction, returning his official greeting with what she thought was a subtle military order of her own. "All present are to be seated immediately!"

Max pulled out a chair and seated himself while Elizabeth announced, "This morning's rations are scrambled eggs, biscuits and gravy, bacon, sourdough toast, orange juice, and coffee." Pouring Max a cup of coffee she seated herself and inspected the table. "Everything seems in order so I'll just bless this food and then we can eat."

Grace completed, she passed the eggs across the table, and asked, "Are you still of the mind to try and save Sam Pritchard or are you simply going to a reenactment?"

Heaping a large spoonful of sausage gravy over two warm buttermilk biscuits, Max replied, "After you came to bed last night I laid there for almost two hours pondering what I should do. There was no doubt in my mind I was going to go this morning, but the thought of saving Sam Pricthard's life, if even possible, weighed heavy on me." Taking a bite of a gravy-covered biscuit he went on, "I'm planning on leaving the farm and crossing the fence before the sun comes up. I don't know what to expect but like you said all I may find is a large group of reenactors. Who knows, I might not even be able to find the young man who paid us that visit yesterday. I'm going to focus on getting to Lee's headquarters where I'm sure there will be several Confederate reenactors from all over the country. I'll just go there and see what happens."

Elizabeth salted her eggs and confirmed, "Well I want you to know that I support you in this adventure you're about to go on. It sounds to me as if you are undecided about whether Sam Pritchard is indeed a reenactor or a ghost."

"I still don't know what to think, but I can tell you this. Being an individual who justifies everything with mathematics there are still some things about this whole situation that do not add up and I'm hoping by going out to the battlefield today this will somehow all be solved."

"I can't wait until you return later this evening," said Elizabeth. "You can tell me all about the reenactors you met. Why, I wouldn't put it past you if you decided to participate in the reenactment today. Have you ever with your father in the past been a part of the third day of battle here at Gettysburg…this Pickett's Charge, I believe you called it?"

"Yes, I have taken part in a Pickett's Charge reenactment. I was fifteen years old and my father decided it was time for me not just to tag along on a reenactment, but that I should participate. There I was, July 3rd, 2008, standing next to my father and the other fellas from his 2nd South Carolina Regiment. At the original battle, there were approximately fifteen thousand men from the south who made the attack. There were only about four thousand of us that day at the reenactment, but it seemed like a lot more than that. We formed up in Spangler's Woods and the order to advance was given. Off we marched across that long, wide field, the sounds of massive cannon fire and then as we drew closer to the Emmittsburg Fence the deadly sound of thousands of Union rifles. Even though it was all make-believe, well, it's like this, as a reenactor, you can easily get caught up in the moment and in your mind, you can be taken back to the time when the actual event took place. As I slowly marched toward the Union line I couldn't even imagine the fear the soldiers on both sides must have experienced." Seeing that he was rambling, he apologized. "Guess I got carried away there. Listen, do you think you could gather up some food for me to take along today? I don't know how long I'll be gone."

Elizabeth pushed herself away from the table and assured her husband,

"I think I can gather something up for you. Some power bars, a banana or two and we have some juice boxes."

Max laughed, "That's very thoughtful but none of those items will do. I have to take food items with me that are consistent with the 1860's. Power bars and juice boxes are out. As far as fruit goes if we have apples I could take a couple of those with me. I don't think soldiers in the Civil War had much access to bananas."

"I just purchased some apples at the market." Picking up a biscuit she suggested, "How about a few of my biscuits and we still have some of that beef jerky in the pantry."

Max agreed, "That sounds great!"

"Well, then just let me get something together." Opening the pantry she joked, "Because you are going to a reenactment I have no fear or worries about you being shot or stabbed with a bayonet and now I can be safe in knowing my man will not starve out there on the battlefield."

Getting up from the table Max finished his juice and turned to walk out of the kitchen. "While you're getting that food together I'll step out into the living room and get the rest of my gear."

Not even two minutes later he stepped back into the kitchen as he adjusted his cartridge belt and bayonet scabbard. Leaning his musket against the refrigerator he turned on the faucet so he could fill his canteen. Looking out the kitchen window at the backyard he saw the last four sections of the fence which were dimly illuminated from a security light mounted on the side of the barn. Screwing the top back on the canteen he took note of the clock above the sink. "With any luck, I should be about halfway to the campsite before the sun is up."

Elizabeth handed him the apples, jerky and biscuits which he placed in his worn haversack, then walked to the fridge, picked up his musket, and displayed himself. "Well, what do you think? Do I look as authentic as Sam Pritchard?"

"Close enough! Your clothing looks old and wrinkled. I think you'll blend in just fine with the others. Now, you best be on your way." Giving him a peck on the cheek she motioned to the door. "I'll walk you out to the porch. If you happen to get back here to the house by six this evening we're having fried chicken. Call me later when you get safely to the campsite."

Max reached into his baggy pants pocket, held up his cell phone, and commented. "This is one of three items I'm taking with me that they did not have during the Civil War." Shrugging he explained, "I might not even be able to call you if it is 1863 out there. There will be no cell towers so my phone will be useless. The other two items I'm taking with me are a small penlight and my Swiss army knife." Placing the phone back in his pocket he saluted Elizabeth, and then in a forced, low manly voice announced, "Well, my dear wife…I'm off to the war."

Elizabeth gently touched the sleeve of his right arm. "God go with you today and I'll see you later on. Now…be on your way!"

Stepping off the low porch, Max started across the partially darkened yard. The moon was bright and cast a pale eerie glow over the landscape. As he approached the fence the moonlight disappeared from a bank of clouds that moved across the vast sky. Ducking through the wooden rails he was now on the other side of the fence…the battlefield side. He looked back at the house as Elizabeth gave him a subtle wave, turned, and went back inside. He took a deep breath and started the climb up the slight rise to the tree line.

At the trees, he stopped and looked back down at his farm. It appeared peaceful with the combination of the barn light and the light from their porch. Before stepping into the dense trees, he took stock of himself and thought. *It doesn't feel any different over here on this side of the fence like Kellem had said. Maybe that feeling was only present when the ghost soldier was in the area.* Moving carefully through the trees the moonlight came and went every few seconds as the clouds continued to move past the moon. He had no idea if he was in 1863. It was too dark for him to see if the woods looked the same as always or not.

Minutes passed and he stepped out of the dark woods and before him was the vast cornfield Sam talked about where his friend, Chester, had been shot down by Yankees. Looking to his right and left, the cloud cover darkened the surrounding countryside once again. Moving slowly into the rows of shoulder-high corn his mind was working overtime as he thought about the fact that if he was indeed back in 1863, then Chester, Sam's friend, was probably still lying dead somewhere in the corn.

Twenty yards into the corn he stubbed his foot on something and went down on his right knee. Turning on the small penlight he had brought along he aimed the slender ray of light toward the area where he had tripped. At first, he saw nothing but dirt and the lower half of the stalks, but then as he moved the thin light to his right, he couldn't believe what he saw, a pair of legs in Confederate gray, the familiar black Brogans on the feet. Pushing the corn to the side, he made his way on his hands and knees to the upper half of the body. He pushed on the body and then tried to roll the soldier over, but the dead weight was too difficult. The light fell on the soldier's ashen face which was turned to the side. His eyes were closed and there was dried blood not only on the right shoulder of the uniform but his neck and around the mouth. The soldier looked young, probably about the same age as Sam. Taking the boy's right-hand Max checked his wrist for a pulse, *Nothing!* Searching the insides of the soldier's shirt sleeves and pant legs for any identification he found nothing. The boy's hat and musket were lying off to the side a few feet away. Reaching for the Confederate hat he found what he was looking for. Pinned on the left underside there was a small section of paper upon which was written, *Chester Blevins– Five Points, Alabama - 47th Alabama Regiment.*

Dropping the hat as if it were possessed, he looked to his right and then the left as he turned off the light. Suddenly, a sobering thought occurred to him. This Chester Blevins had to be one of the two friends Sam mentioned back at the farm. Sam had explained how he and Chester had run from Little Round Top to a cornfield where Chester was shot by Yankees while Sam escaped certain death by running off. According to Sam, this is where he received the bullet wound in his lower leg. A simple math equation entered into his thought process, two plus two equals four and that could not be disputed. This *was the cornfield* and Chester *was the soldier* Sam had talked about who had not only been shot there, but killed. If these things were indeed true then in all actuality *he was in 1863.*

He peered into the eerie dark stocks of corn, a sense of urgency coming over him. If he was in 1863, rather than 2019 he was going to have to be extremely careful. There could be Union soldiers lurking or who were separated from their regiments not only in the corn but the surrounding fields. As long as it was dark the chances of being seen were minimal, but soon the sun would be up and he would no longer have the luxury of the darkness to conceal him.

A crunching sound off to his left caused him to hunker down as he stared into the darkness. There was a few seconds of silence followed by another sound of nearby corn stalks moving, then a more pronounced sound as if someone had run off, the sound fading into the darkness. Taking a sigh of relief Max thought, *Probably just a deer.*

He stood, leaned on his reenactment musket, and then had a frightening revelation. If it was 1863 and the morning of the third day of battle at Gettysburg within a few hours according to history things would begin to heat up and around the battlefield. If he was seen by any Confederates he was confident that aside from the fact he appeared to be in the southern army he could bluff his way through. If on the other hand, he ran into any Union soldiers, more than likely they would shoot rather than ask questions. Looking at the musket in his right hand he spoke in a low tone to himself, "I'm defenseless with this gun. It doesn't even fire live ammunition." Then, he got a crazy idea…a dangerous idea, but at least he would be able to protect himself if need be. Hiding his reenactment musket a few feet away in the corn, he picked up Chester's musket and then bent down to search the boy's cartridge box and cap pouch for any rounds of ammo.

The ever-changing cloud cover had moved on and with the aid of the moonlight, he was able to see what he was doing. Pulling out a small handful of paper-wrapped cartridges he counted the rounds: seventeen. Placing the ammunition in his empty cartridge box he dumped the percussion caps into his cap pouch and picked up the musket. Holding the gun in both hands he admired the weapon and realized he was holding a gun that had been used in actual Civil War combat. What he didn't know was if the gun was loaded. More than likely it wasn't, that is if the story Sam had shared with him was true. Sam had stated that when the Union staged that bayonet charge at Little Round Top he fired his gun and then turned to run. If Chester had done likewise, then they probably wound up in the cornfield with unloaded muskets. The only way he was going to be able to find out if the gun was loaded was to fire the weapon. That could be better accomplished after the sun was up, because when he fired the gun if it turned out to be loaded, then he was going to have to reload the weapon.

He looked down at Chester and thought that the boy should be buried. He didn't have the time or the means to do so at the moment and besides, if it was 1863, eventually the body would be discovered and then buried. He was behind schedule and had to get moving.

Max continued his slow journey through the corn and finally arrived at the edge of the field where he sat down in the damp grass and checked the time on a pocket watch his father had purchased for him as a high school graduation gift. The time was 6:10 and within the next fifteen to twenty minutes the sun would be up. Looking at a section of trees that was the next part of his journey he would be at the dirt road that led to Lee's headquarters. Getting to his feet he decided to try and make the road while it was still dark.

Ten minutes later when he stepped out of the trees, the first light of day was beginning to pierce the darkness. He knew approximately where he was, but had never been out on battlefield property this early in the day. Looking off into the distance he knew Ike Bledsoe's farm was to the left and Lee's headquarters to the right. Looking down at his feet, he suddenly realized he had stepped out of the cornfield further down than when he had hiked out this way with Kellem in the past. Rather than the familiar rough dirt road, there was just matted-down grass and weeds. There was evidence from some noticeable deep hoof ruts that several horses had passed by this way recently. The area looked different than what he remembered. Before when he had been here the grass and weeds had been worn down to the dirt because of the ATVs the park service used to get to this part of the park. Starting up the road he thought that maybe he was too far down and that the park vehicles did not come this far.

He no more than took five steps up the path when he decided it would be better to stay just inside the tree line than out in the open. Slipping into the trees he continued. Fifteen minutes passed when he stopped to take a drink from his canteen. Following two long swigs of water, he thought it best if he checked to see before going any further. Moving back deeper into the trees he came to a small clearing. Sitting on a large tree trunk he took a percussion cap from his satchel and placed the cap on the firing nipple and cocked the hammer. Aiming the musket at a large tree on the other side of the clearing he took a deep breath and squeezed the trigger. There was a clicking sound but as the hammer hit the nipple no shot was fired. Looking at the gun he spoke to himself, "The gun was not loaded."

Reaching into his cartridge box he removed a paper-wrapped cartridge, tore off the top of the paper with his teeth, and dumped the powder down into the barrel. Then, just like he had done on hundreds of occasions while shooting with his father he placed the minie ball down the barrel, removed the ramrod from beneath the barrel, and rammed the ball home. Laying the ramrod against the tree trunk he placed another cap on the nipple, pulled back the hammer, aimed at the tree, and pulled the trigger. The loud noise from the shot caused several nesting birds in the surrounding trees to fly off. Max watched as the bullet sank into the bark of the tree, then satisfied that the gun was in working order, he reloaded the weapon quickly as he had to move on.

He walked back through the trees and felt more confident now that he was armed with a musket that worked, plus he had plenty of ammo. He hoped that he would not be confronted by any Yanks as he didn't feel like shooting anyone. If he did come across some Union boys he would run off if he had the chance. He was not from 1863, but from 2019 and he had no right to shoot at or kill anyone. At the edge of the tree line, he stepped out onto the path when he heard a rumbling sound followed by two short yells…"Yah!"…"Yah!" followed by a shrill human whistle. Looking down the road in the direction of Bledsoe's farm he saw two horses pulling a buckboard wagon emerge from the trees. Standing in the middle of the road he was just about to leap back into the trees when he saw a soldier riding shotgun as he pointed in Max's direction. In the next three seconds, Max recognized their dirty Confederate gray uniforms. Realizing the driver of the team and his companion were not with the Union army Max waved his arms back and forth signaling for the wagon to stop.

The wagon continued and stopped just short of where he stood, the young soldier sitting next to the driver standing as he leveled his musket at Max. The driver, a much older man brought the team to a halt and then reached over and pushed the aimed musket in the boy's hand downward as he ordered, "Hold up, there Nate. He's one of ours!"

The young boy lowered his gun and stared back at Max while the driver, probably in his sixties, spit tobacco juice and then wiped the side of his mouth with his left hand. Grinning, he spoke with a deep southern drawl, "Howdy there youngin'. Where ya be headin'?"

Feeling as if he had passed for a Confederate soldier and in no danger of being shot, Max replied, "Trying my best to get back with my regiment."

The old man spit again and asked, "An' what regiment would that be?"

Standing proudly as any true Confederate would Max answered without missing a beat, "First Army Corps, General James Longstreet commanding, McLaw's Division, General Kershaw's 2nd South Carolina."

Max's confident reply caused the old man to introduce himself and his armed partner. "My name be Preston Fox an' this here young man sittin' next ta me is Nate Peters. We're both from Virginia. Tell ya what. Why don't ya hop up there in the back and we'll run ya back ta the main camp. It's 'bout an hour's walk from here but we can drop ya off there in half the time."

Max nodded in agreement and started to walk toward the back of the buckboard but was stopped when Preston Fox spoke, "Didn't catch yer name there, Son."

"Miller," said Max. "I'm from Charleston, South Carolina."

"Well Miller, hope ya don't mind blood 'cause we got us three southern boys in the back there. Two are dead and the other one is shot up pretty bad, but it's better than walkin' I reckon."

At the back of the buckboard, Max saw two soldiers laying side by side, the wood bed of the wagon stained from the blood of numerous bodies that had been transported either to a gravesite or to a makeshift battlefield hospital. The other soldier who was sitting on the right held his right arm up with the aid of his left, his bloodied right foot turned at an odd angle. Hoisting himself up into the wagon, Max nodded at the wounded soldier who looked to be in his forties. Tipping his hat to the man Max introduced himself, "Max Miller, 2nd South Carolina."

The man winced in pain but responded in a low, painful voice. "Robert Kline…4th Texas." Looking Max up and down the man went on, "After two days of fighting you don't look none the worse. Not a wound on ya. What have ya seen since you've been here?"

Lying, Max explained, "The first day we arrived on the battlefield late in the day when it was all but over. I never fired my gun. Now yesterday, that's a different tale. We formed up just after two o'clock in the afternoon and marched through two fields and then down some road where we fought tooth and nail near some farm for a few hours with the Yanks. As the day wore on they were reinforced and they got the best of us and we retreated into an unorganized mess. It was very confusing. I got lost in the woods and have been wandering around all night long trying to get back to the main body." Looking up the road, Max smiled. "Looks like we'll be there soon." Shaking his head in sympathy Max gazed at the man's wounds. "You look like you've been through hell. Where were you when you got shot?"

"Got hit three times in a matter of seconds when we were retreating across some stream and then a field. The first shot got my left wrist and then the second, my right shoulder, and then the third got me in my right foot. I've been wandering around following our retreat and then through the night. Sometime, I can't say for sure what time it was, but it was and had been dark for some time I just couldn't go any farther so I sat down next to some trees and tried to get some sleep." Holding up his right arm painfully he remarked in amazement. "I'm surprised I didn't bleed out. I guess it was about a half hour ago this here wagon came by and they loaded me up."

"Well for what it's worth," said Max. "I'm glad you didn't die out here in the fields. When we get to headquarters they'll get you patched up."

"Hope so," stammered Robert. "I think my wrist and foot wounds are minor, but I have to face the fact I might lose my right arm."

Max reached across the wagon and gently patted the soldier's left leg as he smiled "Let's hope that doesn't happen."

Robert looked down at the two dead soldiers, frowned, and stated, "If it's the Lord's will I lose my arm well then so be it. At least I'll be better off than these two fellas."

Reaching for his canteen, Max offered, "Care for some water?"

"No thanks. Had my fill when they found me. Don't mean to be rude but I think I'll close my eyes for a spell. Feelin' mighty tired."

They bounced along in the buckboard while Max looked out at the rolling countryside. The trees, the fields, the slight rise here and there in the land itself seemed like it always had but then again, he hadn't spent all that much time out here in this part of the battlefield. Looking at the two dead soldiers two feet away from where he sat, the blood-stained floorboards, and the sleeping, wounded soldier sitting across from him, there was no doubt. *He was in 1863.*

He realized that within ten minutes or so they would arrive at the main Confederate camp. He tried to lay out in his mind his course of action once they arrived. First off, he was going to have to fit in. If anyone even remotely suspected him of not being in the army but yet wearing a Confederate uniform he could be labeled as a spy and be shot on the spot.

Preston brought the team of horses to a halt at the top of a rise. Spitting the chewed-out wad of tobacco in his mouth to the ground he announced, "Here we are boys! General Lee's headquarters."

Max gazed down at the familiar battlefield site that he had been to with his father in the past and then with Kellem. Centered toward the middle of an expansive field sat the widow Mary Thompson's small stone farmhouse where General Lee set up his headquarters during the three-day battle. The house looked the same as Max remembered it to be but the fence in the front yard looked much older, the roof was a bit tattered here and there and the grass around the house had been trampled by thousands of footsteps of the Confederate army. A small barn off to the left had an attached corral that held four horses who were munching on a pile of hay. In every direction, out from the house, there were endless rows of off-white tents that stretched out to meet the wooded areas far beyond the original four-acre property, thousands of Confederate soldiers walking about or sitting at campfires.

As Preston slowly guided the team down the sloping hill Max tapped the sleeping soldier on his leg and assured him. "We're back and before you know it they'll put you back together."

Robert yawned, looked out at the surrounding tents, and frowned. "I think we're in for yet another day of fighting."

Preston, who overheard the remark stated with confidence. "Nah…I don't believe so. It's too hot and both armies have to be worn out. Accordin' ta what's bein' said around camp, we all but ran the Yanks off the first day, but yesterday we took a beatin'. We almost broke through their left flank but we not only were driven back but we suffered a great number of casualties. I, or no one else in this army has any idea what Lee has up his sleeve this mornin' but I for one can't see him backin' down and givin' the last two days ta the Yanks. There will be more bloodshed on both sides before this is over. Lee is not going to run from a fight!"

Max, who already knew what the day held in store for the Confederate army could only shake his head. As they were slowly passing the front of the Thompson farmhouse Max had the crazy thought of just jumping out of the wagon and running up to the door of the house telling the soldiers standing around in the yard that he needed to speak with General Lee. Pulling out his pocket watch he noted it was just after seven in the morning. According to history Lee had awoken at dawn on July 3rd, 1863, and rode out with his staff in search of his ol' warhorse, General Longstreet.

Within the next hour, Lee would lay out his massive attack plan to break the Yankee center. Even if it were possible for him to speak with Lee, the idea that Lee would fail would not be accepted, especially by Max, who wore the uniform of a lowly private in the army. If General Longstreet could not sway Lee's decision, then who could? No one, because it was history. Passing countless tents where soldiers sat around campfires, many of them eating their last meal, Max silently asked himself, *What am I doing here?"*

Preston brought the wagon to a stop short of the dirt road that ran in front of the house as he applied the foot brake when he turned and spoke to Max. "This is where we part ways. I'm off to the right to a field hospital of sorts where we drop off the dead and wounded. I can't say for sure where yer Carolina regiment is located but if ya ask around someone will know."

Max jumped down from the back of the wagon and spoke to the wounded soldier. "God bless you, Robert."

Trying to salute with his left elbow Robert responded, "Looks like my fighting days are over. Maybe they'll send me home. Besides that, I can't see this war going on much longer. You keep your head down, Miller."

With that Preston urged the horses forward with a whistle and the team pulled the wagon to the right up the rutted road. Now, standing alone yards from the house Max thought it best to get moving as if he appeared to know where he was going. Crossing the road he stopped where two men were in the process of unloading bags of grain from a wagon. Approaching the soldiers Max spoke, "Excuse me, but could you boys direct me to where the 47th Alabama is located?"

The soldier in the back of the wagon shrugged as if he didn't know but the other man taking a sack from the back, rubbed his rough beard as if in thought, hesitated, and then answered, "This area all around here is mostly boys from Virginia. If you walk up this road a couple of hundred yards you'll come to a broken down wagon and a pile of old fencing where there is a crossroad. The Texas regiments are on the left, Alabaman's on the right."

Max tipped his hat and replied, "Thank you kindly."

He walked down the dusty road and looked at his watch: almost 7:30. The sun had already been up for an hour and not even two miles away General Robert E. Lee, according to history, was explaining his battle plan for the day to General James Longstreet. Lee thought that the Union army was strong on their right and left flanks but in the middle along Cemetery Ridge, they were the weakest. This is where Longstreet was told by Lee to concentrate approximately fifteen thousand men stretched out in a line nearly a mile and a half in length.

This assault was to be proceeded by a massive artillery attack from one hundred and fifty Confederate cannons which in Lee's mind would break up the Union lines in the middle. Following the hour-long incessant cannonade Longstreet was then to order the nine brigades under his command to move out across a three-quarter mile open field thus breaking the Union center, splitting the northern army in two. From a mathematical point of view, Lee held the advantage of numbers. Lee had twice more cannons on the battlefield and had the Yankees outnumbered two to one as the Union soldiers manning the stone wall numbered sixty-five hundred.

Longstreet would strongly disagree with Lee's plan stating that no fifteen thousand men alive could advance across a three-quarter mile open field and be successful in taking that wall. Longstreet argued strenuously against the attack but Lee was convinced that his plan would succeed. Because of the great respect Longstreet had for Lee, he following the cannonade, ordered the fifteen thousand forward which resulted in nearly 50% casualties for the Southern army. It has been thought and stated by many a historian over the years Lee had made a grave mistake at Gettysburg and that the Union victory there was the turning point of the war.

A few yards down the road, he kicked at an army issue haversack lying in the weeds next to the road. Another few feet and he spotted a discarded canteen and then a bed roll. On the opposite side of the road, he saw a broken musket, another canteen, and a cartridge belt. These were items that men, for some reason had tossed to the side. Maybe they were removed from the dead or wounded. Nonetheless, he found himself staring at several Civil War artifacts that would be worth a lot of money in his world of 2019. But here, in 1863 they were nothing more than remnants of the first two days of battle here at Gettysburg.

On either side of the road next to the trees and even further back in he could see men milling around in small groups or off by themselves. A man sitting on a tree stump gently strummed on a fiddle while a man sitting next to him puffed away at a pipe. Another soldier sat by a tree as he read a Bible and another man appeared to be writing a letter or maybe entering a notation in a journal. Some men appeared to be sleeping in the shade of the trees while others just stared off into the distance.

By this time in the war, all of these men were grizzled veterans. All the deserters and cowards had long since run off. These were men who had seen many a battle. Unlike reenactors who always seemed to be laughing and smiling before and after a reenactment these fighting men wore the look of sadness, having lost friends or comrades. If he was not convinced up to this point that he was back in 1863 he was now! He was in the midst of an army that was ill-fed, clothed, and equipped and yet had experienced many victories. But that was all going to end for many of them on this day, this third day of battle.

The road took a slight bend and there thirty yards up ahead he saw the broken-down wagon and pile of fencing. Approaching the wagon he was about to go to the right when he noticed six riders galloping in his direction, the lead rider on a dappled horse wore a plumed hat, an exceptionally clean Confederate officer's uniform complete with dangling sword and scabbard, and knee-high black spurred boots. Behind him, there were five other riders, all in Confederate gray, the last in line carrying a Confederate flag flapping in the breeze. Stepping to the side to allow the small group of riders to pass he realized that the lead rider had to be one of the many Confederate generals who fought at Gettysburg, the remaining five his field staff. Saluting the lead rider as he approached, the plumb-hatted, bearded man gave him a nod and moved on by, his staff following, leaving a cloud of road dust surrounding Max, who waved at the air trying to clear it. Watching the riders proceed down the road toward General Lee's headquarters Max realized he had just seen a Confederate general. It was not Lee or Longstreet as he knew exactly what they looked like. Could it have been Piclett, Stuart, or maybe even Armistead or Heth?

He proceeded down the side road and stopped where a man sat, his back against a tall oak as he whittled at a piece of wood. "Excuse me there sir, but could you tell me where the 47th Alabama is located?"

The man blew some wood shavings from the stick, pointed down the road, and spoke. "They're down at the end of this here road. You'll have to walk past the 4th and 15th Alabama and then you'll run smack dab into the Forty-Seventh."

Max tipped his hat. "Thank you kindly. God go with you today!"

The man smiled back and replied, "The Good Lord is always with me. He's got me through many a battle but I don't think there'll be any fighting today."

Max walked off and thought about how wrong the soldier was. There would be fighting this day and within the next few hours, the Confederate army would lose thousands of men in a failed attempt to break the Union center.

Thirty yards down the road he turned to the left and there before him on both sides of the road and nestled back in the thick trees there were scattered tents, hundreds of men in Confederate gray walking here and there, sitting around campfires and in general it appeared that no one was in the mood for any more fighting. Moving past the first few tents Max thought that word of Lee's plan of attack for the day had not been passed down to the ranks as of yet. A few yards farther on he saw a small regimental flag fluttering in the breeze: 4th Alabama. Stopping to talk with an older man on crutches Max inquired, "I was wondering if you could direct me to the Forty-Seventh?"

Balancing himself with his right crutch he pointed the other down the road. "Down at the end of the road, you'll find the Forty-Seventh."

Max patted the man on his right shoulder. "Thank you and take care today."

After walking for five minutes Max saw in the distance fifty yards ahead where the road ended at the edge of some woods. Passing a man who was cleaning mud from the bottom of his shoes with a stick, Max asked, "Forty-Seventh?"

Pointing the stick at Max the man replied, "Nope…Fifteenth. See that large pine tree? Well, when you get past there you're in the Forty-Seventh."

Max nodded at the man and then moved on. Passing the tree he began to look to his right and left for any sign of Sam. *This is going to be difficult,* thought Max. *Everyone looks the same!* There were at least two hundred men, all dressed in Confederate gray crossing the road or walking in and out of the tents. Aside from an occasional tall or skinny individual, everyone appeared to be a typical Confederate soldier. Almost at the end of the road, Max decided he was going to have to ask if anyone knew Sam Pritchard.

Two tents from the end of the road Max stopped and walked over to three men seated on the ground around a low campfire. Going down on his haunches, he smiled at the three soldiers and asked politely, "Two questions, is this indeed the 47th Alabama and do you know of a young man by the name of Sam Pritchard?"

The man in the middle who was stirring a frying pan filled with potatoes and onions with a bayonet, looked back at Max, and not recognizing him as one of their own asked skeptically, "Who wants to know?"

Max realized he had to be careful of what he said. "Name's Miller…I'm with the 2nd South Carolina. Grew up with Sam down in Alabama near Five Points. I guess when we were about twelve my father moved our family up to Charleston for better work. Sam and I never saw one another again but we wrote back and forth. The last time I heard from my old friend he wrote that he was joining up with the 47th Alabama and was off to the war. Shortly after, I guess it was a few months, I up and joined the army in South

Carolina. Here it is nearly two years down the road and I just found out the 47th is here at Gettysburg, so I decided to mosey on over here and see if he has survived the war so far, and if he has I'd like to see him."

Stirring the potato-onion concoction the man stabbed a small potato and took a bite then made a face. "Needs more salt."

The soldier on his right reached into an old sack and removing a small handful of salt granules, sprinkled them into the pan and then spoke to Max. "We all know Sam. He's a little young, but he's a good soldier. He was just talking with us a few minutes ago when he and two other men got up to relieve themselves over there in the woods. He should be back shortly."

The third man shrugged and commented in a friendly tone, "Yeah when nature calls!"

Max was about to walk off when he reached into his haversack and removed three of the four biscuits his wife had packed, "I already had me a good breakfast. Throw these biscuits in with your taters."

Each man caught a biscuit and the pan-stirring man held his up and remarked, "I guess you South Carolina fellas are okay…thanks."

Waking toward the trees Max tipped his hat. "Good day to you boys!"

He passed the last tent in line and came to a worn path that led up a slight hill to the trees. Three-quarters up the path he stopped when he saw two soldiers emerge from the trees. He stepped to the side allowing them to pass by when he noticed a third soldier step out of the treeline. The young soldier had his head down as he was busy buttoning up his trousers. The soldier looked up just as he was approaching Max. Max reached out and gently touched the boy's left arm as he inquired, "Sam…Sam Pritchard?"

Sam looked at Max's face but did not recognize him. Removing his hat, Max went on, "It's Max…Max Miller from the farm. Remember, we fed you and my wife bandaged your wounds…remember!"

Sam looked closely at Max and then with a look of concern looked to his right and then the left and asked, "Mr. Miller, what are you doing here and why are you dressed like a Confederate soldier? You said you were not in the army."

Max tried to explain. "This is not an army-issue Confederate uniform. I'm not in the army, this is simply a reenactor uniform."

Looking Max up and down, Sam seemed confused, "I don't under-stand what a reenactor uniform means."

Max turned Sam away from the camp as he continued to try and explain. "This uniform is not that important and I don't have time to explain it to you but there is something very important I must speak to you about. We need to speak in private because there is not much time."

Sam, still confused, replied, "Time for what?"

Max gently guided Sam toward the trees and suggested, "Let's go up there and sit in the shade of the trees as I have something to say you need to hear. It's about Rose. Do you remember when we discussed her when you were at my farm?"

"I do remember that but still, why are you here? This may not be the safest place for you. You are a Pennsylvania farmer dressed in Confederate gray. You could be looked at as a spy. You're in danger here in this camp."

"I know I took a chance in coming here this morning, but the truth is *you* are the one who is in danger."

Walking next to Max toward the tress Sam looked back down at the camp. "Perhaps it would be a good idea to go into the trees where you cannot be seen. It'll be safer there."

They entered the tree line and stepped a few yards into the forest where Max sat down with his back against a tall oak. Sam did likewise a few feet away as he looked back through the trees to make sure they were not followed. Satisfied they were alone he asked, "What is it you have to tell me?"

Max wiped his sweating brow, then answered, "This is going to be hard to explain. I'm not all that sure I even understand any of this, but I'll do my best." Removing the folded document from the Hall of Records from his pants he handed the paper to Sam and explained, "Look at this and tell me what you think."

Sam took the paper and looking at it shrugged. "It looks like a list of names. What does it mean?"

"It's more than just a list of names," said Max. "It's a list of men who were killed here at Gettysburg."

Looking at the paper again, Sam spoke in confusion. "I still don't understand."

Max pointed at the document. "Go down to the sixth name listed and read it."

Counting down the names, Sam read out loud, "Samuel Pritchard." In amazement, he remarked, "Well, I'll be! It would seem there is another soldier with the same name as mine in the army."

Amused, Max smiled and stated, "The name listed there is not another man with the same name as you. That is you! Read the rest of what follows the name."

Sam ran his finger across the typed sentence while reading, "Five Points, Alabama, 47th Alabama Regiment. Died July 3rd, 1863, near Emmittsburg Fence, Pickett's Charge." Looking at Max, Sam replied, "I still don't understand. How could the man mentioned here be me? I'm sitting right here in front of you. I don't understand what this means."

Taking the paper back from Sam, Max looked up into the trees as he took a deep breath. "Let me see if I can explain. All right, how about this? Do you understand what the future is?"

"If you're asking me if I know what the future holds for me or anyone else…no."

"That's not what I'm asking. I'm asking if you know what the word… future means."

"Well, that's pretty simple. Tomorrow is the future and yesterday is the past, and I might add today is the present."

"Now we're getting somewhere," said Max. "Would you agree that not only tomorrow, but next week, next month and next year are indeed the future?"

Sam gave Max a strange look as he answered, "Yes, I would agree with that."

"Now, pay attention," said Max. "It being 1863, ten years from now it will be what…1873?"

Nodding, Sam agreed, "That would be correct and hopefully this war will be over."

"I can guarantee you, Sam, this war will end long before that, but let's stretch this out a bit more. One hundred years from right now it will be 1963…correct?"

"I'm not all that great with numbers but I figure that's probably right. Surely by that time this war will not only be over but long forgotten and all of us who are alive today will also be long gone."

"Don't ask me how I know because we don't have the time to go into all of that, but this war will end in about two years and you're right. We, all of us here today will be dead and in the grave. If we were to add another fifty-six years to that one hundred years I mentioned that would make the year 2019."

Trying to add the years up in his mind Sam surrendered his thoughts, "I guess, if you say so."

"Numbers don't lie and in one hundred and fifty-six years from right now, it will be the year 2019. Now, what am I about to say may seem baffling or impossible but I believe it to be true. When you were at my farm yesterday and you stepped through that fence and entered onto my property you stepped ahead in time one hundred and fifty-six years to the year 2019."

Sam remained silent and just shook his head in disbelief.

Recognizing Sam's skepticism, Max tried his best to explain. "That's why everything seemed so strange to you. You didn't know what a hot dog or a hamburger was, what ketchup and mustard were, and you didn't understand my smoker grill where I cooked the meat. The reason why you didn't know what these things were is that in your world of 1863, none of those things had been invented or even existed."

Sam thought for a moment when he reached into his pocket and pulled out the small plastic pill bottle. "You mean like this container of medicine your wife gave me for the pain?"

Max pointed at the bottle with a sense of *Now I'm getting somewhere*, as he answered, "Exactly! That medicine is from the year 2019 and when you left my farm and stepped back through that fence you came back here in 1863 and you brought that medicine with you. When you came to my farm you stepped into the future, the year 2019, and when you left you came back here to 1863. Do you understand?"

"Once again, I'm not all that good with numbers and I think I understand what you're saying but it doesn't make any sense."

"To be honest with you this doesn't make a lot of sense to me either but yet, it's happening. Now, here is where it gets even more confusing. I'm going to try and answer your question as to why I am here. After you left our farm I got to thinking about how you talked about Rose, the girl who said she would marry you after you returned from the war. Do you remember speaking of her? Why you even showed me a letter she wrote you."

Reaching inside his pocket Sam pulled out the folded letter. "You mean this letter?"

"Yes, and you allowed me to read it. One of the things you told me and my wife was that you had to survive this war by whatever means and you would do anything short of deserting to get back to Five Points and marry her. Do you remember that conversation?"

"I do."

"I was up part of the night thinking about what you said about Rose and that's why I've come. I've come to save you so you can go back home and marry her."

Sam shook his head and replied, "Why would I need you to save me? I've done all right up to this point."

"That you have, but all that is about to end today. Unless you listen to me you're going to die today."

"You've said a lot of strange things to me in the last few minutes, but the idea of me dying today is not going to happen." Turning and nodding down at the camp he went on, "Look at all those soldiers down there. It's a peaceful July morning and it does not appear to me that the army is preparing to fight today. It's too hot and everyone is worn out. It wouldn't surprise me if Lee pulls out of here in the next couple of days."

"Looks can be deceiving," said Max. "You and all those soldiers in the Confederate army may think that nothing is going to happen today but nothing could be farther from the truth. Right now, General Lee, about an hour's march from here out there on the battlefield is explaining his plan of attack for the day with General Longstreet. Soon, the word will come down through the ranks to form up and move out and fifteen thousand southern boys, including the 47th Alabama, will hunker down in a long tree line called Spangler's Woods. After over an hour of shelling from every cannon that Lee can muster you and the others will be ordered to march across a large open field directly into enemy fire. It will be a disaster for Lee and the army will sustain heavy casualties. You will be one of those casualties. It says so right here on this paper."

Sam stood and remarked, "Mr. Miller…you have told me many things here today many of which are just plain hard to believe. You say I'm going to die today when it appears the army is not even prepared to go into battle in the next hour or so as you say. That paper, well it's just that…a piece of paper."

Out of frustration, Max held up the paper and stated, "I'm going to try and explain this from a different angle. When you were at my farm yesterday it was July 2nd and today is July 3rd. Would you agree with that?"

"Yes, today is July 3rd. Earlier this morning I heard some of the men in my regiment talking about how tomorrow will be July 4th…Independence Day."

"All right, so now that we agree that today is July 3rd, 1863, let me point out that the date the paper states that you die is July 3rd, 1863. That's today. It also states you are going to die near the Emmittsburg Fence during Pickett's Charge."

"But how can that even be possible?" said Sam, "I've never even heard of this Emmittsburg Fence. I've heard about Emmitsburg Road a few times around camp but nothing about a fence named the same. I know who General Pickett is. I've even seen him ride through our camp yesterday, but I know nothing of this Pickett's Charge."

"The field you will be ordered to advance across has a long fence you and the others will have to go through or climb over about two-thirds of the way across the field. That is where you are going to die. I do not know if your death will be from cannon fire or by musket. The advance will become known as Pickett's Charge because General Pickett will lead the army in the attack. The reason I have come here today is to save you from dying out there on that field. If you listen to me and do what I say then you can survive this day and possibly the war and return to your hometown and marry Rose. If not, then you will die. There is nothing more I can say to try and explain why I've come here today. It's simply to save your life…at least for today. It's up to you. You have to decide if you want to live or die this day. I can't make that decision for you. If you decide to not believe the things I have told you, well then so be it. I'll just be on my way back to my wife and daughters on my farm and you'll go into battle later today and you will die out there near that fence. There is nothing more I can say. I've done what I feel is the right thing by coming here and telling you this. It's up to you."

Sam reached out and touched Max's right shoulder. "Mr. Miller, I believe you are a good man. I'm not so sure I would have made it back to camp yesterday if it wouldn't have been for the kindness of you and your wife. You gave me water, fed me, and bandaged my wounds. Now, you come to me with this story about the future, this strange piece of paper, and information about a battle that no one here at camp is aware of. I have no reason to believe you would lie to me because you don't seem like that kind of a man but I have to say this whole conversation seems a bit far-fetched. If it turns out that later in the day we are ordered to form up and march off to this Spangler's Woods, well then, I might be more convinced of the things you have told me, but I don't know if that is going to happen."

Reaching for Sam's hand, Max shook it and spoke, "Let's do this. In the next minute, I'm going to walk off through these trees toward Spangler's woods. It'll probably take me about an hour or so before I get there, but when I arrive there I'll hide out in the trees. Later today, and I guarantee you, you will be there with the rest of your regiment, I will find you and then you can decide if you want me to save you or not. If so, then we'll talk about what is to be done. If not, then I'll be on my way back to my farm and that will be that. Agreed?"

Sam returned the handshake and smiled, "That sounds fair."

CHAPTER FORTY

Making his way through the thick trees and underbrush, Max knew if he continued on a westerly course, he would either come out north or south of Spangler's Woods or if he was lucky, he might wind up smack dab in the middle of where Lee's men would form up for battle. Stepping over a fallen tree and pushing low-hanging tree branches from his face he shook his head in wonder. All the time he and his father had walked the various battle sites at Gettysburg and yet he had never been to this isolated part of the park. Stopping, he looked at his timepiece: 8:46. By this time Lee had already passed on to Longstreet his orders for the day. Soon, the word would be given to the army, and they would begin the march over to Spangler's Woods. He was sure he had enough time to get there before the thousands of Confederate soldiers arrived.

Max thought about the strange conversation he had with Sam and wondered if the boy had taken him seriously. He was confident Sam would not share any part of their conversation with anyone in his regiment. *How could he?* Anyone he would confide in who had a lick of sense would think he was off his rocker. No, he would keep Max's version of his death to himself, but when he arrived at Spangler's Woods what would his decision be. Life or death? It was up to Sam.

At the top of a small gully, he stopped and took a drink from his canteen. Splashing a handful of water over his face he looked up at the morning sun filtering down through the trees. It was already hot and he could feel himself sweating profusely in the heavy wool uniform. Moving on he thought about Elizabeth back on the farm. By this time she had already put up the breakfast leftovers, washed up the dirty dishes, and had no doubt fed the twins. He was blessed to have such a wonderful woman for a wife.

Thinking about how empty his life would be without her he started to think about the relationship between Rose and Sam. According to Sam, she had only agreed to marry him when and if he returned from the war. At this point in Sam's young life, he had not seen the love of his life for going on two years. He seemed determined to survive the war to return to Five Points so he could marry her. Would his longing to once again be with her back in Alabama be enough for him to avoid going near the Emmittsburg Fence during the upcoming battle?

Sitting on a tree stump, he wiped his brow and checked the time again; almost 10:00. He had been trekking through the woods for over an hour and a half. He had to be getting close to Spangler's Woods. Taking a swig from his canteen he noticed what appeared to be a clearing in the trees off to his left. Getting up he made his way through forty yards of trees when, sure enough, he came to a large clearing. The ground was sloped near the tree line so he could not see across the large field itself. Walking up the slope he laid down in the low weeds and surveyed the acres of open ground spreading out before him.

Looking to his right and then left the rolling field prevented him from seeing what was in the distance. He couldn't just walk out onto the field as he was not exactly sure where he was. For all he knew he could be behind Union lines. Going back down the slope he leaned his musket against a tall tree and then removed his haversack, canteen, and cartridge belt, laying them on the ground. Taking his binoculars from his sack he searched the tree line for a climbable tree. A few yards down he located a tree with lower branches that would allow him to climb up for a better view of the field. Pushing branches to the side he managed to climb up a good twenty feet where he balanced himself on a sturdy branch. To the south, the field stretched for what he figured nearly two miles where it ended at another grouping of trees. Looking to his right he raised the binoculars to his eyes and there a quarter mile off was the Emmittsburg Fence and just beyond that the low stone wall fronting the center of the Union army.

He surveyed the activity going on behind the wall, there was a long row of cannons, many of which were being manned in preparation for whatever the day held. Union soldiers were stacking ordnance, positioning cannons, and three men, probably officers were gazing through field glasses to the east end of the field. Turning his binoculars in an easterly direction there it was; Spangler's Woods. The activity fifty yards out from the famous tree line appeared very organized. There were already dozens of Confederate cannons lined up, their deadly barrels aimed at the Union defenses nearly a mile to the west. More cannons and caissons were being brought up and rolled into position. To the far left down from the line of cannons, he saw five men grouped, one gazing through field glasses while pointing across the vast field toward the Yankee lines.

Both sides were gearing up for what was to become an epic Civil War battle. Farther back in the trees, he noticed a long line of men in Confederate gray as they walked slowly through the trees where they would wait with thousands of others for the orders to attack. But that was hours away. Looking again to the west at the Union line, Max thought that what he was witnessing was very similar to a reenactment, but much more realistic. Lowering the binoculars he decided to climb down and walk back toward Spangler's Woods. He was just about to step down to a lower branch when he heard voices. Searching the surrounding ground for the voices he froze when he saw two Union soldiers in dirty blue uniforms stop at the base of the tree as they peered out toward the field. Hugging the tree he remained perfectly still, hoping the men would not notice his gear lying on the ground a few yards away.

The taller of the duo looked to his left and right and spoke to his companion. "I'm not so sure we should go any farther. There might be Rebs close by."

The shorter of the two looked through a set of field glasses in the direction of Spangler's Woods and remarked, "General Meade was right. Lee is planning on attacking our center."

The other man shrugged, "That's crazy. Stage an attack across an open field under long-range cannon fire and if they get close enough thousands of aimed muskets. That's suicide!"

The short soldier placed a wad of chewing tobacco in his mouth and replied, "Don't underestimate that ol' fox, General Lee. I've been in this war from the beginning and I've been witness to what he can do with an army. If anyone could march across that field and take out our center that would be Lee. I count about seventy cannons over there right now, but it looks like they are bringing up more." Lowering the glasses he asked, "Do you think we should try and move closer?"

"No, I think we should get back and report what we've seen."

The two soldiers turned and walked past the tree, the tall man's right foot no more than twelve inches from Max's canteen and haversack. Waiting until the two soldiers disappeared in the trees, he climbed down, put his gear back on, and checked once again to make sure the two Yanks were gone.

Thinking to himself, *that was close,* he started to backtrack the way he had just come but tried to stay to the right, angling his progress toward Spangler's Woods, but remaining in the trees.

Minutes passed when he was stopped in his tracks when he noticed a Union soldier a few feet away propped up against a tree. Couching down to avoid being seen Max stared at the soldier who was not moving a muscle. *Maybe he was sleeping?* Realizing that if he was seen by the soldier he could be shot, he reluctantly raised his musket and approached the man. He stepped on a twig which made a sharp snapping sound.

The soldier never flinched. Getting closer, he aimed his musket at the man and prayed he would not have to fight this soldier. Upon getting even closer, the man appeared to be unaware of his approach. Picking up a nearby rock he tossed it in the soldier's direction. There was no reaction. Approaching the man slowly Max suddenly realized the man was not sleeping, *but dead!* His legs were in a spread eagle position, his open canteen laying between the legs, his arms and hands drooped at his side. His face had taken on the pale gray look of death. The eyes were wide open and stared straight ahead, the mouth was open displaying a swollen tongue.

Max searched the surrounding area for the man's musket but it was not to be found. Aside from his canteen, he had no haversack or cartridge belt. Someone had probably stripped him of his gear. He considered searching the soldier for any identification, but at this point what difference would it make? Max stared at the man's deadpan face when he saw three bugs crawl out of the side of the man's mouth. Max suddenly felt nauseous and leaning against a tree he felt as if he were going to vomit. He wretched three times but nothing came up. He was simply left with that horrible aftertaste that one gets when in the process of upchucking.

Taking a long swig from his canteen, he rinsed out the inside of his mouth, spit, and then took a swallow. Looking down at the dead soldier Max thought once again, *What am I doing here? Maybe I should not have come.* Moving off through the trees he wondered that when he got back home was he going to explain to Elizabeth all the horrible things he had seen. It had only been about five hours since he stepped through the fence back at the farm and he had already encountered four dead soldiers, three Confederate and one Union. He knew if he made the upcoming charge he could very well witness hundreds of southern men die as they crossed the deadly field he was now passing by a few yards to his right.

After plowing through the low underbrush and trees for what seemed like a half hour he finally arrived at the edge of the forest, the very left end of the line of Confederate cannons on his right. The last cannon in line was no more than forty-some yards out into the open field. Surveying the activity Max figured he would just walk out of the trees and approach the last section of cannons as Confederate soldiers were walking here and there in between the line of cannons and Spangler's Woods. So far he had managed to pass for a Confederate and of the many soldiers preparing for the assault they had much more on their minds than one of their own stepping out of the woods. Taking a deep breath he thought, *Here we go!*

With his musket balanced on his right shoulder, he stepped from the woods with confidence and crossed the expanse of low weeds. Stopping at the first cannon he got the attention of two young soldiers who were stacking ammunition. "Excuse me, boys. Might you tell me where the 2nd South Carolina Regiment is located?"

The boy closest to him who was holding a cannonball nodded toward the woods to their rear. "I'm not sure if they're here today but if you check back there in those trees someone can probably tell you."

The other soldier gave Max a strange look which caused Max to explain his sudden appearance. Angling his thumb back toward the woods he explained, "Got separated from my regiment during the heat of battle yesterday. Then I wound up getting lost in the woods and I've been wandering around most of the night. Need to get back to my regiment." Looking at the long line of cannons as if he was not aware of what was going on, he inquired, "What's all this?"

The boy holding the cannonball placed it on the top of a pyramid of ammunition and replied, "Seeing as how you've been out in the woods all night, I guess you haven't heard. Lee is planning on attacking the Yankee center. Those who are to make the advance are starting to form up back there in the trees."

The other boy added, "Right now we have over a hundred cannons out here. Lee plans to break up the Yankee lines on the other side of this field. After that, our boys go in. It's a stretch but we must do what we have to."

Saluting with the index finger of his right-hand Max spoke with genuineness, "Good luck today boys."

Max started to walk toward the tree line as he saw yet another regiment of gray-clad soldiers file into position just beyond the edge of the trees. He nodded at three different soldiers he walked by but remained silent. The less attention given him the better. As far as everyone else was concerned he no doubt looked like one of thousands of Confederate men who would gather at Spangler's Woods this day.

Entering the tree line he walked to the left sat down next to a tree and removed his haversack, his musket lying on the ground next to his legs. He checked the time: 11:45 in the morning. With any luck within the next hour or so Sam along with the 47th Alabama would arrive. Removing one of three apples from his haversack he had brought along he also took a folded piece of paper from his pants pocket, a computer printout that he had generated before breakfast back at the farm.

This printout showed the battle formation of all the Confederate regiments during Pickett's Charge. Five Alabama regiments, one of which was the Forty-Seventh, according to history would form up at the far right end of the attacking force. This was a blessing as he did not have to walk up and down the mile-long line of Confederates to locate the Forty-Seventh. If he stayed put Sam would come right to him or at least be within a short distance. Munching on the apple he laid his head back against the tree and closed his eyes. He was nearly at the end of his quest to save Sam Pritchard, but the most difficult part of his plan lay ahead and within the next few hours he should be on his way back to the year 2019, his wife and farm.

His head bobbed forward and brought him out of a short rest. He checked the time, he had dozed off for nearly ten minutes. Taking the last two bites from the apple he tossed the core off into the weeds, stood, and stretched when he noticed a long column of soldiers marching in his direction. When he saw a flag bearing the seal of Alabama he casually walked up to the passing column and asked a soldier, "Pardon me there but would you happen to be the Forty-Seventh?"

The soldier turned and looked back down the line of men and replied, "Nope, we are the Tenth. The Forty-Seventh is farther back down the line. They should be here in the next half hour or so."

Max nodded at the soldier in thanks and then waiting until they passed by he walked to the edge of the trees, the vast field that would soon be the scene of Pickett's Charge spread out before him. Raising the binoculars to his eyes he gazed across the large field. He could not see the Emmittsburg Fence as it was hidden from view due to a natural dip in the landscape in the distance. He could barely make out the low stone wall that fortified the Union position. There, behind the wall was the copse of trees that Lee had ordered Longstreet to concentrate on as the focal point of the men who would advance across the field. He turned his attention to the activity out a distance from the trees he was now standing in. More cannons were being brought up, ammunition was being stacked, and officers staring through field glasses at the Union line on the other end of the long field.

He leaned his musket against a tree and began to think about the mathematics of Pickett's Charge. According to history at one o'clock which was less than an hour off Longstreet would give the order for the Confederate cannon barrage to begin, 150 cannons blasting away at the stone wall three-quarters of a mile off on the other side of the field. The Union forces would answer the southern cannonade with approximately seventy-five cannons of their own. The artillery battle would continue until two o'clock when Longstreet would reluctantly order the nine brigades of soldiers forward, 15,000 men strong. The attack would not even last a full hour as the Confederate army would be turned back suffering nearly 7,500 casualties, approximately 50% of their force, while the North manning the stone wall, 6,500 would only experience 1,500 casualties. By three o'clock the Confederate army, what was left of it, would retreat sadly back to Spangler's Woods. The closest most of the Confederates would get to the stone wall would be about thirty yards, with many a Southern man losing his life near or at the Emmittsburg Fence. When and if he got to speak with Sam Pritchard again he was not going to have the time to explain everything that would happen.

Max snapped out of his mathematical daydreaming when he spotted another Alabama regiment approaching. As he watched the line of soldiers file by he looked to see if he could locate Sam. It was hard to decipher one soldier from the next as they all appeared somewhat the same. Row after row of tired men dressed in Confederate gray. The entire regiment passed by with no sign of Sam. Thinking the regiment may not have been the Forty-Seventh Max decided to trail them into the trees and ask what regiment they were.

He no sooner followed the marching men when off to the side he saw Sam standing, his hat in his hand, his musket in the other. Approaching Sam, Max stuck out his hand, "I didn't see you when you passed by. I wasn't sure if this was the Forty-Seventh or not."

"When we passed, I was on the other side of the column where you could not see me but I saw you standing out there by the edge of the trees. We've been ordered to lay down in the trees near the far edge of the field." Motioning toward two large oaks, Sam suggested, "Com'n, let's go sit and talk."

Max removed his haversack and made himself comfortable as he leaned back against a tree. Looking at Sam who was seated across from him, he asked, "So, what have you decided? Do I hang around here and try to save your life this afternoon or do I just leave and go back to my farm?"

Sam tied his right shoe and answered, "After we talked back at camp and you walked off in the woods saying you would meet me right here in Spangler's Woods I didn't know what I was going to do. At that point, I was not convinced we'd even form up and march over here. I have to say I was still confused about some of the things you told me, while on the other hand, some of the things you said made sense. I guess it was about an hour after you walked off when the word came down through the camp that we were to form up as we were pulling out in fifteen minutes. No one told us why we were forming up or where we were going, but about ten minutes into our forced march the reason became clear as word of Lee's plan for the day spread like wildfire through the ranks. It was just like you said. Lee is planning on attacking the Yankee center out there on the other side of that field. The attack will be proceeded by a massive artillery barrage and then all three divisions which could include as many as twelve to fifteen thousand men will advance across the field. Some of the boys are saying that Longstreet does not agree with Lee, but is going to go ahead anyway because that is what Lee, the commanding general, ordered. When I realized things were turning out just the way you said I figured if you knew all of these things before they happened well then there must be some truth to what you have told me. So, I have decided that I do want to get through this day, survive the war return to Alabama, and marry Rose. So what do we have to do to make this happen?"

"Before I explain my plan, first of all, you need to prepare yourself for what is about to happen. All nine brigades will hunker down back here in the trees and wait for the order to advance. But before that happens you are going to witness something like you've never seen." Looking at his time-piece, Max continued, "It's twelve-ten right now and in about three-quarters of an hour at one o'clock Longstreet will give the order for the cannonade to begin."

Handing the binoculars to Sam, Max explained, "Look through these across the field. You'll see a long low stone wall, several cannons, and hundreds of Yanks preparing for the upcoming assault. Toward the center of the wall, you'll see a small grouping of trees. Those trees and the surrounding area will be the focal point for the 150 cannons Lee has out there in front of us. I'm telling you these things now because when the shelling starts it will get to the point where it will become difficult for us to speak without yelling."

"Do you think so?" asked Sam. "I've been present during other cannon attacks in the past and I'll admit it was loud, but we were still able to hear one another."

"Let me explain," said Max. "An experienced artillery crew can load and fire a cannon three times in a minute. Lee has 150 cannons out there and that means somewhere in the area of 450 shells will be hitting the Union lines every couple minutes out there on the other side of the field. The shelling will last for an hour which means thousands of shells will be fired at the Yankees. The Union guns which amount to about seventy-five will return numerous deadly rounds at us. The noise will be so loud and continuous that the sound will be heard in Harrisburg which is well over thirty-five miles from this spot. It will not only be unusually loud but at times you will not be able to see from the smoke. Many of those soldiers here in the trees will be killed by the Union cannon fire before they even step out onto the field."

In shock, Sam responded, "Well then, maybe we should get out of these trees."

"You have nothing to worry about as long as you're here in the trees. History tells us that you were killed out near the Emmittsburg Fence. You're safe here and as long as we stay away from that fence you have a better-than-average chance of surviving this day."

"And how exactly do we stay away from this fence?"

"That's part of my plan, but a lot of things will happen before we get in the area of the fence." Gesturing toward the field Max explained, "Around two o'clock the shelling will stop and the brigade and regimental officers will give the order for all 15,000 of us to step out onto the field and form up for battle. There will be two lines of formation, the first wave and then the reserves. This double line of the army will stretch for nearly a mile in length."

Pointing to his right Max went on, "The 47th Alabama and the other four Alabama regiments will form up as reserves behind several Virginia regiments down there on the far right of the long column. Shortly after the regiments are formed the order to march will be given and we'll begin our advance across the field. There will still be some sporadic cannon fire but it will be minimal as enough ammunition must be saved to support the army as they approach the enemy defenses. For the first ten to fifteen minutes there will be minimal casualties in our lines because we will be in between long-range and short-range cannon fire and still be too far off to suffer from aimed muskets, kind of a calm before the storm.

"Eventually short-range cannon fire will start to take effect on our lines and gaping holes will be opened in our line of attack because we will be packed together in formation. Groups of ten to twenty men all up and down the line will be blown away by cannon fire and by the time we get close to the fence the mile-long line we started with will be reduced to just a half mile as those still standing will be ordered to fill the gaps.

"All in all the army will be led to the slaughter just as General Longstreet predicted. Just before we get to the fence there will be a dip in the ground and the enemy will not be able to see us as we approach. When we arrive at the top of that rise we will see the fence twenty to thirty yards away. It is here that the order to double-quick will be given and it will be every man for himself to go over, under, or through the fence. Many a Southern man will die on or at that fence line. Union cannons with blow up the fence and the men who crawl over it to pieces and this combined with thousands of aimed Yankee muskets will cut down Lee's men at a horrible rate. Everywhere men will be falling like stalks of wheat."

Sam stared back at Max, remained silent, but then asked, "And at this fence is where I am to die?"

"According to history...yes! I think I have an example that you will be able to understand about how bad it is going to be out there near that fence.

One of the things you shared with me when you were at my farm was when you were at the Battle of Fredericksburg. Do you remember when you told me about what happened there?"

"Yes, I do remember that. It was horrible what went on that day."

"It must have been and I recall you telling me you and your regiment had the assignment to load gun after gun and then hand them up to the Georgia regiments behind that stone wall and how you were saddened about how the Yankees just kept on coming forward and how they were being butchered. Well, it's going to be the same thing today but this time the Yankees have the stone wall, and the Confederates will keep advancing and be cut to pieces. Do you understand how dangerous this charge is?"

"If I didn't up until this point, well I do now. If we are to suffer today like those Yankees did at Fredericksburg then I say this attack is ill-fated."

Max changed the subject, snapped his fingers, and removed two pieces of beef jerky from his haversack, one of which he handed to Sam. "Here, have a piece of jerky."

Sam nodded in agreement as he took a bite and commented, "I haven't had a good piece of jerky since I joined the army." Chewing in satisfaction, he held the remaining jerky up and continued to speak, "My mother used to make jerky back in Five Points. Did your wife make this?"

"No, she purchased this at Weis Market. Weis is this huge grocery store right here in Gettysburg. If I had an opportunity to take you there you would not believe all the food they have. It's kind of a giant version of the general stores that they have here in the 1860s."

Sam took another bite and remarked, "Speaking of your wife. When I was at your farm she struck me as a wonderful woman. She not only patched up my wounds but she seemed like a very religious person. I say this because she knew word for word Psalm 91. There are a lot of people who memorize scripture, but not many Psalm 91 as it is a long scripture."

"My wife is quite religious, far more than I but I do believe in God. I take it you are a religious man, Sam."

"Indeed I am. My father was not much of a believer but my mother was as religious as they come. She read the Bible every morning and evening not only to me but to my two younger brothers and my sister. She took us to church every week at a small Baptist church down the road on the other side of Five Points. My father never went, but he never interfered with how my mother wanted us to be raised. By the time I was nine years old, I had memorized Psalm 91 and I recite it quite often throughout the day. Let me ask you. Does your wife believe you…that you can save me from death on this day?"

"No, I'm afraid she does not agree with me. She has stated that I am going against God's will by trying to save you and that if you were meant to die then I should not interfere. That's why I told you it was up to you to decide if you wanted to live or die this day. I cannot make that decision for you. That is up to you and you have told me you want to survive this day…the entire war and then return to Alabama and marry Rose. Do you still feel that way?"

"Yes, I do. I'd be a fool to say that I want to die. I am still willing to go with whatever your plan is for this day. I don't completely understand everything you have told me, but I do understand that I want to survive."

Max, finishing his jerky, reached into his pocket and removed his pocketknife.

Handing it to Sam, he spoke, "Here, I want you to have this. It's a gift from me to you."

Looking at the strange object Sam asked, "What is it?"

"It's a modern-day pocketknife."

Sam turned the closed knife over in his hand and commented, "I had me a pocketknife when I joined up but I lost it three months into the war."

Max pointed at the knife. "That's called a Swiss Army Knife and you can use it for many other things than just cutting."

Sadly, Sam responded. "I don't have anything of value I can give you."

"That's okay," said Max. "The fact that you have decided to live through this battle is enough of a gift for me."

Sam put the unfinished piece of jerky in his pocket and asked, "You haven't explained to me how I am going to survive this day."

Max checked his timepiece. "You're right on that. In about ten minutes the cannons will begin to sound so I guess I should explain my plan. When we get out there near the Emmittsburg Fence I'll give you a nudge with my elbow. This will be the signal for us to begin. After I nudge you I'll fall as if I'm shot and then you go down on your knee as if to assist me but then you fall to the side like you're shot. We'll lay there motionless for four or five minutes, then we'll crawl off through the low weeds to the trees on our right. After we are in the safety of the trees we'll wait out the remainder of the charge, then you can go back to Spangler's Woods or to Lee's Headquarters. After you leave then I'll hike back through the woods to my farm and that will be the end of it. You will have survived the day and I'll be back in 2019."

"Your plan sounds simple enough but do you think it will work? There will be officers there who will insist we move forward. If we fall off, acting like we have been shot, when we decide to crawl off into the trees don't you think we will be noticed?"

"No, we will not be noticed by any officers, and here's why! By the time we get near the fence, the lines will have already begun to collapse. The smoke will be thick, the noise from cannon and musket fire will be deafening, and men will be falling dead or wounded everywhere you look. The officers, those who are not shot themselves, will have their hands full trying to keep the men in formation. They will not have the time to pay attention to two soldiers crawling off into the trees. At this point, the charge will only last another ten minutes or so. It will be chaos and disorganization on the field. No one will pay us any attention. Once we get to the trees we'll lay up until it's all over. Then, you can walk back to Spangler's Woods or the main encampment. Tomorrow Lee will pull the remainder of his army out of Gettysburg and escape back down into Virginia and you will have survived what went on here. The war lasted for another two years, but in the end, Lee surrendered to General Grant at a place called Appomattox Courthouse down in Virginia."

Surprised, Sam asked, "Are you saying the South will lose the war?"

"Yes, the South will lose but it will take our nation years to recover from all the death and destruction this war has caused."

Sam looked out across the field and asked. "Once again, you speak of things I know nothing of. How is it that you know the ground out there in the field so well? To listen to you one would think you have been there before."

"I have been out there before…many times. I have even made this attack before as a reenactor."

Confused, Sam inquired, "Re-en-act-or. Whatever does that mean? I am not familiar with that word. And, another thing, how could you have made this charge before as it has not happened as of yet?"

Max thought for a moment and then responded. "Have you ever been to a play?"

"No, not really. Well, come to think of it, every year at Christmas the

Baptist church my mother took us to had a yearly play about the birth of Jesus. Local citizens in the town would dress up like Joseph and Mary, the three wise men, and so on. The pastor had a manger built on the stage live animals were brought in and a real live baby was used as Jesus. One year I was even in the play and I had to dress up like a shepherd boy. Some of us were given certain things we had to say."

Max grinned, "You have answered your question as to what a reenactment is. The reason your church and your community had that play every year was to remember and honor the birth of our Savior, Jesus Christ. It's kind of the same thing with a Civil War reenactment. Men like myself dress up at certain times of the year and we play out different battles that happened during the war." Tugging at the sleeve of his uniform, Max explained, "This is not a real Confederate uniform. It was just made to look like one. Just like you dressed up as a shepherd boy, I from time-to-time dress up like a Confederate soldier. The musket that I normally take with me is not a real Civil War musket, but one that was made to appear as one."

Looking at Max's gun Sam asked, "Are you saying the gun you have with you is not real?"

"No, this gun is real. When I go to a reenactment I always take my reenactment musket with me. I had my regular gun with me this morning when I left the farm, but then when I got to the cornfield you told me about where your friend was killed and you were wounded, I found this gun lying next to a dead Confederate soldier. You are probably not going to believe this but that soldier according to a piece of paper pinned inside his hat turned out to be none other than Chester Blevins…your friend. He was shot to death just like you said. I hid my musket in the field and took this gun…Chester's musket."

In amazement, Sam asked, "Then you saw Chester?"

Sadly, Max answered, "Yes, I did and don't ask me how he looked. He was stone cold…dead."

Sam sat quietly and frowned at the mention of his friend, but then spoke, "You've been here before, haven't you…I mean here to this field, these woods, that fence out there where according to you, I died."

"Yes, I've been here many times over the years. My father who is also a reenactor and I have walked every inch of Spangler's Woods, that field out there and the stone wall on the other side. We have been to the Emmittsburg Fence and stood where many a Confederate lost their life. Speaking of the fence. The fence that is out there right now will within the next couple of hours be destroyed. Here's something quite strange. The fence at the edge of my farm is part of the fence that is out there now."

Sam looked at Max in confusion. "How can that possibly be?"

"Well, you see I bought the farm that I now own from an old fella who had a great grandfather many times over who owned this land where the battle will take place today. This very field was part of his property. After the battle was over this man came out here to this field and one of the things he did was to haul back the broken sections of the fence to his farm. Eventually, the fence was reconstructed, placed at the edge of the farm, and believe it or not it still stands today."

"Once again," said Sam, "you speak of things that are difficult for me to understand."

The sound of a cannon being fired reverberated through the trees, then was followed by three more consecutive cannon rounds being fired. Checking his timepiece Max held up his watch and announced, "It's one o'clock and the shelling has begun. You best be getting back to your regiment. You'll be told to stay put in the shelter of the trees until the cannonade is over. Like I said it will be about an hour before you are ordered to form up out there on the field."

Sam stood while asking, "Are you going to come with me?"

"No, I'm going to sit in those trees just off to the right of where your regiment is. Don't worry. When you are ordered to form up I'll get as near to you as possible. Try and relax if you can because once things get underway, there will be no time for relaxation. It's going to be intense and deadly, but if we stick to my plan we'll both make it through this day."

Sam shook Max's hand as he hoisted his musket. "I'll see you in about an hour out there on the field."

Max, returning the handshake grinned, "Count on it!"

Watching Sam walk through the trees to his regiment Max veered off to his right and made himself comfortable in between two large oaks. "Removing all of his equipment he reclined against one of the trees, removed his Brogans, and began to rub his socked feet. Then, taking off his hat he opened his canteen and poured a stream of water down over his hair and onto his sweat-covered face. He took a long drink and then thought about what lay ahead. His plan seemed simple enough as he reviewed what he planned on doing once on the field and then when they approached the fence. If everything went the way he thought it would then within the next hour and a half he and Sam should be safely in the trees on the right of the field away from the horrible battle.

Looking high above into the leafy trees, he thought about the fact that he could leave right now, just slip away into the forest and head back to the farm. When he considered what he and Sam might face out there on the field leaving seemed like a sensible and logical move but then what would Sam think when he did not appear when he stepped out onto the field? No, he would stay and fulfill his promise of saving Sam. If nothing else he always prided himself as a man of his word.

For the next ten minutes, the incessant cannon fire went on and on with no let-up from one cannon to the next. The loud noise of the individual shells seemed to join together, the constant, boom, boom, boom, boom, boom connecting into one long deadly sound to his ringing ears. Looking through the trees to his left, some fifty yards away he cringed as a Yankee shell exploded a few yards back in the tree line, several soldiers catapulted into the air along with their equipment.

Within four seconds of the hit, there was a thudding sound next to his right leg. Looking down in horror he saw the bloody stump of a man's arm, blood, muscle tissue, and bone fragments hanging from the severed limb. His first thought was to pick up the body part and toss it off into the weeds but then he thought that would be disrespectful. Thinking the blast had been way too close for comfort he quickly slipped his feet into his Brogans and picked up his gear. He was moving further into the trees where he would be out of cannon range. Another blast exploded off to their right setting the low brush in the area on fire while two tall trees began to fall in his direction. Running as fast as he could he escaped the loud deafening thud of the tall tree as it hit the ground, limbs, leaves, and branches flung in every direction.

He stood back in the trees and had a fleeting thought about how he should just keep going on through the forest, and make his way back to the cornfield and then the farm. If his father or Kellem were with him they would no doubt agree with his logic, but they were not present. Going down on his right knee he began to tie his shoes. He was still determined to remain on the field of battle and lead Sam to safety.

Another fifteen minutes passed, the ongoing cannon noise something he thought would never end. At the beginning of the cannonade, the smoke drifted off to the east, but the slight breeze in the air shifted and the thick smoke now hung in amongst the trees like an early morning fog. But this was a deadly fog because now one could only hunker down while hearing the approaching Yankee shells. It was like swimming in the dark in a pond full of alligators.

Suddenly, out of the smoke, there appeared a Confederate soldier, a middle-aged man who had tears streaming down the sides of his face. Kneeling next to Max he made the sign of the cross and then spoke, "I've had enough! I'm going back to Virginia. Good luck to you, son!" With that, he was off and disappeared into the trees. Max watched as the man ran off. *A deserter!* He could hardly blame the man.

It was just minutes ago that he was questioning himself about staying. He checked the time: 1:35. According to history, the Confederate shelling would stop at two o'clock. Another twenty-five minutes of cannon hell, but this was just the tip of the iceberg. When the shelling stopped the men would be ordered to form up out on that deadly field and the worst was yet to come for most of them. He figured that many of the men had no idea what awaited them. He felt strange as he realized out of the 15,000 Confederates who would make this charge he and he alone knew what was to come. If he managed to survive the day and get back home to the farm who would believe what he was experiencing? The only person he knew who would possibly understand what he was going through would have to be Kellem and that was only because he had seen Sam Pritchard, the ghost soldier years ago back at the fence on the farm.

Max lowered his head praying, "Dear Lord…I've gone and got myself in quite a fix down here on this old earth. I really can't explain all this but here I am. Forgive me for trying to save Sam as it may just be Your will that he dies on this day. I pray that You will intercede and guide me in what You would have me do."

The next twenty minutes passed slowly as more Confederates hiding in the tree line were blown to bits from Yankee cannon fire. Then, as if by magic the cannonade stopped, the lingering and ongoing noise and smoke slowly drifting off to the west. Max stood and walked to the edge of the woods next to the field when a rider galloped up and down the soldiers in the trees as he announced, "Form up boys! Form up!"

Suddenly there was a long loud drumroll and as if the trees were leaking, hundreds and thousands of men in gray stepped out of Spangler's Woods and fell into position out on the field, the rattling of canteens and bayonets echoing up and down the mile-long line of men. Taking up a position at the far end of the 47th, a soldier on the end stared at Max and then asked, "Never seen you before. You're not with the 47th."

Max stuck out his right hand. "I'm from the 2nd South Carolina and there is no way I'm going to miss this attack."

The man smiled and shook Max's hand as he replied, "Glad to have you with us South Carolina."

Max squeezed the man's hand, "Same to you, Alabama!"

He searched the line of soldiers for Sam and then spotted him six men down in the row in front of him. Sam turned and noticed him as he tipped his hat. Max gave him a thumbs up at which point Sam turned and faced the field. The drums stopped and there was an eerie silence that fell over the Confederate lines.

Up the line, Max saw a rider stop out a few yards from the men, and raising his sword into the air he began to speak. The rider was too far off for Max to hear the exact words but he figured that had to be ol' George Pickett and he already knew what was being said. "Up men and to your posts! Let no man forget today that you are from old Virginia!" This was followed by a loud resounding "Hip. Hip, hoorah!" which was repeated three times, all the while the thousands of Confederate men, waving battle flags, hoisting their muskets, and shaking their fists at the Yankees three-quarters of a mile off.

When the men finally settled down, there was another moment of silence when an officer standing in front of the Virginia regiments which were positioned in front of the Alabama regiments gave another short speech. This then had to be General Armistead. The officer looked up and down the line of soldiers then spoke loudly, "Virginians, Virginians! We fight for our sons and daughters, our friends, our wives, and our sweethearts!" He looked at the rows of soldiers standing before him, remained silent, and then raised his sword high and loudly ordered, "Forward…" He hesitated, then lowered the sword and commended, "March!" Armistead turned and took his first step toward the Yankee lines, the thousands of Confederates stepping out at the resonating drum call to *Advance!*

It was a few seconds before the Alabama regiments stepped out in support of the men from Virginia. This was followed by all one hundred and fifty Confederate cannons firing a single shot each toward the stone wall.

Within a minute the mile-long line of wavering soldiers passed in between the cannons and the artillery crews who waving their hats and cheering, applauded the advancing brigades and regiments forward.

Five minutes out into the field, the cannons now behind them, Max, Sam, and the others marched in close formation, some of the men still cheering. The cannons were now silent and eventually not a man was cheering. Thoughts of what must lie ahead were no doubt starting to invade their minds. Max kept looking to his right and the woods were just a few yards away. *Soon!* He prayed he and Sam would be in the trees away from all the carnage that was to come.

Another ten minutes passed when the silence was pierced by loud cannon fire from the stone wall. The first few shells landed far behind the advancing southern men. In the next two minutes the Yanks had adjusted their cannon range and large gaps were being blown in the Confederate lines. After each direct hit, at the direction of a line officer, the men on either side of a new gap would move sideways to plug the hole. Max looked for Sam but the smoke was too thick for him to see clearly.

Max was temporarily blinded as a shell smashed twenty yards on the far right of the 47th, and several men catapulted up into the air. The Alabama soldier Max had talked with before pulled Max by his sleeve to the left so they could help fill the gap. Even though several southern boys had just lost their lives, it was turning out to be a blessing as Max was now almost directly behind Sam. Two soldiers broke from the Virginia regiment that was in front of them as they lost their nerve and ran for the trees. An officer appeared to yell for them to stop which they did not. He withdrew a pistol, firing at the two deserters, the bullets missing their targets, the two men escaping into the thick trees.

Seconds and minutes passed by quickly and now in between the Yankee cannon fire Max could hear the sound of musket fire coming from the wall. Three Virginia soldiers in front of where he was to his left fell, one a company flag bearer. The man next to the bearer bent down and hoisted the battle flag and continued as they descended into the natural dip in the field near the fence. Walking through the shelter of the lower ground, they were out of sight from the stone wall, musket balls, and cannon fire passing above their heads.

He watched as the Virginians arrived at the top of the crest, many of them falling from enemy fire. Climbing up the crest was difficult as dead or wounded soldiers fell and rolled back down into the dip making it difficult for those pushing forward. At the top of the crest, it was chaos as the formation began to dissolve before his very eyes. It was now every man for himself as officers ordered the men to run to the fence, get over it, and advance to the wall. Max looked for Sam and he spotted him ten yards ahead. As he ran to Sam's side, the soldiers on either side of Sam went down, probably shot to death. *Close enough!* thought Max. Running forward he bumped Sam on his shoulder, the signal for the plan to start. Max instantly went down as if he were shot. Sam, as planned went down on his right knee to assist Max, but then faked being shot himself. Laying in silence Max reached over and gripped Sam's shoulder, the signal to remain perfectly still.

Max waited as the seconds ticked by while several soldiers and two mounted riders passed them by. Laying perfectly still Max could hear the shots from Yankee muskets whiz over their heads. Raising his head slightly, he decided, *Time to go!* Pulling on Sam's right arm he nodded toward the trees, a signal for him to follow.

It took a full five minutes of crawling through the low weeds, all the while enemy fire passed over their heads until they arrived at the edge of the woods. Taking the last few yards on their hands and knees, Max sat against a tall tree and reached out taking Sam by his shoulders as he announced out of breath, "We've made it!"

Sam hid behind an adjacent tree and stared out at the still-raging battle as he gasped for breath while asking, "Now what?"

Max took a drink from his canteen and replied, "We just stay put and wait things out. This should be over in the next ten minutes or so, then you can return to camp and tomorrow you will be pulling out of here with the rest of the army."

Looking back out at the smoke-filled field, Sam asked, "And what of you?"

"I'll be back at my farm with my wife and two daughters."

Sam moved next to Max, his face streaming with tears.

Max bumped Sam on his shoulder with his right fist. "What's wrong? You're safe now."

Sam stood and pulled Max to his feet. "I can't do this, Max…I'm sorry. If I leave my regiment now, why I will never be able to forgive myself? Your wife was right when she said it was wrong to interfere with God's will. If it's His will that I should die today out there near that fence, then His will must be done. I'm going back!" Taking Max's left hand in his right he explained, "Do you remember Psalm 91 and when your wife and I spoke it at your farm?"

Not waiting for a response, Sam went on, "Part of that scripture reads, *'And God will command His angels concerning you to raise you in their hands and prevent you from stubbing your feet against a stone.'* It is my prayer for you and your wife, Max that in the future if you or yours are in danger then God will send an angel to protect you. God bless you, Max. You're a good man." With that, he hoisted his musket and ran back into the field toward the fence. Not even five seconds passed when a loud explosion, followed by dense smoke filled the air.

Max got the strangest feeling that Sam, at that moment died near the fence as history had stated. He thought about venturing out to the field to see if he could locate Sam but thought better of it. He had gone as far as he could go. It was time for him to go back home. He hesitated but then three bullets sank into the tree he was standing near. He needed to leave while he could. Slipping off into the trees he headed northeast in the general direction of where he thought the farm would be.

After walking for just over three hours he found himself standing at the edge of a familiar sight, the cornfield that was no more than a quarter of a mile from the farm. Taking a last drink from his now empty canteen he was ringing wet with perspiration. He checked his timepiece: 6:47, seventeen minutes late for Elizabeth's promised fried chicken dinner. Looking around to see if anyone was watching he slipped into the stalks of corn and in less than three minutes he found Chester Blevins's body. Placing Chester's musket next to the body, Max spoke to the dead soldier. "I tried to save your friend Sam, but things didn't quite work out the way I planned." Raising his eyes toward the heavens Max went on, "Good Lord…I pray that these two men…these two young boys, soldiers that they were who died here on the killing fields of Gettysburg will enter your kingdom!"

He searched the nearby corn stalks, found his reenactment musket, and made his way to the far edge of the field. He still had to walk through a stand of trees before he arrived at the slight hill that overlooked his farm. Setting out on the last leg of his journey home he figured he'd be home by seven-fifteen at the latest.

In the middle of the stand of trees in a relaxed state of mind, he suddenly realized something that made him brace himself into a state of alertness. *He was so close to getting back home but he was not out of the woods just yet!* He figured that he was probably still back in 1863 and would remain there until he crossed the fence in his yard. The thought of being seen by any Yankees now and being shot or captured would be catastrophic after all he had been through. He slowed his pace and became more aware of his surroundings as he made his way slowly through the trees.

Almost through the trees, he found himself breathing heavily as he slowed his pace. He stopped for a moment to catch his breath, then took no more than two steps when he heard two shots ring out. Since he was still in 1863 the shots had to have been fired by soldiers, Union or Confederate he could not be sure. Another shot rang out, but this time it sounded closer. For some reason, the only thing that came to his mind was to *run!* He was only five minutes from the farm and the thought of failing now was erased from his brain as he ran as fast as the heavy Brogans on his feet would allow. He tripped over a log, got up quickly, and stumbled over a small boulder but regained his balance as yet another shot sounded.

He stopped running but kept up a good but careful walking pace as he looked to his right and left for anyone, Yankee or Reb. Reassuring himself he was going to make it, he thought, *Just two more minutes and I'll be out of these trees and then down the rise to the farm.*

It seemed like the longest two minutes he had ever experienced, but then he emerged from the trees, and there at the bottom of the slight rise sat his farm. Taking a deep breath he smiled to himself as the setting below reminded him of a picture postcard: the farmhouse, the barn, his wife's garden, and the fence that bordered 1863 from 2019. Feeling he was now safe he walked down the hill, stopped, and looked back at the trees. No one had followed him. Stepping through the fence he leaned his musket against one of the rails and bent down, his hands on his knees as he was out of breath. Leaning on the top rail he spoke a brief prayer. *"Dear Lord…thank You for getting me through this day. I do not completely understand what I just went through these past few hours, but I guess it doesn't make a difference because now I am home.*

Like an answer from God, Max heard his wife's voice, "Max…Max!"

He turned and saw her running across the yard as fast as her legs would go. He took two steps toward her as she almost leaped into his outstretched arms. Looking into his tired and dirty face she ran her fingers through his hair knocking his hat to the ground. Tears ran down her face as she hugged him tight and kissed him three times.

The greeting over, Max held her by the shoulders and asked, "What's all this with the tears? You told me when I left that you were not the least bit afraid of me crossing the fence on my search for Sam Pritchard?"

"I was not afraid until six thirty rolled around and you had not returned. It's almost seven thirty and you're an hour late. I know how punctual you always are and I began to worry that something terrible may have happened to you." Wiping tears from her face she looked him up and down. "Excuse my French as they say but you look like you've been through hell. What happened out there? Did you manage to find Sam Picthard?"

"I can't explain everything that happened since I left this morning, because I'm not so sure I understand it myself, but I can tell you this. I did locate Sam. When I found him I remembered what you said about how saving Sam might be going against God's will. I realized you were right in what you said, so in talking with Sam, I told him if he wanted to live it would have to be up to him and I could not make that decision for him. He decided to live…to survive the day. Later when we made the charge across that deadly field just before we got to the fence where history tells us he died, we escaped into the woods."

"Then you saved him?"

"No, I don't think I did. At the last moment when we were hiding in the trees and the battle was still raging he had a change of heart and told me you were right. That if it was God's will that he die today, then so be it. He also said he would not be able to live with himself, abandoning his regiment which had been his family for the past two years. He shook my hand, said a short prayer for you and me and then he ran back into the battle. He hadn't left the safety of the trees for more than a few seconds when a cannon shell hit where he ran. I didn't know what to do. I could not go back out to the field to see if he had survived because it was too dangerous. I figured he died just like he was supposed to. I turned and walked away from the remainder of the battle and made my way back here to you, the twins, and the farm. There is a lot more that I saw and experienced and we'd have to stand out here for the next few hours for me to explain it all."

Pulling her husband by his right arm, Elizabeth took control of the moment. "Let's get you in the house. You can get out of this filthy uniform and shower. I set aside a plate for you, two chicken legs and a breast, mashed potatoes, corn, and stuffing. It'll be waiting for you on the table when you come down and then you can tell me all about this adventure of yours."

~ 645 ~

CHAPTER FORTY-ONE

Max, lying on his right side, slowly opened his eyes and gazed at the alarm clock next to the bed: 8:35 Wednesday morning. Sitting on the side of the bed he stretched and looked out the window as the early morning October sun bathed the fence at the edge of the farm. Just up the rise beyond the fence the trees resembled a patchwork of color, nature's quilt of fall leaves, crimson red, bright yellow, and gold, mixed with rusty browns and the ever-brilliant green of the pines. Getting up he thought, *fall is the best time of the year.* Walking to the shower he couldn't believe he had overslept. It was rare when he slept beyond six in the morning.

He stood in front of a floor-length mirror, slipped his socked feet into Cordovan loafers, and examined himself: button-down light blue shirt, grey and blue striped tie, pleated suit pants. Running his fingers through his hair in approval of his appearance he draped his suit coat over his right arm, placed his watch on his wrist and it was down the stairs to the kitchen for breakfast and then it was off to the office for yet another day in the world of finance.

Max entered the country kitchen where he saw Elizabeth busy at the stove. Clearing his throat to get her attention he asked, "What's on the griddle this morning?"

Elizabeth turned, raised a spatula in the air, and announced, "French toast and red potatoes, coffee, and juice. I was just about to go up and roust you out of the sack. Last night before we turned in you said your first client of the day was scheduled for ten o'clock. That gives you about a half hour to get something in your stomach and then it's off to work with you." She placed a breakfast plate and a cup of coffee on the table in front of Max, put her hand on his shoulder, and blessed the food. The blessing complete she sat across from him and sipped at black coffee. "Do you have more than one planned client coming into the office today?"

"I only have two scheduled appointments for the day. The first one at ten is with Janet Whitcomb. She's a new client who just inherited a few hundred thousand from her grandmother's will and she wants to sit down and discuss all the options available for investment. In the afternoon at one o'clock Luke Stemmons, a long-time client, even before I took over the business wants to make some changes to his will. That in itself could take a few hours, so I don't imagine I'll be home much before four o'clock." Cutting off a corner of French toast, Max asked, "What's on your docket for the day?"

Stealing a small piece of potato from his plate she popped it in her mouth and replied, "First of all I have three phone calls to make. I have to call your parents back and let them know that you and I discussed them coming up for Thanksgiving. When I talked with your mother last week she said if they came they'd probably come up a few days before the holiday and then drive back home on the twenty-ninth. I just have to firm everything up with them. The second call is going to be Kellem. After you talked with him last week about the death of his brother last month and then with his sister passing away in her sleep that leaves him down there in Florida by himself. You suggested that we invite him to move back here to the farm for the rest of his days. He seemed open to that and said if things work out he'll more than likely be here just before Thanksgiving so it should be a full house around here on turkey day. The last call I need to make is to Ellen. We've both been so busy lately that we've been out of touch for the last month. We just need to catch up. After that, I plan on talking the girls outside for some fresh air and fall sunshine while I clean out the gutters with that new blower attachment you purchased last week. I'll rake up all the leaves around the house and by then it should be time for me to get supper underway."

Max pushed himself away from the table, stood, and slipped his brief-case over his shoulders while looking at his watch. "Nine thirty-five. Just enough time for me to pick up a coffee at the gas station on my way to town." Giving his wife a peck on the cheek he tickled the twins and gave them both a kiss and headed for the front door. "Be careful today and I'll see you this evening."

Unlocking the rear door to his business, Max hesitated before entering as Detective Vanderway pulled in and parked next to the Jeep. Hopping out the detective waved a good morning at Max, "I was hoping to have a few minutes with you before you get too busy. Can we talk?"

Max held the door open and gestured, "Sure, my first client of the day is not scheduled to be here until around ten. So I have a few spare moments to talk." He flipped on the hallway light and led the detective to the front office where he opened the blinds allowing the bright sunshine to fill the room with light. Max sat on the edge of his desk and offered the detective a chair.

Vanderway sat and apologized, "This should only take a few minutes. It's not a big deal but I thought it's worth mentioning."

Max sipped at his gas station coffee and motioned for the detective to continue. Vanderway crossed his legs and began. "I received a call early this morning from the Manheim Township Sheriff. If you'll recall he and I talked with Simon Buamer twice. Once after he attacked you at Kellem's farm and then we talked with him about the destruction of your business. It seems that of late your old nemesis, Simon, is reported to have gone off the deep end."

"Whatever does that mean?" asked Max.

"That's the same thing I asked the sheriff. He responded that folks in and around the Mennonite community have noticed a drastic change in Baumer's behavior. He has always been known as a shrewd but fair busi-nessman, but right now and for the past few weeks all of his employees at his hardware store have up and quit, saying he has become impossible to work for. His business is falling apart and he is driving everyone nuts over at a farmers market they have over there. He is obsessing over the fact that Elizabeth left the Mennonite faith to marry you. He claims he should have never allowed that to happen. He's making the elders in the community crazy with his constant raving about what happened and that it should not have happened. Last week at this farmers market he got into a knockdown drag out with a couple of male college students who were just simply having a conversation with some Mennonite girls."

Max frowned as he asked, "Do you think he's dangerous?"

"Once again, I asked the sheriff that same question. He answered that Simon Baumer was too smart to do anything foolish. He said he thinks it's just talk, but he thought we should be informed about his current attitude just in case."

Concerned, Max asked, "Just in case…what?"

"The sheriff said he'd keep me posted on how things on his end are going and in the meantime if you or Elizabeth see Baumer over here in our area or if he calls or drops by the farm call me immediately. I doubt if any of those things will happen but just to be safe…heads up!"

Their conversation was interrupted when the front door opened and in walked a tall thirty-ish-something young woman, who upon seeing the detective apologized. "I'm so sorry. I think I'm just a wee bit early."

Max stood and smiled at the woman. "Janet Whitcomb?"

The woman smiled graciously and responded, "Yes and you must be Mr. Miller."

Vanderway realized it was time for him to leave. "I have to be on my way. Make sure you tell Elizabeth about our conversation. I'll call you if anything else comes up." He then shook Max's hand and turned and nodded at Mrs. Whitcomb. "Have a nice day, Ma'am."

Pulling out a chair Max motioned to the woman. "Please have a seat. Make yourself comfortable and then you can tell me all about this inheritance and the money that you want to invest…"

Mrs. Whitcomb, as it turned out, had a lot more questions than Max had anticipated about investments, and she finally left the office at eleven-forty-five. Max hung a BE RIGHT BACK…OUT TO LUNCH sign on the front door, locked up, and then walked up the street to the café for a BLT and chocolate milk. Ten minutes later he returned, and wolfed down his sandwich and milk, leaving him fifteen minutes before Mr. Stemmons showed up. He thought about his conversation with Detective Vanderway and decided to give Elizabeth a call to update her. He tried twice but the line was busy. Placing Mrs. Whitcomb's file in a desk drawer, the front door opened, and his afternoon client arrived.

Elizabeth placed the last of the clean breakfast dishes into a kitchen cabinet while thinking about her conversation with Ellen. She thought about calling Max at work and sharing one of the things Ellen had discussed with her but thought better of it. She did not want to disturb her husband and decided to tell him when he arrived later in the afternoon. She checked the time on the kitchen clock: 1:15. *Time to get after those leaves,* she thought. Slipping a light sweater over her shoulders, the first thing she needed to do was get the twins dressed in their little fall outfits.

Approaching the couch, she reached for the first outfit when there was a knock at the front door. It was not the typical friendly tapping, *I need to borrow a cup of sugar knock,* but three hard knocks...almost as if they were official. Looking at the door she surmised, *Who could that be?*

Before she could even take a step toward the door the three hard wraps came again. Straightening her hair, she started across the living room as she spoke in a loud voice, "Coming!"

The three loud wraps came again and as she opened the door, she was taken completely by surprise. There stood none other than Simon Baumer, his six-foot-six-inch frame filling up the doorway. His feet were encased in muddy work boots, his dress attire that of black pants and a beige shirt complete with black suspenders. The all too familiar Mennonite straw hat sat squarely on his large head. He looked as mean as ever with his scraggly red beard, piercing blue eyes, and set jaw. Staring at one another for what seemed like seconds Elizabeth finally broke the ice, "Simon, what on earth are you doing here?"

Simon looked past her into the interior of the house and then out across the yard, as he spoke sternly, "I've come to take you home, Elizabeth."

Not understanding his meaning, she repeated, "Take me home...why? Did my father send you for me? Is everyone back home all right?"

"This has nothing to do with your family or for that matter anyone in our community. This is about us. I should never have allowed your father to permit you to leave the faith and marry Miller. Your father made a horrible mistake in letting you go out into the world which we for the most part oppose. You were meant to not only be a Mennonite but a Mennonite wife to a man in our community...of our faith. That man is me. I courted you for nearly three months and you never said one time that we should not marry.

I believe you have made an error in judgment. You are to be my wife and that is why I have come."

Elizabeth placed her hands on her hips and shook her head in wonder. "Simon, you must have lost your marbles! I am a married woman with two babies not quite two years old. I have left the faith and happen to be quite happy out here in this world. It's your world that's screwed up, not mine. What makes you think you can waltz over here and take me back home? The law will never allow that."

"You speak of the law of the world outside of our community. Their laws have little to do with how we as Mennonites choose to live our lives. I have more than enough money and I know the correct people that can arrange to have your current marriage annulled. Besides that, this is no way for you to live. This puny little farm is nothing compared to the home that I am prepared to offer you. I can not only support you but your two daughters as well as all of the children that you will give me."

"Simon, enough of this nonsense! You cannot make me go with you. I refuse to go and that's that!"

Baumer reached for her right arm and demanded, "You can come willingly or I can take you by force…your choice!"

Elizabeth jerked away as she stated firmly, "You're hurting my arm. You need to leave this house and this property…now!"

"We'll see about that," barked Simon as he reached for her arm again, but then there was a loud sound like a gunshot, Simon violently drove up against the side wall of the porch where his knees buckled and he sank to the floor. Elizabeth, not sure of what happened held her right hand over her mouth as she saw an ever-growing crimson-red circle of blood staining the back of Simon's shirt. She looked out toward the fence, the barn, and then up into the tree line, but saw no one.

Turning her attention back to Simon she heard a muffled breathing sound as he began to slowly get to his feet. Reaching up he grabbed the porch light for support but his weight pulled the fixture from the wall causing him to slide back down the wall. He was no sooner back down when he began to force himself back to his feet. Turning slowly to face Elizabeth, she could see trickles of blood running down both sides of his open mouth, his eyes seemed to be full of confusion. The front upper right half of his shirt was now soaked with blood. Taking one awkward step he reached for Elizabeth when another loud shot resounded across the back yard, this time a red splotch of blood appeared just below his heart. Simon once again was pitched back against the wall of the porch. Slamming into the wood siding, he slowly slid down the wall to a sitting position, took one last breath, and lowered his chin to his chest.

This time Elizabeth let out a scream which caused the twins to break out in loud wailing. She searched the fence, the barn and the trees for the shooter but there was no one to be seen. Trying to compose herself she reached into her pocket for her cell phone but dropped it to the porch floor, the small device bouncing off Baumer's left leg and down the three steps. Carefully stepping over Simon's right-booted foot which was lying across the threshold, she tripped on the last step and fell to the ground. Ignoring her fall she retrieved her phone and began to call Max but then quickly discovered that the fall to the ground for some reason caused her phone to not work. She turned and ran back up the porch to use their landline inside the house but she tripped over Simon's left foot. Both of the twins were screaming as she got to her feet and raced to the phone next to the couch. She nervously punched in Max's work number and then waited.

He answered on the fourth ring, "Miller Financial Services, Max speaking."

Elizabeth tried to compose herself, but her voice was anything but calm as Max listened to his wife's plea, "Max…please come home…right now! Simon Baumer is here and he's been shot…shot to death I think."

Max could hear his daughters screaming in the background as he stood pressing the phone close to his ear. "Are the twins all right…are you all right?"

"The girls are fine and I'm not harmed in any way…just come home!"

Confused, Max asked, "Who shot Simon?"

The answer came back quickly, "I don't know. There doesn't seem to be anyone around. Just come home!"

"Lock the house and take care of the girls. I'm going to call the police. If they arrive before I do explain to them that I'm on my way. My revolver is up in the kitchen cabinet behind the sugar bowl. There are bullets up there also. Load the gun like I showed you and don't let anyone other than the police in the house. I'll be there in less than ten minutes!"

Luke Stemmons sat in shock after hearing the short phone conversation. He stood and concerned, asked, "Am I to understand that someone has been shot out at your place?"

Max walked to the front door. "At this point, you know as much as I do. Look, I've got to go and take care of my wife and family. I need to lock up and go."

Luke placed his hand on Max's shoulder and assured him, "Look, if there is anything you need or that I can do please let me know."

Opening the door for Luke, Max responded, "Thank you but I need to go."

Max removed his wallet and searched for Vanderway's business card.

Locating the card he punched in the number and surprisingly the detective answered on the second ring, "Detective Vanderway."

Max was stressed but he tried his best not to panic as he spoke, "This is Max. Baumer showed up at my farm. Elizabeth called me and said he'd been shot. She thinks he's dead. I'm leaving right now, please send someone to the farm." Ending the call, he ran down the hall, locked the back door, hopped in his Jeep, and sped down the alley leaving Vanderway staring at his office phone.

Turning to Detective Parks, Vanderway shouted, "Let's go, there's been a shooting over at the Miller farm. On the way over there we need to have a cruiser dispatched to the scene."

Eight minutes later Max turned from the Chambersburg Pike down the long dirt road that led to the farm. Parking next to the barn he saw Baumer's black Caddy parked out behind the barn and a Gettysburg Police cruiser parked on the grass a few yards from the porch. Getting out he ran across the road and the grass but was halted by a uniformed officer. "Hold on there sir! You need to stay back. This is a crime scene."

Max slowed to a walk as he replied, "My name is Maxwell Miller and this is my place. I just called Detective Vanderway about a reported shooting. Have you talked with my wife yet?"

"No sir, we just got here ourselves. Where is your wife and is she all right?"

"She's in the house. I need to go in and make sure she's okay. My two children are in there also."

The officer gestured at the front porch as he suggested, "It would be better if you could enter the house by a different door than the porch. We don't want to disturb any evidence in this area."

Max looked past the officer, where he saw the body sitting against the side wall of the porch. "Is he dead?"

The other officer chimed in, "Yes, he was long gone before we arrived. Do you know the man?"

"If it's who my wife says it is, then yes, I do know him. His name is Simon Baumer, he's a Mennonite farmer from over in Lancaster County. Detective Vanderway knows who he is. I'll talk with him when he arrives. I'm going in through the back door and check on my family."

One of the officers placed his hand on his revolver and suggested, "Just to be on the safe side I'll go in with you just to make sure she's all right. The shooter, as far as we know at this point has not been apprehended. Lead the way."

Walking around the house the officer followed Max and then waited while he unlocked the back door. Opening the door slowly Max shouted, "Elizabeth…it's me, Max, I have an officer with me. We're coming in. Is everything all right?"

Elizabeth's voice sounded from inside the house, "Max…thank God you're here, we're in the living room."

The officer silently motioned that he should go first and that Max should fall in behind him. Max, thinking the officer's decision was uncalled for relented as he realized the man was just doing his job.

They walked slowly through the kitchen and entered the living room where they found Elizabeth seated on the couch cradling one of the girls in her arms the other fast asleep next to her. When she saw Max she got up slowly and went to him. Placing his arms around her he asked, "Are you okay?"

"I'm okay and so are the girls."

Max calmly asked, "Where is my gun?"

Pointing with her free hand at a coffee table in front of the couch, she spoke softly, "It's over there on the table."

Overhearing the conversation the officer asked, "Is there a loaded gun in this house?"

Max walked to the table and he responded, "Yes, it's right here. We keep it in the house for protection."

The officer motioned for Max to move away from the weapon as he asked, "Has the weapon been fired?"

Surprised, Elizabeth answered the question. "Heavens…no! The gun was not taken from the cabinet in the kitchen and loaded until after the shooting. It's been lying right there on the table for the past fifteen minutes or so."

"I'm sorry Mr. and Mrs. Miller, but we are going to have to confiscate this gun as possible evidence."

Elizabeth looked at her husband in confusion and stated, "I don't understand. The gun was not fired. It just sat there on the table."

"It's not that simple folks," pointed out the officer. "A man is lying on your front porch who from what we have seen so far has been shot to death. The shooter has not been apprehended and no weapon has been found. This gun is the only weapon in the vicinity."

Just then Detective Vanderway entered the living room by way of the kitchen and upon seeing the threesome standing by the couch, he, asked, "Is your family all right, Max?"

Max shook the detective's outstretched hand and responded, "Yes, everyone is fine. Your officer here was just about to confiscate our gun, which by the way was not fired. As a matter of fact that gun has not been fired for the past six months since I took it to the firing range. When Elizabeth called me to let me know Baumer had been shot I told her to lock the house, get my gun down from the cabinet in the kitchen, load it, and then not allow anyone in the house other than myself or the police."

"Confiscating this gun falls under standard operating procedure," explained Vanderway. "In a case like this, there has been what appears to be a murder; the shooter is still at large and we have no murder weapon. The gun will be dusted for prints and examined thoroughly. I'm quite sure nothing out of the ordinary will be discovered and your gun will be returned in the next day or so."

Vanderway ordered the officer. "Bag the gun and then give it to Detective Parks who is out on the porch."

The officer removed a pair of white plastic gloves from his pocket, slipped them on, and then with a clear plastic bag he carefully picked up the weapon and placed it gently in the bag.

Nodding at the front window, Vanderway continued with his orders. "Another cruiser just arrived. That gives us four officers available to search the fence, the barn area, and the tree line. Search every inch and see if we can determine where the shooter was positioned. Be careful. The shooter may still be nearby."

After the officer left, Vanderway asked politely, "Is there somewhere we can sit? I need to ask Elizabeth some questions about the events as they occurred."

Elizabeth motioned toward the kitchen. "I think the kitchen table would be best. Besides that, I think I'm going to put on a pot of coffee."

Following Max and Elizabeth to the kitchen Vanderway added, "Coffee sounds good right about now."

Max, grabbing three coffee mugs from above the sink, spoke, "I saw Baumer's car out by the barn."

Removing a notepad from his suitcoat pocket, Vanderway answered, "He must have walked to the house from that point."

"That seems odd," said Elizabeth. "Baumer parked his car near the area where I felt the two shots came from."

Vanderway laid an ink pen next to the pad and explained, "There are always things that seem odd while investigating a case, especially a murder case as this appears to be. I'm no expert when it comes to murder because here in Gettysburg murder is not an everyday, weekly, or monthly occurrence like in larger cities. As a matter of fact, in the last twenty years, I can only recall two murders here in our city. One thing I can assure you of is that there will be no stone left unturned in the investigation of Baumer's murder."

Elizabeth took a seat across from Vanderway at the table and stated, "It'll be a few minutes on the coffee, so I guess we can get started."

Clicking his pen, Vanderway agreed, "All right then…let's begin. Starting at the beginning how did all this unfold?"

"Well, it was all very quick. From the moment I heard a knock at the door up until Simon was shot I bet it was no more than five minutes."

"Can you tell me about what time this all took place?"

Elizabeth estimated. "The last time I looked at the kitchen clock it was one-fifteen. Right after that, I decided to get the twins dressed as I had planned on doing some yard work when I heard this strange knock at the front door."

"What do you mean by strange?"

"We don't get all that many people out this way knocking on our door, but I recall thinking that it was very deliberate…and loud. By the time I got to the door, the knocking occurred two more times. I opened the door and there stood Simon Baumer. Needless to say, I was taken by complete surprise. Baumer was the last person in the world I expected to be on my front porch. At first, he just stood there staring at me. He didn't say a word.

"Finally, I spoke up and asked him what he was doing here and he said he had come to take me home. My initial reaction was that my father had sent Simon to bring me home because something had happened to someone in my family. Simon told me his coming had nothing to do with anyone back home. His coming had to do according to him…with us, meaning he and I. He then went into this tirade about how he should never have allowed my father to permit me to leave our faith and marry Miller… meaning Max. He went on to say that my father had made a horrible mistake in letting me go out into a world that we as Mennonites are opposed to. He said I was a Mennonite woman and that I was to marry a Mennonite man and that *he was that man!* He reminded me that he had courted me for nearly three months and all that time I never said I would not marry him. He explained to me I had made an error in judgment and that I was to be his wife and that is why he had come."

Taking a breath, Elizabeth then continued, "I could not believe what I was hearing and I told him that he had lost his marbles. I was a married woman and had two young daughters. I informed him that he could not just waltz over here and take me back and that the law would never allow that. He persisted in telling me that the laws of the world out here had nothing to do with how we as Mennonites live. He went on to say that he had enough money and knew the right people who could arrange to have my marriage annulled. He told me that he could not only support me and the twins but all of the children I would give him. I then told him that this was nonsense and that I refused to go with him. He then grabbed my arm and told me I could come willingly or by force. I jerked my arm free from him and told him to leave the farm…and now!

"It was then that I heard a loud noise followed by Simon being violently pitched up against the wall of the porch. I saw an ever-growing circle of blood appear on the upper half of his back. Realizing that he had been shot I looked out to the barn and the fence line and then up into the trees up on the ridge, but I saw no one and heard nothing. I turned back to Simon and he had slid down the wall and was on his knees. I remember him trying to get back to his feet but he went down on his knees again and then began to try to stand. He pulled the porch light out of the wall, slowly got to his feet and turned around facing me. He had blood coming from his mouth and he had a look on his face that I pray I will never again see. I did not realize it at the time but he was in his final moments. He raised his arm and tried to reach for me when yet another shot rang out, this time hitting him in the area of his left chest, near the heart. He was catapulted once again back against the porch wall, slid down to the floor, lowered his head and I assume took his last breath and probably died.

"I looked again out to the fence and the barn but saw or heard nothing. I guess what had happened finally took hold of me and I screamed which frightened my two daughters who were now crying. I ran into the house and called Max and told him Simon had been shot and for him to come home. He told me to lock the house, get his gun down from the cabinet in the kitchen, load the weapon, and then not allow anyone other than he and the police to enter. I think it was about ten minutes or so later when the police arrived and then Max got here…and here we now sit with Simon Baumer lying dead on out the front porch." Looking toward the kitchen counter Elizabeth announced, "I believe that coffee is ready now."

As Elizabeth got up Vanderway asked, "Can you recall how much time passed following the first shot that the second shot sounded?"

Elizabeth approached the table with the coffee pot and a tray of cream and sugar as she replied, "Let me think about that. I guess it must have been twenty, twenty-five seconds…maybe thirty."

Vanderway reached for a cup. "That seems odd to me."

Elizabeth, pouring hot coffee into the three mugs, sat as she took a short drink and then lowered her head in guilt. "This may have all been my fault. I may have been able to prevent all this from happening. I was warned that Baumer was acting strange."

Vanderway looked at Max and spoke, "Then you called your wife as I suggested?"

"I did call her twice, but the line was busy both times. My afternoon client showed up so I decided to wait until I got home later in the day to share with Elizabeth what we discussed."

Elizabeth sat her cup down and held her hands out in confusion. "What am I missing here?"

Max jumped in on the conversation. "It would seem that we are all missing something here. When you say you were warned about Baumer's strange behavior what are you referring to?"

"When I talked with my friend Ellen earlier today, she told me all about how Simon was obsessing over the fact that I had left the Mennonite faith and had married you, I thought about calling you at work, but thought I'd wait until you got home."

Max shook his head in absolute wonder as he went on to explain. "Detective Vanderway talked with me this morning when I first arrived at the office. He explained to me no doubt the same thing that Ellen had explained to you…that Simon Baumer was going off the deep end. I tried to call you twice but the line was busy. I guess you were on the phone with Ellen or maybe even Kellem. We were both aware of Baumer's strange behavior yet failed to tell the other."

Elizabeth lowered her head again, and spoke softly, "If I would have called you then maybe we could have prevented this horrible event from happening."

"None of this is your fault," said Max. "If anyone is at fault here it's me. I should have continued to try and get through to you on the phone."

"Look," said Vanderway, "this is no one's fault other than Simon Baumer's. He chose to play with fire, and he got burned…in this case…shot to death. Fortunately, no one other than Baumer was injured. The fact that we all were aware of his strange behavior as of late is water over the dam. The issue now is *who* shot Baumer plus the fact that he or she or whoever it was is still out there at large and that concerns me."

Detective Parks walked into the house as he addressed Vanderway, "Frank…Greenie has arrived and is in the process of bagging up the body. We happened to find a bullet that was lodged in the wall of the porch. I bagged it as evidence and gave it to Greenie along with the Miller's gun. He said he would begin an autopsy this evening and should have the results by no later than tomorrow evening. The boys are still searching the surrounding woods, the fence line, and the barn but so far have turned nothing up in the way of evidence. I have gone over everything on and near the porch with a fine-toothed comb. Do you want me to call in a cleaner?"

"If you're satisfied with the crime scene, let's get the cleaner over here as soon as possible."

Elizabeth, sipping at her coffee, asked, "What on earth is a cleaner?"

Responding, Parks explained, "A cleaner is a police term that refers to an individual or sometimes even a team, depending on what has to be done that goes to a crime scene, like your front porch and cleans up all the blood and the mess that's left behind after the fact."

"There is no reason to call some stranger in to clean off my porch," said Elizabeth, "I am perfectly capable of doing that."

Vanderway excused Parks and then spoke directly to Elizabeth. "You have always struck me as an extremely strong sort of woman and I have no doubt you could stomach cleaning that porch up, but a cleaner does more than just clean up the mess. He or she is trained to look for evidence… something that we may have overlooked, so I do appreciate you're offering to clean the porch, but we'll still go with our cleaner."

He made a note on his pad, then asked his next question, "Did you in any way, Elizabeth, touch Simon's body after you realized he was dead."

"No, I did not. Well, I guess I did. His right foot was laying across the threshold of the porch door which prevented me from locking the house so I shoved his foot to the side with my foot."

"Correct me if I'm wrong but you lived with your parents in a Mennonite community over in Lancaster County for what…over twenty years?"

"That's about right. I lived with them until my father released me from adhering to the Mennonite faith and what we believe in. It was difficult but that was my wish. Things have worked out well for me. I'm married to a wonderful man in Max and I have two beautiful children and then there's this farm. I love living here. This horrible event that took place here has placed a stain on our home, but in time with God's help that will pass and our lives will return to normal."

Vanderway nodded his head in agreement as he continued, "The reason I asked how long you lived with your parents in the Mennonite community is because I'd like to know that over the years how close or familiar were you with Simon Baumer. What I'm asking is that over the years did he have enemies or were there people in the community or even outside of the community that disliked him?"

"Simon was twelve years older than I so growing up as a little girl I knew who he was from worship services and then he was always at the farmer's market. Later on, after his wife died he became quite successful and became a man of great wealth. I never really knew him that well until he started to court me. This lasted about three months and during that time I learned who Simon Baumer was. He was a man who was used to getting his way, but yet I felt he was an honest man. If I had married him he would have been a good provider but I was not in love with him. I have no idea if he had, as you say, any enemies. As far as the Mennonite community is concerned we are pacifists and do not believe in violence. That being said, Simon did have a short fuse when it came to his temperament. I can't imagine anyone in the Mennonite community who would desire that Simon Baumer be shot to death. That's just not how they live their lives. Whoever shot him was no doubt from out here in this world. Now, who that could be I have no idea."

Max suddenly spoke up. "If there was anyone in this world who wanted Baumer to be shot, *that would be me!* I had every reason to shoot this man. He attacked me twice, once here at this farm and then once at Elizabeth's father's farm over in Lancaster. Add to that the fact that he could have very well been the one who was responsible for the destruction of my business and he made our lives miserable for a long period, I could have very well shot him, but I did not. During the time he was shot, I was sitting in my office talking with Luke Stemmons."

Shaking his head in agreement Vanderway stated. "I know that your alibi is solid but still we need to check that out. Do you have a number for this Stemmons?"

Taking his wallet from his suitcoat Max removed a business card. "Yes, I can supply you with his number. He gave me three of his new business cards. You can have this one."

Vanderway placed the card in his coat pocket and continued with his questions. "Who else could have desired that Baumer be eliminated from life? What about Kellem McCulhay? After all, he did fire a shotgun near Baumer and even displayed a revolver when Baumer was here at the farm."

Elizabeth immediately objected, "If you are suggesting that Kellem could have been responsible for Simon's death, well that would be impossible. I talked with him on the phone around eleven this morning. Kellem is in Florida and he would not have had enough time to drive or even fly up here. It couldn't have been Kellem."

Getting up from the table Max walked to the kitchen window, pulled back the lace curtains, looked out, then turned back and spoke to Vanderway. "I've been sitting here in this kitchen thinking about who could have shot Baumer. I could be way off base here, but I think that Kip Griner or the people he worked for or still does could have knocked off Baumer."

Vanderway refilled his coffee as he responded, "That very same thought crossed my mind. The people Griner worked for could have been responsible for Brad Sykes's death and we thought that there was a possibility that they would go after Simon as well. The problem we have here is that how Simon Baumer was killed does not line up with traditional organized crime family hits on people they want to be eliminated. The time frame between the two shots is not consistent with how a hitman would operate. He or she or whoever it may have been, if a hitman, would not hang around for twenty to twenty-five seconds before taking a second shot. I'm not saying they are not responsible but how everything went down, the probability of the shooter being a hitman doesn't seem to fit the crime."

Parks appeared in the kitchen as he addressed Vanderway. "We're finished up out here. The medical examiner took Baumer's body and the evidence we collected. Greenie said he would begin the autopsy this evening and should have some answers for us sometime tomorrow. The officers have not found any evidence of where the shooter fired from. I called the cleaner and he and his crew will be here in about two hours to get the porch cleaned up."

Vanderway closed his pad and stood as he took one last swig of coffee. "Well, I guess that's it for now."

Max walked back to the table and asked, "So what happens next?"

"The investigation will continue. I'm going to give the Manheim Township Sheriff over in Lancaster County a call and let him know about this and see if he has anything on his end that may be of help in this case. I'm also going to call Detective Martinson up in Ithaca and see if he has heard anything more about Kip Griner or those he works for. In the meantime, I am going to leave two officers here for the night. When you consider the fact that the shooter is still on the loose, I'd feel better knowing you have some protection. We'll station one officer outside and the other will remain here in the house. I hope this will not inconvenience you, but I think it's for the best. As soon as we hear something from the medical examiner, we'll be in touch. Try and relax. We appreciate all your cooperation. Talk to you tomorrow."

Vanderway no sooner walked out the back door when Elizabeth standing at the kitchen sink suggested, "We've got some phone calls to make. I need to call my parents and put them at ease. When word of Baumer's death hits the community over there, a lot of folks are going to be concerned over me. You also need to phone your folks and let them in on what happened here."

"If I know my mother," stated Max, "after hearing about the shooting she and my father will either drive or fly up here. I don't think we need to call Kellem at this point as he has enough on his plate right now."

CHAPTER FORTY-TWO

Thursday morning, Max kicked off the sheets, sat on the side of the bed, and looked out the second-floor window at the tree line at the top of the rise beyond the fence. It was a beautiful fall morning, the quilt work of fall color of the leaves nothing short of magnificent. The numbers on the alarm clock showed the time: 7:00. *Time for a quick wake-up shower.*

Bounding down the stairs, he found his mother seated on the wood flooring next to the kitchen cabinets where his twin daughters were banging on assorted pots and pans. Elizabeth stood at the stove while stirring a plastic bowl of batter. Seating himself on the floor next to the girls Max announced, "Good morning, family, where's Dad."

Kate handed a wooden spoon to one of the girls as she answered, "Your father was up and out the door before the sun was even up. He said he was going to climb over the fence and go out to the battlefield. We told him that was not a very good idea as the shooter, whoever they may be might still be out there lurking in the woods. He responded that he had no doubt the shooter was long gone. He left the house at six-fifteen and Elizabeth told him breakfast would be on the table at eight."

Max got up and walked to the stove where he filled a mug with coffee, then started for the front door. "I'm going to go out and sit on the picnic table and wait for Dad. It's such a beautiful morning."

Out on the porch, Max took a drink of coffee and then breathed in a long, deep breath of crisp morning air. Looking at the porch floor and the siding he thought about the fact that less than seventeen hours ago Simon

Baumer had been shot to death not two feet from where he now stood. To look at the porch now, if it was not known there had been a shooting there no one would know. The professional cleaners had done an excellent job of cleaning up the blood and the mess left behind. The only remnant of the murder was the hanging porch light Baumer had pulled out of the wall.

Once across the yard, he sat on the table, his feet resting on one of the wooden benches. From where he sat he had a perfect view of the back of the barn where Baumer had parked his Caddy and then walked to the house. He remembered something Elizabeth said during the questioning with Vanderway and that had been she thought the two shots had come from the same area where Baumer had parked his car and that seemed odd. Vanderway said there could be many odd things about the shooting especially here in Gettysburg where there had not been a murder in years. Looking at the porch Max thought the shooter would have had a clear shot at Baumer no matter when the gun had been fired, be that from the barn area, the fence line, or up on the ridge.

He looked off into the trees and thought about the mathematics of life as he recalled all the things that happened in the past seventeen hours. Simon Baumer had been shot to death, he and Elizabeth were questioned by the police, all of the evidence as far as he knew was collected, the medical examiner bagged up Baumer's body and took it away for an autopsy, the cleaners had erased any traces of the shooting and his parents, after being told about the incident drove through the night arriving at two-fifteen in the early morning.

Suddenly, his father appeared at the edge of a long row of bright yellow trees. Seeing his son at the picnic table Charley waved, jogged down the slight hill and despite his age hopped over the fence like a teenager and walked briskly to the table raising his hands to the sky and acknowledging, "What a glorious fall day it is! Good morning, Son."

Max raised the coffee mug in a toasting fashion and replied, "It is indeed. How far into the battlefield did you go?"

"I walked through two stands of trees and crossed a cornfield. I got as far as a dirt road, but considering the time I turned back. I could be wrong but I think that road might lead to Lee's Headquarters."

"If it's the road I'm thinking of, you're correct. Kellem and I, I guess it was a year or so back, hiked that road over to Lee's Headquarters."

"Speaking of Kellem," said Charley. "Didn't you say last evening when we first arrived that he was moving back to the farm with you and Elizabeth?"

"You heard correctly. His only other surviving brother passed on and then just recently his sister passed away in her sleep. He's all alone down there in Florida and Elizabeth and I agreed he would be better off living here with us."

"I believe you're right on that. The man spent what, eighty-some years living on this farm. It only seems right that now he lives out the remainder of his days where he spent the greater part of his life."

Charley changed the topic and looked at his watch. "According to what your wife informed me of when I left this morning, at eight o'clock, which is in five minutes, breakfast would be on the table. Guess we best head on in."

While crossing the yard, Charley continued to speak, "When we first got in last night and we asked Elizabeth how she was doing despite this shooting she said she was doing okay. You know her much better than Kate and I, so let me ask, considering what happened how is she holding up?"

"When you consider she was standing no more than two feet from Baumer when he was shot, I'd say she is doing quite well. When the detectives left after speaking with us I asked her if she was going to be all right. She told me how much she loves living here on the farm, but that the shooting has placed a stain on this house, in time, even though Simon was shot to death right before her very eyes, and something she will never forget, eventually things will get back to normal. Elizabeth is a strong woman and I feel she'll bounce back just fine."

On the porch, Charley reached out and touched the dangling porch light. "Before the day is out I intend to get this light back in working order. I'm not sure if it needs to be rewired or if we need a new light. Either way, by tonight this porch will be well lit."

Breakfast was over, Elizabeth and Kate were busy at the kitchen sink with the dishes and Charley was out on the porch working on the light. Max, at the side of the house, was raking up a pile of leaves when his cell rang. Digging the phone from his pocket he answered, "Hello."

Following a short conversation, he walked around to the front of the house and approached his father while speaking. "Just got a call from Detective Vanderway. The autopsy has been completed and he and Detective Parks will be dropping by with the results around two this afternoon. He also said the medical examiner was coming along. Doesn't that strike you as strange? On television, whenever the police talk to someone in their home about an autopsy the medical examiner is never present. I just always assumed that after a death the examiner does all his work back at his office or wherever they do that sort of thing."

Charley laid down a screwdriver and pulled the wiring away from the siding as he replied, "I've never in my life been involved in an autopsy so you know as much about the procedure as I do. It's just after eleven now, so that gives you and Elizabeth three hours to prepare for whatever you are to be told."

Max gave his father an odd look. "You're planning on being here… right?"

Charley removed the light from its wiring and responded, "I think maybe not so much. Whatever this detective has to reveal to you is between the police, you, and your wife. Even though your mother and I are quite concerned over the situation I'd kind of feel like we were imposing."

"Nonsense!" objected Max. "I, and I'm sure Elizabeth would want you and mother to be present. There is nothing that could be said to us you cannot hear. We have nothing to hide. You drove through the night to be here with us in this time of need and we appreciate your support, so yes, I want you to be here when the police talk with us?"

Charley grinned, "All right then, we'll sit in with you. In the meantime, I'm going to run into town. This fixture appears to still be good but by the time I rewire the thing it would just be easier to purchase a new one. I'll be back long before the police arrive."

Seated on the couch next to Max, Charley seemed amused as he addressed his wife and Elizabeth who were seated in two wooden chairs. "I don't mean to make light of the importance of this upcoming autopsy meeting with the police and this examiner but was it really necessary to vacuum the carpet and dust all the furniture in this room. And then, on top of that, you two have baked cookies and have prepared coffee and iced tea.

You'd think rather than the police showing up that some close friends are dropping by for a pleasant afternoon."

Elizabeth, arranging a tray of cookies, cream, and sugar bowls on a side table replied as she smiled. "It's just the way I was brought up. No matter how clean your house may be you always straighten things up when you are expecting visitors. Besides, I have a feeling we are going to not only be discussing Simon Baumer's death but possibly what went on inside his body and the effects of the two shots fired. I'm just trying to lighten things up a little when you consider the topic that will be at hand."

Kate stirred some cream into a cup of coffee and added, "I could not agree more. Discussing Simon Baumer's death as far as I'm concerned could be stressful on all of us so I say the pleasant atmosphere Elizabeth is trying to create will no doubt be welcomed by these detectives." A tabletop clock chimed the time at two o'clock. Taking a drink, she announced. "They should be arriving soon."

The words were no sooner out of her mouth when there was a knock at the door. Getting up, Max gestured toward the door. "Right on time!"

Max opened the door and stared at the three visitors as Detective Vanderway reached out and shook his hand. "I hope we will not be an inconvenience for your family today. We should only be here for about an hour or so."

Stepping to the side Max offered, "Please gentlemen…come in."

The trio stepped in and hesitated as Max closed the door at which point, he led them into the living room where he made the introductions. "Detectives Vanderway and Parks, I'd like you to meet my parents Charles and Kate Miller and of course, you already know my wife, Elizabeth. Mom, Dad…these are the detectives who talked with us yesterday." Looking at the third man, Max apologized, "I'm sorry. I don't know your name but you must be the medical examiner."

An older man with long gray hair and a matching mustache introduced himself, "Reginald Green. Those who know me call me Greenie. I have been a physician here in Gettysburg for the past thirty-one years and also have the dubious honor of holding the position as the country medical examiner."

Walking to the couch he extended his hand to Charles. "Charley Miller! We've met before. I believe it has been close to twelve years gone by when we met. You gave a Civil War seminar here in Gettysburg during our yearly reenactment that year. I had always heard you were quite the expert when it came to the history of the war so I attended. I must say your rendition of the generals who were here and how the decisions made during the three-day battle affected the outcome was very interesting. Being a reenactor myself I have to say after hearing you speak that you are without a doubt the most knowledgeable man I have ever met when it comes to the Civil War. I'm glad you're with us here today. There is a possibility your expertise may be of value in assisting us to solve this case."

Charley, who stood and shook the examiner's hand responded in confusion, "I'm afraid you have lost me. I can't imagine how my knowledge of the Civil War could in any way help you to solve your case."

"I'll explain that a little later. If I get into that right now I'd be putting the cart before the horse." Nodding at Elizabeth and Kate, he went on, "If everyone is ready then I believe we should get started."

Elizabeth sat forward, folded her hands on her lap, and politely announced, "We have cookies, coffee, and iced tea if anyone would care for refreshments."

Vanderway, taking a seat in one of three old wooden chairs declined saying he had just recently eaten lunch. Parks and the medical examiner agreed as they both sat.

Placing a small briefcase on the floor at his feet Greenie started the conversation. "The shooting of one Simon Baumer occurred yesterday at approximately one-thirty. During that timeframe, Mr. Baumer was shot twice, resulting in his death." Standing, he asked Parks, "Would you, Detective be so kind and stand next to me as I need a body to demonstrate how the two separate shots affected the victim."

Parks stood and removed his suitcoat which he draped over the back of the chair, while stating, "Ready when you are, Doc!"

Displaying Parks, Green went on to explain, "The human body is very complex so I'll try and keep this as simplistic as I can." Approaching Parks, he placed both of his hands on Park's upper chest. "On either side of the upper chest, we have the lungs, the right, and then the left." Moving his right hand slightly to the right he went on, "And right here in this area is the heart. If you will turn around Detective I will continue."

Parks turned around facing away from everyone while Greenie continued to speak while running his hand down the right side of Park's back. "The human body has what is commonly referred to as a rib cage. There are twelve ribs on either side of one's frame." Starting at the shoulders he slowly ran his index finger down Park's back as he spoke, "Ribs one through seven are what are called true ribs, while ribs eight through ten are false ribs. Ribs eleven and twelve way down here at the bottom of the back are known as floating ribs. Okay, now let's discuss what happened.

"The first shot hit Baumer as he was facing away from the shooter. The bullet entered the body on the upper mid-section of the right side of the back. The bullet, after penetrating the skin and muscle tissue hit rib number three, broke it, and then moved downward fracturing rib number four, then pierced the right lung and embedded itself in the porch wall. This shot forced the victim up against the wall and according to you Elizabeth, he was at that time still moving. Injured seriously, but still breathing and moving. Am I on target so far as you can recall?"

Elizabeth smiled and confirmed, "As I can recall…yes."

Taking Parks by his shoulders, Greenie slowly turned him back around so he was facing everyone in the living room. "Now, you claim Baumer got back to his feet and slowly turned around, now facing the direction you thought the first shot came from. Are we still on the same page?"

Elizabeth looked at Max and responded, "Yes…exactly. Simon had this strange look on his face, a look I hope to never see again."

"The bleeding from the mouth area was due to the damaged lung and the look on Baumer's face was probably caused by shock. He was still conscious and probably realized he had been shot. You also stated that it took him about twenty to twenty-five or so seconds to turn around." He looked to Elizabeth for confirmation.

Responding instantly, she replied, "That is correct."

Greenie held up an index finger as he pointed out. "Remember this because that right there is an important clue." Patting Parks on his arm, he suggested, "You can be seated, Detective." Sitting back down himself he opened his briefcase removed two plastic bags and held them up for all to see. "In my right hand we have the first bullet that was fired…the one we dug out of the wall and in my left we have the second bullet that was lodged in Baumer's back. The first bullet was not the kill shot. This bullet caused severe damage and Baumer would have eventually died depending on how long it was before he received medical attention.

"Now, the second bullet…that was the kill shot and after it hit the heart area it was only a matter of a second or maybe two when Baumer breathed his last. The first bullet, taken from the wall as you will notice has been damaged while the second bullet from his back is still in rather good condition." Getting up he crossed the room and handed the two bags to Charley and asked, "Do these two bullets look familiar?"

Charley reluctantly took the two see-through plastic bags and asked, "Why would these spent bullets look familiar to me? I was in South Carolina when this shooting took place. I don't understand."

Vanderway urged Charley to take a close look. "Please, if you would. just examine the two bullets and tell us what you think."

Relenting, Charley looked at the contents of the two bags and then handed them to Max while stating in absolute amazement, "These appear to be Civil War minie balls."

Max examined the bags and agreed, "I believe my father is correct. These do appear to be minie balls. Now, I understand why you would seek my father's opinion, but these are no doubt modern-day manufactured replicas of Civil War ammunition. I have a number of these down in South Carolina in my father's gun safe."

"Which brings me to my next point," said Greenie. "What type of gun would be capable of firing a modern-day Civil War minie ball?"

Charley was quick to respond. "In most cases, I would say the gun would have to be a replica of a Civil War musket, gun, or rifle as they are referred to."

"Precisely," said Green. "That being said leads us to the answer of why the twenty to twenty-five-second delay between the two shots. The shooter was reloading. Does this make sense Charley?"

"It makes perfect sense. During the Civil War, an experienced soldier was trained to load and fire their musket three times in a minute. Even today, Civil War reenactors in mock battles, utilizing in most cases replicas of actual Civil War muskets load and fire their weapons about three times per minute. There are even contests where reenactors or gun collectors can compete for speed and accuracy using this method. Max and I have attended many of these contests ourselves. Some even use replicated Civil War muskets while hunting."

Max joined in on the conversation and pointed out, "In South Carolina my father currently holds the record for reloading and firing a replicated Civil War musket. He can accomplish this feat in fifty-seven seconds. Myself, well the best I've ever done is right around sixty-three seconds."

Agreeing with both Max and Charley, Greenie explained, "As a reenactor myself I too have competed in these sorts of contests and I have to say that you both are faster than I when it comes to firing and reloading a replicated Civil War musket. Let me ask you this, Charley? Would it be possible to fire a replicated minie ball from anything other than a replicated Civil War musket?"

"In most cases no. But then again there are a lot of strange guns out there that experts can configure to fire different types of ammunition so that is remotely possible but more than likely improbable. I mean, this type of ammunition, meaning mine balls is always shot with a gun or musket that is designed for that particular type of bullet. I suppose a gun could be altered that is not a replicated Civil War musket to shoot minie balls, but once again, that is highly improbable."

"Okay then," said Greenie. "We have established that Simon Baumer was shot to death with replicated Civil War bullets and with a replicated Civil War musket, but this case goes much deeper than that. As a reenactor, like you, I am an expert, not as far as the entire war is concerned, but in one particular area which happens to be Civil War weaponry: muskets, pistols, cannons, ammunition, and the like. The strange fact that Simon Baumer was shot to death with replicated Civil War minie balls by a replicated Civil War musket got me to put my thinking hat on. As a physician and medical examiner, everything is not always as it seems so therefore in many cases we have to turn to science. I hold degrees in pathology and forensics. I ran extensive ballistic reports on these so-called minie balls and what I discovered is just this and I find it quite amazing.

"The minie balls in those bags, the ones used to kill Simon Baumer are not replicated ammunition but the real thing. The report which shows a lack of rifling on this ammunition indicates without the slightest doubt that they were fired from an 1861, possibly '62 Springfield 58 caliber Civil War musket. The proof is irrefutable. These two bullets are nearly one hundred and sixty years old, not to mention that the gun used in firing this ammunition is also at least that old. This throws a different set of circumstances into the mystery of this murder. Who, in killing Simon Baumer would use weaponry and ammunition that is over a century and a half old…and why? Any thoughts gentlemen?"

Charley looked at Max and then responded, "This makes no sense whatsoever. First of all an authentic 1861 or '62 Springfield 58 caliber in most cases would not be fired for the simple reason that anyone who owns one is either a reenactor, collector, or gun enthusiast. I happen to own a '63 Springfield Civil War musket. I met a young man who attended one of my seminars and during our luncheon, he got me off to the side and said he had a Civil War Springfield musket that had been in his family for decades. He wanted to know if I was interested in purchasing the gun. I had always wanted one, so I wrote a check for thirty-two hundred dollars and now and for several years am the proud owner of an 1863 58 caliber Springfield musket. The young man told me as far as he knew the gun had not been fired since the war.

"When I got back home, I took the gun over to Savannah, Georgia where a friend of mine who is a gunsmith lives. I asked him to look the musket over and tell me if it was capable of firing. He told me based on what I had paid for this relic if I attempted to fire the gun, I could be throwing away three thousand dollars. He told me the gun, if fired could misfire, destroying the weapon and possibly blowing up causing severe damage to my face, arms, or hands. He went on to say of all the thousands of Civil War muskets out there that very few are fired and besides that, who in their right mind would fire a collector's item? Myself, why I can't even imagine who would want to shoot Simon Baumer using one hundred and sixty-year-old ammo not to mention a gun over a century and a half old. It just makes no sense."

Parks, who had remained mostly quiet since the meeting had gotten underway, got up and poured himself a glass of iced tea then returned to his seat. "The results of this autopsy as far as the murder weapon has indeed thrown a monkey wrench into our investigation. It's almost as if this case is over and it has just begun. At this point, we don't even know who we should talk to or what direction we should go."

Detective Vanderway added, "What my partner says is true, and unless someone comes forward with information we are at a dead end."

Kate, munching on a cookie asked a question. "Is there no way, no public or official records that indicate who here in Gettysburg or the state owns an actual Springfield whatever Civil War musket? I have always been of the understanding that if an individual purchases a gun of any sort there is a rigorous government or mandated process that must be adhered to before the gun can be purchased."

Charley answered the question immediately, "Yes, there are laws and plenty of documentation about how and who can purchase guns, but not in all cases, especially when it comes to collectors. Sales of guns by private collectors are not monitored as closely as guns sold at gun shops or gun shows. In my case when I purchased my Springfield from that young man, aside from me writing a check and him handing over the musket to me the only paperwork there was, was a document of authenticity. The musket I own along with many other collectible firearms, especially weapons that are extremely old in many cases is unknown by the government. Besides that, even if it were possible to track where all the still non-existent Civil War muskets are located, that would be like searching for a needle in a haystack."

Excepting her husband's explanation she asked her next question, "So as it stands right now the police have no suspects to speak of?"

Vanderway held up four fingers as he responded, "We currently have no suspects but we do have four possible persons of interest and one of them happens to be here with us now, and that's you, Max. You have already admitted when we last talked that you had every reason to want Baumer eliminated from life. The man attacked you not once, but twice. And let's not forget he could very well have been behind the destruction of your business. For a time he made your lives miserable.

"Now, all that being said, the possibility of you being the shooter is impossible. We checked out your alibi and Luke Stemmons stated without a shred of doubt that you and he were seated in your office at the time of the shooting. Then, there's Kellem McCulhay. We know when Baumer came here to this farm looking for you Kellem ran him and his brothers off the property by not only firing a shotgun a few feet from Baumer but then brandishing a revolver. Kellem is more of a person of interest than you Max because he fired a gun in Buamer's direction. But then, Kellem as the shooter is also impossible. Elizabeth told us yesterday she talked by phone to Kellem a couple of hours before the shooting. Kellem was in Florida at the time of the shooting so that leaves us with just two other possibilities, one of which happens to be Harmon Sykes, Brad Sykes' father. Max, I believe both you and Charley have met Mr. Sykes."

"Yes, we did. We met him right here in Gettysburg when I was a freshman in college. He wanted to sue me for a confrontation between his son, Brad and I. Harmon Sykes was straightforward, a man who didn't say that much, but I believe he was a fair and honest man."

Vanderway agreed, "I too have met Mr. Sykes. Once here in town at the college where his son was asked to transfer out because of his unruly behavior as a student. The other time we met was up in Ithaca, New York when we interviewed his son about the destruction of your business. Harmon Sykes was as you say straightforward and seemed honest. But let's not forget that his son was killed in an automobile explosion outside of his business. Brad was his only son and the police in Ithaca felt he was killed because he, for lack of a better phrase, threw a one-time friend of his, Kip Griner, and the people he worked for under the bus. These people in New York don't like that kind of publicity so they eliminated him. Mr. Sykes knew Simon Baumer contacted his son about teaming up with him to get revenge on you. Harmon may have felt Baumer was the catalyst which caused the death of his son."

Charley, not in agreement spoke up, "I find it hard to believe a wealthy man like Harmon Sykes would gun down another man, even an enemy."

Parks interjected the next thought, "We're not saying Sykes pulled the trigger but that with all his money he could have easily hired someone to kill Baumer, but still that's a stretch. Why would Sykes go to the limits of having Baumer shot using an actual Civil War musket and collector ammunition? That seems like overkill, something that is not necessary."

Max snapped his fingers as he suggested, "Maybe Harmon Sykes arranged to have Baumer shot in this fashion to throw suspicion on me. In his mind, there may have been the possibility that as a reenactor I would have access to the type of weapon and ammunition used."

"No, I agree with Detective Parks," said Vanderway. "I feel if it was Sykes his interest would be centered on simply having Baumer killed, the weaponry would make no difference. Myself, well I'm leaning toward Kip Griner and the people he works for as the possible culprits. The type of people Griner is associated with are members of a crime syndicate and if they indeed killed Brad Sykes then it is not out of the question they may have wanted to take Baumer out as well, but the fact Baumer was shot with a 160 year old Springfield 58 caliber musket not to mention actual Civil War ammunition at least in my mind eliminated them as the shooter.

"I say this because organized crime families, when and if they decide to have someone rubbed out, as they say, would send a professional to get the job done. They would not take the time to use an ancient gun and ammunition. More than likely they would use a modern high-powered rifle and the shooter would not have hesitated for twenty-some seconds before taking a second shot.

"How Buamer was shot and the gun used does not fit how an organized crime shooter would operate. And another thing, why was Baumer shot over here in Adams County rather than over in Lancaster County where he lives? One thing we have not discussed and that's the motive for killing Simon Baumer. The fact he was killed right out there on your porch while trying to kidnap you, Elizabeth, and your daughters and take you back to Lancaster County strongly indicates someone knew Baumer was coming here to take you back.

"What other reason could there be for him being shot here? Everyone in the Mennonite community you came from knew that Baumer had recently been obsessing over the fact that you not only left the faith but married outside of the faith when he thought you and he would marry. It could very well turn out that someone from the Mennonite community didn't agree with the way Simon felt, so they followed him over here, and ultimately by shooting him they prevented him from taking you back."

Elizabeth instantly waved off Park's version of what may have happened as she retorted, "Detective, we all realize that you are in search of the truth but any Mennonite involvement is out of the question. I spent a little over twenty years living in the Mennonite faith and without any doubt whatsoever guarantee you that there was no Mennonite involvement in the shooting death of Simon Baumer. Mennonites are pacifists. I know of no Mennonite who owns a gun or even has a desire to fire one. A true Mennonite would not even kill their worst enemy."

"Perhaps you're right," said Parks, "but we as the police have to investigate every possible angle that avails itself to us."

Charley spoke up. "So where do my son and daughter-in-law go from here? The shooter is still out there and the murder weapon has yet to be found. Do you feel they are in any danger?"

Vanderway answered the question. "Mr. Miller…it is my professional opinion that this shooter has accomplished what they sought to do and that was to put an end to Simon Baumer's life. I feel Max and Elizabeth are out of the woods as far as any further danger is concerned. At this point, I would say that all of you need to try and get back to a normal way of life as soon as possible and just simply allow us to do our job. We still have some feelers out there.

"The Ithaca Police are speaking with Harmon Sykes today and told us they would call us if anything regarding Baumer's murder surfaces. I could be wrong but I doubt if anything new will reveal itself. I think talking with Sykes is just another dead end. Also, the Manheim Township police over in Lancaster County have assured us they will continue to ask around the

Mennonite community for any leads. In the meantime, it's just a matter of waiting to see if anything turns up. So, with that, we'll be on our way. If we hear of anything new we'll give you a call. Likewise, if you should stumble onto anything you think may be important, let us know."

Greenie stood with the detectives and put in his final two cents. "I hope our visit this afternoon was not too disturbing or stressful for you folks, but we thought it was important you know the results of the autopsy."

Max stood and walked the three men to the front door as he assured them. "I'm sure we'll be all right. I and the rest of my family are confident in the next few days or weeks that you will get to the bottom of this shooting."

Watching the three cross the yard to where their car was parked, Max closed the door and walked back into the living room where Elizabeth was already gathering up coffee cups and the remaining cookies as she made her way to the kitchen. Charley stood, stretched, and announced. "Well, that was certainly interesting. I think Detective Vanderway was correct in his advice about trying to get back to a normal way of life which is exactly what I intend on doing. I'm going into town to the hardware store to get a new bracket for the porch light. Care to tag along, Max?"

Max declined as he headed for the door. "No I think I'll pass. I'm going to take a short walk around the farm. I've got a lot of thinking to do."

Kate, picking up the cream and sugar bowls, chimed in, "Elizabeth and I need to get busy putting together dinner for this evening. We'll be eating around six-thirty. There is nothing more normal than a good meal."

Charley opened the door and casually waved, "Well, I'm off to town."

Max followed him out the door and added, "And I'm going on that walk."

Charley went to the right and Max to the left, walking to the edge of the farm property where the slight indentation in the earth marked the spot where Kellem had explained to him that at one time there had been a long six-foot deep gully and that one of his past great-grandfathers had buried thirty-three dead Confederate soldiers, which resulted in Kellem's ancestors hearing strange voices. Walking by the area where the gully had been located, Max thought about what Kellem had told him, about how his father growing tired of not only the occasional voices but all the tourists who ventured onto the farm in search of hearing a voice had reported the burial site and that the bodies had been exhumed and moved to a cemetery on the battlefield near town. Kellem's father, then utilizing actual parts of the fencing that had been present during Pickett's Charge rebuilt the fence and placed it at the edge of the farm property along with assorted parts from seven cannons, which allowed his father to construct three cannons placed along the fence line facing the battlefield.

Turning to the left Max followed the fence line while passing the first cannon as he gazed up into the trees at the top of the rise. The wind picked up and leaves from the forest were blowing down the ridge and into the yard. Reaching up, he tried to grasp a leaf here and there but was unsuccessful in capturing one of the bright-colored leaves. Looking up into the trees once again he thought the shooter could have hidden up there in the trees and fired the two shots that took Simon Baumer's life.

Passing the second cannon he looked in the direction of the barn and surmised that the shooter could have stood at the edge of the barn with a clear shot at Baumer on the porch. Continuing down the fence line he thought about the strange results of the autopsy. Baumer had been shot to death not only with an early 1860's Springfield 58 caliber rifle but with ammunition that was at least one hundred and sixty years old. It seemed like someone had not only gone to great lengths to kill Simon but the weaponry used didn't make any sense.

He stopped at the last cannon and something hanging on the third fence down from the end caught his attention. Moving slowly forward he checked to see if anyone was nearby. *Not a soul!* Just short of the fourth post he couldn't believe his eyes, an old canteen suspended by a frayed rope hung from the fence. Reaching out he lifted the old water container and there on the side there was an inscription roughly etched into the wood, *Samuel Pritchard Five Points Alabama 47th Alabama*. Holding the canteen he looked to the right and the left, the barn, and then up into the tree line. *He was alone! Who could have placed the canteen there on the fence?*

He then noticed something on the top of the post. A knife, not just any knife but a Swiss Army knife sticking into a ragged piece of paper. Closely examining the knife he recognized the knife as *his knife!* The corner of the handle was chipped and had been for years. He had given the knife to Sam as a gift and here it was sticking in the fence. Noticing the ragged piece of paper stuck in the top of the fence post he removed the knife and stuck it in the top rail. Picking up the paper he read the written message.

And He will command His angels concerning you and they will raise you in their hands and prevent you from stubbing your foot into a stone.

Thinking back, Max recalled that day when Sam came to visit him and Elizabeth in the backyard and the very words that were written on the paper were part of the scripture Sam and Elizabeth had taken turns quoting word for word. Sticking the paper back on the fence post with the knife he read the inscription on the canteen again and then looked out at the tree line. Suddenly, what had been very confusing became clear as a bell. Taking his cell from his pocket he called Elizabeth. Almost instantly, she answered, "Hello."

Max, trying his best to contain the excitement of what he had discovered explained in a calm voice, "Elizabeth, I need you to come out to the fence down by the picnic table. I have discovered something that you are not going to believe. It's simply amazing. Just tell mom I need you out here for a moment…nothing else."

"All right," said Elizabeth, "I'm on my way."

It wasn't but a few seconds when Max saw her as she bounded down the porch steps and ran across the yard, her long blond hair blowing in the breeze, red and yellow leaves swirling about her head, her apron still tied around her waist. Stopping just short of where Max stood, she took a deep breath, commenting, "I guess I'm not all that used to running. What is it that you have discovered?"

Pointing at the canteen hanging from the fence post Max asked, "Does this canteen look familiar?"

Not sure where her husband was heading she looked at the canteen, shrugged, and remained silent.

Max removed the canteen from the fence and handed it to her while explaining, "There is a rough inscription etched into the side of the canteen. Could you please read it?"

Holding the canteen up she silently read the inscription, then in confusion stated, "Is this not the same canteen that reenactor, Sam Pritchard, had with him the day he visited us here on the farm?"

Max smiled. "The same, and that's not all." Pointing at the knife sticking in the post he explained, "Do you remember that morning when I decided to cross over this fence right here and go back in time to try and save Sam Pritchard?"

"I do recall that."

"One of the things I told you I was taking with me was my Swiss Army knife. When I returned later that day I forgot to mention this to you, but I did not bring this knife back with me. I gave it to Sam as a gift before both of us stepped out in the field where Pickett's Charge was to take place." Gesturing at the knife Max went on, "This is the knife I gave to Sam and I know this because the corner of the plastic handle is chipped. It has been that way for years." Removing the knife from the post he folded it and placed it in his pocket while handing her the note. "The last thing I discovered is this note. If you would, please read what is written."

Elizabeth took the note and read silently, then responded in wonder, "Why this is a small portion of Psalm 91."

"That is exactly correct and not only that part of Psalm but the entire scripture was recited by you and Sam that day he came to our farm. Do you remember that?"

Elizabeth confirmed, "Yes I do."

"When Sam quoted this part of the scripture, he gave me an odd look that day but I didn't think anything of it. That part of Psalm 91 is also the last thing he said to me after I managed to get him off the field of battle just before he decided to run back onto the field and then disappeared in all of the confusion and smoke. When you consider everything we have discovered here today on this fence we have solved the mystery of who shot Simon Baumer!"

Elizabeth stared at her husband and then spoke softly, "As usual, when it comes to this sort of thing, I'm afraid I'm not on the same page as you. What are you saying?"

"I'm saying that none other than Sam Pritchard returned here to our farm and that he shot Simon Baumer. It makes perfect sense. The medical examiner stated without any doubt whatsoever that an 1860s Civil War Springfield rifle and actual Civil War ammunition were used to kill Baumer, both of which Sam had in his possession when he was here at the farm. Vanderway told us that unless someone steps forward with information that leads to the identity of the shooter then this case is at a dead end. Someone, namely Samuel Pritchard, has stepped forward and with all this evidence he left behind here at the fence he has revealed that he shot and killed Simon. This to me is as plain as the nose on my face. There can be no other reasonable explanation for this. Do you now understand?"

Elizabeth handed the note back to Max and stepped through the fence as she stared off into the trees at the top of the ridge. Turning back she leaned on the old fence and shook her head in wonder. "If what you say is true then we have to call Detective Vanderway and explain all of this to him."

Max folded the note and placed it in his pocket, leaned on the opposite side of the fence, and pointed out, "One would think that is the logical thing to do, but if we do that Vanderway nor anyone else will look at our reasoning as logical. You see, we were both wrong when it came to who Samuel Pritchard was. All along you thought he was a reenactor, but that was not who he was. I was also wrong in thinking he was a ghost. He was neither a reenactor nor a ghost. When I first started talking to you about this ghost business you told me as a Mennonite you did not believe in ghosts but you do believe in angels. Turns out that Sam Pritchard was not a reenactor or even a ghost but that he was and is an angel…an angel sent here to protect us, in this case, you, from stubbing your foot into a stone, that stone being Simon Baumer.

"I think we need to keep this to ourselves. We can't mention this to anyone, not Vanderway or the police, not my parents or yours, not even your friend Ellen or even Kellem. Who would believe any of this? If we reveal what we think happened here it will only make things even more complicated. As far as I'm concerned Sam left this canteen, my knife, and the note here for us on the fence so that we can be at peace and that is good enough for me. Are you good with this decision?"

Elizabeth joined him on the farm side of the fence and took both his hands in hers, gave him one of her great smiles, and then stated as she nodded back at the picnic table. "I remember that day when Sam came to visit us, how I patched his wounds and he ate lunch with us and how he and I recited Psalm 91. Ever since I have known you, Max, which is what now… seven years you have always based your life on mathematics and have stated many a time over those years that math always reveals the truth. I guess I look at the world from a different viewpoint than you. Rather than mathematics, as you are well aware, I depend on the Bible for any answers in this life, and a particular scripture comes to mind that puts me at peace with this entire situation. Hebrews 13:2. *Do not forget to entertain strangers, for by doing so some people have entertained angels without knowing it!*"

Author Bio

Gary was born and raised in Williamsport, Pennsylvania. He currently lives in Arnold, Missouri, just outside of St. Louis with his wife Linda and their rescue cat Walter. Gary is a proud grandfather of four and is a member of Connect church in Fenton, Missouri. He is an avid baseball fan and enjoys swimming, spending time at the beach, model railroading, reading, and writing.

Other books By Gary Yeagle

The Road to Williamsport: A true story about a Little League team who won the Little League World Series in 2002. At one time this book was considered for a movie.

Angels Footprints: A short story collection of feel-good stories.

Angels Footsteps II: A collection of even more uplifting stories.

Iron Fist Velvet Glove: A fast-paced Irish thriller set in Belfast Ireland.

The Smokey Mountain Murders: A trilogy of murder mysteries that include Seasons of Death, Echoes of Death, and Shadows of Death

House of Cards: A past history of the St. Louis Cardinals combined with an uplifting fictional story about a young boy who dreams about being a major league pitcher.

Dreamer's Gospel: This book covers the deaths of Marylyn Monroe, President John F. Kennedy, his brother Robert Kennedy, and Jimmy Hoffa. It is a work of fiction packed with actual historical events. A very fast-paced read.

Lowcountry Burn: A murder mystery set in the low country of South Carolina.

Delayed Exposure: A follow-up book to Lowcountry Burn as the story continues with more murders.